TranzCon

Coming Soon

HAHNSREA
the sequel to TranzCon

PRIVATE MEADOWS
the third book in the TranzCon trilogy

TranzCon

- DAVID HULETT WILSON -

Published by DHWBooks 2013

Copyright © David Hulett Wilson, 2013

All rights reserved. No part of this publication may be reproduced, stored in a retrieval system, or transmitted in any form or by any means, electronic, mechanical, photocopying, recording, or otherwise, without the prior permission of both the copyright owner and the above publisher of this book.

This is a work of fiction. All characters, organisations, and events portrayed in this novel are either products of the author's imagination or are used fictitiously.

Paperback ISBN: 978-095758-780-9

Printed and bound by:
Printondemand-worldwide.com
9 Culley Court
Orton Southgate
Peterborough PE2 6XD

www.DavidHWilson.co.uk

To Jean,
who told me to carry on when I was
about to give up.

And not forgetting Claire and Christine
who gave their support.

What happens when a man loses everything?

1
Conference

Tom Hanson hacked off another slice of the delicious bacon and lifted it jerkily up to *his* mouth. Paula Marlow watched and wondered if he was going to complete what he'd been trying to say. But that was always the problem with a working breakfast and a slightly uncoordinated host body, you couldn't always manage to talk and eat at the same time.

The two colleagues had transferred into Port Preston's reception centre only a matter of hours earlier and gone straight into acclimatisation, a process that hadn't been made any easier by the time difference between Vissan and Daluun. "TranzCon lag" they called it. Fortunately Paula had scheduled in an easy day so they'd have time to adjust and relax before the conference started next morning.

Tom emptied his mouth and continued, but really there was nothing more to say. They'd run out of new ideas long before turning in late last evening.

★★★

On his previous and all too brief visits to Daluun Tom had always made the trip down to Nagula on a private VSTOL flight, something a man in his position took for granted. But he'd always promised himself that one day when life was just busy rather than hectic he'd allow a little more time for sightseeing. Well things hadn't slowed down in the slightest, but this time he was going to do it anyway. And after all, the trip on the coastal hydrofoil only took a little over an hour so the jet wouldn't have saved him more than a few minutes.

It was said that the views over the Rickenburg mountains could be stunning if the weather was right so it was by good fortune that the two colleagues had arrived on one of the few days when the region was free from the dank mist which so often shrouded that part of the coastline. And it was as just as amazing as the travel correspondents had said, the views of the snow capped summit of Daniel's Pike far off inland and the smaller peaks which towered over the imposing coast were breathtaking. To say the scenery here was different from what they were used to back at home was understatement in the extreme. When people said the scenery on Daluun was big, they meant "BIG" spelt in capitals.

The kind hearted made the excuse that the views on Vissan included a lot of sky.

★★★

As the sleek craft rounded the headland into Half-Moon Bay Tom and Paula quickly downed their coffees and rushed back out onto the now crowded deck, and straight away they'd felt it, the *gradient*, the magical rise in temperature that swept over a vessel and those on board as it left the open sea to enter Nagula's micro-climate. Tom had read about it, and he'd felt the extra heat in a single hit as he'd stepped down from the VSTOL on his previous trips, but it was as the reports had said, it was something that simply had to be experienced first hand. It was after all the reason the city was there at all.

And there it was - Nagula. A thin crescent of low lying land that curved around the sparkling blue waters of a tranquil lagoon. A tropical paradise in a location which by rights was just a little too far north to be either tropical or a paradise - something which was all too evident just sixty kilometres up the coast in Port Preston.

The city which was now home to more than a quarter of the planet's population had been the first major settlement on the planet, and its location on a wide alluvial plain at the mouth of the Selen river had been chosen for a number of compelling and entirely logical reasons. Raw materials were what Daluun was all about and the mighty river now formed an aquatic highway that linked the busy port with the rich mineral extraction areas far inland.

But for all the big city's wealth and bustle, its industry and commerce, its docks and the shuttle terminal, it was a rainy old place which somehow managed to feel cold and damp even on the sunniest of days. With at least some moisture falling from the gloomily overcast sky for 150 of the planet's 335 day cycle any citizen who'd been there for more than a few months knew all too well that complaining was never a good idea - the alternative to a day of steady drizzle was usually much worse. The city's richest folk had given up long ago and moved down the coast to the almost endless fine weather of the beautiful bay that statistics said had the highest hours of sunshine anywhere in the Union.

Another of the interesting statistics published was that Nagula boasted the highest number of climatologists per head of population anywhere in the Union. A year on location to study first hand the most bizarre mix of climate and weather ever known was without doubt the best off-planet posting in the galaxy. For Tom the chance to witness the fascinating interplay between two conflicting weather systems was simply the cherry on the cake of a job which took him away from home all too often.

As the hydrofoil approached the city's ferry terminal the pilot cut the throttles and the half-plane half-boat settled gently down into the crystal clear water. Then as the craft manoeuvred in towards the dock it turned its passengers broadside on to the show that had run for thousands or even millions of years. High up in the mountains behind the city, angry, billowing storm clouds flashed with lighting and rumbled with thunder, while below them the narrow coastal plain basked in sunlight. A stand-off between rival weather-Gods, or just a quirk of nature? Certainly a spectacle to interest the army of scientists who'd struggled over the years to find an adequate explanation. But Tom knew it wasn't always like this. Once in a while the sea's frontal system would strengthen and push the towering clouds back over the mountain tops lighting up the peaks in a brief interlude of brilliant sunshine. And then just as suddenly the clouds would sweep back seaward to provide natural irrigation for the parched plain below.

Not that there was much plain left, almost every square metre of precious flat land had been covered by something man-made. Only the beaches and the seafront gardens remained as a reminder of a time when nature had reigned unchallenged. And that was Nagula, a century ago no more than an impoverished fishing port and now the planet's capital city. A working city, a holiday resort, a tropical gem, and the home of the rich - all in one. Definitely the place to be. The planet's largest corporations had made a smart move many decades ago when they'd relocated their head offices here. It was true the land and the housing could be expensive, but it was a fabulous place to live and that made the best talent easy to attract. With big business already well entrenched it had seemed logical when the planetary government decided to follow.

And slowly the area changed as wave after wave of new citizens had arrived to demand housing and shopping malls, and then the housing and shopping malls had wrought havoc with the natural beauty of the area. With over two million people now packing themselves into a thin arc of land which swept round the bay, low-rise had become high-rise, and high-rise had become higher as the city's second rank of wealthy residents demanded restoration of the sea-views they'd once enjoyed. The first rank of the wealthy still occupied the better parts of the seafront and the original fishermen's cottages that overlooked the old harbour.

★★★

Just to the south of the ferry terminal where the long sweep of golden sandy beach had already begun to give way to a more rocky shore was a small inlet, a bay within a bay - Malin bay. And overlooking the water stood a rather nice hotel where Tom had stayed before and had liked very much. Perhaps the atmosphere in this more select and secluded part of the city lacked the vibrancy of the down-town areas, but experience had shown that if a guest preferred a good night's sleep to a fun evening out in the clubs and bars this haven of tranquillity could offer more than a few advantages. He stopped and wondered, was it age that was finally getting to him, or had he just been worn down by so many years in a demanding job? It was for certain there were more lines on the overworked face than had been visible on the day he'd been elected.

Lines on *his* face - his own face.

And yet somehow they seemed to be there when he looked in the mirror. Tom was suddenly aware of the body he was using for this trip. Not the same one he'd used on previous visits to Daluun but still a reasonable match for his own.

Almost the same height, slightly lower in weight and waistline, and a nose that was spot-on. The hair had been too long and wavy but it wasn't anything a quick cut couldn't fix. And he'd taken the chance to have a few grey highlights put in where it finished just above the ears. As a top player in his profession he'd learned long ago that age conveyed wisdom, and wisdom commanded respect. When he handed over the reins of power next year he could go back to the boyish looks he'd never really lost.

In fact they'd both done well because his colleague's host was a ringer for her own body back in Jackson, though the knowledge that the woman who owned it was nine years younger said something about the way Paula kept herself so trim. Who'd have ever thought a forty year old mother of two could look like that? Tom had wondered more than once whether Carol might have sent along a few spies to check that their relationship was "business only".

A bell rang outside in the corridor. Ten seconds later it was still ringing. Tom drummed his fingers on the table in annoyance - the most important meeting he'd ever attended was starting in two hours time and now a fire drill. He was tempted to stay sitting at the table but he knew the rules - safety procedures applied to everyone - including the Union's First Minister.

He pulled himself to his feet and walked over to the window. The weather outside looked sunny and warm as was normal for this time of year but he knew from his previous visits that the early morning breeze could be chilly so he pulled his suit jacket on. Paula slipped a light mac over her blouse.

★★★

Outside on the far side of the seafront road the residents of the Malin Bay hotel were gathering at the official muster station where a girl with a clip-board was ticking off names one by one. Tom looked around at the motley collection - men with half shaved faces, women in bath-robes with shampoo still in their hair. Half seven in the morning was not the most popular time for a fire drill.

He found a policeman who fortunately recognised who he was speaking to.

'Is it just a drill officer, because if it is I've got a lot to do before the conference. Is there any way I can get back inside?'

The policeman shook his head. 'I'm sorry sir, but it's a bomb scare. Separatists you know.'

And Tom did know. They were the reason he was there in the first place.

'Well how long before we can get back in?'

The policeman looked at his watch. 'Another ten minutes before the squad get here, and they'll want a couple of hours at least. I wouldn't put much hope of getting back in before ten.'

The word that formed on the minister's lips began with "sh" and ended with "t". The conference was due to start at 10.00 and after the opening address from the Daluun leader he'd be next up. After beaming across 120 light-years to be here there was no way he could turn up late.

A plan formed in his head. He looked over at Paula.

'Can we get hold of the car? We might as well go straight to the hall if we're not going to get back into the room.'

'What about all the notes you prepared? And all the figures too?'

'I'm on it. I've got my opening speech off pat and by the time everyone else has had their say it'll be time for a break. I can get away without the stuff from the room till after twelve. If we get Mr Plod here to give us a call when the hotel's safe to go back inside you can come back in the car and pick it all up. OK?'

She sighed and nodded to show her agreement. Even the exalted post of junior minister meant being the dogsbody sometimes.

***

On the drive to Government Hall Tom realised he hadn't brought a tie from the room but fortunately the one he was able to borrow from the car's chauffeur didn't clash too badly with his shirt. Overall he felt a mess and wondered if he looked it, but maybe no-one would notice. He'd been in worse situations than this.

When the car pulled up outside the hall a man in uniform opened the door, and Tom and Paula stepped out into a blast of hot air neither of them had expected. With property prices in the prime locations going through the roof the seat of government had moved inland to a marginally cheaper district where the last of the plain ran out before the land started rising up into the Rickenburgs. And it was all too obvious that once you moved away from the breeze of the seafront it got very much warmer. Uncomfortably hot would have been a better term. Tom loosened the tie he'd just taken three goes to fasten.

And then he stood and looked up at the building where the conference would be starting in just over an hour. With the last pour of concrete only cured three months ago the building was a futuristic edifice that appeared to be a smaller version of the senate hall in Jackson. But not that much smaller. When he studied the huge dome that arched high overhead a little more carefully he wondered if it might even be an exact copy. But then, if you employed the same architect, you got the same sort of design. Why ditch a winning formula? Or was that the real reason? He looked again and wondered whether the design was telling him, shouting at him, that Daluun could look after its own affairs and had no need of central government.

Walking inside he was hit immediately by the chill of the climate control system. Perhaps just a little too cool but most certainly a relief from the "fry an egg on the pavement" heat that was building up outside. He guessed the hall was being over-cooled in anticipation of the four hundred or more delegates and reporters who would fill it before the conference began, but Belen only knew how much a powerful system like that cost to run on a planet where construction of the first fusion reactor hadn't even started yet.

Taking his seat at the central table a very welcome cup of coffee was immediately poured for him by the gloved hand of an immaculately suited waiter. Sipping the hot liquid carefully to avoid scalding his host's lips he looked around the hall to see if there was anyone he recognised, though he knew the problem would be the same as always - it wasn't every politician or businessman who could find a host who so closely resembled their own body.

★★★

By the time the cup was half empty the hall was beginning to fill up. Obviously some of the other delegates staying in the Malin Bay had had the same idea. But at least getting there early had given Paula and himself time to go through the strategy one final time.

For years now the separatist problem had been getting worse. At first it had been just a few local politicians and business leaders complaining that far too much of the revenue from their planet's booming natural resources industry always ended up on one of the more established worlds. Then more and more of the ordinary citizens had joined in when they'd begun to realise that if Daluun was granted independence there'd be riches for all. With an abundance of the raw materials the Union's massive industrial machine needed to keep running the annual revenue from everything their mineral-rich planet produced would turn them all into overnight millionaires.

But that wasn't the way the Union worked! For centuries it had been enshrined in the constitution that anything *God given* was the property of all. Natural resources were to be shared equally amongst the citizens of the Union. The three planets originally colonised, Vissan, Temenco and Miranda, had each given their own bounty for the benefit of the Union, and now the more recently discovered planets had to do their bit. After all, it had been Union astronomy and exploration missions that had found Daluun in the first place, and Union money that had funded the colonisation.

And then the nature of the argument had changed. The economic basis underlying the desire for independence had shifted to a more political stance. Apparently setting aside the very attractive economic considerations that were surely the driving force for the rank and file of their supporters the separatists had argued that what really mattered was freedom from domination by a life-expired and decadent ruling elite they said was becoming increasingly irrelevant to the lives of the people on Daluun. That was when the bombings had started. And yet the planet already had an appropriate level of self-government. Each planet in the Union had its own administration service to handle affairs which were local in nature or did not require input from central government, and the authority it exercised depended to a large extent on how developed the planet was and how much self-determination its population could be trusted with.

For the past four years Brian Rushmore had been the elected leader of the Daluun parliament. Coming to the planet originally as a senior executive of a major corporation based on

Miranda he'd decided to stay on when his posting ended. And he'd been a popular leader as well as a shrewd politician who'd made a point of knowing exactly what grants, tax-breaks, development aid packages and soft-loans were available. So although Tom saw him as a political ally there was no denying the tough talking businessman had never missed a trick and had always put his adopted planet first when it came to financial matters. But despite his understandable allegiance it was a matter of concern on Vissan that Rushmore might not be returned to power at the forthcoming elections.

He and Tom had spoken by video link almost every week since the day he'd been elected, and Brian had kept him informed of developments. In particular the First Minister had been interested in the rise to prominence of Adam Greenwood and his "Independence for Daluun Movement", a party which its leader claimed was committed to achieving its objectives through peaceful, non-violent means. So no connection at all to those nasty people who thought bombing their way out of the Union was a good idea? There were rumours that suggested otherwise.

In practice the bombings had been more troublesome than dangerous. Security at all Union related institutions had been increased and now the men of violence appeared to rely more on threats - a policy which seemed to work better than actually bombing anything. It only took a phone call to make a threat and there was no need for either the explosives themselves or an operative who'd take the risk of putting them in place.

But even threats had been on the wane in recent months when the party realised that if they were to appeal to the masses, they had to make it clearly understood they shunned any connection with violence. In fact the organisation had seen how democracy itself could be used as a weapon against the power of central government. If a vote was held tomorrow the outcome would almost certainly swing in favour of Daluun ceding from the Union. If central government ruled it was not a matter that could be put to a vote, then where was democracy? Greenwood in a suit was far more dangerous than he'd ever been in a balaclava and flak jacket.

But the leadership election wasn't due to be held until next year so there was still a chance for Rushmore to do something to improve his chances, but for that to happen he had to secure a better deal from the Union - which was something Tom knew he couldn't allow. If he caved in and gave Rushmore what he wanted, matters elsewhere would almost certainly become very difficult indeed. If he offered any kind of special concession to Daluun it was just opening the flood-gates to all the other planets who would ask why they weren't a special case as well.

Erandar was perhaps the biggest of Tom's headaches. The planet was a political hotbed that had never been a strong supporter of the Union. Colonised in the days before FTL had brought journey times down from decades and centuries to months and years, the planet had always been self-supporting with its own mineral resources and manufacturing industries. It had never been much of a net exporter of raw materials although mining had always been an important feature of an economy that paid billions each year in tax revenues. Without a shadow of a doubt, Erandar would be the next in line to ask why it couldn't have a better deal.

And Erandar he could deal with, it was Darius that was the bigger problem. Without the almost endless supply of natural resources the home planets received from Darius, Union industry would quite literally grind to a halt. Politically the planet was a pussycat with massive support for the Union - at the moment. But things could change, especially if it looked like Daluun and Erandar were dipping their fingers in the pot. Why should they deserve special treatment if Darius didn't?

The worst possible scenario by far was if the three mining planets ganged up together. Then what? The government on Vissan would have to give them at least a part of what they were asking for, and that really would be the beginning of the end for whoever was in power. Handing out special treatment to the mining planets meant ignoring what was going on at home, and neglecting the opinions of fifteen billion voters asking why they couldn't be a special case too was political suicide. It truly was the difference between a rock and a hard place.

Why couldn't they all just accept that the cake was big enough for everyone to have a slice? The Union was rich beyond belief but no-one seemed to see it that way, everyone wanted more, never mind who would have to go without to provide it. Somehow Tom knew that this time the problem wasn't going to just blow over.

The mobile in his pocket started to ring. The policeman outside the Malin Beach hotel was calling to tell him the alarm had been another hoax and they'd be allowing people back inside within the next few minutes. Paula was sitting at her place on the first row of seats facing the main conference table. Tom caught her eye and pointed to his phone - she guessed what he was trying to tell her and headed off towards the side exit.

When Tom looked up from his phone he saw Brian Rushmore and his team just arriving. As the big man walked up to the top table the two old friends greeted each other warmly before taking their seats side by side. They both knew they had a long and difficult day ahead.

★★★

As was to be expected on his home soil, the opening address was the privilege of the Daluun leader. Tom's turn would come soon - too soon, even for such an experienced and seasoned player. Feeling slightly nervous Tom ran his mind through the main points he and Paula had identified while he poured himself a glass of water. And he looked hard at the glass because somehow the liquid inside had failed to settle. A series of rings formed on the surface, and then vanished as he picked the glass up from the table. Then he felt a vibration that seemed to come from the ground underneath his chair. What was that then, a resonance from the cooling equipment now more of the compressors had kicked in? Bloody architects, they never got anything right.

Rushmore was still on his feet, telling the gathering how the planet could prosper within the Union and from the noises that issued from the audience many of the local delegates obviously felt the same way.

But then the speaker stopped in mid sentence. Tom felt it too. A movement from underneath, as if the floor of the building had suddenly pushed upwards. For just one moment a hush fell over the hall before cries of alarm began to fill the room.

Then it was still again. Whatever machinery had caused the vibrations had been turned off. Rushmore took a sip of his water, glanced around at the audience, and resumed his speech. A full three minutes must have passed before the movement came again. Almost at the end of his speech he stopped. The sounds from the audience this time were more of surprise than alarm. And then all was still again. The audience quietened so he could continue.

And then the ground shifted. The hall erupted with shouts of panic as the floor seemed to rise up. It was as if the Devil and his demon hoard were underneath making one last effort to break out of hell. Men and women jumped from their seats only to lose balance on a floor that seemed to have come alive. The ground rose up again, the movement stronger this time. Then chunks of masonry began to fall from the ceiling, small ones at first followed by a steady stream of larger pieces. Showering down, landing indiscriminately on whatever or whoever was below. A woman screamed as a block of stone twice her own weight landed just centimetres away. Faster and faster came the deadly rain, and as the blocks hit the floor they broke up into smaller pieces and dust. A choking cloud began to fill the hall.

People not already injured began rushing towards the exits but to no avail. The heavy steel security doors had jammed in their frames and refused to open. With nowhere to go the people trapped in the building were shouting or screaming in panic as the structure fell in on them.

Tom saw what was happening. Rushmore was standing to his side, notes still in his hand, dumbfounded at the scene of chaos unfolding before him.

Tom shouted, 'Brian. Get under the table. It's the only chance.'

All the furniture in the hall had been built using native Jaccan-wood from the local forests and looked solid and strong. The conference table where the senior delegates had been sitting just moments earlier was the largest and strongest of all and fended off the blows dealt out by the rain of concrete and stone.

Watching the mayhem and unbelievable carnage Tom was shaking with fear and his pulse was racing. Calming himself just a little he was able to take smaller breaths, avoiding breathing in too much of the choking, foul tasting dust that swirled like a deadly fog. And then he heard the sound. A creaking, then a mighty crack. The huge dome that had arched majestically overhead gave way. For those underneath who saw tonne after tonne of the concrete structure crashing down it was the last thing they ever saw. Tom and Brian heard smaller pieces clattering down on top of them until a massive block of concrete landed with a thud, and despite its enormous strength the wood of the table cracked and splintered. One of the legs gave way. A second leg creaked and cracked before splintering into pieces and the heavy top dropped down onto the two cowering men. Rushmore called out in pain as the weight pressed down onto his back, crushing his chest hard against the floor. Entombed but free to move just a little Tom crawled towards his friend to see what he could do to help. The man's ribs had been crushed though for the present he was still alive.

Another leg gave way and the table dropped further, this time wedging Tom in position and trapping his left leg. A cracking sound came from the knee as the joint was ripped apart. The agony that seared through the host body was more than he'd ever known. He screamed out loud, he screamed at the top of his voice for someone to help him. While he shouted the pain was somehow held at bay, only to return the instant he stopped. Again and again he called.

And then the sound of falling material stopped. The lifting of the ground that had done so much damage ended quite abruptly. The floor of the hall no longer heaved up and down. Now Tom heard the sounds of a hundred voices - shouting, screaming, calling for help. As best he could he turned his eyes towards his companion. Brian was whimpering, scarcely able to breath, crushed down by the weight of wood and concrete above him.

Always calm in a crisis Tom's mind somehow adjusted to the pain - somehow accepted that the agony he'd felt from his crushed leg just moments ago was now the norm. Then panic set in. He tried to move and couldn't. His head was wedged solidly between the table and the floor. The slightest movement would crack his skull. His body was similarly immobile. He was lying on the right arm and could already feel a buzz of pins and needles from the lack of blood supply. His left arm had been pushed behind his back and was held firmly in place, though he could at least move the fingers. Only the good right leg was free to move. He flexed the knee joint and the leg bent and unbent.

Now he heard a different sound. Voices, but not calling out in pain. A blast of speech from a loud hailer ripped through what remained of the hall. Tom thought he made out the word "help" but the rest was lost amongst the bedlam screaming. He guessed that many more would be trapped or injured like himself.

Brian beside him gave a weak cough. Despite the dust that had blasted him in the face and filled his mouth Tom found a way to speak. 'Brian. Hang on in there. They're bringing help.'

He never expected the man to answer.

Carefully Tom tried to work his left arm out of the position where it was held behind his back. It moved just slightly. Wriggling the fingers he tried pulling the whole arm up towards his shoulder, and it moved just a little more. Somehow he found the strength to turn his upper body. It made just a little more room for the arm to move. Little by little he worked the arm out of its trapped position and round to the front of his body. He reached out toward Brian Rushmore but his hand stopped short. Wriggling the arm just a little more at last a single finger made contact with something soft - and noticeably cool to the touch.

Now he felt the pain from his leg again. The trapped arm he couldn't feel at all.

He felt a cough rising in his throat as his body tried to expel some of the dust that parched the inside of his mouth. The cough came but only made the feeling worse. For just one sip of water he'd have sold his soul. Time passed, but how long, was it hours or only minutes? He tried to concentrate, to think of happier times. Carol, Sophie, Allison - they'd be waiting for him, they needed him. Needed him to be there with them, to be a husband and a father. He'd get through this, he *would* be saved.

Sounds came. Different this time. The sounds of machinery. Engines revving.

The table moved just slightly and now Tom felt a new wave of pain as the wood pushed down onto his skull. Surely it would be crushed any moment, the agony was too much, unbearable. But then slowly the pain was slipping away. The sensations from his body grew less and less, the muscles once tense relaxed. He felt strangely calm, serene. Tired, so tired. When his eyes closed of their own accord, he let them.

2

Elaine And Elodie

The doors slid apart and Bridgette Greaves stepped down onto the platform. 08.26 on the dot, so with the five minutes it would take to walk to the laboratory she'd be exactly one minute late - as always. If the trains could be reliably late as they'd been years ago when she'd started making her regular morning commute she could have caught the earlier one and got to work on time. Not that it mattered for the sake of a minute - the clients were never booked to arrive before 09.00 so there was always enough time to prepare.

Now it was just a case of running the morning gauntlet - the *every* morning gauntlet. Somehow fast food and railways just seemed to go together. Like love and marriage? Chance would be a fine thing. Most of the shops were OK, there was nothing *too* tempting about a triangular sandwich in a chiller cabinet. No, the culprit was always the same - *The Pioneers' Burger Bar*.

And here was the question, the "64,000 HUC to the winner" question. Who the hell ate burger and chips at half eight in the morning anyway? Sadly she recollected that she could think of a woman who could devour one right now, if she wasn't on a diet. Always diets. Bridgette had been on one for at least half a century which was quite an achievement for a woman of thirty seven. No, it wasn't really fifty years, it just felt that long.

But why "Pioneers" anyway? Was there some implication that the original colonists had survived on a diet of burgers? Perhaps Hermione herself had been keen on the occasional Big Bear Double Cheese, with a side order of fries? Though from the photos Bridgette had seen of the grand old lady she appeared to have been a skinny little runt who either never needed to diet in the first place or was anorexically good at it.

She walked by as close as she dared for her morning fix of passive fat inhalation, and popped a sweet in her mouth to sooth the worst of the hunger pangs. Now if only they came in cheeseburger flavour, that really would be something.

Three minutes and thirty seconds later she arrived at the flight of shining marble steps which lead up to the laboratory complex of Spencer Group Research. Twenty seconds to the top as always, and another ten to make an entrance into the impressive potted palm lobby. The final minute was always the least reliable stage of the morning's journey, but that was the way it was with lifts. Precisely seventy seconds late she walked into the lab where she worked with Professor Irving Harris, the revered scientist who'd been her boss for the past four years.

★★★

Elaine Smith and Elodie Simpson first met on the day they started at university. Maybe they'd have got together anyway, but that first morning when the alphabetic lottery pushed two strangers together had turned out to be the catalyst for one of those friendships that just seemed to begin straight away. And by the end of the first week it was as though they'd been pals all their lives.

Both the girls were lookers though no-one would have suggested they could be sisters. Elaine always kept her hair quite short in a boyish style that countered the femininity of her figure in a most alluring way. Elodie in contrast kept her mane long and luxurious, and knew exactly how to draw male attention by nothing more than a gentle toss of her head. When the two of them walked together down the corridors no-one was ever sure if they noticed the way the boys went silent as they passed, but the girls never stopped to chat. It wasn't that they were stand-offish in any way, it was just the way their appearance and demeanour sent out a message that was clear to all recipients, "A-league players only ….. please, and only when it suits us …… thankyou".

As it was for most students getting by on grants and loans, money was always a bit on the tight side, especially for those who chose to study in a capital city like Jackson. There was always just a little too much week left at the end of the money so the girls kept a careful watch on the adverts at the back of the university magazine, scouring the small print for scientific institutions anxious to employ those brave enough to participate in their research. The girls had done it all: given blood, tissue samples, they'd been weighed and measured, they'd taken drugs under test, they'd been brain scanned and had given thousands of answers to all manner of questions. Three weeks ago Elodie had spotted another new ad and today it was happening.

First there'd been the questionnaires to fill in. Standard stuff they'd seen before. Endless sheaves of A4 sheets asking the same old questions. The only new one was an inquiry into whether they knew of any Erandan predecessors in their lineage, which was a "no" in both cases.

Then it'd been the routine tests. Tests to check their hearts were working right, tests to check the blood the hearts pumped had all the right ingredients, and in the right proportions, tests on their eyes, their ears and more or less everything else. But when the pay was on an hourly rate who cared? The longer it took the better it got and the friendly, though rather overweight nurse who carried out most of the tests had made it all seem so easy.

After a short break to down two cups of machine coffee they'd finally come to the real stuff. Dressed only in hospital smocks the big nurse had lead them through to a room containing a pair of huge doughnut scanners. They'd seen that sort of thing before when they'd been brain scanned, but never anything quite as impressive as the equipment here.

The professor greeted them warmly and introduced them to his team: Raf was the computer specialist who'd developed the software that brought the system to life, Marty and Felix were transfer technicians who'd be running and monitoring the mind-swap.

The four men took their places behind a glass screen that separated the control area from the main part of the lab while Bridgette sat at her console between the two scanners. With the guinea pigs safely aboard, motors whirred to move the girls into the scanners. When both beds had stopped they heard the startup "dink", then the faint hum from the big coils that now engulfed their heads. The test took sixteen minutes to run before the two beds motored out to release the specimens back into the land of the living. Now it was just a question of waiting to hear the results.

Two days later the professor rang to say that the test had been a success and the girls were compatible in a new way no-one had even suspected existed until just a matter of months ago. If they chose to, they'd be able to participate in the main experiment, but he made it clear it wasn't something everyone was prepared to do. He would understand if they decided they'd sooner not be involved.

★★★

When the professor had explained to them that the project involved transferring the consciousness of one human subject into the body of another, the girls had gone just a little cold and wondered whether to collect the money they were owed for the initial tests and walk straight out of the door. Perhaps if the professor had put even the slightest pressure on them that's exactly what they would have done. But he'd been so pleasant and charming, he'd sounded sincere when he told them he only worked with volunteers, and he hadn't pressured them for an answer right then and there. On the contrary, he'd refused to accept an answer until they'd had time to discuss the matter in private.

But it had certainly sounded scary. For God's sake, waking up on a laboratory bed to find you'd moved into someone else's body. Weird or what? The first day after the meeting they'd been almost on the verge of phoning the laboratory and telling the prof where he could go, but over the next few days a spirit of adventure had crept in. The money for a whole weekend would be very nice they both agreed, but the change of heart they'd experienced told them that neither of their young lives would be complete unless they actually went ahead with the exchange. Before long they were so excited about the prospect they'd even have paid the nutty professor, though they realised there was no need to tell him so.

★★★

The early part of the week dragged slowly, but at last the big day finally came. Bridgette had met the girls in reception and taken them through the preliminaries. After administering a mild sedative she said would help them through the transfer she lead them back into the room where they'd been scanned eight days earlier. It was the same room and the same equipment she assured them, but this time the two huge scanners looked somehow just a little more imposing.

The first motor whirred and Elodie's head advanced into the scanner until only a tiny fraction of her swanlike neck remained on view. Elaine followed just moments later. The equipment hummed and buzzed as it sprang into life and the girls knew this was really it - the last chance to opt out was only seconds away.

Harris was there, standing behind the big glass window with Raf and the two technicians seated at the bank of consoles behind him. Bridgette was out in the lab attending to the girls and checking the monitors for body functions. When the amber light came on to show the equipment was active she settled herself onto her stool ready to watch for the telltale signs that indicated incompatibility.

'Ready to commence,' Harris called into his microphone. 'Bridgette, how are the ladies doing?'

'I've got No.1 at 79, 95 over 67, cerebral activity 9.6. No.2 at 83, 101 over 75, cerebral activity 9.7. Both ready to go professor.'

'Raf, OK at your end?'

'Scan normal for No.1, just a tad high for No.2. Nothing beyond what we've seen before. Ready to go.'

The amber light winked out and changed to red. Harris watched his equipment as streams of data flooded the screens to show that the transfer was running. Buried deep in the scanners and already lightly sedated the girls slipped rapidly into full unconsciousness as the mind-swap began.

Bridgette knew within seconds that something was wrong. She watched the monitor as Elaine's pulse leapt to 200 and carried on rising. Her blood pressure was way off the scale at

250 over 190. Without even a moment's hesitation she jammed her fist down on the emergency button and raced to the side of the bed to activate the withdrawal mechanism. The motor whirred - and she gasped. Despite the awful nights she'd spent in A&E, or the times she'd sat in ICU with a patient who sadly just wasn't going to make it, nothing had prepared her for what she now saw. She looked down in horror at the girl's face, the once silky flesh now crossed with a mesh of angrily pulsating over-driven blood vessels - and the eyes, oh God her eyeballs, wide and bulging as if ready to burst from their sockets. She ripped off the thin laboratory gown to see the same gruesome picture repeated all the way down the body as it rose and fell, struggling violently to rip itself out of the safety straps.

The speaker blared and she heard the professor's voice calling urgently. 'Bridgette, get her on life support, NOW.'

The nurse shouted back. 'It's not life support she needs professor - her body's going too fast already.'

'Well get her back into the scanner,' he screamed. 'I'm going to reverse the transfer.'

Bridgette pressed the button for the girl to go back into the scanner, but already it was too late. A wash of something hot hit her in the face and she felt the sting as liquid filled her eyes. Blinded she reeled backwards only to fall onto the bed where Elodie lay prone and silent in the other scanner. Bridgette leapt up screaming before dropping heavily to the floor.

Harris raced into the room and instinctively went down to the woman on the floor immediately feeling at her neck for a pulse. She was alive thank God.

Raf was just a moment behind and was already withdrawing the other bed, but he looked down in horror as he saw the lifeless face that came slowly into view as the bed motored out from the scanner.

He shouted. 'Prof, this one needs you. Right away.'

Harris was up in a flash. 'Help me get her onto the floor.'

The skilful fingers felt no pulse. He clasped his hands together and pushed down hard onto the girl's chest. One, two, three, four, five, his face went down onto her mouth and he breathed into her. With no medical training Raf felt helpless and simply stood by in stunned silence watching the girl's chest as it rose and fell. Now Harris was back to the heart, one, two, three, four, five before re-inflating her lungs for a second time.

The two technicians from the control room ran in to join them. Marty pressed the button to withdraw Elaine from the blood spattered scanner, but before the motor had chance to stop he felt the bile as it rose deep inside him. He couldn't help himself as his stomach contents ejected onto the ruined body.

Felix joined Harris on the floor with Elodie and took over cardiac compression leaving the professor to concentrate on the woman's breathing. The two of them worked tirelessly for over twenty minutes before they finally had to accept their efforts had been in vain.

★★★

Three weeks had passed since the fateful morning when Professor Harris's eighteenth mind transfer experiment had gone so horribly wrong. The pathologist who came to examine Elaine's body expressed his indignation that so much damage could be caused by an experiment and immediately called the police to arrest Harris and the technicians. Only after watching the video of the transfer four times did the police agree there was no evidence to indicate that any physical violence had been inflicted on the girl and the injuries she sustained were entirely the result of her own actions. No-one was surprised to find that Elodie's ribs were broken in several places, though that was not the cause of death and was only to be expected after such a prolonged period of CPR. The police left after instructing Harris to discontinue his experimentation programme until a full investigation had been carried out. As if he could have continued after such a terrible disaster.

A specialist medical team carried out post-mortems on both girls, and analysed the records of their final moments, millisecond by millisecond. Elaine had certainly died when her body somehow went into overdrive - the enormous pressure from the manic heart-rate had ruptured blood vessels and destroyed vital organs. The heart that had caused the damage had survived intact, but her lungs, kidneys and liver had literally exploded - wrecking the body from the inside and leaving no chance of recovery from such devastating damage. They agreed the nurse had done her best until she too became a casualty.

Elodie's death was, if anything, an even greater concern. If the reasons for Elaine's death were so obvious and manifold, the reason, if even there was a reason for Elodie's death, was entirely absent. Only the sight of her lifeless body confirmed she was dead at all.

The nurse Bridgette Greaves, the only other person who'd been in the scanner room at the time of the transfer, was still alive and physically stable, though after all these weeks she remained in the coma she'd entered following the blow to the head she'd received when she'd fallen to the floor.

***

Everyone was delighted when Bridgette suddenly opened her eyes and sat up. Millie Patterson her nurse in ICU was taken completely by surprise. Well, after three weeks lying motionless in a coma it wasn't what anyone had expected. Patients who'd been unconscious for that long usually stayed that way, or died.

But then the woman hadn't acted in the way Millie had expected. People who returned to life after weeks in a coma were usually dazed and took a while to recover. Some suffered from amnesia and never returned to normal. But this woman appeared to be fully conscious, and yet she was acting in a very strange way. She'd lifted her hands up to her face and studied them, then she'd felt at her arms, her chest and her face. And then without even the hint of a warning she'd turned herself round and leapt off the bed - only to fall limply to the floor because her muscles had atrophied during the weeks of inactivity.

Straight away Millie called for backup and a orderly rushed in to help get the patient back onto the bed. Fortunately she seemed to be alright despite her fall. Then after just a minute or two composing herself she demanded to be helped out of bed and taken to a mirror. It was an unusual though not unreasonable request.

Millie and the orderly wheeled Bridgette's gurney into the bathroom where a full length mirror was fixed to the wall. With a lot of assistance from the big orderly they helped her off the bed and down onto legs that had regained a little strength but were still quite unsteady. The woman studied her reflection for a moment, as if trying to make sense of what she saw ..... then screamed out loud. Taking no notice of the male orderly standing watching she ripped off her gown and threw it to the floor. She looked again with an expression of disbelief, then dropped sobbing onto the tiles. She made no protest when they helped her back into the bed.

Millie could tell something strange was going on and found an entry in the patient's notes requesting that a Professor Harris should be contacted if the patient awoke, and it gave a number to call.

★★★

It was half an hour later when a panting Harris raced into the room. Bridgette looked up at him from where she lay on the bed. The look he saw in his nurse's eyes were pure venom.

'You Professor. You did this to me.'

She gestured towards her face and flabby arms.

Harris was about to remonstrate, after all Bridgette was the one who'd survived the ordeal, she should be grateful for just being alive. But then he wondered whether things weren't exactly as they appeared. He changed his approach.

'Who are you?' he asked calmly.

'I'm Elaine Smith,' the woman answered, 'who did you think I was?'

★★★

Over two years passed before Harris was able to regain the licence he needed to carry out his mind transfer experiments. Some were surprised he'd got it back so quickly, others were surprised he'd got it back at all. The biggest surprise was that the people funding his research didn't appear to have been put off by everything that had happened. In fact they'd provided him with an increased budget and resources to uncover whatever it was that had gone so wrong.

But in the intervening time Harris and his team hadn't been idle. If the moratorium had ruled out transfers from one subject to another it had allowed for a limited degree of testing on individuals. And with the latest suite of software Raf had developed Harris found there was a lot to be learned from what had become known as a "deep scan", an investigation into the inner workings of the brain that now revealed so much more than just the mind-type of the test subject.

But why were there multiple mind-types at all? Early in the development of mind transfer technology experiments with apes had produced the predictable result that a single mind type existed for a single species. When experiments progressed to using human subjects it had come as a surprise to find that two separate and entirely incompatible mind types existed in what the geneticists had always been sure was a single species, and which by definition had to be a single species since its members were able to interbreed.

So what were the effects of the different mind types? In short there was a total lack of compatibility. Put an Alpha mind into a brain that had previously contained a Beta, and for reasons that still confounded the science Harris had developed, none of the expected linkages were created - the mind experienced no sensations and bodily functions ceased. Exactly the same was true for a Beta mind in an Alpha brain. The only good news was that no long term damage was caused to either the minds or the bodies provided the mismatched transfer was reversed within a few seconds - a happy situation that had come to an abrupt and startling end with the transfer he'd attempted between Elaine and Elodie.

So what was the explanation, could race or species be a factor? And how could that even be possible in a people descended from a single, racially harmonised, group? Had the two mind-types existed in the colonists when they'd arrived 2500 years ago, or had the split occurred some time later?

Only the situation on Erandar gave any clue as to what might possibly have happened.

The discovery of a third mind-type had been made in the year before the Elaine and Elodie incident when a team sent by Harris began testing on Erandar and found a remarkably large proportion of subjects who registered as Alphas, but who in mind-transfer tests proved to be just as incompatible with either Alphas or Betas as those two groups were with each other. Months of development refining the scanning software provided an enhanced level of sensitivity that was able to show the small, but significant, differences between the established mind-type Alpha and the newly found type, now termed "Gamma".

It was possibly the history of the planet which provided an explanation. Erandar had been the first new world to be sub-colonised by the offspring of the original colonists, and the fact that the discovery and conquest had been achieved just four centuries after the first arkship entered Vissan orbit was little short of remarkable. Whether it was fortunate or otherwise for the new residents of Erandar that financial and political problems on Vissan had prevented further contact for hundreds of years had always remained a topic of debate for Union historians, but the result had been the virtual isolation of the planet until the development of FTL nearly two millennia later.

The ship which had taken the colonists to Erandar had carried 25,000 new pioneers on board, a number which should have been enough to avoid the sort of problems which could arise from inbreeding. *Should have*. Unfortunately the outbreak of a virulent plague just a few years into the development of the new colony left less than 5,000 survivors, a much reduced gene-pool. Even so it should still have been enough to minimise the usual range of interbreeding abnormalities, though the geneticists were in agreement that it was worryingly close to the number which could lead to the development of mutations.

So was that the answer then, was the new mind-type a mutation? Other developments in the people of Erandar had certainly occurred, in particular the modern day population benefited considerably from an increased lung capacity that allowed them to capture oxygen from the planet's high-nitrogen atmosphere. It was the very essence of evolution, an advantageous response to a new circumstance.

But what could possibly be gained from the development of a new mind type? What advantage did Gammas have over Alphas? What advantage did Alphas have over Betas? If there was no apparent reason for a change, why change? To create a new mind type thousands of years before the development of the equipment need to detect it seemed nonsensical. But it had happened.

Now the question was, did the knowledge of what had occurred on Erandar lead to an explanation of what had happened to two young women when a transfer between supposedly compatible Alphas had gone so badly wrong? They had to be Alphas because when the scans had been taken the recently upgraded equipment was able to detect easily the differences between Alphas and Gammas. And in any case, the incidence of mind-type Gamma on Vissan was only a tiny percentage of the population and without exception occurred only in subjects who could trace their ancestry back to an immigrant from Erandar.

Harris hoped the answer to his question was "yes". The explanation for what had occurred on Erandar had been the identification of a new mind type, and perhaps a similar explanation might apply to what had happened with Elaine and Elodie. It was possible that one of the girls had not been a true Alpha but a hitherto undiscovered mind type which, as with Gammas, had merely masqueraded as Alpha. If he'd only known before running the transfer he and Raf might have been able to have taken action that would not only have saved the girls' lives but would have advanced his research as well.

Maybe, just maybe, the answer might be locked away in the brain of Bridget Greaves. Bridget, who claimed she was Elaine Smith - it was a most curious and unexplained situation. But that was something that simply was not going to happen, the woman had made it *very* clear she was never going back in a scanner as long as she lived. Harris quite understood her fears.

No, he was going to have to do it the hard way. Part of him groaned when he thought of the task ahead - scanning endless thousands of new subjects, scouring haystack after haystack for one tiny needle, seeking out a difference he knew *had* to be there but which he did not yet understand. Yes, part of him groaned, but the scientist in him was raring to go.

But it wasn't going to be easy. The advantage with the Gammas of Erandar had been that they were present in large numbers and were almost exclusively the residents of a single planet. Now the challenge was to identify another new mind-type which occurred in only a small proportion of the Union's population, and in all likelihood spread further than the bounds of a single planet. A difficult task to be sure, but with a few guesses about exactly what it was he was looking for already in his mind it certainly wasn't impossible.

With Harris's guidance Raf refined and extended the already complex scanning programmes. Harris interpreted the results from the tests he ran on subjects, seeking out the tiny differences that might just be the clue to a new mind-type. Once a tell-tale characteristic had been identified Raf was able to feed the new parameter back into his scanning programmes so that in future the project's bank of super-computers would highlight it automatically. With luck the first few faltering steps would give way to a new march of progress.

After many sleepless nights and a few false trails the team finally struck gold with the identification of a characteristic that occurred consistently in just 0.5% of the population. To Raf's first scanning routine the new mind type appeared to be entirely Alpha. Even the improved version with the ability to spot the Gamma characteristic still showed it as Alpha. But the latest routine picked it out every time - mind type Delta was real.

***

When the authorities finally restored his licence to permit mind-transference experiments to recommence Harris had already built up a useful portfolio of type Delta candidates and was pleased to find that their minds could be swapped from body to body without major problems. It was true that in some cases the "fit" between minds and bodies was poor, but in all cases bodily functions were supported - and in the final reckoning that was what defined a mind type.

So what of the transfer that had gone so wrong? The explanation had to be that it had been a cross between mismatched minds because the unsophisticated scanning routines of the day had been unable to differentiate between an Alpha and a Delta. It went a long way towards explaining the deaths of the two subjects, even a death so horrible as had actually occurred. But why the interaction with an unconnected third party? Theory presented no workable explanation and the idea of repeating the experiment was unthinkable. Sometimes life generated more mysteries than science could ever solve.

3

A Call From Paula

Jon Chandler looked around the room - his room. Not just any room, not just any old office, this was the office of a government minister. Everything about it was just right, everything about it said "Class". The polished oak panelling, the mahogany desk, the tannin smell of row upon row of leather-bound books, the deep pile of the carpet, and the knowledge that just beyond the door which lead into this, the holy of holies, was an entire department: toffee nosed senior civil servants who called him "Sir" and sat when they were offered a seat, row upon row of their underlings, and the vast ranks of the underlings' underlings. All of them at his beck and call. Life at the top was rewarding, very rewarding.

He smiled when he thought of quite a few men and women in the government, now his colleagues whether they liked it or not, who'd tried to keep him out of the party. Maybe their fears that the larger than life ego with its matching playboy lifestyle would drive away the more conservative voters had had some foundation. But others had known that what won votes in the middle ground was charisma and a high media profile. And that was an area where he hadn't disappointed his many followers. His extensive and often expensive love-life had won him regular appearances in the glossy mags that followed celebrities around.

But that had been ages ago - a misspent youth. For over twelve years now he'd been a happily married man - and he'd kept his away matches strictly under wraps.

And although some of the exploits from his earlier days might have put off a few of society's older and more staid members there were many more out there who'd followed his career and knew that the astute business head on the flamboyant shoulders understood better than most how work and pleasure could be kept in their separate camps. "Work hard and play hard" was what his headmaster from long ago had said, and by God it was a motto any true-blooded Chandler would hold dear. The proof of the pudding was, as they said in the eating, and at least a few people must have voted for him because here he was - the well formed alpha-male bum was comfortably ensconced in the sumptuously upholstered seat of power.

So was it enough to have got here? Was it enough to enjoy the power of a senior government position? Had he made the grade? Was it now just an endless round of committees, meetings and business lunches while he held onto the job for long enough to make it into the history books? Emphatically "No". Anyone who knew him would say with absolute honesty it was not. For Jon his post as minister was simply a way to serve, a way to grow even greater success from an already successful organisation. The chance to work late into the night to make sure fourteen billion workers stayed gainfully employed: producing, manufacturing, building, maintaining, repairing, providing services. And if he played his cards carefully there was more than just a chance it might be the stepping stone to greater things.

He was awoken quite suddenly from his reverie. As if punishing him for daring to relax his phone began its irritating warble. He picked up the receiver and held it to his ear - the screen on the desk showed the image of an attractive woman in her early forties - Amey his secretary and PA.

'Mr Chandler. Urgent call for you, from Daluun. A lady.'

Jon's ears pricked up at the mention of Daluun.

'Put her through please.'

There was a brief click and Jon recognised the next voice to speak - Paula Marlow. He knew she was at the conference with Tom.

'Jon, I've got some bad news.'

'Paula, I can hear you clearly, but I'm not getting any video. Can you see me?'

'Sorry Jon, but the link's audio only. It's all I could get.'

'How's it going Paula? Are we making any progress?'

'Jon, I'm afraid the call's got nothing to do with the meeting. We've got other problems at the moment.'

Jon wondered what in hell's name she could be talking about. The threat from the separatists was the biggest danger the Union had faced in over fifteen hundred years. Then his brain clicked in and he guessed the truth, any sort of gathering involving central government was a magnet for another attack.

'Is it another bomb Paula?'

'If you want the good news Jon that's it, it's not a bomb. What we've just experienced here has been an entirely natural event, but it's done more damage than anything the terrorists ever managed. It's been another of those earth tremors they've had down the western coast recently, but this one's been way up the scale and it's devastated the whole of the eastern side of the city. The new Government Hall's in ruins. The central dome just caved in. They're still digging bodies out of the rubble.'

'When did it happen?'

'Mid-morning, just after everyone had assembled ready to start. I'd gone back to the hotel to fetch Tom's notes and that's the only reason I'm alive talking to you now. I got the details from one of the delegates who wasn't too badly injured.'

'Injured? How many?'

'It's not just injuries Jon. There's 177 dead already, Brian Rushmore was one of them.'

Jon was shocked.

'The whole city's in chaos. The local hospitals can't cope so they've been flying people out to Port Preston and Harleston as fast as they can. And they haven't even got them all out yet, there's more of them still trapped under the rubble. No-one knows if they're dead or alive.'

'What about Tom?'

'He was in the seat next to Rushmore so he was right in the worst of it but he's got nine lives that guy. They're saying the only reason he survived was because he managed to crawl underneath the big conference table. It collapsed under the weight of all the concrete that came down from the dome but at least it protected him from being battered to death like some of them were. Seriously Jon, it was a good thing they got him out when they did because he couldn't have lasted much longer.'

'But he's going to pull through?'

'Well he was in a bad way when they got him out. His left leg is broken and they're still X-raying his arm, and he's a mass of cuts and bruises but they took him off the critical just before I phoned you.'

'But Paula, it's only his host who's injured. His own body's safe here in Jackson.'

'It *is* only his host I'll grant you, but if the body had died in there it would have been for keeps. That's what's happened to some of the other delegates who TranzConed in.'

'Somehow that guy was born lucky. When will you be coming back?'

Jon heard an intake of breath from the other end that told him it wasn't going to be quite so easy.

'There are problems Jon. We've been in contact with the host and he's not playing ball. He's got some hot-shot lawyer on board, working on a percentage of whatever he manages to win.'

'Bastard. Can't we do anything?'

'Our lawyer went to see him and his lawyer and explained what had happened, and he made it absolutely clear that none of it was Tom's fault. It's not as though he was doing anything dangerous, that would be outside his contract anyway. So he went through the schedule and offered them twice the standard level of compensation, but they turned him down flat. The guy knows exactly who he's hosting and he's going to milk it for everything he can get.'

'Have they mentioned a figure?'

'Two million.'

'Oh come on, that's just ridiculous. For Belen's sake he signed a contract ……..'

Paula's voice broke in before Jon could say any more.

'Jon, sorry, but he's coming out now. I'll call you back.'

The phone clicked and she was gone.

★★★

By the time Jon turned on his TV the news had moved on to asking why the disaster had happened in the first place. It all centred around the ground tremors, but it just didn't seem possible. There'd been ground tremors recorded on Vissan but in two millennia of monitoring only the most sensitive equipment had ever been able to detect them. There was no way something like that could destroy a building.

The report switched from the studio in Jackson to live video from Daluun. The reporter was interviewing a boffin from the school of geophysics at the university in Port Preston.

'I don't think people elsewhere in the Union appreciate just how much power there is in these tremors. They're orders of magnitude stronger than anything ever recorded on any of the home planets. The whole ground just lifts and shakes and anything man-made falls down. It's due to tectonic plates.'

The reporter was confused. 'Tectonic ..... what?'

'Plates, tectonic plates. They're like islands that ride around deep down in the planet's crust. Normally you wouldn't even notice anything on the surface, but sometimes they collide with each other and then they can cause massive amounts of damage. It's something that happens on young planets - only on young planets.'

The reporter was even more confused. 'I thought Daluun was supposed to be over four billion years old.'

'It is, but that's young as planets go. The home planets are all more than twice that age.'

'But if it's something that could cause such a huge amount of damage, why have we only noticed just recently?'

'That's the question everyone's asking now that something big's happened. The answer is that some people had known for a long time but no-one in authority ever took any notice. They say the fishermen who founded Nagula told stories about the ground moving, but when you remember they were people who stayed in port when there was a full moon because they were afraid of some monster that was going to rise up from the ocean, is it a surprise no-one ever took them seriously.?'

'Yes, but the fishing community moved out decades ago. What about the people who moved in? They can't all have been superstitious types.'

'For some reason we can't even make a guess at the region's been quiet for years. And then just recently it's started happening again, but much stronger than anything anyone had known before.'

'Why hasn't anyone ever carried out a survey?'

The scientist let a tired look show through on his face.

'My department's been investigating ground movements in the coastal area for the past seven years but we've been held back by the lack of equipment. No-one ever thought there was a problem, and "no problem" always means no money to solve it. All we've got at the moment are a few crude monitors the techs knocked up in the workshop - they're better than nothing but it's not a real solution. What we need is a decent budget - in fact if this planet was allowed to keep even half the money it generates from mining there wouldn't be a problem. I blame those clowns in Jackson for what's happened here today.'

'Including the First Minister?'

'Well he's the leader, so he has to shoulder the responsibility.'

'Did you know Mr Hanson is here right now and was injured when the Government Hall collapsed?'

'I assumed he'd be at the conference.'

'Do you think he'll put more money in your direction after today's events?'

'Well he'd be stupid if he didn't, but I think he's left it too late. I'll be voting for Greenwood, he'll get me the money I need.'

4

Mrs Chandler Looks Back

Robert Chandler junior opened his eyes and gazed around the room. Despite the heavy curtains he could see the first rays of the dawn streaming through the gap where the breeze from the open window had blown them apart. Just moments ago he'd been sound asleep but now he was alert, wide awake and ready to take on whatever the new day threw his way. On the other hand, he'd had a busy time the day before so perhaps he owed himself a lie-in. But no, he'd made his mind up, this was no time for sleeping, this was the time to be up and at it, time wasn't there for wasting. He opened his mouth and the scream that issued was little short of ear piercing.

Maureen Chandler rushed into the room and lifted her son out of his cot.

'Oh Bobby, what are we going to do with you?'

She sighed as she looked at the clock, two minutes past five. And Bobby his usual self: hungry, hyper-active and raring to go for another energy draining day. Her mother had told her it got easier after the first one - well she certainly hoped so.

★★★

Seven years later Bobby was a lot nicer to know and was the apple of his father's eye. A clever, bright-eyed boy, full of energy, full of fun, and loving to his parents. In fact all that a mother and father could have hoped for. He was still hyperactive of course, but by now his parents had worked out how to use that feature of his life to their advantage. They kept him busy running around and made sure the little scoundrel had more than enough to do all day, and in the evening they sent him off to his bed worn out and ready for many hours of sleep. And he was under strict orders not to disturb his parents or his siblings until the clock said seven.

When she first knew she was expecting a second baby, Maureen had hoped and prayed that their family might be complete with the arrival of a little girl. It was good that the first-born had been a boy because a man needed a son, and now it would be nice for the next one to be a little girl. She could do her hair in pink ribbons, and they'd play house, and look after dolly - feed her and change her nappy. Then she'd help her mum in the kitchen and it'd be - it'd be just wonderful. So although she never let on to anyone, she was just the tiniest bit sad when the scan said Bobby was going to have a little brother to play with.

Compared to his brother, Andrew Chandler was a very different little animal. As a baby he'd quickly settled down to the idea that when it was dark you slept, and when it was light you scoured the house for things to investigate, usually with the inside of your mouth. Andrew was bright there was no doubt, but so very different from his brother. Bobby had learned to walk by climbing up onto his wobbly young legs, far too soon, and falling over - then getting up, and falling again.

And he did it again and again until finally, by sheer perseverance he didn't fall over any more. Never mind bumps and bruises - they were just an inconvenience a boy had to put up with when there was work to be done.

Andrew was different. He'd sat patiently and observed with the utmost attention to detail as Bobby had marched by, and when his parents were getting just a little worried about their second son's rate of development, he'd simply got up and walked with such confidence they'd have sworn he'd been doing it for years. Now just past his fifth birthday he was a quiet, self-contained boy who took life at a slower pace than his elder brother.

But that wasn't the end of the Chandler clan. Even though Andrew was still only small, Maureen had asked her husband if they could have one more try for the little girl she wanted so badly - and Robert senior had agreed. After all, money wasn't a problem for a family like theirs and the house had enough rooms to accommodate at least one more member.

***

Maureen remembered how she'd held her breath as the cold jelly spread across her stretched stomach and the nurse pushed the probe down onto the goo covered skin. She'd tried for a long time but finally had to report that, because of the way the twins were lying, it was impossible to tell the sex of either. She'd have to wait to find out, just like mothers had had to in ages long past.

The weeks slipped by and the big day finally came when Robert drove her to the hospital, and she was head over heels with joy when she heard the words "It's a girl Mrs Chandler". A girl, she was so happy, and there was still one baby to go. She knew in her heart that two girls was more than she could hope for, so she just laid back and pushed and wasn't in the slightest surprised when the fourth little Chandler was another boy.

Amanda Felicity Knighton Chandler and her brother Jonathan Charles Churchill Chandler were baptised together, and for the whole of their infant lives were like two peas in a pod. Mandy never bothered to notice she was any different from her three brothers, so she wore jeans like them, and she played football with them, and she climbed trees with them, and climbed higher too - even if Martin the gardener had to bring the ladder to get her down again.

As far as the four children were concerned, they were just "the Guys". As the leader, Bobby naturally took the position of "Guy 1", and Andy fell in line as "Guy 2". Jon & Amanda insisted on equal status and neither was prepared to be "Guy 4" even though Amanda told Jon it should be him because he was the youngest. So the twins settled for being "Guy 3 Part 1" and "Guy 3 Part 2", and no-one was ever quite sure which one was which.

Belenfest came round every year and it was in some ways just the tiniest of problems for a little girl because all the usual troop of uncles and aunts could be relied on to provide another couple of dolls or that kind of thing. Some were like babies and cried with a synthesiser voice while others were obviously grown-up women who came with an impressive ensemble of clothes, hats, shoes, accessories, and their absolutely essential ponies. Like the well brought up young lady her parents had wanted her to be she smiled sweetly and thanked them very much. And when her benefactors had finally departed, she packed the dolls back into their boxes, complete with the clothes neatly folded, and put them up on the shelf next to the ones she'd had for her birthday. Boys' toys were much more fun and Jon was always happy to share his.

★★★

By the time Bobby was eight, the Chandler-Wilmott Bank was doing very nicely indeed, and with four children getting bigger by the day it became obvious that more room was going to be needed, so a move up to a new house was decided upon. Jon and Amanda had only the haziest memories of the old house, but Bobby and Andrew remembered, and to them the new residence was the "big house" - and so it was always called.

Perhaps the most prestigious of the Jackson City suburbs, Rosemount was an area which lived up to its name, though only in the springtime when the hillsides were covered in bright cherry blossom. For the rest of the year a variety of green hues swathed the wooded landscape, punctuated only by the occasional grand mansion with its lofty towers and ivy covered walls. As its name suggested the area was certainly a hill, in fact a series of hills and the most popular and expensive plots were those down in the valleys which nestled between the surrounding areas of higher ground. It was in a valley just like this where the big house stood, a majestic old villa built over a hundred years earlier in the style of the time and which offered accommodation that would have put many a small hotel to shame.

And equally impressive were the grounds that surrounded the house. Several hectares of woodland extended in roughly a circle with the grounds close-in laid out to immaculate and well-stocked formal gardens. Terraces, balustrades, stylish urns and statues without arms were the sign of success in Rosemount.

Jon's mother quickly came to love her new home and felt a special affinity for the delightful old summer-house that stood in a commanding position looking down onto the Italianate gardens. So she was sad to hear that the old structure was worn out and would last scarcely more than another year.

Then Maureen's birthday came and she was surprised when the present from her husband came in a large flat envelope. Hastily she tore open the flap and looked inside to find the architect drawn plans for a new building to replace the old one - and then Robert told her the builders would be starting on the job the following week so the work would be finished in time for them to sit together and enjoy the roses as they came into flower. In fact, when the work was finally complete it was clear that, although it did its best to copy the gentile old-world style of the construction it replaced, the new building was quite a lot better. With heating installed and a glassed-in corridor to connect it to the big house it was going to be a lovely place to sit in the cool of the early summer evenings and watch the last rays of the sun as it dropped below the wooded horizon.

The children liked the house too though their father made it very clear they weren't allowed to play in the formal gardens. Balls and boots would do far too much damage to the manicured lawns so the preferred location for games was at the far side of the house in a walled area that might have been home to rows of espalian trees in an era gone by. With a white painted portal and net at either end the area made a creditable football pitch.

But a pitch like that was really a bit big for just two on each side so Bobby found a way through the woods and climbed over the fence into the garden of the house next door to organise a match with the boys who lived there. The offspring of the Freeman family included three brothers, with Steven the eldest about half a year older than Bobby, and the other two a pair of twins about the same age as Andrew. So putting the three of them up against the four Chandlers made for a pretty even contest and the weekly match occupied almost every Saturday afternoon with away games one week at the

Freeman's house and the home game back in the walled garden the week after.

The whole happy scene went on for well over a year until Steven made the bold announcement that girls weren't supposed to play football, and he should know because he'd been playing for years and now he was nearly eleven and a half. Obviously as the senior member of the team he was entitled to lay down the rules, and the order he gave was that Mandy couldn't come to their house anymore. Well Bobby wasn't standing for anything like that and even though Steven was older than him he wasn't afraid and said he was going to fight him for it. Bobby was outraged when the boy told him it didn't matter who won, she still couldn't play so he made it quite clear to the whole team that the ball had been a birthday present from his Uncle Des and if they didn't want Mandy to play they could rely on the fact that he would be taking it home with him.

Edmund and Grahame were Freemans like their brother, so protocol demanded they should support him when important matters were at stake, but they were just slightly disappointed that the games they enjoyed so much were destined to come to an end. So although they never openly said anything that might have undermined the authority of their brother, Bobby welcomed them with open arms the afternoon they trooped up the path through the woods and asked if they could join in. And just to make sure there were no hard feelings they even agreed to let Mandy play on their side. Not to be outdone, Steven announced that in future he would be going to a real football match on Saturdays, and sadly would no longer be available to play with *children*.

Maureen Chandler knew nothing of the involved politics leading up to the change, though she had noticed all the matches were now held in the walled garden and that usually meant she had to clear up after the two Freeman boys as well as her own brood. Now it was late October and the rains that had deserted the region to leave lawns browning in the summer heat had returned in anger, though fortunately for the Rosemount Rovers it had held off that afternoon until almost the end of the match. She held her breath as the door opened and the first of the Guys trooped in leaving a trail of sticky mud right across Mrs Johnson's sparkling kitchen floor. In recent weeks Bobby had become impervious to his mother's scolding, after all, what were they supposed to do when there'd been so much rain? Grown-ups were strange, they never seemed to understand that if you came back clean from football you just weren't doing it right. Tigerstripe looked up, leapt to his feet and made a dash for the sanctuary of the sofa in the room next door - he knew full well the small people weren't allowed in the comfy room till they were clean again. Guy 1 was followed by Guy 2 with the two Guy 3s bringing up the rear. Maureen loved them all, but when she watched four equally mud spattered objects as they stomped into the house she sometimes wondered where the fluffy pink girl she'd wanted so much had gone. Three boys and one tomboy, oh well, perhaps she'd change when she grew up - girls usually did.

David Hulett Wilson

5
Science Fiction Is Bunk

As a boy Jon had been fascinated by "sci-fi" and there was a time when he would read nothing else. He loved the way his heroes teleported down from their space-ships, then they'd shoot each other with ray-guns and travel effortlessly from one end of the galaxy to the other just by disappearing down a worm-hole.

Like so many other children of his generation Andrew had cut his teeth on the same genre, but clever little kid that he was he'd soon seen through it and recognised it for what it was and what it would always be - fiction. And like any good elder brother he was anxious to pass on the knowledge he'd gained, or more importantly the knowledge he'd worked out for himself. In just one afternoon he shattered all Jon's dreams of a wonderful new future. Dematerialising transporters, complete bunk. Worm-holes, total dross. Hyper-space and warp drives, theory did not support such concepts.

But Jon protested that there'd once been a time when faster than light travel had been science fiction, and then the light barrier was broken. Surely that was an example of science fiction coming true?

Andrew had thought about that one for a moment. It was a good point coming from one so young, but undaunted he continued:

'Yes there had been a time when FTL had featured only in fiction, but it was in fact something that had always been there, waiting to be discovered even though the great minds of earlier ages had denied that such a thing could ever be possible.'

Andrew certainly knew his stuff because thousands of years earlier there'd been a man who, for his day, had been seen as a great scientist and who'd had insight greater than any man or woman who'd gone before. He'd observed and, as any good classical physicist would, he'd theorised and he'd presented a totally believable explanation of why the speed of light could never be achieved let alone exceeded. And of course, with the limitations of the technology of his day he'd been right. But in more recent times scientists had agreed that blind acceptance of the great man's theories had held back the development of FTL travel for over a thousand years.

What the man had said was that it was impossible to accelerate anything to the speed of light, and on the basis of action and reaction, if the driving force was slower than the speed of light it followed that the object it was seeking to accelerate could only approach the speed of light and could never equal or exceed it. What he could not have known given the primitive times in which he lived was the essential difference between light and gravity. Unlike light or other electromagnetic emanations gravity was the true fundamental force of the universe. A force which knew no bounds, no speed or time, gravity appeared equally and instantaneously throughout the universe. The secret of the FTL drive had been to harness the power of gravity. Not to create gravity which was found to be impossible, but simply to guide it. By the use of energy in magnitudes almost unimagined by the scientists of earlier ages it had become possible to distort space-time and focus gravity itself. The gravitron drive had been invented.

A complex and power hungry device to build, the operation of the g-drive was simplicity itself. As man-made objects go a starship is large and heavy, though minuscule when compared to the creations of mother nature. Certainly when compared to the grandeur of a planet or a star. But when the gravity of a ship was focussed so that over 99.99% of its mass was directed towards a single distant star it masqueraded as being very massive indeed. In fact it appeared to be orders of magnitude larger than any object ever made by nature itself. And when the two objects were drawn together by an irresistible force the featherweight starship simply "fell" towards the star. Just as gravity was an unlimited force not tied to the mere speed of light, so neither was the new driving force that powered a starship. Light went along at its own pedestrian speed as it had since the universe exploded into existence billions of years before, but now the creations of mankind went much faster. Within limits, so many of the theories postulated by the great man remained true, though as science later realised they were very far from being the whole truth.

6

Jon & Amanda

Jon had watched with interest when his eldest brother brought his new girlfriend up to the big house, and to a boy of twelve the teenaged girl had seemed so grown up. Bobby had been changing too, though for the family who saw him every day it wasn't so easy to notice. It was true he wasn't one of the Guys anymore, but really the Guys didn't exist nowadays. The young man who thought himself almost grown-up didn't bother with Jon & Mandy like he had in the old days, but Jon admired him all the same and couldn't wait to be like him.

But the girlfriend intrigued him. She was a girl in so many ways, and yet she was something different as well. She didn't play games the way children did, but she was kind to him and always said hello. He watched the way she moved, the way she looked like a woman, and he saw how she curved at the back, and at the front too. Jon didn't know what it was that interested him so much, but there was something about her that looked good in a way he couldn't quite explain. Something that made him hold in his breath for just a little too long, and made something in his trousers stir. His young mind tried so hard to fathom the feelings that came to him, exciting and new.

Jon failed to understand it all - Mandy was a girl too, but she wasn't like the girlfriend, she was just his sister and she'd always been there. And it hadn't been so long ago when she'd been happy to come in covered in mud from another football match in the old walled garden. The two of them were still the Guys, or what was left of them. Without Bobby and Andy things were quieter now, but the younger two would play together for hours, two souls who'd never known the abstract concept people called solitude. OK, at school Mandy would go off and play with the girls and he'd be with the boys, but outside school it was just as it had always been.

Sometimes one of them would pick a fight, but it wasn't really about fighting, it was just a scrap, usually about nothing and they'd roll around on the soft carpet of the living room, each one battling valiantly to gain the advantage and get a good wrestling hold because now Mum didn't hold them to her the way she'd done years ago they took pleasure in the closeness of a struggling embrace. First it would be Mandy trying to get her arms around him, then he'd turn the tables and try to pin her down. By now Jon was maybe just a little bigger than his sister, and stronger too, but Mandy could hiss and scratch like Tigerstripe, and when he saw that wild look in her eyes he just knew it said "back off". So romping on the rug was definitely with claws retracted. It had always been that way.

But now there was something different about Mandy too. Jon saw how when she wore a tight tee-shirt the slight swelling of flesh underneath that was so unlike his own, and it was exciting because it *was* unlike his own. The next time they fought he manoeuvred his way round behind her, and in the struggle his hand, ever so accidentally, came up and cupped the squashy mound beneath.

So suddenly that Jon was taken aback, Mandy stopped and sat up. Without a word she turned to face her brother and gave him the sort of look that only a girl could give. Jon and Mandy never romped again.

7

Oh No, Not Me

It was a few hours later when the phone warbled again.

'Mr Chandler, I've got Mr Hanson on the line. Shall I put him through?'

'Straight away Amey. Thanks.'

Jon could see from the blank screen that the circuit was audio-only again, or at least it was coming in his direction.

'Tom, I hear you've had an accident. How's it going?'

The voice he heard was bright and upbeat.

'Operation successful and the patient lived. I take it Paula's filled you in on the details?'

'She explained it. Said it would be some time before you'd be free to travel.'

'That's understatement if I ever heard it. I've got a whole legal army working on it and so far they've not made much progress, but it's early days. My problem now is keeping the Union running. I can handle routine business by phone and I could even do holopresence into the chamber if they didn't mind seeing me laid up like this. But if I'm going to be stuck here for weeks there's no way I can make it to any of my off-planet appointments. Some are more important than others of course. Most of them can just get cancelled or postponed, but there's a biggy coming up. If I can't get there myself we need someone to represent the Union at the Phoenixan accession conference. Someone from the top of the tree.'

Jon's heart skipped a beat when he realised the purpose of Tom's call.

But there was no doubting just how important Phoenix was to the Union. Discovered just fifteen years ago the planet was rumoured to be the home world of the civilisation that had launched the missions to colonise Vissan, Miranda and Temenco. If that failed to make the planet of more than just a little interest then nothing would. For the past decade the Union had operated a Mission on the planet as a step towards opening an embassy and setting up full interplanetary relations, and three years ago the star-liner Lysander had set off from Darius carrying Anthony Cochrane and his diplomatic team - but they'd never arrived. Somehow, somewhere, the ship had gone missing from an established interstellar route and over a year of searching had found nothing. The incident was entirely without precedent.

'Oh no Tom. Not me. You know I don't do swaps.'

Tom paused just long enough to take in a breath.

'Jon, right now my people in Jackson are looking to see who else is available, and there's every chance they'll find someone. All I'm asking at the moment is for you to be the long-stop. If there really isn't anyone else I need a man of the right calibre to back me up, someone I can really rely on. I'm not asking you to make a decision right here and now, I'm just asking you to consider it.'

Jon had already thought, he'd already considered it a thousand times. The answer had been "No" every time, and it was still "No". He was going to tell Tom straight. The voice from the other end came back on the line sounding more urgent than ever.

'Jon, they're pulling the phone out of my hands. They say I've got to rest before I go in for the next operation. I'll call you back when I can.' The line went dead.

Jon pressed a button on the intercom.

'Mr Chandler,' came Amey's reply.

'Did you get a time code on that call?'

'11.25 in the morning Mr Chandler.'

Jon looked at his watch, 14.35 here on Vissan, so the two planets would have synchronised daytime hours for the next few weeks. It was going to be an advantage in the coming days.

8
Bobby & Celia

Years had passed since a group of children had called themselves "the Guys", and now Maureen Chandler could scarcely believe the eldest of her brood was a student entering his second year at university. And the best university on Vissan for a student to read accountancy was the School of Economics in Jackson, so it had been the obvious choice for a young man with an "A-star" in every subject he'd ever taken.

With a home in the outer suburbs it would have been possible for Bobby to have travelled into the city each day, but his father had insisted he should embrace university life to the maximum and take a place in the halls of residence. And that was fun for the first year, but all good things come to an end and for those moving up to their second year, finding a house or flat to share was the order of the day. Although he'd been a regular visitor to his old home Maureen had missed him a lot and suggested he should come back up to the big house to live - then he could move back into halls for his final year. But the idea of living with a group of mates was too much of a temptation, and besides, they wanted a place they could bring girls back to that was well outside the gaze of nosy parents.

And when it came to girls, Bobby had been a star performer right from the very first disco of fresher's week. Confident, good looking, captain of the rugby team, and hunky in the way girls just seemed to like he'd never had any trouble attracting the sort of attention that only females could give. He'd never made anything of the fact that he came from money, but his dates usually found out anyway. Just letting on that your folks lived in Rosemount usually gave the game away.

And it was that type of girl Bobby's father had begun to worry about - gold-diggers. He'd never sought to control how his son lived his life, as long as he devoted enough time to his studies then it was OK to have some fun, and he knew that fun usually meant girls. And that was OK too, provided they were only to play with and not for keeps - so he wasn't too concerned when he started to hear about "Celia this" and "Celia that". Maureen could see straight away that if they wanted to meet their son's latest love they'd have to invite the two of them up to the house.

When Bobby drove Celia up to the big house one Sunday morning his parents realised just what he saw in her. The words pretty and vivacious scarcely did the girl credit. The long dark hair, the aquiline nose, the deep eyes, her sultry looks. The girl was a stunner, Andrew and Jon could vouch for that. Mandy was polite though she kept her distance. And the girl seemed to have some manners, nicely brought up, though somehow she looked just a little out of place in the kind of grand house where a family such as the Chandlers lived.

***

Back in his office on Monday morning Robert Snr was getting increasingly concerned because after spending a few hours on the phone and the internet, nowhere could he find any mention of the girl's family. Bobby had said they lived in Jackson, so he'd asked his colleagues from work and the club, and he'd searched through the directories of all the city firms. But no-one knew anything about a family that went by the name of "McArthur".

Robert called his son on the phone that afternoon when he knew lectures would have finished for the day and fired some pretty frank questions at him. But Bobby was more distant than he'd ever known him. Even at his tender age he was as wily as an old politician, and though the two of them spoke for over an hour, each time the tack of the conversation moved even vaguely towards affairs of the heart, the younger man had skilfully steered back onto another course. Robert Snr knew exactly what his son was telling him - if there'd been anything good to say, he'd have said it.

When six months had passed Robert knew his son was still with the girl although Bobby never mentioned her by name anymore. And it was over three months since she'd last come up to Rosemount. Bobby had tried to explain to his parents how they always made Celia feel uncomfortable even though they made at least an effort to appear friendly and hospitable.

The worst news of all had come from the private detective Robert had hired. He read the report and shook his head. The McArthur family lived in a rented house on the Undercliffe estate and her father worked as a labourer, when he could be bothered - so most of the time the family lived on benefits. Robert didn't know whether to be outraged or just disappointed. For his son to have a girl like that as a plaything was something he might possibly have understood, but if they were still together after all this time, what message did that send? It was beyond his worst nightmares.

When summer came the older Chandlers saw just one ray of hope. Bobby and Pete, a friend from university, had gone travelling together and the detective reported that Celia had stayed in Jackson. Maybe things might be cooling, if only a little? When the boys returned and the final year at university was about to start Maureen begged her son to come back and live at home, but he told her there was no chance, life at the flat was too much fun.

If he'd been concerned before, Robert was worried sick by what his detective reported next - Bobby's two mates never came to the flat anymore, but Celia was often seen to arrive during the day - and she never left until the following morning.

★★★

Bobby graduated and it would have been a surprise to everyone for him to be awarded anything other than a first, so for a while his parents forgot their problems and threw a party for him at the big house. It was quite a do with professional caterers, a well stocked bar and a marquee out on the lawn, and with almost everyone Bobby had ever known in his life in attendance the house and garden hummed with activity. Everyone had fun, and most of them drank rather a lot too so for the first time since the Chandlers had taken up residence there all the bedrooms were pressed into service. *She* was there of course, and *she* stayed the night in Bobby's room - but both Robert and Maureen agreed it was better than them driving back to the flat after downing so many drinks.

With university over and the memory of it fading into the past, Bobby's next move was into the junior position at Chandler-Wilmott that had waited patiently almost since the day he was born. He was well qualified of course, though the joke the staff kept away from the old man was that the fresh-faced youngster would have to work his way up from the bottom - even if it took all afternoon.

But for a while Robert Snr was just a little happier. Now he saw his son every day and was able to get him alone when the two of them went to lunch. Maybe he was even in a position to exert a little pressure on the boy, especially since his career had begun and he needed to look ahead to which way life would take him. Robert tried every which way to bring up the subject of his son's marriage plans, but Bobby would never be drawn into any sort of discussion that involved Celia. He loved and respected his father and knew how easily a discussion might become an argument.

With money coming in now and no longer any need to hide anything about his background it wasn't long before Bobby took a step up in the world and moved from the scruffy student flat to a smart new down-town apartment. As Bobby well knew, his father disliked the modern style, but the location overlooking both Pioneer Gardens and the river was superb. And with the business district just ten minutes walk away the place was ideal for an up and coming young executive.

But this time there was no attempt to conceal the truth. The detective reported that the bellpush in the lobby had the names "Chandler" and "McArthur" by the side of it.

9

Unclean!

The phone warbled. Jon glanced at the time as he picked it up - 19.15 here on Vissan so it was late afternoon on Daluun.

'Mr Chandler, I've got Mr Hanson on the line again.'

'Put him through please Amey.'

Jon heard the click as the line connected. He looked down at the screen and saw that this time the call included video.

'Tom. What's the latest, any progress with the host?'

'Things are looking a *bit* better, all thanks to Paula. We're working on two fronts. Our lawyer's made the host an offer, and it's a good one.'

'How much?'

'Half a million. It's a lot less than he was after but for an ordinary working guy it's still a lot of money.'

'What if he turns it down? What's the other line of attack?'

'Attack - that's a good word Jon. I think you've hit the nail on the head. I've got a man in Jackson who's going to tell him, in a reasonably polite manner, that if he doesn't accept our very generous offer he'll have to swap back for the standard compensation when we eventually get a reclamation order through. And then he's going to check there are no witnesses in earshot before he points out that his body here on Daluun might just have another accident. I wonder how he'd feel if he broke his other leg …. and possibly his good arm into the bargain?'

Jon grinned to himself. He knew that when push came to shove his boss could play hardball with even the heaviest weight opponents, but this plan sounded tougher than normal.

'Would you really do that?'

Jon looked down at the screen, the grinning face he saw there told him the answer was an uncompromising "yes".

'Jon, I don't know if it's still true, but there was a time when you'd have done it.'

Jon frowned. 'Where do you get your gen from?'

'You don't get to be First Minister without listening to the rumours, and then working out which of them are true,' Tom said slyly, as usual giving away slightly less than nothing.

'So you're pretty confident you'll be back then?'

'They've given the host till tomorrow morning to think it over and our lawyer is drafting the agreement for him to sign right now. We'll find out soon, but it's not going to be soon enough.'

Jon felt his heart go thump. 'Why not?'

'Medical reasons, so they tell me. It'll be days before the general anaesthetic wears off and I can't go into a transfer till the body's completely clear. Too many chances of side-effects, or so they tell me. Then the rules say I have to spend a minimum of 48 hours in my own body before I can travel again. It'll be good to get back to Jackson but there's no way I'm going to make it to the Phoenix conference.'

Jon steeled himself to ask the question.

'Have you had any success finding someone represent you?'

The brief silence that followed told him the news wasn't good.

'That's what I'm calling about Jon. Max and Paula were on the phone all the time I was under and so far they haven't come up with anyone suitable.'

'Couldn't you send Marcus?'

'He's on Miranda, in his own body. There's no way he could possibly get there in time.'

'Well what about Stacey?'

'She's with Marcus.'

'Well Felix then.'

'He's on a transfer to Antonby investigating the hydraulic relocation project. And really he's not the right guy for the job.'

The silence was oppressive. Jon guessed Tom was waiting - for as long as it took. What was that technique called, the aggressive use of patience? At last Jon gave in.

'So you're coming back to me then?'

'Jon, I told you earlier I needed someone I could rely on.'

But if all the others can pass the buck, why does it have to be me?'

'Maybe it's just a question of luck. You're the only senior member of the government who's actually on Vissan at the moment, and you're the man I need.'

Jon was about to break in but Tom was too fast.

'Now hear me out on this one, I know what you've said in the past, I know you've never transferred before and you've told me the reasons a thousand times. But come on, if you're going to go further in your career you've just got to get real and use the technology available.'

Jon drew in a deep breath. 'Tom, it's alright for you and all the others, but where do I find a host? I mean, Deltas are scarce enough anyway and my sub-group's about as rare as hen's teeth. You just don't understand how it is for people like me.'

The face on the screen was nodding rapidly.

'OK Jon, I know there's a shortage of Deltas in the galaxy. God works in strange ways but it doesn't mean there's a total absence. Other people like you, Deltas, *can* do it, and they *do* do it. It's not difficult, you find a few people of your own mind-type who are just right for you, one on each planet, put them on a retainer to be available exclusively to you, and then you travel in and out whenever you want. It's not as if you're short of money or anything and it's on expenses anyway.'

If Tom had been looking at his screen right then he'd have seen the worried look on Jon's face.

'Tom, I've been OK up to now travelling in my own body. It's not really that far to Miranda and Temenco, and I did a holopresence meeting on Erandar last week.'

'Jon, we all know how much you enjoy travelling on your liners but you know as well as I do it's out of the question for a journey like this, and there are no holopresence facilities on Phoenix. They never managed to build a working system for themselves and the equipment they ordered from Darius is still somewhere out in space.'

'I don't like it Tom.'

'Liking it isn't part of the job Jon - it's a question of duty. And here's something you need to take on board, if you do right by others, they'll do right by you. And if you didn't pick up on that one I'll make it clear for you. The election's coming up next year and you could be the man to replace me. I've already promised you my support but it's something that works both ways - if you do want to go for it you're going to have to give me your support - right now.'

'Tom, you *know* I want your help. I'm going to need it to stand a chance of getting selected, but there's a limit to what I'm prepared to do. We've been through it all before.'

Jon looked at the screen and saw the customary smile had left the First Minister's face.

'Jon, I'm not going to waste my time arguing. You're my only hope and I'm relying on you. What part of "don't let me down" is giving you a problem?'

Jon mumbled as he searched for an answer.

'Look Jon, I've got to go. The quacks want me to get some rest before the next op and there's one standing next to me tapping his watch. But just one thing before I go, did you know Horace Walton's a D2, and he's on Phoenix right now? He's due back on Vissan any time soon so I'll bet you could use his host. Give him a call and see what he says.'

Jon was more than just a little surprised.

'Horace has a D2 host on Phoenix?'

'A very good one if you ask me, Andrew Westinghouse I think they call him. I was talking to Horace on a video link a few days ago and I'd say the guy was young, handsome and fit. And don't tell anyone I said this, but for a bit of extra dosh he even lets the randy old sod use his body for those things the contract normally excludes. And I'm sure I don't have to explain that one to a man of your accomplishments, Jon.'

The line clicked and the screen went blank. Jon thought about what Tom had said and realised it was true. After the debacle of what had happened last time they were in office the democrats had never really regained the sort of credibility they needed to win another election. Whoever got the Harmony party's blessing was going to be the next First Minister, the most powerful man in the galaxy. And it could be him. He wanted it, he wanted it so badly.

He leaned towards his desk and pushed the button on the intercom.

'Amey.'

'Mr Chandler.'

'Amey, can you make me a booking with TranzCon. I'm going to Phoenix.'

'But Mr Chandler, you said you didn't do mind-swaps. I think you swore on someone's grave.'

'Well things change Amey. I've changed my mind, or at least I've had it changed for me.'

★★★

Back in the quiet of his office Jon leaned back into the big leather chair and thought about the venture he'd just committed himself to. Had he been too hasty? Was he really doing the right thing?

Maybe he might have liked the idea better if he'd been a shareholder in the company who carried out all the mind-swaps and was going to make money out of his trip. But he didn't own a single share in TranzCon. Somehow he'd missed the boat with the company whose business it was to send their clients out across the galaxy by the *Trans*fer of *Cons*ciousness (the switch from "s" to "z" was made on the orders of the marketing department who claimed it made the logo more flashy). It wasn't the sort of slip investors of Jon Chandler's calibre normally made.

Ever since his amazing success with Rapier and all the other acquisitions he'd made in the space transport field, he'd prided himself he was up to date with the latest developments and could sort out the sure-fire winners from the plodders, or at least the plodders from the no-hopers. He kicked himself because TranzCon stock had climbed relentlessly up the index in the week before its launch, and on the first day of service its shares had gone almost through the roof.

But it had been just too outlandish, too risky to put money into. The idea of travelling to other planets by swapping minds with a host body already there at the other end? Surely something so inherently dangerous was never going to get a licence to operate? Even if it did, the first sign of trouble would surely have closed it down. Then where would the investors be? It simply wasn't commercially viable.

As a toy to amuse a few well-funded scientists the idea was fascinating and for many years that was as far as it had gone. For decades they'd known about the technique of swapping minds from body to body ever since a research team had succeeded in carrying out the first consciousness transfer between a pair of experimental chimps. But the word was they'd kept very quiet about how many of their hairy travellers had died before they achieved that first success.

The work went on but even after they'd developed the technique to an acceptably high degree of reliability it was still little more than a curiosity. The only money anyone was ever going to make from swapping chimp minds into other chimp bodies was from making documentaries to sell to the TV channels which specialised in the science and technology fields. Then two of the scientists from the team made the news in a big way when they swapped their own minds. The government wasn't exactly happy about the way they'd flaunted the rules but they'd made a point and had opened the door to experimentation with human volunteers. And that was something that had fired the imaginations of many.

The most obvious application of the technique was travel. The ability to transfer instantaneously to a distant planet was very attractive indeed. Then a number of the Union's richer inhabitants had looked at the idea with interest, particularly the older members who'd seen the possibility of trading in a wrinkled old body for a lower mileage model, with a bit of money changing hands in the process of course.

The first had been slapped down hard when it was admitted that the communication systems of the day were simply not up to the task. Perhaps it might be possible to transfer from one point on a planet's surface to another, or maybe even out as far as a moon, but the GBeam system of intersolar communication lacked the capacity to carry anything as demanding as the gargantuan data flow that was essential for mind-transference. And it was made very clear, the system lacked the potential to ever be developed to the sort of bandwidth needed.

The government had nipped the other application in the bud. "Body theft" as it was termed, would carry a severe penalty whether money was involved or not. The old would have to stick with the established methods of replacing their worn out bodies one piece at a time.

The church was against the whole idea, of course. The mainstream governing body hadn't exactly threatened anyone with excommunication but the radical factions had wasted no time in denouncing the whole business as the work of the Devil. No committed adherent would ever participate in moving their mind to another body. It wasn't what God had intended for her people.

Then there'd been the first human deaths. Two perfectly healthy volunteers who'd previously swapped with other volunteers had died for no apparent reason. When a second pair died in exactly the same way the research had been stopped immediately. And that was it, mind transference was as good as dead on its feet. There would never be any practical application and certainly never any commercial application.

But not everyone had been prepared to give up quite so easily. After a moratorium that was surprisingly brief the research had been allowed to re-commence. How the researchers had ever got their licence back was anyone's guess. How they'd ever found more human guinea pigs was another. Someone with money was greasing palms - maybe. But why?

The first breakthrough came with the discovery of mind types. For an entirely unpredicted and unexplained reason humans possessed a number of separate and incompatible mind-types, a characteristic that had never been detected in any of the animal test subjects. The first two types discovered were termed "Alpha" and "Beta", and it was found that if mind-swaps were always carried out between compatible subjects no deaths occurred. Well almost no deaths. The subsequent discovery of the minority mind-types "Gamma" and "Delta" had followed and went some way towards explaining the deaths that had occurred. Then the designation "Epsilon" had come along to group together the tiny number of renegade minds which stubbornly refused to be categorised.

Something which had been known from an early stage was that a transfer had to be completed within a set time. If the delay was even micro-seconds too long the subjects died. But the team working on this aspect of the research had already postulated the solution and their next efforts proved that their hypothesis had been right. Although the life-force which formed the consciousness of a human being was still something unknown and unquantifiable the memories which went with it were well understood, and it was realised that to function adequately a mind simply did not need access to all the memories with which it was normally associated. All that was needed were the most recent or relevant memories and with the massive advances in computer power that had been made it became possible to sort and filter every thought or experience a person had ever had. Of course there were limits. With access to less than 10% of their memories transfer subjects became confused and unable to function. With 50% available the loss of memories went completely unnoticed, and 25% was a workable compromise.

At a stroke the technique cut the size of the data transfer dramatically and yet the communication bandwidth needed was still much larger than anything in service or being developed. Progress had been made of course, the original GBeam system which had struggled to carry anything more than a very limited throughput of off-line data had been extended over the years by refinements to the modulation techniques employed. In its improved form the beam could handle live video and a couple of TV channels but that was the end of the line - mind-swap transfers were still no more than a dream.

And then a breakthrough came that increased beam capacity by a factor of almost twenty. Overnight the frontiers had been pushed back when the latest development introduced a new generation of wide-band transmitters capable of handling real-time hologram projection along with the standard fare of high bandwidth data, multi-channel TV, and several thousand video calls. And yet it still wasn't enough.

In the end the solution came from a group of consciousness-transfer experts who found that if the mind's activity could be reduced to a level substantially lower than normal the transmission bandwidth required came within the bounds of what the next stage of beam improvements promised it could provide. At last a working system was on the horizon.

Using a pair of heavily sedated chimps as test subjects the first intersolar transfer was carried out using the newly upgraded link between Vissan and Miranda, and it worked.

Just days later the test was repeated with humans. It was true that both travellers were well and truly zonked when they arrived and took four days to recover from the so-called "flat-line" condition to which they had been subjected, but it was still faster than travelling by liner. When a new generation of rapid-clear drugs was developed the prospect of mounting a public service became at least a possibility. After six months of testing the TranzCon company was formed and the service was launched.

Or at least it was for the Alphas who made up 63% of the Union's 30 billion inhabitants and the Betas who made up the next 29%. For the non-mainstream members of the population, travelling by the new service was not so straightforward.

After the Alphas and the Betas, the third largest mind-type group was Gamma, and although its members existed in considerable numbers, the fact that over 99% of their kind lived on a single planet made travelling elsewhere in the Union quite a problem.

Then finally came the Deltas, nature's "also ran" group. The "forgotten few" as the media dubbed them. A people spread equally between the eight habitable planets of the Union but who represented only a tiny proportion of its population. And if that hadn't been bad enough the next phase of research revealed that the mind-type was split into two or possibly three largely incompatible sub-groups.

So what chance was there of finding a host when a person belonged to a mind-type shared by only a few thousand others? Science would have the answer, they'd find a solution to the problem very soon, or at least that was the promise. But so far it hadn't happened.

Jon hated TranzCon. As a rare Delta2 it had made him a mental leper.

10
Jon's Career Choice

Although he'd never appreciated the fact while he was growing up, Jon's future had been mapped out almost since the day he was born. It was the same for all four of the siblings - a private education, university, a move into the family firm, a couple of years to rise up through a carefully selected array of junior positions, and one day the Chandler children would take over from their father, just as Robert Snr had taken over from their grandfather. This time though, there were a few differences, Robert Chandler Snr had four bright, healthy and able children, and that made the situation quite different from what had happened fifteen years earlier when he'd inherited the top job from his father Max.

Max Chandler and Charlie Wilmott had started up their bank to fund a range of projects they thought had been dismissed just a little too quickly by the bigger players of the finance industry. It was history now to say they'd chosen their investments well because seven of the top 100 companies in the Union were ones that Chandler-Wilmott had supported through some difficult early years. The two men had had so much in common back in those early days and had been the best of friends as well as being business partners. As family men they'd both married and looked forward to the days when sons, daughters and heirs would begin to fill their houses. But fate can be cruel and who would have guessed in those days so long ago why luck would visit one, and would pass the other by. Max was blessed with two strong healthy sons, Desmond and Robert, and both boys had showed promise from an early age. Charlie was not so lucky. His first child, a boy, was born with a mental disability, and the second child, a girl, died soon after birth. With a diagnosis of a genetic abnormality from somewhere in the lineage Charlie's wife had told her husband "no more", so sadly he was never father to the heir he'd hoped for. And although he never said as much, he envied his business partner when he brought his young sons into the bank to show them what work was all about.

Although Desmond was perhaps the brighter of the two boys, there was something of the rebel about him, and perhaps it was in his time at university he'd realised he'd never be happy spending thirty years playing second fiddle to his father. So after a couple of years learning his trade in the bank he'd left to start up on his own, and he'd done very well too. And so it was always understood that when Max stood down, control of the bank would go to Robert - the younger brother had never had any competition for the post. It was certainly true the Chandler-Wilmott Bank went on to greater things, particularly with Robert's safe hand on the tiller, and Desmond never begrudged his brother the wealth he accumulated so easily. Neither did he ever regret his own departure from what was surely a steady and comfortable life. He was his own boss, and that was all he would say on the matter.

But this time things were different. Bobby was an exceptionally able boy and could have excelled at any career he'd chosen, so it was without doubt he was going to follow his father and when the time came, he'd assume control of the bank. Then there was Andrew, the next in line. A very different boy everyone agreed, perhaps not as outgoing, but certainly no less bright than his brother. So where did that leave Jon, third son and fourth child? Centuries earlier he'd have been destined for a comfortable life in a country parsonage.

Jon looked at his life, and his future. With his two elder brothers going before him it was plain to see there'd never really be a place for him at the bank. He could do a Desmond and take on some new venture that the family bank was now too big to get involved in. Maybe that was his destiny, but the bank had so much money these days, there really wasn't any need for another entrepreneur to boost the family fortune.

The more he looked, the more he saw that his life could, should and would follow a different course. The careers people at school had made sure he knew all about the jobs a young man like himself would be suited to, a lawyer, an engineer, an architect. All worthy professions to be sure, but one job, one vocation, a calling, stood head and shoulders above the rest. Not an easy course to study, not an easy qualification to get, but for the clever few with the brains and the dogged perseverance, what an opportunity, what a chance to do something real, what a chance to do good for people in their thousands, millions even? The more he looked, the more he knew that the only job he really wanted to do was to be a doctor, a medical doctor.

For weeks he agonised over how he could break the news to his father that going into the family firm was not his choice of profession. Maybe his father would see it as a desertion, a vote of no confidence, a rejection. But Jon knew inside himself it was none of those things. If only he could make his father see it as he saw it. Finally the time came and his heart was thumping madly as Robert Snr closed the door to his study to sit and discuss with his son what it was that was so important that a meeting in private was warranted.

Jon explained it all to his father who listened intently, and to his surprise actually listened until he'd finished. He sat looking into his father's eyes, wondering what the old man was going to say, whether he might actually give his approval, or whether he might throw him out into the street right then. He could scarcely believe his ears when his father's face brightened and he said,

'Jon, I think it's a splendid idea. I did wonder how you were all going to fit in at the bank. And to take up such a wonderful profession, a profession that cares for people. Jon, you have my blessing and you have my support.'

The most wonderful words a son could hope to hear.

But Robert Chandler was not a man who did things by halves. Now Jon's future was mapped out all over again. He'd go to the very best medical school, into a hospital as a junior intern, promotion to registrar, qualify as a surgeon, then a consultant. If Robert Chandler had his way his son would be driving forward the whole of medical science one day. That was Father all over, there was no room for anything mediocre or second rate in his business, or his family.

If there was any part of Jon's decision that Robert wasn't entirely sure about it was the money Jon would make as a doctor. He put it to his son.

'Jon, I respect your choice of career and I will always stand by you, but with young people, they sometimes don't consider the bigger picture. Have you thought about the salary you'll earn as a doctor? It wouldn't be anything like the sort of money you'd make in the banking business.'

In truth Jon hadn't given it much thought at all, though he couldn't lose face by admitting so. Their family GP and other doctors the family knew all seemed to live in nice houses. Perhaps not quite in the same league as the Big House, but still quite a way above average. And surely a qualified doctor would make a good enough living to keep a wife and family. What more did a man need? He told his father that everything was in hand. He'd got it all worked out.

★★★

So after Jon had completed his time at high school he was proud that first day when he'd walked up the steps into the lovely old stone-built hall in the leafy suburbs of Regenswood. Six years he was going to be here, either at the medical school or working in the nearby hospitals, and when he'd finished he'd be a doctor. The very first man in either the Chandler or Knighton families to become a doctor.

Although it had been rebuilt a few times during the intervening millennia, Regenswood was a nice old place with a history that went all the way back to a time just a few years after Hermione Jackson and her team made planet-fall on Vissan. When the pioneers' first settlement had reached an unmanageable size with its massive population of over 15,000, the elders had decided that was about as big as a town ought to be and had drawn up plans for a new community a hundred kilometres to the north-west.

Now that the city which a thousand years later finally dropped the word "Landing" from its official title had grown to the metropolis of over five million souls that was all anyone alive could remember, the distance between Jackson and Regenswood had reduced somewhat, but the sixty km of countryside that still separated the two cities was just right in so many ways. Far enough away that Jon felt comfortable in the knowledge that at last he could live his life outside the watchful gaze of his parents, but close enough that a half hour train-ride would get him back to his home city for the weekend. Though with so much to interest a young man going on down town he often found it easier to stay in Bobby's spare room and borrow the car to drive out to Rosemount for Sunday lunch, sometimes taking his new girlfriend Liz to meet them. Bobby hardly ever went to see his parents these days, and Jon was well aware of the reason.

Liz Stuart was a girl Jon had met at Regenswood when she'd arrived there just as he was starting his second year. His friends always ribbed him he'd just been out to see what he could pull from the new meat on display during fresher's week, and probably they'd been right at the time, though things had developed over the following months until the two young medical students were very much an item.

Robert and Maureen liked their son's choice of girlfriend very much and had welcomed her in with open arms, but that had been confusing to Jon. The way Liz had been so easily accepted had made it all the more obvious that Celia was still not considered a suitable partner for his brother - well not for a first son anyway. Perhaps expectations were lower for those further down the pecking order.

Why they did they have to hate her so badly? Jon could see she was just right for Bobby and he felt happy to know that such a lovely girl might one day become his sister-in-law. If only his parents would allow her to get closer, maybe they might change their minds.

But he knew the story and understood his parent's prejudice. Celia had come from humble beginnings and had missed out on the kind of education the sons and daughters of the rich took for granted - but was that a reason to dislike her so? She and Bobby made such a good couple and it was plain to see they were very much in love. So perhaps it was out of consideration for parents too high in the clouds to accept the idea of a daughter-in-law from the wrong side of the tracks that Bobby & Celia were never formally engaged, though Jon and the others knew they considered themselves to be so. And when two years later the date of their wedding was announced, the tell-tale signs Liz noticed when they stayed for the weekend indicated that maybe the first member of the next generation of the Chandler family might be arriving very soon. Perhaps the only way to tackle a bull was to take it by the horns.

11
Looking For A Host

Knowing what lay ahead of him Jon had found it difficult to settle to any of his regular work. Yes, he'd told Tom he'd be going to Phoenix and at the time he'd really meant it, but that had been in the heat of the moment. Tom hadn't really left him any choice. But what was he to do? Go back on his vow never to embrace the technology that was TranzCon, or accept as inevitable that his only alternative was relegation to the political sidelines? Politically things were quiet on Vissan, in fact things had been quiet on Vissan for hundreds of years and most of what happened here at home could be run by the civil service anyway. Maybe there was more doing on the other home planets, but really not that much. Tom had never been in any doubt about where his efforts were needed most. He'd always seen his role as a leader who got out onto the frontier planets to do his bit towards binding more worlds ever closer, and he was good at it too.

But Tom was an Alpha, the most common mind-type by far. The lucky man had his choice of hosts anywhere in the galaxy. He selected people who looked reasonably like his own body, and he'd worked up a budget to pay for them all to have suits, coats, shirts, ties, shoes and the whole kit'n caboodle in exactly his own style. He liked them to have the same hair and he'd even paid for one balding guy on Erandar to have a transplant because he hated having to wear a wig. With a bit of make-up the image was complete on all eight habitable planets of the Union. And when you saw the main man on TV hundreds of light-years from home you'd have sworn he'd travelled there in his own body.

So Jon knew Tom was right when he said TranzCon was the only practical way to travel for visits to the outer planets. Of course it lacked the style, the splendour, and the comfort of a 1st class passage on a star-liner. But when he stopped and thought of the kind of schedule Tom managed - a summit conference on Temenco, a top level security meeting on Daluun, opening some new building on Antonby, a media briefing on Darius, and back for questions in the house here on Vissan it was clear there were some lifestyles that only TranzCon could support. A week could be a long time in politics, but when a man could travel nearly 700 light-years and still spend Sunday afternoon with a beautiful wife and two lovely daughters Jon wondered if he hadn't considered TranzCon seriously enough. Maybe this was a new beginning for him, but why couldn't God have made him an Alpha like Tom and Stacey, or a Beta like Marcus and Felix?

He typed a few characters in at the keyboard and waited while the screen pulled up a mugshot and a page of spiel. Andrew Westinghouse, resident of Celebration. Tall enough at 1.8 metres, not slim but certainly not fat, nice face, full head of hair, tidy appearance, clean bill of health, and just 37 years old. So what if there were only a few suitable hosts, with one like this who needed more? In any case, and despite his connections with the space transport business he'd wondered what it would be like to travel by TranzCon.

"Go for it Jon" he said to no-one but himself.

12

The Meeting With Bobby

Robert Chandler Snr was just a little surprised to see the sleek red shape that motored up the drive and stopped outside the garage block. He'd seen Bobby at the office earlier that day and the atmosphere had had its usual icy feel, so why would he come calling now?

Having shed the finery of the bespoke suit that was de-rigueur for anyone of his rank at Chandler-Wilmott, the younger man had changed into casual clothes for the evening. As he walked into the room he threw his jacket over the back of the chair and sat down to face his father.

'I've come to discuss an important matter with you,' was his opening gambit.

His father watched him without betraying any sense of emotion. Obviously the matter was important because otherwise his son wouldn't have bothered to drive all the way out to Rosemount.

'We've got all evening Bobby, you can stay for supper if you've got time. I know it's a while since you were here last but you're always welcome. You know that.'

Bobby pulled himself up straight in his chair, not entirely sure how to raise what was clearly a difficult subject. After a few moments he finally spoke.

'I'll come straight to the point Father. I know you've not been happy about my choice of partner these past three years and you've done your best to scare her away, but by now it should be obvious it's not going to work. What I've come to ask you, and I'm only going to ask once, and please understand that I'm not begging, I'm not giving Celia up and I want you and Mum to accept her as your daughter-in-law.'

His father sighed and looked down at the carpet. He'd known before his son had spoken even his first word there was only one subject for them to discuss.

'We left you alone to have your fling Bobby, sow a few wild oats the way young men do. But we always thought that one day you'd want to settle down. We've waited for you and we're still waiting. We'll wait as long as it takes for you to come back into the family, and we'll do everything we can to help you find the right sort of girl, someone from your own background. You've got everything going for you, you could have your pick of any number of girls, clever, rich and beautiful girls. It's only a few years since you were getting on so well with Melissa, and if we spoke to her father I'm sure he'd let bygones by bygones if there was a chance of a union with a family like ours.'

'Melissa's a nice girl.'

'Nice! Melissa's a fabulous girl.'

'OK, OK, she's fabulous. But I didn't love her, I don't love her now and I could never love her.'

'Love!' Robert shouted out loud. 'Who said anything about having to love her? We're trying to build a dynasty here. Money and genes are what matter. Love doesn't come into the kind of marriages we're talking about.'

'But you and Mum, you've always been so happy together. Me and the others all assumed you were in love with each other.'

His father looked him in the eye, fidgeting with his fingers and gently chewing at his lower lip.

'The way it's turned out, your mother and I have been lucky, very lucky. Our families intended us for each other from an early age, and although they never told us so, throughout our childhood and especially when we came into our teenage years they found every reason they could to get us together. We were like cousins though there was no blood relationship, and when we did finally start dating everyone was very pleased. We were manipulated, totally manipulated, though I didn't realise it until many years later. I could have been angry, but why be angry when all they'd done was to angle me into marrying the prettiest, most personable, loving girl on the planet. They did me a favour Bobby, a very big favour indeed - but one I swore I'd never inflict on my own children. You, and Andrew, and Mandy and Jon, I guarantee you'll all be able to choose your own partners.'

'And that's exactly what I'm doing, choosing my own partner.'

'Bobby, Bobby, there's more to it than that, and you know it. You've been grown-up for years, you know the business and you know the social scene as well. You're a society boy, and everyone expects you to marry a society girl. OK you can have some little friends to play with for a few years, but in the end you come home and marry according to your station.'

'And have society children?'

'Yes, and have society children.'

'So why couldn't we bring Celia into our kind of society? She really is a tremendous girl and it's not her fault her parents are poor. With a bit of grooming she'd learn, she's already learned so much. No-one would ever need to know where she came from.'

'Oh you're stupid Bobby. I never thought a child of mine could be so totally stupid. Of course they'll all know where she came from. You know the way the trashy end of the media hound people like us. They'll spot her, they'll dig, they'll have her on the front pages of their so-called magazines before you can blink. You'll make the lot of us into a laughing stock.'

'Father, you've said enough. Now it's your turn to do some listening. I don't give a toss about society, or the press, or building dynasties. I'm in love with Celia and she's in love with me. We want to be together and that's how it's going to be from now on. Either you come on board with the idea or you just keep yourself out of our lives. Am I making myself clear?'

'What about your duty to the family Bobby? If you let the family down, do you still expect them to support you?'

'The family can make its own choices. Some things are important and I'd have hoped the family would have respected the wants and needs of its young people. For Belen's sake, it's not like I just picked the girl up two nights ago. We've been together for years now. Everyone knows Celia, and apart from you as the obvious exception, most people seem to like her.'

'Your mother doesn't like her.'

'Mother does whatever you tell her, and you know it.'

Robert looked annoyed now. He clenched his fists and shook his head.

'So you'd just carry on despite the pain and hurt you're going to cause to those who ought to be closest to you. And I notice you didn't mention money in your fine talk - tell me how you'd feel if you were no longer my principal heir?'

Bobby continued as if he'd been expecting that old chestnut to come up somewhere in the conversation.

'I'd work something out. I'm smart, I know the business and I've got the contacts now. There's more than a few heads of big firms out there with idiot sons and daughters who'd be over the moons to have me on board. OK, perhaps I wouldn't be as rich as you, maybe not at first, and maybe never at all, but you can't threaten me with life on the breadline. You throw me out and I'll land on my feet. You just try it and see if I don't.'

'Bobby, I'll lay it on the line for you. If you go ahead with your ridiculous plan of marrying this, *nobody* she will never be part of *my* family. You will never bring her to this house, you will never be visited by myself or your mother, and I will make sure she is never invited to even one society function.'

'And what about the children Dad, *your* grandchildren?'

'If you are stupid enough to have children with this woman, let me make it clear to you that they will not be *my* grandchildren and they will never become part of the family inheritance. Do you understand?'

Bobby sat fuming. He'd never thought his own father would be so hard to deal with.

'Well I'm glad you've made yourself so plain, Father, because what I came here to tell you this evening is that your first grandchild, in fact a grandson, is already on the way. Celia and I will be marrying in three weeks time and neither you, nor the firm, nor all your money are going to stop us. There'll be invitations to the wedding in the post, and you will choose whether to come, or not. And your choice will affect you more than it will me. OK?'

Robert Snr went pale. 'She doesn't have to have the baby Bobby. There's still time, you can back out of all of this any time you want. We'll call a clinic in the morning, pay the girl off with a few thousand and you can stay in the family. Oh please, Bobby, please.'

'And you'd murder your own unborn grandson? Why the fuck should I want anything more to do with the likes of you? You make me sick with all your stuck up society ways. Maybe there won't be any invites to the wedding after all.'

In a rage now the younger man grabbed his jacket off the chair-back and headed for the heavy oak door, slamming it loudly behind him as he stormed out of the room. Robert heard the powerful sports car revving up, and then the sound of chippings as they flew up from the drive and shot-blasted the garage door.

***

Celia McArthur looked up at the clock. Already half one and still no sign of Bobby. Had he stayed for supper with his parents? Had they ended up breaking open his father's latest single malt, and now he was staying the night? Surely he'd have phoned to say he wasn't going to be back that night? She'd tried his mobile hours ago only to find he'd left it in the charger on the table by the front door. But he could have called on the landline from the house.

She thought of the police, but she'd look silly if he turned up next morning having just slept the night at his own parents' house, the house where he'd grown up. She knew exactly where she stood with the Chandlers, but she was going to have to call them. A few poisoned words down a phone-line couldn't break any bones. God, if she'd had the nerve an hour ago it would all have been easier.

Robert Chandler Snr was deep in slumber when the nagging sound of the phone dragged him rudely awake. Just because he had a phone in the bedroom didn't mean he expected anyone to call it at this hour of the night.

'Chandlers,' he spoke into the handset with a croaky voice.

'Mr Chandler I'm sorry to call you so late, but I'm worried about Bobby.'

Robert heard the words and knew exactly who he was speaking to. What in hell's name did the stupid little tart want at this hour?

'What about my son?'

'Has he stayed the night with you?'

'No he left hours ago,' and a slight feeling of dread crept into Robert's mind.

'Well he's not back home yet. I'm going to call the police.'

'You'll do no such thing. *I* will call the police and *you* will keep out of my family's affairs. Am I making myself clear?'

★★★

The policeman who came to call at the big house as the first rays of the rising sun blazed over the eastern horizon carried the sad expression that told his tale without the need for him to speak. With the feeling that his heart had fallen right down to his feet a grey faced man confirmed a car registration. His wife behind him buried her head in her hands.

The policeman told the couple that two surveillance cameras had clocked an expensive sports coupe at over 200 km/hr in the minutes before the crash. The young man who'd been in the driving seat had been dead on arrival at Jackson General. Fortunately the hydrogen tanks in both vehicles had held or the other party in the accident might not have survived. The driver of the other vehicle was only slightly injured and had called for an ambulance.

The police would give the family more news as soon as they were able.

David Hulett Wilson

13

Drives And Barriers

It was part of the history lessons taught in every school throughout the Union that the human race had not originally been native to any of the habitable planets it now occupied. Clearly that meant they must have come from somewhere else, but where? Despite the huge optical arrays and the fleets of deep space exploration vessels the descendents of the colonists had built, no sign of the original home world had ever been found - before.

The ones who'd conceived the mission to tame the three worlds the Union now knew as the home planets had been well up on their technology, though only to a limit. Despite everything they'd known about science and the nature of the universe, their theories had failed entirely to predict that faster than light travel would ever be possible. Journeys to the stars would take far longer than the lifespan of a mere mortal, so arkships laden with cargoes of cryogenically sleeping passengers had trundled for centuries across the void of interstellar space.

For the early pioneers, every new day had been a challenge. A challenge to hunt and grow food, to construct houses and communal buildings, to find fuel and mineral resources, and occasionally to fight off the fearsome alien beasts that had roamed across the planets twenty five centuries ago. The people back then had been too busy with their lives to stop and think that the old ones had built technological progress into the plans for the colonies they would never see with their own eyes.

So without realising just how controlled were their lives, and loosely following a pre-ordained script, the colonists slowly but surely developed their technology according to the grand plan until the day at last dawned when they became the equals of those who had sent them. It was only when they first exceeded the technology written into the script they opened their eyes to see that for so many centuries they had actually been following a script. And now they were free to progress as they chose.

More centuries passed before the technology came to fruition, but finally the day came when the first experimental vessel powered its way through what had once been seen as a barrier. It was true the first flight only managed less than twice light-speed, and the power it needed was orders of magnitude higher than flawed theories had predicted, but it had proved its point. Then it was only a matter of time before the first feeble gravity lens had been refined into a true gravitron drive and the voyages between the home planets, previously measured in years, fell to months. With the next breakthrough just around the corner the whole scientific community was sure that months would become weeks, though how long would pass before weeks became days no-one was prepared to say, but it would come. One day they were sure it would come.

The engineers of the day took up the challenge and enjoyed success. If it took more power to go faster, they'd provide more power, and more power again. If it took another refinement to the g-drive that drew the ship inexorably towards its distant target, they'd develop it. For a while it worked and ships were pushed to ever higher speeds - until once again they would go no faster. Could it be another barrier?

For a society living in an age of unprecedented peace, and with energy, wealth, and materials beyond the dreams of their forefathers, any so-called barrier that showed itself was surely only a temporary problem. Next time the scientists would not be defeated by great men or women who produced so called *evidence* to prove they had finally come up against a limit. It would only be a matter of time before a way would be found to power right through any obstacle mere nature thought it could put in their way.

But sadly, and despite all the resources, all the money, all the best brains and all their best theories; still the barrier remained.

For a pan-global civilization that had spread itself across an unimaginable range of space, a society where no-one who was anyone in the academic community risked the ridicule that would surely come from saying there was something that couldn't be done, the astronomers looked out into the universe to see its gems, twinkling in the far distance - still almost as remote as they had been to the man who ground the lens of the crudest telescope. The fabled idea of an epic voyage to explore other galaxies remained no more than a dream.

14

A New Start For The Chandlers

When Andrew called him on the phone Jon was dumbstruck to hear the dreadful news. He was on the train to Jackson within the hour and up at Rosemount as fast as the cab could carry him. Lectures would have to wait.

He watched his father as he sat motionless, staring into the empty fireplace, somehow detached from a world that had dealt him such a savage blow. Maureen was up in her bedroom with Mandy by her side. Andrew and Grant, Mandy's new husband, were busy making arrangements with the undertaker.

★★★

A week passed before the police completed their investigations and the family was allowed to bury Bobby's remains. Jon hadn't attended many funerals but he'd worked out for himself that when an old person died the service was the celebration of a long life well lived which had finally come to its due and expected conclusion. But the funeral of a young man with his life still ahead of him, a life so stupidly and needlessly wasted, was surely the saddest event he'd ever experience.

And for one brief moment hostilities were suspended as Robert and Maureen stood side by side with the mother of their unborn grandson, though Jon saw that no words were spoken.

After the long dark car had dropped the mourners back at the house Robert spoke the first words he had uttered since the accident and asked Jon to come into his study with him. What his father had to say surprised him, not so much for what he said, but for what it was he found so important that it should be his first words since the tragic event. He sat in his favourite chair and lifted up his sad face to look at his son.

'Jon, we're going to have to live without Bobby now - we know that. He's gone and I have to live with that for the rest of my days.'

'We all have to live without Bobby Father.'

His father looked at him with sad eyes and spoke softly. 'The burden lies heavier with me than anyone else Jon. I feel responsible. I could have given in, so many times I could have given in. But no, not me, I did what a Chandler does and I stood firm. And now look where it's got me.'

And Jon saw the first trace of a tear in the corner of his father's eye.

'We have to remember him now for what he was and not grieve over what he could have been. We have to think of those wonderful times when you were all so little. You remember those days when you used to troop into the kitchen caked in mud? I suppose I was the lucky one, I saw him every day at work in the office. Your poor mother had already been living without him this past two years. It's like we lost him so long ago, but we kept on hoping that one day he'd come back. And now he's really gone, and for all the family riches and all your medical science, no-one can bring him back. I've grieved for a week as have we all, but now it's time to look to the future. The family has to go on and the firm has to go on.'

Jon nodded in agreement but wondered where the conversation was leading.

'Now you know how proud I was when you told me of your choice to enter such a noble profession, and I'm sure you could make a fine doctor, but things have changed. This is the time when I need my son beside me. Not just for myself, but for the whole of the family, the family who are living now, the ones long gone, and those yet to come. The bank has been a tradition in our family since your grandfather and Charlie set it up all those years ago, and we owe our allegiance to it. I'll put it in as few words as I can, Jon, my son, my treasured son, will you come into the firm with me? Will you take your brother's place?'

Jon stared at his father aghast. 'But what about Andrew? Surely he's the next in line?'

Robert shook his head. 'Andy's a good boy, he's clever and with what he knows about finance and contract law he's a real asset to the bank. And he's a good team player too, but he's a player, he'll never be the leader. There was an extra *something* that Bobby had, like a spark that lit him up from deep inside, and you've got it too Jon. You could take Bobby's place.'

'I can't just suddenly become Bobby. I can't just step in and be a replacement.'

'But you've got what it takes to be a leader Jon. I need you to take over from your brother.'

Jon reflected on the conversation and knew it was true what his father had said, Andrew would never have what it took to be the head of the bank. Bobby had been right for the job, he'd been clever, a natural leader, and as his father's first son it was the role he'd been born for - his birthright. And it was because everyone had known that Bobby would one day take his father's place at the head of the firm that Jon had looked elsewhere for a career. But now he looked forward into the decades yet to come and saw the vision that had visited his father. He knew and accepted that it was himself who was destined to be there running the family firm. And he felt so powerless, it was just as his father had said - three years into his studies, already half-way to becoming a doctor, and despite everything he'd learned, all the medical science known to mankind could never bring back his brother. Could he even be a doctor at all? How would he would feel if he lost a patient? Never in his years of study had he felt such disillusion. And Jon realised, that as well as needing him there to groom as his replacement, his father needed him there to help him through the difficult days ahead. In a single heartbeat his decision was made.

★★★

Although he'd spent the past three years studying medicine, the good news was that Jon's high school qualifications were not too far away from what he needed to switch courses, and with a few favours called in from well placed friends Jon had a place to start at the School of Economics that autumn. But unlike the choice his brother had made, he was going to live at home to be company for his parents in their hour of need.

15

Still Looking For A Host

Meetings - if there was one thing that might possibly have convinced Jon that a life in politics wasn't really for him after all it was the endless round of meetings. Not that meetings alone made politics very much different from business. That morning the perishable goods sub-committee had threatened the virtual end of the kumquat unless drastic action was taken, and taken very soon they were keen to add. And it was straight from one gathering to the next because he knew they were expecting him at another long, boring round of chin-wagging to discuss the agenda for the conference on Phoenix.

At last the ordeal had ended and Jon breathed a sigh of relief as he opened the big oak door that lead through to the peace and tranquillity of his office, but before he'd even had chance to sit down the phone warbled. He picked it up and heard a man's voice at the other end - Michael Heathersett his private secretary.

'Jon, I've got a bit of bad news for you.'

'Is it any worse than the fate of the kumquat?'

The face on the screen looked puzzled.

'They've tagged a sub-committee meeting about legal issues onto the end of the Phoenixan accession conference.'

'And?'

'Well that's Horace Walton's field, so they've asked him to stay on for a few days.'

Jon's heart sank.

'Is this a nice way of telling me that Andrew Westinghouse won't be available after all?'

'Sorry Jon.'

'So where do we go from here then? You know I've all but promised Tom, and there's only another two days till I'm supposed to be there. I'd pinned all my hopes on using Andrew.'

Michael continued. 'I've taken the liberty of asking TranzCon for details of other D2 hosts who might be available. Hopefully the gen will be coming through in a couple of hours, then we can get together and review it.'

Always the competent one Michael. A good looking young man in his mid-thirties. Excellent qualifications, pleasant manner, not tall for a male and he wore his hair in a way which wasn't quite the look people expected from a man in his position, but in his sharp suit he looked every bit the senior civil servant. Here came the big question though, was he going to be able to pull a rabbit out of the hat? What were the chances?

Jon knew the facts and the figures. Statistics were his bag but sadly, in the case of mind types they didn't tell him quite the story he'd hoped to hear. Deltas were pretty thin on the ground anyway, and that was something that was pretty much a constant throughout all the planets of the Union. But when you took into account the fact that the Delta 2 sub-group accounted for less than 5% of all Deltas it gave some idea of just how hard it could be to find a host. Even worse, just because another person was a Delta 2 it didn't follow automatically that they'd make a good host. Some were too young, some too old, some the wrong sex, lots were employed in good jobs they wouldn't give up simply to sell themselves as TranzCon hosts, and some objected to the whole idea of mind swapping either because someone or some organisation had told them it was immoral. Then there were those who were scared of what might happen if things went wrong. As if they did? This time the statistics were on Jon's side - there'd been thousands of TranzCon transfers in the past twelve months and every one of them had gone through without a hitch.

All he needed now was a host so he could find out for himself. And hosts *did* exist, even for Deltas. Take a tiny fraction of a percentage and multiply it by 30 billion, and the result always came out to a nice big healthy number. Vissan, the most populous planet in the Union, could have supplied well over a million hosts. Even insignificant Nehrad with its tiny population had over fourteen hundred.

But the problem for Jon was Phoenix, the strange new world so recently discovered. A world where religious fervour had whipped up opposition to mind scanning and even the state governments took no steps to combat ignorance. Unbelievably, some of the governments even supported the opposition - something which would have been illegal, and certainly unthinkable, anywhere in the Union.

And that was the problem Jon now faced because without widespread deep scanning of the population it was obvious there could be only the scantiest data available to tell TranzCon which of the potential hosts belonged to each mind-type. For the Alphas and Betas there was, as usual, no problem. But for the *forgotten few* suitable hosts were very rare indeed. He simply hadn't realised how rare until Michael sat with him at his desk to review the motley band of individuals the mind-travel company had to offer.

★★★

The first data-sheet off the rather slim pile showed a man who was a D2 it had to be agreed, but there the attraction ended. He was over 80 years old on a planet where male life expectancy was a paltry 93 years. Even worse the poor guy had recently suffered a stroke that had left him unable to walk. It would be bad enough travelling into a good host and finding that the mind-fit was so bad he wouldn't be able to walk, but to know in advance there was no chance - it just wasn't acceptable. Jon screwed up the sheet and dropped it into the bin.

The next sheet showed a D2 male, 71 years old and in good health for his age, but there was a note to say that he'd never indicated any willingness to host a traveller. In his working days he'd run a successful business and had no need of the money. For the likes of Jon who was used to being able to buy whatever he wanted the idea of something, or someone, not being up for sale was quite an annoyance. He put the sheet to one side and asked for the next one. Michael passed it over and Jon stared almost in horror at the photograph …… of …… a woman. The data-sheet showed she was 57 and her mind-profile would make a good fit to his own. Jon shook his head - vigorously.

'No Michael, there's no way I'm taking this one.'

Michael had obviously expected this sort of response and knew it was a time for him to push, just a little.

'Jon, I made a few enquiries and they told me there's no technical reason why you couldn't use a female host. Considering the importance of the trip and the fact it would only be for four days, she might be your only choice.'

Jon spoke calmly, but in a manner that clearly indicated his mind was made up.

'Michael, read my lips - I don't do female, got it? What don't I do?'

'OK Jon, I take your point. We'll concentrate on the male candidates for now, but I'm not shredding this woman's sheet just yet.'

'Do what you like with it, but you know my views on the subject. *I'm* the one who's got to go there, so *I* get the final say. OK? Right then, let's have a look at some more.'

The look on Michael's face told the story even before he spoke.

'That's the end of the good ones.'

Jon gasped. 'They were the good ones? How bad are the bad ones?'

'All that's left are Delta 1s.'

Jon knew the score with D1s. From the aspect of a transferred mind being able to carry out the basic function of keeping the host's body alive, a swap into a D1 was feasible - but at what cost? The fit between a D1 and a D2 was dodgy at the best of times and in too many cases the senses and motor functions failed entirely to map onto each other. It was standard procedure to run a simulation of the travellers' scans against each other before the transfer, but sadly, even the best prediction that TranzCon's compatibility matching service could give offered no guarantees. The chances of travelling into a host to be blind, deaf, wheelchair disabled, quadriplegic, or any combination of those awful conditions were high, very high. Given enough candidates to review there was certainly a chance of finding a D1 who might possibly make an adequate match for a D2, but all they had here was a tiny handful of possibilities.

Jon was almost in despair as Michael passed him the sheets. The best of the bunch was a male aged 45, good looking and in good health, but the deep scan profile indicated a poor fit and both parties would be unable to walk without assistance. It was quite likely they'd both be wheelchair disabled and it was unlikely the host would agree to such a badly matched swap even if he himself was up for it.

The next D1 looked promising at first, 35 years old, tallish, handsome, clean bill of health, but as Jon read further he saw there was a real problem, the number of unquantifiable variants in his deep scan profile was so high that running any kind of compatibility simulation would be meaningless - something that could lead to serious consequences if he was unlucky. And bad luck was what you often got when you trusted things to luck. Another half hour of leafing through prospective hosts was time wasted and finally Jon had had enough.

***

An hour later Michael was back and this time the expression on the man's face showed that perhaps the fabled rabbit might be making its hoped for appearance after all.

'I've been making some enquiries Jon and there's an outside chance we might still be able to find you a host.'

Jon looked expectantly.

'I spoke to Horace and he told me about a host he'd used a couple of times before he found Andrew Westinghouse. I've got his details here - a man called Daren Robinson.'

Jon took the sheets and leafed through them. The details looked good, almost too good to be true. The man was in his early forties, no disabilities, fit and quite good looking. He was perhaps a little on the short side at 1.7 metres though that was scarcely a problem when the predicted mind fit was over 97%.

'He's good. Is he available?'

'That's the big question. The information TranzCon have shows he hasn't worked as a host for over a year, and they've confirmed he's not on their active list right now.'

'But there's only one player in the mind-swap game, so if he's not working for TranzCon it follows that he has to be available. Do they have any contact details for him?'

'They were checking when I last spoke to them.'

'Well get back to them and let me know as soon as you have something.'

16

Robert Chandler 3rd

Seven months after his father had parted from life the next turn of the wheel brought a new Chandler into the world. That he was a Chandler at all was an annoyance to Jon's father, but no-one doubted that Bobby was the boy's father, so no-one challenged the baby's right to the name. Neither did they challenge his right to be Robert, a name that made him Robert Chandler the third.

Without Bobby's income the comfortable life Celia had known had come to an abrupt end and her sojourn in the luxurious apartment overlooking the river was now nothing more than a memory. The rent was way beyond anything a single mother in Celia's situation could even have thought of affording, and now she and the baby were living in hard times.

She'd sold the more expensive pieces of furniture, and except for a few keepsakes, the contents of Bobby's wardrobe. No-one could deny that she needed the money, but she'd burst into a flood of tears when she heard about the most valuable asset her man had left her. Despite the circumstances of the crash the insurance company paid out the write-off value of the expensive car Bobby had died in, and as co-owner she was entitled to the money. When she'd opened the envelope and had seen the cheque stapled neatly to the letter that had made no attempt to express any measure of condolence she'd wanted to throw it in the river and shout to God about the wicked trick she'd played on her. To scream till her voice could scream no more. It was Jon who'd calmed her down and told her to take the money. He told her he'd be able to help with money of his own when he finished at university, but until then she was going to need everything she could get her hands on to pay the rent on a flat in a cheaper area. Bobby would have wanted her to spend her time with their baby son instead of dumping him in a nursery while she went out to work. So she'd agreed, she'd do it for Bobby and for baby Robert.

The rundown little flat over a shop they found was at the opposite end of the luxury scale to her previous address, but it was somewhere to call home. On the edge of Undercliffe it was only a short walk from her parent's home, and with two bedrooms, a kitchen and a small sitting room it was an adequate place to live. Jon had tried hard to be enthusiastic about it but it was by far the worst place he'd ever thought anyone could call a home. Fortunately Celia was less daunted.

★★★

Spending so much of his time down in Jackson now Jon was only a tram ride away from Undercliffe and often came to stay at the little flat, though he always told his parents he was staying with a friend in the halls of residence because he had to work late that day. He'd bring round a takeaway dinner and a bottle of wine and the two of them would sit together and drink themselves into the night. And though he was well aware of the charms that had drawn his brother to this lovely girl, he slept each time in the spare room.

Some afternoons when there were no lectures he'd come round to the flat and they'd take little Robert out and push the buggy round the pond in the local park. Soon the little tyke would be running about feeding bread to the ducks, though that was something for another year. Anyone who'd seen two young people walking together in the afternoon sun would never have thought they were anything other than a married couple, and even though Jon knew so well the reaction he could expect from his parents, the afternoon came when he finally plucked up the courage to ask Celia if she'd be his wife.

From the way her face changed he knew instantly the answer was "no". Stupid man, he'd been romancing just to think this lovely woman could be his. They stopped to sit on a bench and for a moment she looked deep into his eyes, but then she turned away, avoiding his gaze.

'How can you even think about something like that Jon, after everything your family has suffered on my account?'

'You can't blame yourself for Bobby's death. If anyone's to blame it's my father.'

'I know your father hated me, and he still does. He probably always will. But I don't blame him - I just wish he'd acknowledge the existence of his grandson.'

'Give him time. He might. But what about us, is there any chance for me? Could we be together?'

He saw the softness of sorrow in her eyes. At first words wouldn't come, but finally she pulled herself together.

'Jon you're the best, nicest, most generous man alive on the planet, and you're the brother of the man I chose. But you're not Bobby, you could never be Bobby.'

'Wouldn't I do instead, if you can't have Bobby?'

'I know this sounds all wrong Jon, but you'd be second best, and second best is never good enough. But what about Liz? After all this time I thought you were serious about her.'

Jon sat in silence, staring at the ripples on the lake. Finally he turned back to face her.

'I like Liz a lot and we've had some fun. But I'm not sure if she's the woman I want to marry.'

Celia stopped and thought for a moment. And then spoke softly.

'Do you know what I really want? I want us to forget this conversation ever happened. I want things to be just as they were when we came into the park. You're little Robert's uncle and my best friend. Can we keep you just that way? Please Jon, please say yes.'

17

Well Make Him An Offer He Can't Refuse!

Hours had passed since Jon and Michael had sat together to review the hosts TranzCon had offered. The usual ministerial workload had piled up but Jon had been unable to concentrate on anything other than his desperate need to find a host. What the hell had happened to Daren Robinson? Where was the man? Was he going to be available as his host? Finally his anxiety got the better of him - he picked up the phone and tapped in a number.

'How's it going Michael?'

'You mean with Daren?'

'What else is there to discuss?'

'Well the good news is they've found him.'

'Do I take it that's a lead-in to bad news.'

'Knowing you're supposed to be going to Phoenix soon I expect you've been doing some homework about the place.'

'Yes.'

'Well you've probably seen that some of the people there can be a bit strange, or at least they are from our point of view.'

Jon agreed wholeheartedly. 'It's a weird planet, with weird people and some weird systems of government. So far I haven't detected any redeeming features.'

'There's a lot of ignorance there. Ignorance breeds fear, fear fuels radical groups, and none of their governments seem to want to do much about it. Perhaps it's because of the way their little states act as rivals to each other instead of grouping together. It's even worse with the religious organisations. Some of them are putting out the line that occupying the body of another person is a sin against their God. Some of the less educated are even spreading it about that evil spirits will find a way in and take over a body.'

'OK Michael, we know they're all loopy, but how does this fit in with Daren Robinson?'

'What we know now is that the man's a regular church-goer, and that means he's more susceptible than most to pressure from a religious angle. There's a sect who've been targeting people who've acted as hosts and after the last time he worked for TranzCon they tracked him down.'

'With a view to indoctrinating him?'

'Exactly that. They work in two ways. First they identify their target and befriend them. When they've got the target's confidence they come on strong with the religious angle and worry them they'll go to hell unless they repent and make amends for their sins.'

'And you think that's what they've done with Daren?'

'We know so.'

'Does he need the money?'

'He drives a fork-truck in a supermarket warehouse and you can guess it's not the kind of job that pays much.'

'House and family?'

'He lives in a run-down flat as a lodger and pays maintenance to his ex-wife and daughter.'

Jon smiled, he thought perhaps he understood just a little more about Daren Robinson.

'I'll bet he's barely scraping by. He'd love to earn TranzCon rates for a few days but he doesn't want to upset his new friends. But everyone's got their price - he'd do a deal if it was worth enough.'

'How much would you be prepared to offer?'

'Let's see, if he had enough to pay off his wife till the girl's grown up and buy himself a decent place to live ....'

Jon scribbled a figure on a sticky notelet and passed it to Michael. The man had clearly been expecting something big, but the surprise on his face showed he'd underestimated how far his boss was prepared to go.

'The government can't sanction a payment like that Jon. Not even for a senior minister.'

'It's not from the government Michael, it's from me. Try him with it.'

★★★

Michael came back just after lunch and the smile he was trying hard to hide told Jon there might just be some success to report.

'Well the offer worked Jon. He's agreed to be your host.'

Jon smiled. 'That's all I needed to hear. Can you get the contract sorted out so I can travel tomorrow.'

18

The Army

When it came to the time for final exams both Jon and his father were disappointed when he didn't get a first like Bobby had. But nothing was ever said that would have made Jon feel he was in any way less worthy than his brother, and at the end of the day, a 2.1 was still a very good degree.

After that the plan had been to come straight into the family firm, but just as his final year was starting his name had come up in the lottery for national service - a one in ten chance for any fit and healthy young man. Of course they'd agreed to wait for him until his course was complete, but once the degree ceremony was over, boot camp awaited him.

His father told him they could make a few arrangements that would keep the Army off his back for another year or two, and then they'd do the same again till he was thirty when the forces would lose interest. But Jon had thought it all through and told his father the firm would have to wait a little longer. It was only a year after all.

★★★

It was only a few months later that Jon wondered whether he'd made the right decision. Being in the army was hard work, the hardest physical work he'd ever done. But now, when he was still running at the end of 10 klics with a full pack, and the assault course no longer left him gasping for breath, he knew he was in better shape than he'd ever been before. It felt good to be fit, healthy and strong. Then there were the bits he really enjoyed, being able to strip down his gun and re-assemble it, to know every part so intimately the motions came naturally - even in pitch dark. A soldier never knew when that ability might save his life. And then to take aim on the target and put three bullets through the same hole in the mannequin. A natural marksman. But he wondered how he'd feel if it was a real person coming for him - would he still be able to pull the trigger, could he really take another man's life? Hopefully he'd never have to find out.

But those times up on Walridge Plain, out in the cold with his gun on his shoulder and full kit on his back. Advancing by night, keeping low, patiently watching in his night-sight for the telltale movements that marked the enemy, and quickly pulling the trigger before any pang of guilt could stop him. It was all blanks of course, and only laser detection to tell him he'd hit his target. But the knowledge of the hit, the thrill of the kill - now could he do it for real? Possibly.

Two weeks before his year was due to draw to a close his captain called him into the office. He'd shown exemplary ability and the Army was interested in keeping him. If he was prepared to sign on for a career he could transfer to officer training and be commissioned in two years time - how did he feel about that? Jon was high on the thrill of living an active life, and he wanted it, he wanted it so much. Now with success in the palm of his hand, could he give it all up for a suit and a desk? He thought back to that afternoon in the study with his father and remembered the promise he'd made, remembered the roll that was out there waiting for him. Most of all he remembered Bobby. The decision was painful to make but he knew there was only one road ahead. He envied the ordinary guys he'd trained with - free to go their own way.

19

The Transfer

The taxi crawled slowly down Western Avenue though Jon wasn't bothered, he'd allowed enough time to cater for the traffic. Another half a klic to go before arriving at TranzCon's reception centre, and then the action would really start.

All morning he'd been wondering and worrying. He knew that really there was nothing to worry about. All transfers went through without a problem, and in the majority of cases the fit between traveller and host was good enough, at least for a few days if not for a whole lifetime. The prediction of his fit with Daren was very good indeed.

And now it was happening for real. More worrying? No, perhaps it was like a soldier going into battle. When it actually happened there was no room for worry, just the need to go out and fight.

As the car turned into Sutton Street Jon's mobile rang.

'Mr Chandler, this is Peter Carrington, Transmissions Controller in Celebration. I'm afraid I've got to tell you we might have a hitch.

TranzCon

Jon wondered. Since he'd signed the contract to swap with Daren everything had seemed to go so well. They'd both been through their deep scans and medicals and everything was go. What could possibly be going wrong this late in the game?

'So what is the problem? Have you found some incompatibility?'

'It's not like that Mr Chandler. It's just that the host you're transferring into hasn't shown up yet.'

'Perhaps he's just left it a bit late. There's still time for him to arrive.'

'It's not usual for hosts to arrive late. Their contract can start as much as four hours before the transfer so most of them come in early The sooner they're on the payroll, the more money they make.'

Jon thought about this one for a moment.

'I don't know whether you know about the *arrangement* I have with Daren Robinson. I'm paying quite a bit more than the normal hosting fee and it's on a flat rate basis so he'll get the full whack no matter what time he gets to your place. There's no real financial incentive for him to turn up early.'

'I hear what you say Mr Chandler, but I don't want to take the chance. You're probably not aware of how our allocation system works so I'll fill you in. If we want to reserve another transmission slot we have to relinquish the one we've got. If we give up the one we'd booked for 15.27 I can get you another at 18.03. It's only an extra couple of hours so it won't mess your plans up and it buys us a bit of leeway.'

'OK, I follow you and it sounds like the sensible course. What do I do in the meantime?'

'Well you'd be made very welcome at the Reception Centre but I know you're a busy man, so I suggest you go back to your office for a while. I know you're not far away.'

Jon weighed up his options. Going back to the office would be a disappointment now he was so psyched up, but sitting drinking coffee in TranzCon's Reception Centre was going to make the minutes pass by very slowly indeed. And he had a pile of work waiting for him on his desk.

The taxi driver swore quietly under his breathe as Jon asked him to turn the car around.

***

It was coming up to five and the time to head off back to TranzCon had finally arrived. Jon turned off his computer and was walking through the outer office when his mobile rang.

'Mr Chandler - Peter Carrington again. I'm sorry to have to tell you that Daren Robinson still hasn't turned up. He's not answering his landline and his mobile goes straight to voicemail.'

'So what do we do now?'

'We're doing everything we can to locate him but it's the middle of the night here in Celebration and that doesn't help us much. We've got a firm of private investigators on the job and they're already out checking the places he's likely to be. If we turn him up I've got a slot reserved for early tomorrow morning, Vissan time. Under the circumstances it's the best we can do.'

Jon was distinctly annoyed at the treatment he was receiving though he accepted there was nothing more Carrington could do for the moment.

'Does this happen often. I mean, do hosts suddenly go missing?'

'We live in a real world Mr Chandler and things happen. The most common reason for people not turning up is that they've met with some minor accident and they turn up in an A&E somewhere. Hospitals are the first places we check.'

'What if he's just chickened out?'

'It happens I'll agree, but only with first timers. Daren Robinson's hosted eight times now and every time without any problem. As far as I'm aware there hasn't been anything that would have put him off.'

'Look Peter, I doubt whether I'm going to sleep much tonight so I want you to call me the instant you've got any information, and I don't care if its three in the morning. Then we'll go for the next transmission slot you can get.'

'Thankyou for being so understanding Mr Chandler. I can promise we're doing everything we can.'

★★★

Jon wanted to be as close as he could to TranzCon's premises so he stayed at his apartment that night. As he'd predicted, sleep was the last thing on his mind so after he'd finished eating dinner he opened up his laptop and started to trawl through the 169 emails it had received on his behalf since lunchtime. At half five next morning he was dragged out of a dream by his phone ringing.

'Peter Carrington again Mr Chandler.'

In an instant Jon had come to full consciousness.

'Have you got any news?'

The brief silence on the line told Jon that if there was any news it was likely to be bad.

'I'm sorry to have to tell you this Mr Chandler, but Daren Robinson was found dead this morning. We think it happened sometime late last evening but the police have only just released the details to us. You probably know they have to contact a relative before they can disclose anything to people outside the family.'

'How did it happen? Was it an accident?'

'I'm afraid it was anything but an accident. He was found with his arms and legs roped to four stakes in the middle of the bowling green in Dalston Park. And there was a fifth stake driven through his heart.'

Jon was aghast. 'It sounds like some kind of ritual killing.'

'The pathologist's report was that in all likelihood he was already dead when he was staked out. The police broke into his flat and found a lot of blood there ……….'

'And the thing in the park was some kind of statement?'

'I'm afraid so. You've probably heard there are some nutheads around and to be absolutely honest we've received a number of threats in the past year. But this is the first time any real action has happened. The police know the organisation and it's almost a dead cert that someone in the group is responsible for this killing, but they're a close knit band and they'll all have got their alibis sorted. It's not going to be easy to bring anyone to justice.

Jon heard the words but somehow wasn't interested. Finding out who carried out the murder wasn't going to get him to Phoenix.'

'What about me though? Is there anyone else I could use as a host?'

'Mr Chandler, we sent through all the details we had and I'm really sorry there wasn't anyone suitable for you. If we'd known you were prepared to offer a premium there might have been some possibles. If you could give us a few more days there's every chance we could turn someone up.'

Jon cursed and turned off his phone. "A few more days" were days he didn't have.

★★★

With the sun already rising when the call ended there'd been no reason to go back to bed so Jon made himself some breakfast and headed off for an early start in the office. When Michael came in just before eight the two of them sat together and Jon explained the bizarre events that had transpired the previous night.

'What can I say Jon? The term "bad luck" scarcely does it justice.'

'I'd really psyched myself up for it. After everything I'd thought, after everything I'd said, I really was ready to lie down on that couch and travel to Phoenix. You can imagine how I felt.'

The younger man nodded. 'What are you going to do now? Do you have any plans?'

Jon shook his head. 'Daren Robinson was my only hope. Now he's out of the running it's "game over" as far as I'm concerned. Somebody else will have to go to the conference.'

'What about Tom?'

'What about Tom? It's not like I didn't try is it? You can tell him we did everything we could.'

Michael sighed. 'I can tell him, not that it'll do you any good.'

'Well Mr fucking Hanson can fucking lump it. There's only so much a man can do.'

★★★

It was just coming up to eleven when Michael next called.

'Jon, I've just had Peter Carrington on the phone again. He's got a new Delta 2 host we hadn't seen before he thinks might be suitable. He's already run a prediction and the fit's almost 100%. The details will be coming though in a few minutes.'

'Meet me in my office as soon as it arrives.'

★★★

The smile was back on Jon's face when Michael walked into the office clutching a thin sheaf of papers.

'Right then, let's get started.'

Michael held back from the big desk for long enough for Jon to suspect something was amiss.

'Come on then. Let's have a look at *him*.'

The seconds that passed could have been hours.

'*Her*.'

Jon stopped in his tracks.

'I told you Michael I don't ....'

'Jon, you told me that when we both thought a better opportunity was going to come along. And it hasn't.'

'Well it's different now. I've made up my mind - I'm not going.'

'And damn the consequences?'

Michael waited pensively but no words came.

'You don't want to damn the consequences do you?'

Jon shook his head.

'How long till your final deadline for travelling?'

'Six and a half hours, at the outside.'

'And how many other suitable hosts have you got?'

'Why do you ask questions when you already know the answer?'

'I trained as a barrister.'

Jon took the papers and studied the photograph on the front sheet. For just one moment the silence was oppressive. Finally he threw the sheets down onto the desk.

'Call Carrington and tell him to look for some more.'

'Jon, you know there aren't any.'

'Look for them anyway.'

20

Desmond Chandler

During the long summer breaks that all universities enjoyed the lucky ones amongst the students went off to seek adventure. Island hopping in the tropical regions, backpacking in the mountains, exploring the old cities of far off lands, or even flying off to other planets if parents could be persuaded to shell out for the fare. For Jon his holiday, if "holiday" had been the right word, was spoken for well in advance - ten weeks in the bank learning the job from the bottom rung upwards.

Many were the days when it had been a hard slog and he'd wondered whether he'd really made the right choice when his father asked him to come into the family firm. Most of the older members of staff had known him since he was knee high so there was no hiding who he was, and they all knew that one day he was destined to be the boss. But in the nicest possible way they'd taken him into their community and even told him about his Dad's younger days - something he kept in the strictest confidence. Maybe they'd be telling the same stories about him one day.

Now those times were slipping into memory. With university long past and his days in the army at an end, life in the bank was for real and he'd hoped things were going to feel different - but they didn't. With one eye on the screen in front of him and the other on the vista of shiny glass skyscrapers that shone golden in the rays of the late afternoon sun he was thinking how nice it would be to be out in the park with Celia and little Robert - when he jerked suddenly to attention as Robert senior rushed out of his office.

'Jon, I've just had the hospital on the phone. Des has been admitted and he's on the critical list.'

Jon was staggered. Des was older than his father, but only by a few years and really he was in tremendous shape for a man of his age.

'Was it an accident? Do you want me to come with you?'

'They wouldn't say anything on the phone. They just said come quickly. Can you ring your mother and tell her I'll be late.'

'Will you let us know how he is?'

'I'll call you as soon as there's any news.'

Sadly Robert never saw Des alive again. The attack he'd suffered earlier that afternoon had been too much for his failing body and he'd breathed his last gasp even as his brother sat impatiently drumming his fingers in the back of a gridlocked cab on the road to Jackson General.

★★★

Jon turned the car into the access road and drove up to the main entrance. The rain was beating down and yet his father stood out in the open, letting the downpour soak through his clothes. As Jon pulled up alongside he saw the ashen face and knew it meant only one thing. First Bobby and now his only brother. And taken so young, 61 was no age on a world where retirement was at 80 and most of the population went on to 110 or even older.

Desmond had never married, though he'd played with quite a few ladies in his time and had always been one for the high-life. Robert always complained about the antics of his brother, but everyone knew that deep down he envied him, at least in some ways. Always the sensible one, Robert had never enjoyed the flamboyance of his sibling, and Des's decision not to come into the bank with their father had been a controversial one that had caused more than a few stirs in the family. And for the few who knew the inside story, there had even been threats the wayward elder brother might be cut off from his inheritance.

But Desmond was bigger than that, so he called his father's bluff and never held it against him. And then went on to make so much money it no longer mattered whether his father had been bluffing. As a wheeler-dealer he'd excelled and he'd travelled out to the home planets in the days long before travel off-planet had become widespread. And that was how he'd made his money. If copper was cheaper on Temenco than on Miranda, he bought it and shipped it there. If washing machines could be manufactured for fewer man-hours on Miranda than on Vissan, he bought them and shipped them. If machine tools cost less to make on Vissan than on Temenco he bought them and shipped them. There were some who said he'd done more to open up interplanetary trade than any person alive. And when the deals got bigger than he could finance from his own resources, he just phoned up his brother and asked for a loan.

So with his trade empire booming he had plenty of money and always found fun ways of spending it. The big hotels welcomed him with open arms whenever he turned up, in any state of inebriation, and it was almost as if he'd used the casinos as steam valves to blow off excess pressure. Even that wasn't a failsafe way of moving money along because many had been the evening when he'd gone back to his room with more in his pocket than he'd laid down on the table.

Any time Des came to visit at the big house was a happy time. He never came without presents and they were usually something exotic from far away, so he was always popular with his nephews and niece. And Belenfest just wouldn't have been the same without him, and whichever pretty lady the children had been told to call "Auntie" that year.

So Jon and his brother and sister were very sad to hear the news about their favourite uncle though they were pleased to be on the receiving end of his generosity. When Robert finally got the accountants to work out how much the old rogue had left there was quite a bit that had to go back to the financiers who'd provided it in the first place, his penthouse apartment was going to the lady who'd lived in it for the past two years, the taxman was coming in for a useful cut, but it still left over 137 million for his brother, and there were legacies of 200,000 HUC to each of the younger generation - including the new cousin in Kingston the three siblings had never known they'd had.

For Jon the money was a fortune, and his only thought had been how much he'd be able to help Celia and little Robert now. Mandy thought it would be useful, though it wasn't really a lot compared to the divorce settlement she was getting from Grant. Andrew caused consternation with his use of the money, but despite all the emails the three of them sent, none of them ever found out what the cousin on Miranda did with hers.

★★★

Andrew Chandler had graduated from the School of Economics with a very good degree three years earlier and had come into the bank to work with his father. It was while he'd been away on a course about contract legislation he'd met Jemima, the eldest daughter of a society family whose estate in Rosemount almost put the Chandler residence to shame. She was a tall girl with a frame that was slightly too far towards the slim side, and although she could look elegant in the right cut of evening gown, only the kind hearted would have described her as attractive. But it was clear the two of them were a match made in heaven. Robert and Maureen gave their blessing and the couple became engaged, though the wedding was still unplanned. Robert never said too much about his son's potential spouse, and although Jon suspected he wasn't too keen on her personally he knew the old man was extremely interested in the idea of a union with the McGaskill billions.

Shortly after they'd become an item Andrew had moved out of the big house and the couple had taken a very nice apartment on the 63rd floor of an exclusive down-town highrise. The view from their balcony was stunning and it was said that on a clear day it was even possible to see the tops of the tower blocks on the seafront at Keemouth. For a girl from the sort of money a family like the McGaskills took for granted there had never been any question of their daughter having to work, so after university she'd taken the usual step for a society girl who didn't fancy a real career and volunteered for charitable work.

Although 200,000 was small beer to a family like the Chandlers, money was money and Robert knew very well that the way to make the HUCs pile up was to be careful with the cents. So when he heard his son had donated his inheritance to charity, he was many stops beyond simply fuming with rage.

21

One Final Turn Of The Screw

The next time Jon's phone warbled it was Tom again. Didn't that guy ever give up?

'So who've you found to host you at the conference Jon?'

Jon was silent long enough for the message to pass without him needing to speak.

'Look Jon, I'm getting the information here as well. I'm sorry about the guy who was murdered and I agree that none of the other hosts they offered you are ideal. But I know this much, there's at least one who'd do. And for Belen's sake it's only for a four day rental.'

'Tom, I hear what you say, but now Daren's gone there really isn't anyone who'd be acceptable. Not even for just a few days. I know what I promised you earlier, but ………'

'So what you're telling me is, you're not going.'

Jon was glad the line Tom had got was audio only. If he could have seen the expression on his face right then the only word to describe it would have been "sheepish". It wasn't the usual stance a Chandler took.

'Sorry Tom. Really I am.'

'Can I just jog your memory Jon. Do you remember who was supposed to be coming to the meeting here on Daluun?'

Jon had wondered when this one was going to come up. A cold shiver ran through him.

Tom had waited long enough for an answer.

'It was you Jon. You were the one who was coming to Daluun. It would've been your first TranzCon transfer, but you were going to bite the bullet and be a man, weren't you? *Weren't* you?'

Jon struggled to find even one word.

'And who wimped out?'

'Look Tom, it all changed. You know very well the original idea was just to have a meeting about finance. We were offering to fund a few processing plants on Daluun to try and shut the separatists up once and for all. That's my field, it's what I do. But the whole thing went political and you got involved.'

'In my capacity as First Minister? What if someone else was the First Minister Jon, it'd be *their* job wouldn't it?'

He paused just long enough to let his point sink in.

'So someone aspiring to the post could have given it a try, just to see if they had what it took? Am I making myself clear Jon?

Jon shuddered, Tom was right - and he hadn't finished yet.

'So if I hadn't been here on Daluun doing *your* job, who'd have ended up under a pile of rubble wondering if they were going to make it out alive.'

'Well you did get out alive Tom - thank heavens.'

'I did - but some weren't so lucky. I was sitting next to Brian Rushmore and he didn't make it, and there were plenty of others too. And I can tell you, that time down there under that splintering table wasn't pleasant for anyone. My friend was next to me, dying. It took over three hours while I was lying there, helpless. I couldn't even move Jon. I just lay there and listened while he called out in agony, and I don't mind telling you, I was in quite a bit of pain myself. Then he was slowly getting quieter …… until at last the groaning stopped. And that left me more alone than ever. Lying there, wondering if it was going to be my turn next. I know I was in a host body Jon but if you die in a host, that's it, you've gone. Can you imagine how it would've been for Carol, seeing my body walk out of the hotel? Watching *me* heading off to catch a plane to the elevator? Knowing my body was going home, but *I* was never coming back. I gave my all that day Jon. You owe me - big-time. If you want my support in the election next year you can get your ass in gear and TranzCon to Phoenix. If you let me down now you can start clearing your desk when we finish this conversation. Got it ……. Jon?'

Before Jon could find any words there was a click and the line went dead. He sat for a while, lost in thought. At last he picked up the phone and pressed the key to call Michael.

★★★

The young man walked in holding the same sheaf of papers he'd brought into the office two hours earlier. Without a word he laid them down onto the big leather topped desk. Jon scanned his eyes over the details before settling back onto the picture of the host - pretty, small and ……. female. In a nutshell, the diametric opposite of what he needed to make an impression at the conference. Jon looked up and saw that Michael was watching him, waiting for him to make the first move.

'The data says she's a better than average match for my mind.'

'Almost 100%. The people at TranzCon say they've never seen anything like it.'

'And no complications?'

'Clean as a whistle.'

Jon sat for a while. Michael watched as his superior shifted his gaze from the ceiling to the papers, and then out to the view out over the river. A minute passed, neither man spoke.

At last Jon broke the silence. 'Michael, you know what's at stake for me don't you - the top job? You can't believe how much I want to take this opportunity. This is what I gave up my business career for, and now it's dangling, almost in front of my face. I know I don't have to do this trip. I know I could pull out any time. But then what, spend the rest of my life thinking about what could have been? Jon Chandler, the greatest First Minister the Union never had?'

He thought for another few seconds.

'You know I'll never get another chance - this girl's my only hope. Would you think badly of me if I went back on what I said earlier?'

Michael drew in a deep breath. 'Jon, I'll tell you honestly, if you were elected as First Minister it would be good for my career and I won't deny it. But it has to be your own decision and it goes without saying that anything that passes between us here in this room is strictly in confidence.'

Jon sat and stared at the wall for a while. He turned his gaze back towards Michael.

'Call Carrington and ask him to book the first transmission slot he can get.'

22

The Legacy

It was after the dinner had been cleared away that Robert Chandler asked his son to accompany him into his study. Both men knew that such an invitation told the others there were serious matters to be discussed. Maureen and her daughter exchanged glances though neither spoke.

Jon carefully avoided his father's favourite armchair and settled himself down onto the leather trimmed sofa. As his father poured the drinks he gazed out to watch the blaze of crimson glory as the sun slipped down into the woodland that separated the big house from the house where the Freeman boys had lived when they were children. When the show was over he turned his attention back into the room. He could see straight away the serious expression on the older man's face.

'Jon, we have business to discuss. Serious business. I went to the hospital last week and had a consultation with the Doctor who attended Uncle Des just before he died. They carried out a full investigation and the Doctor recommended that I should have a few tests, just to make sure I didn't have the same thing.'

'And no doubt you're going to tell me about the results.'

If the older man was offended by his son's straightforward approach he made no complaint.

'The results came back this morning and that's why I was out of the office. I'm sorry to have to tell you that the news isn't good, I have a morphing xeno-cancer. It's the same condition that killed my brother.'

Although it had been some years since Jon had studied medicine he remembered much more than he'd forgotten.

'It's not fatal though. There must have been some other complication.'

'There is. In your time at Regenswood, did you ever come across a strain of xeno-cancer with a genetic defect?'

Jon shook his head.

'There was one, just one. Out of the 87 xenos they developed, just one had this problem And even then they didn't find out about it until just a few years ago. They used it on Vissan for about 7 years until they found a cheaper way to synthesise it, so about 5% of the population still living have that strain of xeno inside them, but for most people it's not a problem.'

'What does make it a problem? What makes it a problem for you?'

'For most of its target cancers it works fine with a very low morph rate, but for one particular cancer it goes morph in over 75% of cases.'

Jon knew exactly what his father was talking about.

'It's a high morph rate I'll grant you, but the chances of developing the trigger cancer must be tiny.'

But if Jon had looked more carefully he would have seen the greyness in his father's face.

'Tiny for some, but not for all. My profile indicates a 1.7% chance of developing the cancer that makes the xeno go morph, and from what I know today I'd say statistics come true exactly when you'd prefer they didn't. There are another 9000 people in the whole of the Union with the same profile for that cancer and the same xeno inside them. Work out the maths Jon. After me and Des there's another 113 people going to die for the same reason. 115 people out of 30 billion. What odds would you give me for that? Don't you think Des and I drew two of life's short straws.'

Jon understood the mechanism very well. Xeno-cancers, the hunter-killers. Tame super-cancers. They tracked down their target organisms and either took them out completely, or neutralised them. Once in a while they'd respond in an inappropriate manner taking on the characteristics of the target, growing it and using their power to spread it throughout the body. That's why there were anti-morphs - killers for cancer killers.

'So they give you an anti and turn it off. What's there to worry about?'

'The genetic defect in this xeno means it won't respond to the anti when it's morphed due to the cancer we've been talking about. What's worse is that it takes over the anti and uses its power to spread the cancer even faster. As a healthy man I had a one in ten chance of surviving the disease, even with a xeno driving it. My chances of surviving the cure are none at all.'

'What happened when they gave Des the anti?'

'They didn't. He knew something was wrong but he was never a man to see a doctor. He never sought any treatment and he never said anything to us, not even to me, his own brother.'

'If he had, they'd have given him the anti and he'd have died anyway.'

'But if they'd known what the anti was going to do they'd have run some tests before using it on a blood relative, and that might have saved *my* life. As it is, it's as if they'd injected me with poison.'

'What would the cancer have done if it had been unchecked?'

'It goes for parts in the bowel area. Totally operable and tissue replacement would have repaired any damage.'

'Without xenos you might have died of some other cancer.'

'We're a lucky family Jon. Our cancer profile is as low as you could hope for. Des and I would've been better off taking our chances than letting them put those things inside us.'

'What about me, or the others?'

'You're my son so it's likely you've got some indication towards the cancer that's killing me. But I checked with the Doctor, the xeno you and the others have doesn't have the same defect. No-one knows their destiny, but at least we know you and the others won't die for the same reason I will.'

'How long have you got?'

'They reckon Des was dying for about two years. It's different for me, I've got the anti-morph driving the cancer and there's nothing any member of our fine medical profession can do to stop it. If it's numbers you want, possibly a few months, a year at the outside.'

'How will it affect you?'

'Every cell of my body is dying Jon. It shouldn't have been that way, but it is. The bits where it grows fastest will go first.'

'Is there any treatment?'

'Yes, but it'd make my last months hell. If there was any real chance of living I'd let them do it, but to go though all that for an extra couple of weeks. What's the point?'

'Have you ………. ?' A lump welled up in Jon's throat and stopped him from saying more.

'Set up an exit profile? It's with the Doctors. They know when to end it, but you, your mother and your siblings have to sign to say you agree. You'll do it for me won't you Jon?'

Jon looked sadly at his father and nodded. 'Do the others know? Are you going to speak to them?'

'I told your mother when I got home from the hospital. If she's as good as her word I think she'll be telling Mandy right now.'

'And Andrew?'

'He's coming round tomorrow. I'll tell him them.'

'So what happens now?'

'Jon, I'm going to die within just a few months. There's no cure, there's no hope, but I'm going to carry on for as long as I can.'

'Father you don't have to. You could take time off, have an easy life. You could even retire completely.'

Now Jon looked and saw the determination in the older man's face.

'No. It's not going to be like that. I like doing what I do and for a while I'll still be well enough to carry on. The bank's been my life as your mother well knows and I'll keep going as long as I can. You can understand that surely?'

Jon stared at the floor, as if suddenly afraid to look his father in the eye.

'If that's what you want, you know I'll do anything I can to help.'

'I know you will Jon. I know I can rely on you, and that's the other reason I invited you in to speak with me now. I'll be gone soon, we know that now. But it doesn't mean that everything I've worked for has to end. When you think of everything this family has achieved in the last three generations, all that we've striven for. The way we pulled ourselves out of mediocrity to join the ranks of the elite, that will go on Jon. It will go on because you will carry the torch forward and *make* it go on. Our ship will continue to sail and a Chandler will be at the helm. Just as I took over from your grandfather, you will take over from me. I will be with you for as long as I'm able, but now we know what we know, from tomorrow I shall start to move out of the way and you will start to take over.'

'But I've only just joined the business Father. It's really difficult when even the junior clerks know more than me.'

'That's why we've got to start straight away. I've seen the way you look out of the window, and I'll grant you that from the level you've been working at, digging a foxhole out on Walridge Plain would be more fun. But if you could see the business from where I stand you'd know it was every bit as exciting. You don't fire any guns, and you don't go fording rivers in your T39s, but the heat of battle in the boardroom is just as gripping. Life in the army is easy, you can see the enemy from miles away because they're the ones shooting at you. Half your time in the boardroom you spend trying to work out who are the allies and who are the enemy. Tomorrow we make a start, and in a few months time you'll be in the thick of it. Just give me that long to convince you, and God give me those months to be with you.'

Jon just sat there, stunned and amazed. 'Yes, yes we'll do it,' was all he could say.

'But I haven't finished yet. There's more, lots more. If you want to feel the heat of battle you've got to be fully engaged, and to do that you have to be hands-on with the money. All of it. Tomorrow I start to pass over the reins to you and I start to hand over the family wealth as well. There will be complications, but I've worked a few things out and in four months time you will have full control of the Chandler family wealth. If I'm still here I will work for a salary, but you will have control.'

Jon saw what his father was offering, but he knew he was a lightweight, no more than an apprentice to the trade. There was no way he could carry it off. He protested:

'But father, it's all so soon. It's too soon for me to take over.'

'We don't know how long we've got Jon. We have to start straight away and hope the time will be enough.'

Jon was not convinced. For his father it was easy to be accepted as the head of the family and the business. But who was he, the third son and just one of three surviving children.

'But what about Andrew, and Mandy Father?'

Robert nodded knowingly. 'I've thought about them and they're two of the complications I told you about, probably the trickiest too. But there's an easy way to handle those two, we don't tell them.'

'Don't tell them? They'll know soon enough.'

'Eventually, when I'm gone. By then enough time will have passed and you'll be established. They'll have to accept you as the top man.'

Jon protested. 'But that's ...., well it's wrong, ...'

His father cut him off before he could say more. 'Jon, what I'm proposing is not against any law that's been written yet, so it's not fraud or anything like that. I've thought long and hard, and this is how it's going to be.'

Jon listened to everything his father had to say and still it was wrong whether he liked it or not. But he knew his father too well to stand his way. Not right then for certain.

'So what do we do eventually with Andrew and Mandy? And if this had been you and Bobby carving things up, would you be leaving me out as well?'

'Jon, there's an old principle from thousands of years ago they called primogeniture, and what it meant was that the entire estate of a father passed to his eldest son. And bear in mind that in the old days the word "son" meant "son". It didn't mean "son or daughter". To keep together the wealth, the lands, or the political power of a family, everything went to the first-born son and the other children got whatever they could - a commission in the army for the second son and good dowries for the daughters.'

'There is just one thing you're overlooking here father. I am your *third* son. In the sad absence of the first son, everything should pass to the second.'

His father was not in a mood to argue and pressed straight on with the speech he had obviously rehearsed earlier that afternoon.

'Primogeniture has no legal standing in this modern age, and when there are no rules to follow, you make your own. You are the child I have *chosen* and to you will go the full estate of the family. You will become the head of the Chandler family and the burden that responsibility brings is that you must support its other members. Andrew will work for the firm and will receive his salary and his due share of the profits. But mark my words when I tell you, Mandy must not have any substantial wealth in her own name or that pratt of a husband will take half when the divorce is settled.'

'And what about my mother?'

'Your mother has never been involved in the business and has never controlled much wealth. Her father raised her to be a woman of the old school and I confess to the crime of leaving her in that position. She was brought up to the idea that ladies would be supported by the men of the family and she must continue to be able to live in the manner to which she has always been accustomed.'

Jon shook his head in disbelief. 'But Andrew and Mandy are still your children and should get their fair share.'

'I disagree. There's no precedent for it in our family. Did Des ask for his fair share when he chose to go it alone? No he didn't, so your grandfather left the whole of Chandler-Wilmott to me. He put the family business entirely in my hands - the hands of the younger son.'

'But it was Des's own decision to go. This is different - you're not giving the others any choice.'

'I don't think they're entitled to a choice Jon, and it's not as if I'm cutting them off without a bean. Far from it, you will make sure they get their fair share of the money that comes in from the business, but I don't want them owning any of the capital. Look what Andrew did with the inheritance Des left him. I don't trust him to own a major share of the firm while that woman's got control of him. And your sister, I'd expected better from her. Goes off to university and comes back a year later because the work was too hard and she didn't like it? That's not what a Chandler does. I want the firm to be in one safe pair of hands, your hands Jon. Surely you must see this is something that matters a great deal to me? If I didn't think you could live up to my expectations I wouldn't be speaking with you right now. But I'll tell you straight, if you won't take on the responsibility I'll sell the whole firm and then you can all have your own equal shares and do what the hell you want with the money. Why should I care? I'm going to be dead Jon. Won't you even do this for a dying man?'

Jon looked his father in the eye. His plan was bizarre and what he was asking was quite unfair. But he wanted to learn and in his heart he knew he wanted to take control of the firm. This was what they'd spoken of on the day of Bobby's funeral - he'd agreed to take his brother's place and that meant taking the responsibility that went hand in hand with the power. But all this mess about who owned the firm, he could sort that out when his father was gone. For now there was only one answer he could give.

23

The Kidnap

Jon pushed his card into the machine and tapped in the PIN code. When a message came up on screen, "No funds available. Please refer to your bank for details" he was more than a little annoyed. Before he could even pocket the card his phone started ringing. Celia - and the desperation in her voice was clear.

'Jon, you've got to come quickly. Robert's been kidnapped!'

★★★

The cab dropped Jon at the end of the drive and as he walked briskly towards the house he noticed the police-car standing on the road outside. Celia was at the door, sobbing. She showed him into the living room where two men were sitting, one uniformed and the other in plain clothes.

The plain clothes man shook Jon's hand and introduced himself as Detective Inspector Bennett. As they sat down Bennett passed Jon a mobile phone which he recognised as Celia's. He read the text on the screen:

"We have your son. Do not contact the police if you want to see him alive".

Jon passed the phone back and then Bennett spoke.

'Mr Chandler, you are I believe the uncle of Robert Chandler?'

Jon was cool in his response.

'You know I am or you wouldn't be asking.'

Bennett's face betrayed no sign of emotion.

'And you are, I understand, quite a wealthy man Mr Chandler?'

'I have a range of financial interests. There are those who consider me to be wealthy.'

Bennett pressed a few buttons on the phone and passed it back to Jon. He read the text, "Tell Uncle Jon the price is 10 million".

Jon looked the big policeman in the eye.

'What are you doing about getting him back? Have you got any leads?'

'Mr Chandler, you have to understand this is an early stage in our investigations. We have almost nothing to go on at the moment apart from two mobile phone numbers and the locations the texts were sent from. One thing I can tell you, it's a professional job - a different SIM card was used for each text, and both cards were purchased over six months ago.'

'Meaning you can't trace where they were purchased from.'

'That and the fact that people don't normally buy a card to keep it in a drawer for six months. The whole thing was planned some time ago.'

'But you do know where the texts were sent from?'

'Somewhere in central Jackson, from any one of ten thousand people who happened to be there at the time. There's not much chance of identifying anyone from video surveillance but we'll run through the records for the minutes leading up to the transmissions. We'll probably find the SIM cards in a bin in Pioneer Plaza, they won't risk using them more than once. But Mr Chandler, I presume you can understand our main reason for this visit?'

Jon knew all too well, but he saw no reason to make their lives any easier than he had to.

'Go on then, enlighten me.'

'Mr Chandler, you have been implicated as the person who would be able to pay a large ransom, so all your personal funds have been frozen. Right now my colleagues are opening a temporary account for your day to day expenses, and they will of course be making sure that all your regular debits are paid. If I suggested a figure of 2000 HUC a week, I'm sure you'd find that reasonable.'

Jon nodded.

'I must also ask you not to abuse any company accounts you have control of. Each and every business transaction made by anyone in either of the companies you control will be subject to scrutiny. The paperwork will be with you as soon as it's ready, and I'm sure you are aware of the penalties for ignoring these instructions?'

Jon nodded again.

'And I'm sure you don't need me to explain that all your mobiles and landlines, and of course any belonging to Miss McArthur, will be monitored for the time being?'

Jon nodded for the third time.

'Well we're busy people Mr Chandler. If you've no more questions we'll be on our way.'

Jon watched as the two men walked out of the house and the car drove away. When it was out of sight he turned towards Celia. She'd stopped her crying for a moment and he saw his chance to speak.

'What the fuck did you call the police for? Didn't you see what the message said? Which part of "don't call the police" didn't you understand? For Belen's sake, how do we get out of this mess now there's no way of paying the ransom?'

Celia spoke between sobs, she'd already called the police before the two text messages came in. She told him the whole story. The first thing she'd known was that Charlie from next door had come running up the drive and banged on the door. He'd been walking home from school with Robert but he wanted to stop at the shop on the corner, so he was going to run to catch him up. Why Robert couldn't have waited outside she'd no idea, but did anyone understand kids? As Charlie came out of the shop he saw a car stopped next to his friend with its doors open, and then two men were fighting a struggling Robert as they bundled him into the back seat. There was no-one else out in the street and Charlie didn't think the men had seen him, but he recognised the type of car and managed to remember half its registration. The police said they'd already found it abandoned a few km away - obviously they'd done a switch. The elderly couple who owned the car used for the snatch hadn't even missed it by the time it was found, and investigations showed they had no involvement in any wrong-doing.

'But surely you knew it was a kidnap? Why did you call the police?'

'It's my son they've got. Obviously I'm going to call the police!'

Jon saw the problem. Coming from the background she did, Celia had no idea about what action to take following a kidnap. Nobody ever bothered to kidnap children from the area she'd grown up in. His own education had been quite different. People from the wealthier classes learned at an early age the first thing the police would do following a kidnap was to freeze the assets of anyone who could provide the ransom money. If they could stop ransoms being paid, perhaps they could eliminate the reasons for the kidnaps - even if a few of the victims had to die. It was a hard policy and parents had no recourse other than to pray that kidnappers would take someone else's children. Jon felt sick inside when he realised the chances of seeing his nephew alive again were slim, but now wasn't the time to explain the details to Celia. He was still comforting her when the landline phone rang.

He picked it up and answered simply 'Yes'.

'Is that Mr Jon Chandler I'm speaking to?'

Jon had never used Celia's number for any business purpose, nor had he ever given it to any of his friends. He made a guess about the source of the call.

'That is correct.'

'How's it coming with the money Mr Chandler? I'm told you're very close to your nephew.'

'There won't be any money. The police have frozen all my accounts, and they're listening to this call right now.'

'You've been very silly Mr Chandler, going to the police when we told you not to.'

'I think you should understand that the police had already been called before your texts were received. Obviously the boy's mother was going to go to the police when her son went missing.'

'What, doesn't she know the way these things are done?'

'No she doesn't. Now considering there is no chance of you ever getting any ransom money I suggest you just drop the boy off somewhere. If you do that I won't fund any private investigation.'

'Oh Mr Chandler, you know it's not that simple. If we gave him back just like that, the whole business would go tits up.'

'Well what then? What are we supposed to do?'

'I'm sure you'll think of something. It's been nice talking to you Mr Chandler, but I've really got to go now.'

Jon sat by the phone waiting for the next call. It took exactly two minutes.

'Did you get all that?' Jon asked the police monitoring service operator.

'Of course. The call was made from a moving vehicle somewhere between Jackson and Linden.'

★★★

Jon drove up to Rosemount to fetch some clean clothes, and then moved into the spare room at Celia's house - the room where he'd slept so often in happier times. Next morning when he arrived at the office he found an envelope lying on his desk. A quick phone call to the post room confirmed it had been in the company mail-box that morning, and from the lack of a stamp or postmark it had obviously been delivered by hand. He read the message inside, "Buy a mobile and register it with false details. Call the number below. The call will not be answered. Wait for instructions".

★★★

With the new mobile in his hand, Jon's fingers trembled slightly as he tapped in the code. As he'd been told, his call was not answered.

24

Joking With Amey

The past hour had seen a frenzy of activity with the mountain of paperwork needed to support the legality of the forthcoming transfer flying backwards and forwards across the 300 light-years of empty space that separated Vissan from Phoenix. Now with just 90 minutes to go before the slot Carrington had booked Jon was desperately waiting for the final issue to arrive on his desk for signature. After everything he'd been through there was no way he could let mere formalities get in the way.

Something that had done little to quieten his mind had been the revelation by TranzCon that they hadn't carried out a single cross-gender mind-swap since the last act of parliament had required a total re-write of the standard contract. But Jon was undeterred, already well past the point of changing his mind. If they'd told him the only body he could transfer into belonged to a hippopotamus he'd probably have gone along with it.

Then the bloody phone wouldn't stop. Somehow everything needed to be sorted that minute just because he was going to be away for a few days. But then, that was all part and parcel of being a senior minister.

Jon recalled that Amey had put her head round the edge of the door during the last call, so maybe it was an indication there might be something waiting for him. He was about to press the intercom button but decided it would be better if he stretched his legs and grabbed a cup of something hot instead of sitting in his chair inviting the next call to ring the phone off his desk.

Amey looked up as he walked into the outer office and gave him a happy smile. Maybe it was just a little too happy. Something was going on - what?

'Have we got the final documents yet?'

'They came in while you were on the phone Mr Chandler. All the changes our lawyers asked for have been included.'

Surely the exchange must have been a cue for an efficient super-secretary to hand her boss the documents and a pen to sign them with, but Amey did neither.

'So is there a copy for me to sign, then you can scan it and email a copy back to Celebration.'

'There's one more change to make. Some clause they'd missed out earlier.'

'Oh for Belen's sake. Like what for example?'

Jon saw the mischievous smile that came to Amey's face.

'On no account can your host body be used for sex. It's absolutely forbidden - and it isn't negotiable either.'

He gave her an indignant look.

'The thought never crossed my mind. Anyway, just what sort of sex would I be using a body like that for. I hope you're not suggesting having sex with a man.'

The smile turned to a pout. She almost kissed the air in front of her.

'And why not, I do it all the time. Well once a week anyway, or maybe twice if Harry's had a good round at the golf club.'

'Yes but you're a woman.'

'And you'll be a woman too.'

'No, it's not like that at all. I'll be occupying a woman's body, but the person in control will still be a *man*.'

Amey knew not to push the joke too far and turned just a little more serious.

'So go on then, what's she like, this girl you're going to be.'

Jon picked up the data sheet and photos from his in-tray and handed them to Amey. She looked critically at the pictures in the way that only a woman could.

'And how old do you say she is, seventeen?'

Jon shook his head. Once upon a time they used to sack secretaries for being too cheeky.

'Well I'll agree she doesn't look very old, but actually she's twenty two.'

Amey peered at one of the photographs.

'She'd be pretty if it wasn't for the nose.'

'I'm not going there to be *pretty*.'

'If you spent your whole life being female you might find that being attractive gave you a few advantages now and again. Anyway the body's nice. Are you sure people are going to take you seriously when you turn up looking like this?'

'Look, the body's just a vehicle, something to operate from. What's important is the *me* inside. People look through the physical details of your host body and see the real person behind the façade.'

'And how do they know it's you inside the body?'

'They give you a badge to wear.'

'A badge to show that really you're a man?'

'Yes, if you like.'

'And do you wear this badge on your left boob or your right?'

Amey was just about disappearing into a fit of giggles by now.

'I don't think it matters,' Jon replied, striving valiantly to keep his composure.

'Well I can't wait to see the photos.'

'Well I'll look just like the picture you're holding.'

'No, I meant something like you in a little black number with the Phoenixan president kissing your hand and wondering if there was more he could do to cement the new entente.'

Jon looked up to the ceiling shaking his head slowly from side to side and made a little "Tsk" with his tongue.

'Amey, come on just give me a break. I'll agree that for *this* trip I've been railroaded into something that I really didn't want, but it's only until the weekend. And you know what's at stake for me don't you?'

'I've heard rumours.'

'Well if it happens, you'll be coming up to the Peacock Room with me. How does that sound?'

The surprise on Amey's face was clear to see.

'But Emma's the secretary to the First Minister. I'd have thought you'd have been obliged to take her over.'

'OK I agree that's what Tom did, but Charles had only been First Minister for two years before he died so it was logical to leave her in that position. Anyway Emma can work for one of the other ministers so she'll keep her pay and conditions. But look, all this about being First Minister, keep it under your hat.'

'I only wear hats for weddings and funerals.'

'If any of this gets out and I can trace it back to you Amey Sullivan the rest of us might be going to a funeral sooner than you think.'

'And if you do get to be First Minister Mr Chandler, are you going to be old school like Charles, or progressive like Mr Hanson?'

'No, and no again. I'm going to take my own route. I'm not just going to follow where others have lead. But something I can bring to the position is that everyone can be sure I'm not just in it for my own gain - unlike some people who get to high office.'

'I don't know why you came into politics in the first place. If you'd stuck to your business ventures you could have been on your way to being the Union's 28th richest man.'

'Fat chance of that. The 28th richest man is over 50% more wealthy than me and getting richer every day. Anyway, I've just thought of an advantage of being female.'

'I'm glad someone has.'

'Instead of being the 28th richest man, I could be the Union's 12th richest woman.'

'So you're planning on staying on Phoenix for a while then?'

Jon laughed. 'No chance! On Saturday I'll be back here in my own body, and first thing Monday morning you can help me start looking for some really suitable hosts, one on each planet in the Union and then I'll be able to travel around as much as I want.'

'No more ships?'

'Well maybe just the odd trip here or there.'

'But nothing as odd as the one you're off on tomorrow,' and she started her fit of giggling over again.

'Amey, I just wanted to ask you, something.'

'Yes Mr Chandler?'

'Amey, do you have any tips, or words of advice about being a woman.'

She smiled. 'Well for a start, make sure you remember to sit down when you go for a pee.'

Jon sighed. 'I'd sort of worked that one out for myself.'

'Oh, and don't forget to check some man hasn't left the seat up - they do that you know. And don't forget your handbag, there's things in there a woman might need.'

Jon gave a frown. 'No, there won't be anything like that. They've got the girl on some medication to make sure it doesn't happen, well at least not while I'm using her body.'

Amey shook her head and giggled again. 'Good job too. That and a dose of man-flu would probably finish you off. Men, you don't know you're even born most of the time.'

Jon had already given up trying to win in the rapid repartee stakes. "Wimmin" he said under his breath, just loud enough for Amey to hear.

25

The Deal

After Jon arrived back at the big house that evening the new mobile rang.

'Nice to speak to you again Mr Chandler. Look we've been thinking about the situation, and we understand the problem your ladyfriend's been up against, so considering the circumstances, we're prepared to accept a token payment in return for the boy. Shall we say two million?'

Jon was calm this time. 'I don't know who you are, and so far you haven't offered any proof that you've actually got my nephew. Why should I even deal with you?'

'Well the boy's missing isn't he, and how many other ransom demands have you had?'

Jon hesitated, desperately searching for an answer.

'That says it all Mr Chandler. We both know what this business is about and people don't take the risks we do just so they can keep some whiny kid supplied with pizza while he watches TV. That's their parents' job.'

'Well put him on the phone then. Let him speak to me.'

'Just assume we've got him will you Mr Chandler. Now what about the money?'

'Ten million, two million, it really doesn't matter how much. I can't get my hands on that sort of money with all my assets frozen.'

'Oh you must have a bit stashed away the police can't find. Everyone else in Rosemount does.'

Jon knew they were right, but he'd raided most of his secret hoard a few years ago when he needed every cent he could get his hands on to finance a new venture.

'I can get you about 150,000 in gold. That's all I've got access to at the moment.'

'Oh Mr Chandler, you do like a joke - it's not even enough to cover our expenses. Something you might like to consider is that you often get damaged goods when you pay knockdown prices. Am I making myself clear Mr Chandler?'

Jon's voice hardened. 'If you harm the boy I can assure you there will be trouble. When we have him back, or when it's confirmed he's dead, my accounts will be unfrozen. Then I can hire a whole army of investigators to track you down. So I'm giving you another chance - if you send him back now, unharmed, there'll be no follow-up and you can have the ingots as well.'

The phone clicked off.

★★★

Next morning a small parcel arrived at Celia's house. After removing the packing Celia gave a shriek the neighbours heard halfway down the street. When Jon got to the house twenty minutes later he saw the object that had been carefully wrapped in a polythene bag. Forensic tests showed it was the little toe from the left foot of a teenage male. DNA tests showed it belonged to Robert Chandler the third.

In the middle of the afternoon Jon's new mobile rang again.

'Did you get the package this morning Mr Chandler.'

Jon was beyond fury, but he tried hard to sound calm. 'Yes.'

'Do you believe we've got your nephew now?'

'Yes I do, you bastard.'

'Oh Mr Chandler, I'm disappointed in your choice of language - and I thought you were a gent. But look, we're going to cool things down a bit now so you won't have to worry for a few days. The boy is well although you can imagine his foot's still a bit sore. This is the deal Mr Chandler, you've got a week to get the money together or we up the stakes a bit, and you know what I said about damaged goods?'

The phone clicked off.

26

Robert Chandler - Rip

Seven months had passed while Jon worked and learned alongside his father. Robert had been as good as his word and had entered into the spirit of teaching his son everything he would need to know to run the company, but Jon knew full well just how many late evenings and missed weekends it had taken. If he'd thought another twenty years of hard labour were going to pass before he could truly take control he'd have given it all up and gone back to the army, or maybe into medicine. It was only the knowledge of his father's limited life that kept him going. He'd had the right training and the best teacher in the world, and with his determination to succeed he was going to do nothing else.

When his father had taken him into his first board meeting he'd been scared. By the time he sent him in alone he was proud. Proud to be able to take the role his father had groomed him for. Now at just thirty years old he was virtually running the bank on his own, though with his father still watching every move. It was re-assuring that the old man was still there to keep him out of trouble, but undermining too because everyone knew it was still his father who held the real power.

***

Jon had his first chance to practice flying solo when his father was rushed into hospital after suffering a blackout. When the final bars of "Belen my Saviour, pray for me" played twelve days later, he knew he was really on his own. Perhaps his father would be watching from some cloud on high and now was his chance to make the old man proud.

The Knightons had always kept a connection with their home city of Keemouth, so when Maureen's sister moved to a nice apartment at Peter's Haven on the western outskirts Jon's mother had become a regular visitor. The stunning scenery and the way the place nestled in the lee of the cliffs made it a lovely place to sit out and watch as the sun went down while the waves crashed onto the rocks below. There were those who complained that for only five days either side of the solstice did the sun actually set into the sea, and for the rest of the year it dropped down over the inconvenient spit of land chance had chosen to put in its way, but most who lived in the houses and flats overlooking the little bay thought the location idyllic. When the apartment next door became vacant Maureen told her children she'd be spending more time by the coast.

Jon thought about his life up at the big house. Andrew was still down-town with Jemima and Mandy was already deep into her second marriage. Four years had passed since she'd last stayed at her old home. The place was really so much more than he needed right now, but his father had been adamant, the house was to remain - the head of the Chandler family did not live in a flat. And like a castle, or a family seat, the house had to stay in the family, to be passed on from generation to generation. But to come home each evening to twenty seven empty rooms? The fine old mansion that had once played host to the laughter of children was eerie in its deathly hush. Before even the first week of life alone was over, Jon was convinced his old home was haunted.

He had thoughts of getting Celia and his little nephew to come and live with him out in Rosemount, but then he thought back to his mother. She'd never said she was actually moving out, so the big house was still her home. For her to arrive one day and find *her* there would be too much. And what would Liz think when she came to visit? She'd already had her suspicions about Jon and Celia. So what about moving Liz in? It was over a year now since she'd begun her internship at the general hospital in Regenswood and surely she must be looking for a move soon. And there were always vacancies in Jackson. But then, he wondered whether he really wanted her to move in at all.

In any case there were other options. Now he had full access to the family wealth Jon knew he could do better for Celia and Robert. Although she'd transformed the little flat from the squalor he'd seen that first morning Jon had never been happy with the place, and in her brief years with Bobby Celia had picked up a taste for the better things in life. So the three of them had been excited the day they'd looked around a nice bungalow in Merrivale, one of the old residential areas just a few kilometres out from the centre of Jackson. And five weeks later they were moving in.

The district was quiet, and the way big old trees lined the sides of the avenues lent a touch of class to the area, something that was often lacking in the more recently settled outer suburbs. Jon loved everything about the place, it was exactly the right size, the older style was pleasing to the eye, and its former owners had really cared for it. In fact they'd been reluctant to leave but unfortunately their circumstances had changed. Along one side and out at the back the house had a modest sized garden, and the big patio doors in the sitting-room gave a good view out onto the lawn and the border of flowering shrubs and bushes that marked the boundary of the plot. Little Robert was excited about the idea of having his own garden with swings and a slide and looked forward to the day when he could invite some friends round to play.

And it wasn't long before Robert found his first friend. A face peered out from a hole in the hedge and a boy suddenly popped out and ran across the lawn. Little Charlie Harrison from the house next door had been used to having the empty garden as his secret domain and was just a little surprised to find new people there. It was the start of a friendship that was to last for many years.

When Jon came to visit at weekends the two boys were always playing together, so Sunday mornings were spent stalking through the bushes with a bow and arrow to ambush the cowboys in the clearing.

For Jon, so alone in the austerity of his grand mansion Celia's new house seemed just right. Cosy and warm, little more than walking distance from the bank, and only a short cab ride home from the city's theatres and restaurants. He knew he'd always be welcome there, in a happy home filled with laughter. If he could have been more than a guest he'd have been over the moons, but would he dare take the risk of losing what he already had? Sometimes he watched Celia out in the garden and wondered whether enough years had passed for him to have another try.

Liz came to Jackson almost every weekend though even she was just a little spooked by the big house, now so empty, quiet and cold. So most times she'd stayed with her parents, and knowing their slightly old-fashioned views about the younger generation not yet married Jon never presumed to share her bed for the night.

The twists and turns of life, the ups and the downs. Perhaps it had been the relationships with the women in his life that had lead Jon into visiting the town late at night. For a man with money in his pocket, opportunities were always there. For a man who tipped well, the hotel porter had forgotten their faces before the room door had even closed.

27

Arrested!

After the last threat he'd received Jon could think of nothing else apart from getting his nephew back unharmed. He told his people at Rapier and the bank he'd be away for a while and concentrated his efforts on trying to get some money together. It was true he didn't have much stashed away but he knew a good few people who did, and the promise of repayment when the ordeal was over was good enough for most when it came from a Chandler. After nine calls on the new mobile he'd managed to secure 1.2 million. If he could get one and a half the kidnappers might do a deal.

★★★

Jon was sitting in the living room at Celia's house making another call when he heard the doorbell. A minute later Celia showed DI Bennett into the room. The big man sat himself on the sofa and looked Jon in the eye.

'Jonathan Charles Churchill Chandler?'

'That is my name as you well know.'

'Mr Chandler, I have a warrant for your arrest.'

The man handed over a sheaf of papers. Jon read the words on the front sheet.

'I take it from this you've not managed to track down the kidnappers then?'

'They're professionals as you know Mr Chandler, they don't make these things easy for us. Now, are you going to come quietly or shall I call for the heavies?'

'What about my phone call?'

'You can make it from the station while we're sorting out the paperwork.'

Celia had been sitting watching, hoping the policeman was going to give them some good news. She put her head in her hands before looking up again.

'You can't take him away, he's the only one who's doing anything about getting Robert back.'

Jon looked over at her. 'It's OK, I know exactly what they're doing. I'll be back here later when it's all sorted out. You'll be OK. We'll get Robert back.'

Celia felt the tears running down her cheeks as she watched Jon and the DI walking out to the car.

★★★

Jon looked around at the grey walls of the room. Unpainted blockwork, a steel door with a mesh reinforced window, a table bolted to the floor in the middle of the room, and four extremely hard and uncomfortable chairs. Pacing round the room was better than sitting, but there was a limit to how many laps he could do before boredom set in.

Perhaps an hour had passed before he heard a sound and turned towards it - the lock clicked and the cell door opened. DI Bennett and Jon's solicitor, Peter Marks, walked into the room. Bennett sat at one side of the table and gestured for the other two to sit opposite.

'And what exactly is the charge against my client?' the solicitor asked.

'Aiding and abetting a criminal operation,' the DI replied. 'It's a serious crime as you well know Mr Marks.'

'And if you've gone to the trouble of arresting my client, I take it you have some proof of his guilt?'

'As you are no doubt aware, Mr Chandler's nephew has been abducted, and we know that Mr Chandler here was planning to pay a substantial ransom to secure the boy's return.'

'That seems to be an entirely reasonable thing to do. Wouldn't you do the same for someone in your own family.'

'Are you suggesting I should break the law Mr Marks?'

The solicitor changed his tack. 'How is the investigation going detective inspector? Will you be making any arrests soon? How many kidnappings have you solved this year?'

The stonewall look on the policeman's face betrayed no sign of emotion.

'It's a very rare crime as you know Mr Marks. There haven't been any kidnappings this year.'

The lawyer gave a quick glance up at the ceiling and shook his head in disbelief.

'It happens all the time, you know it does.'

'Well we can only solve the crimes that are reported to us.'

'And do you wonder why kidnappings aren't reported to you?'

The big policeman shifted himself round on the hard seat, obviously not at ease with how the case was proceeding.

'With respect Mr Marks, this line of interrogation you're subjecting me to is not getting us anywhere. I suggest we stick to the charge that's been made against Mr Chandler.'

'As you wish. Since you've arrested him it follows that you're going to charge him, and if you're going to charge him you must have some evidence or you're going to look a bit silly when the case comes to court.'

'We have evidence that the accused was attempting to secure funds to pay the ransom demanded. That's enough to secure a conviction, and of course we'll be pressing for the maximum sentence. It wouldn't do for someone to get off lightly just because he was rich enough to buy his way out of justice, would it?'

'Maybe you'd be so good as to share the details of this so-called evidence you have?'

'As you are aware Mr Marks, in cases like these we immediately start monitoring any incoming or outgoing phone calls, or texts, that might be relevant to the case. So the standard ploy of the criminals is to get their victims to acquire another phone which isn't being monitored.'

Peter Marks wrote a brief note in his book. 'So you agree my client is the victim then?'

Bennett ignored the question and continued. 'And our monitoring service became aware of a previously unregistered mobile phone connecting to the network in a cell which could also have provided service to Mr Chandler's office.'

Marks was looking worried now, but he continued. 'And it follows from that, that my client is guilty?'

'There's more, as you can probably appreciate. Still located in the cell that covers Mr Chandler's office, the mobile made a single call. It later received a call in the cell that covers Mr Chandler's home. The mobile then received another call in the cell which covers the house belonging to Miss Celia McArthur, who I'm sure you know of. The most compelling piece of data the police monitoring service collected is that this newly connected mobile moved from cell to cell at almost exactly the same time as the mobile we already know is registered to Mr Chandler. That's very close to proving he had the phone in his possession.'

Peter Marks gave Jon a look he didn't quite understand.

Bennett continued. 'So considering the circumstantial evidence that existed, we sought authorisation to intercept calls on this newly connected mobile, and the transcripts are here.'

He dropped a pile of A4 sheets onto the table.

'Would you like to read them, or shall we continue the discussion?'

Peter Marks picked up the first one and showed it to Jon who nodded.

'You'll have time to go through them in detail of course, but I think it's fair to say that Mr Chandler has been involved in the process of gathering together unregistered sums of cash and gold. And since he has been served with an order that prohibits him from doing that, I don't think we'd have much bother securing a conviction. What do you think Mr Marks?'

'I'd like to speak to my client alone for a while. Would that be OK?'

'You've got ten minutes.'

The big policeman stood up stiffly and walked out of the door.

Jon could see the way his solicitor was looking at him.

'That was a bit silly Jon. Obviously they were going to link the new mobile to you.'

'I didn't know they'd got the technology to trace it like that.'

'Well you know now - just a shame it's too late. He's right in everything he says of course - they've got you by the short and curlies and there's sod all I can do about it. If Bennett goes ahead with charging you it's a non-violent offence so they can't refuse bail, but when it comes to court you're going to lose and you heard what he said about pressing for the maximum sentence. You could go down for somewhere between three to five years.'

Jon's jaw dropped. 'But under the circumstances, surely a citizen is entitled to take action to safeguard his family?'

'That's not the way the law sees it. Preventing ransom payments is the only weapon they've got against kidnapping.'

'Isn't there anything we can do?'

The lawyer thought for a moment before he spoke. 'Well look, Bennett's not really in the business of prosecuting people like you, certainly not anyone as high profile as you. If he offers another way out, any other way out, take it.'

They heard the door and DI Bennett walked back into the room.

'I hope that was enough time Mr Marks?'

'Plenty, thank you. Can you advise me what's going to come next? Do you intend to charge my client?'

Bennett turned to face Jon, his jaws moved together as he bit onto his upper lip.

'Mr Chandler, unless I charge you, I can only hold you here for 24 hours, and I would like you to be with us for a little longer than that. If you'd be prepared to "help us with our enquiries" on a voluntary basis, then I might be able to put off charging you - and maybe the whole matter might just blow over.'

Jon looked over at Peter Marks and saw the way he nodded.

★★★

Celia was beside herself with worry. A week had passed and she'd heard nothing from the police, and nothing from Jon either. She'd called his mobile, she'd tried the offices at Rapier and Chandler-Wilmott, and of course the house in Rosemount too. It was only after making trips to the office and the big house that she was sure enough to call the police and report him as missing, but apart from the deadpan response of the desk sergeant at the central station who took the details, so far there'd been nothing.

Now she looked at the package in front of her - delivered by mail and neatly wrapped in brown paper. It was addressed to Jon and the postmark showed it had come from Linden. She ripped open the paper to see a plastic sandwich box filled with polystyrene chippings. Rooting through the white beads she found a freezer bag with something red inside. The note inside read: "Sorry you've not been in touch with us Mr Chandler. We did warn you that something like this might happen".

With trembling hands Celia picked up the phone and called the number on the card that DI Bennett had left.

28

The Arrival

Jon heard the sound of the motor as it whirred into life. The bed advanced slowly into the scanner blanking out his view of the rest of the room. Just he'd been told he concentrated his gaze on the bright point of light just in front of his face, let his mind go blank - and waited. In a matter of seconds he knew he'd be unconscious, but those first few moments could feel like hours. That was the bit he didn't like.

The process started and almost immediately he felt the mental turmoil, felt the machine as it stirred his memories, sifting, raking, tunnelling down into the recesses of everything he was, everything he'd ever known, setting free a mind that before this moment had known only a single home. Setting it free to begin a journey. Pictures flew into his vision. Some passed, whirlwind fast. Some he grabbed and held for just a moment: a small boy with a grazed knee, a kindly lady washing it with something that stung - Bobby and Andrew kicking a ball - Mandy laughing, opening her presents at Belenf ……….

★★★

David Hulett Wilson

A river flowed. Shafts of sunlight percolated through the leafy canopy high overhead to beam a pattern of sparkling diamonds that danced and shimmered across the glassy surface. A pair of eyes gazed high to the tangle of arching branches that joined overhead. A body floated serenely through a tunnel of green. In joy, Jon called out for only the creatures of the forest to hear, that paradise had found him - at last.

The lazy waters of the big river buoyed him slowly past walls of the dense green jungle which marked the boundaries of the flow. One moment in deep shadow the eyes passed to a clearing where vision was stolen by the scintillating flash of brilliant rays. Dazzled and blinded the eyes were patient as the patina of purple slowly faded. With sight restored he lifted his head to watch a tapestry of heavy hanging roots that passed him slowly by, the dull green swathe interrupted only by the iridescent hues of bright flowers that set the bank ablaze. Far above him the shrieks of parrots pierced the background buzz of insects in their millionfold. The once placid air rushed and rippled as a flash of blue wing whisked by no more than the breadth of a hair from the lightly bearded face, and a luckless fish met the fate it had never known to dread.

Whether there had been existence before the river he would never know. Maybe he had been here for a thousand years, or perhaps this had been his life for only the blink of an eye. The river was here, and here was he. Timeless harmony. How it had always been, how it was, how it would ever be.

Peace reigned. Days passed in the comfort of the gentle current, or maybe only seconds, and yet he knew, somehow, that not all was well. The calm he'd known for so long was broken by an urgency, a sensation he recalled. From when? From an earlier life?

At first it had been no more than a distant rumble. Perhaps thunder from a storm? But the sounds grew louder, the hushed murmurs of the tranquil forest soon forgotten. His eyes were startled as water-birds, knowing of old the impending peril spread heavy beating wings and gave their trust instead to the air. The river, once benign, became a bore, a rip-tide running faster. And faster. Rocks ripped savagely from the deep, as if swords thrust high by hands unseen to split the maelstrom time and time again to an outraged torrent that stormed frantically beneath him. Spray lashed out to deluge the banks that struggled to contain the angry flux. The frenzied roar of the fury drew nearer with every heartbeat.

Now he was swimming, swimming madly, swimming for his life. A gift from the Gods was granted as a rock flashed into view. A strong hand grasped the wet cold pinnacle - only to be ripped painfully away as the impetuous surge pulled him ever onward. Another rock approached. He reached out toward it but the turbulent stream dragged him by, the precious handhold no more than a half millimetre beyond his reach. A chute of water took him, and sped him madly down through the next rapid. His head went under as the flow tumbled him head over heels, over and over again. In desperation he caught a glimpse of the water's surface, so near and yet so far, but he had to try.

Summoning the last reserves from muscles that screamed in pain he powered up though the surging water. At last he broke out from the surface, heart racing, lungs gasping for air, thankful for his salvation - when the tumultuous flow slammed him head-first into a wall of solid stone.

When he next opened his eyes he was clinging to a rock that stood alone in the middle of the course. One hand made contact while his free arm flailed wildly in the current as the river strove with overwhelming force to drag him away.

The last of his strength was failing, but he held on - held onto the rock: held onto life. But how long could he last?

How long before his strength was finally gone? How long before the plunge into the yawning abyss below?

The light, once dull and fading slowly changed. Somehow brighter. The noise of the river abated. A stillness descended. Jon lifted his eyes from the rock to gaze up at the shimmering orb floating gently above him. A sparkling jewel of azure blue. The light revealed only to souls so lost that hope had been abandoned. Was it God's emissary leading him to paradise? Or the Devil's lure to tempt him to hell? He remembered back to an age long past, to words he'd almost forgotten:

"Have faith Jon. Follow the light. Trust ME. Follow".

His grip was weaker now and the keen edge of the rock bit painfully into the red raw fingers. The orb remained, floating serenely in the air above him. Waiting, watching perhaps? In the calm there was time for thought. A change was coming - soon. His fate was in his own hands - the decision had to be his and his alone. He knew, he had to want it, he had to *want* whatever the step before him brought. No matter what it brought.

The fingers parted and the rock slipped away, slowly at first, but faster with every moment.

Now the silence was ripped apart. The thundering crescendo returned and he saw the edge as it approached at breakneck speed, the marker that stood sentinel to the frontier of life. No more than a moment passed before the mighty river became a cascade into the void which opened below as he fell into the empty darkness.

★★★

A body jerked ……. and then was still.

A man in a white coat watched and eased himself forwards until his lips almost kissed the microphone on the desk in front of him. Quietly, as if fearing he might raise the dead from their slumber he spoke no more than a single word, 'Lifesign.'

David Hulett Wilson

29

The Reading Of The Will

Even as the family members grouped together outside James Greene's office Jon watched his brother and sister chatting, and knew there'd be trouble before the morning was over. Their father's old solicitor sat behind a big leather topped desk shuffling files and folders before finally picking up the wax sealed envelope. Andrew and Mandy sat on the chairs next to Jon, watching with expectant eyes.

There was little surprise when James read out the first of the details and told them that 2.5 million HUC would be used to buy an annuity to pay a pension to Maureen Chandler. There were murmurs of discontent when he read out that the big house would be held in trust to be used in perpetuity by his heirs and descendents, but when the old man began to read the next part he stopped to glance through the rest of the papers before he continued. The remainder of the estate of Robert Emerson Chandler would be divided in equal portions between his surviving children. After deducting the 2.5 million needed for the annuity, and making due allowance for the costs of setting up the trust and the settlement of

James' fee, the three heirs would each receive 1,130,000 HUC. The hush that filled the room was oppressive. Jon knew it wouldn't last for long, and he knew there was no escape.

***

The three siblings had only got as far as the reception area when an agitated Mandy asked. 'What's going on Jon? Where's all the money gone?'

Andrew pushed his face closer to his brother's, as though he was ready to threaten violence. 'I think you've got some explaining to do.'

Jon looked at the almost menacing expressions on the faces of his brother and sister and knew the time had come for him to lay his cards out on the table. After all, the channelling of the family fortune in his direction had been his father's wish and he personally had nothing to hide. He drew in a deep breath.

'This is what Father wanted for me, and for us. Now I'll agree that neither of you knew at the time, and this was entirely our father's doing, but a number of months ago the family share of Chandler-Wilmott was put into my sole trust, so it didn't form part of our father's estate. All that was divided up today was what he'd retained personally outside of company funds.'

Jon looked Andrew in the eye and could see straight away that his brother was unhappy with the news he'd heard so far. Without giving him chance to break into the conversation he continued, 'and according to our father's wishes, I am charged with the responsibility of owning it on behalf of the family. I have to tell you that I was against it at first, and I told our father so, but eventually he talked me round.'

'Talked you into taking the whole fucking lot! How much *talking into* do you need, you money grabbing bastard?'

Mandy was not at her most ladylike Jon had to admit.

Andrew spoke. 'So he's effectively made you the head of the family then? What about me?'

Jon could tell his brother was more rattled than he'd ever seen him before.

'As I said, at first I told him it was wrong, but our father asked me to take this role - a role I never sought. But be sure of this, from today onwards the three of us will split the profits from the bank's activities - in equal shares.'

'And how much is that then?', Mandy asked.

'We need to go into the audited accounts to be exact, but we could be looking at about three million a year each. Is that enough to keep you in the manner to which you've become accustomed?'

'It's not a lot compared to what Kasper makes.'

'It's a fortune compared to how ordinary people live.'

'We're not ordinary people Jon, or hadn't you noticed? But what about the capital? The bank alone is worth over 500 million.'

'Of which the Chandlers own 51%.'

Mandy looked puzzled. 'Why so little? I thought we owned it all.'

'When Charlie pulled out of the business, Grandpa had to buy him out. The only way he could raise money like that was to float the company but he always retained a controlling interest. That's why the Chandlers have exactly 51%. Over the years the bank issued more stock so some of the senior people could have a stake, but Father bought in as well so he could keep control.'

'And now you're keeping the whole fucking lot for yourself. Dare we ask who you'll leave it to when you finally pop off? Am I going to have to doff my cap to Celia?'

'Perhaps you'd be civil enough to wait till I've died before carving things up would you.'

Jon noticed that his voice had risen, both in volume and pitch. He let himself calm a little before he continued.

'Anyway, there's no chance of anything major going to Celia. She knows nothing about the business and she isn't a Chandler.'

'Just like me then,' said Mandy.

'Mandy, I know you're Mrs Ormond now, but by blood you're a Chandler.'

'So does that mean the brat might get a cut?'

'He's called Robert and he's your brother's son, so he's a Chandler. Whether he gets a stake will depend on whether he wants to come into the business when he's older. Anyway, although I own the Chandler stake in the bank at the moment, on behalf of all of us I hasten to add, my original thought was that when this day finally came I'd split it up into equal portions. But I've thought about it in these last few days, and after the response I've just got from you and Andy I'm not so sure whether it's the right thing to do.'

'And where do I stand in all this?' Andrew chipped in.

'You're a Chandler and you know the business. If I thought I could rely on you, you could take your share of the firm right now. It's Mandy who's the loose cannon. As she freely admits she knows nothing about the business and she's married into a family who could turn out to be dangerous enemies. How can I risk 17% of the voting rights going to her when Kasper could use it to overrule me on an important issue?'

'Knowing who *I'm* married to, can you risk any voting rights going to me?' his brother asked.

Jon was struggling for answers now. For so many years, all his father had wanted was for his children to marry into the old money dynasties of Jackson. But he'd never thought through the implications of getting so closely into bed with powerful rivals.

'Both of you, this is my decision. For now everything will stay exactly the way it is. All the Chandler shares we own, that's 51% of the voting stock, will remain with me, but you will receive shares of the profits as if you owned an equal third. What I'm going to look into is finding a way of giving you the financial stakes you're entitled to, but without giving away any control. Does that sound reasonable?'

Mandy didn't seem to be happy about the deal.

'So we'd get non-voting stock then. It would be worth less than full-rights stock, but we could sell out if we chose?'

Jon shook his head. 'No - that wouldn't be allowed. We're talking about family restricted stock here. You can only sell to blood relatives of the Chandlers.'

'What about the Knightons?' Mandy asked.

'The rules are written to say "Chandler",' Jon replied.

'So that means the three of us here, and the love-child in Kingston of course,' said Mandy.

'And your children when they come of age,' Jon countered.

'So what you're offering us is stock that has no power, and that can't be sold either. It's not an attractive offer is it?'

Jon saw how the going was getting harder all the time. Next time he spoke his voice was raised.

'Look at my situation then. How can I do anything else? I'll tell you now, before we started this conversation I didn't know how it was going to pan out. I was playing the whole thing by ear, but with the attitude you're taking it's getting easier and easier to make my mind up. I mean, it's not like you're poor or anything, you won't be sleeping rough tonight. You don't even have to make your own dinner because the servants buy it, and cook it, and serve it up to Lady fucking

Muck - on fucking silver plate. And then they wash it all up afterwards. Lets face it, you're not exactly short.'

'And that's your final word?' she almost shouted.

'Its my final word.'

And then Mandy was strangely calm, but there was venom in her voice as she spoke. 'Jon, do you remember a time when you wanted to be a doctor? When you wanted to help people. You almost persuaded me to go into medicine with you, and I'd have done it if I'd got the grades.'

'Got the grades? Got the fucking grades? You never did any work for them. You didn't deserve those grades.'

Jon looked at his sister. She was fuming with rage.

'Did you even think about money in those days when all you wanted was to help people? Now the only thing that matters is *more*. *More* money, *more* profit, *more* wealth. Greed, greed, greed.'

'You just don't understand Mandy. It's got nothing to do with greed. I've got a duty to the shareholders, I have to work hard to make sure they get value from their investment.'

'And who's the biggest shareholder? You're making it for yourself Jon. Well good luck to you and your financial fucking empire. I hope you work yourself into an early grave.'

'Oh piss off Mandy.'

Mandy turned and stormed out of the room.

Jon looked Andrew in the eye. 'And what about you then brother. How do you stand?'

Andrew spoke calmly. 'About a year ago I received the offer of a very good job at Tyndalls, but of course I turned them down. I heard yesterday that the guy they gave the job to hadn't really worked out, so I'll bet it's up for grabs again. Assuming I am accepted, you'll have my resignation on your desk almost immediately. Will that be satisfactory .... sir?'

Jon turned his head away, unable to believe what he was hearing. Why did it have to be this way? He'd been forced to accept whatever his father had wanted, and now with the old man gone only days ago the people he'd once thought so dear weren't prepared to accept the same.

★★★

Two days later Jon found a letter on his desk. He knew what it said even before he opened it. Mandy for her part never spoke to him again. And she never sent a Belenfest card, or even a birthday card though there was no way she could have forgotten the date. And she never spoke to her children about their rich uncle.

Well good riddance to the pair of them. *He* had a job to do, *he* was the one who'd been entrusted with protecting and building the family fortune. *He* knew it was what Grandpa and his father, and Bobby too, would all have done.

30

A Boy By The Roadside

Just like the week before, and the week before that, Ernest Palmer was off on business again. His wife hated Monday mornings when her man climbed into his company car to head off for another week out on the road. Ernest hated it too. Another four nights of faceless motels, another four evenings of meals that always came with too many chips and a sprig of limp salad. But somebody had to keep the business rolling in, somebody had to smile nicely and do their best to enthuse the customers about the virtues of his employer's latest range of industrial valves and pressure regulators. Five more years and he'd be in line for an early retirement package - if they were still offering early retirement in five years time. The radio signal faded as he got further away from Jackson and he was just searching for another station when he saw the hitch-hiker by the side of the road. But somehow the boy didn't quite fit the bill - far too young and no rucksack. He hadn't even stuck his thumb out as Ernest went by.

Any other day Ernest could have driven on - somebody else's problem. But something wasn't quite right and he knew he wouldn't be happy till he he'd been back for a better look. He turned the car round and headed up the road. The boy was still there, but even as Ernest drew up alongside he didn't turn to look, until suddenly he flinched and threw himself to one side. Ernest rushed over to where the boy had fallen.

'Are you alright lad. Did I scare you?'

He watched in surprise as the boy struggled to his feet and set off to run away, but went head-first into the drainage ditch that ran along the far side of the grass verge. Ernest ran after.

'It's OK lad,' he called, 'I only want to help. I saw you there at the side of the road and wondered if anything was wrong.'

Struggling to climb out the boy had only managed to slide further in and was down in the bottom of the ditch now. The flailing limbs finally found a purchase. He got to his feet and staggered a few steps along the channel before hitting the pipe that crossed over at about the same height as his chest. Winded the boy fell back down into the dirty water. Ernest watched from the edge.

'Listen lad, I only want to help but I can see you're scared. You just stay where you are. I've got my phone here and I'm going to call an ambulance. Listen to me while I call them.'

Ernest sat at the top of the ditch trying to talk to the boy who just sat crouched and shivering in the trickle of water, his arms up around his head covering it protectively. What would happen if the ambulance came now and saw him there with the boy cowering in fear? Stupid man, stupid. He should just have driven by. Leave the troublesome youth to someone else. Surely there'd have been a police-car along sooner or later.

'What's your name lad?' he tried again.

'Robert.'

'Do you want me to call your mother Robert? Do you know the number?'

There was no reply.

'It must be cold down there in the water Robert. Come on, climb up the bank and sit here with me. I'm Ernest and I'm not going to hurt you. The ambulance is on its way and it's all going to be OK.'

Ernest saw how the boy was starting to relax, but realised someone must have treated him really badly for him to be so scared. Just as he heard the sound of a siren somewhere in the distance he watched as the boy lifted his arms away from the young head, but when he saw the sightless eyes that stared back at him he almost retched.

31

Rapier

With Jon's steady hand at its helm the Chandler-Wilmott Bank could have continued happily and profitably for many decades. As a reputable organisation with an excellent credit rating its business was to borrow money from the market, and then to lend it out to businesses that needed an injection of funds to fuel their growth. Borrowing was at one rate and lending at another, and in between the bank took out a healthy margin to cover its operational costs. For Jon as the head of the organisation this meant living in the style his father had enjoyed, and his grandfather before him. To say the Chandlers were "comfortable" was quite an understatement.

And the whole thing could have continued in the same manner for years to come, but some days the gift-horse of opportunity comes trotting round the corner.

On the morning when Adam Wexford, an old chum from college days, had invited Jon out for lunch he'd thought little of it. Maybe it was just the chance to catch up, or maybe another business needing money. It was always a simple formula - make a study to see how viable the company was, and if the risks were low enough, lend them the money. But as starter moved into main course Jon realised that what Adam was putting forward was in quite a different league. The sheer scale of the project was so much bigger than anything Chandler-Wilmott had handled before.

★★★

Adam had explained his plan. In his position as Chief Design Engineer in the propulsion systems division of Atlanta, Vissan's largest constructor of passenger space vessels, he'd realised that for decades the progress that had been made was minimal. The heady days when FTL travel had first become viable for civilian ships were long gone. In those days every year that passed had brought with it some new breakthrough or other. Designs had advanced with the development of ever more powerful reactors, lower drag hulls, and higher rated g-drives. On the day when the first of the new generation of tight focus g-lens drives was announced, everyone in the business had known that for space travel it was a turning point.

With travel times to the home planets down to just two weeks for Miranda and three for Temenco a new chapter in the history of the colonised planets had opened. It was no exaggeration to say that the developments in space travel had been directly responsible for the creation of the Union itself.

But as Adam explained, that last major breakthrough had been almost 85 years ago. A time long before he or any of the engineers in his team had even been born. All that had happened since had been a refinement of the technology, gradually squeezing just a little more performance from ships that were almost unchanged from the ones the present population's grand-parents had travelled in.

And the ships themselves had never been popular with the passengers. The designers did their best, but with drag to consider once a vessel went FTL a ship had to be small and streamlined. If the number of passengers was to remain economic it meant each person aboard could only have limited personal space so the standard format included a comfortable seat, a table and a secondary seat for a visitor. At night the whole thing made up into a full length bed which often guaranteed a good night's rest, but there was a limit to how long a passenger could sleep. For planetary flights of 12 hours the space provided would have been luxurious, but for an interstellar journey of 14 days it was like travelling in a galactic sardine tin.

Only the hardy few ever made the three year journey to the outer planets.

Adam explained that as designers they'd reached a dead end. The mass of the ships had been cut by using the latest generation materials, the g-drives had been fully developed for the last two decades, and the power from conventional reactors had been increased as far as technology would allow. Of the three key factors only an increase in the power available would have any significant effect, and to do that they needed a step change in design. He was proposing to put a fusion reactor into space.

Fusion power, the chimera sought by scientists and engineers alike for two millennia. And then the breakthrough had been made just seventeen years ago. Now fusion power met almost the entire demand of the three home planets, boundless energy, almost too cheap to bother metering.

But putting a fusion reactor based power station into space? The idea was preposterous. Building one into a space vessel was the stuff of fantasy. And yet Adam was sure it could be done - all it needed was money, lots of it. Without a doubt the project was the risk of the decade if not the century, but if someone could pull it off the rewards would be almost limitless - something that had most certainly not gone unnoticed by Jon.

But the risk. Was it really worth risking his shirt? Maybe it might just be easier to continue the safe, comfortable life of Chandler-Wilmott's regular business. Maybe that was what his father would have done, but Jon was not his father.

★★★

Two months later Jon and Adam sat together with the rest of the design team to study the feasibility report his people had prepared. Specialists from the Thor corporation had confirmed there was no underlying reason why a fusion reactor could not be built in space, and provided the vessel designers were prepared to take a few steps beyond anything they'd ever done before, there was no reason why the reactor shouldn't be built into a star-ship. It was just going to be very much larger and look more than a little different.

Together with Adam and the vessel architect, Jon had reviewed the computer generated simulation of a ship that was nothing less than a radical departure from anything ever built before. With the huge torus of the fusion reactor at one end, the enormous doughnut ring of the passenger accommodation at the other, and thousands upon thousands of space containers clamped unimaginatively to the hub in-between, the awkward looking beast was something only a mother could love. The 3D image spun around on the screen and Jon couldn't help commenting that he'd seen better looking turkeys. Until now the Union's long range ships had all looked fast and streamlined, speedboats just waiting to scream off into space. This camel of the skies was anything but, though as the architect reassured them, the new ships would be built for power, speed and carrying capacity. Who was ever going to see one from the outside?

If the external view had been something of a disappointment the simulated images of the interior were more encouraging. The first impression was one of space. A view from inside showed the enormous cavern of the accommodation doughnut as it disappeared up and around, only to return from the other direction after a circuit of 3000 metres. A gin palace of a ship where people had freedom to roam, freedom to live real lives. Huge amounts of space for parks, gardens, football pitches, tennis courts, ... even a lake and a golf-course. And the indoor areas would be spacious too. Streets where people could walk about to shop, or choose where they planned dine that night. A theatre, an art gallery, a gymnasium. This was a star-liner that people wouldn't just be *content* to travel in, this was a city in the sky they'd sell their granny into the slave trade just to afford a single ticket.

The input to the meeting from Jon's financial team was less dramatic but no less important. The ship would pay its way.

One of the earlier ideas the team had tossed around had been to simply produce a better ship and let the existing players in the space transport game beat a path to their door. It was almost guaranteed they'd have TMV, Bryant-Winters, Miranda Martyn, Stevenson Deepspace, Darius Lines and the rest queuing up, jostling for position for the right to buy the first ships off the production line. But Jon had wondered if they couldn't go one better by setting up their own space line. It was true the established players had expertise and good-will, but that was all they had. Most of the ships operated by private companies were on long term leases, groundside handling was sub-contracted to specialist companies, access to orbits above the home planets was via the state owned space elevators. Good-will would change hands rapidly once the passengers saw what the new line had to offer, and if the price was right, expertise could be bought in as necessary.

Perhaps the thing that had swung the decision to go it alone was that freight would be a key factor, even for a passenger liner. With the almost limitless power of the new ships, factors such as mass and size were no longer constraints. Of course freight generated far less revenue per kilogramme than carrying passengers, but then freight didn't need looking after or feeding, so the additional costs of a freight operation were no more than loading the ship at one end, and unloading it at the other. And the scale of the operation was almost unbelievable. With the hub of the ship covered in space containers the new passenger liners would be carrying as much freight as seven conventional cargo ships. The figures Jon presented had taken the rest of the team by storm because they showed without a shadow of a doubt that a flight with a full load of freight would still break even without even a single paying passenger on board.

And something Jon had kept to himself was that this new generation ships with their massive freight carrying capability might be the key to opening up the mineral rich outer planets. For the first time in the history of space-flight operations a scheduled service that reached beyond the home planets could really become economic. And once there was a regular service running passenger numbers would build up. And that was the bigger picture because if passenger numbers built up, so would the economies of the planets they visited. Now there was an investment opportunity! In comparison the money to be made from running a space-line was no more than chicken-feed.

***

With the new space-line now registered as "Rapier" things were progressing fast. An order had been placed with Atlanta for construction of the first two ships. Two ship which Jon hoped would be only the forerunners of a vast fleet.

Imposing a blanket of secrecy was something Jon had seen as a useful tool for the new company even though there was no way they could hide the fact that two gigantic ships were being constructed up in low orbit. The first of the fleet, the Hyperion, was well advanced and its hull could even been seen from the surface of Vissan, but keeping people guessing about its details might put the existing lines off their guard, and that was going to give the project quite an advantage.

With two more years to go before the new kid on the block could offer its first flight, the old established lines had several opportunities to prepare themselves for competition from the upstart challenger. Miranda Martyn had already reduced the number of seats on each ship in order to create more open space. TMV were cutting margins to the bone to compete more strongly on price. BWS were offering cut-price deals for anyone who would make a block booking up to ten years into the future.

They weren't going to go down without a fight and Jon knew he needed some means of wrong footing them. So he came up with an interesting ruse. He issued a release to the press that told no lies. He made it clear that with so much power available the new ships would have an extra turn of speed compared to existing passenger vessels so they were more capable of running deep space operations. Then he made references to how business was building up on Daluun and Antonby, both of which desperately needed the support of a scheduled passenger carrying service. And just to complete the subterfuge he ordered a fleet of space-plane shuttles for the ships, a facility everyone knew was only needed for the developing planets that lacked the luxury of the space elevators the home planets enjoyed.

And it worked.

The existing space line companies had stood on the sidelines and watched the project with a mixture of interest and worry, but when the announcement was made that Rapier would be targeting the deep space routes they'd breathed a sigh of relief. In fact they'd laughed out loud that someone was actually having a go in a market they'd always seen as total loser. Once Rapier had gone bust they'd be able to buy up the ships for a bargain price.

★★★

At last the big day came when the new service was due to be launched and Jon knew that despite the inevitable budget over-runs, now was no time to go cent-pinching with publicity. Despite the protests of the others on the board he took the unprecedented step of hiring the Jackson Holopera house for the launch. With the ability to show a massive and brilliant 3-D display that truly made every viewer feel as if he or she was actually out there in space, the Holopera would give Rapier the chance to demonstrate to thousands just how exciting a trip on the new ship could be. Only by witnessing the kind of scene the Holopera was designed to show could anyone really appreciate the space, the luxury, and the comfort without actually going on board. The Hyperion, magnificent in its beauty embodied every aspect that would from now onwards define a new benchmark in space transport. It was quite simply the only way to travel.

Everyone on Rapier's team was holding their breath and crossing their fingers that the day would be the success they'd hoped for. But the butterflies in Jon's stomach were even more active. If his plan worked, this was the day he was about to become the Union's new billionaire. And if it didn't, his next role would be stacking shelves in Vissanmart.

For weeks he'd considered, and thought, calculated and wondered. Was he brave enough? Could he really take such a risk? What if it went wrong? What if his worst fears actually came true? Would he ever be satisfied with himself if he chickened out?

At last his decision had been made, he was going to take the biggest gamble of his life, maybe even the biggest gamble in history. Over the past days he'd set up a group of brokers on all three of the home planets taking advantage of the lucky coincidence that the stock markets on Miranda and Temenco would close just minutes before Rapier's launch at 10.00 AM on Vissan. He knew the rules of course and trading in his own company's shares was a very big no-no, but there were other ways to skin cats. In the hours leading up to the launch his brokers short sold shares in all the existing space-lines quoted on the exchanges. The total came to a staggering 2.5 billion HUC. If the plan worked he was going to be rich, very rich. If the markets didn't respond in the way he hoped he'd be the biggest bankrupt in Union history. There really would be no way of ever paying the debt off - he'd be working for the rest of his days just to make enough to feed himself.

So even while the launch was taking place Jon slipped away to have a look at how the market was reacting. At first things weren't looking too good and even had Rapier falling a few points. Next the shares began to rally and rise, but so did the shares of the other space-lines. With success like that he could be broke before the day ended. But when analysts started doing the sums that would determine the true impact of Rapier's masterstroke the market began to realise that the boost to the travel business the new player could provide was not going to spill over and benefit any of the existing lines. With his nerves jangling Jon watched the screen and studied the figures as they changed, seeing how green turned to red as the established companies dropped, slowly at first and then with ever increasing rapidity as the day wore on.

By the time the stock market closed on Vissan, TMV had fallen over 30% and the others had fared little better. When trading opened on Miranda and Temenco next morning the drop was over 40%, but Jon worried that the stocks might bounce back if the market decided it had over-reacted. He made the calls and bought in to cover the shares he'd sold so heavily just 24 hours earlier.

If he'd had even more confidence he might have done deals for twice the value, or held on longer hoping some of the existing space-lines would fall further, but when he thought about it, raking in almost 800 million HUC for a day's work was a pretty good return. He breathed a sigh of relief as he uncrossed his fingers and toes, then crossed them all again when he called his brokers to put the day's profits into outer planets mining.

32

First Awakening

It came as a surprise, but Jon found he was ……. awake. No more than a moment had passed since he'd lain so deep in a comfortable, happy, dream. A traveller lost in a far off realm, a player in a story so real, yet never to be finished, never to be explained - nor understood. For a while he'd hovered this side and that of the misty edge of sleep, but at last he knew, as every waking dreamer does, the glimpse of a world that had seemed so real was no more than a wraith of a memory.

For a while he'd rested, neither still in sleep nor yet fully awake, but fighting the urge to succumb, fighting so hard against the desire to slip back to the cosy neverland of the dreamworld. He fought, fought to break out into the light. He fought …. but failed.

★★★

Whether the next waking moment came after a minute, or an hour, or maybe even another day, Jon had no way of knowing; but he felt sure that this time of waking would be a little more permanent. He would *make* it more permanent. Playtime was over, it was time to get to grips with acclimatisation to life in the host body.

But after a few minutes of trying to get even the slightest response he began to accept with more than a little disappointment that it wasn't going to be quite as easy as he'd hoped. He knew his mind was working overtime, struggling to map the neural connections of an alien brain, finding the ways in that would allow it to access the body's senses and control its limbs, but it was going to take time.

He probed around to see what he could find. Somewhere amongst the jumble of sensations that invaded his brain was his host body, but as yet he could detect virtually nothing of it. Fuzz,... and Buzz - was all he could feel. It was as though a barrier of pins and needles separated him from life. Vision was no better. Yes, he could see light, an overall canary yellow, rippled like the sheen a walker on a cliff-top might see from a sunward ocean. But not the slightest level of detail. His hearing was no more than a series of dull rumbles.

Maybe he should have been afraid. He prided himself to think that a lesser man *would* have been afraid. But it was like they'd told him it would be, exactly like it. He knew he had to be patient and wait until his mind made sense of the connections into the host body. They would come, most certainly. He had to work at it, that was the other thing he knew, but the hardest thing of all was having to accept there was no substitute for patience. If Jon Chandler's psychological makeup was short on one commodity, it was patience. He was a "do it now" sort of man.

★★★

Sleep had come again, though for how long he'd no idea. Trapped in his private world there were no clocks, though that made the knowledge of his impending deadline all the worse. He had to be up and about, he had to be functional. Yes, they'd explained it all and told him he was cutting things fine, given him lectures about how the assimilation process often took longer for Deltas than for run-of-the mill Alphas and Betas. But he was a busy man, he couldn't just break off from important business. Crazy people, without a doubt they knew about the mechanics of mind transference, but they'd no appreciation of what life in politics was like. But now as he lay there, still almost deaf, blind, and paralysed; he began to wonder whether he should have taken what they'd had to say a little more seriously.

Things were improving though. His ears now registered sounds, though what they were hearing he still couldn't tell. His eyes had seen vague shapes as they'd moved across his field of vision. The pins and needles effect from his host's limbs was lifting just a little and he'd felt it when his arm had been moved by some outside force. He'd tried to respond, even if it was only a wiggle of a finger, but the body remained unresponsive. His eyelids worked - thank heavens for one small mercy. And then he was tired again.

★★★

When he'd next awakened things were getting better. His vision was still fuzzy but his ears had made out the sound of someone speaking his name. Now he was listening to musical scales, some small piece of automated equipment was working his audio functions to the limit.

Progress had been made with his limbs too. He'd thought that trying to move the fingers would have been the obvious place to start, but in fact he'd been wrong. For some hours now he'd been able to lift his arms from the shoulders and flex his elbow joints, but the fingers remained in their state of paralysis.

★★★

Next time he awoke things were definitely looking up. Shortly after opening his eyes two nurses had sat him up in the bed so he could look around. His eyes could at last see with vision that was close to normal, and it didn't go unnoticed that his host's neck was able to support her head. He looked around - it was no surprise to see that he was in what had to be a hospital ward, four beds, curtains that could be pulled round each one independently, stands with drip bottles, tubes, hoses, machines on trolleys with displays that flashed and bleeped. It looked well equipped and up-market. Well it ought to be, the government was paying enough for him to be here.

A doctor had come and examined him, spoken to him though as yet he hadn't been able to reply. Then it had been all the usual tests, banging on the knees and other joints to test their response, shining lights in his eyes, getting him to touch his nose. When the doctor had finished a young woman had arrived soon afterwards and with the help of a big male nurse they'd got him off the bed and onto his host feet. And fortunately the legs had functioned, just about. After an hour he'd progressed to solo status, though with the help of a walking frame - step left, step right, lift the frame and jerk it forwards, then repeat. It took a long time to cross the hospital ward, but only half the time to get back. The woman seemed satisfied, but just as Jon had picked up the challenge she'd announced it was time for him to rest again. He knew she was right though because he'd been asleep almost before his head had touched the pillow.

★★★

Next time he came to consciousness he noticed it was dark outside and he began to wonder exactly how much time had passed. But he didn't have long to wonder. No more than a moment later the acclimatisation team leapt into action again, sitting him up, turning him on the bed, and getting his feet down onto the floor. And this time when he stood up he'd walked almost unaided, though it had given him a laugh to see that just like a toddler still in nappies he was holding onto the finger of the big male nurse.

33

Released

Jon lay on the bed and looked around at the four grey walls that held him prisoner. Mostly the courses between the blockwork were straight and parallel, but just to the side of the door that was the only link between his dungeon and the outside world there was a crack. The crack ran along under one block, then up the vertical gap between that and the next, and then went horizontal again. And so on until it reached the ceiling. Had someone slammed the door too hard, or was it just subsidence? Who cared?

From the date on the newspaper he was too fed up to read anymore of he knew he'd been banged up in the tiny space for eleven days. God only knew how many more might pass before something happened. The most he knew of events was when he'd found a part of a column of the newspaper cut out on page four. When he glanced at the highlights on the front page it read "Boy missing. See page 4 for details".

He turned his head towards the door as he heard the key turn in the lock - by now a familiar sound. Breakfast had been cleared away hours ago and it was still too early for lunch -

what manner of excitement was being visited on him? The uniformed policeman stepped in and spoke:

'Station Sergeant wants to see you. Now.'

Jon pulled on his shoes and followed the cop out into the corridor and up to the main office. The sergeant looked up at him.

'Mr Chandler. DI Bennett says you're free to go. There are no charges. You can collect your stuff down the corridor.'

They gave him his own mobile back but he was informed that the one he'd bought to contact the kidnappers would be kept as evidence. He tried his phone but the battery was dead. Outside in the street he jumped into the first cab he could hail and went straight round to Celia's.

★★★

Celia came to the door and it was obvious she'd been crying.

'Oh Jon, Jon. I tried and tried to call you but you never answered. I didn't know where you'd gone, nobody did.'

'I've been down at the police-station, sitting by myself in a cell this last eleven days. No contact with the outside world.'

'But I called the police. I even reported you missing, but they didn't do anything.'

'It didn't suit the police to let on they were holding me, so they ignored you.'

'But you're here now, thank God.'

'Nobody's told me anything, but I presume from the fact they've let me go it means something must have happened with Robert.'

Celia spoke, but there was no happiness or enthusiasm in her voice, things were far from alright.

'Robert's alive Jon, but he's blind. The bastards blinded him.'

★★★

Celia told him about the package she'd received while he'd been away. She'd called the police and their forensics people had analysed the contents of the plastic bag. Inside they'd found half a little finger and the DNA was a match for Robert's.

Nothing had happened for another four days, and then she'd received a call from the hospital to say they'd got her son. She'd gone along straight away of course. He was healthy and as well as could be expected, except for his eyes, his awful acid burned eyes. His left foot was missing a toe as they knew, just as his right hand was missing half a finger. Those injuries weren't going to change his life, but how was he going to manage now that he was blind?

Bennett had told her Robert had had a note from the kidnappers in his coat pocket when they found him. The police were keeping the original as evidence, but they'd given her a copy. Jon took the sheet that Celia passed to him and read the words: "We might have accepted the money you'd got together Mr Chandler, even if it had been a bit less than we'd originally had in mind. But ignoring us is rude, very rude, and we just sort of lost our tempers with your nephew. If you try to come after us, there's a lady lives on the coast might be a bit unhappy about it".

★★★

Robert was deep in shock after everything he'd been through and was scared at the prospect of facing a very different new world when he got out of hospital.

A woman from the police had sat with him, trying to get him to remember anything at all about what had happened. He told her that when the men had dragged him into the car, the first thing they'd done was to pull a hood over his head, so he'd seen nothing. From the voices he'd realised there were two men at first, but when they changed to a different car there'd been a third. Afterwards he'd been kept in a room without windows and whenever one of the kidnappers had come into the room he'd been wearing a hood with eye-slits so Robert had never been able to see any of their faces. All he could tell her was that one of the men had a Mirandan accent, and another was addressed as "Bo".

34

The Second Day

As the time for his trip to Phoenix had drawn closer Jon had spent some of the intervening hours wondering how it was going to feel living for a few days in his host's very different body. A body that was of his own species, but so totally different from his own that it might have been alien. As a male he had more in common with a little green man from Draxilus Minor - with the emphasis being on "man" rather than "little" or "green".

He'd had a few ideas about how it might feel, but now as he sat half upright on the bed he knew he'd failed to understand exactly how different the whole experience was going to be. The fact that he now existed in the unfamiliar flesh of a female paled into insignificance compared to everything else he'd struggled to cope with. Yes, he now had an adequate degree of control over the girl's hands, arms, legs, and senses, but it had been a hard won uphill battle.

And now the next battle was only just beginning. At long last the doctor in charge of his acclimatisation had deigned to honour him with a visit, but the man didn't seem to be prepared to listen to reason.

'Mr Chandler, we all realise who you are and we know just how important your visit is, really we do. I'll admit to you now that we'd underestimated the time you'd need for acclimatisation, but you have to understand, we had no idea just how good the fit between you and your host was going to be. And I'm sure they must have explained at the office in Jackson that the better the fit, the longer it can take to become one with your host.'

Jon scowled in a way that surely passed on the message that he was anything but sympathetic to the doctor's dilemma.

'But you have to accept that our transfer specialist did suggest an additional twelve hours, just in case there were problems.'

Jon was cross and he wanted the man to know.

'I'm a busy man and twelve hours is a long time for someone with a schedule like mine. A man in my position can't just take another half a day off, not when I'm going to be away for four whole days.'

The beleaguered look on the doctor's face indicated he was having as hard a time with his impatient patient than the patient was with him.

'But it would have allowed us to get started earlier, and in this instance you needed the time. And more.'

'So now I *am* acclimatised, why won't you let me go to the conference? I know I've missed most of the first day but could manage to get there for the last couple of hours.'

The doctor shook his head. 'I'm sorry Mr Chandler. You will have to take my word for it when I tell you it's still too soon. Even now, after all this time you can only just walk unaided and your speech is still slurred. If you relax this evening and then get a long night's sleep I have every confidence you'll be ready to attend the conference tomorrow morning. But now that your vision and hearing are up to scratch there is something we can do to help, we can provide you with a TV monitor with a link to the conference so you can watch the proceedings.'

Jon was furious and tried his best to shout, though all that issued from the girl's vocal cords was a trail of speech that came out a good octave higher than anything he might have considered to be a commanding tone.

'I could have watched the whole thing from my office in Jackson. There's just no point in me even being here.'

'I disagree Mr Chandler. You've done very well to get this far and tomorrow you'll be up to full strength. I know how important the conference is and I realise you'll get there later than you'd hoped, but the people will understand. This facility was set up to cater to the needs of TranzCon travellers and I know for a fact that half the delegates to the conference beamed in during the past few days. And take it from me, they all remember when they had to do it for the first time. They'll be sympathetic, you'll see.'

Jon wasn't convinced. 'It's not sympathy I need doctor. I came to do a job, I came as the representative of the entire Planetary Union. I'm standing in for Tom Hanson and I'm letting him down. Even as I sit here in this bed I'm letting him down. I don't know how much you know about me, but I can tell you, I'm not a man who shirks any duty or lets anyone down.'

The doctor's tone turned harder. Now he spoke in a voice pitched to command authority.

'And I am responsible for your wellbeing, and for the safety of your host's body too. Now I understand full well how important you are, but you will leave this clinic when I say you're ready. And right now you are not ready.'

'Do you realise ....'

'And please Mr Chandler, don't try to pull rank on me. I am the senior physician here, I make the decisions, and TranzCon will back me 100%. This is my field and I know what I'm talking about. This is how it's going to be, you can sit here and watch the conference, or you can sit here and do nothing. At four o'clock we'll do the medicals and get you dressed and then you can relax for an hour. If, in my professional opinion, you're well enough you can go to the hotel, and if not you will stay here for another night. Either way you'll be at the conference when it opens tomorrow morning. That's the best that's on offer, and it's the only offer you're going to get. Now please, it would be easier if we had your co-operation.'

Jon was almost knocked over backwards. How many years had passed since anyone had dared to speak to him like that he just couldn't remember. But deep inside he knew the doctor was right, this was the time for him to accept that others knew better. He was going to achieve more by co-operating. There was another way to achieve his objective and he asked the doctor.

'Can you get me a recording of the whole of the conference?'

The doctor thought for a moment. 'I expect so, under the circumstances.'

'OK then, I'll go along with what you say, but I want to get on with the medicals and stuff right now. Then I'll relax afterwards while I'm skipping through the highlights. Deal?'

The doctor shook his head in disbelief. Most of the patients he looked after had sufficient reverence for his profession that they didn't presume to impose "deals".

'OK, but I'll examine you later and we can decide whether you can go to the hotel or stay here for another night. If that's alright then yes, it's a deal.'

35

Keith Medley

After Robert was released from hospital and started the long task of learning how to adapt to his new life Jon's thoughts turned to finding the men who'd done this awful thing to his nephew. And he couldn't believe the way the police had managed to be so totally useless. Whenever he called they claimed they were still working on the case, but after all the weeks that had passed they still hadn't found a single lead. He knew it was only a matter of time before the case was just conveniently pushed to one side.

★★★

It made Jon sad to even think about what young Robert had been through but he knew the hospital had done absolutely everything they possibly could. Sending his nephew to a specialist clinic had cost far more than ordinary people could ever have afforded, but money wasn't what mattered now. They'd performed the most delicate operations to equip him with everything that cutting edge science could provide. They'd repaired what they could save of his eyes and replaced damaged parts with artificial lenses and retinas that interfaced directly into the visual cortex. One eye was optimised for distance vision so he was able to detect objects and get around. The other was designed for close work and reading, and had a colour sensing area too. A so-called third eye buried deep inside his brain provided a link to electronic systems so he could "see" what was on a specially adapted television or computer screen without the crude resolution of the artificial retinas. But for all their technology, Jon knew it would never be like having real sight. The boy would never really be able to see around him in the way normal people took for granted, never be able to appreciate the colours of a spring garden, never be able to drive a car. And perhaps the most important thing, he'd never achieve his ambition of becoming a doctor.

Jon thought of the threat the kidnappers had made, and it just made him more sure than ever that bringing them to justice was what society needed. Forget the police, they were never going to do anything - useless pratts. He had the money to hire whoever he needed and wasn't going to be put off easily, but his first thoughts had been towards the safety of his family and himself. The security up at the big house, already formidable, was reinforced with an extra line of defence. The old track the Guys had followed down through the woods and over the fence into the Freeman house had been closed off many years ago and now would deny passage to all but the most dedicated terrorist hit-squad. On his advice, his mother and her sister had moved to a nice house a little further inland, but somewhere more secluded and in a location that leant itself to the installation of a high level security system. He'd even contacted Mandy though she was just a little too quick to assure him the Ormond family's security systems were second to none.

Then he wondered how he was going to even make a start finding the people. Just a few weeks earlier he'd threatened to employ an army of investigators, but now he realised that sheer brute force was not the right approach. Too much activity would surely alert the kidnappers to the fact they were being hunted. No, the right solution was to go in softly softly. It needed someone good, but only a single person.

With so many business contacts, many of whom had had cause to use private investigators in the past, Jon had no problem getting recommendations for more good people than he could have shaken a stick at. But the one who appealed to him most was a man who'd been a career soldier and had spent most of his time in the commandos. He proved to be a bit elusive, as people in that sort of role usually were, but eventually Jon was able to track him down.

★★★

When Jon first invited Keith Medley into the summerhouse for a preliminary chat he was impressed with the man, though couldn't help noticing the way the man's presence was just a little unnerving. When the two of them had talked about good old days in the army it had given Jon the chance to take a really good look at his investigator. As he'd seen when the man first walked into the room, Keith was stockily built with a powerful body. He was probably a few centimetres shorter than himself, but Jon had no doubt that the old commando, either by cunning or sheer strength, could have overpowered him any time he'd wanted. Maybe the man chose his appearance for effect, or maybe he simply didn't care, but his hair was too long for a man of his age and he sported a neatly trimmed though entirely unfashionable moustache. And there was something in his eyes that gave Jon the creeps.

Eventually Jon steered the conversation around to the job in hand and he could see that Keith felt the same way he did.

'People like that boss - scum, they just make me sick. When they knew they weren't going to get any money I can imagine them killing the boy, but to do that to him. Animals. They don't deserve to live. Jail would be too good for them.'

'I'm glad we're on the same wavelength Keith. Tell me what sort of approach you'd take to find them, assuming I employed you for the job.'

Jon watched as an even harder expression came to the investigator's face.

'I work from the inside boss. I don't know how much checking up on me you did, but I'll put it up front, I've got form.'

'Form?'

'I've been inside.'

'Inside?'

Keith shook his head in disbelief. He spoke quietly, as if someone was listening in to the conversation. 'In jail boss.'

Jon wasn't sure whether to be shocked or not. 'What did you do?'

'I prefer not to discuss it if that's OK with you, but being in there gave me a glimpse of a different world. If you want to make your way on the wrong side of the law, a few years at the university of crime is all you need to get started. I know these people and the way they work. What I'd do would be to get myself deep inside their organisation and join in with whatever it was they were up to, just to get their confidence. The biggest worry is getting caught for something minor while I was building up my credentials, so something I'd want from you would be a guarantee of your support if I got picked up while I was investigating for you. Either that or I stay on the payroll if I got sent down.'

Jon was amazed at the way the man was prepared to spend time in jail just as long as someone was paying the bills. Obviously there was a very wide gulf between the two of them, but he could certainly go along with the man's requests.

'There's a lot you can do with money Keith. I'd see you were OK, one way or another.'

Keith had clearly got some ideas together and was more than ready to share them. By the time the man was halfway through Jon had made his mind up to employ him.

'So basically I find my way in, do a few small jobs, then when they're ready for me to work on something big I shop them all together part way through another kidnapping. If I can't manage that there's other ways, you know, like picking them off one by one and posting you a few bits as proof. I'll get a result - you can rely on it.'

Jon was just a little concerned at what the investigator had said.

'Look Keith, I don't want you killing people unless it's in self-defence. Understand? You might be the kind of guy who can disappear overnight but I'm high profile these days and I'd be in serious trouble if it looked like I'd put a contract on someone.'

The face smiled, though without humour.

'I'll do what I can boss, but sometimes the only way to win the fight is to take them out.'

Jon continued. 'And I want some feedback on how you're doing. It doesn't have to be an email each week, half nine every Monday morning, but I want to know how things are coming along. If you want you can come up here, or there's plenty of places in town where we could meet.'

'OK boss. Like you say, I can't guarantee regular contact if it's going to put me in a fix, but I'll keep you informed.'

36

Evening Falls

It was early evening when the car left the reception centre and set off for the hotel. Jon sat in the back with Vicky, his allocated personal assistant by his side. She was a pretty girl as Jon had noticed the moment she'd walked into the room. With a mane of long blonde hair tied into a pony-tail that swished alluringly from side to side as she turned her head, and a body to draw the attention of any male eyes it was no exaggeration to say he fancied the pants of her. And yet he knew that in his present manifestation any interest he showed would be so totally inappropriate. It was confusing.

Jon watched as the car left the road and entered the immaculately tree-lined drive which lead into the splendour of the floodlit hotel forecourt. Climbing out of the car he gazed in wonder at the intricate façade high above. With its carved stone statues, pointed arches and soaring spires it was surely something from a different age. The illuminated sign from more recent times read "Elizabeth Hotel", without a doubt the premier establishment of its type in Celebration.

With his luggage following a respectful three paces behind Jon climbed the three steps from the roadway and walked towards entrance where an imposing figure in military uniform opened the door for them to pass through into the lobby. And what a lobby. Jon stood in awe and gazed around at a lobby he could only describe as splendid. The way the polished wood blended with the marble columns. The feel of the "oh so sumptuous" carpet under his feet, paintings, the mirrors, the trees and bushes, the tinkle of the water in the fountain that broke the silence - ever so gently. The hush he'd only experienced before in the most majestic of cathedrals. It was the sort of finish he'd always envisaged for the first class lounges of Rapier's fleet of liners but never quite managed to explain to the designers.

The name on the charge card he'd been issued with said "*Mr* J. Chandler" and yet he didn't feel like "mister" anybody. And he knew that in Jana's body he didn't look it either but fortunately the dignified and unflappable clerk behind the reception desk understood precisely the nature of the diminutive figure in front of him and presented him with a key-card to access the Washington suite located on the third floor.

The checking-in process had taken no more than a minute and a half.

***

Up in the room Vicky snapped open the catches on the case and started to lift the clothes out one by one. Jon watched with interest because apart from the casual clothes they'd given him to wear before he left the hospital he hadn't seen any of the more formal apparel he'd be wearing for official engagements. First out were two women's business suits which Jon carefully noted included trousers rather than skirts. That was something he'd been very keen to stress, female host or not there was no way he was wearing a skirt! Next out came a collection of underwear and casual wear which Vicky stacked neatly into the pigeon-holes next to the hanging section of the wardrobe. It wasn't a lot, but then, he'd only come for a few days. Before she left she reminded him they needed an early start in the morning and suggested he set an alarm.

★★★

Now for the first time in days he had a bit of time on his hands Jon wasn't quite sure what to do with himself. There were things to be done of course, it was just the way he felt right then that he didn't feel like doing any of them. It wasn't as if he was a stranger to being alone in a strange hotel, he'd done it hundreds of times before but this time the sense of isolation was oppressive. He checked his watch and selected conversion to Vissan time. He'd have liked to have given Sylvie a call but he could see that back home it was still the wee hours of the morning. Another four hours would pass before her bedside clock sounded its morning alarm call and by that time he'd probably have settled down to his own sleep.

Room service would have been happy to oblige he knew, but part of the pleasure of a cup of tea was making it for yourself, so he filled the kettle and clicked its switch. He settled himself into a huge armchair which just seemed to swallow up Jana's tiny body. It was so big! How he was supposed to get the girl's feet all the way down onto the floor without sitting right on the edge was beyond him so instead he pulled them up and laid her head with all its tickling mass of hair down onto her arm. And then he was lost to the world again. When he awoke the kettle was already cooling and needed another blast before it was ready to make the tea.

He found the solution to the chair problem lay in the big upholstered stool that occupied the space between the sofa and the other matching armchair. With the girl's feet up on the stool, his cup of tea in hand and no mirror in view to remind him how different this day was from all others he was at last able to sit and relax. Maybe things weren't so bad after all.

Still putting off the work there was to be done he picked up a newspaper from the table by the side of his chair and had been reading for five minutes when he suddenly noticed he was managing more than the headlines without glasses - for the first time in 30 years! It was amazing to have the girl's young eyes that needed no help.

And it wasn't just the eyes which were so different. Before he'd been allowed to leave the hospital they'd run through the usual series of examinations and checks, and perhaps it was then that he'd first become aware of the feeling of vitality and youth the girl' body exuded. His own body back on Vissan was in good shape of course, he'd always found the time to do a bit of working out no matter how busy he'd been. Well perhaps not quite enough in recent years though he'd still been active. But he reflected that decades must have passed since he'd last felt so full of energy. Talk about youth being wasted on the young.

The last event of the day before they'd set of to the hotel had been a visit by Mr Christopher Townsend, TranzCon's legal officer to brief him about the some of the aspects of his stay. Of course Jon already knew most of the details, but signing to confirm his consent to the terms was obligatory. Whether they'd have sent him straight back to Jackson if he'd refused wasn't clear, so with a very shaky hand he'd made a scrawl that was entirely unlike anything anyone might have called a signature.

The first item Townsend had raised concerned his host's privacy. He'd wondered whether it was a joke. Compared to his own position as a minister in possession of a vast range of privileged information it seemed unlikely that the young and unimportant Jana Kell would have many secrets. But none-the-less he had to accept that it was his duty to maintain her confidentiality in the event that any of her memories intruded and became available to him.

Then Townsend had handed him an identity card whose twin pictures showed the host body's face alongside an image of the man Jon really was. His details were cross-referenced in the Phoenixan central records computer to Jana's physical characteristics, in particular to her eyes to ensure that a scan of her iris's would link to details relating to Jon Chandler. An electronic read of the chip embedded in the card would open a file in any security system to explain why his temporary outward appearance was so radically different from that of his true persona.

And nothing happens without money. TranzCon had set up a charge account for Jon's use and included in the package was a charge card and the PIN required to make it work. The facility would be available for the whole of the time he was on Phoenix and would be terminated automatically when confirmation was received from Jackson to advise that his life-force had returned home.

Last of all he'd received a mobile phone, a watch, and a laptop computer. The phone had been programmed with all his usual contact details. The watch was a multi-mode device with the capability of displaying the time here on Phoenix or on any of the Union's eight planets. The computer would allow him real-time access to his documents and emails as well as the government database in Jackson.

With the kit all checked out Jon looked again at his watch and decided it was time for dinner, or at least it was the time when his own body should have been craving food. But he was surprised to find that in the girl's body his usual healthy appetite was largely absent so he ordered a sandwich from room service. And then he thought about what he'd just done. Had he really avoided going down to the restaurant because of lack of hunger, or was it because he was scared to go out into the public rooms of the hotel looking the way he presently did? With people around him, fussing over him, tending to his needs it had all felt so right. And yet now he was far from feeling at ease. Next morning the odd he/she hybrid would be on open display in front of hundred of delegates and for the first time Jon admitted to himself just how much he was dreading it. But that was another day.

37
Bingo!

Jon was pleased with how things were progressing. Keith had taken over the investigation where the police had left off, and his first reports had sounded hopeful. But then there was nothing - days passed, weeks passed. Weeks turned to months, and months passed. Then without warning a text had bleeped in to give him just the slightest reassurance the man was still working on the job. Occasionally Keith got on his motorbike and made a trip up to the big house to report his progress and to collect the stage payments they'd agreed on.

For Jon who'd spent a lot of his time working in the legal end of the finance business it was certainly interesting to hear about the things Keith had been getting up to: burglaries and confidence tricks mainly, with the odd driving job thrown in for good measure. How the man managed it without getting caught Jon was at a loss to know, but then he supposed that a man who had no desperate need of the money could pick and choose his jobs and stick to the ones he felt safe with. Each time they met, Keith stressed how important it was that he worked his way in little by little. It wasn't the sort of job that could be rushed.

After a year had passed Jon was beginning to wonder if Keith was just using him as a meal ticket, until one day a text came in. "Bingo" was all it said.

★★★

The traffic warden was at it again - persecuting mothers who'd just stopped off to deliver their brood to the local school, harassing people popping into the corner shop, sticking his notices on the cars of motorists who'd only left them unattended for thirty seconds. Even the plumber working at No.79 got a ticket and his van was over the end of the drive of the house where he was working. Why the bastards couldn't get proper jobs was something he doubted he'd ever understand.

The warden was typing numbers into his machine as he noticed a schoolgirl go by - walking slowly as her thumbs flitted nimbly over the keys of her phone - obviously navigating her way between the low overhanging branches by radar. He noticed she was tall for her age and skinny as a bean-pole, but her hair was nice and probably as long as the school allowed her to wear it. Her parents must really love her, or at least he hoped they did.

When he was sure there was no-one else around he put his phone to his lips and spoke. Then he followed her up the road, covering himself by looking into the windscreens of the parked cars as he passed by.

Twenty five seconds later a large saloon car drove by and he started to run. The car pulled up by the side of the girl who at first paid it no attention. A man jumped out and grabbed her just as the traffic warden reached him. Five seconds later the two men were diving into the back of the car with a twelve year old girl kicking and struggling for all she was worth.

Roughly the warden pushed her onto the floor behind the front seat and held her head down with his foot as he slipped out of the bright yellow jacket.

The man at the wheel had been watching the street carefully while the action in the back was taking place, and since no-one had been there to see the snatch he drove off at a comfortable pace to avoid drawing unnecessary attention. As he turned the corner he dialled a number on his hands-free phone and spoke.

★★★

A man in a security guard's uniform timed three and a half minutes on his watch before walking out through the car park of a disused factory unit to open the main gate.

Twenty seconds after the guard had disappeared back into the building a car came down the road and drove through the open gate, across the car park, round to the back of the building and in through the open roller-shutter door. The car pulled up alongside a white van as the roller door motored closed.

The driver opened his door and got out, feeling inside his pocket for something. The warden climbed out of the back seat with the girl who by now had her hands ratchet strapped behind her and a hood tied over her head. As the man stood up he might possibly have heard the "snick" of the bullet from a silenced pistol just before it went through his head. He'd never noticed the red dot on his forehead.

The security guard saw what was happening and ran towards the car. Realising his mistake too late he turned and ran back. The red dot settled on the middle of the man's back and the "snick" came from the gun a second time.

The man still inside the car was startled and hurried to get out but as he got to his feet the driver ran round from the back of the car and stood blocking his way. The laser dot from the pistol flicked around a little, a brilliant spot of crimson on the white cotton of his shirt.

'Turn to face the car,' the gunman ordered. Patting the man down the driver pulled a small automatic from the back of the man's trousers, released the magazine and pushed it into his pocket.

The disarmed man took advantage of the driver's brief lapse of concentration and ran over to the girl. He grabbed her and held her in front of him as a shield. Dead she was worth nothing.

'What's up Zack? Did you want all the money for yourself? You don't stand a chance without me. We can do a deal.'

The driver spun round to face the man. 'I don't want the girl, or the money. It's you I'm after Bo. Let her go and you don't have to get hurt.'

The man frowned but kept his cool. 'I knew there was something about you all along. Who're you working for?'

The driver repeated his order. 'Let the girl go.'

Bo put his arm around her neck and pulled her closer.

The driver smiled. 'It's no use Bo, she's not big enough to cover you. Shall I put the bullet through your head like I did with Clem? I'll give you five to let her go. One, two ……'

In a flash Bo lifted the featherweight girl up in front of him to shield his head. It was exactly as the driver had expected. Fighting hard to control the struggling body that was all he had for protection Bo never noticed the gun being lowered away from his chest. A moment later he cried out in pain as the sting of a bullet ripped through the leather of his right shoe and embedded itself in his foot. Cursing out loud he dropped the girl down onto the concrete floor - a muffled scream came from inside the hood. Bo fell to the ground and sat there nursing his bleeding foot. Despite her bonds the girl struggled to her feet and tried to run. Although she narrowly missed the open door of the van she found herself out in the open of the big workshop, and blinded by the hood she realised there was nowhere to go.

The driver watched the proceedings with obvious amusement. The red dot settled back onto the man on the ground.

'Now I've got a clear shot at your head Bo, so I can kill you whenever I need to.'

Bo looked up into the muzzle of the gun. 'Why don't you just get it over with, bastard?'

'I get a bonus for bringing you in alive.'

'I'll double it. We'll get five million for the girl and I'll cut you in for 75. The others won't be collecting so you can have their money.'

The driver shook his head. 'Naw, it's not the money that matters. It's you I don't like. Put these on Bo,' and with his free hand he threw down a pair of handcuffs.

Bo picked up the cuffs and threw them across the workshop. The driver fired a shot into the man's left foot and again he called out in pain.

'I knew you'd do that Bo, so I came prepared.'

The driver put his hand back into the pocket and pulled out a second pair of handcuffs and dangled them in the air in front of Bo.

'Now then Bo, are you going to be a good boy and do as you're told. My gun's still got another ten bullets and as you've seen I'm a very good shot, especially with a laser sight to make it easy. How about if I use nine persuading you to see things my way, then I'll kill you with the last one. OK I'll lose my bonus, but what the hell, I like hearing you scream.

He threw the handcuffs down in front of Bo who was watching the way the red dot was wavering slowly over his left thigh and tracking up towards his groin. Scowling he put one of the rings around his left wrist and then brought his right hand up to the other cuff.

The driver shook his head again. 'Naw stupid, behind your back.'

Bo scowled again and put his hands behind him. The driver heard the sound of the ratchet.

'I hope that really was round your wrist Bo because I'd be a bit pissed off if you were fooling. Turn around and hold your hands out so I can see them.'

Bo shuffled round and lifted up his hands so the driver could see the steel rings were closed around his wrists. Putting the gun down on the ground for a brief moment he clicked the rings tighter.

'Oww, for fucks sake Zack!'

'Stop complaining, or I'll give you something to *really* moan about. Get up and sit on the van floor.'

'Fuck you!'

The driver pulled his leg back and kicked hard at Bo's bleeding left foot. The man screamed out in pain.

'Look shithead, I'm doing you a favour saving bullets. When Zack gives you an order, what do you do Bo?'

Bo scowled again and struggled to his feet before limping over to the van.

'Further into the van. Lift your legs up.'

As the legs came up the driver pulled them together and wrapped three turns of heavy gauge tape around the ankles before pushing the feet and their owner right into the van. Bo sat there helpless and watched while the driver dragged the lifeless corpses of his two former cohorts to the back of the van and lifted them inside. When the doors were closed and locked the driver turned his attention to the girl. By now she was slowly walking away from the van, feeling the way in front of her with an outstretched foot. The driver strode after her, easily catching her up. She screamed as he touched her, but he ignored the noise and grabbed her arm. Pulling a pair of side cutters from his pocket he snipped the straps to free her wrists - then he pushed the barrel of the pistol into her stomach.

'Hold your arms out,' he commanded, 'if you don't I shoot you like I did the others, OK?'

Trembling with fright the girl lifted her arms and held them out at each side.

'Right, I'm watching and just remember, I can see you, but you can't see me. Listen to the sound of the van and after it's gone count to a hundred - then you can take the hood off and go home. Take it off too soon and the next bullet goes through your head. I don't like shooting kids but I do it when I have to. OK?'

A mumble came from inside the hood which the driver took to be her agreement.

★★★

Jon picked up his mobile and accepted the call.

'Package ready for delivery Mr Chandler. Can you be up at the house this afternoon? Alone?'

★★★

Jon watched as the old white van drove up towards the house and stopped on the chippings outside the garages. Keith got out and Jon could see the man was smiling - not an expression he'd seen on the serious face before.

'I didn't get the chance to bring them all in alive Mr Chandler, but I saved the best one for you.'

With that he clicked the catch and pulled open the rear doors. Jon saw the two dead bodies, but the man still breathing was bleeding and was obviously in pain. Keith grabbed the tape that held Bo's legs together and pulled him roughly out of the van. He winced as his feet touched the ground. The look Keith gave him was pure evil.

'Don't worry Bo, they're not going to hurt for long.'

Keith turned to Jon with a satisfied look on his face.

'There you are boss, meet Bo. Boris Stamford if you prefer to know his real name. He used to work for Nathan Holbein. You know, the drug pusher.'

Jon remembered the name well. The trial of the drug baron and his gang had been in the news for quite a few weeks. But that had been years ago.

'Holbein went down for life didn't he?'

'And most of his top people too. Mr Stamford here escaped quite lightly. He wasn't there when the police raided them so he was able to ditch the dope he was peddling. Then he dashed off home to get his private stash only to find the police sitting there waiting. They couldn't pin much on him so the judge gave him the maximum he could for possession.'

'How long was that?'

'Two years. Not long, but long enough to mess up a promising career. When he came out he found some other organisation had stepped in to take over Holbein's territory, and they weren't interested in using any of the old crowd. Didn't trust outsiders.'

'So he needed some other way of making a living. Why didn't he just get a job like most people do?'

Keith shot Jon an incredulous look. How could anyone be so naïve?

'He was doing OK for a while. He was smart and did his research right and he knew the people paying the ransoms wouldn't take the chance of going to the police. If you ask me he'd already made enough for a comfortable retirement, but people get greedy boss. Never know when enough's enough.'

'Are you sure he's the one?'

'You said your nephew told you there was someone called "Bo", and this guy here's in the kidnap business. The way they did the snatch this morning was almost a copy of how they caught young Robert. It's good enough for me.'

Stamford looked up at Jon. 'It's not true, don't listen to him. I've done a few snatches I'll admit that much. But I'm not the one who did that awful thing to your boy.'

Keith looked up at Jon. 'I never told him anything about what happened to Robert.'

Stamford was desperate now. 'I read it in the papers.'

Jon joined in. 'It sounds pretty convincing to me.'

'I take it you're Jon Chandler then.'

Jon hesitated, not sure whether he was giving away too much letting the man know who he was. Maybe he'd done the wrong thing letting Keith bring him up to the house. Keith guessed what was going on in Jon's head.

'It's OK boss, he's going to die soon so it doesn't matter if he knows who you are.'

Jon was pleased to see how Keith had been so successful catching Robert's mutilator, but he was repulsed by the thought of taking a helpless man's life.

'We can't just kill him though. We haven't got any hard evidence.'

'Evidence is for the police boss - justice works in other ways, if you want it to. You don't want scum like that getting off on a technicality do you? After what he did to the boy I thought you'd want to finish him off yourself. We can't leave him alive, so if you don't want to pull the trigger I will.'

Memories of the kidnap were coming back to Jon now. He remembered the way Celia had sobbed and cried in grief when Robert had first been taken, and he thought of her now, having to live every day with the knowledge of what this monster had done. And he remembered the way Stamford had cheeked him on the phone, and the way Bennett had been so high and mighty, locking him up for all that time, the bastard. He felt his heart go "thump" as his teeth clenched tightly together.

'Give me the gun Keith, I think I'm ready.'

Jon took the gun in his hand and felt the once familiar weight of the powerful weapon. As he pulled back the slide to bring a bullet into the chamber he though back to the times out on the army firing range. He remembered the manoeuvres up on Walridge plain when he'd never been quite sure if he'd be able to pull the trigger. Perhaps in a real conflict it would have been easy to fire on a man coming over the top with his gun in his hand - either you shot him or he shot you. But this was cowardly, the man was handcuffed and already in pain. Could he just shoot him in cold blood? And then he thought again about Robert, his whole life wrecked by this low-life standing in front of him. He pushed the gun into Stamford's face and the two men stared at each other.

'Open your mouth, it'll be quicker for you,' he commanded.

Stamford had realised some time ago that life held no future for him, and being shot once by Chandler was a better option than letting Keith torture him first. Resigned to his fate he took the end of the silencer between his teeth. With both eyes closed Jon was spared the sight of the blood and the scraps of brain that spattered onto the inside of the van.

With the deed done he relaxed his grip on the gun and let Keith ease it gently out of his hand. When he opened his eyes and saw the lifeless body on the ground behind the van he stood in stunned silence at the knowledge of what he'd done. Keith saw the way Jon was staring at the corpse.

'He deserved to die boss - you got your revenge, you did the right thing. But it'll be best for both of us if we keep this to ourselves. Not even the boy's mother has to know, OK?'

'What about the bodies, what about the gun?'

'I can dispose of them boss. No problem. Give me a hand with this one will you.'

The two men took the body by the arms and legs and swung it up into the back of the van. Blood spat from the open mouth of what had once been a man. Keith closed the doors and drove a few metres forward before walking calmly back to the still badly shaken Jon.

'Have you got any petrol or paraffin boss?'

Jon pointed. 'There'll be some in the end garage, with the ride-on.'

Keith came back with a five litre can in his hand and began pouring it onto the blood stained chippings. When the ground was thoroughly dowsed he felt in his pocket and brought out a box of matches.

'No DNA for the cops to find boss. Just to be on the safe side.'

They both stepped back from the heat of the flames as the fuel took light.

Still shaking with fear, Jon watched the van as it headed off down the drive. Of all the days in his life he wished he could unlive, all those awful times when Bobby, and his father, and Des had died - this day was by far the worst. He walked over to the summerhouse and fell asleep hours later with an empty whisky bottle lying on the rug beside his chair. Next morning he rang his secretary at the office to say he wouldn't be in for a few days.

★★★

The following evening Keith came back up to the big house and the two men sat together sharing the new bottle of single malt Jon had opened. Although he was still far from happy, Jon had calmed down and realised that now the affair was almost over it was going to be better for both of them if he pulled himself together and got back to a normal life as soon as he could.

First there was the business side to look after. Jon took the bag of gold bars and used notes from the wall safe and handed them over to Keith. He prayed that a day like this would never dawn again.

Maybe Jon was slightly surprised when the man didn't pick up his reward straight away and leave. He seemed quite comfortable and there was nowhere either of them had to be, so Jon offered him a top-up.

Looking over at Keith, glass in hand and obviously in good humour Jon listened to the stories his hired assassin had to tell. He wondered whether the man was luckier than him - the casual way he could kill and walk away without even a thought.

"Everybody dies boss" Keith had said, "people like me just make it happen sooner".

It wasn't an attitude Jon really understood, but he had to agree with the point Keith made about why a supposedly civilised society retained an army and a spacefleet staffed with men and women they'd trained to kill.

Keith told him about how he'd worked his way in with Stamford and his men. He'd started off with a few small robberies and made sure enough people knew about them. Then he'd taken on some driving jobs - and made sure Stamford was going to need another driver. Everyone knew Lou Benson drank too much, and everyone knew he often got into fights afterwards. When he'd beaten the shit out of the guy he claimed had insulted him, and was later found in an alley with his throat cut it was obvious who'd done it. But who was the man he'd fought with? No-one had ever seen the guy before and the police didn't bother themselves too much with what went on at that end of town. Sometimes it was better to let communities look after their own affairs, and if they'd caught the knife killer he'd have denied it anyway, wouldn't he?

When Jon asked Keith straight to his face if he'd been the one who'd knifed Lou, all he'd answered was "Ask no questions. You know the rest boss".

★★★

Mrs Jefferson from No.17 looked out and saw the rusting old van still outside in the street blocking her view and bringing down the tone of the neighbourhood. Who'd left it there she'd no idea, but surely it must have been there for over three weeks now. She called the police to see if it had been abandoned. They promised to call her back.

Two days later she received a call from the central station to tell her that the van she'd reported belonged to a small trader in Reverton who used it every day and the police from the local force had been along that morning to confirm he had it in his yard. When she asked how the same van also managed to be outside her house the police lady said she'd send a patrol car round to check it out when things were quiet.

When the police finally towed the van away and broke into the back they were only moderately surprised to find the three decomposing corpses laid out side by side. The bodies were identified by DNA analysis, and forensics noted that the controls of the vehicle and its door handles had at some time in the recent past been operated by a person wearing surgical gloves. The position of the seat indicated either a male driver or an unusually tall female.

38

On The Third Day

The alarm sounded its irritating note. Jon looked up and saw it was at half six. He'd have happily turned over for another ten minutes but there were things to be done. Vicky would be there at seven and then the hairdresser was due at quarter past so there was no time to lose. Hauling himself out of the bed he noticed how much his balance had improved since the previous evening, something which made standing in the shower a much more relaxed affair than if he'd attempted it the previous evening.

He was just towelling off when the doorbell rang, a couple of minutes early. Vicky was bright and breezy and ready for the day. While she was laying out his clothes Jon noticed how the shoes she'd selected had what appeared to be quite a bit of height in the heel. As with the stipulation that his suits should have trousers he'd specifically requested flat shoes. Vicky explained without being apologetic that a woman of Jana's stature would normally wear much higher heels with a formal outfit and he needed a bit of a boost if he was going to look right. Jon picked one up, studied it carefully and wondered how Jana was going to feel about coming home to a sprained ankle. And then he decided not to make a fuss. After all it wasn't as if he was setting off on a twenty klic route march.

The hairdresser arrived on schedule and set to work straight away, washing, drying and brushing the girl's long fine hair. Finally she braided it into a broad plait up the back which Jon had to agree looked stylish at the same time as being practical.

Dressing wasn't quite the problem he'd expected though he'd still needed some help getting into the unfamiliar bits. The suit was easier and he was pleased to note that felt like the kind of cut and quality he'd come to expect. The usual rule was that if a suit felt right, then it was going to look right too. And his reflection in the mirror confirmed it, though it was disconcerting to gaze into the glass to see a stranger looking out at him.

Breakfast came up to the suite courtesy of room service and as a man to tuck into a hearty meal whenever one was on offer Jon had chosen the full offering, a plateful he'd had no trouble agreeing was the best start to the day he'd ever seen. But it wasn't all good news because he wasn't even halfway through when the girl's stomach gave him a very clear message that even one more mouthful was going to meet with an unwanted response though he took his chances with one final swig of the excellent coffee.

As he was finishing the cup the phone buzzed and Vicky took the call.

'Your car is waiting for you Mr Chandler.'

★★★

It was just after nine as Jon walked into the meeting hall of the Phoenixan government offices complex. The girl at the reception desk, sitting just a little too high up for Jon's liking, knew exactly who he was and issued him with the necessary security badge.

The main part of the conference wasn't due to recommence until eleven so the first action of the day was to get together with the members of the Union diplomatic mission. Apart from Timothy Darling who'd travelled to Phoenix in his own body ten years earlier and two locally recruited aides, the members of the team were all travellers like himself, people who'd popped in for the regulation twenty to thirty days permitted by their TranzCon contracts.

But now Jon's time had come. Here he was, face to face with the team - in a manner of speaking, though not quite. The men seemed nothing short of huge and the two female members of the team were both quite a bit taller than Jana's small frame, an effect made all the more obvious by the elegantly high heels they walked so effortlessly in. If that had been the end of the matter he'd have been happy but he was painfully aware that in their grey pinstripe power skirts they looked both feminine and in control.

Like a small child overwhelmed by the situation he wanted to run away and hide. If only he could have found a host more in keeping with his own self. An Alpha or a Beta would never have had this problem. With more than a little envy he looked over at Horace Walton, standing tall in the handsome body *he* should have been wearing.

Jon knew that with tall frame of his own body he looked imposing at any gathering. Powerful and regal, though he'd always prided himself it was for his position rather than his appearance that people respected him. Now he wasn't so sure, and the feeling he got from the others was that they didn't really see him as part of the team. Time and again he'd tried to attract Timothy's attention, but the man was always too busy to speak to him. Jon was little short of furious, for someone in his position to be repeatedly ignored by the leader of the delegation was downright rudeness.

★★★

The conference itself had gone no better, probably because no-one asked him to do anything. He'd missed his main input on the first day, and now they were no longer interested in what he had to say.

There had been one very minor speech regarding trade matters that was passed his way, but it was no more than a consolation prize. Even that had gone all wrong - the microphone had been set too high and he hadn't managed to adjust it himself. With at least another day to go before his mind gained full control of his host body the girl's small hands fumbled as he'd tried without success to unscrew the knob. It had only taken a moment for a technician to come onto the stage and drop it low enough for him to use, but he knew that vital seconds had been lost. He knew how to work an audience and could recognise the telltale signs that told him how well it was going, so when the first members of his audience began to talk amongst themselves he knew he'd blown it. When he was at last able to start he was quite unnerved and his mind went blank. For a politician of his rank to give a speech almost entirely from notes was almost unheard of. It wasn't something to make a good impression.

After that debacle he'd been happy to go back to his seat and listen to the rest of the speeches. The most he'd had to do all day was applaud when yet another dignitary had said, in another slightly different way to all the others who'd said the same thing before, what a wonderful achievement it would be if Phoenix was to become part of the Union.

39

Blackmail

Jon was sitting reading the paper when the gate entry-phone buzzed to let him know someone wanted to visit the big house. It was unusual because he never brought business back to Rosemount and he always met up with friends at his apartment down town. If it was a cold-caller he'd just send him on his way.

He clicked a switch on the panel and his heart sank when he looked at the screen and saw the face of Keith Medley staring into the camera. Maybe it was a full-moon that night? He'd made it clear to Keith when they'd last met five years ago that just because he'd done well finding his nephew's kidnappers, it didn't make them friends. He'd really hoped he'd never have to meet the man again.

So what did the guy want now, after all this time? He knew Keith wasn't the sort of man who took kindly to being ignored so it was going to be best to speak to him in person - in private. Jon pressed the button for the gate to open.

★★★

Just as they had five years earlier the two men sat and talked together in the summer-house. Keith was lounging in his chair and admiring the gardens while he sipped appreciatively from a glass of Jon's latest single malt. Jon was slightly put off by the way the man appeared to be so comfortable in his house.

The old soldier explained that since the time when he'd done "the job" for Jon things hadn't been going too well and he needed money. Jon asked him what had happened to the money he'd paid him, after all it was more than a working man would have made in ten or even fifteen years. All he would say was that he'd spent it, and now he needed more. Jon tried to make it clear that their contract had been years ago, but despite the brave face he was trying to show, at the back of his mind he was worried, very worried indeed.

'I need more Mr Chandler, and you wouldn't even miss the sort of money that would keep a man like me supplied with all the necessities of life. Every time I watch the TV these days it's all about how your space-line is opening more routes and driving the competition out. And all that money you put into natural resources on the outer planets, I should think you're really coining it now.'

Jon knew he was right, his grandfather and his father had worked so hard to build up the family fortune, and if they could have seen the way his business ventures were going now he didn't know whether they'd have been proud or envious - probably both. He could pay any sum Keith asked for and not even miss it, but that wasn't the point. He was trembling slightly when he replied.

'Just because I've got money Keith, it doesn't mean you can drop by and help yourself any time you fancy. Life just isn't like that.'

Keith looked at him in a way that left Jon unable to fathom the man's thoughts. He remembered back to how he'd found the old commando's gaze slightly disturbing, and in the years that had passed nothing had changed.

'But not everyone has the kind of relationship we do Mr Chandler.'

Jon was shaking less now as he became more irritated.

'And just what sort of relationship do we have Keith?'

'I'll put it to you straight, you're a murderer, and I've got a gun with your DNA and dabs all over it as evidence. That's what sort of relationship we've got Mr Chandler.'

Jon's worst fears had suddenly come true.

'But I thought I paid you to get rid of the bodies and the gun. I saw the van on the TV. What happened with the gun?'

'Let's say I kept it, just in case a day like today ever came round. It's safe and you've no need to worry. As long as I'm around to look after it the police will never find it.'

'What if I was to walk over to the cocktail cabinet and get out the gun I keep there "just in case", and shot you dead? Perhaps your gun would stay hidden and I wouldn't need to worry.'

Keith looked and smiled. Slowly he shook his head.

'No Jon, if you don't mind me calling you Jon. I saw you with a gun in your hand that day when you shot Bo. If that was the best you could do against a handcuffed man, you don't stand a chance against me. And I know you haven't got a gun here because I checked - there are no firearms registered in your name, and a fine law-abiding citizen like Jon Chandler wouldn't take the risk of ten years inside for possession of an unregistered weapon. Am I right?'

Jon knew the old soldier had the measure of him.

'And even if I put a gun in your hand right here and now, you still couldn't shoot me. I'd have fifteen chances to jump you before you got anywhere near pulling the trigger. Do you remember how it used to be in the movies? The bad guy in the black hat would stand there with his gun ready to shoot while he explained to the good guy all the reasons why he was going to kill him.'

'And he gave the good guy a chance to overcome him and turn the tables. There wouldn't have been a happy ending if he hadn't.'

'And do you believe in happy endings Jon?'

'OK then, you've got me over a barrel, at the moment. But what if I got another guy like you to take you out. Fight fire with fire - happy ending for me but not for you. Maybe I'd be better spending my money like that instead of just handing it over.'

'Already thought of it Jon. If I die in let's say *difficult* circumstances, there's someone else who might just make the gun and the story available to the police. And you know the way DI Bennett loves you so much don't you?'

It was pretty much as Jon had expected. Obviously the man was going to cover himself, though he could be bluffing - or maybe not.

'So what are you looking for?'

'Absolute chicken-feed to a man like you Jon. 200k a year and my silence is guaranteed.'

It was as Jon had suspected, Keith wasn't just looking for a one-off payment - this was good old-fashioned blackmail. But it was as the man had said, chicken-feed. Years ago he could have paid it with ease, now he wouldn't even notice if money like that fell through a hole in his trouser pocket.

'What if I was only prepared to pay 100k Keith?'

'It's not enough.'

'What if I just told you to go to hell and then you handed the gun over to the police? You wouldn't get any money at all then.'

'But you'd be going to jail.'

'And you would be too. Maybe we'd be cellmates together.'

'If they catch me Jon - if they catch me. Just think on this, I'm a lot lower profile than you are, and where would you hide anyway? The only places you know to go are five star hotels. In any case, I'd do a bit better in jail than you would, and you know I'm speaking from experience don't you?'

Jon knew he was defeated. It was as he'd said before, Keith had him over a barrel. Angry for leaving himself so open he walked over to the house and went into the study. He moved the picture and turned the tumblers on the wall-safe. Back in the summer-house he handed the wad of notes over to the man, whom he noticed had helped himself to another slug of whisky.

40

Later That Day

When the conference ended Jon wasn't surprised to find that the organisers had laid on a rather nice buffet reception so the delegates could get together on a less formal basis. Considering who he was, and knowing his position in the organisation he represented, he'd naturally assumed that people would be queuing up to speak to him. That was how it usually worked out - it was always good for the ego to be in demand. But after a few short and stilted conversations he soon realised the other delegates were passing him by. There were even times when he'd been left standing alone helping himself to the vast array of tasty finger-food laid out on the buffet table. It was something that had never, ever, happened before.

As he was doing a second lap of the canapés he was surprised when a man he'd never seen before came along and stared quite blatantly at his host body's bust. Bloody cheek of it - Jon felt like offering the guy a photograph though he was becoming aware of the way men would glance at Jana's body in general, and the curves of her shapely bosom in particular. It was as if he could feel the way their eyes scanned around the room in his general direction, and then stopped for precisely one moment too long when they happened to be pointing in his direction. Obviously there was a technique to it because he could feel them looking, and yet when he returned the glance, somehow they'd managed to be looking the other way. Was it paranoia, or was it really happening?

Then the man's face looked down into Jon's eyes and he smiled.

'Jon, Jon Chandler. How nice to see you - and in such a delightful body too. They told me you were using a female host on this trip but I'd expected some old hag, not a little dolly bird. I could scarcely believe it when I saw the photo on your ID badge. How the devil are you?'

Jon was so taken aback he hadn't had chance to take a look at the man's ID badge. Obviously he knew Jon, but for the moment Jon didn't know him. He improvised.

'Yes, how nice to see you.' And then he asked, just a little sheepishly, 'who are you?'

'Oh sorry Jon, I should have introduced myself. This host body is so like my real one that I just assume people will recognise me - Dougie Smith. We were at the perishable goods sub-committee meeting last Thursday.'

In fact Jon could remember almost nothing of the day, but then it hadn't been the most exciting event in town. Maybe it was a memory he'd left behind in his own brain back in Jackson. But he joined in and did his best.

'Oh Dougie, of course I see it now. Your host looks just like your real body, well apart from the skin colour, and I can tell from your speech and your mannerisms it's you. I'm just not very good at this body swapping business.'

'Steady on with the bit about the skin colour Jon - the people here can get a bit touchy about things like that.'

Jon made a note in his mind to discuss the matter further. Dougie continued.

'I'd heard this was your first mind-transfer and really I was quite amazed that someone in your position hadn't travelled before. I did twenty trips last year, and nearly as many the year before.'

Jon wondered why he was having to make excuses for himself, but somehow they seemed to be expected.

'Well I don't know whether they told you, but I'm a Delta 2 and it's not easy to find hosts. There just aren't many of us around and that makes travelling by TranzCon a bit difficult. As you can see, I've had to accept this female as my host and quite frankly it's not working out too well. I suppose you're an Alpha or a Beta.'

'Yes, a Beta. Endless selection of hosts available. I just looked through the website and picked out the one who looked most like me. He's a couple of years older than me, but the body is in excellent shape and the fit is quite good. They said the reflexes wouldn't be sufficiently fast for me to try anything like driving a car, but who cares about driving? I don't come on these trips to drive myself around. A bit of lubrication in the bar and then back to the hotel with a chauffeur at the wheel. Damn sight more fun than staying at home I can tell you.'

'So Dougie, I didn't see you earlier but I'm sure you'd have been announced. Did you actually make it to the conference or did you just drop in for the free booze and nosh?'

The face smiled. 'Guilty as charged Jon. I was supposed to be here right from when it started yesterday morning but TranzCon were having some kind of technical problem. They blamed it on beam strength, said it was too low for the normal type of transfer. They could have put me under to do a flat-liner but that would have left my host here virtually unusable for a couple of days so I decided to wait and see whether the beam was going to come back. In the end I was on the couch, wired up and ready to go for over 30 hours. The instant it was up to full strength they fired me across.'

'So how long ago did you arrive?'

'About three hours.'

After all he'd been through getting to grips with Jana's body Jon could scarcely believe it. To be up and about so soon was amazing.

'And you're standing here talking to me, fully acclimatised and bright as a button? I didn't have anything like such an easy ride.'

'It all comes with experience Jon. The more trips you make, the more your mind works out how to link into the host. So now I just land in the body, wait while they unhook me, sleep for a while, put some clothes on and off I go. No bother at all, especially when you come back into a host you've used before. You'll get used to it after a few more times.'

'If I ever travel this way again.'

Dougie looked him closely in the eye. 'Seriously Jon, to do your job I think you're going to have to. Liners are OK for short haul trips, and they're a great way to travel I'll grant you - we've both had a bit of fun on liners so I should know. But when you're into journeys that would take years on a liner, they just can't compete with TranzCon. Face it old man, TranzCon is the way we'll all be travelling a few years from now and you'll have no choice if you want to stay in your present job.' Then Jon saw the glint in the man's eye. 'Or if you want to go onto higher things.'

Considering that he hadn't made any kind of formal announcement yet Jon wondered just how many people knew about his plans for the next election.

'Look Dougie, it's all very well for you, but just look at me here in this body. I tried this morning, I really tried, but it doesn't convey the image I want to project. It doesn't feel like anyone is taking me seriously. I'm here representing the whole frigging Union for Belen's sake.'

Dougie looked just slightly sympathetic. 'I can see how that's happened Jon, but quite frankly I don't think it's only because you're using a female host - it's probably more because she's a dinky-sized young dolly-bird. Jolly pretty too if you don't mind me saying.'

Despite the smile Jon almost managed to show, inside he was scowling,. Dougie hadn't any idea just how much he *did* mind.

'If she'd been middle-aged and shall we say, not so sexy, I think you'd have done better. Though I'd agree that what you really needed was a male host. We're all so open minded these days, or at least we think we are, but when it comes down to basic instincts there are still people around who've got a problem with cross-gender travel. And then we come back to the age thing. If your host had been twenty years old and male you'd *still* have had a job on your hands. What you need if you want respect are a few grey hairs. Look at me, years ago I was young and keen, and it was an uphill struggle all the way. Now I'm an old codger they hang onto my every word. There's no justice, really there isn't.'

Jon sighed. 'I suppose you're right, to some extent. But I'm sure there's more to it than just age. Tom isn't very old and he's the most revered man in the whole damned galaxy.'

'I'll go along with you on that one Jon, image is important too. Tom always looks right and in your own body you look damned good, not that I fancy you of course - well not in your own body anyway.'

Jon smiled.

'You know what it is that makes the difference, it's height and size. People have always respected big men, and in our own bodies that's you, me, Tom, and quite a few more of our colleagues in government. It's a caveman thing, the bigger the man, the more dinosaurs he dragged home to the cave, and the more heads he knocked together when someone challenged him for his position.'

'Cavemen didn't kill dinosaurs, they died out millions of years before.'

'Well sabre toothed tigers then, or something like that. The point is, big men always got taken seriously back in those days, and it's still true today. Totally ridiculous because there's no reason why a small clever man, or a woman, couldn't be the best leader the galaxy had ever seen. But just look at our history, it hasn't happened so far. To date, all our leaders have been men, and they've all been at least a notch over average size.'

'So you think it's more the fact that my host body is small than that it's female that I've been having trouble?'

'Its definitely a factor. Put everything together, the age, the sex, the small stature, and you can see straight away you're backing a loser. In your own body Jon you're a natural leader, and if you were going to run for First Minister I'd be right in line supporting you. But in this little girl's body, I might possibly take you on as a junior secretary.'

Jon smiled at the thought. 'But only if I agreed to sleep with you first?'

Dougie bellowed with laughter. 'You've got it Jon, you've got it in one. So are we off down to the town to get some action?'

'What sort of a place did you have in mind?'

'Oh come on, the sort of place we've ended up in so many times before.'

'And are we on the pull?'
'Could be.'
'So what about me then? Do you suppose I should be on the pull for men or women?'
'Who cares Jon. Lets get some drinks.'

41

Alan Baker

The thieves never managed to get into the house, but the fact they got through the fence and into the grounds was disturbing enough. What in hell's name did you have to do to make a place secure? For Belen's sake, every house in Rosemount was like a little fortress these days, how much more security did they need?

Alan Baker, the rep from Weston Security was a nice guy and Jon even thought he recognised him from years back, but when? After the two men had chatted for a while he had it worked it out, Alan had been a career soldier for most of his life, and like so many of the older members of his profession he'd ended his service days passing on his knowledge to new recruits. So that had been it, the previous time they'd been face to face Alan had probably been telling him what a useless soldier he was and always would be. Oh well, that was a long time ago and you couldn't hold a grudge forever, not even against a drill sergeant.

Alan told him that after finishing in the army he'd done a couple of years in the police, but he'd never really got on with that outfit so in the end he'd left and moved into the private security business. It wasn't a passport to stardom, but it paid the rent.

After walking round the full length of the perimeter fence the two of them sat together for a cup of coffee and a bit of telling the tale of how it had been in the old days, though neither of them was prepared to describe them as the *good* old days. It was clear that Alan remembered quite a bit more about Walridge Plain than he did.

★★★

Alan called back a couple of days later with the quote from Weston and they agreed on the upgrades the house needed, but he had to apologise that it would be a few weeks before they could get the sub-contractor up there to install the gear.

★★★

Despite all the government business that was taking up so much of his time these days it was turning out to be a busy period up at the big house too and Jon had found himself spending more nights there than was his normal practice. And there was one event coming up that he wasn't looking forward to. It'd been the same every year since *he* had paid a visit.

Jon was sitting in the summer-house when the gate buzzer went, and as he'd expected, the camera showed Keith Medley's menacing face again. In his usual organised fashion he was well prepared and the payola was sitting ready in the safe, all in used notes of course. Keith came in and accepted his usual glass of single malt, but Jon could tell right from the start this wasn't just the normal handover meeting they'd had before. He'd worried himself sick about the day it might happen, and now he had to sit and listen while Keith explained that now Jon Chandler was such an important man in the government, and inflation was running at an all-time high of 1.3%, perhaps an increase might be in order. He thought a million a year would be a reasonable sum.

Jon could afford it of course, if money had been an object for him he'd never have left the management of Rapier to move into politics. But what really worried him was that the man seemed to be even less reliable than he'd been before. The way his hands shook as he accepted the money, and the obvious marks on his arms were a pretty good indication of where the blackmail money had been going. A guy like that could go off the rails any time and shop him whether he paid up or not. The solution that had got them through the past five years was probably not going to last.

★★★

When the security system contractors turned up on a Monday morning three weeks later Alan came with them to supervise, but he found plenty of time to sit with Jon and chat over the inevitable cups of coffee. The more they talked, the more Jon saw that maybe *this* old soldier could offer a chance of solving his latest problem.

Jon came straight out with it and asked Alan how much he made from working for Weston Security, and had to hold himself back from smiling when he heard the answer. For Belen's sake, even his secretary's junior secretary made more than that. On the spot he offered him a job to come on board as his personal security chief.

It was plain to see that Alan must have wondered exactly what the job entailed, but with the salary offer that Jon laid on the table, and the fact that the conditions of employment included one of the cottages on the estate, rent free, the man had little trouble accepting. Alan pointed out he was obliged to give Weston's three months notice, but he'd be spending quite a bit of that time up at Rosemount supervising the work anyway, so Jon told him he could move into the cottage whenever it suited him.

***

After a removal van had dropped its pitifully small load at the cottage Alan became Jon's nearest neighbour, and he made a point of telling him he had a standing invitation to come up to the big house any time he wasn't staying at his apartment down town.

And so it was that Alan came round to share dinner that Saturday night. They chatted about the army, as usual, though that wasn't Jon's primary purpose for the meeting. All day he'd been wondering and worrying. Could he really take the risk of sharing his darkest secrets? What if Alan went straight to the police? But it was clear that if the man was going to be any help he'd have to open up, he'd have to take the chance. Perhaps a few drinks in the summer-house after the meal would make it easier.

It did. Jon told Alan the whole story: the kidnap, everything that had happened to Robert, how Keith Medley had become involved first as his private eye, and then in a slightly different capacity as ruthless assassin. And he made clear the role he himself had taken in the final elimination of Boris Stamford.

Alan looked thoughtful and said that maybe he'd heard something about Keith years ago, and if memory served him it hadn't been anything good. He promised to make a few investigations and see what he could find out.

***

Monday evening found the two men back in the summer-house working their way down the bottle of single malt they'd started two nights before, and it was clear that Alan had uncovered quite a bit.

'What made you employ a man like Medley Jon?' he asked. 'If you'd wanted to put a contract on someone there were much better operators around.'

It sounded as if the old soldier was quite comfortable with the idea of having people terminated.

'My original plan had been to catch the people and then hand them over to the police, so I took him on as an investigator. But somewhere along the way he turned into more, and then, when he put the gun in my hand so I could blast the life out of the bastard who mutilated my nephew …….. well, I just saw everything through a sort of haze. It was like I was in a dream. I didn't really feel like I was killing someone for real.'

Alan nodded knowingly. 'The first time you kill, it's always the hardest.'

'But I trusted him, at first anyway. He was ex-army and really seemed to be right for the job.'

'He was ex-army alright. Did he tell you what he did and how long he'd served?'

'Yes, he said he'd been a sergeant in the commandos and had seen action in the Garanda campaign on Temenco. He served for 19 years, a real career soldier. Surely someone with that sort of record deserves respect, or at least that's what I thought when I took him on.'

'At face value it's true. He was in the service the whole 19 years, but I'll bet he didn't tell you that the last nine were in a military prison.'

'Indeed he did not. What'd he done?'

'They found him guilty of war-crimes after his platoon took some two-bit village.'

'And what did he actually do that was a crime? I mean, all war's pretty messy stuff.'

'He knew the villagers had been collaborating with terrorists who were holed up somewhere in the hills just outside the village so he set about interrogating them, but although his methods were quite inventive the people told him nothing that was of any use. They were probably too scared of what the terrorists would do to risk passing on any information.'

'And then what.'

'He used the sort of tactics the terrorists would use. Fight fire with fire. The ones he didn't think were going to be any use he herded into one of the buildings at gunpoint, and then he torched it. Anyone who tried to get out was machine-gunned. And they were the lucky ones, the rest of them he tortured to have one more go at getting information.'

'Tortured them? Obviously something beyond normal interrogation techniques.'

'A long way beyond. They were tied to chairs and then he cut off their hands and feet, one by one, and left them to bleed to death.'

'Not really a way to get someone's confidence though.'

'No, but if you're watching and you know you're next, it puts quite a bit of pressure on you.'

Jon screwed up his face at the thought.

'The army court-martialled him and sent him to jail, but he wasn't an easy man to manage and the only way they could keep him under control was by putting him on a cocktail of drugs. And as you can imagine, he became addicted.'

'But in the end they let him out?'

'He came to the end of his sentence and they let him go, partly because he appeared to be rehabilitated, and mainly because they wanted rid of him. It was costing the army quite a bit to keep him in jail, so if they could move him out of the military sector the public health service would have to pick up the tab. When he was first back in civilian life his doctor kept him on the same medication they'd given him in prison, and it worked OK for a while. That's when you used him to take out those three guys who kidnapped your nephew - he was relatively stable at that time.'

'So what happened next?'

'They tried to get him off the drugs, but they did it too fast and the man started going to pieces. When he couldn't get his drugs on prescription anymore he discovered he could make do with heroin, and of course he could buy that on the street if he could get enough money.'

'He seemed OK to me, I never realised he was a junkie till just recently.'

'In those days he was getting plenty of work and making enough money to pay for what he needed, but the heroin had side effects and it was dragging him down. It interfered with his work and as he got less investigation work he branched out into other activities, like mugging people. There's scarcely a man alive could take on a guy like that. He could go unarmed against a knife, and he'd even have the edge over most people holding a gun on him. He was lightning fast.'

Jon nodded, it fitted exactly with his own take on Keith.

'When I first met him I could tell he was dangerous, but that's what you expect from a commando. If I tell you the truth, that was part of his appeal because a nice guy wasn't going to get anywhere.'

'Well he's dangerous now and not just in a physical way. Even if you do keep him supplied with money for his drugs it's only a matter of time before he spills the beans, whether he means to or not. With what he knows it could be the end of you and your career, and it might even drag Rapier down too. There's nothing else for it Jon, we've got to take him out.'

'Alan no, I don't want to go down that route again. That's how it all I started. Sometimes when I lie awake at night I want to come clean about it all, I want to go and turn myself in. I'm sure they'd be at least a bit sympathetic if they knew about what happened to Robert.'

When Jon looked up he saw the way Alan was shaking his head.

'No. I wouldn't hope for too much. You engaged the services of a hit-man, and that's a serious enough crime in itself, and then you carried out a murder.'

'But that bastard, he deserved to die.'

'He deserved to be tried in court and be punished according to the law. You took the law into your own hands and carried out an execution. Even if the judge was as lenient as he could be you'd still be looking at twenty years. And then you'd have Keith to worry about. If they ever let him out on the street again he'd come looking for you to take his revenge.'

Jon was struggling to speak.

'You can do whatever you like as long as you don't involve me Jon. But if you want to stay out of jail and make a success of your career, I don't think you've got a choice, really I don't.'

42

Trade Talks

After a session of trawling the bars of Celebration with Dougie it had been quite late when the two friends had finally called time. The old guy had consumed enough booze to put any decent sized man right under the table, and Jon had found out the hard way just how much more receptive Jana's body was to the effects of alcohol. Even though he'd done everything he could to choose soft-drinks, or tip a few shots of whisky into Dougie's glass when he wasn't looking, he'd still downed a fair bit more than the small female body could take. One of the few things he did recall was trying to walk in the awful shoes Vicky had encouraged him into seventeen hours earlier. If there was any reason at all in the galaxy to wish to be born male, the shoes just had to be *it*.

But what a night. When he awoke in his hotel bed next morning he truly had no idea of how he'd got there, and the fact that the girl's body was naked didn't help either. It wasn't something he'd ever been bothered about in his own flesh. What he did know all too well was that his borrowed head was throbbing quite badly and he wished he could give it back to its real owner. But it wasn't to be; even if most of the other delegates had packed up and gone home to Vissan he'd still got another day to do, and from the way he felt right now it wasn't going to be easy.

Staggering uncertainly around in his room Jon wasn't in any mood to tackle the complexity of the kettle, so he called room-service for a pot of their strongest coffee. Fortunately the clock showed just after seven and the trade meeting wasn't due to start till eleven. At least he'd got another couple of hours before he needed to be up.

Perhaps he'd managed to disappear back into the land of nod, or perhaps not, but five minutes later he heard a knock at the door. Room service of course and he was desperate for the coffee. One cup later he had another go at some shut-eye, but it came again - the awful knock at the door. Vicky and the hairdresser had come to get him ready. He told them to go and get some breakfast and come back later. Finally he got another precious hour of badly needed sleep.

By the time the two women had done their work and room-service had delivered a somewhat smaller breakfast than the day before, Jon felt he'd returned to the land of the living and was just a little more cheerful about the prospect of an afternoon to be spent discussing trade agreements. That was what he'd come for after all.

***

Back at the conference hall things weren't so bad because the whole mood of the meeting was more relaxed than the slightly stuffy atmosphere he'd experienced the day before.

For hours the committee had dug into the details of products and services Phoenix could provide for interplanetary trade, but what was becoming clear was just how far they were behind in most areas of technology. As far as Jon could see there wasn't a single manufactured item that matched the quality he'd come to expect from Union industry. Even worse, the level of automation they had available was pathetically low and that meant the cost of their products was going to be unacceptably high. The only items which might possibly have found a market in the Union were some of the planet's highly effective pharmaceutical products that his advisors had told him were usefully in advance of anything the Union had developed so far, and items of specialised mining equipment. If the airless worlds out in the Antonby region were going to become the Union's next source of raw materials a leap in the technology employed was essential if they were going to be developed to their full potential.

But then there was the time it would take to deliver goods from Phoenix. The two year trip to Darius was manageable, and with a population of nearly six billion the planet was certainly a huge market in its own right, but the seven year journey the home planets was going to be a real obstacle.

Despite the problems the delegates had identified it had been a good meeting, and if their enthusiasm was an indicator of the desire they had for the planet to become a Union member then it had achieved a lot. Things had gone very well indeed, even to the point where Jon felt he'd enjoyed himself. In fact it had gone so well there'd been one point when he'd forgotten entirely he was there in Jana's host body. It seemed the other delegates forgot it too so his true personality had had a chance to shine through.

43
Jon & Alan

Jon thought about the situation he now found himself in, and the more he thought, the more he knew that Alan was absolutely right - he had to dispose of Keith Medley. One way or another, the guy had to go. In some ways the decision had made itself because the biggest worry all along had been the extra risk he'd be taking if he let on to anyone else about his involvement in the sordid affair. Now he'd taken Alan into his confidence he had less to lose by going along with the plan.

Alan explained a few things about the intricacies of "causing people to disappear" as he termed it.

'There are three main problems with murder if you don't want to be found out. The first is getting rid of the murder weapon, and that's comparatively easy because usually it's quite small and you can store it for years without it starting to smell. Getting rid of the body is more difficult because it's a lot bigger, it's a lot messier, and after a few days it stinks to high heaven. And it gets worse, unless you're unusually big you can't easily handle a lifeless adult human single handed. Even if you could, what do you do with it?'

Jon was taking it all in, intrigued by how casually his new friend could discuss murder.

'You could bury it of course, but people tend to notice you digging a two metre hole. You could stick it in a freezer, and that's OK till someone goes looking for the ice-cream. Perhaps the best type of murder is just to drive by and shoot them in the street, but then you've got the problem that everyone knows there's been a murder, and surprise surprise, the police are out looking for a murderer.'

'How about dumping them outside someone's house in the back of a van?'

'Like Keith Medley did? Pretty good technique, especially if they can't trace you from the vehicle's details. You have to think of surveillance cameras though, you don't want to be caught on CCTV while you're walking away. But these things pale into insignificance compared to the biggest problem.'

'And that is?'

'The other people who know about it. Whenever you've got someone on board to help you, you've got someone who can shop you. And unless you can get them in as deep as you are, you've got the problem that the police will offer them immunity if they own up. Mark my words, the murder weapon and the body are easy compared to what you do about other people who know too much.'

Jon smiled. 'So maybe my best way out would be to get you to help me, and then bump you off as well? You could even go in the same hole.'

Alan gave him an indignant look.

'Private Chandler, you were sod all use at unarmed combat, and you couldn't even shoot a mannequin let alone a real live human being.'

'And I suppose my hair needed cutting too?'

'Be serious Jon. Anyway, you don't need to worry about me. I'm on your side.'

'You make it sound as though you've got some personal involvement?'

'I hate the Keith Medley's of this world Jon. I hate anyone who gives the military a bad name. Just sticking a psycho like that in jail for a few years wasn't any sort of solution. I know we've come to, shall we say, an agreement, but you need to understand that my heart's in it too.'

★★★

The next time the two of them were together they considered the options available and what was likely to work best. Jon had worried about the gun he'd used to shoot Boris Stamford. If it was true what Keith had said about someone else passing it on to the police in the event of his death, simply disposing of the man might not solve the problem. Alan thought about that one.

'From what we know about him, he's not the sort of man who has many friends. Certainly not people he could trust or confide in. So on the one hand there's a strong chance he's just bluffing, buying himself some insurance against you putting a contract on him.'

'And on the other?'

'Unfortunately, he could be telling the truth. Either way it'd be safer if we could get control of the gun. Even if Medley was still alive, without the gun he wouldn't have as much to blackmail you with.'

'But that's exactly why he's not going to give it up.'

'Consider his motives though. What's the main thing he's after? The *only* thing he's after?'

'Money.'

'So how much do you think you'd have to offer to get him to hand the gun over?'

'Well, he's asking me for a million a year, and he's got perhaps another sixty or seventy years to live, unless he kills himself with all the drugs he's taking. But assuming he lives a long time, maybe he'd want sixty or seventy million in total. Although …….. if he had twenty or thirty million to set up a sinking fund, invested right it could pay him a million a year for the rest of his life.'

Alan was almost in stitches listening to what his new employer was saying.

'Jon, you know a lot about money I'll grant you, but you don't know much about the Keith Medley's of this world. Unlike financiers they don't live their lives trying to predict how the market's going to behave years into the future. If you offered him five million he'd snatch your hand off. But anyway, you've got room to manoeuvre, you could put five on the table and see if he went for it. If he turned it down, barter a bit. Even if he took you for double you'd still come a long way short of your twenty million figure.'

'So then I'd have the gun, but Keith would still be around to tell the tale to anyone he chose. Even after shelling out a lot of dosh I still couldn't guarantee his silence.'

'The gun's only step one. We're offering him a baited hook. He has to come up here to bring it and collect the money, and here's a big plus, he's comfortable coming here.'

Jon was looking worried again. 'Then what?'

'And then you shoot him. Simple as that.'

'Me? What chance do I stand? He told me himself he could take me out before I could even pull a trigger, and I believed him. I still do. But you Alan, you were in the army for years. You could do it.'

The old soldier smiled. 'I shot a lot of targets in my time, but how many people do you suppose I actually killed?'

Jon thought about it and quickly realised that in a peacetime army the occasions when real action happened were few and far between.

'OK, I take your point, but I'm still not sure. If we worked together we might stand a chance.'

'No Jon. Keith's used to coming here and finding you on your own. If there was anyone else around he'd smell a rat.'

'But what if you were hidden away and shot him from somewhere concealed?'

'From what you told me you always met together here in the summer house. Just look at the place. Talk about minimalist décor - there isn't anywhere for a man to hide and if you moved into the main house it might make him suspicious.'

'Where do we get a gun from?'

'No problem there Jon. I can get a brand new unregistered pistol, and it'd be completely untraceable.'

'And what if I can't shoot him?'

'You have to. You shot Stamford didn't you?'

Jon nodded.

'You didn't have to shoot him, but you did. You just filled your mind with reasons to hate him, and the bullet came out of the end of the gun. Keith won't give you time for doubt. You'll shoot him, sure as eggs are eggs.'

Jon wondered but said nothing. He watched as Alan paced around the room looking at the few items of furniture and the positions of the lights.

'What do you do when Keith comes in here?'

'We sit in the chairs overlooking the garden, and usually we drink whisky.'

'Do you go to this cocktail bar to get the drinks?'

'That's where everything's stored. I fill the ice bucket from the fridge and bring it over to the table along with the bottle.'

Alan looked thoughtful again. He picked up a chair, climbed up to the lamp above the cocktail bar and changed its angle so it pointed further out into the room.

'Walk up to the bar Jon.'

Jon was intrigued - he got up and did as he was asked.

'Does the light shine in your eyes as you walk towards me?'

'Yes, it's quite blinding really.'

'Good. We've got a plan.'

He walked around on the floor looking at the polished wood and lifting the loose-lay rugs in a few places.

'What's under the floor?'

'How should I know? I'm not a builder.'

'Neither am I but I know a bit about how you put a house together. This is a ground floor room with a wooden floor and that's just a bit unusual these days. I'll bet the whole summer house is a traditional construction with the outer brick wall rising up from concrete footings set about a metre or so down. The space in between the walls and below the boards will just be the soil that was here before the house was built. Have you got any tools?'

'I expect there are some in one of the outhouses. When the family lived here we used to have some maintenance guys who looked after the place, but these days I just bring in contractors when I need them.'

'Lets go and have a look.'

★★★

Half an hour later the two men walked back into the summer-house armed with a saw, a set of chisels, a big hammer and a torch. Alan rolled back the heavy rug that covered the centre of the room and set to work on the floorboards. When he'd managed to lift the first board he shone the torch down and called Jon to come and have a look. Jon peered down into the gloomy undercroft, not quite sure what he was supposed to be looking at.

'It's just like I expected Jon. The floor of the house is about a metre above the ground outside so it gets a better view of the garden, and the gap under the boards inside is the same. Then it's just bare soil.'

'So what?'

'You know I told you that getting rid of the body was the second hardest thing? Well this is where we dispose of it. Anywhere else on the whole planet someone would notice you digging a big hole, and even if they didn't the police would spot a freshly dug grave somewhere out in the woods. But no-one would even think of looking under the living room floor, especially if you weren't even suspected of anything. It's perfect.'

★★★

Saturday evening was coming round again just a little too quickly for Jon's liking. But it came anyway and he wasn't surprised when the gate panel buzzed and the face he'd expected to see came up on the screen. When the throbbing of the bike's big engine had stopped and the rider laid down his helmet, the two men greeted each other coolly in their usual manner - a stand-off that recognised their roles as acquaintances drawn together for business reasons only.

It was clear that Keith liked the big house quite a lot and he certainly enjoyed sitting on the sofa by the patio windows that looked out onto the beautifully tended gardens, especially with a drink in his hand. Jon got straight to business and told him he'd thought about the request for more money, but that he'd considered the idea of offering a single sum in full and final payment - provided of course he handed over the gun. It was clear Keith hadn't been expecting it, but when Jon suggested he'd be able to afford a place of his own with a garden and a big comfortable sofa he showed more than a little interest. He thought about the idea for a while before asking the all important question.

'How much did you have in mind?'

Jon was in his element when money was the subject. Not a poker player alive could have read the emotion that came from lips which formed the words, "Four million".

Keith frowned and shook his head.

'Oh come on Jon, you'd be paying me that in just a few years. If you really wanted me to be interested in the deal you'd have to put a bit more on the table than that. What's money to a man like you anyway?'

It occurred to Jon that if Alan's plan succeeded the scheme wouldn't cost him anything at all. So as long as he wasn't so free with money that Keith suspected something was up he could actually offer as much as the man asked for.

When the two of them finally shook hands the sum agreed was eight million HUC.

★★★

When Saturday came round again Jon was getting nervous, particularly when Alan proudly showed him the shiny new Brandt revolver.

'Why a revolver Alan? I'd been expecting an automatic.'

Alan weighed the gun in his hand, spinning the magazine and listening to the perfectly oiled action.

'It's lighter for one thing, but the main advantage is it's more accurate. There's so much moving metal in an automatic it can spoil your aim unless you're ready for it. OK a revolver's only got six bullets, but you'll only be needing the first one.'

TranzCon

He walked over to the cocktail bar and pulled open the top drawer. After moving the contents around a bit he cocked the hammer and placed the weapon inside next to the ice tongs. It fitted in perfectly.

After half an hour Alan was still busy, making preparations. Jon had been puzzled as he'd watched Alan pour away most of the contents of a dark glass bottle of single malt, and then he'd made a pot of tea in the little kitchenette at the back of the summer-house. That in itself was no surprise because he knew the security man preferred it to coffee, but he'd been intrigued to see Alan pour it into a jug and put it in the fridge. An hour later he took out and poured it carefully into a whisky bottle he'd fished out of the bin earlier.

'Method in the madness Jon, we need Keith to drink as much strong stuff as you can pour down him, and we need you to be stone cold, so you'll start off with some of this tea.'

He poured out a glass and held it up to the light.

'Look at that eh. Pretty convincing don't you think? Just make sure Keith doesn't get to taste your tipple.'

★★★

When Alan finally left there were still two hours to go before Keith was due to arrive and Jon sat anxiously on the sofa, wondering if he could really go ahead with the plan his security man had so carefully devised. He wanted to start on the whisky there and then, the real stuff, but he knew this was one evening in his life when he had to stay as sober as he could. He tried to watch TV but found himself staring out of the window. He tried to read but after half an hour he was still looking at the same page. For most of his life, time had conspired to pass in the blink of an eye - now it was grinding.

The clock chimed seven and Jon knew the evening show was due to roll up its curtain very soon. Half-past came and he waited for the buzzer to summon him. The minutes dragged and still he was waiting. At ten minutes to eight he nearly jumped off the sofa when the call finally came.

From the summer-house window he could see across the grounds to the gap in the hedge that flanked the southern side of the garden, and he caught sight of the motorbike as it flashed past. Two minutes later he met the rider at the door and the two of them walked over to the summer-house. Now, after weeks of planning it was finally happening, and he was strangely calm - the jitters that had churned his stomach most of the afternoon had departed the instant Keith arrived.

Keith took off the boots and heavy leathers he used for riding and the two of them sat together on the sofa. Jon drained the last of the tea Alan had prepared into his whisky tumbler and added another two cubes of ice. He picked up the other bottle and showed Keith the label.

'Single malt for you?' speaking to the man as if he were an old friend.

When the glass was half-full the man raised his hand. Jon carried on pouring for a millisecond longer. They chatted for a while and Jon made a point of finishing his tea and refilling the glasses from the bottle before getting up from the table.

'I'll get the money. It's all in the study.'

As he walked over to the main part of the house he wondered what Keith would be doing while he was away. If he snooped around and found the revolver in the cocktail cabinet drawer the game was up. But there was no way of knowing what the man was doing. Hope was all he had now.

As they'd agreed, half the money was in high denomination notes and the other half in precious stones, but it still came to quite a load and Jon wondered how Keith had planned to take it all home on a motorbike. And what if he was robbed that night? The good news was that it wasn't much of a worry when the sort of punk who mugged easy targets in the street left the likes of Keith Medley well alone.

Jon laid the payment down on the table in front of the sofa and made a gesture of pushing it halfway towards Keith. He looked expectantly at the man. Keith picked up the rucksack he'd been wearing and laid it down on the table. He put one hand inside and the cloth he withdrew clearly showed the shape of a gun. He laid it on the table and pulled back the edges of the cloth. And there it lay, the big automatic they'd used the day Jon had executed Bo. Keith put his hand back into the bag and pulled out another cloth with the silencer and the laser sight inside.

'Is this really it Keith?'

Keith nodded. 'This is it. For what you're paying I don't need to cheat you.'

Jon lifted the gun in its cloth and studied it. Everything about it told him it was the one he'd used that day to kill Boris Stamford. When he was satisfied he put the gun back down on the table.

'OK then, a deal's a deal. Take your money.'

Keith began to bundle the notes into the rucksack. Jon picked up the bottle and gestured in Keith's direction.

'One for the road?'

Without waiting for an answer Jon poured the last drain from Alan's carefully prepared bottle into the man's glass. It only splashed over the bottom.

'Never mind, there's more where that came from.'

Jon was nervous as he stood up from the sofa and walked over to the cocktail bar. His hands were shaking as he pulled the tray of ice-cubes out of the freezer and began popping them out into the bucket. Quietly he slid open the drawer behind the bar and looked down at the revolver lying there where Alan had left it.

'I've got two bottles here Keith,' he called, 'one's twelve years old and the other's fifteen. Come and see which one you fancy.'

Keith had finished stashing the loot into the rucksack and got up to walk over to the bar. In the glare from the lamp over the bar Jon watched as the heavy muscled frame walked slowly towards him. The man had a menacing appearance even when he was being friendly and Jon shuddered to think what it would be like to be on the wrong end of his anger. If he fired the gun and missed he was likely to find out.

Acting as naturally as he could Jon took hold of the tongs and began lifting cubes into the two glasses, watching as Keith approached. He wanted to do it right then, the man was near enough now but he was afraid, afraid he wouldn't manage to fire. Keith reached the bar and Jon held out the bottle of fifteen year old single malt for the man to take. He put his hand around the neck and studied the label.

Jon looked at Keith and saw how he'd given his attention to the whisky bottle. Now was the time, while he was distracted. He lowered his hand into the open drawer. Quietly he lifted out the revolver and levelled it at his foe. Keith was too close for him to miss, he just had to pull the trigger - "Pull the trigger Jon!". The voice in his head was screaming "for fuck's sake do it now - pull the trigger NOW!" but his hand froze. Muscles failed to respond and the finger sat motionless.

Somehow sensing not all was right Keith looked up from the bottle to find himself staring into the barrel of the revolver. It took no more than a heartbeat for the old soldier to understand his peril. The bottle fell from his hands and with a scream of rage he pushed the whole cocktail bar towards Jon, knocking him backwards as the polished wood cabinet fell onto his body and pinned him to the floor. The cocked gun jerked in his hand and fired, the sound deafening in the confines of the small building.

Jon never saw how the bullet ripped through the thin frame of the cocktail bar. He never knew how the wood had splintered as it passed through. But the man on the other side felt the burn as the slug entered his chest and passed through his heart. It was the last thing he ever felt. Jon shouted out in pain as 95 kilos of the old commando's body added its bulk to the weight of the cocktail bar already crushing down onto his legs.

For two hours Jon lay there, trapped under the remains of the bar and unable to move. The searing pain in his right leg had faded to numbness, and then he heard the sound of a vehicle's wheels crunching across the chippings of the driveway. A minute later Alan walked into the room and stared around at the scene of devastation. Quickly he ran over to the cocktail bar and dragged the big soldier's body off. With the weight no longer on the light wooden frame Jon was able to lift it enough to pull out his aching legs.

★★★

When morning came Jon woke to a throbbing feeling that was coming from his right leg. He looked down the bed and saw how the limb was bandaged, just as Alan had left it the night before. When he climbed out of the bed and tried to walk the leg was painful but it took his weight. At least it wasn't broken.

At his slow pace it took longer than normal to make the short trip over to the summer-house. When he arrived Alan was already there lifting floorboards from the area usually covered by the big rug. He looked up at Jon.

'How's the leg?'

'Painful, but I can walk on it.'

'You were lucky not to lose it. What happened last night?'

'I couldn't do it Alan. I tried but I couldn't do it.'
'But Keith's dead. How did that happen?'
'It was an accident in the end.'

Alan shook his head in disbelief.

'A man's dead from a gunshot wound and there's a matching revolver with your DNA and dabs on it - and you say he died because of an accident? Try telling that to the judge Jon. Come on, we've got a hole to dig.'

All that morning the two men took turns to hack out the ground below the summerhouse floor and shovel the soil to the side of the hole. By mid-day the hole was almost two metres deep and a sweating and weary Jon was relieved when he heard Alan announce it was enough. Together with the blood-soaked clothing they lowered the body down into the hole, and Alan carefully laid the two guns beside it. After searching around on the floor Alan found the bullet that had gone through Keith's body and threw it into the hole. Between them they broke up the remains of the ruined cocktail bar and dropped the bits down on top of the body. When at last the deed was done another two hours of not quite so hard labour saw the grave filled in again. With the floorboards laid back down and nailed into place no-one would ever have to know what lay beneath.

Despite the chaos Alan had seen when he'd walked in the night before the mess wasn't too difficult to clean up. Most of it was broken glass from the bottles that had smashed and spilled when the cabinet hit the floor. By now the lighter spirits had evaporated long ago though the heavier liqueurs had left a sticky stain as their contents had run out. By good chance, Keith's body had fallen onto the polished wooden boards so none of his blood had stained the heavy woollen rug, though even that was something Jon could have disposed of. Half an hour's scrubbing with some products they found in the cleaner's cupboard was all it took to remove the obvious signs of what had happened the evening before.

'They'll find DNA evidence if they ever look Jon. We can't scrub the floor that clean.'

For the first time in fifteen hours Jon managed a smile.

'Why would they even need to look in a house where a respectable man lives alone?'

★★★

It was later that evening, not long after dusk, when Alan put on Keith's boots, leathers and helmet, and with the rucksack that had so recently contained a fortune on his back rode the big motorbike to the square outside the converted house where the man rented a small flat. He pulled the bike onto its stand, walked up the steps, put the key in the outer door and disappeared from view.

Up in the flat he stripped out of the leathers and hung them neatly on the back of the main door. After he'd found some casual clothes in the wardrobe he made himself a cup of tea and switched on the TV - just loud enough for the neighbours to hear. He slept the night in the flat and about half ten next morning pulled some of Keith's clothes on, stepped out of the door and set off down the road towards the Lazy Eagle bar where his research had shown Keith often went for brunch - and his first drink of the day. Except that Alan walked straight past. He walked into the big DIY store round the corner and headed for the toilet where he changed out of Keith's clothes and into the ones he'd been carrying in his rucksack. He looked casually around the store, bought a small hacksaw for cash and went back out into the street. An hour later he was across town on the metro and met Jon in the Grill House for a steak and a beer. They drove back out to the big house in the small car which Jon kept for the times he needed to travel around Jackson without drawing too much attention.

***

Keith wasn't the kind of man who'd had many friends, and with no regular work to go to no-one noticed his absence for quite some time. In the end he was only missed after the landlord called round two weeks later to remind him the rent was due. He'd seen Keith's motorbike parked outside in the square so he thought it strange that the man never answered the door. Finally he went in using his pass key and found the place deserted. It all looked so normal with the helmet and leathers hanging in the hallway and the pile of unwashed dishes lying in the sink. He knew a bit about Keith's background and knew his tenant was a man who might possibly choose to disappear quickly, so he never bothered to report him missing. He collected as much of the decent stuff in the flat as possible and sold it to recoup some of the money he was owed.

The only thing he wondered about when Keith never came back, was how the man could have gone off and left behind the motorbike he loved so dearly.

***

Jon had been devastated by the whole affair, but he had to admit he'd actually got away with it. And now that Keith Medley was no longer part of his life he could sleep just a little easier at night. Of course, now there was another person who had the drop on him, but he felt a lot more comfortable knowing it was Alan. And six weeks later when Alan finally came on board as his security chief he felt more comfortable still.

44

The Return Home

After the meeting had ended the car took Jon back to his hotel and he had the time to relax with a cup of tea because there was still an hour to go before dinner. If he'd known earlier they were going to finish quite so soon he could have called TranzCon and made arrangements to transfer home that evening, but life felt good now and the Elizabeth Hotel was splendid in ways that put its counterparts in Jackson to shame. Perhaps this was something the planet could export: the comfort, the service, the food, the whole ambience. Just sitting there, drinking it in was bliss. There was no reason to hurry home - being "back on the beam" next morning would be soon enough.

But what about TranzCon as a way to travel? Would he ever do it again? He thought for a while and wondered whether he'd been just a little hasty with his earlier dismissals. After all it was exactly as Tom had said, not being able to travel by TranzCon was a real disadvantage for a man in his position. Certainly for a man in the position he was keen on winning. Yes he'd had problems with the girl's body being inappropriate to his needs, but this was a one off, never to be repeated. If he could do like Dougie had said and find a selection of hosts with bodies more in keeping with his own, men who were tall and looked good in top-notch suits, then he'd get the respect he deserved. It would take a bit of money to find the right sort of hosts, but what was money other than a tool?

When dinner was over Jon did eventually give in to the tumbler of malt whisky on the rocks he'd promised he'd never touch again till the day he died, but he went to bed a happy man. The excitement of knowing that the morning would bring with it his trip back home was too much though and for a while he was unable to settle. He put the light back on and picked up the magazine he'd been reading earlier, but somehow he couldn't concentrate on that either. He just sat there mulling things over, wondering how things would be when he got home. Wondering about Sylvie.

Beautiful Sylvie, 42 now and lovelier than ever, the most amazing woman who'd ever walked the surface of Vissan. She was tall and willowy, with long dark hair and blemish-free deep brown skin. And those beguiling dark eyes set in a face that could have launched a whole fleet of ships. Had it been love at first sight when they'd met? He remembered the way she'd turned him on and it was obvious she'd had the same chemistry for him because sex was just "wow", right from that first night. Though he had to admit that, as a young man, he'd somehow expected "wow" was going to happen anyway.

It hadn't been so many years earlier at medical school that Liz had been the girl in his life, though somehow he'd never really felt passionate about her. Maybe you didn't in those young days when emotions were still so new, so volatile. The two of them had had fabulous sex, but somehow he'd never really loved her. It was as though he hadn't been able to love her.

Maybe it'd been Celia who'd come between them? Celia, the girl he'd loved more than he'd felt able to say, and she'd never really appreciated just how very special she was to him. Maybe if Celia had never come into his life he might have made it with Liz, but it wasn't to be. He'd been sad when they'd finally parted, but only a little sad. So where was she now? She got married a few years after splitting up and was blissfully happy with a loving husband and a house full of children.

And that had been the start of what Jon thought of as his *wilderness* years. Crazy times of hopping from bed to bed, always a new girl on the go, always some wild party on his yacht, the stupid challenges the men made to each other - swimming down under the keel with far too many drinks inside them. If there'd been any justice in the world he'd have drowned every weekend that summer. With his work at Rapier and the bank demanding so much by day, and the way he'd partied by night, his life was just going too fast for him to want anything as mundane as love. But maybe deep down, love was the only thing he'd really needed. Sylvie came and rescued him just when he needed her most.

Of course he'd guessed even then that a woman so beautiful, and so clever too, was going to be trouble - but maybe that had been part of her allure. The more he saw her, the more he knew he had to have her, like a drug he was high on. But Jon was a good catch too, good looking, strong, tall, powerful and rich - the sort of formula that could draw in even a woman who could have her choice of men.

Jon had been beside himself with joy when she agreed to be his wife - she was everything he'd ever hoped for. How long was it now, fourteen years since they'd first met, and twelve since they'd married?

David Hulett Wilson

Back in the days when the two lovebirds had first met she'd been working as a doctor. But the role of a provincial GP was never going to be enough for am ambitious young woman and it wasn't long before she'd taken a position with Larson Medical Services – the largest hospital group on Vissan and a major player in the Union. Gradually she'd slipped away from practicing medicine and moved towards the business side of the industry, and it wasn't long before the people in charge had seen her potential and given her the chance to prove herself as the firm's new director of sales.

Being promoted to such a senior position so young was a fantastic thing and it gave her a terrific boost in confidence, though it did lead to a few problems on the financial front. After working for such a short time, and continually dogged by the student loans that had to be repaid, she'd never had the chance to accumulate much capital. Now with all the lucrative share options that came her way every cent she could spare got recycled back into the company. One day she was going to be rich, but for a while, living with hardly a bean in her pocket was just how it had to be. And as a point of honour she'd refused to accept any help from Jon, though she did let him bail her brother out when his construction company was suffering from cash-flow problems. It was only a few million and it was the sort of thing you did for family. Jon would have been happy to have just given him the money, but a man has his pride so he never suggested it wasn't to be repaid.

That had been long ago and as the years passed things had changed, things had cooled. He'd still found her attractive, most certainly, but when two hectic lifestyles pulled them so mercilessly apart and there was hardly an evening they spent in together it had felt as though life had taken them down separate roads. On the few occasions when they'd actually managed to get together they'd both been both dog tired.

Maybe they should have had children. Perhaps he might have been able to persuade her to take a step back from her high-flying role in LMS, at least for a few years. After all she'd only been thirty when they'd married so there were plenty of years for them to start a family. But no, her career was just taking off and in the end it won the battle over maternal instinct.

And it wasn't as though Jon's career was letting up either. With the busy pace of life in high office that demanded his body and soul for twenty hours of every day it was probably only the chances he got to relax on off-planet business trips that had saved him from slipping off into an early grave. A brief sojourn on one of the big liners to catch up with life, time to take a walk round the gardens and smell the flowers, time to sit in the bars overlooking the parkland enjoying a long cool beer after running a couple of laps of the ship. Time to remember the part of his life he'd neglected for far too long. If Sylvie had been able to accompany him on a few of the trips maybe it might all have been different.

He'd had some fun on the liners too. That trip to Miranda six years ago when he'd bumped into Katrina had been the start of it. She was lonely and he was horny, and it had just gone on from there. Somehow it had lead him back into his old ways.

After that he'd managed to arrange for some girl or other to be there for him on almost every trip. At first he'd managed to hide it from Sylvie, but it's a small galaxy and word gets around. So when she'd confronted him with eye witness reports he'd been man enough to give her a full confession. He'd tried to explain, the girls on the ships, they were just toys to play with. Who could blame him if he took advantage of a bit of meaningless fun now and again? She was the woman he loved and he'd always come back to her. And he knew there'd been at least one little indiscretion on her side too so the pair of them had agreed a truce.

And it had worked, for a few years. They'd made time in their busy schedules to find opportunities to spend a few weekends together, and they'd enjoyed their evenings in, even if the "wow" wasn't shouted quite so loudly as once it had been.

Looking back he could see it all more clearly now. Perhaps it'd been when Tom Hanson had first come on the scene that things had started to change. Jon had ignored the young upstart in those days and put his support behind "good old" Charles Beaumont in the leadership elections. And he'd been rewarded well because his political fortunes had advanced considerably when Harmony took the election by a landslide. But back then no-one had had any idea how little time would pass before Charles fell ill and despite the old trooper's valiant attempts to fight back he was in and out of hospital for months before he finally accepted he was going to have to stand down. OK he'd been 75, but that was no age these days and everyone had expected him to make it through at least one term in office.

There'd only been one real contender for the top job, so when the charismatic young rival took centre-stage Jon felt straight away he'd been side-lined and wondered whether he'd be out of the executive completely at the next reshuffle. But then it had all turned around, Tom had started to appreciate the qualities Jon brought to the job, and slowly the two men had begun to warm to each other. Despite all the political differences they'd once had they found many reasons to be friends rather than just colleagues. So many times they'd attended functions together, sometimes just the two of them, but often as a foursome when Sylvie and Carol were able to make it. Before long it had progressed to dinner parties and weekends on his yacht.

All good innocent fun of course, and when the trips to the opera had started it was obviously no different. If he admitted the truth, Jon didn't care for the highbrow end himself, but Tom and Carol were both keen fans and had talked Sylvie into going along with them. By the time the first performance had ended she'd announced that opera was the love of her life, and after that the three of them had made trips out to a performance almost every week.

When Tom and Carol made the headlines by going for a trial separation the visits to the opera continued, and as Jon had noted the number of patrons had reduced, but only by one.

Maybe it had been a sense of paranoia that had lead him to read up about the storyline of the latest production the two of them had been to see, but his suspicions were confirmed when Sylvie couldn't manage to answer even the most basic questions about the performance she'd seen the night before. Perhaps he should have seen it coming, perhaps he should have tried harder to put some spark back into the relationship, but when he was so busy with his job it wasn't easy to find time for the woman in his life.

But now he felt different. The experience of the last few days had changed him. Why exactly he wasn't sure. The problem of intrusion from host memories was a fact that had to be accepted by all TranzCon travellers, but it shouldn't have had any effect so early in a transfer. Maybe it was the female hormones flowing through his host bloodstream that were to be thanked. Maybe with softer, more caring thoughts he'd been able to see things in a different light.

Maybe things could change when he got home, if he tried, if he really worked at it. He'd have a try, he really would.

As the magazine slipped slowly down onto the duvet the host's head dropped down into the mess of her golden tresses - for the very last time.

★★★

The sound came again, but he was too tired to notice. Time to sleep, "go away". He turned onto the girl's other side but still the sound droned on. Slowly he opened his eyes and looked at the clock, five minutes after three - why was he asleep in the afternoon? He sank back down into the pillow, but the noise persisted - like the buzz of an insect, trapped behind glass it could neither see nor understand. Next there was a banging at the door: someone was trying to get into his room. After a minute the pass key turned in the lock and an immaculately suited hotel porter stepped briskly in.

'Mr Chandler, I apologise most profoundly for waking you like this, but I am told it is a matter of the utmost urgency. It is vital that you answer the telephone.'

Jon sat up in the bed. What in hell's name was going on? Then suddenly aware that his host's womanly charms were on full display he pulled the duvet up around her body before picking up the phone. Michael's voice came through the receiver.

'Jon, thank God I've finally got you. You've got to get up and get ready - right now!'

But Jon was weary.

'Michael, it's three in the morning here. What *is* going on?'

'Jon it's the beam. It's way down in strength and losing more with every hour. TranzCon don't know how much longer they've got to get you across. Get some clothes on and get down there fast. Don't bother taking anything, the people on Phoenix will sort it all out.'

Jon was slowly coming to consciousness.

TranzCon

'Have you made arrangements with them?'

'Yes, it's all fixed. There's a car down at reception waiting for you right now. But the other thing you've got to understand is that the beam's already lost a lot of strength. They're going to have to send you across flat-line. There's a doctor in the car and he'll start putting you under on the way to the reception centre. You'll be unconscious by the time you get there, but trust them, they're going to look after everything.'

By now Jon was fully awake and aware of the urgency of his situation. He thought back to what Dougie had told him earlier. He rallied himself and spoke.

'OK Michael. All in hand. I'm on my way,' and in his haste he dropped the receiver by the bedside, failing entirely to get it back onto its cradle.

The hotel porter was still there in the room, trying quite hard to keep track of the proceedings while averting his gaze from the naked young female climbing out of bed.

'They said there was no need for clothes sir, but I suggest you should wear your robe.'

The man held the garment open for Jon to slip the girl's arms into and both of them were a little more comfortable when the strap was tied. They stepped out into the corridor and Jon had already turned in the direction of the lift when the porter told him with a politeness that failed entirely to co-ordinate with the urgency of his message:

'And they suggested you ran sir.'

Knowing the boundless energy of the girl's young body, Jon burst into sprint down the corridor but had to struggle with the robe to stop it from flying open. God only knew what he looked like, but that wasn't the issue right then. Another porter was standing with the lift doors open ready to receive him and a moment later they were inside and descending. Another sprint across the lobby took him out into the cool night air and into the back of a dark limousine. As he settled the girl's body into the seat Jon turned to see a man beside him on the back seat preparing a hypodermic syringe.

'Good morning Mr Chandler, allow me to introduce myself. I am Dr. Atkinson from the medical department. I'm sorry we have to meet under circumstances like this, but I expect they've already explained the importance of my task.'

'Yes, yes they called me from Vissan. Please go ahead.'

'Could you slip the sleeve of your robe down please.'

Jon loosened the strap and slid the robe off the girl's right shoulder. He felt the sting as the needle went in and by the time he'd restored Jana's modesty the reality of the world was already beginning to slip away.

★★★

Jon gazed out into the distance and saw it far away, moving across the horizon. The blue light. Heading towards him at unbelievable speed. A moment passed before it flashed past his face and dived into the water. He knew his mission - to follow, to follow with unquestioning faith. He sucked in a last gulp of air and dived under the waves. With powerful strokes he chased the light down through the clear water, down through the limbo area where neither surface nor bottom was visible, down to where he could just make out - the outline of a wreck. Perhaps an old wrecked liner, lying in majestic splendour, bathed in the eerie green glow that was the only light to penetrate so deep into Neptune's kingdom.

The blue light lead the way through a glassless opening to where half a century earlier a master had once stood, barking orders, striving in vain to save the beleaguered vessel that was to him no less than a mistress. With the big ship neither upright nor completely on its side, once within the steel boundaries of the hull there was no up, and there was no down. But still Jon followed. He passed through a companionway, turned into a long dim corridor that had not felt the touch of the sun's rays since the events of that dramatic day so long ago.

There was no time to tarry and he resumed his powerful stroke until seconds later he burst out from the confinement of the walkway to the expanse of what seemed to him a measureless cavern. The blue light was there in front of him, so near now and yet still so far. Tantalisingly close. As he swam toward it the light moved further away. Jon followed. At the end of the room he passed into a smaller room, then a corridor. At the end of the corridor was a door with a window. The blue light slipped effortlessly through. But to Jon the door was solid. He grasped the handle and pulled. It turned slightly but when he pushed against the door it was firmly wedged. He braced himself and pushed harder. He pushed with all his strength and it moved, but only a crack. Far in the distance he could see the blue light, slipping away and beginning to fade - then it was lost from sight. Now Jon was alone and he knew the peril of his situation. He had done his duty - he had trusted and followed, never once thinking to question why. Now he was here, lost in the ship, deep under the sea, without air. WITHOUT AIR!

His lungs were bursting. Aching, hoping, for the feel of just one more breath. In desperation he swam back to the big room, searching everywhere for the way out he knew had to be there - somewhere. A tiny shaft of green light from the sea bottom filtered in through a porthole. He swam towards it and looked out at the freedom of the ocean beyond. But the opening was too small for him to squeeze through, even to save his own life. He panicked again at the pain deep in his chest. His lungs were aching for air and yet he knew that here so deep there was no air.

Then he felt the pain slipping away, the sense of panic abated leaving him strangely calm. He floated high in the water above what must once have been a dance-floor and watched as a sad faced grouper swam by, staring him in the eye, though with little interest. The loss of pain turned to euphoria - why should he need air at all? Then he realised the truth - he was dying.

In an instant the burning agony he'd felt from his lungs returned. The pain nagged at him, stronger than ever. In desperation he swam in all directions, searching - searching for the way out he knew had to be there. At last, release, he was free and swam for all he was worth, but horror took him when he found himself back at the door. As he peered through the glass he saw a faint glow - the blue light had returned. Then a face appeared at the window, the face of a woman, eerie in the dim light, the bubbles of a final breath rising from her open mouth. Jon saw the fear in eyes that pleaded with him to save her. Now she was hammering on the door, hammering so hard. Jon tried one more time, he pushed, he pulled, he pulled with all his strength but it was without hope.

Startled Jon looked up to see the blue light hovering serenely above him. And there behind it the green glow from the ocean outside filtered in through a jagged gash in the ship's side. At last a way through, a way out. Freedom. But the way through was small and he felt the pang of pain as a ripped shard of metal pierced his belly as he squeezed through. But at last he was free. He struck out for the surface, rippling and silvery above him, yet still so far. Too far. With the very last of his precious reserves pumping into screaming muscles he powered up through the warm shallows until at last he broke out from the surface in a fountain of foam. Gasping in the precious air he gulped it down. In shock he felt his body tense and jerk.

45

In The Hospital

A body jerked violently before it slumped back onto the bed - apparently gasping for breath. The technician watching spoke into his microphone:

'Lifesign - as if you could have missed it. What the hell happened in there?'

His colleague watching from the control room came on the intercom.

'Transit dream. God only knows what they get up to but it's no surprise for a flat-liner.'

★★★

Jon opened his eyes and stared up to see a ceiling covered in lights. His vision was fuzzy at first but rapidly pulled into focus. He looked at the pipes and cables running overhead. When he turned his head to the side he saw machines, their lights flashing in sequence, traces on scopes, beds and the usual paraphernalia that told him he was in a hospital. Then he remembered, he'd been through the transfer. This was home, this was the reception centre in Jackson.

A voice called out "Doctor come quickly, bed three. Patient coming round". Jon heard the sound and wondered if it was himself they were talking about. A man in a white coat walked over to the bed and looked down at him, roughly pulling his eyes open to examine the pupils. A female voice was calling "Hello. Are you back with us?".

Jon struggled to speak, but all that came out was a grunt. He tried again, but sleep overtook him before he could manage even a single word.

★★★

When he next awoke he opened his eyes and turned his head to look around. As he'd suspected he was in a hospital ward, lying on a bed and connected into a spider's web of tubes and wires. The nurse watching attentively by his bedside saw the movement. She checked the readings on her equipment before she leaned over and spoke into his ear.

'Welcome home Jana.'

Jon's heart skipped a beat. Why had the nurse called him "Jana"? His arm, he could feel his left arm and could move it, and the right one too. Suspiciously he lifted his hand up to his chest. It almost recoiled in horror as it settled onto the soft pillow of flesh that lay under the hospital gown. Another hand went down to his crotch and confirmed his worst fear. The transfer hadn't worked!

The doctor came back and carried out a few tests. He appeared to be satisfied that all was well.

In his still slightly groggy state Jon had co-operated as best he could, and from somewhere found the presence of mind to speak.

'You think I'm Jana Kell don't you?'

The doctor looked down. Jon saw how he nodded and smiled.

'You are indeed Jana Kell and I'm pleased to be able to tell you, you're in very good shape even after being so heavily sedated for the transfer. It's a bit of a strain on the system, but for a fit young body like yours it was no problem. We'll give you another hour to get yourself together and then you'll be ready to move on. You can have something to eat if you like. How's that?'

Jon was in shock. 'But I'm not Jana. The transfer didn't work.'

The doctor nodded knowingly.

'The information we had from TranzCon was that they'd had to use flat-line to get you across, but it all went as planned. They did warn us though that you might possibly suffer a little confusion when you woke up. Sometimes travellers aren't quite sure who they are when they first come round. When you're up and about we'll discharge you and then you'll be going back to TranzCon. They've got specialists who're much better informed about that sort of thing than we are here.'

'And exactly where is "here"?'

'This is the King Charles hospital in Celebration. After you transferred back from Vissan the people at TranzCon knew it would be quite some time before you recovered full consciousness, so they sent you along for us to look after you in our ICU. But you can rest assured, it's all in a day's work and you're absolutely fine.'

★★★

An hour later Jon was up and showered but now he had a question to ask.

'What's this mark down my front?' He ran the girl's finger down a line of red that followed from just below her breasts to a few centimetres below her navel.

The doctor took a close look. He picked up the girl's right hand and inspected the fingernails.

'My guess is you scratched yourself. The TranzCon people said you were almost fitting when you came through and it's possible you've done yourself a bit of damage. I'll give you some cream to put on it.'

Jon gazed at the mark and wondered.

46

Back To TranzCon

After his time-out from life Jon had almost no idea how late it was and obviously the hospital had made something of a miscalculation. When the ambulance arrived at the TranzCon centre the office had closed for the night and only the receptionist and a security guard were still on duty. The girl at the desk pointed out that he was lucky to have found anyone there at all because with the beam off-line there was no need for them to stay open longer than normal office hours.

When Jon told her about how his transfer back to Vissan had failed the girl checked on her computer and told him that, as far as she could see from the database, the man *she* had hosted had successfully transferred back three days earlier, just before the beam went down. It followed that Jana Kell had returned here to her own body in Celebration.

Jon picked up on the argument and in the end the girl agreed that a small number of transferees suffered from a state of confusion, especially after going through a flat-line transfer. From what she knew, the condition cleared up quite quickly by itself. She checked the screen again and told him there was no note or anything to say there'd been any indication of this condition arising from the Chandler/Kell transfer. She suggested he should go home for the evening and come back next morning when he'd be able to speak to a specialist.

When Jon protested he'd no idea where "home" might be the girl told him they'd be locking the office up in a few minutes and didn't have any overnight accommodation at the moment, so there was nothing they could do to help. Then she noticed he was still wearing a hospital gown and slippers and after doing another check on her computer she told him they had some of *her* belongings there ready for collection.

Jon needed some proper clothes and some money, so the logical thing was to collect Jana's stuff. The girl gave the security man a slip of paper and he disappeared out through a pair of swing-doors. A minute later the doors swung open again as he came back carrying a small holdall bag. Jon looked through and found a pair of shoes, a set of casual clothes and some underwear but not much else. In addition to the holdall there was a coat hung on a rack. Jon rifled through the pockets but apart from a collection of used tissues found they were empty.

What he really wanted was the identity card they'd given him that said he was a TranzCon traveller being hosted by Jana Kell. As far as he could remember he'd left it behind in the room on the night they'd rushed to the reception centre in the limousine, so perhaps it might be there at the hotel.

Jon tried the side pockets of the holdall but to his surprise found no money, cards, keys, or even a mobile phone. He reasoned that Jana had to live somewhere so she was bound to have some keys if nothing else. The girl checked the computer again and told him Jana had deposited a handbag as well, but it had been locked in the safe and couldn't be retrieved till next morning.

The only bit of good news was that he was entitled to a taxi ride home - wherever that was.

★★★

Apart from the hospital, the only place Jon had stayed overnight was the Elizabeth Hotel, so it was the obvious place to go. The destination made no difference to the cab driver who was just going to charge a standard rate to TranzCon's account.

★★★

The splendidly suited clerk at the reception desk checked some details on the hotel computer and advised him that Jon Chandler who'd been hosted by Miss Jana Kell had checked out in an emergency a few days ago. A lady from TranzCon had phoned to authorise payment of the account and had told them Mr Chandler would not be returning. The woman had also asked them to pack up Mr Chandler's temporary belongings for Miss Kell to collect. The clothes were part of the hosting package though Jon wondered whether the deal ran to the hardware items like the phone and the laptop.

The clerk asked to be excused for a moment and disappeared into a room behind the reception desk. After just a few seconds he came back with Jon's suitcase which he carried to a opening in the desk before snapping his fingers to summon a porter.

'Can I call you a cab Miss Kell?'

'A cab to where exactly?'

'Well to your home I presume. That's usually where people go at this time of night.'

'I think I'd need more than a cab to get home. Since I've been unable to travel back to Vissan I really don't have anywhere to go, and the only place I know on Phoenix is this hotel.'

The clerk checked his computer and advised him that he had a number of rooms vacant and *she* could check in for the night if *she* wished. Jon knew he hadn't got much money, but then he remembered there would be his temporary charge card somewhere among his stuff. The porter carried the case over to one of the lobby tables where Jon opened it and started to look through the contents. Underneath the laptop he found his mobile phone, the business suit he'd worn, the casual clothes, and a pile of underwear, now mostly dirty. Feeling through the suit's jacket pockets he finally found the charge card and 25 Phen in cash. He handed the card over and the man pushed it into a machine.

'Please look into the screen Miss Kell'.

Jon felt the scan as it washed over the girl's irises, and a thought suddenly struck him. The clerk pulled the card out of the machine and was reading the details that had come up on the screen.

'I'm sorry Miss Kell, but this card was issued for the sole use of Mr Chandler. Because he's now returned to Vissan there are instructions for me destroy it. Do you have any other means of payment?'

Jon watched as the clerk took a large pair of scissors from a drawer and snipped the precious piece of plastic into several pieces. He flicked through the meagre amount of cash and guessed it wasn't going to go very far at an establishment like the Elizabeth. There was no possible way he could afford to stay here, but since he'd nowhere else to go, the opulence of even the hotel lobby with its sumptuous couches looked more than inviting. The idea of a meal in the hotel restaurant sounded good to his rumbling stomach, but he was well aware of the prices they charged, and for the first time since he'd been a student he encountered the odd experience of knowing there was something he couldn't afford. The idea of ordering a meal and simply not paying entered his head but he guessed that that sort of action would only to lead to trouble. When the media got hold of the story that a senior politician had left a posh restaurant without paying the bill it was hardly going to help his election prospects.

***

Out in the town Jon found that 10 Phen went quite a lot further in the local burger bar than it did in the Windsor Brasserie and he returned with a suitably full stomach. When he'd collected his case from the desk he wandered through the empty lobby, checked he was out of sight of the reception desk and found a big leather upholstered sofa he could settle down on for the night. But first he had some calls to make and fortunately the phone was prepared to work for anyone who knew its PIN number.

His first try was to Horace Walton and he was relieved when he heard the phone answered. Horace would be able to help him get things back together and it was even possible he was upstairs in one of the hotel bedrooms. Jon listened to the voice on the other end and it was definitely Horace on the line, but he soon picked up that it was the real owner of the host body and not Horace. And the man wasn't too happy about being woken so late at night. The useful piece of information Jon deduced from the conversation was that the host had returned back from Vissan four days ago, so at least Horace had succeeded in getting home. Lucky Horace.

As far as Jon could remember, Dougie had been due to travel before Horace, so it was almost certain he'd be back on Vissan as well.

The only other person he knew to call was Timothy Darling. As the de-facto ambassador to Phoenix, if anyone was going to be able to help it would be him. Anxiously he found the entry for the man's number and pressed the button. A recorded voice came on the line to tell the caller that Mr Darling was on a transfer to Vissan and would be back the following Monday morning, a date which Jon noted had already passed. He cursed himself for forgetting that the whole delegation had travelled on to Jackson for another meeting. He ought to have remembered because the appointment was in his own diary. It was a logical deduction that if Timothy wasn't back by now he was stuck on Vissan - just as Jon was stuck here on Phoenix.

He locked the keypad and tucked the phone away in the pocket of the girl's jeans. It was getting late and he was tired now so he plumped up one of the cushions and settled himself down. Just before he dropped off he noticed how Jana's body was able to stretch out full length on the sofa. His own long body would have been doubled up uncomfortably. Well there had to be some advantage to being small.

★★★

How long had passed before Jon heard the voice that wrenched him out of sleep he didn't know, but he wasn't happy to be disturbed. He looked up at the smartly uniformed porter hoping for an apology, or at least an explanation, but he quickly saw that the boot was on the other foot.

'I'm sorry Miss - you can't sleep here. The hotel is private property. I'll have to ask you to leave.'

Jon came to his senses faster than he'd expected. Perhaps he hadn't been asleep for very long.

'Leave to go where exactly?'

'That's not the hotel's problem Miss. You have to leave or I'll be forced to call the police.'

Jon was tired and all he wanted to do was sleep. He yawned.

'Well then you'd better call them. I expect they'll provide me with a bed for the night.'

'It might be a bed in a cell Miss.'

'A bed's a bed. Who cares where it is?'

The porter walked away for a minute or two and came back with the clerk from the desk. The Elizabeth wasn't the sort of hotel that enjoyed having any flavour of blue lights flashing outside, so the clerk used a little discretion and instructed the porter to take Jon and his luggage up to a vacant room they had available on the 2nd floor.

As he settled down in his bed, Jon realised that the staff had actually been as nice as anyone could have been about an interloper in their hotel. He made a mental note to remember to pay for the room and thank them after he got back to Jackson.

47

The Specialist

Jon stirred in the "oh so comfortable" bed. How many times he'd turned over, promising to get up in a minute's time he couldn't count, but the bedside clock showed it was past nine when he finally crawled out.

He picked up the mobile phone from the bedside table and saw there'd been a missed call about an hour earlier. There was a text message as well: TranzCon had made an appointment for him to see their specialist at 11.00. Hooray for something.

★★★

After showering he dressed in one of the business suits he'd worn at the conference and spent the last of his rapidly dwindling supply of cash on breakfast. At 10.30 the doorman called him a cab and just minutes later the car was pulling up outside the main entrance of the TranzCon office. With all his money gone he told the driver that TranzCon were going to pay - he'd go in and make arrangements. The driver threatened to call the police if Jon tried to get out without paying, but he wasn't a man to be bullied. He pulled out the mobile and called TranzCon's reception to explain his problem. Moments later the receptionist walked down the steps and handed two notes to the driver. Jon got out and the car screeched away, the driver cursing under his breath.

The staff in TranzCon's office were pleasant, in fact very pleasant. They gave him a seat and offered him a cup of coffee. At the stroke of eleven, give or take a few seconds, a tall woman in a dark power suit stepped out from a set of double doors and walked up to the reception desk. The girl pointed in Jon's direction. The woman walked over to where Jon was seated, still finishing his coffee.

'Miss Kell, how nice to meet you. When you've finished your coffee would you come this way please?'

The coffee had cooled to glugging temperature so Jon swallowed the last mouthful quickly, anxious to see what could be done to get him out of his predicament.

The woman set off in front and lead the way to a small cubicle office a few doors down the corridor. She introduced herself as Barbara King, TranzCon's client liaison officer. She'd picked up *her* file and was aware of the circumstances.

Jon quickly sussed that Ms King was a woman who was accustomed to being patient in the extreme, whether the recipient deserved it or not. It took nearly ten minutes of pleasantries and platitudes before she could be pressed into giving up even a single snippet of information. The beam was still down and had been since shortly after *Jana's* arrival back on Phoenix, but things were looking hopeful because a limited degree of communication had been restored and the beam was now working on basic telemetry. She went on to explain that there had been over twenty periods in the previous year when they'd lost reception for more than an hour. It was nothing unusual and they were hoping to get normal service back any time soon.

Jon asked her, 'You said there was basic telemetry, so if there's any communication at all can we get a message through to my people on Vissan? If we can they'll be able to confirm that I didn't actually make it back when I tried to transfer last week.'

Ms King went on to explain that all that was available at the moment was a service channel and that was being used by engineers working on the system. Unfortunately there was no bandwidth available for ordinary service users, not even for an influential customer such as TranzCon. So at present they had no facility to send anything off-planet. She suggested *she* should send a basic text email via the public network as this would be stacked in the buffer ready to be transmitted the instant any capacity became available.

Jon moved the conversation back to his present circumstances. He told her about how he'd gone into the transfer. He described the dream sequence and explained how he'd followed the blue light. Finally he'd passed out and the next thing he'd known was when he'd woken up in hospital to find he was still on Phoenix. Ms King agreed that his experience had been indicative of being in the transfer process because a high proportion of travellers had recalled seeing a blue light or some other phenomenon that had lead them through. There was however no scientific explanation for it.

Ms King shifted her chair over to the computer terminal on the desk and logged on. After a few seconds of navigating through a few screens she turned the display round so Jon could see it. It took him a while to work out exactly what he was looking at, but at last he could seen that the screen did show that a traveller had been received into Jana Kell's body within seconds of a communication being received from Vissan to say that Jana Kell's life-force had been transmitted.

'It's a positive indication that the transfer took place Miss Kell.'

The air of authority with which she spoke was absolute. There could be no doubting the truth of her words. Jon wasn't so sure. Positive indication or not he was in no position to simply accept what she said.

'So was there some sort of signal from Vissan to let you know they'd received Jon Chandler's life-force?'

'Yes, we received an initial confirmation from Vissan just before the beam went down. At the moment we're waiting for the final confirmation that Jon Chandler arrived back in his own body without any complications.'

'So let me get this straight, you've got an *initial* confirmation, but you still have to receive a *final* confirmation?'

The woman nodded.

'And until you do you can't be absolutely certain that the life-force received on Vissan was actually that of Jon Chandler'.

Ms King drew in a breath that somehow indicated she was getting tired of having to explain things to people who lacked even the most basic degree of knowledge about how mind-transference worked.

'Miss Kell, it is standard procedure that all TranzCon trips between all planets are co-ordinated so that only a single transfer ever takes place at any one time. That trip has to be completed before the next one can start and this ensures that only two life-forces can be in transit at any one time. So with only two hosts in the whole of the galaxy open to the reception of travelling life-forces, and only two life-forces in motion, it follows that they have to settle into their correct bodies. Nothing is left to chance.'

Jon still wasn't convinced. Since he still occupied Jana's body, there was no way he could possibly accept Ms King's so-called assurances.

'I can see the logic in your argument and I'll agree there couldn't be any mix up with a sort of hi-tech crossed-line that brought a life-force from somewhere else into a host. But just imagine what would happen if the life-forces couldn't get through. What if they simply settled back into the host bodies they'd just come from?'

Ms King clearly expected that the customers of her company would be prepared to accept what she told them without delving too deeply into the science of mind transfers. In a voice which clearly indicated that his allocation of patience was now dangerously close to being fully expended she explained to him.

'TranzCon has been providing a commercial service for fifteen years now with many thousands of transfers taking place each year. What you are suggesting is something that has never happened. Every travelling life-force has its own destination, and it never, ever, comes back to the host it has just left.'

Jon asked again about the confirmation messages. Ms King explained that this was done as a matter of routine because it "handed over the baton" so the next TranzCon trip could go ahead. The purpose was more that of allowing the next transfer to go ahead than confirming correct receipt of a traveller because the initial advice was adequate indication that a traveller had been received. The only difference on Jon's trip had been that the beam had gone down so soon after the transfer that there hadn't been the chance to send or receive the final confirmation notices. There was one on its way from Vissan of course. It was in the system even as they spoke and since it was a priority communication it would come across to the reception centre in Celebration the instant the beam came back on line.

Jon wondered about this one for a moment.

'So right now the whole of TranzCon's galaxy-wide operation is being held up waiting for a missing confirmation signal?'

Jon watched Ms King's face and the expression he saw told him he'd got her on the run. She thought about the question for a moment and the hesitation in her voice said more than her words.

'I'm assuming that our people on Vissan did actually receive the signal from our installation here in Celebration, so they'll be carrying on as normal. Except of course for not being able to send any travellers to Phoenix while the beam from Darius is out of service.'

'But you told me the final confirmation signal hadn't been received yet. What if the same happened on Vissan? They could be held up waiting for the signal.'

'No, it's not possible. If communication with one of the remote stations was lost for several days, they would resume normal working after a safety period long enough to ensure that the transfer had been completed.'

'Or after they were sure the transfer had failed?'

'Miss Kell, please accept the explanation you've been given. There simply is no indication that any transfer has failed.'

Jon was getting annoyed now and was close to shouting, though he guessed it would only lose him points.

'Well, me still being here on Phoenix is a pretty good indication isn't it?'

Jon saw how the placid image Ms King had projected so strongly just fifteen minutes earlier was beginning to give way to an obvious irritation. She stood up and asked to be excused for a minute or two. Jon looked at the computer terminal and was aching to put his fingers onto the keyboard so he could search for the information he was sure was there - but he held himself back from interfering.

The door opened and Ms King strutted back in, the heels of her shoes clicking noisily on the tiled floor.

'Miss Kell, I can see I've not been able to convince you that you were correctly received back here in Celebration so I'm trying to contact one of our specialist physicians. If you are able to wait for an hour the doctor will be available to see you.'

Jon had nowhere else to go and nothing else to do. He made himself comfortable in the reception area while the girl from the desk brought him another round of coffee and biscuits.

48

Jon Sees A Doctor

After Jon had finished his coffee and spent a while browsing through a back issue of the company magazine a woman in a nurse's uniform walked into reception and called for "Jana Kell". Jon wondered if they might be getting off on the wrong foot if he accepted the summons, but he'd waited for nearly an hour and if he wanted to see the doctor he was going to have to go for it.

The nurse lead him down the same corridor he'd walked along earlier in the day and past the room where Ms King had spoken with him. She showed him into an office where a young man in a white coat was seated behind a desk. The man stood to greet him and invited him to have a seat.

The conversation began with the doctor's admission that with no beam in service he didn't have a lot to do at that moment. Normally he'd have been busy checking on travellers' medical conditions before and after transmission, so it was fortunate that he had the time to see *her* without an appointment.

Jon looked down at the desk and saw that the doctor had his file open in front of him. After flicking a few pages and reading for a few minutes the man looked up, which Jon took as his cue to tell the story all over again about how he'd gone into the transfer, followed the blue light and finally woken up back in Jana's body here on Phoenix.

Despite his youth, the doctor had obviously listened very carefully when they'd given the lecture on gaining the upper hand by adopting a calm and serious manner.

'Miss Kell, I've studied your case and I've heard what you've had to say. You seem quite adamant that you are still Jon Chandler, the man whose life-force you hosted. But as my colleague explained to you earlier, the evidence we have here at TranzCon shows that Jon Chandler did actually transfer back to Vissan without any complications.'

Jon was exasperated now and let it show.

'And yet I'm still here! The proof you keep offering isn't worth a bean while the beam is down and you know it. You don't have the final confirmation to tell whether or not my life-force was actually received on Vissan.'

'Miss Kell, I agree with you about the final confirmation, but we have the initial report and it's never been wrong before. Now as you're no doubt aware, here on Phoenix we're new to the Union's TranzCon system, and I am not by training a psychiatrist, but I do have quite a detailed knowledge of the psychotic conditions which can, in a tiny number of cases I hasten to add, result from TranzCon transfers.'

'Including those that go wrong?'

The calm manner was still holding.

'There is absolutely no evidence to suggest this transfer has gone wrong Miss Kell. Now I see from the file that both yourself and Mr Chandler were going through a transfer for the first time, am I right?'

Jon nodded.

'And your transfer back from Vissan was carried out under flat-line conditions where both travellers were heavily sedated. What you probably don't know is that there is a condition which has occurred following a relatively small number of transfers which we term "spirit image retention". The word "spirit" in this case being something of an informal term to describe the life-force which is the essence of any sentient being. The likelihood of this occurring is increased when one or both of the travellers are going through for the first time, or if they are sedated for the transfer.'

'And spirit image retention is what exactly?'

'It's a condition where an image of the hosted mind remains in the brain for a while after the transfer. It means that a traveller can be left with the feeling that he or she is still the person who occupied their body during the hosting period. The good news is that the condition clears itself up after a short time, usually after no more than a couple of days. The even better news is that there's a clause in the contract you signed which allows you to claim an allowance for any day you have to miss work due to a condition which arose as a direct result of the transfer in which you participated. It's not the full amount you got paid for the days you were on Vissan in Jon Chandler's body, but it should compensate you for any loss of earnings. What job do you do Miss Kell.'

The first answer that came into Jon's head was "how the fuck should I know", but he realised he'd retain more credibility if he kept cool.

'I know very well what job Jon Chandler does, but I know nothing, nothing at all, about Jana Kell or her life.'

The doctor had obviously expected a reply along these lines and remained on track.

'What I suggest Miss Kell is that you go home, get plenty of rest, and sleep as long as you need at night. Have a holiday at TranzCon's expense. You'll probably wake up tomorrow morning with no idea you'd ever thought you were Jon Chandler. But look, it's very much in TranzCon's interests to make sure that everyone who works for us is well looked after, so if your symptoms persist call this office and I can arrange an appointment for you to see our resident psychiatrist. He's an expert in these matters.'

Jon was about to speak, but he hesitated for just one moment and the doctor continued.

'Now I know you're going to say again that you're not Jana Kell, but just give your brain the time it needs to get back to normal.'

Jon had to admit that what the guy had said had been very convincing. With the doctor's calm and authoritative manner he could even have believed him. Was there a chance he might even be right? Was *he* going to wake up tomorrow morning knowing *he* was Jana Kell after all?

★★★

The nurse came back in and escorted Jon to the reception area where he remembered about Jana's missing handbag. It wasn't that he actually wanted to be the owner of one - in fact it was about the last thing he wanted to be seen dead with. It was more that it might contain some vital information. He asked the girl on the desk who promised it would be retrieved straight away, and she suggested he took a seat while he waited.

And while he sat he wondered about how the next few days were going to pan out. The doctor had said about waking up next morning, so the first question was, exactly *where* was he going to wake up? Where was he going to go without money and in a city he had no knowledge of? Without some cash or a valid charge card there was no way he could go back to the Elizabeth Hotel. Comfortable though the room had been he could hardly ask them for a second night of free board and lodging.

But then he reasoned, the real Jana Kell had to live somewhere, quite possibly somewhere in the local area. Everyone he'd spoken to since waking up back on Phoenix had insisted he was Jana Kell so they couldn't really complain if he found the girl's home and took it over for a day or two. Well, that was assuming he could find out exactly where "home" was. Celebration was a big city and all he'd seen of it so far were a few streets in the central area.

The girl on the desk waved in his direction.

'Miss Kell, I've got your handbag from security. Can you check the contents and sign for it please.'

The girl handed him a brown leather bag that almost shouted *woman* to anyone who observed the carrier. Jon stared at the object for a moment before deciding he was being stupid. He picked it up by the handles and carried it over to the table where he'd drunk so much coffee earlier that morning. He took the items out one by one: 15 Phen in cash, two keys on a ring, a mobile phone, a small notebook, a packet of paper tissues, a lipstick, and what he'd really being hoping to find, a small plastic wallet with three cards and the added bonus of a folded 20 Phen note inside. He checked through the plastic, an ATM debit card, a credit card, and an ID card with a picture of Jana. The absence of a driving licence told its own story.

Jon scanned through the notebook to see if there were any details that might be useful, but even with the wonderful young eyes that had years to go before they would need the help of an optician he could hardly read Jana's atrocious scribble.

He piled all the bits into the bag and took it back to the desk. The girl smiled again.

'Is everything in order Miss Kell? I'll just need you to sign the form to say you received it.'

She turned a sheet of paper round and pushed it over to Jon's side of the desk. Jon had already found that writing with the host body's facilities was quite difficult. Her left hand was absolutely useless when it came to anything intricate and he himself had only the vaguest idea of how to write right-handed. But he picked up the pen and had a try. Something not entirely unlike a signature came off the girl's fingertips, though it looked nothing like the one he'd seen on her ID card. The girl took the form without even a second glance at what he'd written, tore off the top sheet and pushed it into a filing tray before handing a pink under-copy to Jon.

Just as he was about to ask whether she'd any record of Jana's address on file he noticed the typed details on the form. In the space below her name there was an address, and if that wasn't where she lived what else could it be? He studied the details and the words "Flat 6" obviously indicated she lived in a block of flats, or perhaps a converted house, but the road and area details meant nothing to him.

He asked the receptionist about sending an email and of course she pointed out that nothing could go off-planet with the beam still out of service, but she invited him to put one into the system ready to go when it was back on line. Fortunately Jon discovered the girl's fingers better at typing than they had been at writing and it only took thirty seconds to tap out a quick message to Michael. At least he'd be establishing contact with Vissan the instant the public service came back on line.

★★★

Out in the street Jon felt just a little conspicuous standing there with his handbag on view for all to see. Just because the passers-by saw a woman didn't mean he didn't feel like a man. Fortunately it wasn't long before the taxi arrived - he opened the door and climbed in. He passed the form to the driver for him to read.

'That's Rokham Park area isn't it?'

Jon hadn't the faintest idea.

The cab crawled slowly through the busy streets while Jon wondered what he was going to find when he arrived at his destination. From the fact that the girl's title was "Miss" he deduced she was unmarried, but that didn't mean she lived alone. What if she lived with a boyfriend, or even her parents? How would they react to the presence of a stranger in their house? Surely they'd spot he wasn't really Jana. Maybe he could explain Jana's unusual behaviour with the same "spirit image retention" story the doctor had just used. Maybe he should just avoid any contact and go off to bed like the doctor had said.

The taxi had been going for about ten minutes before Jon noticed they'd left behind the high-rise buildings of the city centre and were now in an area of large old terraced townhouses. The appearance was that of a district that at one time might have been very much the place to live but was now down on its luck. The long established old trees down each side of the street gave the area an aura of sophistication, but Jon couldn't help noticing the peeling paintwork on the houses, the rubbish that lay in piles by the sides of the road, and the way lines of washing hung out from the upstairs windows.

After turning into one of the side-roads the taxi came to rest outside one of the big houses. Peering over into the front Jon could see the meter read 4 Phen and 45 cents. He handed over a 5 Phen note and got out before the driver could offer any change.

49

The Flat

As the taxi drove off Jon looked up at the house in front of him. The number above the front door fitted in with the number on the pink form so he walked up the short flight of stairs and into the porch. By the side of the glass panelled front door he saw a row of pushbuttons, each with a name adjacent. The button for Flat 6 said "J. Kell" next to it. He was home, but still very unsure of what he was going to find.

He tried the first of the keys but it wouldn't even push into the lock. He tried the second one which slid in and turned easily. The door swung open with a creak. As with what he'd seen out in the street, the paintwork in the entrance lobby looked as if it had seen better days but the tatty appearance didn't necessarily mean there was anything unsound about the house - it just needed a bit of sprucing up. It was a reasonable deduction that the people who lived here lacked money to spend on mere decoration and in many ways it reminded him of his student days.

Standing in the lobby he looked around. The single door he saw had a "1" on it. Then there was a corridor running towards the back of the house, and a flight of stairs leading up to the next level. Logic suggested that Flat 6 would be upstairs. The first floor landing gave access to rooms 3, 4 and 5, so it looked like Flat 6 was going to be up the next flight on the attic level.

On the top landing he found a single door with a big number "6" painted on it. He tried the first key that had been rejected by the lock downstairs. The key fitted, the door opened and he stepped inside.

A slight whiff of a smell hit him, but it wasn't bad. The left-over odours from last week's cooking. He opened the window to let some fresh air in.

Looking around he saw the flat was small and untidy, and he noted the way the ceiling sloped towards the edges of the room. But then, he'd already worked out it was the attic floor. If he'd been there in his own body the low ceilings would have made it almost impossible for him to stand upright anywhere other than in the centre of the room, but for Jana's smaller frame much more of the floor area was useful space.

From the main room he stepped through an open archway into the smallest, and probably the least hygienic kitchen he'd ever seen. Back in the main room a door lead through into a bedroom, and from the far side of the bedroom another door opened into a small shower room with a toilet. With only a single bedroom and one double bed it wasn't the sort of place she could have shared with family or a housemate, but it didn't rule out a boyfriend.

To Jon's eye the whole place was a complete and utter mess. Clothes were draped over the backs of chairs, half-read magazines covered holes in the threadbare carpet, tables were liberally covered with empty coffee mugs and plates still showing the signs of whatever meal they'd been used for several days ago. In the kitchen he filled an electric kettle, settled it onto its stand and pushed down the switch.

While the kettle was heating he looked round the rest of the flat. Lots of junk but nothing he might possibly have wanted. A shelf in the bathroom was overloaded with all the bottles, sprays, jars and tins that women seemed unable to live without, and he noticed the absence of any toiletries aimed at men. After a quick look along the shelf and in the mirror fronted cabinet he was relieved to find that the only razor on display was pink .... and only a single toothbrush stood in the holder.

The kettle clicked off so he went to make his drink. Finding no clean mugs in any of the cupboards he picked the least disgusting example off a side-table and gave it a wash in water he soon decided was never going to run hot. A box in the cupboard above the sink yielded its last two tea-bags and one went into the mug. He filled it to the brim. The fridge was mostly devoid of anything resembling food, and when he put his nose to the bottle of milk it was clear the semi-solid contents would be going down the sink straight away.

Even in his student days he'd never lived like this.

A landline phone was lying on the floor so he picked up the receiver and listened - nothing - although he noted the instrument was plugged in. Fortunately he had the phone they'd given him and now he had the girl's mobile as well.

He took his drink and as he settled down into a big easy chair he was immediately surprised by the way the girl's feet were whisked off the floor as he fell further into the chair than he'd expected. He climbed back out and sat on the edge of the seat as he rummaged around in the holdall for Jana's mobile.

The phone was off so he pressed the button on the top. The screen lit up and showed a small amount of battery life remaining, but it was waiting for a code number to activate it.

For no reason he could explain an idea came to him. He took the back cover off the phone and there on the battery was a sticky label with 4 digits on it. He typed them into the phone but the number was rejected. He put the digits in back to front and got "Code Accepted". Very secure he didn't think, but thank heavens the girl had made it easy for him. He scrolled down through the address book and looked at the entries - presumably a list of her family and friends.

After finishing his tea Jon went back to the kitchen and searched through the cupboards and the fridge to see if there was anything available to eat. With only 30 Phen to his name he might have to live off whatever was lurking there till he could find a way of getting hold of some money.

The business suit he'd put on at the hotel that morning wasn't really the sort of thing to wear around the flat, and he remembered the underwear he had on was still the same as he'd worn at the final session of the conference, and that had been days ago. He walked through to the bedroom and looked for some reasonably suitable clothes. It was a fair bet that anything on the floor was waiting for its turn in the wash, and for the stuff hanging over the backs of chairs he thought it better to assume the same. So he looked through the big old wardrobe and the enormous chest of drawers, and what caught his eye was the obvious poles apart mixture of the clothes he found. Some of the garments were quite basic, ordinary everyday stuff a twenty-something woman might wear, while others were anything but. The ensemble included some raunchy looking garments he was sure went a long way beyond what most women would wear for normal purposes. It made him wonder just exactly what the girl did for a living.

He went back to the unisex department and selected a tee-shirt, a pair of jeans and a pair of comfortable flat shoes to wear.

After he'd found how to turn on the heating system he looked around the flat and couldn't help noticing how its untidiness annoyed him intensely. The fact that he was only going to be there for a couple of days somehow didn't seem relevant, so he set about clearing up a bit. After an hour he'd washed up all the mugs and plates, hustled the clothing that was strewn around into a laundry basket, stacked the magazines into tidy piles and had even given most of the surfaces a once over with a duster he'd found in the cupboard under the sink. There was a vacuum cleaner in one cupboard, but he'd have a go at the carpets some other time.

That night he cooked himself a meal - pasta shells with tomato ketchup and some oily fish out of a tin. Haute cuisine it wasn't, but it filled a hole.

50

The Sandwich

When dawn broke next morning and Jon opened his eyes to gaze around the bedroom at Jana's flat he was not at all surprised to find that nothing had changed. No miraculous revelation had come to him in his sleep. No realisation he was Jana Kell after all.

Deep inside he wondered whether things would have been easier if he had woken to find the doctor's explanation about spirit image retention had been true after all. The man had made a very good case that *he* was actually Jana. But it was too weird, he really felt like he was Jon. Perhaps he could understand how one male could be confused about being in another male body, but Jana's female body, lovely though it was to look at, felt so alien to be inside. Maybe more days had to pass before the prediction finally came true, but somehow he doubted it.

★★★

There was nothing in the flat that anyone would actually have called breakfast so Jon made himself another cup of black tea and finished off the last of the pasta in sauce from the night before.

After an hour spent vacuuming he sat and wondered how he was going to pass the time between now and the beam coming back on line. Five minutes of sitting in the chair had left him bored so he decided to go back to TranzCon and see the doctor to tell him the memory retention condition hadn't cleared itself up yet.

The cab to Jana's house had cost 5 Phen, so it was clear that a trip into the city and back would take far too much of the money he had left. But then he remembered, he'd seen buses going up and down the main road before the taxi had turned off. Not that he'd much idea what to do with a bus.

Fortunately for Jon, none of the others at the stop noticed that the young woman standing there with them was getting quite nervous, especially when the bus came round the corner and there were only seconds to go before they were due to board. In fact Jon was happy to be at the back of the queue because it meant he'd have a few moments to watch what the others did before his turn came. When he'd stepped on board and put a Phen note on the tray and asked for a ticket to "city" he was beginning to relax, or at least he was until he found there were no seats left and he had to stand. For heaven's sake, it was dangerous enough having a seat without a safety belt, but standing there with ten big men lined up ready to fall on him when the bus stopped was scary. Didn't the planet have any safety standards?

As the bus made its way to the centre Jon thought back to his youth and tried to remember when he'd last been on a bus. Maybe it was one of the memories that hadn't come over with him in the transfer because try as he might he truly had no recollection.

★★★

It took some time to get through the busy streets, but the bus went all the way into the city and stopped on a road where almost all the people got off, so Jon reasoned this was where he'd been heading for. His first stop was a newspaper stand where he bought a map, and fortunately the TranzCon office was only a few streets away.

The girl at the desk recognised him from the day before and treated him to another instalment of her "on demand" smile. When he asked whether there'd been any progress with the beam she logged onto GBeam's operational site to check the latest status. Jon held his breath as he watched the screen load but he could have saved himself the trouble. The beam was still down, but the news hadn't exactly come as a surprise. Even worse, the basic telemetry that had been working the day before had also been off-line since the early hours of the morning. As before, they were still very hopeful that normal service would be back any time soon, but hopeful wasn't getting him home. What was that old saying, "if wishes were horses then beggars would ride"?

He explained his situation and asked whether it would be possible to see the doctor again. The girl checked the screen and told him the doctor had a lot of leave owing, so with not much to do he'd decided to take a few days off. He was due to come in at the beginning of next week so Jon could make an appointment to see him then.

The next item on the agenda was getting hold of some money so Jon asked the girl whether he could expect any payment for Jana's services as a host. She told him it was probably in the system right then and would be credited to *her* account as soon as the beam came back on line. It wasn't exactly what he'd hoped to hear so he asked her if TranzCon could give him an advance. He'd obviously gone a stop beyond what the computer was able to tell her and he experienced something close to a feeling of success when she smiled again and picked up the phone.

For most of the call it was obvious that the girl was listening to someone on the other end, so after the first ten seconds Jon lost track of the conversation. After the phone was back on its cradle the girl told him it was something that could only be authorised at the company's head office in Jackson, something they couldn't arrange until the beam came back on line. He was beginning to wonder how the planet had survived for so long without a channel of communication to the rest of the galaxy.

★★★

When Jon left TranzCon's office there was still plenty of day left and the weather was warm, so he decided to walk back to Rokham Park, partly to save the bus fare, and partly to find his way around and get a better look at the area where Jana lived.

He knew the route home was only a few klics and that was only if he'd stuck to the main roads, but he was in a mood to explore and found a shortcut that took him past a row of interesting shops, including a takeaway that issued its tantalising odours out into the street. For the first time in his life Jon was on the verge of hallucinating over a kebab - the thought of ordering one and legging it was getting more attractive by the minute.

The last shop in the row was a mini supermarket and hunger was finally getting the better of him. But now he had a plan. He walked into the shop, took one of the small trolleys from the stack and ambled slowly up and down the aisles taking the occasional tin or packet from the shelves while he checked which bits of the store couldn't be seen from the checkout desk. With the girl's heart thumping he went to the open fridge display, took out a sandwich and peeled off the wrapper. Carefully he slunk back to the bit of the shop that was hidden from view and made short work of the sandwich before pushing the empty wrapper in behind a stack of toilet rolls. Now he had to get out of the shop. Trying to look as though butter wouldn't melt in his mouth he dumped the half-full trolley at the end of an aisle and walked past the people queuing at the checkout. The girl there watched him pass but made no comment. He was mightily relieved when he made it out onto the street without being challenged. Crime had never been his thing.

51

Shopping

Next morning Jon considered his situation. If he was going to stay alive until the beam came back on line he was going to have to eat. Helping himself to one free sandwich was all very well, but how many times could he get away with it before the local shopkeepers began to notice? He needed access to money and his only hope was to try and use Jana's bank cards, either to spend in shops or to access cash direct. He opened the handbag and took out the plastic wallet. For a minute he stared at the two plastic cards and the banknote lying side by side on the table and wondered. Stealing wasn't the sort of thing he'd ever contemplated before, but what was he supposed to do if he couldn't get at his own money?

He pulled on the girl's coat and headed off towards the city, though he made a point of avoiding the street with the mini-supermarket and the tempting kebab shop. As he came closer to the centre he saw a building which from its imposing stone construction was obviously a bank. Major financial institutions didn't seem to vary much from one side of the galaxy to the other. To the side of the main entrance he saw a hole in the wall with an ATM tucked away inside.

After finding a bench to sit on he scoured the notebook he'd found in Jana's handbag, and just inside the back cover he saw a four digit number written in the corner all by itself. It was worth a try.

He took the debit card out of the wallet and slid it into the cash machine. After telling him he was entitled to free cash withdrawals the screen switched to one inviting him to enter his PIN. He typed in the one from the book - and it was rejected.

Shit, think Jon.

He gave it another try with the sequence reversed - and still it was refused.

Shit again.

Now clutching at straws he reversed the first pair of digits, and did the same with the second. The message came up to tell him his card had been retained. Shit, shit, shit! Clearly his own version of logic did not map onto Jana's.

He looked in the wallet and saw he still had her credit card, but he realised he was going to have to be more careful before he risked using that. Reluctantly he unfolded the banknote. He'd been hoping to keep it in reserve until things got desperate. And they were.

★★★

Walking back towards his temporary home Jon came across another mini supermarket quite similar to the one he'd robbed the day before. It wasn't the cleanest and brightest of establishments but the thought of the almost empty cupboards back at the flat made his stomach rumble. He took a trolley, thought better of it and switched it for a basket before heading off round the store gazing longingly at the tempting items on display, all the while knowing he could barely afford even the most basic essentials. Never in his life had he been this hard up.

For a man of Jon's considerable ability, making a financial analysis of the wares available was easy and he found that the most calories for the "Phen in your pocket" came from eating pasta in tomato sauce, though budget sausages and a white sliced loaf ran a close second. Sadly a bottle of "own brand" whisky at 13 Phen was way beyond his budget. He bought as much food as 20 Phen would run to and wondered what would happen if it ran out before he was able to access more money. Did they really have soup kitchens or were they just something from the history books?

★★★

After getting up the stairs with his shopping and packing his purchases into the kitchen cupboard Jon turned his thoughts to acquiring more money. Although Jana's debit card had been swallowed up by the ATM he still had her credit card. He just had to find a way of making it work.

After he'd eaten another filling though uninspiring dish of what was rapidly becoming a staple diet he set off round the little flat on a mission of discovery. He searched through Jana's purse, through the drawers and the magazine rack, rifled through a box he found on top of the wardrobe and collected together anything which looked official in the slightest way.

Perhaps the best find had been a drawer stuffed full of papers. It wasn't exactly a sophisticated filing system - the old stuff was at the bottom of the pile and the latest stuff on the top. And it was clear that when the pile had got too high for the drawer to close, she'd started new pile in the next drawer. It wasn't quite the administrative efficiency that came so naturally to Amey.

After wading through hundreds of randomly ordered documents Jon finally struck gold and found a cache of financial statements together with a wad of PIN number notification forms all stapled neatly together. Wow, a staple - obviously a technology upgrade. He checked the account number and it corresponded with the credit card he still had. All he had to do now was to put the sheets in date order to see which was the last one Jana had received.

***

After sleeping through another very comfortable night Jon rose none too early and enjoyed a breakfast of toast and marmalade, and actually had some milk in his cup of coffee.

Bursting with anticipation, full of hope and with the girl's fingers crossed he set off down to the local shops and found an ATM. He was going to give the credit card two goes with the number he'd found, and then retrieve it if it wasn't accepted. The machine accepted the card in the usual way. He put the number in and waited, and waited. How relieved he was when the screen lit up to display a range of options, words just couldn't describe. Before the machine had a chance to change its mind he pushed the button to take out 200 Phen. With the notes carefully stuffed into an inside pocket he asked the machine for another service and selected a balance check. With the 200 Phen he'd just drawn out the account stood at 2906 Phen in debt. With a credit limit of 3000 the card was only going to get him another 94 before it ran the curtain down.

***

Full of enthusiasm after his success Jon decided there had to be more he could do. Although Jana's credit card account was badly overdrawn there was a chance there might be some money in her bank account. He'd lost the card in the ATM it was true, but now he had a full set of Jana's relevant details at his fingertips he could phone her bank and ask them to issue a replacement. Even if they were using a voice recognition system as part of their security system the present operator of Jana Kell's vocal chords would still be accepted.

He checked the number on the sheet and dialled it into Jana's phone. After negotiating the minefield of options and only listening to seven minutes of recorded music, Jon finally ascended to the nirvana of being able to speak to a real human being. He was very surprised when the man told him that, according to Phoenix Central Records, Jana Kell was on a TranzCon transfer to Vissan while her body on Phoenix was being used to host a traveller from Vissan. The real human being regretted that the bank was unable to accept *her* request for a replacement card.

As soon as he'd rung off Jon's thoughts were somewhere along the lines of "what the fuck's going on?" His problem in the last few days had been trying to persuade TranzCon and any other interested parties that he was still here on Phoenix. Now the double whammy was that here was a database that insisted Jana Kell was on Vissan. A simple inversion of its logic told him Jon Chandler had to be on Phoenix, or at least he was as far as Central Records were concerned.

He thought about it for a while, trying to work out how he could turn the situation to his advantage. If he couldn't get a card in Jana's name because she was on Vissan, perhaps he could get a card in his own name because Jon Chandler was on Phoenix. With the major Union institutions gearing themselves up to grab a slice of the action in the newly discovered Phoenixan market his own bank had recently snapped up the Standard Credit Universal Bank here on Phoenix. It was the obvious place to start.

Jon opened up the laptop and told it to search for a network. Although Jana had no computer or internet connection of her own Jon was amused to find that one of the neighbours had a wifi connection that they hadn't bothered to password protect, just like his own system at home. It was only the difference between the isolation of a grand mansion in Rosemount and a house where ten people lived under a single roof that got him on line.

After logging onto the SCU website, filling in four pages of information, ticking a seemingly endless number of boxes, and giving what he hoped were correct answers to a stream of security questions a confirmation screen came up to tell him his card would be delivered within ten working days. The PIN number would of course be delivered separately. Easy when you knew how.

52

The Doctor

On Monday morning Jon was out of bed early and a hurried bite of breakfast later was off on the bus into the city.

The girl on the reception desk at TranzCon was her usual smiley self, but when he asked her about the beam she frowned and told him there'd been no news since the last time he'd been there. She invited him to have a seat while he waited to see the doctor.

★★★

Jon could see that the doctor was just a little perturbed to find that his diagnosis of how spirit image retention would clear itself up after a few days had so far been wrong. But the man did admit he knew little of the problem and had no real idea how long the symptoms might last.

Jon told him. 'I think that if I was deep scanned you could use the information to show exactly who I am. If it shows that I'm Jon Chandler then it would allow me to be recognised as my true self. I'd have access to my own funds and would at least be able to live more comfortably while I'm waiting for the problem with the beam to be solved. But if it proves I'm Jana Kell, then I promise you, I'll do my best to accept it and get on with her life.'

The doctor thought about what his patient had said, and from the way he nodded his head enthusiastically Jon wondered whether he might actually be making some progress.

'Miss Kell, or Mr Chandler depending on who you actually turn out to be, I think you're right in what you say, and as a former TranzCon traveller having medical problems directly related to your transfer you are most certainly entitled to whatever help we can give you. However, I have to tell you, before TranzCon can carry out a scan for such a purpose it is a mandatory requirement for you to be examined by a psychiatrist. If he recommends that you should have a deep scan then TranzCon will carry this out at no cost to yourself. Is that OK?'

Jon confirmed that it was, though he was slightly disappointed to then be informed that before he would be allowed to see the psychiatrist at TranzCon's expense a total of 21 days had to pass since the date of the transfer. With eight days already gone it meant waiting another thirteen, but then as he remembered, while he was stuck here on Phoenix he wasn't exactly short of time.

53

Jasmine & Arnie

After he left the TranzCon office Jon went back to the little flat for a bite to eat. With the girl's stomach re-charged he decided there was plenty of day left so he'd go out and have a look to see what there was to do in the surrounding area. He'd been to Rokham Park two days ago and decided it was worth another visit, especially since the weather was unseasonably good that day. He strolled around the flowerbeds, bright yellow with the spring daffodils, the bowling greens where the old folks were enjoying a quiet afternoon, and the pond where the children ran around feeding the ducks and trying hard to stay out of the way of the geese and the big white birds with the long necks he'd never seen before.

At one time the park must have been the grounds of the old hall that stood almost in the centre of the park and now functioned as the offices of the city administration's parks and gardens department. The owner from long ago had chosen his position well because the big stone building stood on ground raised several metres higher than the rest of the surrounding land, which gave the benches around the edge a commanding view over the nearby parts of the city. It was a bit of luck that he found a seat on one of the benches facing towards the south-west because it allowed him to admire the view while he sat basking in the warmth of the late afternoon sunshine.

He'd been resting there for about half an hour and was just thinking of getting up to have another look at the duck-pond when an eye-catching young woman with a small dog in tow came up to his bench and spoke.

'Hi Jana, how's it going? I thought you were going to give me a call when you got back. Was it exciting being on another planet?'

Jon looked up at her and was amazed. He could see that underneath the aura she projected to the world she might have been acceptably pretty, but the way she was garbed in such a darkly bizarre costume topped off by a head of purple spiky hair was somehow at odds with what nature had planned. As she came closer Jon could see the garish makeup she wore and the items of jewellery that extruded from several parts of her face in ways the Good Lady had surely never intended for her finest creation. He wondered whether she'd done it to make herself more attractive - or less. Heightwise she was about as tall as Jana, and as far as her clothes revealed she had a similar figure; but otherwise the two women were as different as chalk and cheese.

It was obvious the girl thought she was speaking to the real Jana.

'No, I'm sorry, I know this is Jana Kell's body, but I'm a TranzCon traveller using her as a host.'

The girl studied him carefully, as if trying to see inside his head.

'The mind traveller from Vissan?' I thought that was supposed to be all over by now?'

Jon was calm when he replied. After all, it hadn't been his choice to still be here on Phoenix.

'I am as you say the mind-traveller from Vissan and I came here to use Jana's body as a host for five days. But you probably know the communication beam between this planet and Darius isn't working at the moment, so Jana and I haven't been able to transfer back to our own bodies. Are you one of her friends?'

And he felt stupid even as he said it because if she hadn't been she wouldn't have stopped to talk. The girl took the spare seat halfway along the bench and introduced herself:

'I'm Jasmine Kell, Jana's sister.'

For a senior politician normally at ease meeting dignitaries of the highest rank Jon was suddenly thrown and the only reply he could manage came out with a stammer:

'Very pleased to meet you Jasmine.'

He wondered whether the next few minutes were going to be just a little difficult. Until then his thoughts had all centred around when he was going to be able to get home, and now he was face to face with a woman who had a vested interest in getting rid of him. He hadn't considered the people who might want to see Jana again.

The girl continued, 'What exactly happened?'

Jon told her the story that so far only he had believed was true.

'We tried to travel back just as the beam was failing, and one of my colleagues who went just before me got across. I had a dream and I thought I'd made it, but when I woke up I found I was still here on Phoenix, and still in your sister's body of course. Jana's still on Vissan living in my body and I'm sure she's hoping to get home just as much as I am. The trouble is, because I went through the process of the transfer, all the people at TranzCon have assumed it had worked as planned and now they won't accept who I really am. So I've had to take over more of Jana's life than I'd planned.'

'It sounds stupid to me. If Jana's not back then she's not back. Why don't you just go and tell them who you are?'

'Believe me I've tried, but it's no use.'

And then Jon realised, Jasmine had recognised in an instant that the life-force inside her sister's body was not that of her sister. He wondered whether to take her along to the reception centre to see if she could give him some support.

'It's amazing that someone like you who knows the real Jana can understand my situation so easily.'

'Why should it be amazing? I've known her for the last 22 years so I know whether I'm talking to my sister or not. And you can't believe how much I want her back. What are the chances of it all getting going again?'

'They keep insisting they're working on it and it's only a matter of time, but so far nothing's happened. To carry out a transfer they need a lot of beam strength, but even if they only managed basic communications I'd be able to get some support from my people on Vissan. And of course I want to get home - I've got a job to get back to, and my wife will be missing me.'

A frown came over Jasmine's face.

'A wife? You've got a wife?'

Jon shrugged.

'Yes. It's quite normal. Lots of men have wives.'

Jasmine was obviously taken aback. 'So that means that the *you* inside my sister's body is actually a man? Somehow I'd just assumed the traveller would be another woman.'

Jon felt there was a moral judgement coming, though from Jasmine's appearance she didn't look as if she was a pillar of the straight-laced community.

'Well it's unusual I'll grant you, but Jana and I both share a rare mind type and she was the only suitable host available. If you're her sister there's a strong chance you're a Delta as well so you could make good money if you worked as a host.'

'What, let some dirty old man into my body for him to run his filthy hands all over me - or worse. What if he went out and got me pregnant, or caught something? No chance of that thank you very much.'

'Well it's not guaranteed to be a man, there are lots of women travelling as well. Anyway, the traveller isn't allowed to use the host body for sex.'

'And what's to stop them?'

'Well the contract they sign. What else?'

'If it was me I'd want something more than a piece of paper for protection. Being locked in a chastity belt would be a good starting point. Did Jana know there was going to be man in her body?'

'Yes, she knew all along. I don't mind telling you I've found quite a few problems with a cross-sex mind transfer, but it was necessary for my diplomatic mission.'

'Diplomatic mission - just who are you?'

Jon told her and she whistled.

'I just can't imagine it. This mind transfer thing is seriously weird, and it's not just you either, I can't imagine a girl like Jana being a man.'

'Well she's still a woman underneath even though she's occupying my male body. But she's got people there to help her with any problems that might come up. She's probably amazed at being so tall, and she might even be having fun seeing what it would be like to grow a beard. In any case she's living in five star luxury while I'm in her scruffy little flat.'

'Scruffy little flat?' The girl's voice took on an indignant tone. 'I think it's a nice little flat, and Jana keeps it really clean.'

Jon wondered how bad a place would have to be before Jasmine considered it to be dirty, but that wasn't the issue right now.

Jasmine looked thoughtful and then she spoke, 'I suppose it's OK, for a while at least. So Mr Mind Traveller, what do I call you?'

'My real name is Jon, Jon Chandler.'

He'd already told her what his position in the government was, but he wondered if there might be just a hint that she recognised the name. She didn't, but then again he only knew the names of a handful of Phoenixan politicians.

The dog had seen something small and furry it would like to have killed and tugged hard at its lead. Jasmine pulled him back.

'Arnie, come and talk to the nice lady here.'

Jon watched as the little dog jumped up and planted a big lick right across his host's face before he'd had time to protect himself.

'Well at least Arnie still thinks you're Jana. He likes you and that's important.'

Jon looked at the dog and wondered about the significance of Jasmine's statement.

'Why's that?'

'Well Jon, you've taken over my sister's body, and her flat, so you won't have any problem taking Arnie back will you?'

'What do you mean taking him back? No-one told me anything about a dog.'

'Arnie was our Mum's dog but she had to give him up when she went into the nursing home. I can't have him cos it says no pets in my lease, so Jana agreed to have him. I've looked after him for the last two weeks because of your mind-swap thing and now the landlord's complaining. If you can't have him I've got to take him to the vet.'

Jon was suddenly suspicious of the girl's motives.

'What for?'

'To be put to sleep of course. There's nothing else I can do if I want to keep a roof over my head.'

Jon looked down at the poor little pooch as it stared sadly up into his eyes. It was almost as if he'd understood every word his mistress had said and knew he might be munching his way through just one last meaty supper before chemical death claimed him and his little doggy life-force set off on its final journey to little doggy heaven. It wasn't a decision Jon wanted anyone to take on his account. After all he did have some experience with dogs, Uncle Des had had one years ago so Jon knew a bit about peaceful co-existence with comrades of the canine variety. And in any case it was only for a few days till the beam came back on line. He thought about it for a moment before agreeing to take him in.

'Hi there Jas, hi Jana.'

Jon looked up to see a young man who'd come up from behind the bench and put his arm around Jasmine. From the way he kissed her it seemed pretty clear the two of them were an item. He walked round the end of the bench and sat himself down next to Jasmine.

She put him straight, 'No Gary, it's not Jana yet. It's still that mind traveller she swapped with. I'll explain it to you on the way home. Jon, I'll come round tomorrow morning and bring the rest of Arnie's stuff. OK?'

The two of them got up together and walked away holding hands. Jon sat dumbstruck with the little dog on the end of its lead. If anyone had told him that morning he was going to be a dog owner before the sun went down he wouldn't have believed them.

★★★

Next morning Jon was just finishing his cup of coffee when he heard a bell ring. When there was no-one outside the door of the flat he guessed the bell must be connected to the button he'd seen outside the building's main entrance door. He'd never lived anywhere that was multiple occupancy before, but it was obvious when he thought about it. He trotted down the stairs and noticed the way Arnie was catching him up fast. Obviously the excitement of discovering who could be at the front door was an important part of a dog's day.

The two of them arrived in the entrance together and Arnie jumped up trying to look through the frosted glass while he *woof*ed in a small dog sort of way. Jon opened the door to find Jasmine standing on the step. She didn't wait to be invited and stepped into the entrance hall with Arnie jumping up at her excitedly.

She accepted the offer of a coffee, so Jon made a second one for himself while Jasmine unpacked her bag. Out came a couple of stainless steel bowls, a brush and a varied selection of toys. Arnie grabbed one and went off squeaking it noisily.

'When you can't stand the racket anymore, put the ones with squeakers up somewhere he can't reach.'

'Which of the other ones have got the squeakers in them?'

She smiled. 'You'll find out.'

They sat watching Arnie playing on the floor as they sipped the hot coffee, and then Jon noticed the way Jasmine was watching him. He looked at her, his expression obviously asking for her thoughts.

'It's just weird sitting here looking at my sister, and knowing it's not my sister.'

Jon tried to re-assure her. 'You'll have her back - just as soon as the beam comes on line. Look, something I was thinking about overnight after I got back here with Arnie, would you really have had him put down?'

Jasmine smiled in an apologetic sort of way.

'Sorry Jon, that was just a bit of a bluff to put some pressure on you. But I needed to because seriously there wasn't anywhere else for him to go and the landlord came along the other day waving a copy of the tenancy agreement in front of my face and kept jabbing his finger on the bit where it said "No Pets". The only other thing I could've done would've been to move somewhere else. But there's another reason I couldn't keep him - in two days time I'm starting a new job so I won't be here to look after him.'

'So you are moving then?'

She smiled. 'I'm going into space - how about that? I've got a job with a company who're refurbishing some old starliner up in orbit.'

Jon was interested. He knew most of the big ships in service - certainly the ones from years back.

'Do you know what it's called?'

She fumbled in her pocket and pulled out a phone. She pressed a few buttons then read from the screen, 'It's called the Hyperion.'

Jon sat speechless. He'd heard that a ship carrying freight was coming to Phoenix, or had arrived by now, but no-one had mentioned it by name. The Hyperion, his Hyperion, the ship that got him started in the space transportation business. Could it really be thirty years since Rapier's first liner had taken the business by storm? He remembered they'd pensioned the old ship off when the first of the new liners with tru-grav started coming off the production line. Its new owners had replaced a lot of the drive equipment and put it into service as a long range freighter. He was genuinely intrigued when he asked:

'So what are they doing with the ship now?'

'The new owners want to start a passenger service to Darius as well as carrying freight, but the old facilities on board are years out of date and need a complete refurbishment. This company I'm working for, Knight Aerospace, has got the contract to do the work.'

Jon looked at her and wondered. She didn't look the type but appearances could be deceptive.

'Are you trained in some branch of space tech?'

She gave a laugh. 'Not me, worse luck. Jana and I never got much schooling. I'm just doing some cleaning, and sorting out the bedrooms to make them nice for the passengers. It's going to be a slog putting in long shifts but the money's better than anything I could get here in Celebration.'

'Have you been up into space before?'

'Never. I'm looking forward to the flight up, and being weightless.'

'Be careful with the weightless bit, it's fun in some ways, but don't travel on a full stomach because you might regret it. Did you know the main reason for people requiring medical attention in the space passenger business is because of inhaling their own vomit and nearly choking to death? And most incidents happen to first-timers because they don't know what they're in for.'

Jon watched the expression on Jasmine's face and saw how her skin turned noticeably green. There was definitely an extra dimension to having the otherwise unattractive pale pasty skin that seemed to be the norm here on Phoenix.

'Thanks for the advice Jon, I can see I'm going to need it. Look, I've got loads to do and I'm on the space-plane tomorrow evening, but I'll give you a call when I get back.'

'It might be Jana who's back by then.'

'Even better. It's been really strange meeting you Jon, but I've had a good think about it all, and really I don't mind. But you just look after my sister's body will you.'

'What, you mean keep my filthy hands to myself? I'll do my best.'

She bared her teeth and made claws at him. He put his hands up to defend himself. Arnie bolted under the table.

'You're getting the hang of being my sister Jon.'

She rushed over, gave him a hug and headed for the door.

'I'll see myself out,' she called.

54

The Bank Card

It was about a week later when Jon and Arnie arrived back from the park that he checked Jana's mail-box and found an official looking envelope nestling amongst the usual round of promotions and mail-shots. He flexed it in his hands and part of it didn't bend. It was a good sign.

Up in the flat he opened the envelope to find a folded A4 sheet inside showing the letterhead of the Standard Credit Universal bank at the top, and what to him was a very attractive piece of plastic stuck on near the bottom. With the PIN number that had arrived in the post the previous day he now had a set. This was what he'd been waiting for.

Then he saw that a second sheet had been stapled to the first. The letter explained that although SCU had temporarily accepted his request for a new bank card they'd written to advise that since they hadn't been able to contact his branch on Vissan they had imposed a spending limit of 200 Phen per day, subject to a maximum withdrawal of 1000 Phen per week. It was a standard security procedure and had been done for his own protection If he considered the limit was insufficient he should make an appointment for a meeting at the bank to request a higher amount.

It was clear to Jon that with his present appearance a face to face meeting was unlikely to convince the manager he was speaking with the real Jon Chandler.

But 1000 Phen. Wow! Compared to the money he normally spent each week at home on Vissan it was only a mere pittance. But from his experience of leading a close to penniless existence here on Phoenix the ability to draw so much every day and every week was going to make him rich, in a very minor way. Perhaps for the first time in his life Jon realised that it was necessary to go without money to really appreciate what it could do for you.

55

The Shrink

Although Dr Morris was retained by TranzCon as their "resident" psychiatrist Jon discovered that in fact he was an independent practitioner who operated from his own premises quite a long way out of town in what he'd recently come to know was the better end of the city. Fortunately he was able to take a bus down town and catch a tram to within a few minutes walk of the doctor's consulting rooms.

The lady on reception was older than those who tended to be employed for the equivalent roles in larger establishments and Jon was just slightly intimidated by what appeared to be her ruthless efficiency. But at least she didn't smile too much, if at all. She took Jon's name and gestured towards a door with the words "Waiting Room" stencilled on it. After about ten minutes a smallish man, perhaps in his early sixties, stepped into the room and introduced himself.

★★★

Jon found that, unlike the movies he'd seen over the years the doctor did not invite him to lie down on a couch but simply offered him a chair. The man was obviously in possession of a copy of Jon's file so he knew the details of his circumstances quite well.

'You are Mr Jon Chandler?' It was phrased as a question. 'I take it you'd be happier if I called you that?'

Jon nodded in agreement.

'Mr Chandler, it has now been three weeks since you regained consciousness after the TranzCon transfer to Vissan that you claim failed to take place. I see from the notes here that TranzCon's own doctor saw you soon after the transfer and told you a little about the condition we call spirit image retention. And I see that he suggested the condition might clear itself up if you gave it chance. From the fact you are here talking to me now it appears that you still believe yourself to be Jon Chandler.'

'That is correct Doctor. I have never been more certain that I am Jon Chandler, and more to the point, I have never been more certain that I am *not* Jana Kell.'

Morris nodded. 'And I see from your notes that you claim to remember a great deal of information about Jon Chandler.'

'I can recall every aspect of my life.'

Morris shook his head. 'No Mr Chandler. Even if you are who you say you are, you would only recall around 25% of your memories because that is all you would have brought with you over the beam. But I'd agree that the lack of the missing memories would not appear obvious to you. So this feeling that you are the man that Jana Kell hosted, it could be because you really are Jon Chandler, or it could be because you are Jana Kell and have retained access to information that remained in your brain following the transfer.'

Jon thought about the statement for a brief moment. If he'd ever heard a man hedging his bets surely this was it.

'Is it normal for a host to retain information about the person they hosted? I thought any memories belonging to the person being hosted were unavailable to the host, and vice-versa of course.'

'That is the normal situation, though I've made a study of a number of case histories from TranzCon's operations over the past 15 years and it is clear there have been a few instances when information has, shall we say, leaked through so it became available to the host.'

'But in that case the host would have knowledge of both themselves and the person they had hosted. In my case that has not happened because I have no knowledge of Jana Kell other than what I've picked up from three weeks of living in her flat.'

'So you say, but we only have your word for it that you can recall nothing of Jana Kell's life.'

'If I was Jana Kell, why would I hide knowledge about myself?'

'You could be attempting to make some sort of claim against Jon Chandler. It happens from time to time when there is such a disparity between the wealth of the traveller and the wealth of the host.'

Jon was forced to accept that it was a credible motive. He decided it might be time to change his tack a little.

'Something I know about transfers is that they are generally limited to thirty days and that is because, in the initial weeks at least, the incoming and controlling life-force so totally dominates the nature of the host brain that nothing feeds back to the controlling life-force. Am I right?'

'Indeed you are Mr Chandler.'

'But if a transfer went on for long enough, eventually the basic nature of the host brain and body would begin to infiltrate the controlling life-force and influence a whole range of actions and responses.'

Morris nodded.

'But the time when the effect starts to make itself felt is normally after about sixty days, and that was why the permitted maximum length of time for a TranzCon transfer was set at thirty days, because it gave an acceptable safety margin.'

Jon looked expectantly at the doctor.

'Yes Mr Chandler, that is exactly right.'

'So here we are on the twenty ninth day since I first arrived on Phoenix and took control of Jana Kell's body, and it follows that until now the part of her mind which remains resident in her brain could not have started to have any effect on my mind, though it might do if I remained in this body for some weeks longer.'

'And the point you are making Mr Chandler?'

'The point I'm making is that, although there could come a time when I start succumbing to thoughts and desires which come from Jana Kell's mind if I don't manage to transfer back to Vissan, so far my own life-force remains in charge. My mind has not been infiltrated by my host so there is no confusion, I know exactly who I am.'

'That is of course assuming you are Jon Chandler and that it is *your* mind that would be infiltrated by Jana Kell's mind. But the alternative scenario we have to consider is that you are actually Jana Kell and your mind is still being controlled by a residual image of the mind you hosted. The effect would be much stronger in the early stages just after the minds had transferred back to their correct bodies. Now, continuing for a moment with the assumption you are Jana Kell, the time you have been suffering from spirit image retention is almost unprecedented because all the experiences we have recorded to date indicate that the condition normally abates within the first few days and is gone completely within two weeks, even in the most extreme cases.'

Jon nodded, but wondered what point the psychiatrist was angling towards.

'But a complicating factor with this transfer is that Jon Chandler is a very rich, powerful, and intelligent man while Jana Kell is, and I'm sorry to have to put it so bluntly, just an ordinary person. In fact a woman with no formal education beyond the state minimum. Although Jana should not feel inferior because the mind her body hosted was so much more powerful than her own, that fact could most certainly have had an effect on the time her mind would take to recover from the spirit image retention condition. A further factor is that both Jon Chandler and Jana Kell were first time travellers and this can also have an effect because neither brain had had a chance to learn how to protect itself against the influences of the mind being hosted. So the incoming life-forces could have left deeper *imprints* in the brains of the hosts. On top of all this, I see from your notes that both Jon Chandler and Jana Kell are Delta mind-type.'

'It's because of being a Delta2 that I had to accept a female host. Any other type of mind would not have supported my life-force.'

'Yes Mr Chandler, I am a specialist in these matters so I am well aware of mind types. But the undeniable fact is you are both Deltas.'

'Does it make a difference compared to other transfers?'

'Perhaps. Compared to the usual transfers between Alphas and Betas there is little history of transfers between Deltas. So it would be within the bounds of science to expect that a far higher incidence of extra-ordinary conditions might arise following a transfer between two Deltas. At present we simply do not know, but the possibility has to be considered.'

Jon was getting impatient that the whole procedure was taking so long.

'So if any of what you're telling me is true, it makes it all the more important that you and TranzCon should find some means of determining exactly who I am.'

'Mr Chandler, we have to take things one step at a time. Eliminating psychosis as a complicating factor will go a long way towards proving who you are.'

'So can we go ahead with your tests?'

'Yes, of course, that is what I have been engaged to do.'

★★★

And the doctor did his tests. He started with simple co-ordination tests such as tracking a finger, or touching the girl's nose. He examined the girl's eyes and ears and finally got onto the main tests where he showed Jon ink-stain pictures and asked him a barrage of questions. After the tests were complete Jon asked him what his diagnosis was.

'Mr Chandler every response you gave indicates that you are completely sane. At first glance it does not appear there is anything wrong with your mental health.'

'I can feel a "but" coming on.'

'Indeed there is. Because of your insistence that you are Jon Chandler, in the face of all the evidence to the contrary, this could indicate the presence of a psychotic condition.'

Jon chewed over what the man was telling him, and rapidly came to a rather unhappy conclusion.

'So if I accepted that I was Jana Kell I'd be sane, but because I'm insisting that I'm Jon Chandler I'm a nut.'

'Please, please; we don't use terms like that these days. And I have to stress that your claim that you are Jon Chandler does not in itself prove that a psychotic condition exists.'

'But it's an indication?'

'It is, as you say, an indication.'

'So has the test proved whether I am Jon Chandler or Jana Kell?'

'Unfortunately, the test by itself cannot prove anything either way.'

Jon was rapidly becoming exasperated. Without actually planning to take any action he might later regret his eyes were scanning the room for something breakable to throw at the wall.

'So what was the purpose of it?'

'We have to do everything we can to investigate the problem, and that is what I have done today.'

Jon was close to shouting, but gave himself a moment to calm before he spoke. The psychiatrist was patient in the extreme and studied his client in a manner that could only be described as annoying.

'But we're still no nearer to an actual outcome than when I arrived here. Now my time while I'm here on Phoenix isn't as valuable as it would normally be if I was in Jackson, but I do need to make some progress. From what I've been told, a deep scan would be able to answer a lot of questions, and I understand you are able to authorise one. In fact my primary reason for coming here today was to meet TranzCon's requirements for carrying out another scan.'

The expression on the man's face lightened noticeably.

'Mr Chandler, I have no hesitation in agreeing to your request and am happy to oblige. If a deep scan will clear up the present confusion, then it is warranted.'

Jon watched as the doctor scribbled some notes on a form and signed it.

★★★

It had all taken an inordinate amount of time to obtain a single piece of paper that he'd thought he was entitled to in the first place. And as he left Jon noticed from the clock in the reception area that precisely ninety minutes had passed since he'd gone into the psychiatrist's room. Hmmmm. He wondered whether a standard consultation was one and a half hours, so to earn his fee the doctor had had to spin the appointment out to fill up the time. If so the doctor's shooting was right on target. Jon wondered whether cynicism was one of the faculties that had come with him through the transfer.

He took the tram back to the city centre and walked to the TranzCon office with the precious form in his hand. The girl at reception greeted him with her customary smile and accepted the form which she scribbled on and stamped. She studied her computer screen and told him they could offer him an appointment at 10.00 AM in three days time. After that he'd need to make a repeat appointment with Dr Morris.

Jon accepted the offered appointment without question, but wondered why it was going to take so long considering that the company had no travellers filling up their schedule right then.

56

The Purchase

It was the standard morning routine. Out of bed, kettle on, quick wash, make coffee, sit down to breakfast, clean teeth, put clothes on. But here on Phoenix there was one more activity on the list - take medication. In particular the pills the doctor had given him when he first arrived and suggested it might be a good idea if he didn't forget to take them. Jon surveyed the back of the blister pack and saw six empty pockets - only the one at the end was still filled. He popped it and placed the two tone torpedo into the girl's mouth. For a moment the capsule felt sticky on her tongue until saliva melted the outer coating, and then the little tube slipped easily down her throat.

He looked in the drawer of the dressing table for the next pack - except there wasn't one. Well it wasn't immediately obvious anyway. He rummaged around. The pretty face frowned - it wasn't logical. Everything in its place - and a place for everything. That was how it was supposed to be, that was the way Jon Chandler ran his life.

He walked through to the bathroom and checked the wall cabinet - no pills. He thought about the packet - large blue letters on a yellow background. Easy enough to spot. He checked the cabinet again just to make sure. What about the bathroom window ledge? Or the drawers in the kitchen? Or the cupboards, or the wardrobe? Half an hour later Jon had turned the little flat upside down and inside out, and still there were no pills.

He switched to a different approach and found the calendar that hung on the back of the bedroom door. A shiver ran down the girl's back as Jon did the maths. There *were* no more pills to look for - no matter how hard he looked.

If the beam was going to come back on line quite soon it wasn't even going to matter, well not to Jon anyway. But the chances of getting home seemed to be getting less with every day that passed. The chances of him still being here in a week, or a fortnight, or a month, were high. Worryingly high. And right then he could hardly bring himself to think the word *month* without realising its full significance.

He turned toward the mirror and looked at his host body. Even after five weeks it still came as a shock to see a stranger looking out from the mirror. The face, so pretty and feminine, the curve of her hips, the swell of her breasts - everything so womanly. And then there were the bits you couldn't see just by looking in the mirror - the bits that worked away in the background. Oh Belen! What was he going to do?

★★★

It didn't take a genius to work out that unless he could get more of the medication to stop the process, sometime quite soon Jana's body was going to revert to what had been its *situation normal* for the past decade: preparing itself each month to grow a foetus if an egg was fertilised, and disposing of the womb lining if it wasn't. Right then he couldn't think which was worse, well not in the early stages anyway.

He weighed up his options. Find out which doctor Jana was registered with, that was easy enough, make an appointment, no problem at all, and ask for another batch of the pills - it wasn't going to work. The doctor would check the records to find that Jana had returned to her own body. And then what, tell him not to be such a silly girl? "That's what happens when you're female - get used to it".

The idea of getting a repeat prescription by doing a smash and grab on the local pharmacy flashed through his head, but even if he knew what to look for it was a non-starter. It'd be just the same except he'd be in jail.

He thought back to those times when he and Mandy were just coming into their teens - one twin able to breeze through puberty, or at least his mother seemed to think it was that easy, and the other having to take the bull of adulthood by the horns. He'd never really felt that much sympathy for his sister back then. Now he realised what she must have been going through in those days of knowing - and yet not knowing.

He cheered up temporarily when he considered there could be a real chance he was going to get home after all. Well no-one had ruled out the possibility, but maybe he ought to start facing facts. Just in case. But he was so badly prepared - no idea what to expect. How would he know what was happening or when it was going to happen? And not even his mother there to help him through the initiation to a club he didn't really want to join.

He sat and wondered, wondered and worried for a while before he felt his practical hat settling into place - "come on Jon, pull yourself together" he told himself. Work the figures out - close on thirty billion people in the Union, thirty two if you added in the ones on Phoenix - half of them female.

Average lifespan one hundred and twenty years, reproductive years about forty, so that made five billion females involved, give or take the odd ten million, and how many of them died each month? None, or was he absolutely sure of that? They all seemed to manage somehow - a bit of pain, a bit of blood. His time in the army had psyched him up for that, it was something that happened to soldiers whenever there was real conflict. The conclusion that he should be a man about it seemed logical if inappropriate.

He climbed out of the chair and headed for the bathroom. His recollection of living with females was that there was always a box of "women's things" on the window ledge, except that here in Jana's flat there wasn't. So he hunted around and found what he was looking for in the cupboard just outside the bathroom door - but the box was noticeably light as he picked it up. Inside just two of the little tubes leaned against the cardboard side and slid down to the bottom as he moved the box. How many the girl's body would need he truly had no idea, but the guess that it was more than two was an easy one to make. He read the details on the box and made a mental note of them.

★★★

Although he knew he could buy more or less anything down at the supermarket, somehow it was all a bit too out in the open, so the corner shop looked like it might be a little more user-friendly even if its prices were higher. He steeled himself, walked in, picked up a basket and looked around. Fortunately there were no men in the shop and the other women there took no notice of him at all, little suspecting the presence of an outsider in their midst. He went through to the rack at the back of the shop, quickly located the product the girl had used - off the shelf, into the basket. Easy bit over, now all he had to do was to take it to the till and pay. The girl at the checkout didn't give him or his purchase a second glance.

57
The Scan

As any child waiting for Belenfest to arrive can tell you, some days just go on forever. And for Jon, knowing the scan was so close but still so far aware was torture. But even minutes that drag slowly by finally pass and everything comes to those who wait.

After enjoying a leisurely breakfast and a trip to the park with Arnie, Jon took the bus down town to TranzCon's office.

The young doctor he'd met on the first day of his quest to have his true identity recognised greeted him and took him into his office to explain the procedure they'd be carrying out, not that it was any more complicated than the time he'd been into a scanner for the transfer from Vissan.

★★★

The assistant handed Jon a medical gown and showed him into a cubicle to undress, and it was only a few minutes later he was laying on the bed while two technicians wired him up to the equipment.

A whine came as a motor started up and the bed moved his head forwards into the scanner array. For just a brief moment there was silence, and then the scanner began to hum. Jon remembered back to the time when he'd transferred from his own body on Vissan and felt the same sequence beginning.

Something he knew of the TranzCon transfer process was that, despite the immense data handling capacity of the beam, he had "come over" with only a small proportion of his own memories. In contrast, everything Jana had experienced in her whole life remained in her brain whether her consciousness was there to access it or not, so it was logical that far more of the memories in there would be Jana's rather than his own.

For the intruder temporarily resident in the brain, the host's memories would normally be hidden from view, almost as if they weren't there at all. But with the unstoppable force of the scanner, a mental whirlwind that raced through the girl's brain, stirring and sifting the contents as it went, each and every memory would be opened up. Everything she'd ever known would be laid bare. The whole process would be over and done in little more than a minute, but to the mind being scanned it would seem as if hours had passed.

And afterwards there would be hardly a recollection of anything his conscious mind had seen. Perhaps one or two snapshots from her past would fix into his memory, but no more than this.

At last the devastation ended. Jon heard the motor again as the bed pulled him back out of the scanner array. As the mental buzz subsided a picture formed in his mind, the reflection from a mirror that showed a pretty seven year old in a pink gingham dress.

★★★

Back in reception Jon was getting his things together ready to leave but he remembered to ask when TranzCon would be ready to analyse the data from the scan and come up with a result. "A result" - he was excited just to think that in just a few days time the scan would have done its work and proved he was Jon Chandler. OK, it wouldn't get him home to Vissan, but at least it would make his life here on Phoenix more agreeable.

He went over to the desk and asked the girl. 'Do I have to make an appoint with you to get the results of the scan, or will I be seeing Dr Morris again?'

The girl was surprised at his question and informed him there was no delay at all in processing the data. The results were available straight away and a specialist had been booked to meet with him in half an hours time.

For ten minutes while he browsed through the latest edition of the company magazine and enjoyed a cup of coffee Jon had had one eye on the doors he knew connected the reception area to the corridor where the offices were located. So he was surprised when a lady in a lab coat approached from the other direction and sat next to him.

Mrs Imogen Daniels must have been somewhere in her forties. Her face showed a friendly smile that went hand in hand with an air of knowledgeable authority in a way that seemed to come naturally to some women. Men always had to look more serious if they wanted to command respect. She explained her role in TranzCon, she wasn't a doctor or a psychiatrist but was a mind transfer analyst who would be able to interpret the findings of Jon's scan. When he'd finished his drink she showed him through to one of the featureless interview rooms he was getting to know quite well.

No sooner had they both sat down before Mrs Daniels got down to the business in hand. Flipping backwards and forwards through several reams of computer printout and pointing to the display on the computer monitor she explained feature after feature using an unfamiliar vocabulary that was almost meaningless to Jon. He watched and listened carefully in case there was anything a mere layman might understand.

There wasn't.

His mind began to wander and he realised he wasn't taking anything in. He was going to have to ask her to explain things in more simple terms, but how do you stop a professional in full flow? At last he plucked up the courage. The woman's face showed a look that was more disappointment than annoyance or anger.

The scan had revealed memories from a mixture of two separate life-forces, but it was difficult to say which memories related to the resident mind and which had been imported during the transfer. What she could tell him was that she'd found a large number of memories compatible with the life of a female in her early twenties, and a substantial number of memories compatible with a male in his fifties. Well that wasn't exactly a surprise. In fact it told him nothing at all he couldn't have guessed weeks ago. An explanation in simple terms provided a simplistic answer. Maybe if he'd been able to understand the detailed analysis it might have meant more.

And in all the time she'd been speaking she'd never moved even a centimetre towards giving him the result he so desperately needed to hear. The bottom line was all that really mattered. Maybe she felt it was necessary to do a big build up before launching into to the finale. The thought running through his head was "oh for Belen's sake, just get on with it", but he knew a less confrontational approach would be more appropriate.

'Mrs Daniels, I've listened to you as carefully as I can. You've explained about the memories, and I accept there is a limit to what you can deduce from them, but what about the analysis of the mind itself, what does that tell you? I'll come straight to the point, does it tell you whether I'm Jon Chandler or Jana Kell?'

She stopped leafing through the printout and spun her chair towards him. The smile that had come so easily just minutes before was less obvious.

'Miss Kell, I'm sorry but you have to understand it's not quite as easy as you seem to think. Despite the best efforts of many eminent researchers we still have no way of understanding anything of the life-force that makes up a sentient being. I thought I'd explained that earlier. Future generations will probably look back on where we are now as something of a technological stone-age. We've learned a lot, we've catalogued a huge range of causes and effects, but so far we haven't managed to delve into the inner workings of the mind. So many hidden truths remain simply that. So instead of attempting to analyse the mind itself we compare it against other minds using complex simulation routines, and within limits we can predict how it will behave under a range of scenarios. But with data from only a single mind there's isn't a lot we can do. So I'm sorry if this comes as something of a disappointment, but there is no quick and easy answer to your question.'

Jon was puzzled.

'But surely, you can run the new scan against earlier scans of Jon Chandler or Jana Kell. Surely you'd be able to tell which one it was the closer match.'

She nodded enthusiastically.

'Yes, of course. That's exactly what a comparison run would show. But at the moment we're not able to do one. The data is all held on the mainframe in Jackson so with the beam out of service we can't get access to any earlier scans.'

Jon was starting to get worried now.

'I can understand that the scan of Jon Chandler is probably only available on the computer in Jackson, but surely you must have a copy of Jana Kell's scan because you initially made it here. With even one of the earlier scans to compare the new one against you'd be able to make a judgement about whose mind is here in Jana's head.'

She shook her head. 'No, I'm sorry, it doesn't work like that. We had the original scan from Jana Kell of course, but we only held it on our equipment for a short time. Then it was deleted after her life-force had been transmitted to Vissan. You have to understand, the data file a scan creates is unbelievably huge and we need the space in memory to process the next traveller. In the next few weeks we'll be commissioning a new computer complex with vastly increased storage capacity but it's not in service yet. The equipment only arrived from Darius a few weeks ago.'

Now Jon was devastated. The hopes he'd been high on for the past three days had vanished in a moment. Only the cold-turkey let-down remained. He was silent for a minute or two while the news sank in.

'So that's it? Until the beam comes back on-line you really don't have any way of confirming whether I'm Jon Chandler.'

'I'm sorry, but we weren't advised that the purpose of the scan was to establish an identity. Anyone here could have told you it wasn't going to be possible until the beam from Darius comes back on-line.'

'So why didn't you tell this to Dr Morris?'

'Dr Morris put in a request for a deep scan to be carried out, and that is what we did. At no time did we promise the sort of service you and the doctor obviously expected. But that's hardly our fault is it? It all rides on the progress they're making getting the beam back. TranzCon is a *user* of the beam, not the provider of the service. We're not the ones who're to blame.'

Jon's mind was in a daze. He said goodbye and walked out into the street, ignoring the calls from the receptionist.

★★★

With his hopes dashed Jon wandered aimlessly around the streets of Celebration, scarcely taking in anything of his surroundings. The main street was busy with shoppers and workers from offices going out to lunch and he shunned the bustle and noise. He wandered on to quieter streets going nowhere in particular. Only when he reached the city's commercial and business hub did he actually take much notice of where he was. A glimmer of hope stirred inside him as he ambled through familiar territory - despite the vast distance that separated Celebration from his real home on Vissan.

And yet he felt at home here as he walked past the lines of elegant skyscrapers, their glittering facades reflecting a golden hue in the afternoon sunshine. Looking up at one particularly magnificent edifice he knew that high up in the penthouse, where the offices looked out over the towering cathedrals to wealth that made up the financial district would be the sumptuous suite where the CEO of some megacorporation sat in regal splendour, presiding over an empire that spread its wealth and power over every one of the little states on this strange world. This was what Jon Chandler did, this was the sort of job that made him what he was. Surely such a thought could never have occurred to a *nothing* like Jana. He knew then exactly who he was. No scan could ever prove otherwise.

Being here on Phoenix wasn't in itself so bad. He had food to eat and a roof over his head. He was in no immediate danger. But he was bored! Thoroughly, absolutely and totally bored. What Jon Chandler needed was the challenge of a high powered job, a job at the very pinnacle of power. Oh how he'd loved that life. The steely calm way he'd made decisions involving millions of HUC, hundreds of millions of HUC. The icy way he'd devastated lives as he'd signed the papers to close down another lame-duck division that wasn't paying its way. The way he'd risked capital in new ventures to re-absorb the heads that had rolled the week before.

This was a life worth living. This was a job he could do. All he needed was a card for the elevator, and a desk with a neatly engraved brass nameplate to remind minions he was the head of finance, or some other grandiose title.

But what were the chances of breaking into such a world for a person everyone saw as a twenty two year old girl without even a single qualification to her name? How close to zero did a guess have to be?

And it wasn't just the qualifications that counted. He knew it now though it wasn't something he'd ever understood before, there'd been so much more to the success that had made him such a wealthy man. When he'd started work at Chandler-Wilmott he'd been little more than twenty two himself. And yet, even on that very first day, he'd been *somebody*. Not because of his qualifications or what he could do, but because he was his father's son. If he hadn't been the chosen one, the next-in-line to an already successful dynasty, he might never have made it in business. Certainly not to the dizzy heights he'd been groomed to expect as his birthright.

To be sure he'd been born with a silver spoon in his mouth, and his father and grandfather would have been proud of the way he'd upgraded, first to gold, and then to platinum. But now he realised that to fly from a nest already close to the top of the cliff was easy.

Just a moment ago he'd felt at least some sense of optimism about his situation. Everyone truly believed the beam would be back on-line anytime soon, then he'd be going home, courtesy of TranzCon. Next morning he'd stride proudly into the office and listen to Michael and Amey as they read out the endless list of his meetings and appointments, briefed him on business in the senate and who he'd be lunching with. Just a few short weeks ago his busy, stressful, exhilarating life had all been real, but now he wondered whether it was already something from the past. Would he, could he, ever get back?

Jon looked around at the street, the faceless masses shuffling by, the hopeless dropouts huddled for warmth in the doorways, "Sleeping Rough", or so their signs said. Now he saw life as it appeared to those who came into the world without the advantages of money and power. What if this was all he had to look forward to? What if he was stuck here on this planet forever?

Now he understood Celia's situation. Jana's physical presence was lovely he knew, and if some rich and well connected boy had driven by in his flashy red sports car, would she have turned him down?

Jon cast a sad eye up at the mirrored side of the block before setting off back to his host's squalid little flat.

58

It's A Dog's Life

After the disappointment that had hit him so hard Jon had recovered somewhat and was fighting back. That was what the men of his family did. What would his business associates have thought of him being beaten by a mere setback? The mighty Jon Chandler brought down by a technical hitch? It was true he was anxious to get home, but there was absolutely nothing he could do to get the beam to come back on line. He just had to hope the engineers and technicians working on the equipment would somehow turn up trumps.

But life wasn't so bad he had to agree. With money coming in now he could afford to live, and eat. The landlord was happy now the rent was up to date. And he'd got Celebration, a city of unparalleled beauty that lived up to its name. It was without doubt a city of sky-high buildings and a bustling business centre, but equally it was a city of parks which brought nature within reach of its two million inhabitants. Whether it was by chance or design that the place had been built nestling in the safe lee of seven low hills was something debated by the historians, but the result it had achieved was extraordinary. Yes it was true that the wide low valley where the big river that flowed out from the metropolis passed through land that had surely been an industrial wasteland in an earlier epoch, but the meandering streams that flowed down to their confluences with the big river were a different matter. Six lovely riverine valleys followed their becks downstream, flowing under a heavy canopy of dense green woodland, bursting out into open meadows, or running down through the dams and millponds which were all that remained from an age of water-power, hundreds, even thousands of years ago.

Country lanes followed the valleys for part of their routes, usually hidden up in the trees, yet plunging down the steep sides to cross the stream, almost as an insult to the unspoilt nature of the tranquil valleys. And throughout the length of each gentle stream there followed paths for the walkers and riders who sought to commune with nature. Those who lived the life of the big city, yet yearned for a chance to forget the world of commerce and industry were well served.

Jon had never known that such a life even existed, yet now he was a convert. For those who came out to play on the days when the workers of this world were busy at their desks, their lathes and their laboratories, these lucky few saw the valleys at their pristine best when peace was at its most peaceful. And Jon had a friend to help him in his pursuit of pleasure, an undemanding friend who required nothing more than to run on the paths laid for walking, and to chase the odd rabbit or three when the normally timid animals dared venture just a little too close. Arnie was a lovely little dog, so full of life, and despite his advancing years he could still give any bunny that fancied its chances a run for its money.

How strange to be a dog. Fat and well when food was plentiful, hungry when it wasn't. Scared when there was danger, but unable to worry over threats that had yet to occur. A passenger in life rather than the pilot. Innocent. The world seen through Arnie's eyes had shown Jon how it was possible to live life at a different pace. Until the day he'd travelled to Phoenix, his whole life had been a race against time. Homework to do at school, studying late into the night at university, army life kicked into gear before six every morning, and once he'd been sucked into the family business and Rapier, every single day of his life had been consumed just keeping the show on the road - and never any let-up for weekends. Then he'd moved into politics, and if it wasn't enough being a senior minister he knew the role he'd set his sights on would demand almost his very soul.

Now he had time to smell the roses.

And there were roses, pink, yellow, white, and the ones he liked best of all, the deepest shade of crimson. They'd never smelled so good, their colours had never shone so bright. Even the buzzing of the insects, busy in the blooms, was crisp and clear in a way he could remember only vaguely from younger days. Everything about the young, vital, body was a delight - so healthy, so full of life and energy. Here on a fine spring morning the sense of "good to be alive" made him want to run and jump, to shout out loud that he was actually enjoying his host's life. Maybe being "stuck" here on Phoenix was the best thing that had ever happened to him.

It was just that today was subtly different from the ones that had passed recently.

When he'd first arrived after coming through the transfer he'd noticed straight away the colder weather, so different from the balmy summer days he'd left behind on Vissan. Five weeks ago this part of Phoenix had still been emerging from the grey days of a long cold winter, before spring had a chance to show its hand. Spring, so often a time of rapid change. So different to autumn, the season which bore witness to the slow, steady progression of the year. Like a clock ticking away the seconds, so autumn marked the passage from the warmth of long summer days, every day just a little cooler, a little shorter, perhaps a little rainier than the one that had preceded it, until finally the first frosts of winter arrived. In contrast, spring was the manic depressive of the seasons. Some days still so dark and cold, almost indistinguishable from the winter that had held the land in its icy grip, and then with a suddenness that could scarcely have been predicted, the land burst out into the heat of a summer's day.

When he'd woken that morning Jon had felt the change, had been unable to not notice the way the temperature had soared a clear ten degrees above where it had been the day before. A glance out into the street had shown how the people passing by had reacted. In a moment heavy coats had been abandoned, left hanging in wardrobes, or on pegs by the door. Discarded and forgotten, well at least until the brief spell of warm weather had passed and the seasonal norm returned.

As Jon had left the house, Arnie pulling anxiously on the leash in his haste to get to the park, he'd realised how things had changed. Without the coats and jumpers that had granted at least some degree of anonymity he felt almost naked.

He thought back to a Belenfest long ago when the massed ranks of the Knighton clan had descended on the big house to help with the celebrations, how they'd greeted the children so warmly only to find how last year's little girl had blossomed into this year's young woman. Jon hadn't understood, but Mandy had been embarrassed. Now he knew why. With nothing more than the thin tee-shirt that was all the day's warmth needed it was as if the girl's body was on view for all to see.

As a man it hadn't been something he'd even thought about, certainly never worried about. Many had been the high summer day when he and his friends had marched about with their shirts slung over their shoulders, and if the manly chests on open display had caught the eye of some pretty girls, then so much the better. They were *always* on the lookout for pretty girls.

Now it was as though the roles had changed, the hunter had become the prey. Maybe Jana herself might have taken delight in the admiring glances that swept, sometimes just a little too slowly over her female form, but for Jon the feeling was scary.

The sudden sound of shouting broke his reverie. Just trying to be friendly Arnie was terrorising a small girl on a trike and her mother, a woman only a few years older than Jana, was trying to chase him off. Jon ran up to pull the dog away but just as he was busy apologising his phone rang. He fumbled in the pocket of his jeans and pulled it out still ringing. Anxiously he pressed the key to accept the call.

The smile failed to arrive through an audio-only connection but he could tell from the sound of her voice it was the receptionist from TranzCon. After he'd left the office almost in a daze three days earlier she'd called later to say that after having a scan it was usual to have a repeat appointment with the psychiatrist. She'd heard from the practice a few minutes ago that Dr Morris had had a cancellation. If Jon could be there in an hour's time he'd be able to see him straight away.

Knowing how much of a non-event the scan had been Jon wondered just what could possibly be achieved by seeing

Morris again. But on the other hand, why not? If the man could help in any way it was worth a try.

In his days of exploring Jon had picked up a fair idea of how the countryside around Celebration was laid out, and had even got the hang of a few bus-routes. If he caught a No.16 it would take him within a couple of minutes walk of Morris's consulting room. The only unknown was whether they'd allow a dog on the bus.

★★★

The receptionist was not cheered by the idea of having a dog to look after but agreed that Arnie could go out in the garden as long as he didn't dig up the new bedding plants. Jon assured her that he'd *never* do a thing like that and hustled the dog out through the door as she held it open. To be honest he hadn't the slightest idea whether Arnie's response to inactivity might be to dig anything up, but his days as a minister had taught the lesson that there were times when you had to promise things you weren't entirely sure you could deliver.

A few minutes later Morris put his head round the door of the waiting room and invited Jon into his room.

Doctor and patient sat together in what was almost a re-enactment of their first meeting ten days earlier and discussed the inconclusive outcome of the deep scan. The psychiatrist admitted that since TranzCon was quite a new development as far as Phoenix was concerned he'd been unaware of the limitations of mind scanning. For what it was worth he expressed his regret, but told Jon he hoped the beam would come on line soon so the whole matter could be sorted out once and for all.

Morris moved the conversation over to the question of whether the life-force of Jon Chandler had actually managed to travel back to Vissan, though he made it clear he had an open mind about the matter and was prepared to accept that the girl sitting opposite him was actually who *she* claimed to be. He admitted he'd been doing a bit of digging and had come up with a few relevant details. From the evidence he'd found in TranzCon's database there hadn't been a single instance of a life-force returning to the body it had just left - which was exactly as Mrs Daniels had said. Since the company had carried out 15,958 transfers in the twelve months covered by the data, the chances of Jon's story being true were very low indeed. The figures also claimed that only 0.02% of travellers had experienced a period of spirit image retention that had lasted longer than 24 hours, though Jon quickly calculated that meant it had occurred in a statistically unreliable group of just three cases.

But facts were facts, and if the statistics were to be believed the chances that Jon Chandler's life-force had whisked out into the ether and then returned to the body it had come from were only slightly in excess of none at all. It was an event that was totally unprecedented and the evidence available pointed to the fact that he really was Jana Kell.

Jon was almost beginning to believe the story himself, but no matter how hard he tried to convince himself he was a delusional Jana Kell, he still felt he was Jon Chandler. After all, the fundamental requirement of an unprecedented event was that it was something that hadn't happened before. There was always a first time for everything.

He was deep in thought when Morris next spoke.

'Mr Chandler, as you can see I have limited facilities here, but I do much of my work at the Marion Clinic and I could offer you a continuation of my services if you were to become an in-patient there. It's a private facility and I don't mind admitting it's quite expensive, but TranzCon would meet the costs. I checked with them this morning.'

Jon was just a little suspicious and played for time.

'I don't know the Marion, but I'm suspecting it's a mental hospital.'

Morris stroked his chin and turned his gaze towards the ceiling.

'These days we prefer to call it, a psychiatric clinic.'

Jon smiled.

'But its purpose is the same isn't it? I can imagine what they'd do there, lock me up and fill me so full of drugs I *really* wouldn't know who I was. Thanks, but no thanks.'

Morris looked back towards Jon.

'It is your choice Mr Chandler, and if you do change your mind you can always phone me. Just call the main TranzCon number and they'll be able to put you through.'

'And that's it then?'

Morris shrugged. 'I am truly sorry we have not been able to help you more than we have, but you must understand, there is nothing more we can do unless you are prepared to give the clinic a try.'

★★★

Jon thanked the doctor and left, remembering to pick up Arnie on the way out. From the glimpse he saw of the garden the little dog must have passed his time sitting on the grass or sleeping because there was no sign of devastation. The receptionist made no comment.

59

Trouble Brewing?

As Jon strolled along gazing in near disbelief at an array of animals he could scarcely comprehend he realised that after two weeks of unbroken warm weather he no longer felt quite so self-conscious about how he appeared to the world. Men looked, as men would do, but as long as they were doing nothing more he was safe. So with a mind that was just a little more at ease he was able to enjoy the way spring had transformed the city, bringing it alive with colour. He looked around at flowerbeds and bushes bursting into life, and the sprouting of leaves on the trees that had brought a welcome return to a land of green. Cycles, everything had to go in cycles. It was only the long months of a bare and barren winter that made people truly appreciate the glory of warmer times.

In search of something to do other than walk Arnie in the park Jon had taken himself off on a tram ride out to Celebration's city zoo, way over on the far side of the city. With a ten minute stop at the city terminus the journey had taken almost an hour, but the ride was comfortable and the fare cheap. He hadn't been to anything like a zoo since the time he'd gone with Celia and Robert to the wildlife park out in the countryside near Linden. That must have been over thirty years ago, a thought which brought both happy and sad memories into his mind. Perhaps if he'd married a woman who'd been more focussed on family than a career he might have seen zoos and all manner of child friendly places - instead of offices and meeting rooms. And then another thought came into his mind, a thought which hurt just a little. Maybe if he'd been at home playing with the grand-children he'd never had he wouldn't have found it necessary to travel way out across the galaxy. Maybe he'd never have known anything of the life of Jana Kell.

Somehow the thought spoiled the rest of his day.

***

By the time the tram had got him back to the city centre the bus service out to Rokham Park had dropped to one an hour and as luck wouldn't have it that day he'd arrived at the stop just in time to see a big blue rear end disappearing round the corner. There was no point hanging around for the next one because he could walk it in twenty minutes, despite being just a little tired from his long day out.

But luck was still not on his side that evening and as he trudged past the rows of deserted shops the skies opened and drenched him to the skin. Well the day had been so nice when he'd set out he hadn't thought to take any sort of clothing for rain. By the time he'd fumbled with the key in the lock and climbed the stairs to the haven of Flat 6 he was not best pleased. Despite the nice time he'd had, somehow he'd been on edge all day even before the rain had started - ratty for no reason at all. When Arnie jumped up to welcome him home it had been almost the final straw and for just one second he'd had to hold himself back from kicking the little stupid little mutt.

Dinner was already in the fridge - the leftovers from last night's meal, just as that had been the leftovers from the day before. He left the meal heating in the microwave while he changed out of his wet stuff and ran the dryer over the girl's long hair. Fifteen minutes later he was in front of the TV chasing away the last pangs of hunger. At last his appetite had made it to Phoenix though how it had got there without the beam he couldn't think. Was it even possible for a physical feeling to come through a transfer?

Then came a decision - should he get on with the washing up, or just settle back in the chair for the evening? The slug option was tempting but there was still ten minutes to go before the programme he wanted to watch, so he decided he'd at least make a start, even if he didn't manage to finish the drying up. He set to and was washing the pots when one of the soapy plates slipped out of his hand and dropped back into the bowl. He heard a sound as it dropped beneath the surface and guessed something down there in the bowl had broken. "Shit" he exclaimed, to no-one but himself.

Putting his hand down into the water to investigate he suddenly felt the sharpest of pains. He pulled it out quickly to see blood dripping down into the suds, turning the inside of the bowl to a bright crimson foam. He called out in pain and with the frustration of knowing he'd done what so easily could have been avoided. In his anger he grabbed a clean plate from the rack and smashed it down on the draining board. The sight of the broken plate annoyed him even more and he grabbed a cup and threw it across the room. It hit the wall and exploded into a hundred pieces. The sight and sound of the cup breaking only drove him onwards into a madness he'd never known before.

With every smash his anger rose and he grabbed each item of crockery one at a time, breaking them in ever more violent ways. Only when the bowl and the rack were empty did he turn his attention away to look for some other inanimate object on which to vent his anger.

And then he realised his stupidity. He bashed his hands down onto the draining board, and banged again and again until both of them throbbed with pain. And all the while he cursed out loud, caring nothing for the neighbours below. Finally he stopped when the girl's legs gave way and he slumped down onto the lino - and burst into tears.

He hadn't cried since he was nine.

And that wasn't the end of it. Any time at all it happened again. The slightest thing that went wrong, *anything* that went wrong, slipped him back off into the madness. This wasn't the real Jon, this wasn't how he lived his life - this was life living him.

David Hulett Wilson

60

Any Progress?

Jon had been out to the park with Arnie and on their way home they'd stopped off at the corner shop to pick up a few tins of dog food. While he was in the queue waiting to pay he noticed a magazine on a rack by the side of the till. The front cover showed a picture of an ultraband transmitter floating majestically in the stillness of space with the crescent of Delano, the Phoenixan moon, placed artistically in the background. Whether the photo was real or the result of some neat software Jon couldn't say, but the headline that read "Beam Off-Line for 1000 years" was more than simply eye-catching. He wondered about the reliability of a trashy rag, but there was no way his day would be complete without reading it.

When Arnie was tucking ravenously into his disgusting bowl of sloppy meat Jon sat himself down in what had become his favourite chair and opened the pages of the magazine. He scouted through the contents page discovering, as so many before him had, that the words so large on the front cover were close to impossible to locate inside the magazine. Finally he spotted what he was looking for and flicked to the pages he hoped were going to be overly pessimistic.

The article revealed with self-appointed authority the latest speculations of their well connected but undisclosed source working deep under cover in the ivy covered halls of academia. For thousands of years the region of space out towards Darius had been densely packed with a concentration of particles that had almost completely cut off Union space from Phoenix - and not, Jon noted, the other way around. Back in the days when telescopes had been the only means of discovering the remoter regions of space the so-called cloud had blocked some areas of the galaxy from view, and now it was blocking the transmissions of the gravitron beam as well.

On the planets which later became the early members of the Union, technological advance had been rapid in the early days after colonisation and it had been only a matter of time before larger and larger telescopes were developed to probe the universe, hundreds of lightyears out into space. But for over two thousand years, sightings in the areas beyond Darius had been strictly limited compared to the discoveries made in the other directions. Then entirely by chance, when such a sighting had been least expected, an old telescope relocated from Vissan to Darius had *discovered* Phoenix.

The article went on to paint a scene of a huge cloud of matter drifting slowly for millions of years through space. All that had happened on the day of the discovery was that a brief parting of the cloud had opened up in the area of space between Darius and Phoenix. Compared to the age of the universe, the fifteen years that passed before the cloud reformed to close off the opening was a single tick of the clock that had run since the beginning of time. No-one doubted that other gaps in the cloud might one day open to allow Darius to be seen once more, but who could tell if it was going to be in a hundred years, a thousand years, or maybe not even for a million years.

It seemed quite likely that the article was based on little more than speculation, but nonetheless its tone worried him deeply. No-one could say for sure if it was right, but neither could they say it was wrong. The thousand years claimed by the article still sounded unnecessarily pessimistic, but compared to a human lifespan of little more than a single century, even a hundred years was depressing enough.

★★★

It was becoming obvious to Jon that if he was ever going to get home he needed to know more about the progress GBeam were making to get the service back on line. The media didn't say much now it wasn't hot news any more, and the only reports on progress were relegated to a few lines buried deep inside the newspapers, just before the obituaries.

Was there really a chance, or was it hopeless? As far as most citizens of Phoenix were concerned the only issue was knowing when they were going to be able to get back to viewing the Union soaps they'd got hooked on. But to Jon the difference meant quite a lot more. What he needed was an inside source of information, but that was easier said than done. Breaking in at dead of night to infiltrate the company's secrets was a sure fire way of being given the opportunity to do a detailed study of the inside of four grey walls, so whatever he did had to be legal. Well, *legalish* if not entirely above board. But what? If Jana had possessed any relevant technical qualifications he might have been able to get a job there, and the money would have been useful too. But with all the education she had to offer he knew he'd be lucky to get in as a cleaner.

Then an idea came into his head. He remembered back to a time at university when the students had been tasked with choosing an organisation to study, and then making an attempt to get the company to invite them inside. The answer was obvious, all he needed were the balls to lie convincingly enough.

He fired up the laptop and checked a few addresses from the internet and the next time he was in town he stopped into the Grenville Massey technical college. The staff in the admissions department were more than happy to supply him with a whole carrier-bag full of information about the courses he could study there, and he thanked them very much. On the way home he spent most of his daily allowance buying a scanner/printer and a pack of the store's best quality paper. It took a bit of work to kick the software into submission, but later that evening he was able to turn out quite passable letter-headed stationary for the college, including a full colour representation of two lions rampant, something called a portcullis and a motto in some archaic language.

From the course literature he'd accumulated he chose "Communications Engineering" and made a note of all the lecturers whose names it might be useful to drop if the occasion demanded. Finally he wrote a very pleasant letter asking for the opportunity to come and see what went on at the heart of the most important communications centre on the planet. And he signed it "Amanda Knighton".

***

A few days later as he was coming back from an early morning walk with Arnie Jon checked the mailbox for Flat 6 and found a letter inside. The first line of the address read "Ms A. Knighton" so he knew it could only have come from one source. Upstairs in the flat he ripped the envelope open and there inside was what he'd been hoping to see - an invitation to visit GBeam, with a date set for Friday the following week.

61

Lady Day

A few weeks after the twins' thirteenth birthday a stranger came to call at the big house. Someone unknown, though not unexpected. Feared just a little, but welcome non-the-less. The fulfilment of a desire to leave an age of innocence behind. For one of the young Chandlers she would herald the dawn of a new life, and perhaps a hope for the future.

Now Jon knew, this time when the friend came to visit, she was looking for him.

★★★

The box of "things" had stood on the window sill for long enough now that Jon was able to think the word "tampon" even if he wasn't prepared to say it out loud yet. He could feel something was happening deep inside the girl's body and somehow he knew it was going to happen soon, but what exactly? The enemy unseen was the scariest of all.

For days now poor Arnie hadn't been getting much exercise because Jon had felt tied to the flat, unwilling to go far from the sanctuary of a toilet, running water and a fresh change of clothes. But when was it going to happen? He was scared half to death, so the first time he felt a throb of something deep inside he actually felt a sense of relief. But when he looked there was no blood, not yet anyway.

Then he thought of how stupid he'd been, for fuck's sake, why hadn't he asked Jasmine? He knew the answer already, he didn't want to. It was happening now and he'd find out soon enough.

There was some pain. Sometimes a dull ache that seemed to spread through the whole of the girl's abdomen, and sometime a bit of a spasm. Not that bad, but bad enough that all he could do was to sit on the sofa and stare at the wallpaper. When blood actually arrived he felt as though a weight had been lifted from him.

62
Jasmine's Shift

The phone rang. Jon wondered why people always waited till the person they were trying to contact was busy with something, like cleaning their teeth. Quickly he spat out the white fluid and rushed through to the sitting room. Jasmine wanted to meet him, so Jon suggested her place in half an hour. He needed to take Arnie out so they'd be able to come through the park. Jasmine changed it to 45 minutes because she needed to get some stuff from the shops.

★★★

In the end it was Jon who got there first because when he rang the bell there was no reply. He pulled out his mobile to give her a try, but before he could even dial the number Gary came up from behind and gave him a hug. Jon looked at him wondering whether to remonstrate, but decided it was better to let it go.

The young man walked up to the door, felt in his pocket and said something under his breath that might possibly have been "shit". Jon watched as he bent down to the flowerpot by the side of the door and pulled the plant and the soil out with his right hand while his left hand went in and brought out a package of cooking foil. He turned back towards Jon.

'Emergency key, just in case. Keep it to yourself.'

A couple of minutes later Jasmine arrived and Jon could see straight away that she looked a little downhearted. After the sisterly hug that Jon enjoyed more than any sister ever had she explained the reason why.

'It's our mother Jon, well mine and Jana's. The nursing home phoned yesterday to tell me she's on the critical list. She could go any time. I need to be with her so I'll be staying at the home for a while.'

Jon told her how sad he was to hear the news, but although he occupied Jana's body and certainly sympathised with Jasmine, the girls' mother was no relation so it was not for him to get involved.

Jasmine explained her problem.

'I'm due to go back up to the Hyperion for my shift next Wednesday and I don't want to lose the job. But if I'm at Mum's place there's no way I can make it.'

Jon saw straight away the reason she'd wanted to see him.

'I think I can work out what this is all about. You want me to take your place on the ship?'

Jasmine's face brightened a little.

'You're a mind-reader Jon. Will you do it?'

It wasn't a voluntary action, but an observer would have seen the girl's eyebrows raise.

'Well it worries me just a bit because I'm not sure I can pull off being you. But I'll tell you now, I'd give anything to be able to go back up and see my old ship, even if I do have to work.'

'You can have the money for the work you do Jon, that's OK. What's important to me is that you keep the job going so I can take over when it's my next shift.'

'OK then, but you're going to have to tell me all about what you do there, and I'll need to know about the people I'm working for and working with. Even if I manage to look like you some of them might spot a change in personality.'

'Well it helps that they don't know I've got a twin sister, so what're they going to think when you're a bit different. The worst they can do is to test you for drugs, and, well …. I assume you don't do drugs, so you'll be clean. Tell them your mother's seriously ill, that'll explain it. They can check the details and find it's true.'

'What about Arnie? He's going to need feeding and walking.'

'I'll take him with me, Mum'll be pleased to see her little dog.'

★★★

Jasmine explained everything about her job, joining the shuttle-flight up to the ship, security procedures, who were the key staff, where they ate and where they slept. All standard stuff Jon would have to know. The job was nothing complicated, but he already knew that. She continued.

'The big thing is, you're going to have to look like me - the hair, the clothes and everything. But on the other hand, we don't want you going about looking like me for days on end so if you come round to the flat I'll do you a makeover the night before you go up into orbit. You can even sleep here so the security camera outside sees you leaving from the right place next morning.'

Jon still had no idea why Jasmine had chosen to make herself look so different from her sister. Maybe after years of being mistaken for her she'd suddenly had the idea of making herself as different as possible. Perhaps he'd ask her sometime.

'Are you planning on cutting Jana's hair short?' he asked.

'Oh sod, I hadn't thought about that. It'd take months to grow again and Jana's going to be a bit narked if she comes back to find it all chopped off. Look, I often wear a hat, so if we just trim it a bit and dye it black you can wear the hat and people won't notice anything different. And if anyone sees you with long hair you can say you always had it like that under the hat.'

'And what about the facial hardware? Jana's not going to want holes all over her face.'

'Sod again. Look we'll just get you some big earrings and if anyone asks, tell them the holes were going septic and you're letting them heal up.'

'What if they get close enough to see there aren't any holes?'

'If they get *that* close you could try taking them to bed.'

***

On his way back home Jon wondered about what he was letting himself in for. Going up to the ship was no problem, and he was desperate for the chance to get back on board, but apart from his recent efforts with Jana's flat the last time he'd done any cleaning was while he was living in a student house. That was 37 years ago and he hadn't been very good at it. What a cleaner he was going to turn out to be.

63

GBeam

The date set by GBeam for Jon's visit had worked out quite well in the end even though he now knew it would be his final day on the planet before heading up into orbit. He dressed the girl's body up a little smarter than normal, but really it only went as far as putting on her best jeans instead of her dog walkers. After all, Amanda Knighton was supposed to be a student so he didn't want to overdo things.

★★★

Jon had prepared himself by putting together a questionnaire and had printed off several copies to use as the basis for his interviews. Now all he needed were a few co-operative members of GBeam's staff to supply the data to fill them in. People were peculiar. It was funny how they'd supply information for something official like a questionnaire that they would otherwise jealously guard.

★★★

Most of the staff in the office at were friendly, though he could see there were some who'd be too busy everyday between now and the end of the universe to bother with a mere student. He just had to hope that he'd find one or two who really knew what they were on about who had half an hour to spare. And then he realised, if he did find the person he was after they would almost certainly be male because only a man was going to fall for the charms of the pretty girl who'd come to chat to him. For the first time Jon began to appreciate the power an attractive woman possessed. The ability to get what she wanted using methods quite different from the way he was used to operating was obviously a very useful talent, and he wondered how many times he'd fallen for that ploy himself.

After speaking with a few people that morning the next on the list the receptionist had suggested was a Dr James Grant - almost certainly another of the balding or grey-haired old profs the place seemed have in abundance. As it turned out he couldn't have been more wrong because the man who walked into the room was no older than his late twenties, and the healthy mop of ginger locks that adorned the young head showed no signs of blocking up any plugholes for a few years yet. The man's luxuriant beard gave him a slightly geeky look and Jon quickly sussed that he wasn't quite as confident as the older men he'd met, but he was pleasant to talk to and was quite forthcoming with a few useful snippets of information.

When the questionnaire was complete the man could have got up and walked out as the others had done, but this one didn't seem to be in a hurry to leave. Jon played along and as they spoke he was aware of the way James had noticed the girl's attractive body because he saw how the man lost track of what he was saying each time he curled a lock of Jana's long hair around her finger. And after the first time he'd taken a deep breath as he'd re-settled the girl's body into the chair he decided he'd better not do it again in case the guy had a small accident.

After the extended interview had gone on for another fifteen minutes Jon had begun to get the distinct impression that James was coming up with more and more information just to keep things going. With no experience in matters like these, well not from this side of the net anyway, Jon was desperate to encourage the man, though equally he didn't want to overdo it. When James finally plucked up the courage to suggest he'd be able to tell *her* more if they met after work sometime Jon knew the fish was on the line, so it was more than just a little annoying that he needed that evening to get ready for his trip up to the Hyperion.

With a bit of quick thinking he told James he had to go and visit his sick mother while his sister was away at work. But he set a date for them to meet afterwards.

64

The Hyperion

With clothes he could best describe as *striking* and makeup that was garish, Jon felt more conspicuous than ever. The thought "if only your mother could see you now" came into his head, but he hustled it quickly into the back cupboard of his mind so it could pass some time with the resident skeletons.

Doing his best to ignore the stares of the passengers travelling with him in the train he looked out of the window and watched the world as it sped by. Ever since he'd first arrived on Phoenix he'd kept to the original contract and not ventured beyond the city limits of Celebration, and now he was taking his host body quite a bit further than anyone had expected. But after all the time he'd been stuck here he felt justified in varying the terms just a little.

The train traced its route through the former industrial wasteland of the city, now redeveloped as shopping malls and trading estates before reaching the inter-city line where it quickly accelerated up to its maximum speed of 350 km/hour. Even so, it would still take almost two hours to reach

Celebration's Interplanetary spaceport. It wasn't quite as local to the city as its name might have suggested.

Once beyond the city's boundary the line headed out into the countryside where only the occasional farmhouse or smallholding told the watching passenger that here was a land not entirely as the good Lady had intended. Jon watched the scenery as it flashed by and could hardly believe what he saw.

Green. It was all so impossibly green.

For eyes that had grown up accustomed to the reddy-purplish tinge of the vegetation native to Vissan the bright emerald landscape of Phoenix was a truly amazing sight. The rain that had fallen just before dawn only heightened the effect and now with the midday sun high overhead the farmland that raced by outside the windows of the train made Jon stare in wonder. He promised himself he'd make some trips out to see the land as it really was when he got back down from orbit.

Feeling nervous he checked his pockets again to make sure he'd got everything. The picture on the security card showed a woman with dark hair, makeup that was well OTT, and quite a few items of facial metalwork that were somehow supposed to enhance a woman's appearance. Was it changing times that had left him behind, or was it just this planet? The diamond stud in the nose he could possibly have gone along with, but the things in the eyebrows were just downright ugly. Ignoring the more obvious features of the disguise Jasmine had chosen for him to wear he looked hard at the photo to see how her face compared with her sister's. There were a few differences he had to agree - Jasmine's nose was straight and true, something that gave her face a prettiness that the slight kink in Jana's stole away. Even her teeth at the front were just that little bit straighter. It was funny how fate had smiled more on one supposedly identical twin than the other, but the differences were minimal. If he kept the girl's lips together and angled her face just slightly to the right even the most observant of recognition programmes would be fooled.

He'd get the chance to find out soon. If his nerve held he'd be on the spaceplane in just a few hours time, and the flight up into space wasn't something he'd ever experienced before. After the first of the elevators had gone into service on Miranda a few years before he was born it had been the end of the line for conventional methods of reaching orbit, at least as far as the home planets were concerned. Not many more years had passed before they'd opened elevators on the first of the outer planets, and now only Daluun, Antonby and Nehrad required shuttle spaceplanes to gain access to long range vessels. This trip was going to be both exciting and exhilarating.

★★★

The train entered a cutting and dived down into the tunnel that ran underneath Celebration Interplanetary and almost immediately it began to decelerate. Jon knew the station was just minutes away so he collected his belongings together ready to disembark.

Stepping out into the station that lay deep under the spaceport he followed the signs that lead him to the escalators that brought him back up into the daylight. From what Jasmine had told him the KAL terminal was way over on the western side of the port and he'd need to catch the company bus to get there. The right stop took a bit of finding but the collection of "KAL" coats standing waiting inside a shelter told him he'd come to the right place. The people paid him only the slightest attention as he joined them.

It was no surprise to find the group included more men than women, and almost all of them appeared to be older than Jana and Jasmine, but each face in the line wore the same weary expression that said no-one was looking forward to another ten days hard slog.

A few minutes later a battered looking bus appeared from round the corner and pulled up at the stop. The yellow and blue livery down each side advertised to all who saw it that the vehicle belonged to Knight Aerospace, though in truth the condition of the old machine made a statement about the company the management might have preferred to have kept under wraps. The line of workers shuffled up to the doors and climbed aboard. The doors gave a wheeze and the bus lurched into motion.

★★★

Ten minutes later the vehicle jerked to a halt and disgorged its travellers outside KAL's private and minimalist terminal. The entry to the building was unrestricted but as he'd been told to expect, just inside the entrance of the building stood a line of automated security barriers. Jon joined on at the back of the queue.

The security card went in and a light came on to say the machine was accessing its data. Jon looked straight into the camera that motored itself down to align with the girl's face. This was the first test and Jon was already a little nervous. When fifteen seconds had passed without any kind of response he felt the girl's heart beating heavily. After thirty seconds he was ready to turn and run away, wondering whether the machine had made a silent call to security and a heavily armed counter-terrorist hit-squad was on its way to arrest him. He breathed a sigh of relief when the machine emitted a satisfying "beep" and the two halves of the glass barrier in front of him slid apart.

Taking his cue from the more experienced travellers he followed the throng through the lounge until they reached another set of doors which lead back out into the open. A ride on a more modern vehicle took them out to a pad where stood the sleek shape of the Knightsky II - the big spacebird that was to complete their commute into orbit.

Jon joined the line waiting patiently at the bottom of the stairs. Then at last it was his turn and he climbed up, ducked in through the low hatch and stowed his rucksack in the luggage cage. By the time he was in his seat and had clicked all five ends of the complicated harness together the hatches had closed and the engines were whining into life. When the revs increased the plane taxied slowly off its stand and headed out to the runway. And stopped.

In silence the whole plane waited, listening carefully to the sound of the engines and the change in note that told them they were ready to depart. The plane moved forward, slowly at first. Then came the roar as the engines burst into life. Jon felt the push in his back as the speed increased, and then the lifting sensation as the craft pulled up into the air to begin its ascent.

From its external appearance the spaceplane was similar to those that had been in use throughout the Union for hundreds of years. Once a design had been fully developed and optimised there was nowhere to go. Perhaps the biggest difference was that this craft used more basic Phoenixan technology and was still running on liquid fuel whereas the more modern Union spaceplanes operated on ultrafuel, a solid substance with over fifteen times the energy density of liquid fuels. The main disadvantage of its capsule packaging was that only what was on board when the plane left the ground was available to boost it up into orbit. In contrast a liquid fuelled plane could get off the ground fairly light and take on the bulk of its load once it was in the air.

The climb to 12,000 metres where they met the tanker was quite leisurely and no faster than the flight of a conventional airliner. When the tanks were full and the larger plane had dropped away Jon heard the engine note rise and the plane resumed its climb until it reached 25,000 metres - and then there was silence as the compressors shut down. Only an eerie whistle from the thin air that rushed past the fuselage penetrated into the passenger cabin. But the calm was only brief. When the engines re-ignited on their stored supply of liquid oxygen the acceleration that followed was almost bone-crushing. The nose pulled up to a crazy angle and the plane began its climb out of the atmosphere and up into orbit.

When the acceleration finally ended and the noise of the engines subsided once again the experience had changed completely. Now the girl's stomach felt as if it wanted to float up to the ceiling to join the archipelago of sandwich crumbs he saw bobbing weightlessly just above his head. He watched them as they hung in the air, moving upwards, slowly at first, then putting on a spurt as the overhead filter-vent sucked them in.

★★★

Jasmine had told him quite a lot about the work she'd been doing on the ship and the people she'd been working with. Most of the time she did her work alone so none her co-workers knew her very well and were unlikely to spot Jon as an interloper. And that summed up life on board. A job in orbit sounded glamorous, but working, sleeping and eating were the only activities anyone ever undertook on their tour of duty. The long hours of toil left little time for socialising and the supervisors who checked up on the workers throughout the day were quick to point out that anyone who didn't like it could easily be replaced. For every one of the workers on board a dozen hopefuls were waiting to take their place.

When the pilot made the announcement that the plane would be docking soon Jon turned away from the window and studied the seatback screen in front of him. There was the Hyperion, dead ahead, shining like a bright star in the sunlight. Thirty years ago the new breed of fusion powered ships had looked so odd and had even been considered ugly compared to the established designs of the day. And yet over the years opinions had changed. Anyone who'd ever seen a ship from close quarters had come to associate the look with power, opulence and majesty. For Jon it was always a moment of pride. He'd seen the Hyperion and her sister ships so many times, and yet somehow he always looked out with awe at the way the huge vessel looked magnificent, hanging in the sky, the vast annuli of its reactor torus and accommodation ring turning slowly around and around.

The spaceplane slowed as it approached the docking bay in the rotating hub of the ship. Then came the nauseating feeling as the wingtip thrusters fired and the rotation of the hub stopped - or rather the Knightsky II had joined the same carousel. With careful slowness the nose of the plane edged into the docking bay until the passengers felt a jolt as the docking clamps bumped into place.

And that was the easy bit over. Now it was back to the scramble for the luggage and the hatch, and the good old fun of trying to get around in weightless conditions. Fortunately the task of exiting the plane was made easier by the grab-rail that had lowered from the ceiling and now the passengers were rising up out of their seats to get a firm grip. Jon waited his turn before joining the line and as he reached the luggage cage he pointed to Jasmine's rucksack so the stewardess could pass it up to him. In freefall the rucksack weighed nothing at all so he hooked the strap round the girl's left foot and towed it behind him into the hub of the liner.

Outside the plane the grab-rail split into two separate routes so Jon chose the branch that appeared to have the least number of people on it. Now he was in the queue for the clock-on machines and there was nothing to do but wait patiently in line. Finally his turn came and he pulled himself over to the machine, pushed the security card into the slot, posed for the camera, and listened for the bleep that told him and the company's accounting system that Jasmine Kell was back on the payroll.

Taking hold of the grab-rail again Jon pulled himself along to the cabin of the spoke elevator. Why it was he'd never known, but everything that had indicated which way was supposed to be "up" in the docking bay and the hub's entrance hall suddenly turned through 180 degrees when he reached the elevator - the seats appeared to be on the ceiling. If a stomach wasn't feeling too happy before its owner floated into the elevator the sudden reversal of up and down was probably going to be the final straw, and "accidents" had been known to happen.

At last the cabin was full and Jon felt the slight jog as the journey out to the rim began, and with every metre the capsule travelled he experienced the strange sensation as the gravity created by the Hyperion's rotation slowly built up. When the effect had reached its peak at 75% of Vissan standard the terms "up" and "down" re-assumed their conventional meanings - and the seats that had appeared to be on the ceiling turned out to be on the floor after all.

★★★

As he walked out of the elevator into the vast open space of the accommodation doughnut Jon looked up in wonder at the amazing interior of Rapier's first ship and remembered back to his last journey on one of the old Hyperion class vessels. As always the view presented to a passenger coming on board was simply weird until the brain adjusted and made allowances for what the eyes were telling it. The immense cavern that seemed to be flat in one local position curved up and away in both directions until the line of the inner surface cut off the view of the far distance.

The modern tru-grav ships that had replaced the Hyperion class were so different with their single flat decks that provided a range of advantages compared to the older ships. Without the rotating motion of the accommodation ring, ball sports had instantly become possible and the largest craft now boasted their own golf-course. Within a few years the new design of ship had become a standard feature on the home planets runs and many of the busier routes to the outers, so it was only on the less trafficked routes that the last few examples of the earlier ships were still to be found in passenger carrying service. But the older ships were far from life-expired and many of them were still in service, though most operated as unmanned freighters.

A major player in the transport services of their own planetary system Phoenix Space Logistics had seen a gap in the market and set up an intersolar division to provide a service between their home planet and Darius. All they'd needed was a ship, but with business building up on the Union's outer-planets routes the chances of getting hold of one of the latest generation vessels were slim. In any case, the projected passenger numbers on the Phoenix route would never have generated sufficient revenue to pay back the huge cost of a brand new liner. So the answer to both problems had been obvious - they'd bought up an old freighter for what was reported to be a bargain basement price, and now they were in the process of refurbishing it to its former glory.

Jon gazed around at his old ship and wished he had the time right then and there to set off on a mission of re-discovery. But he was here to work so it was something that would have to wait. He groaned at the thought of tomorrow's

06.00 AM start - it was a lot earlier than he'd needed to be up for quite a while.

The food in the workers' canteen was basic, but it filled a hole and it was free. As he left he picked up a couple of sandwiches to eat for breakfast next morning. Now he just had to find his way to somewhere Jasmine called home. She'd given him instructions to help him find his way to the three blocks where she'd been working and in any case there were direction signs to guide anyone making the journey on foot. He could have taken the shuttle-rail to speed up his journey, but the pleasure of a walk in the warmth of the evening, watching as he went the circumferential light tube as it dimmed down to its night-time illumination level was much more fun. Finally he arrived at Myrtle block and climbed the stairs to the first floor - and there as promised was the room where Jasmine had stayed on her visits to the ship.

In the positions he'd held over the years, both within Rapier and now in his ministerial role Jon had never considered any class of travel other than First, so apart from a brief look round when the Hyperion had first been commissioned he'd not too much idea of what to expect in Standard. But he had to admit, it wasn't bad. The room was large and well equipped though it lacked the separate bedroom and living area that were to be expected in First. The carpet had a deep, soft pile, the sofa was big and comfy looking, and over on the far side of the coffee table was a huge chair that rocked and swivelled. Or at least it would have for someone whose feet reached all the way to the floor. The bed at the far end of the room was almost a prairie of sleeping accommodation. For only a little over half the cost of travelling in First this lower class offered a very good deal indeed. Perhaps the biggest drawback was that the accommodation blocks here in Standard went up to six floors whereas those in First never went higher than four. It was true that the top floors often had better views, but with their closer proximity to the ship's hub the gravity effect was noticeably reduced so they were unpopular with most passengers and the ones on the lower floors always filled up first.

★★★

Morning came - far too soon. Jon yawned and stretched when the alarm went off. He'd have given anything for another half-hour of shut-eye but he knew he had to get up and get on with the job. Jasmine had warned him that the time he was most likely to see a supervisor was early on the first day of a new shift, and instant dismissals were not unknown.

Twenty minutes was more than enough for a cup of coffee and a sandwich, but it didn't leave much time to apply the make-up he needed to pass as Jana's twin.

As Jasmine had explained the task before him was in Juniper, Myrtle and Rose blocks: cleaning the rooms ready for occupation, checking on the condition of the carpets, curtains, beds, mattresses, bedding, and towels; and ordering up any replacements she thought were necessary. Sometimes the rooms would need a full redecoration, so another part of her work was to assess the condition and decide whether to call in the team for a full job, or to just do a bit of touching up of the paintwork herself. All the workers had been made well aware of how tight the budget was so the instruction was to save money wherever possible, especially in Standard class where Phoenix Intersolar had adopted the idea of presenting a trendy "old hotel" look. In any case, Jasmine and her counterparts had a vested interest in keeping as much of the well-paying work to themselves.

Work - that was the bit about the jaunt into space Jon hadn't fancied. In his life in business and then in politics he'd been no stranger to burning the midnight oil, so long hours didn't bother him. But cleaning? Actually getting his hands dirty? It wasn't something he was keen on, and after ten minutes of pushing a vacuum up and down he was already starting to get bored. He looked at his watch and wondered how long it would be before he could justify stopping for his first coffee break.

Perhaps it was the first hour that was hardest because as the day went by he started to get more of a feel for the job and saw some purpose to his work. After doing a check on some of the rooms in Rose block which were just as they'd been left years ago when the ship had been converted to its role as a freighter he could see exactly what needed to be done. The rooms hadn't been trashed of course, the kind of person who travelled interstellar wasn't into anything like that, but he could see the way the relentless wear and tear had reduced them to a condition he could best describe as jaded. By the time his day's work ended Jon was feeling very much better about the whole thing and had taken on board the old idea that if a job was worth doing, it was worth doing well. And he was tired from his labours so he was certainly ready for a sit down and a meal in the canteen that evening.

When supper was over there were still a few hours free before he needed to get off to bed, so at last he had a chance to explore round the ship. Of course there was far too much to see in just a single evening, but if he did a bit each day he'd have visited the whole of the ship before it was time to board the shuttle-flight back down to Phoenix.

He headed out from the canteen wondering which way to go. There was so much to see but the obvious place to start was the downtown area so he took the shuttle-rail to save a little time and got off just outside the Holopera house. Rapier had been lucky thirty years ago because the technology to put on mass performances of all the great operas using hologram players and scenery had come to fruition just a couple of years earlier. There'd been many who'd dismissed the whole thing as a gimmick, and others who'd complained it was doing real opera performers out of a job, though no-one could deny that the actors got royalties each time their performance was played. A star-liner was never going to carry an entire opera cast anyway so the idea of bringing the hologram projection system on board had been a masterstroke.

And of course the hall hadn't catered only for high end culture. The technology lent itself just as readily to any kind of performance that could be recorded, so rock concerts and musical shows were among the other popular events available to long haul passengers. There was always some performance to enjoy every night of a voyage on the new Hyperion class ships. How much business it had taken from Rapier's rivals Jon couldn't even have guessed.

Walking on, he passed through the maze of tiny streets that clustered around the market area of an old grand city that had been frozen in time for hundreds of years. The little boutique shops, the arts and crafts stores, and the market stalls stood in stark contrast to the glitzy shopping mall he knew was just a little further down the street, though its modern features were carefully hidden from the gaze of the shoppers in the old town.

Then there were the restaurants, the wonderful, fabulous eating houses that Rapier had become famous for. Food was always something quite amazing on the big star-liners with virtually every form of cuisine available, and served in such a varied array of establishments. The most prestigious of the first class restaurants served nothing less than five course haute cuisine every night of the week, accompanied by entertainment from a holo-projected cabaret. At the other end of the scale a passenger could enjoy a pie and a beer in a traditional pub, or perhaps a nice salad and a glass of wine on the terrace of one of the chic bars that overlooked the parkland. For lunches the stall in the park where passengers could order a picnic to enjoy out on the lawn was always popular on the days when irrigation wasn't scheduled for daylight hours.

The irrigation, that had been a laugh. With so much parkland in need of water and a fusion reactor turning it out by the megalitre the obvious method would have been to supply it through a normal system of drip-feeders and sprinklers during the night hours when no-one was around. Then the idea of pouring it down from a high level system had been put forward, and the more the designers had thought about it, the more they'd liked it. Although it had seemed ridiculous at first the idea of experiencing what looked and felt like proper wet rainfall had only added to the real-life effect the ship was attempting to project. What had really surprised Rapier's management once the "sky-irrigation" system had gone into service was that more people came out to walk in the park on days when rainfall was scheduled than bothered to turn out for the endless days of predictably warm summer weather. And it had also meant a lucrative sideline for the shops selling umbrellas and wellie boots. But as they'd found out quite quickly, the secret of success was choosing the right ratio of wet days to dry days because if there were too many it spoiled the fun.

Heading off down a side alley Jon came to the little place that had been his favourite haunt on so many trips - the tavern where a traditional musical evening was guaranteed every night of the week. Oh if he could only go back to one of those times when he'd staggered back to his suite with several glasses of strong stout inside him.

Time was getting on so he decided to leave the smarter end of the town for another night and doubled back to the street and out into the gardens. When they'd originally planned everything they could do with the space and power of the new ships they'd thought mainly of indoor activities, as if the ship was going to be merely a top hotel with a shopping mall and a sports complex attached. But then they'd realised that the area the passengers would actually need for living, eating or recreation was only a few percent of the space available. But what to do with all the rest? In the end the answer was simple, give the passengers a taste of the great outdoors. So the gardens had always been spectacular, beds with row upon row of prize blooms, immaculately trimmed hedges, flowering shrubs, perfect lawns, urns and statues, the pretty pond with its flock of hologram ducks swimming out by a tree covered island, big wide promenade walks, and small meandering paths that headed off into the woodlands. With guaranteed weather every day passengers had even begun to wonder whether Rapier's recreation of real life was better than real life itself.

Jon walked on - he knew what he was looking for, the fruit and vegetable garden. With space being so freely available they'd even hit on the idea of growing food for the journey, though the accountants had quickly pointed out it was never going to be an economic activity. But people liked to wander around the area and plan the healthy meals they were going to change over to, starting that very evening. There'd been just one minor scandal when the news had leaked out that almost three quarters of the produce described as "garden fresh" had actually been loaded into the ship's freezers at the previous stop, but all in all the veg garden had been a rip-roaring success.

Well it was all part of the business plan. If it was necessary for someone to spend years of their life travelling through space, then Rapier's philosophy had been that those years ought to be the most pleasurable possible. When one of the many media critics had complained it was as if they were trying to create mini-planets that flew through space the marketing team at Rapier had wholeheartedly agreed and used the idea as part of their next advertising campaign.

The only significant failure had been in the ball games area. One of the early ideas had been to provide tennis courts, a five-a-side football field and even a pitch and putt golf-course - but it hadn't worked. With the artificial gravity on board being provided by the rotation of the ship, the trajectory that a ball in flight thought was a straight line was very much at odds with what the human brain had learned to expect. But they'd never forgotten the idea and now the latest ships with tru-grav featured all the activities Rapier had planned for their first generation of liners.

If ball games had been a non-starter for the Hyperion class, any other type of sport was possible so there was a circumferential track running the around the doughnut for those who chose to take their exercise on bikes or roller-blades, or for those who simply wanted to walk or run. And then there'd been the climbing wall featuring actual rocks and the slightly unrealistic feature that the going got easier as the climber went up towards the levels closer to the hub where the gravity effect was beginning to drop off.

It'd been so much fun back in those old days when the whole industry of luxury travel was in its heyday, the days before the new upstart TranzCon brashly pushed its way in to steal away the richest of the clientele. Jon sighed. If only he could have stepped out of his present life into memories of what had gone by so long ago. If only he could be transported back into those exciting days that were now slipping away into the mists of time.

Looking up to what passed as the sky he could see the illumination level was dropping and knew he'd been out for longer than he'd planned. Tomorrow would bring another long hard shift, and boy did he need some sleep. He jumped on the counter-rotation line of the shuttle-rail and rode the car back to the stop outside Myrtle block.

★★★

Next evening when Jon came out for his instalment of exploration his original plan had been to have a look at the shopping mall and the gym area, but it was as if some unseen force was guiding him towards the control and administration complex. Obviously he wasn't going to risk getting into any sort of trouble venturing into areas that were off limits to someone of a cleaner's lowly rank, but no-one could blame him for putting his head round the door to take peek inside.

He knew that once a ship was out in space the flight-deck was strictly off limits to the passengers, apart from the weekly guided tour, but while so much work was going on refurbishing the ship it was likely the whole area might be open for technicians to buzz in and out. Trying hard to remember the layout he searched around and eventually found his way into the forward observation lounge he knew was just one stop along from the flight-deck. But after a session of gently pushing doors to see which ones were locked failed to get him into the room he really wanted to visit he decided he'd have to make do with a look round the outer part of the command centre.

Although not the holy of holies, the room Jon eventually found his way into was only slightly less impressive. He looked down the seemingly endless rows of computer displays and was hit by a thought he could only describe as mischievous. He sat down at one of the terminals and typed in the log-on code he'd been issued with all those years ago when the ship was undergoing commissioning trials. The screen came up with a window asking for his password, which to his surprise he actually remembered. And the system accepted it! He was dumbstruck with the realisation that he now had high level access to all the systems on board, even the control complex, the fusion reactor and the astral navigation system. Obviously the ship's many owners had added new authorised people over the years, but somehow they'd never bothered to delete those who no longer needed access. It was something he was going to have to mention to Rapier's head of operations when he got back home.

Quickly he logged off in case someone stumbled across him meddling and demanded to know what the hell he was doing.

★★★

The alarm sounded its brazen note - again - and Jon knew the time to get up for the tenth early morning in a row had arrived. The work had been hard, but it had gone well and he'd even begun to enjoy it in the last couple of days, even to the point where he wished he could come back up and do it all over again. But it was Jasmine's job and he knew she needed the money so she'd be the one coming up next time. Now there was just one final shift to get through before he was back on the spaceplane, sitting by one of the tiny windows and watching the spectacular views as the craft made its re-entry back into the atmosphere. And he was looking forward to seeing Jasmine and Arnie too.

★★★

That evening when his work was done Jon packed his stuff into the rucksack and joined his co-workers going off-shift in the queue for the elevator. The doors opened, he found a seat and strapped himself in, and then it was the same as always - the seats that had looked right when he got into the cabin were all back on the ceiling by the time it got up to the hub. Weird, weird every single time - it was a good job he wasn't planning on eating before he got down to Phoenix because the girl's stomach was already feeling just a little queasy. He floated out and joined the people on the grab-rail waiting for their chance to clock off.

Jon's turn finally came and he pushed the card into the slot - the beep came as he'd hoped and the barrier slid open in front of him. It was just as Jasmine had said, there was more security getting off the ship than getting on, but with all the shuttles that came and went it was the only way the company could guarantee their workers would actually clock-off.

Getting on board the Knightsky II Jon just managed to grab the last window seat though it was probably only because the woman who'd had her eye on it had lost her grip on the grab-rail and was now attempting an impression of a featherless bird up at the top of the cabin. Once she got close to the ceiling she'd be able to push herself off and get back down, but for a vital twenty seconds she was out of the equation. Whether she'd looked daggers at the girl who'd nabbed her chosen place Jon never knew since he'd made a point of gazing out of the window the instant he'd got his harness fastened. A spectacular drop back into the atmosphere was coming in just a few minutes and he didn't want to miss a moment of it.

65

The Date

When the Knightsky landed and the workers were trooping off into the terminal Jon realised his time on the Hyperion had been a welcome distraction, but the life that now passed for normal was waiting for him back here on Phoenix. Nettles had to be grasped. One thing that had nagged at him during his last few days on the ship was the date he'd arranged with James because it was coming up soon and he was quite simply dreading it. He was on the verge of phoning to call it off, but how could he do it without offending the young man? He didn't think the excuse of washing the girl's hair would carry much cred.

In some ways he wanted to go ahead with the plan - the whole event was an essential fact finding mission and James did seem to be nice. But how comfortable could he be with the idea of being one to one with a horny young man while he went around looking the way Jana usually did? It was like getting ready to light a fire by dowsing yourself in petrol.

And what was the horny young man going to want from the pretty young woman? Jon knew all too well what he'd want so the thought of being on the receiving end filled him with dread. Then again, maybe he was worrying too much. Maybe James would be pleased just to be out with a girl and would be happy for things to be platonic - well at least for a first date. Maybe he was going to expect a kiss? Jon wasn't into kissing men, even the ones without beards. Perhaps he might have to let him plonk one on Jana's lips, but there was no way he was going to respond. And if the guy tried so much as sticking his tongue in the girl's mouth he'd get the bloody thing bitten right off!

What if James just couldn't control himself? He might be safe enough while they were out in public, but what if he invited himself in for coffee - when coffee was the last thing on his mind? Jon knew that in Jana's small body there was absolutely nothing he could do to fight off a fully grown male. Oh God, was this the way women had felt when they were getting ready to go out with him? Maybe he should just call the whole thing off. Call it off - and then do what, sit in front of the TV wondering about all the gen he could have picked up from James?

No, it had to be done. Steel yourself man, we're going over the top!

★★★

Having a shower and blow-drying the girl's long hair was all essential stuff though Jon knew it was just putting off the inevitable. For weeks now he'd been happy wearing jeans, or company issue overalls while he was working on the ship. But now he needed to dress up just a bit more, and he knew he was going to have to look through the drawers he'd carefully ignored until now.

He wondered about wearing a skirt, Jana certainly seemed to have a good selection. He wasn't keen on the idea at all because he'd feel stupid in one even if the onlookers just saw a woman doing things that women normally did. But what clinched it was that for a woman of Jana's height to wear a skirt some substantial heels would be essential. And that was an absolute no-no.

Checking through the wardrobe he found a pair or trousers he liked - cropped at the bottom and very stylish, in a casual sort of way. But there was no doubt they were quite a bit tighter than the jeans he'd worn so much and when he tried pulling them on over the girl's very feminine behind they proved to be quite a challenge. But in the end he made it and when he stood in front of the mirror they looked good, really good. The girl's heart skipped a beat when Jon realised just how good they did look.

Then there was a top to sort out. Fortunately Jana had a good selection and he finally decided on a nice sleeveless ribbed one with an intriguing design over the front - and the way the material pulled tight over the girl's boobs was almost immoral. Jon looked at the view of *herself* in the mirror. The immaculately brushed blond hair that hung alluringly down the girl's back, the smile from the blemish-free face, the way her feminine curves pushed out the tee-shirt. Lucky boy who was going to get his hands on that! And then he realised what he was thinking and stopped abruptly - he was scaring himself to death.

The weather was warmer now that summer had finally arrived, but the evenings could still cool down quite a bit so he needed something to go over the top. Looking through the wardrobe again he found a light coloured jacket that pulled in very nicely at the waist. And it had the advantage of hiding the line of Jana's feminine shape, so he'd be able to tone things down a bit if he needed to - like riding home in James' car for example.

★★★

It was just after seven that evening when Jon jumped to his feet and shouted a few words his mother would have preferred not to hear. James would be coming to call in twenty minutes and he remembered that the name by the side of the bell push said "Jana Kell". If James saw that name he might make some connection to Jana, or to Jon Chandler, and then the game would be up. Or he might even think he'd got the wrong house and go looking elsewhere.

Jon grabbed some paper and a pen and quickly printed, as neatly as he could manage with the girl's awkward right-handed writing "Amanda Knighton". He rushed downstairs and slipped the paper into the plastic covered slot next to the bell push.

Back upstairs in the flat he couldn't settle. No matter how hard he tried to stay calm the girl's heart was racing, and then he heard a sound outside. He looked out through the window and saw the car that had just drawn up - the time was exactly half seven. He watched as a young man got out and walked towards the front door. This was it, there was no turning back.

★★★

On his walks with Arnie, Jon had passed some nice looking bars and restaurants, and there was one which had particularly appealed to him, although he had to admit he didn't really know how to get there by road. Fortunately James knew the area quite well so it wasn't long before the two of them were sitting at a table in the garden of an old half-timbered coaching house that overlooked the green wooded valley Jon had come to love in the past few weeks. These days he wasn't one for the noise and bustle of the city, and although Jana's shapely body might have been welcomed at a bar down town he knew that wasn't his sort of place.

James was obviously relieved that the pretty girl sitting by his side had chosen a peaceful location where they could chat quietly and drink a few long cool beers in the warmth of the early summer evening. He told Jon how he'd graduated in Communications Engineering five years ago and had then joined GBeam straight out of university. Now he was part of the team that operated the orbital transmitter and receiver installations and monitored the performance of the beam. When he'd first joined he'd been working on the old narrow-band equipment, and then he'd spent some time on the new ultraband transmitter doing commissioning work after it had arrived two years ago. There was no doubt he knew as much about the system as anyone on Phoenix.

Of course, he was a most polite young man and he did pause to ask a few questions about "Amanda", but having few convincing answers to give, Jon was happy to pass on to the real business of the evening. James was obviously keen on his chosen subject so there was no difficulty steering the conversation round to the problems they were still having with the beam.

It was encouraging to hear that an investigative mission had set off a week ago to carry out a series of tests to establish why the beam no longer functioned. The vessel being used was the original narrow band GBeam transmitter that had arrived from Darius eleven years earlier and the plan was to travel towards Darius in stages and attempt transmissions back to the Phoenix ultraband receiver. The latest news was good because they'd already had a report from the ship at its first test point. A full strength signal had been received and now the ship was heading on to the second test point. The process was methodical, but Jon could see that it was going to take years before any meaningful result was obtained.

'So what could be blocking the signal?' Jon asked. 'I've been reading the bulletins and they've been speculating about a mystery planet which has suddenly got in the way. The other one is the idea of some alien race building an obstacle out in space to block the beam.'

James smiled before he spoke.

'Well, some unaccounted-for celestial object big enough to block the beam would certainly be the sort of thing that space-lane surveys couldn't have failed to find because a collision with something like that would be fatal for a ship and its crew. It's just not a real possibility. Even if there was a planet somewhere out there in interstellar space, which no-one seriously believes anyway, it would only have taken a few minutes to transit through the beam, and then it would be gone. As for the aliens, the so-called little green men? Well in thousands of years of exploration the Union has never found a non-humanoid race.'

'Except for the Meren.'

'Who?'

'Those six limbed creatures they found when they were searching for new habitable planets.'

'OK, except for the Meren, but they're still at a primitive stage, and we're not even sure if they've got what it takes to progress to a technologically advanced society, even given hundreds of thousands of years.'

'But it proves there are other races out there in the galaxy. Some of them could be technologically advanced.'

'It's possible, but so far we haven't seen any. And why would they make an attack on human society by blocking the communication beam between two planets? What would be the point?'

'They could have blocked all the beams, and we wouldn't even know about it.'

James was obviously becoming just a little exasperated.

'Mandy, yes it's true, I agree, but its not a likely method of making first contact is it?'

'What if they're building something in space and don't know they're blocking our beam?'

'But what are the chances? They just happen to pick the bit of space our beam passes through. Come on, the chances of winning the lottery jackpot three weeks running are far greater than the chance of that idea being true.'

'Could it be one of the transmitters losing power?'

Now James looked thoughtful.

'It was the first thing we thought of. We carried out all the standard tests, and our transmitter is working 100%. That's a fact.'

'So you could be transmitting fine from this end, but there might be a problem with the transmitter at Darius.'

James looked very serious as he thought for a brief moment.

'They could replace and re-commission every major component within 36 hours, that's part of the design. After that there's no reason they wouldn't be back at full power. Anyway, they've got an old narrow band transmitter still in orbit and if they'd got a serious problem with the main transmitter they'd put the old one back into service.'

'Would that work with an ultraband unit at this end.'

'It'd work fine. The units would agree on their best data rate and the ultraband would just work below its capacity. We couldn't do TranzCon with that setup, but we'd have communications.'

'So if it's not the transmitter, what else could it be?'

'The simplest explanation is that there's just a bit too much of what there normally is out in space, and it's blocking our beam.'

'But there isn't anything out in space, it's just ….. well ……. space.'

'You'd be surprised,' James said. 'There's more stuff out there than you'd think, especially in our local patch between here and Darius.'

'Is this the dark matter the media keep talking about? They're all coming up with this idea of a sort of cloud that's drifted in. Could something like that really block the beam?'

'Dark matter's a bit of an outdated term and we know much more about it these days, but even before you get down to the sub-atomic level there's quite a lot of real matter to contend with.'

'Like what?'

'Interstellar microparticles. Admittedly not much per cubic km, but there's a lot of cubic kms out there and something we know from the data collected by sampling missions is that the region between Phoenix and Darius is quite dirty as interstellar space goes, and that's what the media seem to have latched onto.'

'And is it true?'

'It's true that there are some regions of interstellar space with over eight times the particle density we'd normally expect but the affected areas are quite small as a proportion of the total route length so they don't cause any significant degradation of beam strength. The beam has to pass through some interplanetary space at each end and the density there is about ten times higher than the average for interstellar space, but the distance is a tiny proportion of the total route length so it doesn't have any noticeable effect. In any case the particle density of the route is a static situation. It would take thousands of years for it to change by any measurable degree.'

'How about if it's like the media said, but instead of the dust cloud having drifted in, what's happened is it's been there for thousands of years, then part of it thinned for a few years, then it closed up again. That would explain why the astronomers hadn't been able to see Phoenix until 15 years ago.'

'It's a great theory but I'm sure it's not true. Spotting planets way across the galaxy is a tricky business at the best of times and my guess is that it was the move of the optical array to Darius that allowed them to see Phoenix.'

'Couldn't our astronomers have seen Darius from here?'

'If we'd been looking we might have, but we weren't looking. Without FTL drive to go and visit what we'd found there was no point exploring anything beyond our own solar system.'

'So if there's been no measurable change in the particle density, how come the beam used to work and now it doesn't?'

James looked up into the branches of the big oak tree that towered over the garden. After a moment he looked down, turned towards the girl by his side and gazed deep into Jana's eyes. Jon was almost expecting a proposal of marriage, but he had to stifle a laugh when the young man spoke.

'Let's start off walking before we try running. If we consider the static situation we might learn something. The samples we have indicate an average particle spacing of 1.6 kilometres, and an average mass of 0.3 milligrams. That's not much per km, but consider the beam width and then think of travelling a whole lightyear through it. An ultraband tight focus beam is about 250 metres across, so that makes an area of somewhere in the region of 50,000 square metres. Lightspeed is about 300,000 kilometres per second, so with 8760 hours in a standard year, and 3600 seconds in an hour, that makes a lightyear about .... 9.5 thousand billion kilometres.'

Jon was a pretty bright guy, but he stared in amazement at James' ability to do maths in his head. His admiration wavered just slightly when the young man took out his phone and started tapping numbers into the keyboard. Obviously there were some calculations that went too far even for a genius. James looked up from the little screen.

'So when you take a lightyear of beam, you've got a volume of 473 billion cubic kilometres, and with an average particle density of one per 4 cubic km that gives you 118 billion particles. Multiply that by the average particle weight and you get 35.5 Tonnes of debris in the way, and that's just in one lightyear. For the full route from Darius to Phoenix it comes to 2840 Tonnes, and that's passing through what at first sight is empty space, and the mass loading is crucial to the operation of the beam. Every particle gets thrown about as the gravity wave passes through, and it helps itself to a tiny bit of energy as it does. By the time 2840 Tonnes of particles have each extracted their own infinitesimally small amount of energy, the end result is that between them they've taken out rather a lot, and that leaves a lot less signal to be detected by the receiving station. But look at it another way, if there really was nothing there you'd be able to send a beam right across the galaxy with nothing more than a decent sized torch battery.'

Jon was amazed by the calculation and didn't doubt the accuracy of the result.

'And just how much mass in the path of the beam can the equipment accept before you lose the signal?

'It depends to some extent on the nature of the particles in the way, but the normally accepted limit before signal strength drops too low is somewhere between 3000 and 3200 Tonnes.'

'So with a loading of 2840 Tonnes there wasn't much margin in reserve?'

'The margin was well below GBeam's normal design figure but for most purposes it was workable. You have to understand it's not just a straightforward matter of sustained total signal loss. The usual considerations are the data rate we can push through and the number of service dropouts we get. Fortunately the total data conveyance between Darius and here is low so we could keep plenty of stuff in the buffers and that kept TV and other non-real-time functions going. You probably won't have noticed because you don't make calls to planets in the Union, but the pricing structure makes emails and data quite cheap but it puts a loading on live phone-calls.'

Jon nodded. 'Limiting the total number of real-time calls. Would I be right in thinking that was so the number of calls interrupted by dropouts was lower?'

'Exactly. It was all aimed at keeping the number of complaints down. The only problem we had was with TranzCon.'

'Why just with TranzCon? What makes it different from other transmissions.'

'TranzCon doesn't take very long, but it's a huge transmission and they need almost the whole of the bandwidth, even with the latest generation of ultraband equipment. In fact the only services which continue during a TranzCon transfer are service telemetry and diplomatic phone calls, and even those have their video frozen at the critical moment.'

'Are you telling me that the only real reason for going to ultraband was to make TranzCon possible?'

James nodded enthusiastically.

'Absolutely. Without TranzCon there would never have been any reason to go beyond wideband anywhere in the Union. And for communication purposes the link between Darius and Phoenix was entirely adequate using the old narrowband transmitter. Of course, you can do TranzCon on wideband, but only under flat-line conditions, and travellers don't like it because even the experienced ones get knocked out for hours, and that's using the rapid dispersal drugs they developed specially for the purpose. Novices can take days before they're up and about.'

Jon thought back to the days he'd been laid up when he first arrived on Phoenix but quickly remembered to say nothing.

'Why are there dropouts if the operation is within limits?'

'We don't really know. We assume it's due to fluctuations in the loading on the beam that reduces the operating margin.'

'I thought you said the loading was static. There shouldn't be any change to the margin.'

'It's as I said before, the loading due to *real* matter is static. It's the 3 and 4sub loading that varies. We won't have any useful data for a few years yet because the ships that took the samples weren't equipped to monitor at those levels.'

'What's 3 and 4sub loading?'

'Do you know about 3sub and 4sub matter? Particles that are below the level of "real" matter?'

'Nothing. I've never even heard of them.'

'I'll take you through it, but first we've got to do a bit of ground-work.'

'Try me.'

'You know about atoms, the things that make up all real matter?'

Jon nodded.

'And you probably know about electrons, protons and neutrons, the particles that make up the atoms?'

Jon nodded again.

'And perhaps you've heard of some of the particles from the next level down? Quarks, hadrons or neutrinos?'

Jon nodded again. The lecture wasn't exciting but he hoped it was going to lead to something he needed to know.

'For a long time we only knew about the first two levels of particles down from real matter and if we were still depending on the science developed here on Phoenix that's all we'd know. Our scientists had worked out a lot but from what we know now their knowledge was only at a shallow level and many things in our understanding of the universe just didn't seem to fit together. Then the Union came along and everything changed. It was a hard pill to swallow but we had to admit they were far more advanced, and fortunately for us they didn't mind sharing their knowledge. In the system they use they call the first level of sub-atomic particles "sub", the next level down are "2sub", and now we know about "3sub" which are the building blocks of 2sub particles, and "4sub" which are the building blocks of the 3sub particles. So far no-one's come up with "5sub", but it's only a matter of time.'

'So how do all these particles affect the gravitron beam?'

'They're only particles in a very loose sense. What we know now is that the old demarcation between matter and energy just doesn't apply at this level, they're something we can't really comprehend.'

'And these really are what we used to call "Dark Matter"? The stuff that makes up 75% of everything in the universe?'

'Exactly right, except it's not dark, and strictly speaking it's not matter either, though for the lack of a better name we still call it that.'

'But it really exists?'

'It really does exist and there's lots of it, more than you can imagine. It's all around us, here on the planet or anywhere up in space.'

'But we can't see it?'

'We're not equipped to see it. You might even say that God, if he really exists, had hidden it from us. We just don't need to know about it.'

Jon picked up on the comment - he'd heard that the people of Phoenix had a male God. It was a radical idea, but that was something they could discuss another night.

'And yet we put huge efforts, and budgets, into finding out about what we didn't need to know in the first place.'

James was searching for an answer, but finally he spoke.

'I suppose we're just, you know, curious.'

'OK then, I accept what you say about these particles, but do they answer the original question and tell us why the beam to Darius doesn't work anymore?'

'All in good time Mandy. We're not trying to do a PhD over a drink, but you've got to get up to speed on some of the basics before you can understand the answer.'

Deep inside the grey matter matrix of Jana's brain Jon somehow shook his head. This guy really knew how to talk to girls, or perhaps not.

'For a start, we've got to cover the actions they have on things that affect us, like why light and radio waves go at one fixed speed and no faster.'

For someone who owned a large stake in a fleet of ships that travelled many times faster than light Jon had to admit he had sometimes wondered why light insisted on going so slowly.

'And why do they?'

'It's because of the interaction with 3sub particles. Normally any object in space, or an electromagnetic wave transmission is unaffected by any form of drag that would slow it down. So sub-light ships get up to speed and then they don't need any more power until they reach their destination. But it's not because there's nothing there to slow them, it's because they don't interact with it. It passes through them, and they pass through it. Well that works for a while, but if the object or transmission tries to go above what we call the speed of light, it stimulates a reaction in the 3sub matter.'

'Like what?'

'The particles are neither matter nor energy as we know them, and the best description we have is that they change between the two stages on a continuous basis.'

'They spend half their time as energy and half as matter?'

'Not quite, they spend *some* of their time as energy and the rest as matter. What's important is the ratio of time they spend in each of the two states. In every area of the universe there has to be a balance between matter and energy, so if something comes along to try and inject more energy, the 3sub particles compensate and spend more of their time as matter. They're still changing state all the time of course, but now they appear as matter for longer than they appear as energy. It's all in tiny amounts of course, but when you put quadrillions of them together the mass builds up and they begin to exhibit a level of gravity you can actually measure.'

Jon stifled a yawn, but tried to look interested.

'And that does what exactly?'

'Mandy, come on. It's the fundamental principle of the whole reaction! They exhibit gravity and attach themselves to the particles of the wave passing through.'

'How do they attach themselves to a wave? It's just energy.'

'Look Mandy, I'm sorry if I'm going on a bit, but I'm trying to help you to understand. I know you don't have the background but I'm doing my best. Waves are particles, and particles are waves. When you understand physics at the 3sub level it all begins to make sense.'

Jon felt the girl's brain start to spin. He wasn't sure if he was glad or sorry he didn't have that level of understanding.

'You were explaining why light always goes at exactly the same speed.'

'It's because of the reaction with the 3sub matter, it's a sort of avalanche. All the way up to lightspeed the 3sub matter has no effect, but then its like pulling the trigger on a gun. If the wave exceeds lightspeed by even the slightest amount it starts the reaction and the wave begins to collect 3sub particles in their matter state.'

'And that slows the wave down?'

'You're beginning to get it.'

'So why doesn't the wave just stop?'

'As it triggers the formation of more matter particles its energy is absorbed and it slows down, but when it slows down the 3sub matter particles revert to their energy state and give energy back to the wave.'

'So if the wave exceeds lightspeed it gets slowed down, and if it slows below lightspeed it gets accelerated?'

'It's a perfect control loop. Wave propagations always go at exactly the same speed. It's a fundamental property of 3sub matter.'

'So go on then, if lightspeed can't be exceeded, how come star-liners can go much faster?'

'A long time ago they talked about the so-called "light barrier" as if it was something that couldn't be broken, and yet even in the stone-age of particle physics the scientists of the day succeeded in accelerating beams of neutrinos to faster than the speed of light. For the first time they'd got the machinery to inject unprecedented levels of energy and they used it. They found that when you gave a neutrino enough power it could push right through the light barrier. The hinge-pin of science was overthrown in an afternoon. And it didn't just apply to neutrinos, the same principle held true all the way up to real matter and beyond.'

'You just put in so much power that the "drag" from the 3sub particles is overcome?'

'That's it. A complicated problem with a simple solution.'

'So how come they hit a real barrier at Hx2? Why won't more energy push us through that barrier so our ships could go infinitely fast?'

'The science to explain that one goes down to the next level, but it's actually no more complicated. A speed a little over what we call Hx2 just happens to be the trigger point where 4sub matter does very much the same thing as 3sub does at lightspeed. Particles remain in their matter state for longer and they drag down the speed of whatever it was that stimulated them to spend more time as matter.'

'But you said before, the light barrier was overcome just by pushing in more energy. Why can't we do the same at the Hx2 barrier?'

'No-one said you can't. It's theoretically possible, you just need enough power.'

Jon was getting interested now, the idea of a new generation of star-liners charging through the Hx2 barrier sounded like his next way of making money. Maybe a service like that could even be a rival to TranzCon. He asked the all-important question.

'How much power is enough?'

James grinned and Jon could tell it wasn't leading to the answer he was hoping to hear.

'Have a guess at this one. How did the power needed to push through the light barrier compare to the power needed for sub-light travel?'

Jon shrugged the girl's shoulders. 'You can't compare them because you didn't need power for sustained travel below lightspeed.'

'Oh but you did, it's just that it was so little that no-one noticed. Well not until they started to undertake journeys of hundreds of lightyears. Then they found that the journeys took just a little longer than they'd expected, and the reason in every case was because the ships had slowly decelerated. I'll come to the point, the power needed to exceed lightspeed was trillions of times more than the power needed for sub-light travel.'

Jon's heart sank. He guessed what James was trying to tell him.

'And I take it the power you'd need to push beyond Hx2 would be trillions of times more than that.'

'Exactly. And if you really could build a star liner with trillions of fusion reactors on board, it wouldn't do you any good because now it'd be so heavy you'd need trillions more to overcome the extra mass.'

'So Hx2 really is a barrier then?'

'It's not a barrier as far as we scientists are concerned, and it wouldn't be a barrier if we could develop a power source with a far higher output than our present generation of fusion reactors. But given the limitations of the technology we have to work with, it might as well be a barrier.'

'OK then mister, we've been through the basics. Are you finally going to tell me why the beam doesn't work anymore?'

'Yes, we're almost there. You know how I said that in their matter state, particles exhibited gravity?'

Jon was getting good at nodding.

'Well if you have enough power or some other stimulus available you can influence a gravity wave. If you couldn't there'd never have been a gravitron beam in the first place.'

'But does a gravity wave stimulate the avalanche effect in the 3sub and 4sub matter?'

'No, only an object or an electromagnetic wave does that. With gravity waves it's a more basic explanation. The 3 and 4sub matter does its usual thing of spending some of its time as energy and some of its time as matter, and while matter is almost unaffected by the passage of a gravity wave, the gravity wave passing through *is* affected, but only in a straightforward linear manner. In the same way as real matter affects a gravity wave, the 3sub and 4sub matter extracts tiny amounts of energy. The result is the same as with real matter, the wave is attenuated, and if it's attenuated too much, not enough of it gets through to the receiver to be detected.'

'But James, we're back to the same place as we were before. If there was all this 3sub and 4sub matter attenuating the beam, it would never have worked in the first place. Something must have changed.'

'I said the situation with real matter hadn't changed, and that's almost true for the sub and 2sub particles. But as far as our knowledge goes at the moment, it doesn't appear to be true for the 3 and 4 level particles.'

'What you're saying is that the level of attenuation due to 3 and 4sub matter is variable in some way. What makes it vary?'

'We don't know, we just don't know. There's nothing to hold them back and virtually no limit to the speed they can travel, so 4sub particles could be in flux around the universe and the density in any one place could vary from time to time.'

'Why would they do that?'

'Who knows? There's another theory though.'

Jon sighed. It was all getting too much and he wished he'd stayed in. A glass of wine in his hand, Arnie on his knee and something on the TV would have been infinitely preferable to what he'd let himself in for. But he had to go on, he had to battle through until an explanation finally showed its true colours. If James had been listening he'd have heard the weariness in his date's voice.

'Let's hear it.'

'Some very knowledgeable people have put forward the idea that the 4sub particle density, or at least its nature, could be affected by the residue ejected from star-liner fusion reactors.'

'But there's nothing comes out of a fusion reactor. All the waste products have some value and are either used or stored on board.'

'And so the Union scientists used to think, but it's not true. In fact a fusion reactor is a massive generator of high energy 4sub particles.'

'How do they get out of the reactor?'

'How do they get out! They just pass through the shielding walls. There's nothing in existence you could put in their way.'

'But surely there's so much 4sub matter out there already the "exhaust" from a fusion reactor would make almost no difference at all.'

'Mandy, you were looking for something that had changed, and this is it. This is the only change that's happened and it's significant. For one thing the total number of 4sub particles in any volume of space is increased and that has some effect, but the main action is that the new particles have so much energy they trigger the existing ones into spending more time as matter. It's as if matter had just winked into existence, and with the beam already on the edge of its operational margin it's a critical situation.'

'An accident waiting to happen?'

'Exactly.'

'I know they can't directly monitor space itself, but I assume GBeam monitors the signal strength and its fluctuations.'

'We do. We keep a continuous record of the signal strength and quality, and that's a good guide to the condition of space between the transmitters.'

'Do I take it that major users of the beam, like TranzCon, would get regular status updates from GBeam.'

'Yes, it goes without saying - I'm one of the people responsible for doing it. I collate the data obtained from operations and send it over the beam to TranzCon's HQ.'

'So TranzCon's main office in Jackson knew just how dicey the link from Darius to Phoenix was, and yet they still operated their service?'

'They knew the figures, and they knew there were risks. They had a team of medics on hand for every transfer - just in case. The story was they were there to administer the drugs they needed for flat-line transfers if the beam strength got too low, but really they were there to provide emergency help if there were any problems.'

'And were there any problems?'

'They never made the news public, but there were rumours from time to time. I heard about a heart-stop when a dropout occurred just as a transfer was going through. It was nothing the medics couldn't handle and the traveller had no memory of it, so they just hushed it up. Nothing got leaked to the media of course.'

'But what about all the other GBeam links. The beam from Vissan to Darius is over 200 lightyears and I never heard of it dropping out at all.'

'It just shows you how good the PR department is doesn't it? When that route first opened as a single link it was virtually unusable and even more problematic than our link to Darius was before it went down ten weeks ago. It was only when they added the first relay station they started to get any worthwhile service, and now it operates as three legs with each section similar to the distance between Darius and Phoenix. With two relays in service the real matter mass loading on each leg is under 1000 Tonnes and that gives a signal margin better than 3 to 1. That's the design target for all the links operated by GBeam, or it was until they commissioned the one to Phoenix.'

'Why do you need such a big margin? Wouldn't 2 to 1 be enough?'

'It would, but we don't have any problem providing more, so to be on the safe side we *do* provide more.'

'How much do you really need?'

'Well, solar activity can put a 5% loading on the beam, and attenuation of the beam in interstellar space could be up to 30% compared to design conditions, so if there was solar trouble at both ends we'd need an extra 40% transmission power.'

'Other things could fail though. What would happen if a transmitter went down while a transfer was going through?'

'It's a very unlikely mode of failure because the system has such a high level of redundancy. Every beam transmitter station has two independent sets of transmission equipment on line at any time, and two sets of receiver equipment. And each transmitter or receiver has a standby that can come on line in less than a second. Every GBeam station has been like that since they started running TranzCon over wideband.'

'But what about the reactors? There's only one at each station so a sudden loss of power could shut both sets of equipment down at once.'

'It could, but it doesn't. The thing about reactors is they don't fail very often, and on the rare occasions when they do, they always give us some warning before they actually lose power. It's not permitted to do TranzCon transfers if there are any unresolved alarm conditions, and the shortest time they ever recorded from generation of an alarm to loss of power was over five times longer than the time to complete a TranzCon transfer.'

'What if a failure happened in a shorter time? There has to be a first time for everything.'

'It's possible, it's just extremely unlikely. The Union's been operating fusion reactors for over 100 years now and the shortest time they ever recorded from alarm to failure was 7 seconds. And most failure times have been well over 20 seconds so there's always been more than enough time for the operators to complete a transfer. They've engineered out all the problems - transferring by TranzCon over a GBeam link is the most reliable means of transport human civilisation has ever known. Get on a bus and you're really taking your life in your hands.'

It was all very believable but Jon knew from personal experience that failures still happened so he took the chance to ask a very relevant question.

'I know you've explained about how reliable the system is, but what would happen if a total failure really did occur just as a transfer was taking place? Would the travellers die?'

James stopped and thought for a moment.

'It's something that's never happened so there's no hard evidence to fall back on, and I'm not a transfer specialist but I do know a little about the subject. Something we don't really know is what constitutes the soul of a sentient being, the "life-force" that gets transmitted. Memories we understand and can easily identify, and when we transmit them, the life-force just somehow tags along. Exactly what the life-force is no-one really knows, but compared to the size of the memories it's reckoned to be something quite small.'

'So if it's small compared to the memories, can we assume it gets transmitted instantaneously?'

'That's the popular opinion. Memories can get split up if there's an interruption, but the life-force always ends up in one body or the other.'

'And no-one dies. But what if the beam was interrupted at *exactly* the instant the life-force was going across. What would happen to it?'

'All this is speculation, no-one knows for sure.'

'But what's your best guess?'

'Well, assuming it's really quite small and takes no time to transmit, it's either in one place or another, so if the failure happened after it had gone across you wouldn't even notice there'd been a problem.'

'And if the failure happened before it had gone across, what would happen then?'

'Presumably it would go back to where it had come from. Maybe it might have floated around in the ether for half a split second, but eventually it has to find a home so it would go back.'

Jon was on a roll. At last someone had admitted there was at least a chance a life-force really could go back to where it had come from.

He asked the all important question. 'And has anything like that ever happened?'

'No. It's never been recorded, but that doesn't mean it couldn't happen.'

Jon's heart sank. When he looked up James was watching him with obvious concern.

'Is everything alright Mandy?'

'It's OK, it's something I once heard. Maybe it was just a story.'

James got up and went into the building to get another round of drinks while Jon collected himself. By the time the young man arrived back at the table he was fully recovered and ready to get back to business.

'We've established that the transmitters can't fail, and there's almost no chance of power failure from the reactors, and most GBeam links operate with a massive signal margin, so all in all we've proved there's no way any part of your wonderful system can fail, apart from the fact that we've lost contact with the rest of the galaxy. So tell me this, how come the link between here and Darius operates with a margin so far below the normal standard?'

'It's entirely political. I don't know if you know much about our new friends in the Union, but they've been technologically advanced for close on two thousand years and they've enjoyed political stability for nearly as long. The outcome is that they've got into the habit of making their decisions to suit a very long timescale, but the downside is that when something new and unexpected turns up, they don't react quite as well as you might have hoped. Their discovery of an advanced, populated planet caught them unawares, and that's us here on Phoenix I'm talking about. No-one has admitted any underlying motive, but it's probably because of our historic importance they wanted to establish diplomatic relations as soon as possible.'

'I think I know the story. Popular opinion is that Phoenix was the planet that launched the arkships which came to colonise the three Home Planets. In fact it was the cradle of human life.'

'It may well be true and the people in the Union seem to support the idea, but since we lost our history in the interregnum we have no record of it.'

'If you believe what they tell you.'

James gave Jon a hard look, as if he were trying to see the workings inside Jana's mind.

'You're a suspicious beast for one so young.'

'I try to keep up with politics.'

'Politics! Yes. The Union First Minister himself, you know that Hanson bloke, he put his spoke in and told GBeam he wanted to get a link capable of supporting TranzCon into service ASAP using whatever they'd got available right then and there. GBeam told him they could achieve communications within three years, but they were looking at closer to ten to get a TranzCon service going. He told them it wasn't good enough and they replied that it would take that long if he wanted one that conformed to established safety standards. The standards laid down just eight years earlier by the government lead by his predecessor.'

'So what was the outcome of that?'

'This is all pretty secret stuff Mandy, so don't go putting this in anything you write. The Union's central government, well Hanson I presume, put a lot of pressure on GBeam. They told them they'd break up GBeam's monopoly and support a competitor if they didn't play ball. You know what they're like, politicians and their meddling ways.'

Jon couldn't believe his ears - it really wasn't what he wanted to hear and he wondered why he'd known nothing about it. Before he had a chance to speak, James continued.

'GBeam were shit scared about what Hanson had threatened them with, so they looked into what they could do. They had a brand new pair of ultrabeam transmitters that had been constructed and pre-commissioned in Vissan orbit, and they were due to set off within days to somewhere or other in Union space to upgrade the link to one of the outer planets.'

'I think I can see what's coming here.'

'And I can confirm you're right. Very slyly and with Hanson pushing them, they re-allocated the transmitters to the link between Darius and Phoenix and sent them off at Hx2 in the opposite direction to the way they should have gone. They'd been in space for over a year before the people from that other planet, Antonby I think it was, even found out. They were pretty narked as you can imagine and Hanson was getting a tough time from them. They even started making noises about pulling out of the Union if the transmitters weren't turned around right there and then. Hanson was between a rock and a hard place and desperate to make amends, so he pushed the money through to underwrite GBeam placing new contracts for a pair of transmitters to replace the ones he'd hijacked. Amazing how much power that guy has - there's no-one on Phoenix could authorise government spending just like that. At the same time he'd got the results of the Darius to Phoenix route survey which showed the route wasn't going to be viable as a single link so he supported the order for a further two relay stations and made it clear they were to take priority over the replacement Antonby transmitters.'

Jon was pretty narked himself. He should have been informed about what was going on with so much government money going towards the support of a private enterprise. Rapier hadn't received a single cent, not even when they'd had the problem that almost brought the company down.

'So presumably the relays got built and must be in space somewhere. In fact they must be arriving at Darius any day soon and then you'll have the signal boost you need to break through whatever it is that's blocking the beam.'

James shook his head. 'Again, political gerrymandering. The people from Antonby had been furious that their first pair of ultraband transmitters had been nicked, so when they heard the news about the delay to the replacements they kicked up a fuss. In the end Hanson had to back down and change the order so the replacements for the Antonby link would be constructed before they started work on the Darius to Phoenix relays. There was a lot of overtime worked and the contractor turned the project around in double quick time and after they'd shipped out the Antonby transmitters they got to work on the relays, but even then the problems weren't over. While they were building them a number of technological improvements came up and they had the option of upgrading them to the new Ultra2band standard even though it was going to push the programme back by nearly a year. Then they had some problems with the new kit so they got delayed even longer.'

'And where are the relays for the Darius to Phoenix link right now?'

'Somewhere out in space between Vissan and Darius but they're not even due to arrive there for another three years, and then they'll have to travel to their final positions. That's another eight months for the one near Darius and sixteen for the one that's closer to Phoenix. Even then it'll take a few months to commission them, so don't expect much to happen for another five years.'

'Do you think the relays will solve the problem?'

'Basically we'll be swamping the link with power. We'll be so far above the margin I can't imagine it not working.'

'So that's the timescale is it? No chance of any improvement before that?'

'Who knows? Things might just clear up by themselves and the beam could become useable from time to time, at least for communications if not for TranzCon. But if you want it with a guarantee, you'll have to wait for the new relays. After all, five years isn't long in the grand scheme of things.'

Jon considered the statement and thought about how he needed to get back to his real life right now if he was going to stand a chance in the elections. No-one had ever been remembered for saying that half a decade was a long time in politics.

***

The journey home in James' car had been just a little tense for Jon and he wondered how the rest of the evening was going to play out. Was he simply going to get dropped off by the door, or was James going to want to come in for the coffee Jon was duty-bound to offer? And then what, more chat or the obligatory half-hour of octopus wrestling Jon remembered so fondly from his student days? It was just that now the tables were turned, somehow the idea didn't seem so appealing.

***

Jon put the kettle on while James looked around the flat, obviously more enthused by the squalid little hovel than he was.

'It's a really nice place this Mandy, and so close to town too. I wish I could find a place like it.'

Jon carried the drinks through to the sitting room - full-leaded coffee for the bearded one and de-caff tea for himself. He sat down on the sofa and wondered what was next on the agenda.

James had lightened up just a little from the hard talk of the earlier part of the evening and had progressed onto any male's favourite subject - himself. The talking only stopped when an arm went round the girl's back and Jon felt the man's hot breath just a little too close to Jana's face. In some ways he genuinely felt for the young man and didn't want him to go home empty handed, but he wished the real Jana was there to deliver the goods. Perhaps the alcohol they'd drunk that evening helped when Jon pushed the girls lips towards the offered kiss.

The next minutes were a blur, the face had responded and was pressed into Jana's. Jon did his best to show willing but it was hard going. Next came the creeping hand, onto Jana's stomach then tracking up towards her breasts. Jon knew the response pretty well, a firm grasp to move it away, but with the testosterone flowing freely it didn't hold James back from trying again. And again.

At last the young man's ardour was assuaged and the petting session came to an end. How much time had passed Jon wasn't sure but the ordeal had been just a little too long. Still, things hadn't gone too far and at least Jana wasn't going to have to come home to the expectation of tiny feet pattering on the landing. Perhaps the price paid was reasonable after all.

It was well after midnight when James finally left the flat and made his way down the stairs. He'd already asked if they could meet again but Jon had been non-committal on that one. Yes it was a good idea to keep such a valuable source of information on tap, but a second date would almost certainly imply that the young man had gained an acceptance that might lead to activities of an even more involved nature, and that wasn't something Jon was prepared to consider right then. In any case, playing hard to get would keep the boy keen.

66

The Beam Is Restored

If anyone had been watching carefully at 03.27 that morning they might have seen the slight flicker of a readout that told them there was activity on the communication beam that had once linked Darius and Phoenix. The dozing technician's routine job had become pointless since the beam had been lost almost twelve weeks earlier, so there was little point in him continuing to monitor the system. In any case, the supervisory would log any events for him to review before he went off shift next morning.

The signal strength was so low the beam was scarcely working at all, but in a blistering burst of focussed gravity waves, 137.9 TB of data transferred before the line went silent again 1.93 seconds later. The transmit buffer on Darius was still 99.97% full, but at least a few things had got through.

A lot of the stuff was simply snatches of TV from weeks ago when the viewer's screens had frozen in the middle of a programme. Some bits were emails patiently waiting their turn to get through when low cost bandwidth came available. Some was high priority real-time data from phone conversations in progress at the instant when the beam went down. And some was from the computers of big corporations that worked in the background to keep their galaxy-wide databases synchronised. There was no pattern or order to what got through, there was no consideration of what tiny amounts of data might have been the most important. It was a digital lottery, no more, and no less.

4139 items of information were passed on to the Phoenixan Central Records Agency, and 137 of those were passed on to the Standard Credit Universal Bank. 19 items were routed to the main branch in Celebration, and one of them set a flag to alert an operator when the dayshift came on duty at 08.30.

67

The Application

Next morning Jon woke early and grabbed a quick breakfast before taking Arnie out to the local park. His head was spinning with everything James had told him and he needed the fresh, clean air of the park to clear his head and get a few things straight.

Only days earlier he'd been thinking it wouldn't be long until it was all over and he'd be going home to Vissan. He'd been relying on it. The beam had failed so suddenly - and logically it could come back just as suddenly. The people at TranzCon said it had happened before, many times. Obviously coming back to full strength would be nice so he could travel home, but even if it only came back at a low level he'd be able to get an email across. Just one lousy email to Vissan was all it needed to get things moving.

Over the weeks while he'd lived in Jana's flat Jon had watched the TV news every day and checked the internet to see if there was any progress with GBeam getting comms back on line. But it was always the same - nothing to report. In fact the loss of the beam had almost dropped out of the news completely, a few lines hidden away in the technical sections of the weekend editions was all they bothered to print. And the news Jon was hoping for would be on the front page.

And where now was his real life, his career and his ambition? Back on Vissan the hectic pace of Union politics would be running at its usual rate. He missed the buzz and excitement. He missed the life that kept him working till midnight, and later. OK, the staff in his department could handle most problems, he knew that. He'd recruited nearly all of them, and they were first class people. His deputy could sign off the smaller things and the major items would go to Tom, assuming he was back home by now. It wasn't as though he needed to keep working to bring money in each month or his family would starve, because to say he had more than enough money for a comfortable life was understatement in the extreme. His body in Jackson was getting older of course and some of the best times of his life were probably passing him by, including the opportunity that was coming his way when Tom left office in just four months time. And the more he thought about it, the more he realised that was his main concern - his life was slipping away without him living it.

Then he thought back to the Hyperion, up there in space, glinting, gleaming majestically as it orbited high above the planet. Another month and the magnificent old liner would begin its two year voyage back to Darius. Two years. It was a long time to spend in space but compared to the alternatives he'd considered it offered a more certain result than staying on Phoenix and praying for the beam to come back soon.

Jon knew his destiny lay on the ship. But how would he get on it? With the drip-feed of money that was all the bank allowed him it could take him years to save enough for even a standard class passage. Travelling First class as he'd always done before was no more than a pipe-dream.

Then he remembered, when he'd first heard the news of the Hyperion's planned return to Darius he'd seen adverts for crew members. Well clearly he had no expertise as operational space crew either in his real life or his time here as Jana, but there were so many other jobs that needed doing on board what was essentially a mobile hotel: cleaning, kitchen work, serving in shops, waiting in the restaurants. Not that he had any experience of doing those jobs either, but the further down the scale you went the less they'd be looking for any formal qualifications.

His decision was made. He would join the crew in whatever menial position the ship's owners could offer him. It was true he'd have missed the elections this time round, but there would be other chances. All was most certainly not lost.

★★★

Next morning Jon was up bright and early, which was something of a change from his new-found habit of lying in until well after eight. He found some clothes that were a bit smarter than the jeans he normally wore, had a shower and washed the girl's long hair. After blowing it dry he spent a whole half hour brushing it through till it hung freely and shone with a deep lustre. Hair like Jana's was high maintenance, but he had to admit it looked good when it was freshly washed and cared for. First appearances mattered and he was pleased with the way the girl's body could be turned out to look so nice.

Leaving Arnie on guard duty in the flat he walked to the main road and caught a bus to the city terminus before beginning his search for the offices of Phoenix Intersolar. Fortunately they were only a few minutes walk away.

★★★

The girl at the desk smiled pleasantly as Jon walked into the plush glass and marble foyer with its almost compulsory forest of potted plants. He told her his reason for visiting and she handed him a sheaf of forms to complete.

Feeling just a little down-hearted by how easily he'd been dealt with Jon scanned through page after page of questions, and saw that each one was just a little more taxing than the one that preceded it. Obviously he had to apply as if he was Jana Kell, so the name and address came easily, but after that the going got harder. Back at the flat he'd been through some of Jana's early life from certificates and photos as well as getting some useful information from Jasmine, but sadly the story of girl's short life was not an inspiring résumé. So although he could manage the bits about the schools she'd attended, the fact that the qualifications she'd obtained could be summarised in a single four letter word was something he'd sooner have kept to himself. Trying to fill in details of the jobs she'd held down was even more depressing, and questions that enquired about the number of years she'd worked for each employer and the final salary she'd received were little more than irrelevances. The best he could offer was a week working on the refurbishment of the Hyperion, but even that had been Jasmine's job and he thought it unlikely they'd be impressed with an admission of how he'd surreptitiously gained access to their lovely new ship posing as his own sister.

It was hopeless. There was nothing he'd seen of Jana's life so far that would actually recommend her as an employee - in any role. It was without much hope he handed the form to the girl at the desk. She thanked him for his application and assured him that the HR department would be in contact if a suitable vacancy arose.

68

Investigated

With no work to go to since the accession conference had ended almost three months ago Jon had few reasons to jump out of bed just because an alarm had gone off. Not that there were any reasons to set one in the first place. He'd just finished yet another long lie-in and was eating his breakfast when he heard the doorbell ring. It was unusual because the only person who'd ever called before was Jasmine, and he knew she'd just gone back up to the Hyperion to start her next shift.

With Arnie chasing excitedly behind him Jon went down the stairs to the entrance hall and saw the silhouettes of two people standing outside the frosted glass window. He opened the door to see a pair of men, both heavily built. He looked them up and down. From the way they wore jackets and ties while failing to look smart to any noticeable degree gave him a hint as to who they might be.

The man who appeared to be the older of the duo spoke. 'Miss Jana Kell?'

Jon thought about the question before giving his reply.

'There are those who insist on calling me Jana Kell'.

The man looked at him quizzically.

'I'll take that as a "yes" then. Miss Kell we are police officers from the fraud squad, based here in Celebration, Detective Constables Haigh and Longland.'

Jon didn't like the sound of it one bit. When the bill was being polite it was only the lead-in to something problematic.

'Is there some way I can help you?'

'We have a warrant to search your premises. Would you please come and sit in the car while my colleague does his job.'

Jon looked at the piece of paper and saw that it was as the man had said, a search warrant.

'Do I have any right to refuse you entry?'

'None at all.'

'Are you going to tell me what is this all about?'

'If you come down to the car I'll tell you what I know.'

'Why don't we all go back up to the flat?'

'I'm afraid my colleague has the right to work without your presence, and that's the way he prefers it. So if you'd come along to the car please, Miss.'

'What about the dog?'

The big policeman looked down at Arnie.

'Bring it with you, but make sure it stays off the seats.'

Girl and dog followed DC Haigh down the steps to the road outside where a large dark car was parked on the single yellow line. He opened the rear door and ushered them in. When the door was closed behind him Jon gave the handle a try, and as he'd expected, it didn't open. A pair of horizontal bars separating the front seat from the back made escape impossible so Jon resigned himself to the status of prisoner. Hopefully it was only going to be temporary.

Haigh left Jon and Arnie locked in the car while he walked back up the steps to speak to his colleague, and a couple of minutes passed before he returned and sat himself in the front passenger seat.

'Miss Kell, as I explained to you earlier, we are from the fraud squad and we are here today to investigate an anomaly communicated to us by the Standard Credit Universal Bank. Can I ask you if you have an account with them?'

Jon wondered just how to answer the question. His own account was with SCU, but so far they were investigating Jana Kell. He reasoned that the answer should be "no I don't".

The man's face betrayed no emotion as he moved onto his next question.

'And can you tell me whether you know a Mr Jon Chandler?'

Jon answered with absolute truth. 'Yes, I know him very well.'

'And does Mr Chandler live here with you?'

'In a way, yes he does.'

Haigh looked puzzled. A straight "yes" or "no" would have suited him better.

'Miss Kell, this is a serious crime we are investigating and I think that as things progress you'll find it will be to your advantage to be as helpful as possible. Let me put it another way, we are aware that you were a TranzCon host to Mr Chandler who arrived here and occupied your body approximately twelve weeks ago. Is this true or false?'

'True.'

'And I take it you are also aware that Mr Chandler returned to his home on Vissan at the same time as you returned here to Phoenix.'

For weeks now the issue of whether Jon had actually made it back home had not arisen, but he groaned to himself that the old chestnut had come up again. He shook the girl's head and sighed.

'Jon Chandler did not succeed in returning to Vissan, and from that single fact you will be able to deduce that the person you are talking to right now is Jon Chandler.'

The policeman shook his head. Something about the look on his face told Jon he'd been preparing himself for this discussion for quite some time.

'Miss Kell, would you agree with me if I told you that our records show that eight weeks ago you made a claim to be Jon Chandler and received psychiatric counselling to help you come to terms with the fact that you were suffering from a condition known as spirit image retention?'

Jon was just considering his next reply when Haigh's phone rang. He listened for a few moments before he spoke.

'Miss Kell, we'd like you to come down to the station to help us with our enquiries.'

Jon smiled at the man's choice of phrase - he thought it was only something they said in old movies.

'Are you arresting me?'

'At the moment Miss Kell, we are simply asking for your co-operation.'

'And if I don't feel minded to come with you?'

Haigh lifted a small leather pouch into view so Jon could see it.

'Do you know what these are?'

'They're handcuffs.'

'Correct, and regulations oblige me to put them on anyone I arrest, I have no discretion in this matter. I can tell you now that it is almost certain we have sufficient evidence to make an arrest right here, so you'll be coming to the station anyway, with or without the handcuffs. Something you might like to consider is that if the records show you co-operated willingly, it might help you to get bail if you are charged. So what's it going to be, the easy way or the hard way?'

Jon saw he had no option other than to go with the man, and it wasn't as though he'd any pressing engagements that morning.

'OK then I'll come with you, of my own free will.'

'Thankyou Miss Kell, that's what we like to hear.'

A movement attracted Jon's attention and he looked out of the car's window to see DC Longland walking carefully down the steps outside the house with a large cardboard box in his arms. Haigh got out to open the boot for him and a moment later they climbed back into the front seats.

★★★

The journey into the city centre took about ten minutes before the car turned off onto a side street and headed down a ramp into a low-roofed underground garage. Five minutes later the three occupants were in a lift which brought them up into the hall of a modern building fronted by a row of large picture windows that looked out onto the street. Towards the back of the hall Jon saw a desk with a uniformed officer standing behind. They walked over and Haigh wrote something on a pad of paper that he handed over.

The sergeant looked up at Jon. 'Name?'

'Jonathan Charles Churchill Chandler.'

Haigh glared at him, obviously making no effort to hide his irritation.

'Miss Kell, you're not making this any easier for yourself you know. Will you answer the sergeant's question and give him your real name please.'

'I *am* Jon Chandler. I *am* the minister for Trans-Union trade, and I *am* on an official visit to Phoenix.'

The desk sergeant looked at him, 'your name please MISS.'

'That is my name, and I'd be pleased if you'd stop calling me "Miss".'

'Look *Miss*. Jon Chandler is a man's name and you are obviously a woman. You can't be Jon Chandler.'

Jon was agitated now. He knew what he knew and wasn't going to be put off easily. He drew in a breath before launching into his tirade.

'The host body I occupy is female and that would explain why you are under the impression you are looking at a woman. If you were to ask the name of the host body I occupy then it is as you already know "Jana Kell".'

Jon watched as the desk sergeant wrote on the pad "Jana Kell". He was furious but he knew that an outburst at this stage was not going to help his situation. The rest of the form filling went a little easier now it appeared that Jon was co-operating just a little. And he accepted their offer regarding the allocation of a public defence attorney before a policewoman took him down to the cell block and ushered him into a stark bare room that lacked any form of window. He noted that the design didn't seem to change much wherever you went and his mind slipped back to the time he remembered all too well when DI Bennett had locked him up for having the money to pay the ransom for his nephew Robert.

★★★

Two hours of boredom passed before Jon heard sounds outside in the corridor. The door of the cell opened and a young man in a smart three-piece suit stepped inside. And what a surprise he was.

In the time since he'd arrived on Phoenix Jon had become used to the idea that most of the people he saw in Celebration had the same unattractive, pasty white skin as Jana, while others were dark brown or even black. So he noticed immediately that this young man had exactly the mid-brown skin tone of the average Union citizen. And yet he was

Phoenixan. Perhaps it was prejudice based entirely on the man's colour rather than for any real reason, but Jon warmed to him immediately. The man threw his jacket over the back of the chair opposite Jon and took a seat.

'Good afternoon Miss Kell. I am Mr Kamar and as I'm sure you've guessed, I have been appointed as your attorney.'

Jon looked at him and worried slightly when he saw how young the man was because "young" in a lawyer often equated to "inexperienced". Back at home he'd have had the sharpest legal eagle in the business, but even with the money he'd been able to access here on Phoenix he still didn't have anything like enough to employ a seasoned lawyer.

Jon began. 'Many people insist on calling me Jana Kell because I continue to use her body as a host, but for official matters I would prefer to be called by my proper name.'

Kamar was ahead of him.

'Which is Jon Chandler I believe. They told me the story and showed me your file. It is no concern of mine what you choose to be called but I suggest that if the police refer to you as "Jana Kell" and they are obviously talking to you, then you should respond. But let's get down to business, we have to look at the facts and then work out a defence to the charges they are preparing upstairs.'

Kamar explained to Jon that he'd arrived at the police station about an hour earlier and he was very sorry to have to leave his client waiting but it was better that he investigated the case first of all. He told Jon what he'd found out so far. The two officers from the fraud squad had collected some evidence from his flat that morning and were proposing to charge him with the dual offences of identity theft and bank fraud. The allegation was that *she* had purported to be Jon Chandler and had used information *she* remembered about this man whom she'd hosted to obtain a bank card in his name. *She* had then gone on to use the card to withdraw funds in excess of 7000 Phen from Jon Chandler's personal bank account and to purchase goods from a number of retail outlets.

Jon considered the evidence. 'Well if I wasn't Jon Chandler I'd be guilty of quite a bit wouldn't I?'

'That is the problem you're now facing. Your only line of defence against the charges is based on being able to prove that you *are* Jon Chandler, and from what I've seen in the files you haven't had much success with that.'

'But if I took the alternative line and said I was Jana Kell they'd have no trouble finding me guilty as charged and sending me off to jail, so it doesn't appear that I've got any real choice. I have to continue with the line of being Jon Chandler. For Belen's sake, no-one's ever suffered from spirit image retention for this long. If I am Jana Kell I deserve to go in the record books.'

Kamar thought about it for a moment before he spoke.

'You recall that Dr Morris invited you to check into his nice comfortable private psychiatric clinic, and the bills would have been paid by TranzCon.'

Jon nodded.

'Well if you manage to persuade a court not to send you to jail because you're Jon Chandler you might end up in a secure mental hospital if they think you're delusional. They're not nice places and they come with the problem that the sentence could be indefinite.'

'So it comes back to the fact that the only way out is to succeed in proving that I'm Jon Chandler. I still don't have a choice do I?'

★★★

Kamar left after about an hour, but before he went he told Jon there was a meeting set for later that afternoon. Without his phone and with no view of the outside world Jon had no idea of the time, but an age seemed to have passed before the policewoman came and escorted him from the cell. Upstairs in the meeting room Haigh was waiting. He was pleasant enough and ordered a cup of coffee for Jon.

A few minutes later the door opened again and two men Jon hadn't seen before walked in and took seats at the table. They were followed by a face Jon recognised from somewhere, though he was unable to put a name to the man. He watched as one of the newcomers pulled a laptop from his case and set it up on the table. Just before they were ready to start Kamar rushed in and grabbed the last chair.

DC Haigh made the introductions. The two men that Jon hadn't met before were Detective Sergeant Mills from the central fraud office, and Mr Carlson, a handwriting expert whose services were retained by the police. The man Jon had recognised turned out to be Townsend, the lawyer from TranzCon. Jon noticed when Haigh passed a small remote control to DS Mills.

Haigh heaved the cardboard box Jon had seen earlier in the day up onto the table and lifted out a pile of papers and Jon's laptop computer. He arranged some of the papers neatly in piles and stood the computer to one side. He began his presentation:

'This is the evidence we recovered from Miss Kell's flat earlier today. The papers relate to a bank account in the name of Jon Chandler, and the laptop contains clear indications that it has been used to make an application for a debit card on the account of Jon Chandler. There are bank statements which show that the card was used for purchases and to withdraw funds during the period after Mr Chandler had travelled back to his home on Vissan. Miss Kell, do you accept that these papers and the laptop computer are yours and were in your flat this morning.'

Jon could see there was no point in denying the obvious.

'They are mine and they were in Jana Kell's flat this morning.'

If Haigh noticed the difference between what he'd asked and what Jon had replied he ignored it.

'Well it appears to me Miss Kell that they are evidence to prove that you stole the identity of Jon Chandler and then used this stolen identity to steal money from his account. Do you have any comment to make regarding the charges which are laid against you.'

Jon could see it was going badly, but he knew the line he had to take.

'Well the whole thing is easily explained. I was entitled to obtain bank cards for my own bank account and I was entitled to withdraw money from that account. I need money to live here on Phoenix while I'm waiting for the beam to come back on line so I can travel home to Vissan.'

'If you wanted money Miss Kell, why didn't you go out and get a job like most people?'

After all the trouble he'd had just staying alive the question was like waving a red rag to a bull. Now Jon was getting annoyed and the irritation showed in the way he spoke.

'I already have a job that pays far better than anything I could find here. I am as we speak still receiving my salary and in any case it is a requirement of my position in the government that I do not take on any additional forms of paid employment. I presume you've looked me up in the who's who of Union politics?'

'Yes Miss Kell, we are well aware of who Mr Chandler is and we know you claim to be him. But we are also aware of the fact that no person or organisation here on Phoenix supports this claim of yours.'

'And what about people or organisations elsewhere in the galaxy? On Union planets for example?'

'You know very well that while the beam is out of service we are unable to obtain any information from an off-planet source.'

Kamar, biding his time until now cut into the exchanges.

'And without this vital information it would appear that at the present time you are not in a position to lay any charges against my client.'

DS Mills spoke for the first time.

'On the contrary Mr Kamar, we believe we have more than enough evidence available here to dismiss Jana Kell's claim to be Jon Chandler. In which case it would be correct to lay the charges against her.'

Kamar continued. 'So far you have presented some details which show that my client carried out a number of actions, and if she is actually Jana Kell then it appears that she has broken the law. But if *he* is, as *he* claims to be, actually Jon Chandler, then he was entitled to do the things he did. Whether or not my client is guilty of anything depends entirely on his or her real identity, and that is something which cannot be proved either way while the communication beam is off line.'

Mills was not thrown by what Kamar said - it was likely he had expected the defence to come from that direction.

'Well we have one piece of evidence to confirm that the woman sitting here is in fact Jana Kell. Miss Kell, would you please sign this piece of paper.'

Jon took the pen in the girl's right hand and signed "Jon Chandler". The people watching looked annoyed, but then he expected they would be.

Haigh spoke. 'Its OK, we need one signature for each name and we were going to ask her to write "Jon Chandler" next anyway.' He passed the paper back to Jon. 'Miss Kell, will you please write the words "Jana Kell", whether that is your name or not.'

Jon picked up the pen in his right hand and wrote as Haigh had asked - if he refused now he would obviously be failing to co-operate. Mills passed the two sheets of paper to Carlson and asked him to give his comments. Carlson ran a hand-scanner over the two signatures and told them he would be a few minutes before he was able to say anything about the latest findings.

Mills spoke to Jon again. 'Miss Kell, if I was to assume for just two minutes that you are, as you claim to be, Jon Chandler what would you say?'

'I'd say thankyou very much for believing me.'

'So it follows that Jana Kell, or at least her life-force, is still on Vissan, presumably occupying the body of Jon Chandler. Am I right?'

Jon was getting concerned with the line of questioning, but he could do nothing other than confirm what the policeman had said.

'Yes, you are correct. Miss Kell's life-force is occupying my body on Vissan.'

'So if I then went on to point out that we have evidence of twenty seven instances of a credit card in the name of Jana Kell being used during the period while she was absent from this planet, what would you say to that?'

Kamar saw what was happening and broke in.

'My client objects to this line of questioning. Are you now making an accusation over and above the charges we are discussing here.'

'Just trying to establish the facts Mr Kamar,' Mills said, cool as a cucumber and pleased things were going his way. 'So

Miss Kell, Jana, or Jon, or whoever you really are, are you comfortable?'

Jon had no idea of the line the detective was taking.

'Comfortable? In what way?'

'You appear to be quite at ease with your outward appearance, your appearance as a woman. I would have assumed that a person who was by nature male would be, shall we say, less comfortable.'

Jon drew in a breath before he spoke.

'This is the appearance that circumstances have landed me with for what I am hoping is only a temporary period. I've done my best to get on with some sort of life, but I have not adopted more of a female role than was absolutely necessary.'

'But still, you are wearing women's clothes.'

'I am wearing the clothes I found in Jana's flat. They are the right size for her frame, I didn't have to go out spending piles of money I haven't got buying other clothes, and the ones I choose to wear are about as unisex as you could find.' Jon stood up. 'Take a look.'

Jon almost felt the policeman's eyes as they dropped away from his and washed over the girl's perfect young body. In a room full of men where *he* was the only female he felt vulnerable and alone. Mills waited until Jon had sat back in his chair before he continued.

'Except for your underwear Miss Kell, which I suggest to you is feminine.'

Jon was indignant now.

'I'm wearing a bra, if that's what you mean. It's more comfortable for a body that has breasts and the overall image I present in public draws less attention than if I didn't wear one. Practicality, nothing more and nothing less. Suggesting that I'm comfortable wearing these clothes proves nothing at all.'

'But you're comfortable, being a woman aren't you? More comfortable than a person who was really a man inside?'

'Detective Mills, for over twelve weeks now I've been living here on Phoenix occupying the role of Jana Kell and I agree that I'm surviving quite well, but I can assure you it wasn't like that at first.'

Mills nodded in a disturbing way but did not pursue the line. He called over to his subordinate.

'DC Haigh, can you dim the lights please.'

Mills operated the remote control that had been lying on the desk in front of him.

'Miss Kell, we have here some video footage from the security surveillance cameras in a store you visited. Have a look and see if you remember.'

Jon watched as the screen flickered into life. He saw a figure which was unmistakably himself in Jana's body, though exactly which shop it was he couldn't say.

Mills broke in. 'This is from the security camera in a mini market in the Rokham Park area close to Jana Kell's flat. What you can see here is a woman buying a feminine hygiene product. Watch carefully. She knows exactly what she wants, she chooses her purchase in a deliberate manner, and I might add, with a degree of confidence that a male shopper would simply not have had.'

Kamar spoke up. 'But does that prove anything?'

Mills turned to face the darker skinned man. 'Mr Kamar, TranzCon received a life-force into the body of Jana Kell, and that combination of body and mind now appears to act in an entirely female manner. It's the strongest possible indication that the person we have been observing is actually female, in mind as well as body. We're not considering the case of more than one male or more than one female being involved are we?'

Mills scanned around at the faces in the room. No-one was disagreeing with his latest offering of logic.

'So if we have a female presence in the body of Jana Kell, and no-one is trying to suggest it might be a woman other than Jana Kell because no other woman is involved, then this life-force really is Jana Kell, and not as she keeps insisting, the life-force of Jon Chandler. But look, we're not the only ones who're convinced. Miss Kell, I have here a report which states that you were examined by the psychiatrist Dr Morris who found you were suffering from a condition called spirit image retention, and as a direct result of this condition you continue to believe you are Jon Chandler even after his life-force has left Jana Kell's body. Is that correct?'

Jon sat and waited for the man to continue.

'Is that correct Miss Kell?' he repeated.

'You know it's correct.'

'Yes I do, and there were a number of consultations with TranzCon's own staff as well as Dr Morris when they tried as hard as they could to help you, and they would still have been helping you except that you declined to accept a continuation of their services.'

Jon knew it was going badly and wished Kamar had said more.

'Dr Morris was offering me a place locked up in his local loony bin. There was no way I was going voluntarily into a place like that.'

'But even so, you agree that it was yourself who broke off from the course of treatment?'

'Yes, if you like, but it doesn't change anything. Despite everything you have said and despite the interesting video you showed us, it remains that I am Jon Chandler and I always will be, no matter what body you happen to see me in.'

Carlson caught the detective's eye and the older man gestured towards him.

'Do you have any results yet Mr Carlson?'

The man leaned over the table and handed a form to Jon.

'Do you recognise this Miss Kell?'

Jon looked and saw it was the form he had signed to accept the caution given by Townsend. 'Yes,' he replied in a non-committal manner.

Carlson showed him another form.

'And do you recognise this Miss Kell?'

Jon looked. 'I can see it's a form from the TranzCon company, but I don't recognise it, and the signature isn't mine.'

Carlson lifted his head and gazed around at the assembled group. His voice had a ring of smugness as he spoke. 'What you see here is in fact the original form signed by Jana Kell when she agreed to host a traveller for TranzCon.'

Mills rejoined the conversation. 'And what do you make of the latest signatures. How do they compare with those we already had?'

'We have here the original TranzCon consent form which was most definitely signed by Jana Kell since it had to be completed before the transfer with Jon Chandler could take place. We also have a form that was signed in the presence of Mr Townsend, and we have the two signatures given today.'

'And what analysis do you make of these?'

A hush fell over the room.

'All the signatures were made by the same hand. There has been an obvious attempt to disguise some of them, and it may well have fooled someone without specialist knowledge. But for myself, and with assistance from handwriting analysis software, the resemblance is clear.'

'There is no doubt? You are sure that all the signatures were made by the same person?'

'Yes, I am sure.'

Mills looked Jon in the eye. 'I think you have to agree that this is conclusive evidence that you are indeed Jana Kell.'

Jon sighed. 'Something which has become clear to me since I arrived on Phoenix and took over Jana Kell's body is that the way the hand writes is governed by the muscles in the hand and the tone of those muscles. I am, and always have been, left handed ……..'

'And yet we saw you just a few minutes ago writing with your right hand,' Mills interjected.

Jon continued. *'In my own body* I am and always have been left handed, but in Jana Kell's body the left hand lacks the necessary muscle tone to form legible writing. So for someone like myself who was, as most left-handers often are, reasonably ambidextrous, it has been easier to use the facilities provided by the host body together with the mental sub-routines that are available to the occupying life-force on a sub-conscious level and to write using my host's right hand. Since my own style of handwriting depends on the mental sub-routines in my own body's brain and on the muscles in my left hand, it follows that I am largely unable to influence the way my host body's right hand operates. In fact I am less able to influence it than a person who normally writes with their right hand would be.'

Mills smiled and shook his head slowly.

'It's an interesting defence that's all I can say. Now Miss Kell, or Mr Chandler, from the way you speak, one would assume you were an expert in these matters. But as we know, Miss Kell is a lady of little formal education, and although we know that Jon Chandler is a highly educated man, in fact there is no evidence that he has any specialist knowledge in this field. Would you say that was correct?'

Jon knew the man was talking from hard facts available to anyone who chose to look him up in the on-line encyclopaedia. There was no point trying to shoot him down on the point.

'Detective Mills, you are correct in what you say, but it isn't difficult for a layman to gain a good grasp of small sections of technical knowledge, so in this respect I must ask you to understand that I do know what I am talking about. Coming back to the previous discussion about the appearance of the writing I produce when I am using Jana Kell's hand, I think that what has been presented by Mr Carlson is conclusive evidence that the signatures were made by the same *physical* hand but, and I stress this, not necessarily with the same life-force occupying the body. I'm sure there must be some previous case when handwriting was analysed and it was found that the traveller's signature was similar to that of the host.'

Haigh grinned. 'I think you're clutching at straws Miss Kell. What we have uncovered during our investigations is that you were able to fool several computer security systems, and this was partly because you had knowledge of Jon Chandler's personal details.'

'Which you would expect me to have since I am Jon Chandler.'

Mills shook his head. 'No Miss Kell. We're tending towards the view that you had this knowledge because you illegally accessed memories which had become available to you after Jon Chandler's life-force had left your body.' He looked towards the man sitting to his left. 'Isn't that correct Mr Townsend?'

Townsend took his cue and entered the proceedings. 'That is absolutely true Detective. After the period of hosting Jon Chandler, Miss Kell could have become party to some or all of the memories of the life-force her body had hosted. It is something which happens from time to time and, although we are unable to prevent it, we can seek to ensure that such knowledge is not used in an illegal manner. Before they travel, a lawyer has a meeting with every traveller or host and the function of this is to warn them of the consequences of using any memories from their counterpart either to their own advantage, or to the disadvantage of the counterpart. This caution would have been given to Jon Chandler before he left Vissan, and I personally gave it to Jana Kell before she left Phoenix. It's standard company procedure, no caution, or no signature to say the caution has been accepted, no transfer.'

Mills liked what he'd heard and the expression on his face had turned to one of satisfaction that the law was about to be upheld.

He continued. 'As I was saying Miss Kell, you fooled the security systems partly because you had knowledge of Jon Chandler's personal details, and partly, in fact mainly, because for a time no final confirmation of Jon Chandler's transfer back to Vissan had been received. Now, I've been checking on laws introduced in the Union fifteen years ago to cover TranzCon transfers which allow a traveller to be given the benefit of the doubt about who they are until their identity can be finally proved. There is no equivalent law here on Phoenix though the interim agreement is that the authorities on this planet will operate voluntarily in accordance with Union law until such time as a law of our own can be passed. Now, in this case there was a period when the identity of the person here was genuinely in doubt because final confirmation of the transfer had not been received, and this was due to the loss of the beam communication with Darius and thus with Vissan. But when the final confirmation of the transfer was received, it became clear that the life-force we know as Jon Chandler had been received back on Vissan…….'

Jon looked up in alarm. 'Final confirmation. What final confirmation?'

Mills was smiling as he spoke. 'The beam came back on line during the early morning of the 12th of June, and final confirmation of the transfer back was received as a result. I have a printout from the Central Records Agency database to prove this fact. And that is something I want to emphasise, is now a fact.'

Jon was stunned. If the beam had come back on line, why hadn't he been able to use it to travel home, or at least to send emails? He was agitated when he spoke.

'So why wasn't this important information made public? And why aren't we now in communication with the Union?'

'I have no idea Miss Kell. As far as the latest news goes the beam is not on-line, though there was obviously a time when it was. And as I was saying before I was interrupted, at the same time as the life-force of Jon Chandler was received back on Vissan, the life-force of Jana Kell was received back into her own body here on Phoenix. Now, I don't claim to be an expert on TranzCon transfers, but something which is common knowledge is that a body with no life-force, no spirit or soul to use more religious terms, would be dead after a matter of seconds unless it was artificially supported by machines.'

Mills looked around, all the faces round the table apart from Jon appeared to be giving approval.

He continued. 'So the very fact that Miss Kell here is able to walk, talk and reason would appear to be proof positive that the body of Jana Kell actually contains a soul or life-force. And since the life-force of Jon Chandler was received back on his home planet of Vissan, the only soul or life-force that could possibly be resident in Jana Kell's body, is that of Jana Kell. You don't have to be an expert to work that one out.'

Jon's thoughts were in disarray. Before he had a chance to reply Mills re-entered the conversation wearing the look of a chess grandmaster going in for the final move.

'Miss Kell, I think this is a classic case of "Tell it to the Judge". There is not a doubt in my mind that you should face the charges of identity theft and bank fraud.'

★★★

After a second session with the sergeant at the desk Jon was formally arrested and the policewoman took him back down to the cell where he'd been locked up earlier that day. If the cold grey décor had worried him before, now it filled him with dread.

For over an hour he sat motionless and dumbstruck until he heard the clank of the heavy door and the policewoman ushered Kamar into the cell. The man sat himself down and went straight to work.

'I've been doing a bit of finding out and it's interesting stuff. You were able to gain access to Jon Chandler's bank account because Central Records had not received any communication to advise that his life-force had been received back on Vissan. Apparently they don't take any notice of the initial confirmation because it's something that's internal to TranzCon. They only go on the final confirmation that comes afterwards.'

Jon was confused. 'But they never got the final confirmation. It wasn't received at the time of the transfer and the beam's been down all these weeks. How could it have been received?'

'It turns out it was received. The beam did come back on line, but only at low strength, and only for a very short time in the early hours of the 12th of June. Because of the lack of a signal for so many weeks the communications centre was largely closed down and my contact there tells me the technician on duty was dozing and slept right through the brief period while the beam was back on-line. Not that it would have made any difference if he'd been awake.'

'So the beam was up for long enough for some communication to be received here and passed on to Central Records?'

'And then onto Standard Credit Universal who belatedly accepted they'd issued a bank card to a person who wasn't present on the planet at the time when they'd issued it. It flagged up an anomaly and it was just part of their standard procedure to carry out an investigation. When they'd confirmed there'd been a breach of their security protocols they called in the fraud office.'

Jon saw a ray of hope. 'But look, I put an email in the system to my people on Vissan. So if communications were restored, even for a short time, it might be that they are already taking action to get me back home.'

'That may well be the case, but so far we haven't been able to get any details of which communications were received and which were not. And we don't even know whether there was any transmission in the other direction. In any case, without working beam communications there isn't anything your people on Vissan could do even if they had received your email. But this isn't helping your immediate situation. Mills has registered the proposed charges and tomorrow morning you'll be coming up in front of a magistrate to be formally charged.'

'And what happens then?'

'As part of the hearing, which should only take a few minutes, you will be asked to confirm your identity.'

'Which one, Jana Kell or Jon Chandler?'

'That's exactly the point we have to discuss. If you continue your claim to be Jon Chandler, Mills will counter it with a raft of so-called evidence to show that you're suffering from mental instability, and in that case the magistrate will probably have you committed to a secure psychiatric facility until the date of your hearing.'

Jon saw where his lawyer was leading.

'And if I go along with the idea of being Jana Kell?'

'Then you'll probably get bail. Everything Mills is laying against you is for non-violent offences, so provided you go along with it all, confirm your identity and accept the charges, I'm fairly sure you'll walk out of the court.'

'But even if they're prepared to grant bail, how much money will they want? As you're aware I have very little access to money here on Phoenix, and we can be sure they won't be giving me my bank card back.'

'The standard rule is that bail is set at a sum equal to six months gross income.'

'So if I was Jon Chandler my bail would run to many millions, but as Jana Kell I don't have any income at all.'

'In which case there is a default minimum of 2000 Phen.'

'Which I could possibly get hold of.'

'So are we agreed then, you're going to go with confirming you're Jana Kell?'

'Well it's OK for now, especially if it means I can get bail, but when it comes to the main hearing, an acceptance that I am Jana is tantamount to an admission of guilt.'

Kamar nodded his head. 'We're going to have to work on your defence, but just because you accept the identity of Jana

Kell tomorrow doesn't mean you can't change your mind and return to your claim of being Jon Chandler later.'

'Except they'll jump on the fact there was a time when I did accept I was Jana Kell.'

'It's a problem I agree, but you can take it from me that if you press your claim to be Jon Chandler tomorrow morning, you'll be escorted out of the courtroom either in handcuffs or a strait jacket.'

Jon shuddered at the thought. 'OK then, just for tomorrow, I'm Jana Kell. So what do we do?'

Kamar presented him with a sheaf of papers and for the next thirty minutes they sat there filling in the details. Jon didn't like the idea of putting in writing what was obviously an acceptance he was Jana Kell, but what could he do?

When the paperwork was finished, he spoke to Kamar again. 'If I do get convicted, what sort of sentence am I likely to get?'

'If you accept the charges as made, plead guilty and make no protest to be Jon Chandler, the likely sentence for the card fraud would be two years in prison. And for identity theft you'd probably get three on top of that.'

Jon shook the girl's head in disbelief. Five years! Five years without even putting up a fight for God's sake.

'What if I continued to accept I was Jana but pleaded not guilty so they'd have to consider the evidence?'

'They would indeed. But just think about this, the sentence you could expect might be anything up to double, probably around seven to eight years for the two offences together. And bear in mind that if you *do* fight the case as Jana Kell, you don't really stand much of a chance of getting off, so it's hardly worth pleading not guilty.'

Jon held his head in his hands. 'So really the only real defence is to make a stand that I'm Jon Chandler after all?'

'That's about it, but I'm afraid there's worse to come.'

Jon turned the girl's face up to look at the bare concrete ceiling.

'How could it possibly get worse?'

'If you press your case to be Jon Chandler they'll bring up the evidence Mills hinted at during the meeting. You'd have to agree that over the past weeks you'd been accessing a credit card account in the name of Jana Kell.'

'Mainly to put money in I'd point out.'

'But not always to pay in. In any case, you accessed an account in someone else's name whether you paid in or drew out.'

'And what will come of that?'

'They'll probably press the same charge of identity theft, but in that case it would be the theft of Jana Kell's identity. And they might even make something of the mental instability issue so you might find yourself in the psychiatric facility.'

'Oh for fuck's sake! So what you're saying is I'm screwed either way.'

'I'm sorry, it's not a good situation. I wish I could do more to help you, I really do, but we're backed into a corner. Even if they dropped all the charges we've been discussing today, did you know they've got you on video stealing a sandwich from a supermarket?'

'Go on then, how many years do I get for that?'

'A month's community service.'

Jon managed a weak smile.

'That I could handle. But what's with all the surveillance? Were they already watching me for something? I mean, had the girl been guilty of some crime before she did the TranzCon swap with me?'

It suddenly occurred to Jon that the girl might have been in trouble even before the swap and had found a way of escaping punishment by transferring to his body on Vissan and then refusing to come back. But no, that couldn't be the case - Michael had told him before his dash from the hotel that the girl was already flat-lined on the couch ready for the transfer back.

'Jon, or Jana, there is something else you need to know about. It all hinges around DS Mills, and more to the point his younger brother who's a constable in the uniformed branch.'

'So what's the big deal, lots of families serve in the police?'

'His brother was badly embarrassed regarding a false arrest he made, and because of it he's just failed to make sergeant.'

'And how does that affect me?'

'The arrest he was embarrassed about concerned a certain Miss Jana Kell.'

Somehow Jon had guessed and had just been waiting for Kamar to say it.

'But if Jana had actually been a criminal with a record, she wouldn't have been considered as a TranzCon host would she? Even being charged with something would have shown up in a search. You know what they say, "where there's smoke there's fire".'

'I fully agree, she wouldn't have been accepted as a host. She was in some trouble but she wasn't convicted because she got off on a technicality. They scrubbed the charges completely so there was nothing returned by the search TranzCon made.'

'So tell me what happened.'

'There used to be a club, Benni's they called it, and it was the hot place to go, except the word to the wise was you walked past if you saw a police car or an ambulance outside. The place was doing some really big trade until about three months ago when it got raided and closed down.'

'What was the reason for closing it?'

'Well they did all the usual stuff, drinks, loud music, dancing girls, bright lights, and sometimes the customers got a bit drunk and fights broke out, so they were always getting shut down for a week or two as a penalty until they cleaned up their act. But what finished them off was prostitution.'

'Why should that come into it?'

'Because it's immoral of course.'

Jon couldn't believe what he was hearing.

'Not on a Union planet it isn't. Whether something is moral or not is a personal decision, and it's been enshrined in citizens' rights for hundreds of years.'

Now it was Kamar's turn to look surprised.

'I know that with Phoenix coming into the Union I'm going to have to bull up on some new laws, but just lately I've been so busy I haven't had the time. But what you're telling me is that people can do just whatever they like on Union planets, no matter how disgusting the man or woman in the street might find it?'

Jon was confused at the way a seemingly intelligent man was so unable to understand.

'Well no, of course not. There are things which are specifically against the law, so you can't do those, but you can't be fined or sent to jail for doing something just because it doesn't suit the opinions of a minority. If something is so bad that the planetary government passes a law against it, then obviously you can't do it without risking prosecution, but prostitution isn't in that category. Of course, prostitutes are always in court but that's because they're notoriously bad at keeping their books up to date and they get done for tax evasion.'

Kamar looked horrified. 'They tax prostitution?'

'They tax any legal money making activity: manufacturing, services, property sales, and in this case leisure. But carry on with what you were saying about the club.'

Kamar obviously had more to say on the morality issue but thought better of it.

'Well at the club they had a lot of pretty girls. Dancers and hostesses, you know the type who come and chat up the men and get them to stay longer and buy more drinks.'

Jon nodded, he'd known quite a few clubs exactly like the one Kamar was describing.

'Well Jana Kell was one of these girls, and so was her sister Jasmine who I believe you know. One night the police did a stealth raid and came to see if they could pick up girls who'd have sex with them for payment.'

'Sounds like the cops have a real hard job in this town. So they got them to ask for payment and then they busted them?'

'No, they were more interested in closing the whole place down - permanently. They didn't bust any of the girls that night, but the officers from the raid came back the next night and picked out the girls they'd slept with, and then they busted the girls and the club at the same time.'

'So how do Jana and Jasmine come into this?'

'Well Jasmine had been one of the girls an undercover policeman had slept with, but it was Jana who was in the club the next night. So she was the one they arrested.'

Jon smiled and almost laughed out loud.

'They couldn't tell the difference between them? But look, I've met Jasmine and she looks quite different to this body.'

'I've done some checking and I'll grant you the appearance she's presenting at the moment is very different, but at the time of the raid the two girls were ringers for each other - they are identical twins you know. The police were watching Jana after the incident because they were convinced she was involved in a vice racket, so Jasmine changed her appearance to be as different from Jana as she could manage. You just have a good look at her next time you see her. So anyway, they took the girls from the club down to the station and set up some identity parades for the officers to pick them out under controlled conditions. Jasmine got a lawyer on the job and he made sure she was on the identity parade standing side by side with her sister. They were hoping that with no positive identification they'd have to let them both go.'

'So Jana got off on a technicality because she couldn't be identified?'

'Well not quite. What seems to have happened is that the police were wise to which sister was which and the officer in question had been tipped off. He picked out Jana who they'd arrested instead of Jasmine because he knew she'd been drafted in to fill up the identity parade. But Jana wasn't the one he slept with. Of course if he'd picked out Jasmine who he'd actually slept with he'd have been wrong too because she wasn't the one who'd been arrested.'

'Neat. And I just have this little suspicion at the back of my mind that the officer in question was a certain PC Mills?'

'Got it in one. On the night when the cops did their raid Jana had been over on the other side of Celebration visiting her mother who's ill in a nursing home. And she could prove it too because some of the staff saw her and most of them can tell the difference between the two sisters. All the other girls were carted off and charged, but Jana and Jasmine walked free. And what's more, the police had to provide a written apology and erase the deep scan they'd done of Jana when they arrested her.'

'They did a deep scan?'

'As you probably know, there's a lot of resistance here to deep scanning but the authorities want to catalogue as many people as they can, so they brought in a law that allows them to scan anyone who's arrested. But if someone isn't charged, or is acquitted, they have to erase the scan.'

'So that explains how Jana came to know she was a Delta 2.'

'Exactly, and as it happened there was an advertising campaign going on to try and recruit people with rare mind-types as TranzCon hosts.'

'And that's why Jana became available. She appeared quite suddenly because on the first day we started looking for a host she wasn't on the list. So presumably Jasmine's a Delta 2 as well. Why didn't she put herself forward as a TranzCon host.'

'Because she's got a criminal record.'

'For what?'

'For prostitution of course - she served six months when she was just eighteen. She must need the money pretty badly if she's still on the game after serving time. They'll send her down for a year if she gets caught again'

'Poor girl. What about Jana?'

'She hasn't got any record, but that doesn't prove she hasn't worked as a prostitute.'

'But on the TranzCon application form it asks questions about things like that. They won't take anyone who's been involved with the sex trade.'

'And of course everyone answers everything absolutely honestly each time.'

Jon smiled. 'OK, point taken.'

'Look Jon.'

Jon noticed that Kamar had called him Jon rather than Jana and hadn't evaded using a name the way he had done before.

'Yes.'

'Jon, I'm coming around to the idea that you've been telling the truth about still being the traveller from Vissan.'

'So what's made your mind up?'

'Well I've just told you a lot of things about Jana and her sister, and I was watching you, picking up clues. It's something you have to learn if you want to be a successful lawyer. Every time I told you a piece of information you gave a reaction as if it was news to you. I don't think anyone could have been so genuine if they'd already known about what it was they were hearing.'

'Well I'm pleased there's at least one other person on the planet who believes in me.'

'Who's the other one?'

'Jasmine. She took precisely ten seconds to work out that I was still the "mind traveller" as she described me. Perhaps we should arrange for the judge to get to know me so he'll be convinced who I really am.'

'Nice idea, but it's not going to happen. Anyway, I think we're both agreed that the best policy for tomorrow is to go along with being Jana. Then we'll have a few weeks to work out a defence, and of course there's always the chance that the beam might come back on-line, even if it's only at sufficient strength for communications. The police will bring you to the courthouse tomorrow morning and I'll be waiting for you.'

★★★

When Kamar departed and the policewoman had banged the heavy door shut Jon was almost in shock at the knowledge that he was locked in. Fear rose up inside him and he began to worry that the building might catch fire leaving him trapped. Whether it was a reaction that had stirred in his own mind or something that came from his host he wasn't sure. In his own body he hadn't been keen on being confined anywhere though he'd never considered himself to be claustrophobic.

After a while the feeling subsided and for hours he sat there, staring at the wall and feeling bored. Then he remembered about Arnie. They'd left the little dog in the back of the police car down in the underground car park, but he'd had so much on his mind since then he'd completely forgotten. Reaching for his mobile phone was almost an instinct, but of course there was no mobile to reach for and banging on the cell door produced no response.

Later on he felt sleepy enough to nod off on the thin mattress, but his night's sleep was far from peaceful.

***

Jon awoke but how long he'd been asleep or whether it was morning he'd no idea. Sleep failed to return so after a while he got up and sat on the bed, and to his reckoning it must have been about a fortnight later when breakfast finally arrived. When the policewoman came to take back the tray she told him they'd be along to fetch him in half an hour, so he needed to be ready by then. As if there was anything at all he needed to do.

Precisely why it was necessary for two burly policemen to escort a harmless looking girl weighing barely more than fifty kilos dripping wet to court in handcuffs wasn't clear to Jon, but he wasn't in the business of upsetting anyone that morning so he made no protest. Anyway, what really mattered today was whether he'd be wearing the handcuffs on the way out of court. The thought of more nights alone in the creepy greyness of the cell was more than he could stand.

As the entourage came up into the entrance foyer of the courthouse building Jon saw Kamar waiting there. The lawyer tagged on behind as they walked to the waiting area outside the courtrooms.

The short hearing went just as Kamar had predicted, though DS Mills was visibly disappointed to hear Jon confirm his identity as Jana Kell. Perhaps the man had wanted more of a fight.

The charges were made and the date of the trial was set for just over a week's time. Bail was granted in the surety of 2000 Phen, but subject to the requirement for Jon to report to his local police station every alternate day and for him to surrender Jana's passport. But even this requirement was dropped when the Central Records computer confirmed that no passport had ever been issued to Jana Kell. The police had opposed bail as Kamar expected, but the magistrate took no notice.

Jon paid the bail using Jana's credit card, leaving the account with virtually no funds available. With his other sources of money closed off he wondered exactly what he was going to live on for the time between now and the trial, but that was the least of his worries. He thought of how things might be just nine days into the future when the trial was over. Would he be walking out to a prison van handcuffed between the two policeman? The elation of being granted bail had evaporated just a little too quickly.

69

The Meeting With TranzCon

With worries for the future on hold for a while the only thing on Jon's mind as he walked away from the courthouse was to wonder what had happened to Arnie. Was the little dog still shut up in the back of the police car - surely not?

Back at the police station the desk sergeant told him the dog had been sent out to a pet-minding service and there would be a 20 Phen charge for one night's care and food. Jon found a bus to take him to the kennels way out on the edge of the city and paid the account using some of the precious credit limit that was all he had left on Jana's card. Then the two of them set out for a long walk home - Arnie needed the chance to run and he needed some time to think.

When six weary feet finally climbed the steps up to the second floor and staggered into Jana's little flat the pair of them collapsed one after the other into the favourite chair. With the little furry bundle curled up on his lap Jon felt safe for the first time in two days and wondered whether the dog had spent as bad a night as he had. Little Arnie, so loving, so trusting, so forgiving after being dumped into kennels overnight, and so unaware of the impending peril that faced his master, or as nature had it right then, maybe his mistress. After everything that had been said, after all the evidence the police had put forward, especially the final confirmation of the transfer they'd somehow received from Jackson, he was confused and not really sure of anything.

Maybe he was Jana after all? Maybe it was as they'd been trying to tell *her* for so many weeks. Jon Chandler had been no more than a passing event in *her* life, an event that had messed up *her* mind so badly *she* didn't even know who *she* was anymore. Was it possible?

★★★

By the time morning came round again Jon felt more like himself, though he remembered all too well the confusion he'd experienced the previous evening. Maybe that was how it would happen? Maybe he'd remember his true self in brief snatches that came more and more frequently until finally they joined together, and at last he'd truly know who he was - who *she* was. But for now he felt like Jon.

As he was eating breakfast his mobile rang. Kamar had arranged a meeting with TranzCon for first thing after lunch and he needed Jon to be there.

★★★

Back in the featureless interview room Jon sat side by side with Kamar while Mrs Daniels sat opposite. The woman began the meeting:

'As I explained to you on the phone Mr Kamar, the initial advice of a transfer having taken place is an internal communication within TranzCon and this is issued purely for operational reasons. We then have twelve hours to make a formal confirmation that the transfer took place and this goes out as an official notification that two people have moved to new locations in the galaxy. TranzCon are obliged to do this by Union law, and as you are no doubt aware, our operation on Phoenix is following the same requirements until we have legislation of our own.'

Kamar looked convinced, though as Jon knew, the whole story hadn't been told yet. He asked the question that was on his mind. 'But what if you're still not sure after twelve hours, what do you do then?'

Mrs Daniels was quick to answer. 'This is something which happens from time to time, particularly with people making transfers for the first time, and in many cases where the transfer has been carried out under flat-line conditions. In these cases we issue a notice of indeterminate status, and this buys us a further twelve hours before we either have to give a final confirmation or renew the notice of indeterminate status.'

'And how do the authorities react to the notice of indeterminate status when they can't say for certain which state or planet someone is in or on?'

'Legally they have to accept it, and in practice it's rarely a problem because usually it means the traveller in question is asleep or incapacitated. If that is the case they're not able to participate in any of the usual activities which make it necessary for the authorities to know where they are. Things like making financial transactions or business deals - you can't do them unless you're up and about, and if you're up and about then it's possible to make a final confirmation.'

Kamar obviously had a question, but he took a few moments to consider his position before he came in. 'The traveller here, whether he's Jon or she's Jana, told me that the transfer in this case took place under flat-line conditions. Am I right?'

'You are correct.'

'And for a pair of inexperienced Delta group travellers going through under flat-line conditions, what are the chances they could have been up and about within twelve hours?'

'Almost nil. I'd have been surprised if either of them could have managed it in twice that long.'

Kamar continued. 'And yet the timestamp on the final confirmation signal TranzCon belatedly received was within twelve hours of the transfer.'

Kamar handed Mrs Daniels a sheet of printout. Her face looked as though she could have been pushed over backward with nothing stronger than a feather. Kumar looked at her for an answer.

'It's impossible, it should have been a notice of indeterminate status.'

Kamar drove his point home. 'What if they'd got it wrong? Could they have sent another signal to move the travellers down to indeterminate status? What if that signal had been transmitted later, after the brief window when the beam came back on-line?'

If the woman had been brought down to the ground just seconds ago she'd now had chance to remount the high horse she was accustomed to riding.

'There are no recorded incidents of TranzCon ever having got it wrong.'

'But you accepted just now that the signal they sent was impossible. So go on, tell me truthfully, is there a chance there's another signal somewhere in the system, maybe stuck in a buffer somewhere that we haven't received yet? Could there really be a signal out there which is going to downgrade the travellers' status to indeterminate?'

Mrs Daniels was backed into a corner now. She almost stammered as she spoke.

'Well yes, …. yes there is that possibility.'

Kamar came in for the kill.

'And if that possibility exists, no-one here on this planet can say for certain whether the traveller sitting in this room with us now is Jana Kell or Jon Chandler.'

★★★

Jon and Kamar went for a coffee afterwards to discuss the progress they'd made. Kamar told him of his plan to ask the court for a suspension until Jon's true status could be confirmed once and for all, because as they both knew, that couldn't be until the beam came back on-line. When that happened the truth would come out one way or another, and until then Jon could remain on bail from the magistrate's court.

Jon wondered whether his money would have been wasted on a hot-shot lawyer.

70

Rejected

With the worry of knowing the fate that might be waiting for him never far from his mind Jon's life was quite a lot less happy than it had been just a few days earlier. But until it happened normal life had to go on.

He was just coming in from the shops when he stopped in the entrance hall to check the mail box. At first he thought it was empty, but the girl's hand touched on something. A single envelope was lurking there at the back of the box. The girl's heart skipped a beat when he read the return address on the back of the envelope.

Up in the flat he opened it and read the contents. It wasn't good news. Phoenix Intersolar had replied in a standard format to tell him that unfortunately on this occasion his application for employment had not been successful, but they would be pleased to consider him if a suitable post arose in the future. The human resources assistant Ms E. Watson had obviously signed it with her own hand. He made a mental note to add another item to the list of disadvantages of being called Jon.

What clicked with him at that moment, was that none of the jobs listed in the letter included any of those he'd had in mind for a young female applicant. Jobs like being a cleaner, a chambermaid, a kitchen assistant, or a waitress. Perhaps he'd applied to the wrong division of PI? Perhaps he'd applied for a post on the operational space crew after all and had been rejected due to Jana's lack of training or qualifications.

There was a contact number on the letter heading so Jon decided he'd ring up to see whether there had been a mistake. Fortunately the number was a direct dial for Ms Watson and Jon was elated when a female voice came from the other end. *Elizabeth* was pleased to speak to him and she confirmed that Jon's application had been made to the correct department, but she told him that the all the categories of employment he'd referred to were allocated to something she called "prisoner-crew".

Jon didn't understand the term so she went on to explain - certain low risk prisoners could be given the chance to serve part of their sentences working for their keep in menial roles. The job title meant exactly what it said and the posts were only open to non-violent offenders who'd already served at least a quarter of their sentence.

When Jon told her how desperate he was to get to Darius she made a joke about him going out to commit a crime just so he could sign on as a member of the prisoner-crew because there were a few categories where they still had some vacancies. At first Jon laughed with her, but the memory of the night he'd spent locked up and the prospect of there being more like that worried him more than he cared to admit.

The woman rang off and Jon knew that this time he had to accept that the Hyperion would be leaving without him. But his old ship was just the first of many that would make the passage over the coming years, and a ship operated by a Union company would most certainly not be allowed to cut its costs by using what amounted to slave-labour. Maybe next time he'd stand a better chance of a job.

71

Jasmine Returns

Jon knew Jasmine had come down from the Hyperion a few days earlier and it had been his intention to go round and see her after she'd had time for a good long lie-in. But what with being locked up in the cells or busy with Kamar there hadn't been a chance for them to meet up. Now after everything he'd found out in the past few days he'd more than one bone to pick with her.

When he arrived at the flat he rang the doorbell and banged on the glass panelling so hard he hurt the girl's hand. When nothing had happened after ten seconds he rang the bell again. After a few seconds he saw a dark shape move behind the door before it opened.

Jasmine stood there in her dressing gown looking tired. 'OK, OK. I'm here. What's the hurry?'

Jon was pleased to see her, though he wasn't prepared to forget the anger that was bubbling inside. He followed her in and pushed the door closed behind him. Jasmine crashed onto the sofa. Jon took the easy chair.

'The hurry is that I want to talk to you about a few important matters. Don't you think you ought to have told me about your little vendetta with DS Mills?'

Jasmine propped herself up on a cushion, suddenly alert.

'Look Jon, any connection we had with that bastard is strictly to do with me and Jana. You can keep your nose out of our business. OK?'

Jon gave a snort. 'I'd be only too happy to, but I've been locked up in a police cell thanks to the antics of you and your sister. Why didn't you warn me about him?'

'I thought the whole thing was over. We won, he lost, case closed.'

'That one might be closed, but Mr Plod's not forgotten it. He's had his eye on you and Jana every day since, just waiting for one of you to step out of line. That's why you changed your appearance so much isn't it?'

She nodded. 'It's true, but he's got to catch us stepping out of line first. There shouldn't have been any trouble.'

Jon was starting to get rattled and let it show. 'Well there is, and it all comes down to me still being stuck here on this dung heap of a world. No-one but you will believe I'm Jon Chandler, and now it's getting me into some serious trouble. I'm out on bail for now but next week there's a serious chance they're either sending me to jail or a mental hospital.'

Jasmine pulled herself upright in the chair. 'So what have you actually done?'

Jon told her the whole story, how he'd been able to access his own bank account because the Central Records computer wasn't up to date, how there'd been a brief spurt of communication that appeared to show Jon Chandler had returned home, and how they were prosecuting him now because they all insisted he was Jana.

'Well Jon, I'm sorry but you can see their point can't you. And really, it's not due to anything that Jana did is it?'

'OK, but it's only gone this far because Mills wants to send one of the Kell sisters down. He doesn't give a toss who's living in the body, he just wants to see the flesh in jail. Is that fair on me? If I'd known about him I might have had the chance to be more careful. Anyway, the whole sodding thing comes down to you being on the game. You told me a lot of reasons why you wouldn't do a TranzCon transfer and all the while you knew you'd never be allowed to work as a host because you'd got a criminal record. If you hadn't been getting screwed for money I wouldn't be in this mess right now.'

Jasmine leaned forward and looked him in the eye. Jon saw the anger on her face, heard the venom in the normally soft voice, and wondered whether he'd poked open a hornet's nest.

'And do you suppose I don't hate myself every time I have to do it. Every single fucking time? And what about Gary, how do you suppose he feels knowing his woman gets used by other men?'

Jon just looked, without knowing what to say.

'And you, you little prude, what help have you been? None, no fucking help at all. Little miss goody twoshoes wouldn't even drop her precious pants one lousy fucking time so her mother could have a decent place to live in her dying days. Have you even seen the kind of place they send you when you've got no money? Well have you?' she shouted. 'It's all down to me isn't it? I've got to keep on doing it till either she's dead or they cart me off to jail again. And I'll get a year next time, you know that. How does it make you feel to know your sister will risk a year inside when you're not prepared to do even the slightest thing to help?'

Jon heard what she was saying and guessed it was an argument that must have passed between the two sisters many times in the past. He didn't know what to think, he didn't know whether he should respect Jana for sticking to her principles, or Jasmine for doing whatever she'd had to to get the money they so desperately needed. And what was real life for so many suddenly came home to him in a way he could never have imagined before. For the whole of his life money had been a toy, something to be played with, something you used to make more. And when people wanted it from you, you handed it over, as much as they wanted, never needing to count how much, never needing to count how much was left. There was always more, always enough, always more than enough. And here was this poor girl who sold the most precious possession a woman owned, and just for money. Not money to spend on a lavish lifestyle, not money for clothes or jewels, just the money to support her closest family.

In that moment, and for the first time in his life Jon hated the wealth he'd had, he hated his father for being rich, he hated him for passing on the greed he'd learned as a child, for tutoring his own children in the ways of making more, and more, for no reason other than to be rich.

He looked over at Jasmine, she was holding her head in her hands now, weeping quietly. Not daring to speak Jon watched in silence for some minutes before she spoke again.

'Jon I'm sorry, I know it's you I'm talking to and not Jana. I shouldn't have involved you in our family affairs.'

'It's OK Jasmine, it's OK. I didn't know and I involved myself. I should have respected your family and kept myself out of what doesn't concern me. Look, I'm building up some money now, I can pay something towards your mother's stay.'

'Don't insult me Jon, this isn't to do with you. If the only way I have of getting money is to work on my back, then that's what I'll do. God knows it's not for many more years. It might only be for months, and when it's over, not even one more time. With God as my witness I tell you, not even once!'

Jon slipped over to the sofa and put his arm around the crying girl. He waited until he thought the time was right to speak again.

'You know Jana is due to get some money for being a TranzCon host don't you? And it's a lot more than normal because she's a rare mind type. Perhaps this is what she was doing to contribute towards keeping your mother. I think the money will have come into her account by now. If we can find a way of getting it out you can have it. For your mother.'

Jasmine wiped the tears from her eyes. 'OK, OK. I'll take what would have been Jana's, and nothing more. You understand how it is, do you Jon?'

And Jon did understand. For the first time in his life he'd glimpsed how things were for the ordinary people. The poor ones, the insignificant ones he'd hardly noticed before. He saw how they had pride. Even in poverty they still had pride. Now his life had changed, everything had changed. He felt nothing but respect for this girl who'd sold herself as a plaything for men. And he thought of all the playthings he'd used over the years and hated himself. She deserved the money more than he did, of that he had no doubt.

72

The Meeting With Kamar

With the trial looming ever closer Jon was pleased that Kamar was working hard on the case, and when the man phoned to ask him to come in for a meeting he was on the next bus.

Kamar's office was anything but a grand affair though it fitted well with the aspirations of a young lawyer just getting his career off the ground. The room where they met was dark with shadows cast by the high shelves of legal tomes that surrounded them. There was scarcely room for a chair in on the other side of the lawyer's desk.

Kamar shuffled a wad of papers and turned them towards his client. Since the meeting with TranzCon he'd been doing more research into Jon's indeterminate status and was convinced that using it in court was the best approach they could take. Jon would claim to be himself and they would ask for the trial to be postponed until a reconfirmation of his status could be obtained.

But as so often happens, some silver linings have clouds because when he'd heard the long and short of his situation

Jon's happy disposition reverted to the glum expression he'd worn the week before.

Kamar explained. 'Establishing indeterminate status means they can't prosecute you for any crime. That's the good news.'

Jon looked expectantly. 'And the bad?'

'For anything other than a non-violent crime the police would have the right to hold you in custody.'

Jon was puzzled. 'That sounds reasonable. If that's the bad news I think I can take it.'

Kamar shook his head. 'It's almost certain we can get a ruling of indeterminate status but in this state it makes you an *illegal*.'

'An illegal?'

'An illegal immigrant. I know a bit about how things are organised in the Union. Somehow, in a way we could scarcely imagine here on Phoenix, you've managed to build a society of 30 billion people that travels freely between eight occupied planets and hundreds of airless worlds. And it's also a society that's remarkably equal in terms of wealth.'

'Some are more equal than others.'

Kamar looked puzzled, as if he hadn't understood the expression.

'Here on Phoenix there are many separate states. As an emissary of the Union you've only dealt with the most advanced and richest of the states, but I can assure you there are places where people live in poverty.'

'Why does the government allow it?'

'The government of this state tries hard to support the poorer countries, but it's always an uphill struggle. The poorer states don't want to be patronised, and they're fearful of political motives. And of course there's always so many things at home that need money, so any government that spends too much abroad runs the risk of being voted out at the next election.'

Jon understood exactly what Kamar meant.

'Well what happens is, the people from the poor states are always looking for a better life and they know they can find it, or at least they think they can find it, in the rich states.'

Jon's eyes lit up at the thought.

'I'd do it if I was one of them.'

'That's what millions of people think, but consider this, if too many were allowed to come in they'd swamp our economy. The government has to impose an annual quota, and once it's filled, no more are allowed in.'

Jon was up to speed now. 'As an entrepreneur I think I can see an opportunity here.'

'And you're right. Smuggling people into the rich states is big business.'

'And those who manage to get in without official permission are called "Illegals".'

'Exactly.'

'But how does that affect me? I don't want to sound too smug about it, but I think we're all agreed that the Union is a rather bigger fish than all the states of Phoenix put together. It's in a totally different league to these poor states you're speaking about. I mean, it's not as if I'm here to steal anyone's job.'

'That's easy to agree, but it doesn't mean the Union enjoys any different status. The major states here on Phoenix have living, working and travel agreements that allow freedom of movement for their citizens. The Union isn't party to any such agreement.'

'But surely, I can't be an illegal because this body belongs to a citizen of this state.'

'But to claim the rights that go with the body you'd have to agree you were Jana Kell, and then the court wouldn't be waiting for confirmation of your status. You could be tried for the crimes she's committed and sent to jail. Maybe the whole thing might get overturned once communications were re-established, but in the meantime you'd be spending your time in custody.'

'Yes, I see the problem. But tell me this, how is it that anyone who comes here from the Union isn't immediately treated as one of these "illegals"?'

'In the absence of any formal framework there's an interim agreement for Union people to stay up to thirty days at a time. That covers anyone who comes on a TranzCon transfer.'

'What about Timothy Darling?'

'He's a special case. He has diplomatic status and can stay until the Union is asked to withdraw him. It's the same with any of his staff who're here in their own bodies.'

'So as a government minister, surely I'd be entitled to diplomatic status.'

'If we could prove you were Jon Chandler then yes. All it would take would be a few emails, but without the beam there's no way.'

'So assuming I am one of these illegals. What happens to me?'

'The normal procedure is to return them to the state from which they came.'

Jon smiled. 'And that's exactly what I want. All I need is for someone to arrange it for me.'

'But as we both know, it can't be done at the moment.'

'So I'll have to stay and wait until it can be done. Problem solved!'

'I don't think you understand what's involved Jon. You wouldn't be free to come and go as you please. They have the right to hold you in custody until they can deport you. It would be secure accommodation rather than jail, but you'd still be locked up.'

Jon was furious now. 'And what if holding a Union government minister effectively in jail lead to some sort of diplomatic incident? I don't know if you follow Union politics but I'm in a good position to take over as First Minister next year and I'll have more power than you could possibly imagine. I might just veto the Phoenixan application to join us. There's quite a lobby who think there's nothing to be gained from throwing money at a useless mudball like this heap of shit you call a planet. I could gain quite a bit of support if I switched horses.'

Kamar looked at him. Jon noticed the changed expression on the dark face.

'If I'd been in any doubt as to your real identity before Jon, I can tell you I'm not now.'

Jon looked perplexed. 'Why's that?'

'Because a 22 year old girl wouldn't harbour malicious ideas like that.'

Jon thought for a moment and looked ashamed. This was his problem, something he had to solve by himself. Slapping a whole planet in the face for what was after all just a minor inconvenience wasn't the answer for a politician of his calibre. In that moment Jon felt very small. He realised that what happened to him over the coming months wasn't part of the big picture. Somehow it left him abandoned by his own people, and yet there was another feeling in there somewhere, a feeling that had somehow set him free. Free from the responsibilities of the position he held. And free to operate in a way he'd never considered before.

73

The Decision

Almost three months had passed since the fateful day when Jon had laid himself down in TranzCon's scanner for the unsuccessful attempt to get home to Vissan. Back in his old life he'd made so many liner trips out to Temenco and Miranda so he was used to being away, but this had been his longest absence by far and now he was almost crazy to get home. If only the beam would work again, just for one day. It had worked to get him here, so why couldn't it just work once more? Eventually they'd overcome the problem but years would pass before he stood any chance of getting away.

And now he had another worry to contend with. If the people who ran this state got their way he was destined to spend a lot of that time incarcerated in one way or another. He wondered why people in authority always seemed to want to lock him up. What could it possibly achieve? But he knew this much, it was one thing to be taken away from his life and career on Vissan, it was another to have to live here on Phoenix in Jana's lovely, but entirely unsuitable body, it was one more thing to have to live in poverty, never really knowing where the next meal was coming from, but to live as a prisoner? The loss of his personal freedom was one step more than he could manage.

His thoughts turned back to the Hyperion. How he wished he'd been able to get a job on board so he could have travelled to Darius. The ship was due to leave orbit in just over a week, if only there was a way he could be on it.

And then a thought crossed his mind. The kind of thought he'd never entertained before. He smiled. The easiest decisions were always the ones that made themselves.

Just four weeks ago he'd posed as Jasmine to cover her shift up on the ship. And he could do it again. He'd get back up there and stow away. Three decades ago he'd known the Hyperion like the back of his hand and he knew that little had changed. If anyone could find a hideyhole somewhere on board it was him. Even if he was discovered en-route all was not lost because there was no way the captain was going to turn his star liner round to return a single stowaway. The journey would be the longest he'd ever undertaken, and two years was a serious chunk of anyone's life, but compared to the alternatives it was the best option available.

The more he thought about it, the more he knew it was his only sure way of getting home, and his only sure way of staying out of jail. And then there was something else that tugged at him from deep inside, a sense of adventure. He wanted to do it, just for the hell of it.

★★★

Now he'd decided on his course of action Jon needed a plan to stand a chance of getting away. Ambling slowly round the park with Arnie he'd put his plan together like the pieces of a jigsaw. It was going to work, he just had to take it one step at a time.

Of course he was going to miss Arnie, but he'd be parted from the little dog if he stayed on Phoenix and they sent him to jail. Stupid to even think of ending his life three hundred lightyears from home just because of a dog. Sorry Arnie.

Back in the flat with a cup of tea in hand he reviewed his plan and put a little more meat on the bones. He'd gone through how he was going to get up to the ship at least a dozen times and now the scheme was close to fool-proof. The biggest flaw in his plan was finding enough money to buy food on board. The free sandwich trick he'd worked in the local shop might work once or twice, but if he tried it every day for a hundred weeks he was sure to get caught.

And even the money he had was running out. After being caught using the card for his own bank account, that source of funds had been closed down. And too much of the money he'd saved in cash had gone to pay his bail.

Then a thought came into the girl's head. He'd lost Jana's bank card when it had been swallowed by the machine, and his application for a replacement had been rejected because Central Records had insisted that Jana was still on Vissan. Now he'd been caught after Central Records had relayed the information to his bank that Jon Chandler had succeeded in travelling home. It simply wasn't fair, but perhaps there might be something in there he could use to his advantage. If Jon was on Vissan, Jana had to be on Phoenix, and if Jana was on Phoenix it followed that her bank would be ready and willing to issue a new debit card. He had the details, he had the signature and he had the irises. But even before he'd had chance to celebrate he knew it wasn't going to work - it would take too long to get a card sent by post. The ship was leaving in just over a week and he was hoping to be a long way out in space before the postman dropped the precious envelope on the mat.

But then he thought, maybe there might be a way after all.

Walking back to the flat he stopped at an ATM and did a check on Jana's credit card account. There wasn't much left before it was going to hit the credit limit again, but he drew it out anyway. After they got back home he told Arnie to be good and left the flat alone to jump on a bus into the city. He found the branch of the Phoenix Mutual Bank that had been on Jana's statements about half a kilometre's walk from the central terminus.

After standing in a queue for a few minutes his turn came up and he explained his problem to the friendly young man at the enquiry desk. He passed over a form for Jon to complete, and after queuing a second time he passed it back. The man checked the details and told him his new card would be there to collect in ten days time. Why did everything always take ten days?

Jon tried his luck. 'Is there any way I can draw out some money before the card comes?'

The look on the man's face told Jon the answer was going to be a good one.

'Yes of course, here in your own branch you can fill in a cheque form and the cashier will pay you over the counter. But until you've got your card there's a daily withdrawal limit of 200 Phen. I hope that will be alright for you?'

Jon would have preferred more, but what else could he do? If he drew the maximum amount every day he might just accumulate enough. The man helped him with the cheque and he took it to the cashier's window. A slip of paper whirred up out of the printer. The girl put it on top of the notes she'd just counted and pushed the pile under the security barrier. Jon whistled as quietly as he could when he looked at the slip and saw that the payment due from TranzCon had arrived in

Jana's account. It obviously included the premium for rare mind-types.

74

Fooled You!

Three days came and three days went. Each morning Jon made the trip down town to draw out his allowance and now it was time for the next part of his plan. Back at Jana's flat he picked up the phone and dialled. He could hear it ringing at the other end but no-one was picking up. Half an hour later he tried the number again and this time Jasmine's voice came on the line.

'Hi, it's Jon.'

'How's it going Jon. Any closer to getting home?'

'The short answer's "No", but there's a chance they might be able to acknowledge that I'm Jon Chandler. There's a lab they've set up with some of the equipment that arrived from Darius and they can do a new type of deep scan that could prove who I really am. The trouble is, it uses so much computer power they can only run it at off-peak times when the network's quiet, so they need me to go in and stay overnight.' Jon rejoiced at his ability to lie convincingly.

'I think I can see the problem Jon, you need someone to look after Arnie?'

'Spot on. What I'm thinking is you could avoid upsetting your landlord by coming round here and staying overnight. Bring Gary as well, I won't be needing the place.'

'OK, sounds good. When's it happening?'

'The first run is tomorrow night, and then they need to do another one the next night so they can compare them to see if anything's changed in-between.'

'Right, so it's two nights then. Shouldn't be a problem though. Will you be back during the day?'

'No the place is right out by Woodbridge so it's a bit of a trek. Anyway I think they've got something else they want to do with me during the day, and I'll need a few hours sleep too. But I'll be back with you Thursday evening and I'll take over Arnie again. OK?'

'I'll see you in the morning then. Half-ten OK?'

★★★

Jon was up early next morning and it was just after seven when he walked into the local police station to report as part of his bail conditions. Whether the officer on the desk knew what time it was Jon neither knew nor cared, but he didn't seem bothered. He signed his initials against Jana's name on the sheet. Job done - tick.

From the police station into the city was only a few minutes on the bus so by nine he was already in the queue outside the central branch of Phoenix Mutual. If the cashiers there were getting suspicious about the visits he made to withdraw his daily allowance, so far they'd never made any comment.

Back at the flat Jon pulled Jana's holdall bag down from the top of the wardrobe and packed a few clothes for two nights away. Anything more might cause Jasmine to wonder about his plan. He pushed the chest of drawers away from the wall and pulled back the carpet to reveal his stash of cash money. 1000 Phen in low value notes looked like quite a lot but he knew it wasn't going to be enough. If only there'd been time for more trips to the bank.

***

It was going on eleven when Jasmine and Gary finally arrived, and it wasn't a moment too soon if he was going to make it on time. He grabbed the holdall and headed for the door.

'Sorry about this guys, but I've got to dash. I've boiled the kettle for you if you want some coffee.'

'No that's OK. Has Arnie been out this morning?'

'Only out in the garden. I didn't have time to take him for a walk.'

'OK then, we'll start off with a trip to the park and we'll see you Thursday night.'

'And if they recognise me as Jon Chandler, I'm taking you both out for something posh.'

'And if not, it's spag bol again?'

Jon smiled. 'That's about it, but I can run to a bottle of wine this week.'

Trying to look calm Jon took one last look around the little flat that had become home, and at the people who'd been his friends. Part of him wanted to stay, another part wanted to tell them about his plan to escape, but he knew neither was an option. He pulled the door closed behind him and headed off down the stairs.

***

Out in the street Jon wasted no time racing round to Jasmines flat as fast as the encumbrance of the holdall bag would let him. He pulled the plant out of its pot and to his relief the foil package with the key inside was still there. If it hadn't he'd have had to have broken in, and that might have alerted the neighbours. For all his talents Jon was not an accomplished burglar.

TranzCon

Quickly he pulled open drawer after drawer, knowing exactly what it was he was searching for but not really having any idea where Jasmine kept it. Suddenly he had a flash of inspiration and switched to looking through her clothes. It didn't take him long to find the overalls she wore for work on the ship and a quick frisk found a stiff bit in one of the pockets. The zip pulled open and to his relief there was her passport, the door access swipecard, and the white and blue ID card that was going to get him on board the Hyperion. Whether he kissed the card or the picture of Jasmine he wasn't sure. He pulled the overall out of the wardrobe and shoved the documents back into the pocket.

Jon knew Jasmine had a rucksack because he'd used it to carry his stuff up to the ship when he'd taken her shift. He found it stuffed behind the sofa and dragged it off to the bedroom to fill with more clothes from the wardrobe. Next he was off to the kitchen - he pulled open the drawer next to the sink and took out the can opener and a spoon.

Now it was coming to the hardest bit. He ripped off his outer clothes and stuffed them in the rucksack before heading for the bathroom. He found the dye Jasmine used to keep her hair dark in the wall cabinet and within minutes he was rinsing it through Jana's normally golden locks. He had to look like the picture on the ID card or someone would smell a rat.

Knowing how tight he was for time there was no chance to do the kind of makeup job Jasmine had done on him when he went up to the Hyperion before, but he found the heavy earrings he'd worn. As quickly as he could he pulled on some of Jasmine's garish garb and looked at himself in the mirror - it wasn't brilliant but it would do for going to work.

For his final act he pushed closed all the drawers he'd opened and tried to leave the place just as he'd found it an hour earlier, though with the amount of junk that was normally lying around he wondered if anyone would even notice if the flat had been ransacked.

The rucksack was already heavy as he pulled it up onto the girl's small back and headed off out of the door. Carefully he wrapped up the door key and put it back into the plant pot.

Down at the corner shop he bought a dozen tins of meat stew, a multi-way screwdriver and a selection of books and magazines. It would all feel very heavy in the rucksack but he knew every bit of his load was going to be necessary.

Time was too tight for the bus and he could barely walk with the weight of the rucksack on the girl's back, so in an act of extravagance that went beyond anything he'd afforded since the day he'd been bounced back to Phoenix he stopped a taxi and directed the driver to the city's rail station.

75

The Stowaway

It had been touch and go whether he was going to make it to the station for the 13.15 train, and the one that left half an hour later might not have reached the spaceport in time for his flight, so the girl's heart had thumped madly as Jon had raced along the platform and hauled the heavy rucksack in through the first set of doors. Before he'd even had chance to look for a seat the doors had slid closed behind him. Talk about cutting it fine, but at least he could relax for a couple of hours now.

★★★

What the excuse was this time no-one bothered to say, but when the train pulled into Celebration Interplanetary it was over fifteen minutes behind schedule, something which would have been almost unthinkable on Vissan or any of the other home planets. But it meant he needed to run again.

Run! It was a nice idea but with the weight of the big rucksack bearing down on Jana's small frame and swaying from side to side he could barely walk. More than ever he longed for the sheer size and strength of his own body so far away - but then, getting his own body back was what this jaunt was all about.

"We're getting there Jon" he kept on telling himself, but it did nothing to assuage the girl's failing and aching muscles.

Considering the short distance it had to travel, the bus to KAL's terminal building took an age and time was still not on Jon's side, but at least a few minutes sitting down gave him a chance to recover. The doors opened with their customary wheeze and he struggled off, made a valiant attempt to swing the rucksack up only to lose his balance and watch as the heavy bag slumped onto the ground. Fortunately there was nothing breakable inside and luck was on his side when one of Jasmine's co-workers helped him get the weight up onto the girl's back.

Going through the doors into the entrance lobby Jon tried to act as calmly as he could when he joined the queue for the security barrier. "Just another woman going to work" - he hoped that was what his fellow travellers were seeing.

At last it was his turn. The card went into the slot followed by the usual delay, but it did its work and the barrier slid open. Quickly he rushed through the lounge to the shuttle bus that was waiting to take the small band of workers out to the Knightsky II.

★★★

Getting on board the spaceplane was almost a repeat performance of the trip before but with so few people on the flight now that most of the work on the big ship was done he had no trouble getting a window seat. He clicked in the ends of the five point harness and shut the girl's eyes. He was absolutely exhausted, though at this time in the middle of the afternoon it was no surprise to find that sleep failed to come. Or at least he hadn't thought he'd been to sleep, but when the next thing he knew was the massive push in his back as the craft accelerated to escape velocity he knew he must have dropped off for quite some time because he'd missed the whole refuelling exercise.

★★★

The arrival into the docking bay was as precise as the time before and Jon guessed the manoeuvre had been performed by the auto-pilot. The docking clamps bumped into place and soon he was on the grab-rail, heading for the hatch that would take them out into the Hyperion's hub. Slowly he edged along till he came to the luggage cage and eased out the big rucksack, now in freefall and lighter than the lightest feather though still possessing a lot of inertia. He remembered he'd have to compensate for the mass when he stopped to join the queue for the clock-on machines. Bull-dozering your fellow passengers out of the way was not the best way of making friends.

Once the workers had clocked-on and were back on the payroll the urgency of the situation dissipated and the rest of the procedure was more relaxed. Back on the rail they filed one by one into the elevator and strapped themselves into the seats that still appeared to be on the ceiling. Five more minutes and they were down to the main accommodation level and the rucksack was heavy again, though not quite as bone crushing as it had been down on the planet. But it was still much more than the girl's small frame could manage for any distance so he decided to do things the easy way and jumped on the shuttle-rail. Travelling just a single stop took no time at all, and then he was struggling with his burden again for the two minute walk to Juniper Block. When he finally staggered in through the doors to the hallway the girl's knees were almost buckling under the weight, but at last his goal was in sight.

Up on the top floor landing Jon went straight to the walk-in linen store and with a sigh of thanks he swung the rucksack down onto the carpet. He hid his books and the tins of stew under a pile of spare duvets and prayed that no-one would find them before he had chance to move them to the destination he had in mind.

The pass-card worked its magic and in a moment he was in through the door of the room Jasmine had last used. In the relative safety of the room he stripped off and changed into the working overalls he'd brought from her flat. Now he looked the part though he accepted there were still so many risks to be run before the ship was safely out into space. If it all went wrong now he was really in trouble.

According to Celebration time it was late in the day and the lighting level on the ship had dropped to its night-time minimum, so most of the workers would be in bed now getting some well earned rest before their long shifts began next morning. That said, he knew there were some parts of the work that had fallen behind and in the final frantic hours it was true to say that the ship never slept. He just had to hope there was no-one in the areas he needed to visit.

From the Standard class blocks where Juniper was located it was almost half a lap of the accommodation doughnut round to the outer command centre, so Jon hopped back on the shuttle-rail to speed things up. He went straight to the control room and checked it for strangers before finding himself a terminal with a clear view of the entrance doorway. Even if someone came in there was still a chance he might get away with his plan.

Just as it had the time before, the command computer recognised his log-on and he searched through a few pages before he came across what he'd been hoping to find - a list of all the code operated locks on board. Quickly homing in on the lift-motor room at the top of Juniper Block he memorised the code and logged off before anyone had the chance to find him there and ask what in hell's name a cleaner thought she was doing in a restricted area.

Back on the top floor of Juniper block Jon stepped out of the lift, noted its number and wedged the door open with a mop in the way the cleaners so often did. He called the other lift and immobilised it with a brush. Anyone heading for the top floor now had six floors to climb so they wouldn't be around for a few minutes yet.

Jon knew he mustn't be found out at this critical stage in his plan so he listened carefully at the top of the stairs before entering the security code on the lift-motor room's access keypad. The lock bleeped and he heard the sound of the bolt as it motored back. As he pulled the door open he knew the action would be recorded by the ship's monitoring system, but if he was lucky no-one would notice or send a security team to investigate at this time of night.

He stepped into the doorway, found the right bit for his screwdriver and quickly unfastened the cover of the door control box set into the architrave. He spent a few seconds checking inside, tracing each wire back to the incoming cable. With several of the girl's toes crossed he pulled one of the small cores away from its terminal and pushed it onto the nearby spare - a small but subtle change that meant the door would always appear closed to the ship's security system. He held the cover in place over the box and fed the screws back in one by one. If he'd got it right his next stop would be Darius.

He stepped back onto the landing outside the lift and listened at the stairs again, still nothing. He stepped back into the lift-motor room, pulled the door closed behind him, and let out a gasp of breath that felt as if it had been in the girl's lungs since he'd left her flat. Heading up the stairs to the motor equipment floor he saw the two motors and their gearboxes directly over the lift-shafts, and as expected a bank of electrical panels mounted on the opposite wall. Although the room was quite large the space taken up by stairs and the equipment was more than he'd bargained on and the only flat space for his makeshift bed was going to be the narrow corridor between the motors and the panels. But it was enough, as long as he didn't reach out in the night and shut something off.

Then at the end of the room he saw a door he hadn't remembered. The girl's heart missed a beat. If it lead to another room or formed part of a thoroughfare to somewhere the techs needed to access, the motor room wasn't going to be the seldom visited dead end he'd been hoping for. And if that really was the case he'd need to start looking for somewhere else to hide. Pensively he tried the handle - it wasn't locked and the door pushed open in front of him and he found himself standing on the flat roof of the block. He walked over to the parapet wall and looked over, then suddenly pulled back when he realised that anyone down on the ground could have seen him.

But this wasn't what he'd come to do. He hurried back to the door and into the lift-motor room, stared at the electrical panels, found the controller for lift-motor No.1 and quickly tripped off its circuit breaker. Seconds later he left the motor room and pulled the door closed behind him. In the stillness and quiet of the empty accommodation block he heard the sound of the bolt as it motored home.

When he took the brush out from the door of lift No.2 it closed as he'd expected, but the lift stayed where it was on the top floor. Obviously no-one had called it while he'd been working. He pulled the mop out from the door of lift No.1 and it sat there, dark and lifeless.

Down on the ground floor of the block there was a phone. Jon tapped in the number for the command centre and reported the *failed* lift to the speech recognition system that was handling calls at this late hour of the night. Hopefully the duty technician was a shift worker and would come straight away.

Back on the top floor he disappeared into the bedroom but was careful to leave the door ajar so he'd hear the bing of the lift when the car arrived. With a duster ready in his hand in case he was discovered by a supervisor he waited in silence.

Over an hour passed before he heard the sound of the lift arriving. He rushed out just in time to see a young man in overalls carrying a tool-bag as he stepped out onto the landing.

'That's the one that's not working,' Jon said, pointing to the lift which obviously wasn't working.

'Are you the one who reported it?'

'Yes, I found it with the door open and the light off this evening when I came on shift.'

'Up here on the top floor.'

'Exactly where it is now.'

The man flipped open his handheld terminal and typed in the code from the label on the lift-motor room door. A number came up on the screen and he punched it into the access keypad. The bolt motored back and he pulled the door open. Now Jon was relieved - when the man put in his report the security system would be satisfied there'd been a valid reason for the door being open. The man went in and up the stairs two at a time, easy for legs that were young and long in the lower gravity of the top floor. A couple of minutes later he bounced back down with a smile on his face.

'No problem at all, just the breaker tripped out. Nothing obvious so I've reset it, and if it holds in for the next day and a half it'll do for me. After that it'll be up to the flight maintenance crew.'

'Are you nearly finished then?'

The young man nodded. 'Yeah. Been a good job this one and I'm sorry to see the ship go, but I heard they're buying another, so maybe we can do it all over again. Are you finished as well?'

The two of them chatted for a while and Jon wondered whether the guy was hoping for a date. He even wondered about arranging something just as an extra line of cover, but before he got chance to say anything the man's phone rang. He listened for a few seconds before pressing the off button and stashing it back into his pocket. He took a look at Jana's pretty face, probably wondering if he might get the chance to see her again before the ship left for Darius.

'Sorry. It was nice talking to you but there's real trouble this time. Just when we thought we'd got it cracked things seem to be going wrong all over the ship.'

He stepped into the now working lift and was gone.

Jon turned back to the door, punched in the code and spent the next few minutes moving his belongings up into the room that was to be home for the next two years. Certainly the floor space was smaller than the room he might have been destined to inhabit, but it had the advantage that the door opened when *he* chose and not just when someone came to unlock it.

But, tired as he was, his work was still far from over. There'd be more than enough time to rest just a few hours from now and it was better to get everything done while his fellow workers were sleeping. He scoured the nearby buildings and found as many discarded drinking water bottles as he could, filled them up from the taps in the top floor bedroom and stacked them carefully in the lift-motor room.

Now he looked around the room, it was already crowded with his belongings and knew that if anyone came back to check on the lifts again he'd be discovered for certain. But this wasn't a time for worrying, he had to hope and put his trust in luck. Next on the list was a bucket and some bin bags, things that were pretty easy for a cleaner to find.

The work had been a slog but at last it was coming to an end and the final item on his list was finding a bed. He'd known all along that getting hold of as much spare bedding as he needed was no problem unless they were going to be packed to capacity, and from the way they'd been advertising passages at ever reducing rates it was fairly clear the ship was going to be a long way short of full.

If the bedding had been easy to find, locating a mattress wasn't. Taking one off a bed was an option he'd considered though he knew it was something that would surely be noticed. But he'd still got a trick up his sleeve. He remembered the furniture they'd brought into the rooms when he'd been up on the ship covering Jasmine's shift. Each of the rooms was effectively a mini-suite and had a sofa as well as a separate bed, but they'd put bed-settees in some rooms because that was all the supplier could provide in time. He just had to find one.

The room he was using was the obvious place to start but no luck, it was only a standard sofa. He tried all the rooms on the top floor before moving down to the floor below but in the end he'd got all the way down on the first floor before he found what he was looking for. It took all the girl's strength for him to pull open the sofa-bed and drag out the folded-up bed mattress. With luck no-one would ever notice it was missing, even if the room was occupied.

Now it was done and he was ready. Tomorrow was going to be a big day and after a hard night's work he was desperate for rest. He walked down the stairs from the lift-motor room and into his top floor bedroom for one last night of comfort.

★★★

Or maybe that should have been *half-night* of comfort because his labours had taken him a long way into the small hours of the morning and it was just three hours later when he awoke to the sound of his alarm. Bleary eyed and weary he dragged himself out of bed and stood under the shower to try and wake himself up just a little. Finally he changed the bed-sheets and wiped out the shower so he'd leave no trace of his presence. Now he had a plane to catch.

Taking just the minimum with him in his now very light rucksack he headed for the spoke elevator and rode it up to the free-fall of the hub. Pulling himself along the grab-rail he made it to the security barrier and pushed Jasmine's card into the slot. The beep let him know Jasmine Kell was off the payroll again and the barriers slid open to let him through.

The spaceplane was late and hadn't arrived yet so he made his way up to the observation lounge to sit and wait. Grumbling slightly about the extra sleep he could have enjoyed he gazed out into the darkness and scanned around to see if he could be the first to spot the tiny point of light that moved against the background. For another ten minutes the room was almost silent, and then a man's voice called out:

'There, there it is!'

Jon looked out to where the man was pointing, but try as he might there was nothing he could make out, yet. Another two minutes passed before Jon saw the faint twinkling far out in the darkness. Two minutes more and the ship was clearly visible, approaching slowly - turning gently round and around. Then he saw the puffs of gas from the wingtip thrusters and the rotation stopped.

For the next ten minutes Jon watched as the spaceplane manoeuvred ever closer and saw the nose as it pushed its way into the loading bay. Clamps bumped in, umbilicals slid out to attach themselves to ports in the fuselage and the boarding tube extended to latch itself onto the seals around the hatch. Now it was time to get down to the loading area if he wanted a window seat for the flight back down to the surface, a space-eye view of the planet he hoped he'd never see again.

★★★

Depending on the weather conditions in its upper reaches re-entry to the atmosphere can be quite an unpleasant affair, and from the buffeting the spaceplane received on the way down this one was going to score pretty high on the chart. A few people had reached for their sick-bags though fortunately only one had been put to use. But the views over Celebration as they approached the spaceport from a clear blue sky were quite splendid in the early-afternoon sun. When the ship finally came to rest on the loading apron Jon sat in his seat and watched as the other passengers grabbed their belongings and joined the queue for the door. Well for people travelling in their own time there was no reason to hang about. He was the odd man out, he had all the time in the world.

When the last few workers from the ship were just disappearing out of the hatch Jon walked along to the exit and casually pulled his rucksack out of the cage. Even with the full gravity of the planet pulling at it the bag was so much lighter than before, not that he had far to carry it.

The shuttle bus took them to the lounge and Jon watched as the throng formed themselves into queues once again, each traveller anxious for the chance to push their card in so the final security barrier would part to let them through. But Jon had other plans - he headed for the toilets and found himself a cubicle. Anxiously he checked his watch because now timing was everything - it had to be right.

An hour passed and no-one else had come into the toilet in all that time. After another half-hour hard plastic seat was getting to be just a little uncomfortable so he stood up for a few minutes. Then came the sounds he'd waited for - women coming in for a last chance wee before they got on board. Facilities on the spaceplane for females were strictly for emergencies only, especially once the craft had reached orbit and freefall began. Casually he opened the cubicle door and washed the girl's hands.

Back out in the lounge he joined the queue that was forming for the bus. Fifteen minutes later he was back on board the Knightsky II, though this time the plane was busier and he didn't manage to get a window seat, but looking out at the view was far from a priority on this leg of the journey. He looked around at his fellow travellers. Everyone in the cabin with him was just a little subdued at the thought of going back to the grind, so despite the plane being full the ambience on board was noticeable quieter than it had been on the trip down. Just another routine commute to work. He was relieved to see that no-one took the slightest notice of him.

The take-off and climb went as planned. The re-fuelling procedure was immaculate in its precision. But the push into orbit was as exhilarating as ever and the views of the planet from space were breathtaking, though only for the lucky ones with window seats.

When the Hyperion was in sight and the spaceplane had commenced its docking manoeuvre Jon reached in the pocket in front of him and pulled out his sick-bag. As he'd been taught long ago he pulled the straps over his head, patted the sticky seal around the edges of the girl's mouth, and remembered to breath only through her nose. He pressed the call button and watched the cabin attendant as she floated over to check whether he'd got it fitted correctly. Throwing up in freefall was always bad news and could even be dangerous for people in range of the discharge.

'Not too good?'

Jon looked up at her as she hovered gracefully above him. He shook the girl's head slowly, being careful to not let on how well he was actually feeling.

'OK, stay in your seat till everyone else is off and avoid any more motion than necessary. Go steady on your way into the elevator, wait for an empty car and keep your bag on till you get back down into grav, just in case. Any problems, give me another call.'

As he'd been instructed Jon waited until the last of the passengers had disappeared through the hatch before floating up to the grab-rail and heading for the luggage cage. He hooked the rucksack strap around his left foot and followed the rail out of the hatch and into the hub. Taking his time he pulled himself along to one of the now deserted clock-on machines, but just as he brought the card up towards the slot he turned it back to front before he pushed it in - just a bit of play acting in case the security cameras were watching because nobody ever went on board without clocking on, well not unless they wanted to work for free.

★★★

Back out in the open on the main accommodation level Jon took the shuttle rail to Juniper Block, a repeat of his journey 24 hours earlier. He took the lift up to the top floor and his first stop was the bedroom he'd used the night before.

Standing in the shower he worked the shampoo into the girl's long hair and watched the dark stains as they ran off into a puddle around her feet before disappearing down the drain-hole. So much of the inky liquid ran off into the shower tray that he really thought it had all gone, so he was quite disappointed when he stepped out to look in the mirror - it scarcely looked as if any had washed out at all. The second time he washed the girl's hair still more of the colour came out, but it took a whole six washes before the suds turned white and the lovely golden shade began to show through. If security suspected there was a stowaway on board they'd be looking for Jasmine not Jana, and the switch from dark hair to blonde was his trump card.

With the last remnants of the dye cleaned up and the shower wiped dry the time had come for Jon to relinquish the comfort of the bedroom and take refuge up in the lift-motor room. He swung the rucksack up onto the girl's back, walked out of the room, tapped in the security code and headed up the stairs. The only thing for him to do now was to sit and wait - and hope - and worry. Three more days to go before the ship left orbit and he knew all too well that the sound of the door opening might be the death-knell for his plan. Now it was tins of cold stew for meals and a bucket for slops until the ship was out into space and up to hyperlight. At least if they found him after that he'd still be going to Darius, even if it did mean doing the journey in the brig.

76

Where's Jana?

Jasmine Kell curled up on the sofa with Arnie by her side, the little dog's furry head lying peacefully on her lap. There'd been no word from Jon and the system said his phone was turned off. Still off, after so long. She looked at Gary and then at her watch.

'I was sure Jon would've been back by now. He was due hours ago. What do you think could've happened?'

Gary was getting irritated now. His girlfriend had been whittling and worrying for hours, and all because of a virtual stranger too.

'I told you before Jas, there's nothing to worry about. He's probably ended up having to stay longer for the tests and you know what they're like in places like that, they don't even allow you to turn your phone on let alone make a call.'

'Yea, but I'm sure he could have got to a landline.'

'But not if he's got his head stuck in a scanner. Look it's not a problem, we'll make some dinner, enough for three, and if he turns up we all eat together. If not we can spend another night here and he'll be along in the morning. We can't go back to our place and leave Arnie can we?'

'OK. One more night and if he's not contacted us by tomorrow morning we start doing a bit of finding out and give this clinic place a ring.'

***

Morning came and found Jasmine back on the sofa, phonebook in one hand and mobile in the other. She made call after call but was getting nowhere.

Her first try had been to TranzCon and after she'd managed to fight her way through all the menu options she'd hung on for half an hour listening to some tedious music before she'd finally managed to speak to a real human being. The woman at the other end had tried to connect her to someone who might possibly have known about Jon Chandler, but the person she was after wasn't in that day.

Next she started looking up clinics to find one that fitted the description of what Jon had told her, but then she remembered the place was new so it was quite likely it wouldn't be in any of the phone books. She needed the laptop from her flat and was just putting her coat on when the doorbell rang. Obviously it wasn't Jon because he'd got a key, but it could be Gary coming back from the shops.

With Arnie hot on her heels she walked down the stairs and opened the door - two policemen in uniform. What the hell did those bastards want?

'Miss Kell?' the officer enquired.

'Yes, what about it?' She hadn't done anything wrong and saw no reason to be polite.

'Miss Kell we have a warrant for your arrest and instructions to take you into custody.'

Jasmine gave them the look she reserved for anyone in authority before she spoke.

'Oh yea, and what have I done this time?'

The taller of the officers spoke. 'It seems pretty obvious to me, Miss, that you've forgotten all about your court hearing at 10.00 this morning. It's Justice Hargreaves on today and he'll probably give you an extra couple of years just for messing him around. He's set a new date and he's not taking the chance you might not turn up a second time.'

A thought came into Jasmine's head. 'Who is it you want, Jana Kell or Jasmine Kell?'

'Jana Kell of course. This is her flat isn't it?'

Jasmine panicked. She turned to run back to the stairs but the cop grabbed her arm and held it firm while his colleague snapped a handcuff round her slim wrist.

'Jana Kell, you are under arrest.'

★★★

When they'd dragged her into the police station she'd been worried. When they'd pushed her into the featureless grey cell she'd been truly afraid. How she'd ever endured six months of it she'd no idea - she couldn't really remember much from that part of her life. And no matter how much she'd protested, the cops weren't listening and kept on insisting she was Jana, including pulling up photographs on their computer which they insisted proved who she was even though they were obviously of her sister.

Every time the policewoman had brought her anything to eat, or to clear it away she'd tried to reason with her, but she'd just ignored her. Sobbing, she lay down on the bed and watched the hours of the night go slowly by without sleep to help them pass.

★★★

The next day had been no better and the second sleepless night was worse than the first. When the policewoman told her she'd thirty minutes to get ready before they took her to court she was totally confused. Being called *Jon* by the brown-skinned lawyer at the courthouse only made it worse. Everything was in a daze and the sight of the courtroom brought back old memories which scared her.

A man at the front of the court spoke for a while, and then she heard the brown-skinned man say "Not Guilty".

Another man started to speak and asked her whether she was Jana Kell which she denied. The man asked her if she was Jon Chandler which she also denied. There was a lot of talking and then the lawyer had lead her out of the big room to somewhere they could sit together.

'Jon, what the hell's going on. Our whole defence is based on you claiming to be Jon Chandler and now you've just denied it.'

'But I'm not Jon Chandler and I'm not my sister Jana. Didn't the man tell me I was supposed to tell the truth?'

'If you're not Jana, who are you?'

'I'm Jasmine Kell, my sister, I mean Jana's sister.'

'So if you're not Jana, do you know where Jana is?'

'She, I mean he, he's gone to some clinic for a scan. They're going to be able to prove he's really Jon Chandler.'

Kamar wondered about what the girl had just said. Surely if it was true Jon would have told him.

'Well he never told me anything about having another scan, and it's fundamental to the case, so I'd have known about it. Is there anywhere else he could have gone?'

Jasmine was waking up just a little now and heard the question. She started to answer but suddenly a realisation came over her. She stopped speaking and sat motionless, staring at the wall. Kamar was getting desperate and even started shouting at her.

★★★

When the court re-convened the defendant simply stood staring straight in front of her. The judge and the lawyers plagued her with questions, yet she stood in the dock with an expressionless face, and said …….. nothing. Nothing at all.

The case was suspended pending a report from a specialist and the defendant was transferred to the secure wing of the Thomas Petbow psychiatric hospital.

David Hulett Wilson

77

Gary Comes Home

Gary Benham arrived back at the flat with two heavy bags of shopping and pressed the bell for Flat 6. As he stood at the door he could see Arnie through the frosted glass, jumping up and down excitedly. But Jasmine didn't come to let him in. He rang the bell again and Arnie started barking.

After five minutes he was getting just a little pissed off, so he called her mobile. No reply.

He pressed the bell for Flat 1 and a woman in her late twenties came to the door.

'I'm Gary and I'm staying upstairs in Flat 6 - I forgot my key,' and he pushed past without waiting to see whether his hurried explanation was going to be accepted.

The woman wondered whether she should threaten to call the police, but it was obvious the little dog knew the man - presumably he was the boyfriend of the girl who lived upstairs.

Arnie raced up the stairs after Gary and the two of them stepped into the flat through the open door. Everything was just as it had been when he'd left earlier, except for the lack of Jasmine. Where could she have gone and why wasn't she answering her phone? Why hadn't she left a message? Why hadn't she taken Arnie? If she couldn't take Arnie, why had she left him running around outside the flat instead of shutting him in? Maybe she'd been called away suddenly, perhaps her mother was ill again?

He tried the phone again and heard it somewhere in the room before it went onto voicemail. There it was, underneath a magazine on the coffee table. Now that really *wasn't* like Jasmine, she'd have taken her phone with her if nothing else. Nothing made any sense.

He sat and waited in the flat, but by mid-afternoon there was still no sign. He left a note on the dining table before he put Arnie on his lead and the two of them went round to their own flat, but there was no sign that anyone had been there. It was a mystery.

Back at Jana's flat, when Jasmine hadn't turned up by evening he was starting to worry. An hour later he phoned the police to ask whether they had any information about a Miss Jasmine Kell. Nothing. Next he scrolled through Jasmine's phone to find the number for her mother's nursing home. But no luck there either, they hadn't seen her since her last visit five days ago.

***

At half eight next morning Gary phoned the police to report Jasmine Kell as a missing person.

78

Captain O'connor

The smartly uniformed figure looked around at his new office. Nicely appointed and very much in keeping with his status, though as so many of his colleagues had commented, the styles popular in the Union 30 years earlier weren't quite as pleasing to the eye as the interiors of some of the Phoenixan ships he'd commanded before. And he'd commanded more than a few. He'd spent his whole career in one branch or another of the spaceflight business.

Like so many of his fellows he'd started off in the military where he'd quickly risen through the ranks to take command of his own patrol ship. But active service is a young man's game and when he'd been promoted and transferred to a comfortable desk job he'd decided that perhaps spacefleet wasn't quite the career he'd once hoped for.

Out in civilian life it was a different story. He'd been pleased to discover the high regard the rapidly expanding spaceline business held for a man with his abilities, and now he was proud to have been appointed to his new role as master of the Hyperion. Liam James O'Connor, the first Phoenixan captain of an FTL star-liner. Maybe it had come just a little too late in his career because he knew that when he'd completed this mission to Darius it would be well past the date he'd planned to hang up his hat for the very last time.

But what a swan-song - to travel faster than light! To race the immense distance to Darius in just two years. "Hyper by 2" they called it, but in layman's terms it meant forty whole lightyears could be spanned in just twelve months. That was Union technology for you. He wondered why all the fine scientists on his home world had failed to develop FTL. Perhaps they might have succeeded if the pan-Phoenixan space agency had ever got the funding it so desperately needed.

So here he was, captain of an FTL ship, never been FTL himself, and in command of a crew who'd never been FTL either. He knew it sounded like a joke, but really it wasn't a problem. Most of the complication of operating a ship like the Hyperion came in the sub-light manoeuvres at each end of the journey. The FTL leg operated under pre-programmed automatic control so the only extra bit was pressing the button that told the ship it was time to go hyperlight, and how much training did a man need for that?

When it had started out on its journey from Darius 27 months ago the Hyperion had been no more than a robot piloted freighter and the job Liam had originally been recruited for was to fly out to intercept it after it had dropped out of hyperlight, and then to fly it into Phoenixan orbit. With a handpicked crew experienced in sub-light operations to back him up the team had trained on simulators and notched up thousands of hours of flight time. So even before they'd stepped on board for the very first time they were familiar with every function of the sophisticated control system.

And that was as far as it had been supposed to go. A nice little earner to keep him busy for his last few years before retirement. Then it had all turned around when PSL had realised there was money to be made carrying passengers as well as freight - and that meant the ship had to fly with a full crew on board. Rules were rules. With only one captain and crew trained to operate the newly acquired ship, the company knew that for the first trip at least it was a seller's market when it came to staffing. And although at first O'Connor had said "no" to the idea of a four year round trip, when he'd looked at the figure on the bottom line of the paycheck his company was offering he'd realised it was an offer he simply couldn't refuse. And the chance of a three week holiday on the planet everyone called the jewel of the galaxy was the cherry on the cake.

The phone on his desk buzzed. There had to be a first time for everything. Liam lifted the receiver and listened for a few seconds - Lloyd Green, chief of security at Celebration Interplanetary. He put the phone on loudspeaker so he could drink his coffee while he talked.

When Lloyd had finished his opening gambit he replied. 'So what you're saying is, there's a woman from the cleaning team still on board my ship.'

The sound from the other end began with a rather long "errrrr" before changing to words that carried meaning.

'Well, depending on what's really true Liam, not exactly on the ship.'

O'Connor wiped a drop of coffee from his beard.

'So, if she's not on the ship why are you bothering me? We leave in two days time and I've got a mountain of paperwork to push along.'

This time the silence that followed was more disconcerting than the meaningless "errrrr".

'But we can't be certain she's *not* on the ship either.'
'Perhaps you'd better tell me more Lloyd.'

'OK then, her name is Jasmine Kell and she was part of the cleaning and refurbishment team. She's done five trips up to the ship now and she's done her work well without any complaint from her supervisor.'

'I can feel there's a "but" coming on.'

'Ten days ago she left the ship apparently having completed her duties, but a week later she flew back up.'

'She could have been recalled to finish something off. We don't know everything KAL are up to, and I don't think they even know themselves. That crowd would do better running a circus.'

'Her supervisor says not, but as you say they've never really had a grip on the work. Anyway, the girl flew up on the spaceplane and clocked on. The following day she clocked off and we presume she flew back down to the surface.'

'So that confirms it then, she's not on my ship.'

'Well that's where the problem comes, she's not recorded as having left the terminal building here at the spaceport.'

'So either she's somewhere in the terminal building or the exit barrier failed to record her leaving the terminal. Either way she's not on my ship.'

The line went silent for a moment.

'Liam, the first thing we did when the computer threw her up as an anomaly was to search the terminal, but you know what it's like, the entrance lobby, security barriers, the waiting lounge and the toilets. It only took fifteen minutes for security to confirm she's not in there.'

'So she's somewhere groundside but not in the terminal.'

'She only had Level 3 security, so she wouldn't be allowed to be anywhere other than the terminal, the bus or the lounge. But we've got groundside security alerted to her possible presence, including restricted areas.'

'And did you check whether she went home? That would be the most obvious place to look for her. Or you could try phoning her.'

'We tried her landline and just got voicemail.'

'And her mobile?'

'We don't have a mobile number for her, and when security went round to her flat there was no answer. The neighbours said she'd left a couple of days ago and they hadn't seen her since.'

'And have you tried the police?'

'They have no record of any investigation regarding a Jasmine Kell, and it's too soon for anyone to have reported her as missing.'

'OK then, the girl's done a disappearing act, and your conclusion is she's hiding on the ship to get a free ride to Darius?'

'Exactly.'

'Well you don't need me to tell you the regulations. If there was positive proof there was a stowaway on board you could require a full search of the ship and hold its departure for up to five days. And PSL would have to pick up the tab for the delay. As it is she's just done a bunk without there being any proof she's on board, so unless you want to pick up the tab for holding a star-liner in orbit, all I'm offering is a quick check over the ship - and if we don't find her we leave on schedule. In any case it'll give my security guys something to do and get them familiar with their patch. But look, we're only going to search the areas her pass would have allowed her access to - anywhere that needed higher clearance we're just going to assume she couldn't have got in there. And of course we'll be on the lookout for her during the flight so if she shows herself we'll pick her up. Then she can wile away the hours in the SA Block. One thing's for certain though, she won't be getting off at Darius and if she really is on board and doesn't show herself she'll just stay on the ship for the trip back here. If she's so desperate to get away she's prepared to spend four years in space just to get back to where she came from, then all I can think is she's in serious trouble with the law. And you say you've checked with the police?'

'The girl served time four years ago for a non-violent offence, but at the moment there are no convictions or pending prosecutions. She's clean.'

'OK, I'll get onto security and they can spend some time checking out the ship, but whether we find her or not, we're leaving on time.'

★★★

Jon heard a noise and looked up from his book. He could clearly hear voices somewhere below him so he crept over to the grill that looked down on the area in front of the lifts - two uniformed men, armed as far as he could see. He watched as they opened each of the top floor rooms in turn. One man stood at the door while the other went into the room. When they'd finished with the last of the rooms they headed off down the stairs.

Jon wondered to himself, a routine inspection prior to departure, or were they looking for him? Or perhaps there might be another stowaway, that was something he hadn't considered before. Anyway, they'd gone for now. He just hoped that was it, but he noticed the way the girl's heart was beating hard.

David Hulett Wilson

79

The Hyperion Leaves Orbit

Jon felt the motion and knew what it meant - the ship was starting its manoeuvre out of orbit and building up speed. Within twenty minutes gravity had shifted to a crazy angle, and it was going to get worse before it got better. He looked at the mattress strapped to the wall and knew that soon he'd be pressed deep into its padding, and hopefully it was going to be enough. It wasn't exactly a purpose designed couch in the acceleration accommodation suite.

With Phoenix now already far behind, the big ship began its run down out of the ecliptic plane picking up speed with every Megametre it flew. Jon looked at his watch - within 12 hours it would be far enough from the star and the planets of the solar system to begin the main phase of its acceleration run. Within 18 hours they'd be FTL.

★★★

Ten hours passed before the shift in gravity eased and Jon knew they were coasting before the run up to hyperlight. This was the last chance to eat, if you thought you could stomach anything, and for him the last chance for bathroom facilities that consisted of no more than a bucket. He hoped it wasn't going to spill when the next gravity shift came.

An hour passed and the g-drive engaged. Gravity shifted and Jon wasted no time getting the girl's body into position against the mattress. If he didn't do it now he'd be stuck wherever the massive G force left him - and the worry was that something hard or sharp would pierce Jana's body leaving her to bleed to death before the ship reached Hx2. Welcome to steerage.

As he positioned himself in front of the mattress he thought of the lucky passengers in their body-form couches, sedated if they chose, intravenous nutrient supply and on-line entertainment to pass the dreadful hours of crushing acceleration. He felt the girl's body respond as the motion pushed it down into the mattress. Now his journey had really begun.

80

Visiting Time

Jasmine Kell sat up, climbed down from the bed where she'd been lying, walked over to the emergency call button, and pressed it. Slowly she walked back to the bed and sat on the edge. She knew there was no time to lie down.

Twenty five seconds later the orderly rushed into the room and saw there was no emergency - just the mad woman sitting on the bed, more or less as she'd been for the past five days. Before he could say anything the woman spoke.

'Mills. Call Detective Mills please. I have something important to tell him.' And then she was silent again.

★★★

DS Mills was busy with his work. Police business never ended and he had a backlog of cases to handle, so he was furious at the thought the mad woman could summon him so easily. And yet if she was ready to talk he had to be there to listen, and he very much wanted to hear what she had to say. He pulled on his coat and closed the door.

★★★

The orderly lead the big policeman down one corridor and then another. A flight of stairs and then another corridor. How did anyone ever find their way in a maze like this? The orderly rattled his bunch of keys and unlocked yet another door, and diligently locked it behind them when they'd passed through. Mills was impressed with the security though he felt just a little uneasy knowing his route back to the real world was controlled by someone else. He was used to being the one who held the keys.

The two men stopped outside a heavy metal door and the orderly opened the viewing flap to look in.

'She's sitting on the bed just like before. She's scarcely moved in days - take a look.'

Mills stepped up to the flap and saw the woman, as impassive as before, and wondered whether his visit was going to be wasted. But he'd come all this way, he might as well go in and see if she was prepared to say something. The orderly unlocked the door and Mills stepped inside. He saw the eerie way the eyes watched him, the unblinking way they followed him as he walked across the room. He pulled up a chair to the side of the bed, looked into the mad eyes and waited.

He didn't have to wait long. 'Ha, ha, ... ha. Ha, ha ... fucking ha.'

Mills jumped to his feet and strode towards her but knowing the security camera had the two of them in full view he resisted the impulse to slap her across the face.

'What the hell are you on about you stupid bitch?'

'He's gone.'

'Who's gone?'

'The mind traveller, Jon Chandler. He's on the Hyperion right now.'

'Jon Chandler! He's the man you were claiming to be before you changed your story.'

Jasmine shook her head. 'The man my sister was claiming to be. She's on the Hyperion - and she's not *she*, she's *he*.'

Mills drew in a breath. 'Are you still claiming you're not Jana Kell? If you're fucking with me you'll be in the nick just for wasting police time - if they ever let you out of this place.'

She looked at him and smiled.

'I never claimed to be Jana: that was something you and the wigs in the court decided. I am now just as I have always been, Jasmine Kell. My sister's body is being used by the mind-traveller and he's on his way to Darius.'

'You little bitch, you helped him get away.'

Just a hint of a smile came to her lips, but faded again before she spoke.

'No, he fooled me, and he fooled you too. He knew that if he asked for my help I'd end up in trouble when the shit hit the fan. So he didn't ask for my help - he fooled us all and helped himself.'

Mills pulled out his mobile and frantically searched through the contacts list. He pressed the transmit button. After a few seconds he spoke.

'Get a signal out to the Hyperion - now. Jana Kell's stowed away on board. Get that bloody ship back here - NOW!'

He turned back to Jasmine. 'So if you didn't help him, when did you know he'd gone?'

'So it's him now is it? You've finally accepted the mind-traveller didn't get back to his home.'

'Him, her - I don't give a fuck. When did you know he'd gone?'

'In the court, when the judge asked me where I thought Jana was.'

'And you didn't tell us.'

'I told you no lies, and you were all busy deciding I was mad. Would you have listened if I'd told you?'

Mills was fuming with rage now, but was lost for words.

Jasmine continued. 'I wanted my sister back and without the beam for Jon to travel home on, my sister wasn't coming back, was she? In two years time the Hyperion will enter Darius orbit. Then Jon Chandler will go back to his own body, and my sister will come back to hers. And then she'll travel back to Phoenix. It's going to take time, four long years, but one day I'll have my sister back.'

Mills stared at her, shaking his head. 'You knew it was him in Jana's body all along didn't you?'

'Of course. I knew from the very first minute I met him. And was there a single day when he didn't claim to be Jon Chandler?'

'Yes, in the magistrate's court when he got bail. He confirmed he was Jana Kell.'

'And he walked free from the court.'

'The bastard lied and walked free. I had him and he walked free.'

'And if he'd claimed to be Jon Chandler, what then?'

'He'd have been in this place.'

'So what would you have done?'

Mills was lost for words.

'When you go will you tell them I'm ready to see Mr Kamar, please.'

★★★

An urgent tight beam radio transmission was issued from Phoenix space agency headquarters to the Hyperion to advise them that Jana Kell, a wanted criminal, was on board. The ship was ordered to turn around immediately and return to Phoenix.

Just doing his duty, the operator knew even as he transmitted the message it would never be received. Well not for hundreds of years anyway. The Hyperion was already FTL and increasing the distance from his signal with every microsecond that passed.

***

After the angry call he'd received from DS Mills, Kamar made arrangements to visit the woman he'd thought was his client in the Thomas Petbow hospital. After bringing in Gary Benham and Mrs Irene Kell who'd travelled all the way across the city in an ambulance, the police finally accepted that the woman they'd incarcerated was Jasmine Kell. The same Jasmine Kell who'd been reported to them as a missing person five days earlier.

With no charges laid against her Jasmine was released immediately, but Kamar told her that wasn't quite the end of it. It only took a couple of phone calls, and when he suggested to DS Mills it would be good court experience for him to bring a prosecution for wrongful arrest and false imprisonment the police agreed to pay his fees and make an ex-gratia payment to his client's sister.

81

Life On The Ship

Once the ship was up to speed and out into interstellar space there was no chance of turning back. Jon relaxed just a little and decided that now was the right time for him to come out of hiding. It would never be completely safe for him to be out in the public areas of the ship, but from his days with Rapier he knew the fundamental mistake that stowaways usually made was to stay stowed away. Surprisingly, it made them easier to find. OK, they were hard to find while they were hidden, but when a new face suddenly appeared weeks after the last port had been visited, it was either someone who'd been in the sick bay - or a stowaway. They all came out sooner or later.

So if he came out into the open now and mingled with the genuine passengers, right at the start of the trip when no-one knew anyone else, the pretty girl with the blond hair would become a normal sight. No-one would even notice her, apart from the way the males of the species usually noticed pretty girls with blond hair.

And there was the fall-back position that even if they did catch him now, there was no way he'd be getting off the ship before they got to Darius. Marooning stowaways on deserted asteroids had never been an option for the captains of starliners.

In the long boring hours while he'd been hidden away Jon had noticed the illuminated displays on the equipment panels in the lift-motor room and had wondered what the figures meant. Gradually he'd realised that two of the figures were indicators to show which floor each lift had stopped at, so he'd been able to keep note of how many visits there'd been to the top floor of the block. So many times when he'd heard the motor start up he'd watched, and although the lift rarely stopped at the first floor, only once had it gone as high as the fifth. And never in all the time he'd been watching had it once come all the way up to the sixth. Well he knew the top floor rooms with their reduced gravity effect were never as popular as those lower down, so it was logical that if the ship wasn't full to capacity the empty rooms would be those on the higher floors. His plan was to keep the situation under observation for another couple of days and then take a chance on moving into an empty room.

At last he was ready and crawled over to make a check through the ventilator grill over the entrance to the lift. Looking down onto the landing below he could see there was no-one about on the top floor, and when both lifts stopped at the ground floor he ventured out for the first time in a week. Life in the lift-motor room was getting to be boring, and a bit smelly too.

Out in the open area of the Hyperion for the first time Jon took a stroll through the park and was pleased to see they'd refilled the lake now the acceleration period was over, and the hologram ducks had been turned on too. It was silly he knew, but he'd missed them when he was up on the ship doing Jasmine's refurbishment work.

As he made his way over to the shopping area he stopped outside the security office and was just a little amused to see the "wanted" poster pinned up on a placard outside. The black hair, the garish makeup and the outlandish clothes were more than just familiar. The placard told passers-by that security were hoping to interview a missing woman by the name of "Jasmine Kell". Jon made a note to remember he was "Amanda" if he spoke to any of the other passengers, just in case they linked the name Jana to Jasmine.

But the main problem was, as he'd known before he came on board, food. So many restaurants, cafes, and bars. Traditional food, themed dishes, sizzling cholesterol laden breakfasts. Full meals, light meals, snacks. All the most delicious fare the discerning traveller could desire.

All sorts of offers would have been made to the passengers, with some of them on all-inclusive deals, while others would only have limited meals included in their ticket price. On the many trips he'd made in his career Jon hadn't known much about the establishments lower down the scale because he'd usually eaten his meals in one of the first class restaurants. The only exceptions to his rule had been the times he'd slummed it in the pub.

Now he looked in through the doors and wondered what it would be like to have a real plate of hot food laid in front of him. The girl's mouth was drooling at the thought. But he knew full well that without a passenger's ID card to gain entry, sampling the smells from outside in the street was as close as he was going to get.

In his days of isolation he'd counted up the cash he'd been able to bring on board, and it came to just under 1900 Phen. He'd done the maths and it came to three Phen a day, a pitifully small amount. And food wasn't the only thing he was going to need. If he'd had more time to prepare he could have got his hands on more, but when there was a ship to be caught, what other choice had he had?

He considered his options. Stealing food was out because they'd catch him within days. Scouting around the bins behind the restaurants could turn up some tasty titbits, but it would be like wearing a big neon sign that shouted out loud to all who saw it "I'm the stowaway". It was going to be a long, lean, slimming journey.

But there was good news too, just a little. The ship wasn't all smart restaurants and expensive cafes. There were cheaper places where a passenger could eat, and the stalls had sandwiches for sale, though at five Phen a go even those were beyond Jon's budget. If he ran out of money before they got to Darius there were just two choices available: either he'd starve or he'd have to give himself up to security.

Taking out the first of the precious notes Jon bought a packet of rolls and a cheap tub of runny cheese and carried them off to the park. Rain wasn't scheduled till next week, so lunch by the pond was as good as it was going to get.

As he sat there dipping his bread into the tub he watched as two young women came by pushing a trolley laden with spades, rakes & hoes. They stopped by a bed of spring flowers and one girl clicked on the trolley's brake while the other unloaded some of the tools. They could have been regular gardeners, but the featureless blue and white hooped overalls they wore told a different story. Jon realised what he was looking at, "prisoner-crew". Slave labour - but at least they got regular meals.

82

A Month Came, And A Month Went

In the first four weeks of the trip the passengers began to adjust to their lives on board, and together with the crew, everyone on the Hyperion found a routine that suited them. The curious ones who'd never travelled on a big ship before set off to explore their new environment. Some chose the shops as a way to pass the time. Ladies liked to be pampered in the spas and salons. The sporty types worked out in the gym, or jogged around the circumferential track. The industrious ones were deep into their courses of study. Others just chose to sit in the park and read.

Evenings brought a change to the pace of life when people sought out the terraces high above the gardens to sit in the warm still air and enjoy a beer or a glass of wine. And everyone enjoyed the cuisine of the galaxy class restaurants.

Almost everyone. Even after so short a time in space Jon had already noticed the way the girl's body had lost weight, and he was becoming bored with the same staple diet day in day out. But if he was to still be eating when the ship arrived at Darius, there was no other way.

And he was just a little bored with the lack of company too. Despite the thousands of people on their way to the same destination he passed his days with a life that avoided too much interaction with his fellow travellers. Since the poster showing Jasmine's metal-adorned face had first been displayed outside the security office a popular game amongst the passengers had been "Spot the Stowaway", so he hadn't dared let anyone get close enough to discover who he really was. And in his opinion the romance traditionally associated with the role was considerably overplayed, particularly in the case of someone for whom it wasn't a game. It brought other disadvantages too. Access to the gyms and swimming pools, the big screen cinemas, the theatres and the Holopera was based on a passenger's class of travel, so entry always required the presentation of an ID card pass. Something that Jon didn't have.

But still, there were so many things to do. The parks and the gardens were beautiful, and the endless summer days offered by the strictly controlled environment allowed a life that could be spent almost entirely outdoors. It was true that in the accommodation doughnut of a star-liner racing through the endless void of interstellar space the term "Al fresco" had a slightly different meaning, but to anyone who was actually there, it certainly felt as if they were outdoors.

When evening fell and the overhead light tube dimmed down to its night-time level the ship's entertainment moved indoors and the nightlife began, for those with cards or money. But a big part of the experience had always been the act of deciding where to go, so for Jon, just walking around, enjoying the tantalising smells that emanated from the many eating places, feeling the beat from the discos and night-clubs, listening to the music that flowed out into the streets, or drinking in the electric atmosphere, was only one stop away from being able to enjoy the fun first-hand.

On several occasions groups of young men had called over to the pretty girl they'd seen walking by herself, inviting him to go and join them - and he'd been sorely tempted. The chance to sit with people having fun, downing just slightly more than enough to keep sobriety at bay, chatting and laughing, drinking toasts to nothing at all. Jon would have loved to join in and help them move along their magnum of bubbly, but he guessed it might also have lead to the opportunity to repay their generosity in kind later on - a price he wasn't willing to pay.

After the first few nights he'd found it was easier to sit in his room and watch a movie. At least that was free.

And that was one part of life on the ship that had gone Jon's way. After his first few days in the lift-motor room he'd quickly come to realise that making it his home for the whole two years of the voyage was not a serious option. The space was cramped of course, he'd known that when he'd chosen it as his hidey-hole, and apart from the cleaner's bucket that functioned as a toilet it lacked any form of sanitation. But the biggest problem was one he'd never expected - every time one of the lift motors had started up he'd been wrenched out of even the soundest sleep. One night he'd almost got as far as clicking off the circuit breakers to shut the machines down, even though his action would have brought with it a sure-fire guarantee of being discovered when the technician arrived to sort out the problem.

So when he was absolutely sure that all the top floor rooms in Juniper Block were vacant he'd used his cleaner's pass-card to have a look round, and he'd selected the one with the best views out over the parkland. And now life was considerably more pleasant. Having proper bathroom facilities was essential, the oh-so-comfortable bed was delightful, and the TV gave him access to every film, soap or documentary ever made in the Union as well as being a terminal to access the ship's computer network.

With the room not officially in service the chambermaids never visited, so after the first few weeks Jon had gone out to help himself to clean towels and bedding from the linen store. And by chance he'd found the place where the staff kept the supplies of tea and coffee to replenish the rooms. But sadly the stock for the mini-bars was all kept securely under lock and key.

But things were working out and he could console himself with the knowledge that his life was getting back on track. It was only a matter of time before the ship entered orbit at Darius and then he'd be going back to his real life. Jana herself would have to do the two year trip back to Phoenix, but he'd make sure she was OK - in fact more than just OK, he'd buy her a First-class ticket.

But one thing troubled him - day after day. Out here in the void on an old ship like the Hyperion that wasn't equipped to intercept GBeam transmissions there was no contact with the rest of humanity. Anything could be happening out there in the Union and he wondered time and time again whether the beam that linked Phoenix to the rest of the galaxy might miraculously have come back on line. There was even a chance it had come back within hours of the Hyperion leaving orbit. Maybe, just maybe, he could have been in communication weeks ago and by now he'd have been back home in Rosemount.

There really was no way of knowing until the ship got to Darius.

83

"To Be Or Not To Be", Is Not The Whole Question

Months came and months went. Now the score was ten. Without doubt it had been a long time to be out in space, and yet the ship wasn't even half-way to its destination. Jon had begun to ask whether some people went mad on long space voyages. He was even beginning to wonder if it hadn't happened already, to himself.

But in so many ways he was bearing up. With time on his hands and a mind too active to settle for a life of idleness he'd spent whole evenings with the TV console's keyboard perched on the girl's lap while he browsed through the Hyperion's vast on-line encyclopaedia. The topic he'd found most interesting concerned his own situation in general, and how he'd got into it in particular.

Following the threads from page to page he'd read about the breakthroughs made thirty years ago by the scientists who'd pioneered the development of mind-transfer technology. It was fascinating stuff and he hadn't failed to notice that the chapters about the effects of long term consciousness transfers were highly relevant to his own situation. But it had come as a shock to see that when an article had said "long term" it had been talking about the case of a transferred mind living in a host body for longer than sixty days. Jon realised that after all the time he'd spent in Jana's body on Phoenix and here on the ship, there was no doubt that the term "long" applied to him.

Something he hadn't fully appreciated on the day he'd agreed to go on the TranzCon transfer into Jana's body was that only a relatively small proportion of a traveller's memories went with him or her. The amount varied from person to person, and the quality of the GBeam connection used had an influence too, but for a traveller to bring with them more than a quarter of everything they'd ever known was a rare occurrence. For Jon it meant that three quarters of his memories were missing, and yet try as he might, he hadn't noticed any blank areas in his experience of life. There'd been things, "remembrances" that had flashed briefly into view in the moments as he'd risen from the depths of sleep. Thoughts just on the edge of consciousness that had floated so close, and yet remained just beyond where his mind could reach. Whether they were dreams or a plea to call back a lost memory he'd been unable to tell.

It was in the world of dreams where his lines of defence had been weakest. The conscious mind with all its logic and rationality rejected as foreign anything that must surely have come from outwith its realm. But dreams were infinitely unpredictable, every one of them a voyage into the unknown. Dreams had never signed up to abide by any rules. So who could say whether a dream had arisen within the consciousness that had travelled into the host brain, or whether it might instead be something trawled up from deep within the id, something that belonged only to the host, something *old* that went back to a time before the transfer?

But what of the psychotic conditions that could arise? Research had found it was the mixing of memories from different sources that caused many of the problems associated with mind transfers. In the short-term the condition showed itself as spirit image retention, the usually benign meld of the returned consciousness with thought patterns, or "relics" as they were termed, that were left over from the mind which had recently departed. In fact the departing mind always left relics, but only in a small percentage of cases was the mental scar they caused severe enough to create confusion in the returned host mind as it strove to re-establish itself. It was accepted by TranzCon and the mind transfer industry regulator that spirit image retention could, and would occur, but the condition was well understood and *always* abated given enough time. Jon read the word again, "always".

The next chapter showed Jon he'd had the good news first because the more sinister manifestation of "mind intrusion" could drive a person to insanity. Mind intrusion, the effect of a long term transfer where a remnant of the life-force native to the host body began to expunge the consciousness of the traveller. As the article made plain, this more serious condition was an entirely different matter because few subjects ever made a full recovery.

Despite the tiny number of tests ever carried out, the mechanism was adequately understood. In the early weeks of a transfer the overwhelming power of the incoming mind swamped entirely any messages arising from the native mind's resident thought patterns. Put another way, the incoming mind was able to protect itself against rejection by the host, but only for a limited time. After a longer period of occupation the tables turned, and slowly the insidious force of the native mind began to regain control of the territory in which it had once reigned supreme. In every case studied, the longer the incoming mind had remained in place, the more it had become prey to the will of the native mind. One by one, native thoughts penetrated the defences of the incoming mind until the consciousness that *flowed* in the host brain was unsure of whether it was the mind of the traveller or the mind of the host. It was a battle of wills where the native mind, fighting on home ground, often won. Often won, though not always. For a number of little understood reasons, some incoming minds remained dominant no matter how much time had passed. Unfortunately for science, the moratorium put in place to save the lives of test subjects had virtually ended that line of research.

For Jon who freely admitted he'd been driven to the point of questioning his own identity this was all highly relevant and seemed to be a more likely scenario than the simple case of spirit image retention which Dr Morris and the specialists at TranzCon had blamed for his failure to accept he was Jana Kell.

Perhaps this other condition had already occurred? Could Jon, or maybe Jana, be a victim of mind intrusion? But how could that possibly be? In the early days of the transfer there simply hadn't been time for mind intrusion to have occurred, and in any case, the effects of mind intrusion should surely have made whoever was in the host body feel more and more as if they were *Jana*. And that wasn't how Jon felt. He *was* Jon Chandler. There was no uncertainty, there could be no debate. In all the months he'd lived in Jana's body his knowledge of his true identity hadn't faded, not even slightly. It was true to say there'd been the occasional emotional outbursts that were so unlike his own calm and collected responses to the situations life threw up, but in all likelihood they could be put down to the roller-coaster ride of the chemical changes that raged through Jana's female metabolism.

So could there be some other explanation? The unfortunate answer was "yes". After reading through three times to make sure he'd fully understood its implications Jon wished he'd left the whole can of worms sealed tight. It was only a hypothesis since no relevant event had ever been recorded, but the accuracy with which it seemed to apply to his own condition made him wonder if the idea might actually be true. The hypothesis suggested that a returning consciousness could slip into a coma leaving an *image* of the departed life-force not only still resident, but gaining strength with every day that passed. A force that remembered who it was and established itself as the dominant life-force. Even if the native consciousness one day arose from its coma it would simply find that the battle for supremacy was already lost.

And as the article had gone on to say, the occurrence of a coma condition would be far more likely when the brain of the host had been forced into a regressive state by the drugs administered prior to a flat-line transfer.

Jon felt an icy chill that crept over him. Something that had nagged at his soul over the long months as the Hyperion had flown through space. Was it possible? Could it really have happened? On that night when he'd dreamt of a girl dying in the watery depths of a wrecked ship, had his mind made its way back into his body? Was the real Jon Chandler on Vissan even now as the Hyperion sped towards Darius? Was the real Jon Chandler already the Union's first minister, the most powerful man in the galaxy? But if that was true, who was he? Was the "Jon" life-force here in Jana Kell's body no more than an inferior copy that had usurped power in the void left by the absence of the host's true mind? What if he got to Darius and contacted *his* people on Vissan only to be told that Jon

Chandler was alive and well after arriving back there two years earlier?

One part of him was anxious to find out, almost desperate to get to Darius straight away. But another part wanted to put off that day as long as it could, afraid of what he might find.

84

Terry

Now the Hyperion had passed the mid-way point of its journey Jon was encouraged by the idea that both he and the big ship were getting closer to their destination. Though with eleven months still to go the great day was still a long way off.

As he'd found out early in the trip, survival through the tedium of the long months out in space was helped by setting a routine, and following it religiously. So part of his regimen was to run a few laps of the circumferential path every day, and on Tuesdays he always did it mid-afternoon because it fitted in with having a shower and washing the girl's long hair before going to the weekly lecture in the evening - one of the few free activities available to him.

Today had been a good day and he'd managed three circuits of the ship without stopping for a break, so lady-like or not it meant he'd built up quite a sweat. Now he was back in his room, luxuriating in the steam and the hot pulsating jets that blasted from the shower - when he thought he heard a noise. An unfamiliar noise, a noise that came when there should have been silence. He recognised the sound of the main door closing, and knew straight away that someone had come in from the corridor outside. Quickly he turned off the shower, reached out and pulled the light cord, though it was only as he stood there in the dark he realised the fan was going to keep running for at least another minute. If the intruder came into the bathroom now it was a dead giveaway. Jon stood in the shower cubicle trying to be as quiet as he could, yet shaking with fear as he strained to hear what was going on out in the main room. Was this how it happened he wondered? Did all stowaways get discovered in the end, and now, today, was it his turn? He breathed a sigh of relief when the fan clicked off, but he quickly saw it was far from the end of his troubles.

A crack of light from the main room shone in as the door swung open. A click and the light came back on, and the fan too. At least the sound would hide any sounds he made now. He heard footsteps and wondered whether he was visible behind the curtain. He watched as a dark shape moved between the light and the sanctuary of his tiny space. The footsteps came closer, but passed him by. He let out the breath he'd held for a few seconds too long.

In a flash the curtain was whisked away leaving him there in the shower, exposed and naked. Whether the reaction to put one arm up over the girl's breasts, and the other down to cover her furry patch was his, or something that came from deep within the girl's sub-conscious Jon was never going to know. But he stood there shivering with fright as a man surveyed him carefully.

'Well now, what have we here? They didn't tell me the room came with its own pretty girl.'

'Get out! Get out of my room right now or I'll call security,' Jon bluffed.

'Well I'm really sorry Miss if I disturbed you, but the information they gave me said this room hadn't been occupied since we left orbit, and that's over a year now. Why don't you get some clothes on, and then we can discuss it.'

He stepped out of the room and closed the door behind him.

Jon felt the girl's heart as it hammered inside the small chest. He had no idea what to think - he'd been discovered and this was it. The game was up. But then he thought again, it was only this one man who'd found him. And this was an important point, he hadn't been wearing a uniform, so presumably he was only a passenger and not someone in a position of authority. But even that was bad enough. He calmed himself enough to think. He needed a plan, but what were the choices? He could rush out and try to make it to the main door before the man caught him From the size and age of the guy, Jon knew the girl's young fit body could outrun him, but then where would he go? Where would he go in just a white bathrobe? It wasn't an option, he was going to have to stay, going to have to meet the man face to face and negotiate the best terms he could. Maybe the man wouldn't give him away to the ship's security people, but which part of heaven was he living in to hope for that?

★★★

Jon dried the girl's body off and slipped on the robe making sure it was pulled close together at the top. With no idea what awaited him on the other side he turned the knob and opened the door. The man was loafing there in one of the sumptuous chairs, his feet up on the stool. Swallowed up by the size of the chair it wasn't easy to tell how big he was, but Jon could see he was quite large with a round, red face, and just a few thin strands of hair draped over the top of an otherwise bald head. Maybe somewhere in his fifties? Late fifties?

'Come on in Miss, I made you a cup of tea. Is that OK, or would you prefer coffee?'

'Tea's fine. Thankyou Mr …….'

'Terry. Terry's the name. And you are?'

Desperately searching for a handle Jon fell back to the alter-ego that now seemed so familiar. 'Amanda, but people call me Mandy.'

Terry sat forward and smiled. 'Now I'm really sorry I burst in on your like that Mandy, but the accommodation services people told me the room wasn't occupied, so my plan was to move in.'

'But haven't you already got a room?'

'I had one, in Myrtle Block. Top floor like this one. I like the low grav up here, most people don't. You must like it too.'

'Yes, it's fine. Are you moving out of Myrtle?'

'One of the lifts had been out of service since we left orbit, and then the other one broke down two days ago. They say they can't fix either of them till they get some parts from Darius, and I don't like the idea of climbing six flights every time I come home. They told me there were plenty of top floor rooms available and I could have one here in Juniper. They gave me the access cards to all of them and told me to take my pick. This was the first I looked at and it was a real surprise to find you in the shower, gave me quite a shock.'

Jon wondered whether Terry had any idea how shocking the experience had been. But now, for a moment, things didn't seem so bad. The man was pleasant and he was apologetic too. He'd taken a good long look at Jana's naked body, but Jon knew men - given the chance, who wouldn't? He relaxed a little. Maybe Terry would assume accommodation services had made a mistake and go off to have a look at the other rooms on offer? But surely, when he got back to the office he'd tell them one of the rooms they'd sent him to look at was occupied. Then how long would it be before someone came round to investigate, especially on a ship with a stowaway on board? Jon faced the facts, he was screwed whether Terry took this room or asked for another.

An idea flashed through his mind.

'I was supposed to be in Rose Block, but the showers on the top floor wouldn't work. They said I could use this room till they got the plumbing fixed. They must have forgotten.'

'Which room were you in?'

'63.'

'That'll be on the top floor too?'

'Yes. I like being high up. It's quieter.'

'Well that's funny because they told me the whole of the top floor of Rose was vacant too, but I chose this block because the view's better. But do you know what Mandy, I think I know you - I've seen your face before.'

Jon felt the shiver that ran down the girl's back. Her voice was just a little unsteady as he spoke. 'Maybe you've just seen me out around the ship? I go out in the park every day.'

Terry shook his head from side to side.

'No, I think it was somewhere else. You know that stowaway girl they've all been looking for? Well I can see you've got blond hair Mandy, and without that whacky makeup you look different. But if I was trying to stow away, I'd change my appearance too. I can see it now, and I'm not a man to forget a face as pretty as yours. Yup, you're the girl on the poster outside the security office aren't you? Jasmine somebody?'

Jon knew then that the game was up. For months he'd happily breezed about wherever he chose, anywhere on the ship, out in the open where everyone could see him. And yet he'd always known the day would come sometime when his secret would be uncovered. Terry knew exactly who the girl was and there was no way of hiding it. Maybe salvation would come if he made a full confession?

Jon gave a sigh before he spoke. 'You're right Terry. I'm Jasmine Kell, I'm the stowaway.'

Terry had been smiling before, but now his face lit up. He was animated when he spoke.

'So maybe I should call security and have them come over to pick you up? It's my duty as a law-abiding passenger …. .'

The pause was for effect only.

'But look, it doesn't have to be that way. I figure you and I could be friends, real good friends. Then I wouldn't have to turn you in. How does that sound?'

Jon felt the girl's blood run cold - he knew exactly how it sounded.

'What're you doing stowing away on the ship anyway?' Terry asked.

'I just wanted to get to Darius, but I couldn't afford the fare.'

'And how do you suppose a stowaway's going to get off the ship when we get into orbit? Security's bound to catch you.'

'I've got friends I can contact. They'll help me.'

'I could help you.'

Jon sat on the edge of the seat and sipped at his tea. The two of them sat in silence for a few seconds before Jon picked up his top and a pair of jeans and walked off into the bathroom. He felt Terry's eyes following him as he went.

Two minutes later Jon came back into the room, just a little more confident now the girl's body was properly clothed. Terry chatted away and despite the menacing threat the man posed Jon could see he was trying to be friendly. He did his best to join in with the conversation, but the most he could manage was a few stilted "yes" and "no" answers. After a while Terry changed the tack of the conversation.

'How do stowaways go on for food Jasmine? Have you been eating well?'

At last there was something he could speak about in all honesty.

'I don't have much money, but I've been getting enough to eat. Just about enough anyway.'

Terry smiled. 'Bet you haven't seen a real steak for ages though? Bet you'd like one if I called room service?'

The big man let his tongue slide over his lips. Whether it was unconscious or not Jon wasn't sure but he tasted the juices that seeped into the girl's mouth. And as if on cue, her stomach gave a low rumble. Whatever was going to happen to him, it was going to happen anyway. He might as well go along with the idea of a steak supper. What was that old phrase, "the condemned man ate a hearty breakfast".

Terry turned on the TV and called up the menu from the BBQ Diner. Jon stared open mouthed at the screen. For thirteen months he'd known the menus were there, he'd just never dared to look before.

'How about the first one on the list Jas? Fillet steak, with fries, onion rings, mushrooms and tomatoes? Red wine to wash it down?'

Jon worried that he was drooling. 'Yes, red wine. Lovely.'

Terry got up and headed for the phone, and as he climbed out of the chair Jon could see the stomach that overhung his trouser belt. Obviously it was no stranger to rich food.

'OK then, I'll give them a call, and how about a little something to finish the evening off with. I don't really know what you ladies go for.'

"I can believe that" Jon thought to himself - and then realised he was being unkind.

'I'd like a single malt, on the rocks please.'

Terry lifted one leg and slapped his hand down on the thigh.

'Well I'll be damned - a girl who likes whisky! I didn't know there were any around. Jasmine, you're my kind of girl.'

★★★

When the door-chime pealed Jon let Terry go to collect their delivery. He stepped back into the room and pulled out the bottle of wine before offering the bag in Jon's direction. He obviously expected the female to do the rest, though the way Jon felt right then it wasn't difficult to accept the duty. The hard job was going to be getting the food onto the plates before he started devouring it.

Sitting on the sofa next to Terry Jon looked down at the big oval plate in front of him and knew he'd underestimated the portion size. Hungry as he was he still wondered where he was going to put all that food. He knew how easily satisfied the girl's small stomach could be, even when it was crying out for food. In his own body he'd have finished it off and still had room for more, so it came as a surprise when he actually ate the lot. He must have been hungrier than he'd allowed himself to think. The red wine slipped down very easily too, maybe even a little too easily. And that brought a thought into his head. Having an idea of what was in store for him Jon began to wonder whether the next part of the evening was going to be easier if he was stone-cold sober, or several sheets to the wind. But as Terry drained the last of the bottle into his glass he realised the decision had made itself already. The big man got up from the table and grabbed the bottle of whisky from the sideboard.

'There's some ice in the freezer compartment Jas. Can you bring us some?'

Jon got up and did as he was told.

When he came back into the main room Terry was sitting on the sofa, bottle in hand and two heavy cut crystal glasses on the coffee table in front of him. He poured out the golden fluid in a way that reminded Jon of happy days gone by. The liquid splashed around the glass before it finally settled and Jon could see in a moment the man was into generous measures. He walked over, put the dish of ice-cubes on the table, and moved off towards the easy chair on the other side of the room. Terry used a pair of tongues to pick up the cubes one by one, and dropped them into the glasses. They crackled and spat as they made contact with the liquid in a way Jon remembered from a time that seemed so long ago. When the man had finished his labours he looked around and saw Jon, sitting alone. He tapped the empty sofa seat beside him.

'I thought it'd be nice if we sat together Jasmine.'

The man was still acting in a really friendly way, but Jon reasoned that might stop quite suddenly if he didn't go along with his plans. He walked back and took the seat he'd been offered. When the first drink came his way he downed it before the ice had chance to melt. Terry smiled and topped up the glass. When he put the bottle down again, he picked up the remote control.

'I fancy watching a movie Jasmine. How about you?'

Jon nodded and struggled to squeeze out a few words. The unexpected stay of execution had taken him by surprise.

Jon let Terry make his mind up what to watch. Something with action and a car-chase was obviously what the man went for, and Jon noticed he wasn't enough of a gentleman to ask *his girl* if she'd prefer a chick flick with a bit of romance in it - which under the circumstances was a long way down his wish-list.

The film started and Terry topped the glasses again. Jon wondered - if he could get enough whisky down the guy's neck he might just fall asleep there on the sofa. Or if he was really lucky the ship might hit an un-catalogued interstellar asteroid before the credits started to roll. Maybe he could slip out of the door while Terry was dozing, but then where would he go? Another eleven months in his lift-motor room hideaway, without food or water?

When the movie finally ended Terry was sound asleep, though part way through he'd pulled Jon over to him and had his arm tightly round the girl's slim waist. Carefully Jon unwrapped the arm and got up off the sofa. Was this his chance, could he grab some stuff and make a break for it? What would Terry do if he escaped - just let him go? More likely he'd call security or try to track him down. The odds weren't good. He left Terry where he was and went to bed in the bath-robe.

***

The following morning Terry was pretty spruce considering the amount of booze he'd tipped down his neck the previous night. Jon was suffering though and the room was still tending to spin a bit if he lost concentration.

They sat at the little dining table facing each other, cups of coffee in hand.

'Well that was really pleasant evening Jasmine. Nice to have your company, and look, I'd like you to be here again this evening if that's OK with you?'

Jon wasn't sure what to say. The silence was almost oppressive.

Terry's voice took on a stronger tone. *'If that's OK with you Jasmine?'*

Jon stumbled over the words. 'Yes, yes Terry it's fine. I'll ….. look forward to it.'

Terry leaned towards him until his face was almost touching Jana's.

'Because if it isn't fine, you know I've got my duty to do don't you? It's a big ship I'll grant you, biggest I've ever been on, but there's only so many places a girl could hide. So if you want to enjoy a few more steak suppers, you'd better be here. OK?'

Jon knew he had no alternative. Terry had been friendly, he'd fed him, he'd bought him more drinks than he'd enjoyed for over a year, and all he'd wanted to do was fall asleep in front of a film with a girl in his arms. And of course he was holding all the trump cards.

'OK Terry. I'll be here.'

★★★

Jon was on his favourite bench enjoying the perennially warm weather while he watched the couples as they sat together eating their picnics. Couples? He wondered if that was how Terry saw himself with Jana? Or if he didn't right now, was that the next step? Was that how he saw their *relationship* progressing? He'd been so friendly, and yet he'd been menacing too. No violence of course, there was no need to resort to violence. He already had full control of Jon and his life here on the ship. You'd only let your dog off its leash if you were sure it was going to come back.

Jon thought back to the day before. Just this time the previous morning he'd been free. Free to come and go as he chose. Penniless and starving, but free. Now it had all changed, his days of precious freedom had vanished - in a moment.

He sat on the bench and watched as two security guards strolled by. Those guys had a good job - no thefts, no murders, no fights - well sometimes the odd fight amongst the prisoner-crew, usually the males - but they were on the ship in strictly limited numbers. Apart from that the job was a doddle. Would the day dawn when they came to arrest him? Would it brighten their otherwise dull afternoon? After all this time in space the girl's face was well known around the ship and many had been the time when those same security men had even said a polite "good morning" to him as he'd strolled around the park. Boy were those two going to have egg on their faces when their boss found out they'd walked right past the stowaway every day for over a year.

Jon focussed on his new situation, discovered, but still evading capture. Discovered but not betrayed. Not betrayed as long as he played Terry's game. But what did Terry want from him? Last night he'd been quite a gent. He hadn't known there was a woman in the shower of a room that was supposed to be unoccupied, and he'd left *her* alone to get dried and decent as soon as *she* could. He'd wanted to talk, men always did. The conversation had been one sided, but it hadn't been unpleasant. Then he'd put his arm around the girl's waist, nothing more. What was the harm in that? And then he'd slept on the sofa leaving Jon alone in the bed.

Jon was confused, Terry hadn't wanted sex at all. Perhaps for a man in his late fifties he wasn't interested anymore. But that one didn't wash, back in Jackson, Jon had his own late fifties body and he certainly wasn't ready to give up that hobby - not yet anyway.

It had been another pleasant day out in the park, but now he watched the lighting as it began to dim down to the golden sheen of its evening glow. Now was the time for him to go back to the room. Time to go back to spend another evening with Terry. He thought again about his hideaway and the prospect of eleven months of incarceration. With a heavy heart he turned for "home".

★★★

Back in the room, Terry was in good spirits even if Jon wasn't.

'Hi there Jasmine. Great to see you, and I must say how nice you're looking.'

Jon tried hard to give the man a smile, but it wasn't in him.

'Want a glass of champagne? It's the real stuff, not that Union rubbish.'

Jon decided to join in. The more the guy drank, the less were the chances of anything happening that evening - and the less he'd notice if it did. Terry topped up the glass after the foam had subsided and offered it in Jon's direction. Jon put it to his lips and tasted. As he'd found at the conference, Phoenixan champagne had something of an edge over even the best vintages from Erandar. Maybe that could be another trading prospect for Phoenix? Though under the circumstances right then, marketing wasn't something he needed to dwell on.

As before Terry indicated that the seat next to him was vacant, and as before Jon was in no position to decline the offer. Terry talked, something he seemed good at and told Jon all about his business ventures on Phoenix and how he was going to expand with branches on Darius where there was good money to be made.

Just as the heavy glass bottle went bottom up in the ice-bucket Jon heard a knock on the door but left Terry to answer it. Dinner had arrived, complete with its own bottle of red.

When the supper ended Terry stood up and fetched the whisky. Jon accepted a glass and drank it down just a little too eagerly. The evening wore on and the level in the bottle went down. And as the level went down, so Terry pulled him just that little bit closer. When the round red face pushed itself onto the girl's lips for a heavy wet kiss Jon wanted to retch. When he felt a hand cupping Jana's breast he wanted to scream and run away. When the big arms picked him up and carried him over to the bed he wanted to die.

***

How long passed before he looked around and saw he was lying on the bed, naked, Jon had no way of knowing, though it seemed as if an age had passed. Everything was fuzzy, but he thought he remembered the big man helping him out of his clothes. Now Terry was busy, for a while, but when the pawing and groping stopped Jon knew it was the calm before the storm. He felt a knee that pushed against the girl's leg and left her open and vulnerable in a way Jon had never truly understood before.

Then it came, the probing in the girl's groin. Then the push of the stiff member as it worked its way inside. Desperately he tried to recall the things they'd told him, "the body remembers, the body knows what to do". If he could just relax and let Jana's body take over it would be alright. But with the fear and fright that filled his mind there was no lubrication and the pain that came as Terry pushed brutally inside made him scream out loud - something the man seemed to accept as praise of his technique. Up and down, in and out, time and time again. It felt to Jon as if the girl's defenceless body was being ripped apart. He was being raped, and not a thing he could do about it. And it just went on and on. Then as the pain was rising beyond the point of endurance Jon prayed to God, please, please let it stop, please let it stop now. At that moment he felt the change as Terry gave a gasp, and his muscles tensed - for a moment. He was still deep inside, but at least the thrusting had stopped.

With the weight of the big man crushing down on Jana's small frame, Jon heard the breathing as it dropped from the rapid gasping of just seconds ago to a slow rhythmic pace. Under the mountain of flesh he lay there in shock, scarcely able to breath.

How much time would pass before Terry awoke Jon couldn't guess but he knew he couldn't last long down there. He wriggled to find a place where the man's weight wasn't bearing down quite as much, and heard Terry's breathing change again. With all the girl's strength he gave a push, and Terry began to slip sideways. The bed creaked as the heavy flesh made contact with the mattress, and Jon breathed a sigh of relief. Terry, half awake, grasped Jana's body round the waist and fell back asleep.

Terry woke half an hour later and was elated, and well he might be. But Jon could feel pain. Pain he'd never known before. He knew the girl's body was damaged and when he tried to get out of bed it came as no surprise to find he could hardly walk. And there was blood even though the girl's period wasn't due for a few more days.

If the guy asked him how it had been for *her*, his chances of getting the bedside table smashed over his head were excellent.

★★★

The next morning Jon was free to go off and spend the day as he chose, just as long as he returned faithfully to his master that evening. Walking only slowly around the gardens he looked at the two security guards as they passed and the idea of surrendering himself to them right then seemed suddenly attractive. But still he couldn't bring himself to do it - not yet.

That evening when Terry started to come on strong again Jon knew he was going to have to say something or the girl's body was going to need medical attention. And there was no way he could manage to see a doctor without being found out as the stowaway.

As the lovemaking that felt more like a wrestling match started over again, a deep seated need finally gave him the courage to speak.

'Terry?'

'What is it my little love?'

'Terry, you're a big man you know, and you were a bit rough with me last night. You hurt me a lot and I don't think I can manage it again, not just yet.'

Jon had to admit the man did look genuinely concerned and was certainly taking him seriously. Maybe he was going to get a night off.

'That's OK Jasmine, there are other ways a girl can please her man.'

Jon felt the girl's face turn green when he considered the options.

★★★

Morning came again and Jon thought back with disgust to the night before. A long cool glass of orange juice improved matters and by the time breakfast was over he was ready to go out for another brief interlude of freedom. He was surprised how fast the girl's body had recovered, but still a few twinges of pain came as he walked. She wasn't ready for a repeat of the performance yet even though Jon knew the alternative that awaited him.

The day dragged. Somehow the simple pleasures he'd enjoyed so many times before no longer had the same appeal. The times he'd sat and let endless days pass by as he'd watched others walking around the park. The times he'd smelled the flowers and the scent of the new-mown grass, or felt the warm breeze as it played around the girls bare legs. Now the only thing on his mind was the obligation to return to his master.

Evening came and as he rode the lift back up to the sixth floor of Juniper Block he began to wonder whether Terry was going to accept that he was still unable to have sex after two days recovering. So he changed to another tack.

'Terry?'

'Yes my love?'

Jon lied although he knew his story was soon to come true anyway.

'Terry, I'm sorry if you're going to be disappointed, but something's started. It's that time when it's not quite right for a woman to have sex.'

★★★

The next day came and for the first time Jon was actually pleased to see the sight of blood - his line of defence. But how many days could he keep the man at bay? With almost eleven months still to go before the ship arrived at Darius, buying time day by day wasn't going to work. With a sense of fear he kept watch on the dwindling number of tampons left in the box - and for the first time he was actually beginning to dread the girl's period coming to an end.

★★★

Five days passed and the time for him to bite the bullet was coming. That night he was going to have to let Terry have his way again. What else could he do? Well there was one thing at least and a trip to the pharmacy saw him better prepared than he had been the previous time.

When he got back up to the sixth floor that evening Terry was there waiting, and he had champagne again - obviously there was something to celebrate. Jon took as many glasses as the man offered - the longer he kept him drinking the longer the inevitable was postponed. By the time the moment came Jon was flying high on the fizz Terry had plied him with, and with a fingerscoop of the slippery jelly from the jar he'd bought inside he found he could endure the ordeal without too much physical pain.

★★★

It was only five when Jon awoke, but somehow he knew his night's sleep had ended. Although with Terry there in bed beside him there was nothing he could do but lie awake and ponder.

Another three days had passed and the novelty wasn't wearing off yet, so he'd had no choice other than to let Terry use Jana's body every evening. He shuddered when he thought of how the real Jasmine Kell made her living. It was true he was getting fed, and plied with drink - he was living in a comfortable room, and most important of all he was buying Terry's silence, but the cost was high. Jon wondered exactly when *high* was going to become *too high*.

And then a deeper thought worried and nagged at him. He knew very well that when a male and a female had unprotected sex something often happened as a result. And in their evening chats Terry had told him all about his family life: two boys from his first marriage and a girl from the second. The guy wasn't firing blanks. And for the first time Jon saw one part of life from a very different perspective. This was a Phoenixan ship operating under Phoenixan laws - laws that by Union standards were almost pre-historic. Religion was strong on the strange new planet and contraception was forbidden except by a doctor's prescription. If he dared to see a doctor the game would be up. And if he didn't ....

The more Jon thought about his situation, the more he worried. It was early in the girl's cycle and he knew it was too soon for anything to happen just yet, but sooner or later her body was going to catch. If it didn't happen this month there was next time, and the time after too. He thought back to an article that had run in the New Vissanian a few years earlier where he'd been featured as the galaxy's luckiest man. What would they say now? If they could see him in a few weeks time, not only a sex slave and plaything, but expecting a baby as well? He held Jana's head in her hands. Oh for Belen's sake, how had he ever got into a mess like this?

★★★

So what if it happened, what if the worst really did happen? What then? He didn't need a calendar to work out that with over ten months still to go before the Hyperion completed its journey there was time enough for Jana's body to take a new life to full term. If the thought of living in her body while a parasite grew inside wasn't bad enough, the thought of what happened afterwards was worse and absolutely guaranteed his discovery as a stowaway. If they'd been closer to Darius, maybe there'd have been the chance of doing a transfer back home and leaving the real Jana to have the baby. If he put enough money her way she'd surely accept. Everyone had their price, if you paid enough.

For days Jon agonised over what he had to do. Finally he was sure. He was out of options and there was only one course left open. He lay there on the bed until Terry stirred and the day could begin.

★★★

Jon finished his breakfast and went off to get dressed. This morning was different from any that had gone before, but playing the game he kissed Terry with as much passion he could muster - which wasn't a lot. As he stepped out of the room he walked past the lift, tapped in the code for the lift-motor room and headed up the stairs.

Silently he sat above the ventilator grill watching. Hours passed but when Terry came out of the room and disappeared into the lift Jon came back down and went into the room. Carefully he collected together everything he owned, stashed it into the rucksack and hauled it up to the lift-motor room. He took the cleaner's pass out of his pocket and the money he had left and slid them behind the safety notice on the wall by the side of the electrical panels.

David Hulett Wilson

Stepping out of the door he closed it behind him and pressed the button to call the lift. He felt the motion as the car descended and the jolt as it came to rest. As he pushed the door and walked out of Juniper Jon wasn't sure whether his feeling was one of elation or release, but he knew a milestone in his life had been passed.

Fortunately the day wasn't scheduled for rain so he was able to spend some time out in the park, out in the tiny patch of captive nature that had helped him find at least a modicum of happiness during the long months while the ship had been out in space. As he walked around the fruit and veg garden he watched the prisoner-crew workers in their blue and white overalls and wondered where the next hours would see him. Would they send him out to work like this, or would they keep him under lock and key?

85

The Surrender

When the heat of the day was past and the light had started dimming down towards evening Jon knew the time had come. Taking in a final look at the antics of the hologram ducks he set off in the direction of the administration area. But as he walked along he wondered whether he was doing the right thing. Twice he'd stopped and almost turned around. It wasn't too late. He could change his mind and go back to Terry. There were parts of their *arrangement* he could manage now he'd got the physical side sorted out. But it was the longer term consequences he could not, and would not accept.

Could there be a solution? He found a bench and sat down to think. Could he make a deal with Terry - sex only on the *safe* days of Jana's cycle? But how safe was safe? He remembered the words of a famous doctor, "we have a technical term for women who rely on natural methods of contraception - we call them mothers". It wasn't a chance he was prepared to take. Spending the next ten months in jail was his only option.

★★★

The two regular day-shift guys were sitting happily in the security office after another event-free day. Jon walked in and saw them there, cups of tea in hand, a plate of biscuits on the table. One of the men was slightly tubby, a friendly faced man who must have been somewhere in his early forties. The other was a bit skinny and probably about thirty or so. Jon looked at the two of them and wondered just how effective they'd be if it came to a real incident. From what he'd seen of the ship's security service so far they'd probably have been at full stretch taking tickets on the door of a jumble sale.

The older man gesticulated towards the empty chair on the opposite side of the desk.

'Good afternoon Miss, always a pleasure to see you. Is there anything we can do to help?'

Jon sat down in the vacant chair and made himself comfortable. This was his last chance to chicken out, and he knew it. It took a big swallow before he finally managed to speak.

'I'm the stowaway, ... and I'm here to surrender myself to you.'

It was almost comical to see the way the two men nearly choked on their biscuits. The older one composed himself, he'd been caught out, but now he'd seen through the prank.

'Oh you do like a joke Miss. Now come on, what can we do for you?'

'I *AM* the stow-away and I'm here to surrender myself to you,' Jon repeated. 'Why don't you get the wanted poster down from the wall outside and have a look.'

The younger man got up and walked out of the office. A few seconds later he rushed back in with the poster in his hand. He held it up to the side of Jana's face and looked from one to the other a few times before passing it to the older man.

'There is some resemblance. See what you think Bill.'

Bill looked took the poster and studied the image carefully.

'The hair's darker in the picture, and she looks different without that odd makeup. But you can see her features. She's a dead ringer!'

The two men looked each other in the eye. Jon could almost hear the two brains thinking "oh shit" just milliseconds apart.

'She was the girl we were looking for just before we left orbit, and we've walked past her every morning since leaving Phoenix.'

Bill looked over at the younger man. 'Have you got her details Doug?'

Doug walked over to one of the filing cabinets and pulled open a drawer. After a few moments of sheafing through the ordered ranks of neatly archived papers he called out:

'Got it! Jasmine Kell, she was a cleaner on the ship while it was being refurbished. She went missing just before we left for Darius.'

Jon broke into the exchange. 'I'm *Jana* Kell. Jasmine's my twin sister and I want to make it clear right here and now that Jasmine had no involvement in helping me stow away.'

'OK, OK. It doesn't really matter whether you're Jana or Jasmine, as long as we've caught you. We always get our man …… or woman.'

Jon continued. 'And I want to make it clear that I surrendered to you of my own accord, and I made no attempt to resist arrest.'

'Arrest, yes, Doug we've got to arrest her. Can you ….., you know what.'

Doug opened another drawer and pulled out a pair of handcuffs. Jon wondered whether they might have rusted up from disuse though it wasn't really a worry, even for cheap Phoenixan stainless.

'Sorry Miss, but it's regulations.'

Jon looked on impassively - he'd expected it anyway. The man took the girl's right hand and carefully closed one ring of the cuffs down onto the wrist before snapping the other onto the metal frame of the chair. Now he was their prisoner, the deed was done. Now there really was no going back. Jana's chest rose as he breathed a sigh of relief.

Bill spoke up. 'Doug, will you make the lady a cup of something hot while I go and see if the Purser's free?' He opened the door and stepped out.

Doug clicked on the kettle and started arranging a mug and a spoon. 'Tea or coffee Miss?'

'Tea please.'

'Milk and sugar, how many spoons?'

'Milk, no sugar thanks.'

When the tea was poured the man brought it over and placed the mug on a small table to the righthand side of Jon's chair. He thought about the arrangement for a moment and moved it round to the left so Jon could reach it with his free hand.

But the uneasy peace didn't last long. Before Jon could take even his first sip Bill marched back into the office followed by another man, who from the military regalia he wore must surely have been at least an admiral. The man pulled up a chair and sat himself down.

'Good afternoon Miss Kell, I am Stuart Robertson, ship's Purser and head of security. Now, from what my team here tells me you've been stowing away on our ship for over a year. We need you to tell us why you stowed away, where you've been hiding, and what's made you give yourself up now?'

Jon went through the whole story. Truthfully he told them about the lift-motor room in Juniper Block, and then lied that he'd had to give himself up because he'd run out of money and needed food. Being a well-fed prisoner seemed more attractive than life as a starving stowaway. Robertson and Bill left the room, closing the door behind them. Jon sat and drank his cup of tea.

★★★

It was about half an hour later when Robertson and Bill walked back into the security office.

'Well we've found your little hideaway, exactly as you described it. How did you manage to get in there in the first place.'

Cool as a cucumber, Jon continued his lie. 'A guy came to mend the lift, and I saw the code he put in to get into the equipment room.'

Robertson went over to the computer and logged on. He spent a few minutes trawling through something or other before he spoke.

'That was while the ship was being refurbished, a couple of days before we left orbit. Have you been on board since that time?'

Now Jon told them the truth, he explained how he'd come up to the ship posing as Jasmine, and then decided to stow away using information he'd gained earlier.

'And why did you stow away in the first place Miss Kell. It seems to be a bit of an extreme thing to risk because all it's going to do is leave you in space as a prisoner. We've another ten months to run before the ship gets to Darius. Then we'll be in orbit for a month and after that it's another two years back to Phoenix where we'll hand you over to the authorities. And they'll put you in jail for a few more years I shouldn't wonder. You're going to spend years in custody, and all for what?'

Jon shook the girl's head. 'You wouldn't believe me if I told you.'

'Try me.'

Jon breathed a sigh, he wasn't short of time so he told the man who he really was and the tale of his failed transfer back to Vissan.

Finally he concluded his story, 'and with you listening now, it's going to add another three to the list of people who don't believe me. The reason for my journey to Darius is to get back in contact with my office in Jackson, then they will make arrangements for me to TranzCon back to Vissan. The real Jana Kell will take over her own body again and travel back to Phoenix with you on this ship, but as a passenger, not a prisoner. Ten more months gentlemen, and then we'll be at Darius orbit. Then you'll have the chance to find out I'm telling the truth. Now, I'll offer you a deal Mr Robertson. If you let me travel the rest of the journey as a passenger, when we get to Darius I'll pay Phoenix Intersolar double the cost of the fare for the whole trip, and what's more, I'll pay you and your security team a substantial bonus for being so reasonable about it.'

Jon saw the way Robertson was looking at him.

When the man said, 'well it certainly sounds plausible. It would explain why you were prepared to take such a risk,' Jon was sure he was getting somewhere. Then the Purser continued, 'but look, I'm in a situation here, I've got a stowaway on board, and I presume that if you'd had access to the sort of money you'd need to buy a ticket before we left Phoenix, you'd have paid to come as a passenger.'

Jon accepted that the logic was undeniable. 'You are absolutely right.'

Robertson continued. 'And the fact you did not pay indicates that you did not have access to that kind of money. And more to the point, at the present time you still have no access to any money.'

Jon was forced to agree. 'That's right. They wouldn't let me draw anything from my own bank accounts, so I was very short of money.'

'So considering that you don't actually have any money to pay the fare, or to pay the bribe you've just offered a senior member of the ship's staff, the Captain's not going to be happy with me if I just let you move into a room and start running up a bill for everything else.'

Jon was worried now. 'But I can pay it all back when we get to Darius.'

'And what if you can't? What if this is just a load of cock and bull? Miss Kell, there is only one decision I can make, and that is for you to complete the journey to Darius in the secure accommodation block. But I've heard what you've said and I'll promise you this, when we get into orbit at Darius you will be given the opportunity to make contact with whoever you think it is can help you. If they can substantiate your story then you will be allowed to disembark and go down to the surface. This will of course be subject to your people on Vissan paying the standard fare for your passage.'

Jon's spirits sank once again - a prisoner for the next ten months. He wondered about buying Phoenix Intersolar and sacking Robertson when he got home, but that wasn't going to get him anywhere right now. And threatening to do it was only going to make things worse.

'Is that really fair though, putting me in jail for ten months and then expecting me to pay for the privilege?'

'Miss Kell, it may surprise you, but it costs us far more to keep a prisoner in the SA Block than it does to have them as a passenger. You'll have somewhere to live and you'll have food to eat, and from what you told me just now you'll be eating far better than when you were a stowaway. Am I right?'

Jon nodded.

'And of course you'll get to Darius at the same time as all the passengers on the ship who've paid a lot of money for the privilege. How good a deal can someone in your position expect?' Robertson looked at Jon for a reply. 'Do you have anything to say Miss Kell?'

Jon just looked and shook his head.

'OK then, it's decided. Doug, Bill, take her down to the SA Block and I'll pass the news on to the Captain.'

86
Porridge

The sight of two security men and a handcuffed young woman trooping across the park to the shuttle rail station drew a bit of attention, but with no news of anything outside the ship for over a year the excitement level on board was close to zero so any kind of spectacle drew a crowd. Jon ignored the stares and had one last look at the wide open spaces and wondered if he'd ever see them again.

A couple of stops along the line Doug and Bill lead their prisoner out of the shuttle car and transferred to a lift that took them down to the sub-main deck level - an area that was off-limits to passengers. When the doors slid open Jon looked out onto a featureless corridor that was grey and bare. "Functional" was the word that sprang to mind, a stark contrast to the polished wood and deep-pile splendour of the ship's passenger areas. The trio walked along until they reached a heavy steel door bearing two signs. The upper one read, "Secure Accommodation - Authorised Personnel Only". The one below read "Female Division".

After Bill had tapped in a code at the keypad Jon and the two guards entered a small ante-room with a second door at the far end and a large armoured glass window down one side of the room that gave the new resident a first glimpse of his new home.

When the outer door swung closed its lock gave a click, then a green light came on above the inner door. Doug pushed it open and lead Jon out into a large room perhaps eight metres wide and ten metres long. With harsh metallic walls, grey tiled floor, and illumination from a pattern of strip fluorescents each safe from harm inside its own wire cage the place didn't appear to qualify for any design awards. To one side of the room stood a collection of plastic and tubular steel dining tables, each with four matching chairs. On the other side of the room four rows of more comfortable seats were arranged in front of a television set. The only other item of furniture was an open rack of dog-eared second-hand books.

When the inner door had closed securely behind them Doug unlocked the prisoner's handcuffs, and Jon noted that to secure the girls slim wrists they'd had to close them down to their tightest setting. If Jana's hands had been just one size smaller he'd have been able to pull them out and escape, but to where? There was nowhere to go and in any case Jon realised his future now depended on how well he could please his jailers. Escaping was not an option.

With the handcuffs packed away back into their leather pouch Doug looked up and scanned his eyes around the empty room. 'Where are the SA Block people? I thought there was supposed to be someone here to meet us.'

Bill was struggling to get some response from his phone which didn't seem too keen to work in this part of the ship. 'I called the woman in charge before we left the office. She said she'd be here when we arrived.'

TranzCon

'Well we can't leave the girl here on her own. We'll have to wait.'

Doug pulled three of the uncomfortable looking chairs away from a table and the group sat down. Jon was already bored after his first thirty seconds in custody, but he noticed how Bill and Doug carried on chatting without a care in the world. The drone finally stopped when Bill got up to see if there was a kettle and some water to fill it, and then in the quiet of the room Jon heard a sound. He looked up and saw a movement through the glass window of the ante-room. The outer door opened and a woman walked in. As she stood waiting for the interlock to operate she turned to look into the room and Jon was able to get a good look at her: thin, tall, and with the most serious face Jon had ever seen on a woman. She didn't appear to be particularly pleased to be there, though Jon had to admit, neither was he. Only Bill and Doug seemed to be enjoying their day.

When the door opened she walked over to the seated group and looked down at the two security men. 'Thankyou for bringing the prisoner down. I can handle things from here.'

The guards recognised their dismissal and got up to leave. Jon watched the way Doug offered a swipe-card up to a reader mounted on the wall to the side of the door. The unit bleeped then he punched in a code before the inner door opened to let them into the ante-room. Once the door had closed and a second code had been entered the outer door opened to let them out into the ship.

The woman seated herself on a chair opposite Jon and surveyed her new charge in a way that seemed to imply she could look inside the girl's head. Presumably she fancied herself as something of an expert in the field of interrogation.

'I've been briefed about this incident by Mr Robertson the Purser. I understand you're Jana Kell. Is that correct?'

The greeting lacked any form of warmth.

Jon confirmed his identity as Jana. Insisting he was someone else was not going to help his situation right then.

The woman continued. 'My name is Ms Lincoln and I am a senior officer in the ship's security services management team. One of my functions is to be responsible for inmates in the secure accommodation block.'

Just then another movement caught Jon's eye and he looked towards the ante-room. Coming in through the outer door was a huge dark-skinned woman. On a ship populated almost entirely by the usual pasty white faced Phoenixans her dark brown features made her stand out from the crowd. It was for certain her skin was a more pleasing colour though her facial features were not attractive. He reflected that he'd never really been able to get to the bottom of why the natives of Phoenix came in so many different varieties, though he remembered that Dougie Smith had known but never got around to explaining it to him.

When the interlock clicked the woman opened the inner door and walked, or more precisely she waddled, up to where Jon was sitting with Ms Lincoln. Without taking even the time for a polite "hello" Ms Lincoln went straight back to business.

'Miss Kell, this is Mrs Beeson. She will be in charge of you and any other inmates of the female division of the secure accommodation block during the hours while you are not locked in your cell. You will obey, immediately and without question, any instruction she gives you. Is that understood?'

Jon nodded.

Ms Lincoln raised her voice a decibel or two and spoke slowly, as if addressing an imbecile.

'I asked you whether that was understood.'

Now that Jon understood that his non-verbal response hadn't ticked the right box he replied. 'Yes.' But being unsure of how the woman might choose to be addressed added, 'Miss.'

'Yes *Madame*,' came the response. 'You will at all times address senior female staff as "Madame"'

Whether this was the woman's best effort at making friends Jon wasn't sure, but he wondered whether he might be able to do something about her, or any other "Madames" on board when he got back to Vissan. Phoenix Intersolar had been pretty smart with their idea of bringing an extra ship onto the Darius run, and what's more they'd done it all on a shoestring budget and in double quick time with their hastily refurbished old liner. Mentally Jon kicked himself. It was an opportunity Rapier should have seen. Perhaps when he got home he could buy PI to get a toehold in the market this side of Darius. But no - here was a better idea. He could take one of the line's older ships off a less profitable route and transfer it to Phoenix, then he could operate in direct competition with PI. With a bit of cross subsidy hidden away by some creative accountancy it would only be a matter of time before the upstart went under, and then he could buy the Hyperion from the Receiver for a rock-bottom price. Either way he could dispatch the "Madames" of the enterprise to wherever he chose. Even better, there was no doubt the woman controlled the finances of the secure accommodation service, so with a new assistant moved in as her deputy there was every chance they could fabricate a case of embezzlement. Then the woman could swap sides and wile away some time in her own institution.

Suddenly Jon was jerked out of his reverie.

'Miss Kell! Are you listening?' Ms Lincoln almost shouted. 'I was explaining the emergency evacuation procedures in case the captain gives the order to abandon ship, and you were lightyears away. Did you hear what I said?'

'Yes ……. Madame.' Jon struggled to keep a smile from breaking out on the girl's face. Yes, he'd deal with her and any other Madame who crossed him.

'Well I'm a busy woman. I have work to attend to. I will leave you with Mrs Beeson and she will explain the rules and find you a place in a cell.'

Jon watched her go. Despite all the centuries of research and the promises of breakthroughs yet to come, even the mega-budget scientific design forces of the Union had failed to create a humanoid robot that actually worked. He wondered if they'd been looking in the wrong places for their inspiration.

Jon turned back to the dark skinned woman. If Ms Lincoln had been skinny and severe, her assistant seemed to be exactly the opposite both in size and her general demeanour. Jon could see the way a smile was never far from her strangely featured face.

She started by stressing that her full name had to be used if anyone official was around, but to prisoners she was "Bee". It sounded like a good start.

★★★

As an opening gambit Bee explained the rules of the house. The day began at 06.30 when prisoners would rise, followed by breakfast at 7.00. Lunch would be at 12.00 and dinner at 17.30. Prisoners would clear away and wash up after all meals. Apart from Sundays, each morning would be spent cleaning the secure accommodation facility until lunch. In the afternoon prisoners would have free time until dinner and then at 20.00 they would go to their cells to be locked down for the night. Reading was permitted until the lights went out at 22.00. Talking between prisoners was permitted at mealtimes, and in the afternoons and evenings until lockdown.

Infringements of the rules would in all cases be punished either by an increase in the inmate's sentence or a spell in solitary confinement.

The second item on the agenda was a tour of the facilities. Jon had already seen what there was to see of the main room with its tables, chairs and TV set. To the side beyond the dining area was a serving hatch and a door that lead into a kitchen area. The facility was clearly designed to meet the needs of a large number of inmates, but Bee pointed out that with only a single prisoner in residence in the female division, and only two men in the male division next door, they wouldn't actually be doing any cooking here. Instead the food would come down from the crew kitchen which probably meant it would be stone cold by the time it arrived. Fortunately the kitchen was equipped with a microwave.

At the back of the main room were seven almost identical doors arranged side by side. Bee showed him inside the first one, the shower and toilets block. The second one was marked "Storeroom - Authorised Personnel Only".

'We'll be coming back here to get you kitted out.'

The third gave access to a mini-gym with a running machine and an exercise bike. The fourth lead into a small room with two computer terminals on desks. The fifth room made Jon laugh - a table tennis table and a pair of bats. What a marvellous provision for a single prisoner. The sixth door opened into a corridor with ten heavy looking doors of its own - five down each side.

'Cell block. This is where you'll be spending your nights.'

And then she turned away to head back to the store-room.

'What's behind the next door?' Jon asked.

'Solitary confinement cells.'

'Can we see inside?'

She shook her head. 'Trust me, you don't want to see inside. Just hope you never do.'

★★★

Back at the store-room door Bee pulled out her bunch of keys, unlocked the door and ushered Jon inside. Running most of the way across the middle of the room was a shop-style counter and the wall behind was purpose built with rows of compartments, each containing items of clothing.

Bee walked behind the counter and as she turned to face Jon a thought struck him, she was going to ask what size of clothing the girl took. Well Jon Chandler knew very well what his own measurements were, but they were for another body a long way from here. What size the girl took he'd no idea because he'd just helped himself to whatever was in Jana's wardrobe.

Bee peered over the counter. She looked him up and down and nodded her head in satisfaction.

'Apart from the shoes, we got just four sizes of everything in here. How about if I put you down as small for everything?'

Without waiting for a reply she walked along to the end of the rack and looked up at a top shelf that was exactly too high for her to reach. Walking back to the other side of the room she picked up a folding step-ladder, carried it over to the rack and climbed up to get what she needed.

Back down on the ground she dumped a pile of clothes onto the counter. Jon looked through them: two short-sleeved tee-shirts, two pairs of trousers, a jacket that zipped up the front, four pairs of socks, two bras, and four pairs of pants. All were in the same fetching shade of orange, including the bras and the pants. He hadn't been particularly surprised to see an orange prison uniform, it seemed to be de-rigueur anywhere in the galaxy, but co-ordinated orange underwear? Surely that was taking the idea a bit far.

'Lets see one of your shoes.' Bee called.

Jon took the left one off and passed it over the counter. Bee looked inside and handed it back, then bent down to rummage under the counter. She came back up with a box and lifted out two heavy lace-up boots in light tan leather. Although they were only part of the ensemble not actually in the standard shade of penal orange Jon couldn't help noticing the way they toned quite well with the rest of the uniform.

'You can change into your stuff in your cell. Then bring all your regular clothes out with you when I unlock you in the morning.'

'What happens to my own clothes?'

'They get put into storage. You get them back when they let you out.'

★★★

Struggling to carry all the bits of his new outfit and a book Bee had suggested he take from the rack, Jon followed his captor into the main room and then back to the door that lead into the cell-block. Inside the corridor Bee unlocked the first door on the left and gestured for him to step inside.

'When we're full it's two to a cell. But for now you got your own private room, and that's first class as far as secure accommodation's concerned. Only one thing you need to know,' she pointed to a break-glass station with a red button inside, 'if there's an emergency you press this button. If it's not an emergency then you're in trouble.'

And with that she clanged the door shut.

Jon looked around. The cell where he was to destined to spend his next ten and a half hours was about three metres square and uninspiring with walls of unpainted metal, a grey tiled floor, and a narrow single bed down each side. Beyond the beds stood a half-height panel that gave a minimal degree of privacy to a toilet on one side, and a washbasin on the other.

To match the walls, the bed-frames and the panel were bare metal, though the toilet and washbasin stood out in slightly brighter stainless. Looking up, the rather low grey metal ceiling was exactly two metres above the grey tiled floor and the only features it possessed were a ventilation louvre and a wire cage containing a pair of fluorescent tubes that shone with a cold blue light to accentuate the grimness of the already grim surroundings. The door which separated the room from the rest of humanity for was heavy and metallic with a spyglass at eye level and a drop down flap at hand height.

It was sometime later when the main lights went out that Jon noticed a smaller fitting inside the cage next to the pair of fluorescents. The glow was just enough for him move around the cell without tripping over, but it was clear the time for reading had ended.

And that was when he felt so very alone. As he lay sleepless on the thin mattress he was almost in despair. Tears welled in the girl's eyes and a thought came into his mind, an idea that shocked him more than he cared to admit - he actually missed Terry and his warm embrace.

★★★

Morning arrived with the strident blare of a horn outside in the corridor and the flickering on of the two fluorescent tubes. Jon opened his eyes and resigned himself to the fact that the few hours of sleep he'd managed to get were over, so he climbed out of bed and washed at the steel basin before dressing in the horrible orange garb. Fortunately the furnishings of the room did not include a mirror.

When Bee came to unlock the cell door he was ready to go and as the two of them walked into the main room he recognised the appetising smell straight away and tried to remember when he'd last tucked into a full cooked breakfast. Terry was a man who'd enjoyed his food more than most, but even he'd only gone for a slice of toast in the morning, perhaps to make up for the indulgence of the evening before.

With a sausage, a rasher of bacon, two slices of toast and a ladleful of beans on his plate it was without a doubt the best start to the day Jon had tucked into for quite a while, and he wondered whether it was food like this that had lead Bee to overdo things just a bit. Life on board the ship could be a bit monotonous and with the excellent food everyone else had enjoyed for the past fourteen months the opportunities for putting on a bit of extra weight were excellent.

Although she wasn't sharing the food he ate, Bee sat at the table with him and watched. Had she already eaten, or was she on a diet but took pleasure just from the sight and smell of food? Jon tried to strike up a conversation several times, but although the woman still wore her friendly smile he met with no response. Finally she spoke to tell him that fraternisation between staff and the inmates was not permitted, and pointed to a camera fixed to a bracket high up on the wall. Anyone could be watching and she didn't want to risk getting into trouble.

With Bee supervising the solitary prisoner from behind her magazine Jon worked hard that morning at the unfamiliar task of cleaning away the dust that had settled in the unused prison during the long months since the ship had left orbit. When at last the clock showed it was mid-day he was both tired and hungry but a bowl of soup, a packet of sandwiches and a cup of tea filled the girl's stomach to bursting point. But then after he'd washed up the plates he knew he'd reached the time when boredom would come calling. This was Day 1 of three hundred, give or take a few.

***

Dinner came and to Jon's delight he found the dish of the day was lamb casserole. There was no choice, but with food like this who needed one? Although his life in the SA Block was severely restricted one thing was clear, he was going to eat far better than he had during most of his days of freedom. All that was missing was a nice bottle of wine to wash it down.

87

All Of A Sudden - Nothing Happened

Days came and days went. Each one brought with it the same pointless ritual and Jon wondered seven times each week whether he was going to end up brain-dead before the ship reached Darius. But he took heart when he studied the calendar - if it was to be believed they were due to arrive in two months time. Just sixty more days before he could call Vissan and get back to the life he'd known so long ago, the life he could scarcely remember. His task now was to stay sane until the ordeal was over.

The food he'd eaten had been good and he'd assumed it was the standard fare provided to the crew. The girl's weight had increased by a kilo or two since he'd arrived in the SA Block, but then she'd been on the thin side after so many months of living on not quite enough. And although the meals Terry had provided had been very welcome, they hadn't been enough in number to fatten her up.

He'd made good use of the SA Block's facilities too and every afternoon he'd done at least an hour on one of the exercise machines. With the girl's eyes closed he'd tried to imagine himself running round the circumferential track, but the lack of scents and smells from the gardens, or the sounds of people enjoying an afternoon in the park meant the illusion never held for more than a few minutes. But at least he could take a pride in keeping the girl's body trim, fit, and healthy. Jana would be pleased with it when they transferred back to their own flesh.

Emboldened by the knowledge that as long as he wasn't directly abusive, no punishment would result, Jon had argued for an improvement in his circumstances. He'd made a complaint to Ms Lincoln that he was being held effectively in solitary confinement because with no company other than Bee, who continued with her refusal to be drawn into even the most simple of conversations, he was effectively in a state of sensory deprivation. And that was something he knew was only permitted as a punishment for a maximum period of 28 days. The answer that he wasn't in solitary confinement, he was a single prisoner, was scarcely acceptable. When he'd pressed the point Ms Lincoln had threatened that if he continued with his line he *would* be put into solitary confinement. Whether that was actually going to be any worse Jon wasn't prepared to find out.

88

Darius

The next fifty days dragged slowly by and Jon's eyes were always on the calendar, willing them to speed up. Which they didn't.

The weekly excitement came in a single hit when Ms Lincoln came to inspect the Block, her staff, and the prisoner. And it was on the day she came to visit that the sour faced harridan took a shift of supervision while Bee had the day off. It was quite an achievement, but Jon awarded her the prize for being even less fun to spend time with than Bee. The woman just sat at the computer all day, getting on with her work and saying nothing. Not a single word issued from the thin lips - ever. Even if the exchanges permitted between them were strictly controlled, at least Bee had some warmth about her.

The seclusion of the almost empty dungeon had been relieved just once when a girl from the prisoner-crew, a kitchen helper, had been sentenced to spend time in the SA Block as punishment for helping herself to tasty morsels from the first class cuisine. But her sentence was just for a single week and that precious time when he'd had company had passed all too soon.

When she'd first arrived in the SA Block, Jon had decided it would be better not to burden her with his stock story of being a mind-traveller from Vissan. Bitter experience had shown that approach never got him very far. So he went along with the idea of being Jana and listened avidly to her endless recollections of boyfriends and relationships, rock groups and parties, shoes and clothes, make-up and accessories. So many things he'd heard in that week a man would never be party to. She was a nice girl in many ways, but sadly forgettable, as was her name - which he couldn't remember.

Despite the isolation, madness had not descended on him yet and as far as he could see the only possible reason was that the ship's proximity to its destination was filling him with hope. From the computer console he'd watched impatiently as the Hyperion drew ever closer to Darius. With the ship at hyperlight and still so far away there was no chance of visual contact yet, but he'd watched the recorded approaches from previous runs, and on the diagram that showed the ship's position between Phoenix and Darius it was almost impossible to see there was any distance still to go. When Bee announced they would be going to deceleration stations in just a few hours Jon was happy for the first time in months. The dream he'd pursued for over eighty long light-years would at last be coming true.

89

Arrival In Orbit

With the Hyperion now running below lightspeed as it entered the Darian solar system there was at last live video of the approach available for all to see on the ship's entertainment network. Even before he applied any magnification Jon could already see a bright spot far in the distance, a spot lost among a vast ocean of stars that shone with the steady untwinkling light of interstellar space. And yet he knew that this one was special - Darius - one tiny sparkling jewel lost in an endless sea of nothing. A fertile planet, a life-giving planet, a rich planet. Perhaps the most blessed of any in the Union, and home to over five billion souls.

In just a few days the ship would be coming into orbit and the lucky people not banged up in the SA Block would be able to make their way up to the observation lounges to look down on its seas of swirling clouds, its deep blue oceans, dusty ochre deserts and the deep green of its rain-forests. Jon would be able to see it on the computer console of course, and he could call up thousands of hours of video taken from space during previous arrivals, but it wasn't quite the same as seeing it "for real". Apart from the knowledge they'd arrived it wouldn't be any different to watching a recording, though the significance of actually being there was far from lost on him.

But getting a view of the beautiful planet wasn't the only thing Jon was looking forward to. Even before they took up their position in orbit he knew the portal would open to allow the ship real-time communication to Darius. And by the power of the gravitron beam, communication to Vissan and the rest of the Union as well - instantaneous communication that would finally set him free. The moment he'd waited so long for was coming at last.

★★★

By the following afternoon an unmagnified view from the console showed how Darius had grown to a huge bright disk directly ahead of the ship. Finally there was the announcement he'd waited to hear: "Ladies and gentlemen - we now have limited communications reception from the surface. Full communication facilities are expected by 23.00 tomorrow night".

Even though the paying passengers had completed their journey and would soon be boarding their spaceplanes for the shuttle-trip to the elevator, Jon knew they'd all be anxious to get back in contact with families, friends, and business contacts as soon as they possibly could. For two years they'd all been together, literally in the same boat, and neither the rich nor the poor amongst them had had access to any form of communication with the galaxy outside. For an old ship like the Hyperion, the ability to communicate from deep space was something that was simply not available, so it was obvious that as soon as it came within range of transmissions from orbital stations the networks were going to be busy, very busy. From the almost total lack of response Jon got from the console in the SA Block it was clear that the prisoners on board had been allocated only a low priority. Time and again he tried and failed to get a channel.

Finally it was just after the evening meal was over and washed up that Jon went back to the console for one more try, and to his delight a channel came free almost straight away. With the girl's heart racing on a fix of excitement he wasted no time grabbing it. He logged in, as his real self of course, and clicked the *Send/Receive* button. Probably because of the limited data rate it took a few moments to complete, but there on the screen he saw something that dumbfounded him - there were no emails for Jon Chandler. Not a single one. He couldn't believe it. In his hectic life on Vissan he'd usually received over a hundred emails every working day, so extrapolating from that there should have been thousands upon thousands stored in the system. All of them just waiting for the day they could finally complete the journey to their intended recipient.

Bee put her head round the corner of the computer room door and called to Jon, 'two more minutes Jana.' After all the long months he'd spent waiting to get in contact with home! And now, just when he was so close it would all be stolen away. But he knew there was no point arguing, it would only get him into trouble.

Quickly in his final moments on-line Jon typed a short email to Michael Heathersett, and with a heavy heart he logged off. Bee stood and watched as he walked to his cell, and when the door banged shut, somehow the featureless room felt even more claustrophobic than normal. But he consoled himself with the knowledge that tomorrow he'd be back in email contact, and hopefully it wouldn't be long before speech circuits came available.

★★★

But knowing his quest was almost over, Jon was too excited to sleep so he lay awake for most of the night, planning and wondering, thinking about getting home. Thinking about the high flying career that had been on hold for so long. Thinking about Sylvie and wondering if the two of them could rescue something of the love they'd once known. The best of those times had been good, so very very good. His life in Jana's body had taught him a lot, shown him how life appeared when viewed from another angle, and now he was ready to change. Ready to make changes so he could be with Sylvie, ready to spend time with her, ready to give her the love he'd always known she deserved.

Tomorrow there'd be a reply from Michael and his journey home could begin. Praying wasn't something he'd done for many years, but that night as he lay awake he prayed, prayed that at last his hopes and dreams would soon be coming true.

90

Hannah

Morning came and brought a surprise. Jon's cell was unlocked by Ms Lincoln even though it wasn't supposed to be her shift for another three days. The sour-faced woman spoke just enough to tell him Bee had called in sick that morning. And that was another surprise, the big black woman was as strong as an ox and in all the time he'd been locked up in the SA Block she'd never missed a single duty.

But it had messed up his plans just a little. Now was the time he needed to get in contact with his people on Vissan and there was just a chance Bee might have allowed a little bending of the rules so he could have had his mid-morning break sitting in front of the computer. He knew that with Ms Lincoln in charge there was no point even suggesting it. He'd just have to wait until after lunch.

★★★

When afternoon came Jon wasted no time at all getting into the computer room and logging on. This was it, this was the moment he'd waited so long for. But again he was out of luck.

All the transmission channels were busy, though there was a bit of good news - ever since communications had been established the ship had been receiving downloads from the orbital network and the update of the on-board database was now complete. Everything that had happened in the past two years while the Hyperion had been out in space was now available to users on the ship: every film, every soap, every documentary, every news broadcast, and every website. All just waiting to be accessed.

What was obvious from the first website he found was that the Democrats under Joseph Brennan now formed the government, so Harmony must have lost the election. And that came as a surprise because at one time his party had been so far ahead in the polls they ought to have had it in the bag. He wondered whether his own absence from Vissan at a critical time had been instrumental in the defeat.

The situation on Daluun had made the news more than a few times. In the power vacuum left by the death of the charismatic Brian Rushmore, the Independence for Daluun Movement leader Adam Greenwood had been elected almost unopposed. And then the man had surprised the entire Union by not pressing ahead with the only item on his party's short manifesto. In defence of what appeared to be a U-turn change of policy he had advised reporters that an increased willingness by central government to keep Daluun on-side had made it advantageous for his planet's position to remain unchanged "for the present time".

The man had certainly shown himself to be a highly adept political player after negotiating a new deal for his planet. All existing loans, aid packages, and grants would be consolidated into a soft loan which would be extended to fund the building of new infrastructure including mineral processing plants, five fusion reactor power stations and the construction of a space-elevator. Economists agreed that the projects made sense because with on-planet refinement the total mass of materials to be lifted into orbit and transported to the home planets would be reduced considerably. In addition the government would underwrite a private loan to support Daluun's acquisition of its own fleet of Hx2 freight transport ships.

The loan would be repaid using money from increased prices the Union would pay for Daluun raw and primary processed mineral resources. Given the necessary time to come to fruition the policy would yield benefits for every one of the planet's growing population, but to buy himself time and goodwill Greenwood put a "feel-good" element into his budget and cut local income and point of sales taxes by a quarter.

When asked how the hike in material costs was going to affect industry on the home planets Brennan changed the question, and in the way that a man faced with an ultimatum often responds, replied that the Union was pleased to support in whatever way it could Daluun's desire for greater regional autonomy. And there was a photograph of the two politicians shaking hands, but it was clear to see which of them sported the broadest grin.

And then there was the beam. For so long Jon had wondered whether the GBeam might have come back on line the day the Hyperion left orbit, but he needn't have worried - his long journey through space had not been in vain. Communications on the Darius to Phoenix link was now possible, though everything sent between the two planets was subject to a delay of several weeks while a pair of courier ships shuttled between beam transmitters stationed on either side of the so-called dust cloud. And here was the important news, with only these interim arrangements in place, TranzCon travel between Phoenix and the Union remained out of the question.

The next article was about Phoenix. Entry to full membership of the Union had been suspended for a further six months due to the continuing communication problems. The government on Vissan was taking the matter seriously though and had awarded the planet associate status following its final adoption of a raft of laws and legislation needed to bring it in line with Union practices. The upgrade to full membership would be no more than a rubber stamping exercise and Jon guessed that the real reason for the delay was so the great and good of the Union could TranzCon to Phoenix for the big ceremony.

The computer beeped to let Jon know a transmission channel had come available so he grabbed it straight away. He was disappointed to see there was no email reply from Michael, but then a thought struck him. He opened a window to the galactic time and date interface routine, which told him it was Sunday morning on Vissan. Of all the lousy luck, two years in space and they had to turn up at the weekend. But at least he was going to be able to send a few emails, though he was just a little annoyed when he found his address book was a total blank. It went without saying that he couldn't recall many addresses from memory, and with nothing in his "In" box there was nothing to reply to.

Well at least he could remember Sylvie's addresses at Larsen and at home, and he knew she checked them every few hours wherever she was, weekend or not. It was always working hours somewhere in the Union.

★★★

The rest of the day had been completely uneventful. Jon had kept watch on the computer to check for incoming emails and had used the rest of his afternoon and evening to get more up to date with a mixture of news and the latest technical developments.

He was sad when Ms Lincoln came into the computer room and made the expected announcement that his day had ended. There was always tomorrow, but for Jon patience was now a scarce commodity and morning seemed a very long way off.

★★★

Morning eventually came, but things were much the same as the previous day. There was still no sign of Bee so Ms Lincoln was on duty again. Not that it made much difference to Jon, so after his usual high cholesterol start to the day he set to work cleaning the already spotless SA Block while Ms Lincoln filled her time with staring at her laptop and making endless numbers of calls on her phone.

About an hour later Jon heard a noise and looked up from his work. A male security guard was escorting an attractive young woman into the SA Block. In fact, if Jana's eyes didn't deceive him, the new prisoner was an *extremely* attractive looking young woman. She was taller than Jana with short hair in a tomboy style that contrasted with her lovely face and her slim though perfect figure. But the way it all went together - all Jon could think was "wow". He could see from the blue and white hooped uniform she wore that she was a member of the prisoner-crew, but he wondered whether in her real life she'd been a model or a movie star. She was obviously in some sort of trouble because she was in the SA Block.

Words passed between Ms Lincoln and the guard and he left a moment later leaving her to unlock the handcuffs from the new inmate's slim wrists. Completely ignoring the fact there was another person who might have expected to be introduced to a new arrival the older woman lead the girl over to the store-room, unlocked the door and ushered her inside. As she disappeared from view Jon noticed the clothes she was wearing, the pattern and colour were the same as he'd seen the ship's gardeners in, but they'd had overalls and heavy boots while this girl was wearing a blouse and a skirt. Knowing the limited range of jobs available for prisoner-crew he guessed she'd been working either as a chambermaid or a waitress.

Quarter of an hour later the two women re-appeared, the new girl looking only slightly less attractive in a colourful prison uniform that clashed quite badly with her pale skinned Phoenixan colouring. But the fact that any woman could look good in the awful get-up was quite amazing.

Ms Lincoln pulled the store-room door closed behind her and lead Hannah over to where Jon was sitting.

'Jana, this is Hannah. She'll be keeping you company for the next couple of weeks.'

Maybe she'd had more to say but she broke off to answer her phone.

For Jon it was like being sixteen again, when girls had just been invented. After all the long months he'd spent virtually alone he was really, really, really going to enjoy having a friend to spend some time with. And what a friend too, she wasn't just attractive, she was stunning. There was something about her that made his heart skip a beat. He watched the way she smiled, the way she moved, the way she touched her hair. And the way she tipped her head to one side as she looked at him was nothing short of seductive, a look that was somehow just a little more than a woman should have shown another woman. Maybe it was just her way.

He jerked suddenly to attention. Conversation Jon! Don't just stand there with your host's tongue hanging out, think of something to say!

'Welcome to the SA Block.' His brain fumbled for something better.

She smiled. 'Thank you. I take it there's just the two of us at the moment.'

'Just us prisoners. Usually we have Mrs Beeson as supervisor but she's off sick at the moment.'

'Chosen her day well hasn't she?'

'Why do you say that?'

'I don't know if you've heard, but there's been some trouble in the prisoner-crew quarters.'

Jon made it very clear that here in the SA Block the inmates never heard anything about what was going on in the rest of the ship. But he made it clear he was keen to hear anything she had to tell him.

'You know we've arrived in orbit around Darius, well we were having a bit of a party to celebrate.'

Jon was surprised. 'Why the celebration, as prisoner-crew they won't let you off the ship to go down to the surface?'

'It's the half-way mark. Lots of the people will have finished their sentences by the time we get back to Phoenix, so it's a big step. Anyway, some of the guys got their hands on a crate of plonk and when they'd got a few drinks inside them they decided they needed some girls to help the proceedings along. And they knew a way through the ventilation ducts into the female quarters and most of the girls were pleased to see them. We put some music on and it was really great. Best time we've had since we left Phoenix.'

'And how long did that go on before your jailers came to break it all up?'

'Well they leave us alone most of the time. Treat us more like proper people than convicts, but they keep tabs on what we're doing. One of the guards came in and saw the guys there and all of us having a party. She shouted at the top of her voice for us to turn the music off and go to our rooms, but we were having too much fun and everyone just ignored her.'

'That was brave of you.'

'Stupid more like. She came back a few minutes later with a load of male security blokes who stormed the place with a baton charge. It was absolute mayhem, they were laying into the guys because they weren't supposed to be there. All the girls started running for our rooms, and it was good job too because it was then that the real fight broke out. At first the guys had thought it was just a show of strength to get them to go back to their own quarters. They'd known it couldn't last and were just making the most of the time they'd got, but they didn't expect security to be quite so heavy handed, and that's when they started fighting back. And bear in mind this is a load of guys who'd been putting booze away for hours so they were itching for a fight. The security people were better equipped, but they were outnumbered five to one and some of the guards got knocked about pretty badly. The others retreated but it was obvious they were going to come back with reinforcements. The guys realised there was going to be more trouble so they climbed back into the vent ducts and crawled through to their own quarters - thought that if they pretended they'd been sitting quietly in their rooms the guards wouldn't be able to prove anything. When a riot squad stormed the male quarters the guys barricaded themselves in their rooms. I don't know what happened after that because we all got locked up but I'm guessing that some sort of siege has been going on overnight - that's what Ms Lincoln's been dealing with.'

Jon was astounded.

'Well that's the event of the trip. I can see the male section of the SA Block's going to be full for quite some time, but it doesn't explain why you're here. I thought you said all the girls were locked in their rooms?'

'What happened to me was something entirely different. It was earlier on before the trouble started. We were all having fun, drinking and dancing, but there was this guy who kept on bothering me - not that it's anything unusual. But this guy wasn't picking up on any messages. He'd been drinking like there was no tomorrow, and you know what men get like when they've had a few.'

Jon nodded. He knew.

'We were supposed to be dancing but he spent most of the time trying to snog me. He kept putting his arm round my waist and I suppose that wasn't too bad, but then his hands started wandering. So I told him to stop, but he wasn't taking "no" for an answer.'

'So what did you do?'

'I changed my tactics and turned to face him. Then I pulled him towards me and gave him a big kiss.'

'Which he enjoyed no doubt?'

'For a while.'

'Why only for a while?'

'Because I'd only done it to put him off his guard. That was when I rammed my knee up in the place where men don't like having knees rammed. Only I think I did it a bit too hard because this morning he was still in pain and they had to call the doctor to see to him. Now he's made an official complaint against me, and here I am.'

'How long did they give you?'

'Three weeks, assuming they don't have to amputate. If he loses his bollocks I can see me staying on in here for most of the trip home. Honestly, I'd no idea I was going to hurt him so much. But what about you? What did you do to end up in secure accommodation?'

'I'm the stowaway they were looking for when we left Phoenix. They caught me ten months ago, and I've been stuck in here ever since. It's a boring, pointless existence, but I get fed and I stay alive.'

'Ten months, it's a long time to be locked up.'

Jon watched as her eyes scanned round the grey depressing room. Was she wondering if she might be staying here for longer than just a few weeks?

'The first nine were the worst.'

She smiled. 'Like pregnancy.'

Jon stopped in his tracks, that was another of the "P" words he wasn't keen on.

'What's it like working here on the ship as prisoner-crew?'

She though for a moment. 'It's pretty good. For sure it's better than rotting in jail back on Phoenix. We have to work of course, but it's not hard and there'll be over four years of my sentence gone by the time we get home.'

'How long was your sentence?'

'Five years.'

'What about time off for good behaviour.'

Hannah gave Jon a slightly incredulous look. 'You don't get any time off with GMS. How come you didn't know that?'

'GMS?'

'Guaranteed minimum sentencing. What planet have you been living on? The sentence you serve assumes you're going to be a model prisoner, and you get time added on for bad behaviour. So if I'd kept my nose clean I could have been out just four months after we get back. Now I could end up with an even longer sentence. I've really screwed up.'

'What did you do to get sentenced in the first place?'

'It's a long story and it goes a long way back. You could say it started when I was five years old.'

Jon wasn't in a hurry, they'd got plenty of time.

'Five years old. What happened so long ago to land you in jail now?'

'Well I'd just started school and as you'd expect, my mum took me there in the morning and came to collect me in the afternoon. Well one day she didn't come, and after an age she still hadn't come so one of the teachers looked up our address and said she'd walk home with me to see if mum was there. We got to the house and rang the bell but there was no reply. The teacher tried the front door but it was locked, so we went through the side gate into the garden. There was no-one in the garden but the patio doors were open so we went inside and I burst out into tears when I saw my mum lying on the floor.'

'Was she dead?'

'At first we thought so, but the teacher found she was still breathing so she called an ambulance. It came a few minutes later with all its blue lights and sirens going, but there wasn't anyone to look after me so I had to go with them to the hospital. They sat me down with a nurse to look after me and then they came to say that mum had been ill but she was going to be OK. She was sleeping but I could go and see her. I remember it so clearly. It looked like she was just asleep, but sadly she wasn't completely right. She was never going to be completely right. All I knew at the time was that mummy was coming home from hospital, but she was still going to be ill. What they told me years later was that she'd had a stroke that left her badly disabled. In the short term it meant that my dad had to cut his hours at work so he could spend time looking after mum, and me. And doing all the meals and housework too.'

'And did your mum get better.'

'She improved a bit at first, but she never got properly better. She could never walk without a frame, and she hardly ever went outdoors. The furthest she would go was out into the garden. She never did much either: she watched TV, or she read, or she just stared at the wall for hours on end. She was OK to be left on her own for a few hours so that fitted in with dad going back to work full-time and me being at school when I was a few years older.'

'I'm very sorry about your mum, but it still doesn't explain you being here now.'

'Well it left me as a five year old girl effectively with no mother, but a father who loved me dearly, and the more time we spent together, the more he loved me. The only thing was, for all that my father loved me so much it didn't mean he was prepared to compromise on any of his own pastimes. He just took me along and expected me to join in.'

'And exactly what were his pastimes?'

'He was interested in owning guns, firing guns, going to gun exhibitions, using guns for target shooting, using them for hunting - and he did a bit of fishing on the side.'

'All good *man* stuff, but not exactly the kind of thing to interest a little girl.'

'No, but it meant we could spend a lot of time together. I remember times when we were off fishing and I'd take my colouring books or would find things to play at. And of course I was always excited when dad pulled a fish out, so it didn't take long before I had my own rod and I started catching my own. At ten I won the girls section of the junior angling league.'

'So you were really good by then?'

'I was quite good, but I was helped by being the only entrant in the category.'

'I can see the problem. What about the hunting?'

'I can remember when dad bought me my first "gun". I think I was the only girl on the planet who was excited about getting an air-rifle for her birthday. We took it out in the garden and fired off hundreds of pellets, and after a few weeks I could hit the bull with nine shots out of ten. But the shooting wasn't the whole of it, dad used to go off on trips with his mates and he just took me along. For years before I was big enough to handle a firearm of my own I used to follow him through the woods as he stalked deer. I didn't shoot but I learned a lot about hunting. Then when I was big enough he bought me my own rifle and I stalked my own, and brought them down with a single shot.'

'And what age were you then?'

'That was when I was about fifteen.'

'Weren't you interested in the sort of things other girls were interested in? Didn't you have a boyfriend?'

'I don't know. I just didn't have much interest in girlie things. I didn't have a boyfriend, but I did have lots of friends who were boys.'

'Who were they?'

'The sons of the other hunters. It's a bit of a father and son thing. They all brought their sons along and we were all mates together.'

'Did it ever get any further than that?'

'There was one I kissed, in the woods near the camp, but it didn't do anything for me. No spark inside.'

'Did you take it any further?'

'The boy I kissed was Tom, Tom Sullivan and it was funny because he and I were rivals.'

'Rivals in what way?'

'We competed against each other in sharp-shooting contests. Early on in my shooting career they'd said I couldn't compete against the boys and had to be in a girl's competition.'

'Sounds logical.'

'But the problem was I was the only entrant most of the time. Just like it'd been with the fishing.'

'So you must have won a lot of cups?'

'What my dad agreed with the club was, if I was the only entrant in the girl's section, then I'd be allowed to compete with the boys.'

'And you were a crack shot, so you won against the boys?'

'I could out-shoot most of them, but not all. There were some pretty good shots in our club, in particular the one I could never quite manage to beat. Guess who, Tom Sullivan of course. So I sort of looked up to him.'

'And did he like you?'

'He respected me for being a good shot, and I'm sure he saw me as a girl, so he made his play when we were off on a trip one weekend.'

'And that's when you decided there was no spark?'

'It just didn't do anything for me.'

'But you enjoyed the hunting and the camaraderie?'

'Yes, very much, I just felt that I was one of the group. My father's son who happened to be a girl.'

'It all sounds like fun, but still it doesn't explain why you're here right now.'

'OK, OK. The next thing that happened was that after so many years of being ill, so many years of being a non-presence in my life, my mother finally died.'

'Were you upset?'

'Yes, of course, but it only affected me for a few days. By the time the funeral was over I'd almost forgotten her.'

'That sounds a bit harsh.'

Jon was frowning as he looked towards her, but she turned away, refused to meet his gaze.

She was silent for a while before she next spoke.

'Jana, she'd scarcely been in my life for any of the time I could remember. She was *ill* all my life, and I just accepted her death. Whatever.'

'I'm sorry Hannah, I shouldn't have said that.'

'No, it's OK, it's me. Next autumn I went away to start college, and with me and mum out of the way that was when my father decided he'd be able to go off on more adventurous hunting trips. It was just as I was coming to the end of my first year that he flew off on some trip to go and hunt bears. There were four of them on the trip and they were all really experienced, and they had a guide with them who knew the bears and their habits. They shot a few bears in the company of the guide, and then they went off on their own to hunt, and that night my father didn't return to the camp. By morning he still hadn't come back so they set off to scour the woods.'

'And did they find him?'

'They trekked through the woods and they called on their walkie-talkies until they heard a reply coming through the forest. They trekked over and found his radio lying on the ground. As they searched around further they found bits of his equipment, and then his rifle, and finally they found his mutilated body. Obviously killed by a bear and partially eaten. I'm glad I wasn't there to see it. I never even looked in his coffin when they brought it home.'

'So he was killed in a bear attack?'

'If ever a man died with his boots on, it was my dad. He died doing what he loved so I suppose I shouldn't be too sad. He knew the risks, or at least he thought he did. He knew deer hunting for sure, but at least the deer don't come and jump you when your rifle jams.'

'Was that how he died?'

'They think so. It was the first thing they checked. Of course it only took seconds for a man so experienced with guns to sort it, but those were seconds he didn't have.'

'And that left you all alone in the world?'

'All alone, and worse than that, I had no money either.'

'Didn't you parents leave you anything?'

'I got the contents of the house, for what they were worth, but my parents had always rented because dad never had the money to buy after he cut his hours to look after me and mum. Then there was a bit of insurance money, but it wasn't much. There was no way I could carry on at college so I had to drop out and look for a job.'

'How old were you then?'

'Twenty one. I had a lucky break though because my uncle, that's my mother's brother, asked me if I'd like to come and work for him.'

'And what did he do?'

'He ran a wine importing company together with my aunt. My cousin had been working there as well, a real family firm setup. But she was just leaving to have a baby so there was a vacancy they had to fill.'

'So you fell on your feet then?'

'In more ways than one, because they even took me into their home. It was great because there was a self-contained granny flat out at the back that my cousin had stayed in before she was married. I just moved in. My uncle and aunt were great too, they loved me like a daughter, but they left me alone to live my own life as well.'

'Best of both worlds then?'

'Yes, and the job was fine too. I was handling the import shipping documentation, and arranging all the transport and customs declarations. It wasn't a high powered job, but it was a job you needed some brains to do.'

'So how long did you work there?'

'In total about eighteen months.'

'What happened then?'

Jon saw the pained expression that fell over the lovely face.

'Everything went wrong. The business was in two parts, there was the original business of importing high quality wines from top vineyards, but it hadn't been viable on its own because the turnover was too low. So they'd branched out into importing cheaper wines as well. They were well connected in the business and even had some contracts with vineyards to buy their entire production. Then they'd import it in bulk, and bottle it at their own place.'

'And was it good wine?'

'Some of it was plonk. They bought it for next to nothing and sold it at rock bottom prices and still made a profit. They had to sell thousands of bottles to get the money in, but there was a ready market for drinkable wine at prices the masses could afford.'

'So that was quite basic stuff?'

'That wine was, but what they'd also found was that some of their vineyards were producing wines that were definitely a cut above the ordinary stuff. Not all of them, and not in every year. And in some cases it even depended on which part of the vineyard the wine came from.'

'So they'd got some pretty good wine coming in as well?'

'Yes, but the problem was they didn't have a market for it. The brand they used for their own wine was associated with basic stuff, piled high and sold cheap. They always handled the top wines under a different brand so people wouldn't make any connection between the two.'

'They could have introduced another brand to handle better quality wine.'

'And that's what they did, but it isn't the only thing they did. They went into the counterfeit wine business as well.'

'And what was that exactly?'

'They selected the very best of their own production, and after bottling it they laid it down for a few years. And this is thousands of bottles, tens of thousands, we're talking about here.'

'Sounds OK, you mature the wine then it sell for more money.'

'Yes they did that, to some extent. But what they also did was to open a few bottles to decide which of their *fine* wines each batch tasted most like. After all, they were both experts in that field - they had the *nose*.'

'Uh oh. I think I can see what's coming here.'

'Yep, they printed all their own labels for the basic wine in-house, so it was no sweat to turn out copies of the labels from the top vineyards. When you think of the way they make it so hard to counterfeit banknotes, labels are easy-peasy, and worth so much more if you play your cards right.'

'So some of the supposedly best quality wines going out were their own production, and not the bottles they'd imported from the famous vineyards?'

'You've got it.'

'But what about the taste and the quality, didn't they get any complaints?'

'This shows just how well they were doing their job. They got more complaints about the real wine than they did about the bogus stuff. When they *did* get complaints about their own wine they replaced it case for case, and always with the pukka stuff of course, just in case someone brought in an independent expert.'

'But surely there'd be some discrepancy between the number of bottles they imported and the number they sold?'

'No, they'd thought of that one too. For every case of bogus wine that went out to be sold, they laid down a case of the real stuff.'

'So how did that make them any money?'

'Well the rest of the business was doing OK by then and they didn't really need to make any money from the counterfeit operation. So they just built up a stockpile of the real top quality wines.'

'But there had to come a stage when they were going to sell them?'

'Yes, of course. Obviously, the top wines they held back were those from vintage years, so with age those wines were going to become worth more and more.'

'You've still got to sell them to make money though.'

'And that's exactly what they were going to do, but before that happened they were going to end the bogus wine production and conveniently have a fire to lose some of the records about how much wine they'd actually imported. Then they'd release the stockpile onto the market and make megabucks. And of course it would all be the real stuff so even if anyone had wondered where it'd come from they wouldn't have been able to find fault with it.'

'And did you know about this operation?'

'At first I didn't, but with the job I was doing there was no way I could fail to become aware of it.'

'Wasn't that dangerous for your uncle and aunt?'

'It was a risk I think they were prepared to take, and that was probably why they'd wanted someone from inside the family to do the job. They knew I'd find out one day, but by then I'd be so deeply into the scam that I'd have a vested interest in keeping quiet. But I think it took them by surprise that I found out so soon.'

'So what did they say?'

'I never confronted them, I just told them I'd be leaving and gave in my notice.'

'Did they know the reason why?'

'They never said, but I think they knew.'

'Did you go to the police and report them?'

'No, but by God I wish I had done because I wouldn't be here now. They'd been running the scam for the best part of ten years and the whole thing had been beautifully covered up. But then there was some problem with the number of bottles of the cheap wine they were paying duty on. I think they were running some other dodgy deal selling more cases of the plonk than they actually declared to the revenue people. But I didn't know anything about that operation.'

'So what happened?'

'Some bright spark at the revenue department decided to do an investigation. Fortunately for my uncle and aunt he found their tax affairs were absolutely in order, or at least they'd cooked the books well enough that it looked like the tax was in order. The problem was, the guy accidentally stumbled on the bogus top quality wine scam. The revenue came en-masse and raided the offices, and all the cellars too. Then the police came and arrested my uncle and aunt, me and the rest of the staff.'

'But you weren't running the scam and until recently you'd known nothing of it.'

'And that's exactly the line the revenue took with the rest of the staff. There was no doubt that some of them had known what was going on, but there was no way of proving it. They treated me differently because I was family, and technically I was living at the same address even though I had my own flat. They just extrapolated from a few facts that there was no doubt I would have known about everything that was going on. And they also picked up on the fact that I was paid a bit more than my job was really worth.'

'What about your cousin who'd done the job before you?'

'They didn't pick up on her immediately, and when they finally did start to investigate former employees, especially family employees, they found her and the baby gone. To this day we've no idea where they went, and if her husband knows he's not telling.'

'So you ended up in jail?'

'My uncle and aunt were sentenced to ten years each, and I got five. I did five months inside and then the job on the ship came up. I put in an application and that was accepted partly because I was in for a non-violent offence, and partly because I was female. They prefer women as prisoner-crew, less trouble.'

'Still unfair though.'

'Completely unfair, but what can I do about it? No-one's on my side, and no-one believes me. But I'm a survivor and the job here on the ship hasn't been too bad.'

They were disturbed when Ms Lincoln's phone rang again. She listened for a while before suddenly rushing over to where Jon and Hannah were sitting.

'You two, both of you. Emergency lock-down. Go to your cells straight away.'

Hannah chirped up. 'I haven't got a cell yet. You said you'd allocate one later.'

The woman was clearly flustered. 'Well go to the cell block anyway, I'll unlock one for you.'

They got up and walked over to the door that lead into the cell-block corridor. Jon took the opportunity to saunter along as slowly as he could - anything he could do to annoy Ms Lincoln was worth the effort.

'Come on Kell. Hurry up.'

Jon didn't, but he kept a close watch on Hannah in front of him. If the girl had looked nice while she was sitting down, she was fantastic standing up. He watched the way her long silky figure ran down from her swan-like neck, past her majestic back, past the curves of the shapely bottom to her perfectly formed legs. Even in the orange uniform she was the most gorgeous woman he'd ever seen.

Jon was just outside the door into the cell-block corridor when he saw Ms Lincoln walk past the first cell and stop outside the second. He watched as her hand felt in one pocket, then the other. Next she was patting herself down, presumably looking for her keys. She said something under her breath that Jon didn't quite catch before running back out into the main room and over to the store-room door. Watching her tugging frantically at the obviously locked door was just a little comical and Jon had to struggle to keep a straight face. After another curse she broke off from the futile task and rushed back into the corridor. She pointed to the open door of Jon's cell.

'Hannah, get in there. Kell, you too, and do please hurry up.'

Jon took his time and followed Hannah in through the open doorway. Ms Lincoln set the door to auto-lock and pulled it closed.

Jon looked around at the cell he knew so well. Just the same as always, but somehow smaller with a second occupant taking up some of the strictly limited space. Something male stirred within him, like an animal preparing to defend its territory. And that was just a little surprising because in recent months he'd noticed how his attitude to life now lacked a lot of the aggression he'd once felt. It was silly really because if he had to share his cell with someone he couldn't think of anyone better than the girl sitting half a metre along the bed from him.

It was Hannah who spoke first. 'What do you suppose this is all about?'

Jon smiled at the thought. 'Item one, silly woman's left her keys locked in the store-room. Item two, I'll bet there's been some more trouble in the prisoner-crew quarters.'

Then there was a brief silence. For Jon it was as if Hannah was a guest in his home and he was expected to provide the entertainment. But of course he had nothing to offer, even the book he'd been reading was outside in the main room. He was almost apologetic when he spoke.

'I'm not used to being banged up during the day. I don't mind it at night because that's what always happens, but it's spoiled my routine and now I'm not sure what to do.'

Hannah shuffled herself up closer. 'I can think of something we could do to pass the time.' She took Jana's hand in hers, lifted it to her lips and gave it a kiss, ever so gentle, as if it hadn't been there at all.

And that was all it took. By one simple action Hannah had declared her hand and shown she wanted Jana in the way a woman sometimes wants a woman. For Jon it was different, he wanted *her* in the way a *man* wants a woman. He struggled to push the thought out of his head. And yet why should he fight against it? He felt the way the girl's breath was coming, and the "horny without a horn" feeling that showed Jana's body was becoming aroused. The animal passion inside him wanted her so badly - wanted to touch, to hold, caress. One hand went round her slim waist and the other settled gently on her right buttock. He pulled her to him and started to kiss the back of her neck. She turned within his grasp and pulled him closer. She pushed her face into Jana's and kissed the soft lips with a passion Jon had rarely felt before. One of her hands was on Jana's buttock and the other felt the soft flesh of her breast. Then she lifted both hands up to Jana's head, digging her fingers into the girl's neck as she pulled him harder into the embrace.

With a roughness Jon hadn't expected from a woman she pushed him down on the bed and fell down on top. He remembered all too painfully the crushing weight of Terry as he'd used Jana's little body as his toy, but Hannah was light as a feather. And the difference was he *wanted* her, he wanted her so much.

She pushed her face down on Jana's once again, and when Jon felt her tongue pushing rudely into the girl's mouth he just wanted his own male body right then so he could thrust up into her. Again he felt the horny feeling, his mind struggling to make sense of the crazy body that gave him the feeling he was huge, rigid and ready to penetrate even though it lacked the essential equipment.

Hannah was frantic now. She pulled up Jon's tee-shirt and pushed her face down onto the orange bra. With an action so swift and accurate he could hardly believe she pushed a hand down behind Jana's back and somehow the bra just came away. Jon felt the pleasure as his lover took the girl's nipples, gently, oh ever so gently, one at a time in her mouth, teasing playfully with her tongue. Now he was arching his back, pushing the girl's breasts up into Hannah's face. His hands fumbled under her tee-shirt to unhook her bra. Whether it was luck or skill he neither knew nor cared as the bra came undone first try and he pulled his hands round to feel the soft weight of her breasts as they fell out and filled his cupped hands. Oh God, oh God, it felt so good.

Hannah's hand went down to his trousers ripping madly at the buckle of the belt. Jon lifted the girl's bottom so she could slide them down, and now he felt her hand stroking, pressing through the thin material of the pants. She pushed her hand down under the elastic, her expert fingers probing, feeling, pushing their way past the girl's fur and deep inside. In a moment she was on Jana's special place, touching, teasing, pressing, pressing in exactly the right way to drive Jana's body into waves of ecstasy. Jon was in heaven. So many times, so many times he'd made love as a man and prided himself he could pleasure a woman, but never had he felt his body come alive as Jana's had now to the skilful touch of this girl. Thoughts of his own body far away, always so close in every waking moment of the long months he'd whiled away were forgotten as he blessed the moment he'd dared take the risk of that first touch, that first kiss.

But there was still more to come.

The fingers were still working hard as he felt the first tingle in Jana's vagina. It spread out to her buttocks, up into her breasts and down her legs until even the girl's toes felt the sparkle from within. Jon gasped harder and harder as the feeling within him rose. The room around him had reduced to a blur, everything hazy, everything going hazy. Just seconds ago he could have controlled it, could have told it no, this was wrong. But now he was helpless, he was putty in her hands, he shouted out in delight as the wave of pleasure overtook him and the climax shook every muscle in Jana's body. He gasped for breath. If only this moment would last forever. He wanted Hannah for his own. Wanted to love her, to keep her, to be his for ever. Nothing else mattered, it just didn't matter. Nothing mattered anymore. He closed his eyes and lay there in bliss.

'WHAT IN HELL'S NAME IS GOING ON HERE?' a stentorian voice demanded. The expression Ms Lincoln wore in that moment would have beaten back the charge of a raging bull. Jon was scared. In less than a heartbeat the wave of pleasure he'd more than just enjoyed had vanished.

'Get up, get up now, both of you.'

She grabbed Hannah's arm roughly and dragged her off the bed, then spoke to Jon in a menacing tone.

'You wait for me here Kell. I'll deal with you later.'

91

The Piper Must Be Paid

Jon watched as the recently recovered Bee walked into his cell and laid an arrangement of shiny steel rings and links down on the bed beside him. She stood there looking down at him, tut-tutting and shaking her head.

'Oh Miss Jana, you've done it now. The Captain's not going to be happy about this. Whatever were you thinking of?'

★★★

Leaving the SA Block for a visit to the open spaces of the ship was something Jon had dreamed of on so many of the endless nights he'd spent locked in his cell. But he was all too aware that this exit did not bring with it the freedom he'd hoped for. With two closely joined cuffs for the prisoner's wrists and a third on the end of a longer section of chain that connected him to the 90 kg bulk of his guard, Jon accepted as a fact that he'd no more chance of escape than little Arnie had had when he'd put him on his lead. Not that there was anywhere to escape to. It wasn't as if he was going to run to the airlock and *escape* out into the inky black vacuum of space.

The corridor outside secure accommodation lead to the lift, and the lift took them up to the ship's main deck. And handcuffed and guarded or not, it was a fantastic feeling for Jon. To be out in the open for the first time in ten months, to gaze around the vast curving cavern, to smell the freshly cut grass, to hear the sounds of other people, talking and laughing. He'd almost forgotten a life like this existed.

The shuttle-rail carried them round to the ship's administration area and then they were back into the usual maze of corridors and intersections. Brighter and more friendly than the no-nonsense grey hues of the SA Block it had to be admitted, but lacking the ambience of the open space they'd so recently left.

Bee pushed a door open and lead her captive into what was clearly a waiting area furnished with comfortably padded benches along each wall. And there on the far side of the room he saw Hannah, orange clad and handcuffed like himself. But with a chain that connected her to the impassive and humourless Ms Lincoln she'd obviously drawn the short straw. Hannah looked over and gave him just a hint of a smile.

Perhaps fifteen minutes had passed before Jon heard a call that came over a speaker system:

"Hannah Symonds please".

Ms Lincoln stood up and lead her charge out through a pair of double doors. Five minutes later they re-appeared and walked slowly over to where Jon was sitting with Bee. Jon would have like to have spoken to Hannah to ask how things had gone, but in his present situation he wasn't prepared to take the risk of upsetting the sour-faced woman on the other end of the chain. So he just sat and looked at the lovely girl in front of him. More than ever he wanted to leap up and hug her, hold her tight and kiss her, but they were already in enough trouble.

Bee took charge of Hannah while Ms Lincoln sat herself down on the seat beside Jon and clicked the steel cuff closed around her wrist.

Another minute passed before the loudspeaker barked into life a second time:

"Jana Kell please". It was time for them to go on parade.

The double doors from the waiting area lead into a larger room where an oldish looking man sat at a desk raised about a metre above the rest of his courtroom. A woman to his left sat at an intermediate level, and Stuart Robertson the Purser was there on the right.

'Prisoner - bow your head to the court,' Ms Lincoln commanded.

Jon lowered his head deferentially. Liam O'Connor sat and scrutinised the young woman in front of him before he spoke.

'Read the charges please.'

The woman to his right stood up to address the assembly.

'Sexual relations between secure accommodation inmates of the same gender sir.'

The Captain looked back at Jon, expressionless but obviously unhappy with the heinous crime that had been committed on his ship.

'How do you plead?'

Earlier that morning Ms Lincoln had visited Jon to explain the court procedure. It was beyond doubt that the two lovers had broken the rules and she warned that if he tried to protest his innocence the only possible outcome would be to cause annoyance to the Captain. And since O'Connor was judge, jury and executioner while his ship was in space it was a risk a mere prisoner would do better to avoid. As a minimum he could expect the inevitable punishment to be doubled.

For Jon it might have been an advantage if they'd told him the rules before he'd met Hannah, but would it have stopped him? He hoped not, but he knew there was only one answer he could give. He looked up at the Captain and spoke the words his jailer had told him to say:

'Guilty sir.'

The Captain was not a man to waste words and had probably decided on the sentence he was going to hand down before the court proceedings had even begun.

'Solitary confinement - 28 days,' was all he had to say.

Ms Lincoln tugged on the chain that joined Jon to her and they left the room to head back to the shuttle rail. Jon thought about it, 28 days in solitary. He wondered how bad it could be considering that for most of the time he'd spent in the SA Block he'd effectively been in solitary anyway.

★★★

Back in the SA Block with the two heavy doors that separated the prison from the rest of the ship safely locked Ms Lincoln freed the girl's wrists and then took Jon across the main room to the door he'd never seen open before. She turned her key in the lock and lead him inside.

At first sight the corridor looked no different from the one which accessed the normal cells, though Jon quickly noticed this one had its five steel doors down one side only.

The woman lead him past the first door, and Jon guessed why. At the second door she stopped, turned a key in the lock and pulled it open. She gestured for him to go inside, and the sight he saw there made him shiver. Surely this was no more than a store-cupboard. The first metre of the cell behind the door was low at only two metres high, but then the room extended at a lower level in a metre wide tunnel.

The door banged closed and Jon heard the turn of the key in the lock.

In the dim light he surveyed his new domain, his home for almost the whole of the coming month. The room was tiny in the extreme, but was he going to be confined to this tiny space all the time? Was he here in this one room for the whole of the sentence, or would they let him out to exercise, or to eat his meals? Would they let him out to shower?

He looked around. On the right-hand side of the full-height the part of the cell was a toilet pan, and to the left a washbasin with a single tap. As with the fittings installed in other parts of the SA Block the toilet and washbasin were in a brighter stainless finish, but the walls, floor and ceiling were in the standard monotone of unpainted grey. Overhead there was the obligatory wire cage containing a pair of short fluorescent tubes, though only one was on.

And this was it - solitary confinement. In the absence of a more comfortable seat Jon perched himself on the edge of the toilet pan and looked around in despair. After a couple of minutes the toilet seat was beginning to get uncomfortable so he moved down onto the floor, but the floor was cold. Searching around he found a thin mattress and a rough blanket in the tunnel section of the cell, so he pulled them out to make a seat.

Hours passed, but with no means of measuring the passage of time Jon had no idea of whether it was supposed to be day or night. After a while he began to doze, but woke up with a start as the girl's body started to slip over. So he unrolled the mattress back down into the darkness of the tunnel to make up a rather cold, hard and uncomfortable bed.

★★★

It was with a degree of sadness that Jon awoke from the happiest of dreams. Sleep was the only practical alternative to the boredom of his cell, and yet there was a limit to how much of it a person could do in a day. Or a night. Was it day, or was it night? Had he been asleep for eight hours, or just a few minutes? But whether it was supposed to be morning or not he'd no reason to get up, so he just lay there restless until the cell's lights suddenly flickered up to full brightness and a blast of a horn out in the corridor told him that the day had officially begun. He guessed it was half six but accepted that his judgement was no more than a guess. There was still nothing to get up for, but he got up anyway.

Standing unclothed at the steel wash-basin Jon found out the hard way that the single tap was single for a reason, so he had a remarkably quick wash in ice-cold water before pulling back on the clothes he'd slept in. Now he needed what usually came next - the tasty sausage and bacon breakfast that had made his life in captivity just slightly bearable, but somehow it was an easy guess that it wouldn't be happening this morning. In fact he'd no idea when any food would be coming his way, but from the way the girl's stomach was gurgling in anticipation he really hoped it was going to be soon.

Standing in the square metre of full-height space immediately behind the cell door he looked around and was surprised to see that in the brighter light there was a feature he'd missed when he'd first arrived. Just above the washbasin there was an alcove set into the wall and there appeared to be something inside. Reaching up as far as the girl's arm would stretch he felt a shape that lurked at the back of the recess - a book. If it was, at least he'd have something to read. It took a further stretch to get a grasp on the heavy tome and he pulled it out to find himself holding a copy of the "Holy Message", the standard text of Phoenix's predominant religion.

But then he looked around again. There was another aspect to seeing the cell in full light. It had been disturbingly small in the dim light of the previous evening, but now the constrained dimensions seemed even smaller, as if that was even possible. And then he thought of the cells in the other division of the SA Block, and how it would feel if he was there in his own male body. It was a reasonable guess to think the cells would be no larger than this one, and yet big men would be penned up in them. More than a few would have been unable to stand to full height anywhere in the cell, and most men would have had to take care to avoid hitting their head on the wire cage that protected the lights. This was cruel, this was not how things had been on *his* Hyperion. Or had they? He'd never bothered to find out whether there was any form of cell block on board, and yet it was obvious a ship needed some means of containing or punishing its troublemakers.

With nothing better to do he picked up the copy of the "Holy Message" and started browsing through the musings of an unfamiliar male God. After five minutes he was losing interest. After ten he threw the wretched book at the wall.

And then an eternity passed. When he got tired of standing he rolled up the mattress and sat down for a while. Then he tried a session of lying down before the girl's legs became restless and he needed to stand up again. When boredom reached its most boring he picked up the Holy Message from where it had landed and read through the first three chapters. And then he heard a noise out in the corridor. He turned round and looked at the door.

Just seconds later the flap which had been closed before was opening and on the shelf he saw a tray being pushed through. No words were spoken, but he could see from the dark hands holding the handles that it was Bee out there in the corridor. He took the tray from her and the flap closed. Without a doubt food had come at last. Lunch! The most exciting thing that had happened since he'd arrived.

The meal consisted of two covered bowls, a spoon, and an empty glass. Sitting on the edge of the toilet pan Jon balanced the tray on the girl's knee. He steadied it with one hand while he lifted the lid of the first bowl and saw some kind of greyish substance lying in the bottom. He lifted a spoonful to his lips and tasted. It was cold. From the texture of the mush there was a chance it might have been mashed potato, but it was the first time in his life he'd eaten food that truly tasted of nothing at all. The second bowl contained a selection of equally cold vegetables which were just a little better. He was hungry though and reasoned that eating whatever he was offered was best if he wanted to stay healthy. But the meal was so completely unappetising he noticed he'd stopped eating long before the food was gone.

Perhaps dinner would be better. Perhaps it might be hot. Perhaps he was hoping for too much.

His afternoon was filled with a mixture of sitting reading, standing reading, sitting doing nothing and standing doing nothing. And all the while he was listening for the slightest sound outside in the corridor that might indicate his next meal was on its way. After several hours he decided to have a second go at what remained from lunch and was surprised to find that it had actually improved. He sat for another hour or so, hoping more food was going to arrive soon. It was only when the lighting dimmed down to its lower level that he finally accepted no dinner was coming. Here in solitary the excitement of the day came in a single hit.

After a while he rolled out the mattress and tried to sleep, but an hour later was still lying there wide awake. And while he lay thinking an awful thought struck him, what were the chances he'd be let out to use the computer or the phone? He'd been promised he'd be able to make his call to Vissan, but that was before he'd been sentenced to solitary.

Realising his new predicament Jon lowered the girl's body down to the slight padding of the mattress and dropped the head into her hands. This would be his life for the next month, and by the time he was released back into the regular SA Block the Hyperion would already have left orbit to start its trip home to Phoenix. The long awaited prize of communication with the rest of the galaxy would be lost and gone for another two years. Of all the stupid, stupid, stupid things he could have done, just when so much was at stake. Two long years in space just to make a single phone call and he'd blown it, blown it completely. And for what, a quick romp with a pretty girl? And from a man's perspective he'd not even been able to make love to her properly.

And then what? After another two years of travelling back to the God forsaken planet he'd be in the same situation as when he'd left: courts wanting to convict him, policemen and psychiatrists wanting to lock him up. Everything he'd planned so carefully, the risks he'd taken, the years of his life he'd invested in this all important project, and now it had all been for nothing. The emotion that washed over him flowed up from deep within. He laid his head down on the pillow and cried until the girl's tears ran out.

***

Next morning Jon awoke but it was long before the sounding of the horn that signalled the start of the new day. Even when the horn blasted out its note and the lights came up to full brightness he still stayed lying there in his bed. What was the point of getting up? What was the point of anything?

But in the end there was a limit to how much time he could spend horizontal and finally he got up. But he wasn't going to wash. The water was so cold it was unpleasant to wash in, and somehow his failure to conform was a token protest against the evil people who'd lured him into this situation.

By the time the day's single meal had been delivered and eaten he was feeling just a little less depressed, but the idea of being in any way happy with his life was just not going to happen. Not today anyway.

When the lights dimmed down to indicate that evening had come round again he unrolled the mattress with the intention of trying to sleep, but hours later he was still awake, mulling over how stupid he'd been.

★★★

Morning came again. The fact that the horn had woken him had to mean that sometime during the long empty hours of the night he must have fallen off to sleep. How many days had he been in here now? How many mornings had he woken up in the tiny cell? After thinking back he decided this had to be his fourth day, and it was disturbing to think that after so short a time he was already beginning to lose track.

And that was when he decided enough was enough. Yes he'd blown at least one of his chances of getting home, but there was still another chance of salvation. He'd managed to get an email into the system and it was likely that even now Michael was making progress towards securing his release. Once it had been revealed that the Hyperion's unfortunate stowaway and prisoner was in fact a senior member of the Union's government they'd have to release him from solitary, and from the SA Block too. Knowing the power that a man in his position could wield they'd be stupid to do otherwise.

So why hadn't it happened yet?

It didn't help his mood to have to accept that here in the tiny cell there was no way of knowing. All he could do was wait patiently, but how could he be patient when his whole life hung in the balance? But they couldn't keep him banged up like this forever. One day Jon Chandler would be out, and then it would all be different. Even if the Hyperion had left orbit by the time they let him out there was still a chance he'd be able to get the ship turned round.

With hope back in his heart Jon was back up to full strength. They would not grind him down. Solitary confinement would not defeat a man like Jon Chandler. Today was his fourth day in the hell-hole, but by God he'd fight back.

And so he made a plan. Every morning at the sound of the horn he'd be out of bed. No lingering, no lie-in. Then he'd strip off and wash, no matter how cold the water was. Then it would be straight into a regime of exercise: marching on the spot to the count of two thousand, one hundred push-ups, one hundred sit-ups, and back to marching on the spot and round again till he'd built up a sweat and was exhausted. Then he'd eat half his lunch, then there'd be a few hours of singing songs he knew, or reciting out loud the rhymes he'd been taught as a child. Finally he'd eat the second half of his meal and read a few chapters of the Holy book for an hour before going to bed - tired and ready for sleep.

And he'd keep track of how time was passing. His day had three fixed points in it: the horn in the morning, the delivery of lunch, and the dimming of the lights in the evening. He'd count the passage of the days as well. Each morning as he climbed out of bed he'd tear a page out of the Holy Message. Maybe the Phoenixan God would punish him for even thinking of committing such a blasphemy, but he'd pray to Belen and her Holy Mother. They'd sort out any upstart male God.

★★★

It was on the 17th day that things had first started to go wrong. Or was it the 18th? Or maybe the 19th? Some days he'd forgotten to tear out the daily page as he'd climbed out of bed, so then he'd torn it out after getting washed. But then he'd wondered, could it be he'd remembered to tear the page out when he got up, and then he'd torn out a second. He tried to remember back, but with so many days being exactly the same as the one before, there was nothing salient in his life, nothing he could get a handle on. When he'd tried asking Bee how many days had passed she'd ignored him completely.

And he was having trouble doing his exercises. With the lack of nourishment from the slop they called food he was getting light-headed if he tried doing anything physical before lunch, and when the meal finally came he was so starving hungry he'd wolfed the lot down in one go. And that had left him hungry later in the day.

Whether it was the lack of food or just boredom he couldn't be sure, but his mind had started playing tricks on him. Although he was completely alone in his cell, he'd thought he'd seen a movement in the corner of his eye. But when he'd turned to look, nothing had changed - or had it?. Then he'd seen it again, he was sure he'd seen it. The walls, already too close for comfort were moving, moving towards him, pushing in, making the tiny room even smaller. If they moved any closer he'd be crushed. He'd tried to reason with himself, tried to tell himself it wasn't true. The walls weren't moving, he just had to try and believe they weren't really moving. But he had to be sure. He'd stood in the centre of the tiny space with his back to the door and stretched the girl's arms to full span - and had been surprised to find that no matter how hard he tried he was unable to reach both walls at once. But the instant he'd let his concentration lapse, the walls had started moving again.

Now it was happening again. Jon felt the girl's breath as it came in anxious gasps - being so alone, helpless, unable to move beyond the heavy steel door that kept him prisoner, it was ……, it was. ……… frightening. In fear he started banging on the cell door. He banged till the girl's small hands began to hurt but no-one heard, or if they heard they took no action. He looked around for the break-glass, the emergency button he knew had to be there. But in this cell there was no emergency button.

And the nightmare had followed him into his sleep as well. The dream had come so many times, in so many different guises, and yet the ending had always been the same. Out in the sweetly scented land of a spring meadow. Running through the long grass, feeling the wild flowers as they'd brushed against his bare legs. Arnie was behind him, barking wildly. Then he'd almost tripped over the little dog as it'd raced around in front, but that was just part of the fun. And then he'd stopped, just stopped in his tracks. The super-sensitive nose had gone down to take in the heady whiff of some creature that had passed by hours ago. Perhaps a rabbit, or a hare? Maybe a badger or a fox? Arnie had raced around like a being possessed, then suddenly taken off down the creature's hole. But then something had gone wrong and now the little dog was calling, yelping in fear. No matter what it took Jon had to save him. Pushing himself down into the hole it had magically opened up to somewhere much larger than it had appeared from the surface, almost like an underground cavern. And yet with every metre he ran the walls had begun to press in - the rocky ceiling had closed in lower and lower. And yet he'd carried on, first just stooped over, then crawling on his hands and knees. But he had to go on, the plaintive sounds of the dog were coming from just a little further down the tunnel. At last the top of the tunnel pushed down onto his back and he was forced onto his belly to wriggle and squirm. Then the sides narrowed, trapping his arms and legs until he was unable to move - buried alive - entombed under tonnes of crushing mud and rocks. And he'd screamed out loud.

His life was saved by the sound of the horn outside in the corridor, then the lights had flickered up to full brightness. And there was the mighty Jon Chandler, sweating, shivering and panting on the mattress in the tiny cell. How many more days, how many more nights could he stand this mental torture?

For hours he'd lain there on the thin mattress, reluctant to stay in his bed, but unwilling to move. Scared lest the walls closed in on him again. And then he heard a sound. There was only one sound he ever heard that came from outwith his own domain, but surely he hadn't lain in bed right through till lunchtime? But still there was a sound. He knew the sound the flap made as it opened, but this time the sound was different. This was a sound he remembered from long, long ago. The sound of a key in a lock. The noise as the key turned, the squeal of hinges as the cell door swung open. And there was Bee, standing in the corridor, holding the door open, inviting him to come out from the tiny dungeon.

Like a child not yet walking Jon had crawled out and hugged onto the stockinged leg, and cried in gratitude for his release.

★★★

After a shower and the first decent meal he'd eaten in a month Jon was getting back up to strength. The ability to walk around and move freely was a major factor too. He knew he'd never forget the dreadful time he'd spent alone in the cell, but somehow it was already in the past. Something to be left behind.

Now there was real business to attend to. In spite of his fears, the ship was still in orbit around Darius for a few hours longer. The crew were running through the pre-flight checks and after just a couple more shuttle runs the last of the passengers would be on board. Six hours was the deadline, then it would all change as the ship started it's two year flight back to Phoenix. But it meant he still had a chance to contact home.

92

The Call

Despite the dust and grime that had built up in the SA Block while the worker had been elsewhere suffering from claustrophobia Bee hadn't immediately set him onto cleaning duties. Knowing that her prisoner would be there to provide cheap labour for the next two years, tomorrow would be soon enough. So he just sat around enjoying the open space.

But despite his inactivity he hadn't been allowed into the computer room, rules were rules and not to be broken. But it just so frustrating, knowing the equipment was sitting there waiting for him but he wasn't allowed to use it. He was itching to have another go at getting in contact, but with only another hour to go before lunch it wasn't worth getting into trouble about. Upsetting his guard now would really screw things up.

At last his time came. He wolfed his lunch in a moment and rushed into the computer room. He logged on and waited for the system to respond, but when the programme had fully loaded he couldn't believe the girl's eyes. There still wasn't a single email for Jon Chandler. What the hell was happening, why had no-one replied? He checked the clock on the screen and after running the time and date interface routine saw it was 10.00 in Jackson, on a Tuesday. The timing couldn't have been better. Quickly he typed in an email to Michael and pressed the "Send/Receive" button, but the email stayed stubbornly in the pending box. He tried again. Then he noticed a red symbol next to his email. When he clicked on it a box opened, and the message inside read, "User does not have transmission rights. Please contact your network administrator".

So he tried the system in phone mode, without success. Although he could ring any extension within the ship, try as he might he was unable to engage an external channel.

He logged onto the ships operational system with the ID he'd been given three decades earlier and found that everything was as it should be. He could check on the status of all manner of items around the ship. He could shut down the fusion reactor if he chose. He could even have started to pilot the ship out of orbit. For sure the safety automatics would have stopped him crashing it down into the planet's atmosphere, but he could have headed off into space and set a course for the home planets. Not that that would have got him anywhere - the ship's real pilot would have spotted what was happened and locked him out. And then what, they'd have traced the intrusion to this terminal in the SA Block, and then he'd be looking at another spell in solitary. And he wasn't going back into solitary again. With God and Belen as his witnesses, he swore he was never going back into solitary again.

But this was crazy. If he'd got such amazing power at his fingertips, why couldn't he send just one simple email? He got up from the terminal and walked out into the main room of the block where his guard was getting up to date with two hundred TV episodes she'd missed while they'd been out in space.

'Bee, I have to make a phone call, or at least send an email. It's absolutely vital.'

She pressed the pause button and looked up.

'I'm sorry Jana, it's not permitted. You've done your time in solitary, but you're still a prisoner and your privileges don't include making phone calls.'

He recalled she'd not been party to the agreement made at the meeting with Stuart Robertson.

'But I was promised by the Purser that I'd have the chance to get in contact with my people on Vissan when we got to Darius. There's still time if I make the call now.'

'OK, I'll call him. But don't get your hopes up.'

The big woman pulled her phone out of her pocket and chose a number from the memory. Jon followed most of the call and it didn't sound good. She put the phone back in her pocket and shook her head.

'Mr Prentice says no. It's not permitted for prisoners to make phone calls or send emails off the ship.'

'Who the fuck's Mr Prentice? Stuart Robertson's the Purser!'

Bee shook her head. 'Mr Robertson left the ship a week ago to take up a land-based post in Phoenix Intersolar's Darius office. Mr Prentice is his replacement. He came on board just a couple of days ago.'

'Well call him back tell him I need to see him. It's absolutely vital.'

***

To say the meeting with the *new* Purser had been a disappointment was quite an understatement. The man had made it very clear that a prisoner's privileges had never extended to transmitting any information off the ship and he couldn't understand why the man he'd replaced had ever entered into such an agreement. The rules were quite clear on the matter - it was not negotiable.

Jon's heart had sunk down into Jana's light tan boots. He'd been so near, and yet he was still so far. Here they were, still in full communication with Darius and the rest of the Union, but not for much longer. Precious minutes were ticking by. He had to do something, but what?

Then a thought came to him. It was a high stakes gamble, but what else did a man do when the chips were down? Bee was engrossed in her soaps and there was no-one else around, so he logged back into the ship's system It took less than a minute for him to track down the access code for the SA Block door, though he knew it was useless without a swipe-card - and where would he get one of those? His chances of wrestling Bee for hers were absolutely zero. And then he spotted something on the screen. It couldn't have been more obvious if it had said "get out of jail free" next to it. For essential safety reasons, if a fire alarm was in operation the SA Block's main door would open in response to an emergency code, and it would do so without the need for a card. This was it, he had a chance, but did he have the guts to go through with it? Could he live with himself if he didn't?

With the girl's heart beating hard Jon walked back out into the main room. Three hours back to back had been all Bee could manage and now he saw her lying there, eyes closed, slouched in her chair with the TV still playing. Quietly he crept past and went into the kitchen. He opened the cutlery drawer, took out the largest serving spoon he could find and with all the strength he could muster rammed the handle into the fire alarm call-point. The glass shattered. The wail of the siren pierced through the calm that had reigned just seconds earlier. He grabbed a fire extinguisher and got it ready in his hand.

'Bee, Bee come quick, fire, fire!' he shouted.

Still in a daze the big woman jumped out of her chair and ran to the kitchen. As she rounded the corner Jon banged the extinguisher's plunger down and the foam began to mix. He aimed the nozzle straight at the dark face and felt the reaction of the powerful jet as it arced across the room. Instinctively, Bee put her hands up to protect herself but it was too late, her eyes were already full of the stinging, blinding foam. Jon dropped the extinguisher and left it spraying its contents out across the kitchen floor.

Now there was no going back. The plan was happening and he was already in too deep to bale out. Getting caught now not only meant not getting home it meant going back into solitary, and for Jon that wasn't an option. He ran to the inner door of the ante-room and quickly tapped in the emergency code, the lock whirred and he pulled the door open. He raced in and pulled the door closed behind him to release the interlock to the outer door. He knew the foam wouldn't last long and through the window he could already see Bee was running towards the door as fast as the bulk of her body allowed. He knew that once he'd exited from the ante-room into the corridor outside she'd follow him through as soon as the interlock permitted.

But now he was in his element - the tables had turned. In his days of freedom he'd made good use of the girl's fit young body and taken it out to run lap after lap of the circumferential track. Even in the SA Block he'd spent hours every day on the exercise machines. If Bee was thinking she could catch him by running after him, she could think again. She didn't stand a chance.

The sub-deck level was off limits to passengers and there were few reasons why any of the crew needed to be there except in emergencies. And there was one, but Jon had factored it into his plan. A blaze on a star-liner was very serious indeed so Jon knew the fire-fighters would arrive at the SA Block in less than a minute, even if it was only to investigate a false alarm. But he knew the ship too, and unless there'd been a major redesign of its services they'd be coming from the direction of the admin area, so he turned in the opposite direction even though it meant running the long way round the doughnut.

Eight minutes later and gasping for breath he arrived at the elevator he knew lead up into the standard class accommodation area, but he didn't take the elevator. If he came up onto a floor where people were waiting he'd be obvious in the bright orange prison garb and trapped. Instead he climbed the stairs until he came to the door that lead out onto the main deck level. He gave himself a minute to get some breath back, opened the door and poked his head out. If he was in luck there'd be no-one around.

With a new lease of life from his short rest he sprinted across the open ground and into the entrance of Juniper Block. The display showed one of the lifts was at the ground floor. He jammed the girl's finger onto the button and dived in, pushing the button for the fourth floor as he went. The security system could log the lift movements he knew so going all the way to the sixth floor would give him away. The door opened and he thanked the stars the landing was empty. With a bit of luck there'd be no-one about on the upper floors with the ship so lightly loaded.

Gasping for breath Jon raced out onto the sixth floor landing that had once been so familiar. Hoping they hadn't changed the code he punched in the access number for the lift-motor room. The girl's heart almost skipped a beat as he heard the sound of the bolt drawing back. Now, he was safe, for a while at least.

★★★

The money he'd had left and his cleaner's access card were still where he'd left them months ago. Well it wasn't often anyone ever needed to go into the equipment room, and even if they did, why would they bother to search behind a safety notice? He headed back down the stairs and out onto the landing. The card still worked. He ran into the room, pushed the door closed behind him and breathed a sigh of relief. It was good to be back in the place he'd called home for so many months

He sat the girl's body down in the chair that had once been his favourite, and with the phone on his lap he selected an outside circuit - easy from the passenger accommodation. Using his ministerial code to make sure he didn't get diverted to one of the minions in the department he called Michael Heathersett's direct line. He waited for the call to connect, but the steady tone that came back told him the line was busy.

He disconnected and called Sylvie at the house in Rosemount. He waited, ... and waited. At first it sounded like the call was connecting, but his heart sank as he read the message that came up on the phone's screen "This number is no longer in service".

He tried her mobile and it was answered almost immediately, but it wasn't Sylvie's face that appeared. A rather cross looking man came on the screen to tell him this had been his private number for over a year and he didn't want to be bothered by friends of the previous user.

He moved on and tried Tom, but got same "out of service" response. He tried party headquarters and was relieved to see Emma's smiling face. She'd been Tom's private secretary so if anyone could get hold of him it was her. She was her usual efficient self and got straight to the point.

'I'm sorry miss, but Mr Hanson is no longer connected with the Harmony party. I'm surprised you didn't know that.'

'I've been on a long space crossing and we've only just got comms,' Jon explained.

'He left after completing his term as first minister and that was over two years ago. You should look back through the bulletins, it tells the whole story.' Jon thanked her and rang off.

No call back from Michael yet, so he pressed the recall button to try him again. This time he was in luck and he watched as the screen flickered and a familiar face came into view - but it wasn't Michael's. Jon put his thumb over the camera lens before he spoke. He heard the voice on the other end and saw Amey's lovely face, slightly unsettled by the lack of video.

'Hello, who is this please?'

'Hi Amey, it's that man with the badge on his left boob.'

He heard laughter from the phone, but he noticed the way it stopped, quite abruptly. There was a brief pause before the woman spoke again.

'Caller, I can put you through to Michael now.'

The screen changed and the next face to appear was the man he'd been hoping to get on his first call. Jon was glad, so very glad to see him.

'Michael, great to see you. It's been so long. How are things on Vissan? I gather there's been an election.'

'Who is this speaking please?'

'It's Jon, Jon Chandler. I used to be the minister for trade, as if you didn't know.'

'Caller it sounds as if I am speaking with a woman, and that would be inconsistent with the name "Jon". Are you able to activate the camera on your handset please?'

Jon remembered he still had his thumb over the lens. He moved his hand and now he knew Michael could see him, or *her* if he was to go entirely by the image the man would see. But Michael knew very well that he'd gone to Phoenix to be hosted by a female, so why was he so slow on the uptake? Perhaps it had been such a long time. For Jon, getting home had been the only thing on his mind for over two years, but he knew all too well that government life with its hustle and bustle had gone on as normal for the people in Jackson. It was up to him to understand Michael's position.

'OK Michael, here you are. As you can clearly see you are looking at the face of Jana Kell, the woman who was supposed to host me for five days when I went on a transfer to Phoenix over two years ago. As you know the beam went down soon after I arrived on Phoenix and I've been stuck in Jana's body all this time, but I can assure you the person speaking is me, Jon Chandler.'

Michael looked at the image on his screen without a trace of a smile.

'Miss Kell. I was afraid something like this was going to happen, and of course I knew the Hyperion had entered Darius orbit so I'd expected your call. In fact I'd expected it a month ago.'

'Michael, I know that communication with Phoenix has been established, so presumably my emails got through.'

'I did indeed receive a number of emails, some of which were sent from Mr Chandler's laptop computer and were encrypted with his ministerial privilege code. Miss Kell, you have to understand that just because you once hosted a senior member of the government it does not mean you are entitled to use his security codes - even if he gave you the details, which I am sure he didn't.'

'But Michael, this is me, Jon speaking. I accept the fact that I'm not actually the minister anymore, but I'm not Jana Kell either, I'm just being hosted by her - still being hosted by her even after all this time and now I need your help to get home. I'm in a lot of trouble here and I need your support, urgently.'

Michael continued almost as if he hadn't heard a word Jon had said.

'Miss Kell, after I received the first email you sent I made some investigations. Of course it took many months to get a reply from Phoenix, but eventually I got one.'

'Yes?' Jon was getting just a little worried now.

'The TranzCon people on Phoenix sent me a report which explained your problem.'

'Problem? I've had plenty of problems for sure, but exactly what were TranzCon telling you?'

'The psychiatric report showed a degree of spirit image retention within your brain which caused you to believe you were still Jon Chandler, the man who you had hosted for five days until he returned to Vissan.'

Jon was alarmed - what the hell was going on? He knew what they'd told him on Phoenix about spirit image retention, but he knew who he was for God's sake.

'Michael. I know who I am and I'm telling you now - I *am* Jon Chandler, the former Minister for Trans-Union Trade.'

'I'm sorry Miss Kell, you are *not* Jon Chandler. You were advised to seek medical help for your condition and you took no notice of what you were told.'

'Michael. I really, really, really am Jon Chandler. You know so much about me, and the business we used to handle.

Go on, ask me anything, anything at all. I can prove to you who I am.'

'Miss Kell, they said that in addition to the spirit image retention which caused you to believe you were Jon Chandler, you also had an amazing degree of memory retention following the TranzCon transfer. Because of this it is almost certain you know much more about Jon Chandler than I do, so obviously you could answer any question I could possibly ask. If only you had continued with the psychiatric treatment Dr Morris offered he might have been able to get to the bottom of your neurosis. You were by all accounts a very interesting case because he'd never known a personality so strong that it could imprint itself so firmly after just five days.'

This wasn't going at all well. Apart from Jasmine who'd known straight away she wasn't talking to her sister Jon hadn't been able to convince anyone on Phoenix he wasn't Jana. Now he couldn't even convince Michael. But here was a new line to try, Michael had said that Jon had returned to Vissan.

'Michael, you said Jon Chandler had returned to Vissan?'

'Yes, he came back a few hours before he was due, and I think it was because the beam strength had been very low, but I'm sure you know all that.'

Well that rang true to some extent. Jon had indeed attempted to travel back at a time when the beam was falling in strength, but what could have happened? He'd wondered before whether some mysterious mechanism had cloned his mind so there were separate versions of *him* occupying two different bodies, one on Vissan and the other here on the Hyperion. But then he had a thought, if Michael was playing games with him, he'd turn the tables and play a game of his own.

'So, Michael, would it be possible for me to speak to Mr Chandler? Do you have a number for him?'

The image on the screen shook its head.

'Miss Kell, I am very sorry to tell you that Mr Chandler is no longer with us. Sadly he passed away just minutes after transferring back into his own body. It was something to do with having to make the transfer under flat-line conditions.'

Jon felt the blood run cold in the girl's veins, "Oh my Lady in heaven! My body died. My body died ..... and they all think it was me in there when it died". He thought back to the transfer dream - it had happened more than two long years in the past, but the memory was still as bright in his mind as if it had happened yesterday. He remembered the feeling as he'd been turned back, and then how he'd seen the girl's anguished face at the window, desperate to get through.

Michael's voice came again. 'Miss Kell, are you alright? I am sorry to have to tell you this news and I'm sorry you are having problems.'

Jon let out the last of a breath and shook his head.

'Oh boy have I got problems now. Michael, can't you just try to believe that the *me* here on the Hyperion, the *me* talking to you now really is Jon Chandler. Please Michael, please - can't you understand it was Jana Kell who died there in my body?'

'I really am sorry Miss Kell, but there isn't anything more I can do for you.'

Jon had an idea. 'How do I know you're telling the truth Michael, how should I know I'm really dead?'

'I presume you have access to full communications while you're in orbit?'

'For a little while longer, the ship's leaving for Phoenix later today.'

'Well I suggest you go into some of the old bulletin pages so you can read the articles about how Mr Chandler died. If it will help you come to terms with your situation, then I urge you to read as much as you can. I'll warn you though, it turns out the good and great Mr Chandler wasn't quite the wonderful man we'd all thought he was. If he or his life-force was somehow still alive right now he'd do well to keep a low profile. Have a look at the web, it's all there.'

Jon wondered what the hell the man was talking about, but if it was a lead he had to follow it.

'OK Michael, OK I'll have a look, but it's crazy.'

'Miss Kell, there is one more thing. I realised when you sent the first email that Mr Chandler's ministerial account was still open, so I closed it and thus it will no longer work. Unfortunately I had neglected to cancel his telephone priority access code but I will be doing that as soon as we conclude this conversation. So please do not attempt to use any privilege facilities you may think you still have access to. Goodbye Miss Kell. I really hope things turn out better for you.'

'Goodbye Michael.'

The screen went blank. Jon sat there in the chair - dazed, dumbstruck. His eyes stared at the light in front of him. He couldn't move, he just sat there and let the light from the screen burn into the girl's retinas.

After a while he started to pull himself together. If he was dead, well if his body was dead, well if Jon Chandler's body was dead, what was he now? What was "dead" anyway? *What* are you when you're dead? *Where* are you when you're dead? Is there a God, is there a heaven, is there a hell? Is there just nothing? Is it all a dream, or perhaps a nightmare, that goes on and on? All Jon knew was, that the *me* that was there on the Hyperion in a body everyone called Jana Kell was very much alive. Someone was dead, but it wasn't him. He couldn't convince people who he was, but the life-force inside, the *soul* that was Jon Chandler, he knew the truth.

But something occurred to him. When Amey had put him through to Michael she'd been laughing at first, and then she'd stopped so suddenly. It was almost as though she'd known she wasn't supposed to laugh. And she'd referred to Michael by his first name. But surely a secretary of Amey's experience when addressing a stranger would have referred to him as "Mr Heathersett", or maybe "Mr Chandler's private secretary". It was odd, very odd.

93

I Read The News Today

Jon looked around at the room that had once been home. It was obviously ready to receive an occupant, though he reasoned that if no-one was in a top floor room by now when all the passengers were on board it was probably going to be vacant for the rest of the trip - depending on how the lifts and the plumbing held up.

The ship's security team would without a doubt be scouring the ship for Jana Kell by now, but he knew just how effective that bunch could be when they put their minds to it. It was a good bet they'd start with the public areas which didn't need any form of security device to gain access. Then they'd move onto the passenger accommodation areas, and given enough time they'd search every one of the unoccupied rooms on the ship. So they were bound to find him sooner or later, but knowing the scale of the task and the fact that there was nothing in their records to link him to this room he could probably stay here undetected for several days. Or at least until hunger drove him back out into the open - he didn't dare go to a shop even though he'd still got a little money left.

He checked the kitchen and found everything was stocked and ready for the occupant who almost certainly wasn't coming, so he put the kettle on and made himself a cup of tea. And when he'd curled up in the big easy chair it was more than just comfortable, it was bliss. But as he sat there mulling over what had happened he was troubled by his conversations with Amey and Michael. People he'd known so well, and yet they'd let him down just when he needed them most. Two years in space trying to get back to his own body at home, and where was he now? Further away than he could ever have believed.

He switched the TV to computer mode and ran a search for newspapers on the day when TranzCon had tried to send him back to Vissan. It didn't take long and he found his death had been the headline news in all of them. The first he read was the Jackson Herald:

> "Politicians of all hues are today mourning the death of Jon Chandler, formerly the Minister for Trans-Union Trade. Mr Chandler had travelled via a TranzCon transfer to the recently discovered planet, Phoenix, to represent first minister Tom Hanson at a series of talks aimed at bringing the planet closer to the Union. On the night before Mr Chandler was due to transfer back to Vissan rapid fluctuations in the strength of the Gravitron beam between Phoenix and Darius made it necessary for him to be summoned from his bed in the middle of the night for an emergency transfer, and because of the poor beam strength this had to be carried out under so-called "flat-line" conditions where body and brain functions are reduced to just the minimum needed to support life. Sadly Mr Chandler's body was unable to withstand the rigours of the heavily sedated condition, and despite valiant attempts to revive him he passed away just minutes after arriving

> back on Vissan. Present at his bedside were his wife Sylvie and first minister Tom Hanson who confirmed that it was indeed the life-force of Jon Chandler occupying his body when he died. Because the beam to Phoenix is temporarily unavailable there has been no final confirmation of whether Mr Chandler's host is well, but an initial report was received in the final seconds while the beam was in service to confirm that her life-force had been received back on Phoenix."

Well it fitted with what Michael had told him whether it was true or not. More reports were carried by the Galactic Courier:

> "The life-force of Jon Chandler, Union minister for trade, arrived back in his own body at 05.13 this morning via a TranzCon transfer carried out under so-called "flat-line" conditions. Just moments after his arrival Mr Chandler's body went into cardiac arrest and a crash team standing by was called to attempt a re-start of his heart. Despite the best efforts of the team, the heavy level of sedation made a revival impossible and at 05.24 his body was pronounced dead. As with all deaths following consciousness transfer, a full autopsy and post-life brain scan will be carried out. When beam communications are restored the TranzCon facility on Phoenix will be asked to carry out a deep scan of Jana Kell, the woman who hosted Mr Chandler on his trip."

> "Tom Hanson, the Union's first minister, told our reporter that Jon Chandler was a fine man who had worked tirelessly towards the goal of uniting the planets of the Union. He was utterly devastated to lose such a trusted colleague and close friend."

> "Sylvie Chandler, wife of the former Union minister for trade was seen leaving Jackson's TranzCon Terminal this

morning in the company of Thomas Hanson, the first minister, but declined to give any comment. According to our reporter she stared impassively ahead as she slipped into the back of Mr Hanson's official limousine."

"The body of Jon Chandler, the former minister for Trans-Union Trade who died earlier this morning will be transferred to the Neural Unit of Jackson Central Hospital where an investigation into the cause of his death will be carried out."

For the rest of the day all the papers said pretty much the same thing and by the time the late editions were coming out they'd already moved onto obituaries, and Jon could see they were gearing up to feature the story of his life and how he'd risen to his position of wealth and power. He scanned forward a few days to see what the post-life scan had found:

"The Coroner's report was released this morning and showed that Jon Chandler, the former minister for trade, died of a massive heart attack which occurred as a result of a blocked coronary artery. A medical spokesman advised our reporter that under normal circumstances a condition like this would not have been fatal, but the level of sedation that had been necessary to carry out the TranzCon transfer under flat-line conditions had been so severe that despite the efforts of the crash team Mr Chandler never regained consciousness. In the minutes immediately following the transfer the team was simply unable to fight against the life-sign suppressing drugs that had been used. A spokesperson told reporters 'If Mr Chandler had been able to hang on for another half hour it might have been a different story because the level of the fast-clearing drugs left in his system would have fallen by a factor of four, so there was every chance he might have pulled through'."

> "The autopsy carried out on the late Jon Chandler, the former minister for trade, found he had a pre-existing heart condition which left him extremely vulnerable in the event of a flat-line transfer. His body had withstood the transfer to Phoenix just five days earlier but this was carried out with full beam strength and needed only a light level of sedation. If his condition had been made known to the TranzCon medical team on Phoenix there would have been no attempt to carry out the return transfer under flat-line conditions."

But the next few reports took a rather different line:

> "Speculation has mounted that the body of Jon Chandler, the former minister for trade, died while still occupied by the life-force of Miss Jana Kell who hosted Mr Chandler on his important diplomatic mission to Phoenix earlier this month. The speculation arose when it was revealed that a deep scan of Mr Chandler's brain had not been carried out to confirm his identity. Because the beam to Phoenix remains unavailable there has been no confirmation that the life-force received there was actually that of Miss Kell."

> "Thomas Hanson, the first minister, today held a media conference to confirm that he was present at the TranzCon arrival of his friend and colleague Jon Chandler. Although Mr Chandler died just a few minutes later, Mr Hanson and Mr Chandler's wife Sylvie who was also present confirmed that the mind resident in Jon Chandler's body in the moments after the transfer was indeed his own life-force and not that of his host Miss Jana Kell of Phoenix."

Then the reports took on a worrying tone:

> "A man in that sort of condition should not have even been thinking of travelling by TranzCon. He got through on

a full strength signal of course, but going flat-line, it was madness, almost suicide."

"It is quite inexcusable that Jon Chandler was allowed to take this risk himself, and to subject an unknowing host to what could so easily have been fatal for her. He had only recently undergone a detailed medical examination and the report clearly showed that Mr Chandler was a very sick man indeed. His condition could certainly have been rectified though it would have put him out of action for a number of weeks. Obviously he thought that was too long for him to wait and went ahead with his trip to Phoenix regardless of his medical condition and the consequences. The only thing Jon Chandler cared about more than money was the furthering of his political career."

"A police spokesman told our reporter 'It is totally unacceptable to subject yourself to that sort of risk, and to risk the life of another person is immoral, totally immoral. In many ways it is a good thing for Jon Chandler that he was the one who died that morning because if it had been his host who had been trapped in his dying body we would now have been chasing his life-force on a murder charge."

"As with all potential TranzCon travellers, Jon Chandler had been required to complete the necessary paperwork and it is clear from the forms made public this morning that he denied knowledge of any medical condition which would have prevented him from travelling by TranzCon. And he signed his name at the bottom. For heaven's sake, the man had only that day received a report from Larson Medical Services to tell him about his true condition. What is more the police found it open on his desk. Self-certification, it's a joke. You can be sure that in future my department will be pressing for a full medical for each and every TranzCon traveller."

They kept on referring to the medical report Jon had been waiting for, and they even said it had been on his desk. It was true he'd been waiting for it, and from what he now knew he'd most certainly have called off the trip to Phoenix straight away. He'd never wanted to go in the first place and the report would have been the excuse he needed for not going. Even Tom Hanson couldn't have complained in the face of a report like that.

But then came the next phase of the story, the investigation into everything Jon had ever done to see how many juicy titbits they could squeeze out to feed to the masses. Jon was taken aback to find the biggest blow came from Sylvie herself:

> "In a surprise interview given by Sylvie Chandler, wife of the former minister for trade, she shocked listeners by revealing that their marriage had been on the rocks for years and had only continued because of pressure put on her and her family by her late husband. She cited over four hundred cases of marital rape and told reporters about the diseases he'd brought home from his frolics with good-time girls while he was away travelling on star-liners run by his own company. The thought of having sex with him after he'd been 'screwing pox-ridden sluts' (sic) was simply disgusting. When asked why she'd never started divorce proceedings she told reporters that her husband had threatened to bankrupt her brother by calling in a loan he'd made to his failing construction company some years earlier. To protect her brother and his family she'd had no option but to stay with her husband until she could raise the money to pay off the debt. She continued and told our reporter that she and her husband had not been out together for years, and it had been a life of hell sharing his

> creepy old house on the few occasions when they had been together."

Jon sat there, reading the awful words in shock and awe. He read on and saw that, although she'd wanted to end the marriage for some time, she'd admitted that early on in their relationship there had been some good years. But now that her husband was dead at least something good had come of it because with her inheritance she would immediately be cancelling her brother's debt.

Then the biggest blow of all came:

> "Alan Baker, former security chief to the late Jon Chandler today revealed that his employer had confessed to him how he had hired professional hitman Keith Medley to murder two men he believed were responsible for the kidnapping and mutilation of his nephew Robert. Baker went on to tell our reporter how Chandler then shot dead the leader of the gang in a cowardly execution. Mr Baker said he could understood how angered Chandler must surely have been following such inhumane treatment of his nephew, but as an ex-policeman he had to stress how important it was that citizens should not try to take the law into their own hands."

But there was more:

> "With Medley's drug habit fuelled by the money he received for the killings commissioned by former minister for Trans-Union Trade Jon Chandler, the hitman became increasingly unreliable. Fearing he might release damaging information Mr Chandler went on to shoot him and bury his body in a grave underneath an outbuilding to his impressive home in the fashionable suburb of Rosemount."

Jon noticed the way the man he had thought was his friend had been careful to leave himself out of the story and had told the media he'd only come on board as an employee some weeks after the shooting of Keith Medley. The article went on:

> "A police spokesman advised that the body of hitman Keith Medley had been exhumed from the grave Jon Chandler dug underneath his summer-house. Together with the decaying remains they found two illegal handguns: a 9 mm automatic and a revolver. Analysis of the two weapons showed they had been used for the murders of Boris Stamford and Keith Medley. DNA analysis of bloodstains on the guns showed close matches to Jon Chandler's stored profile."

Jon understood to some extent how Alan must have felt, losing his job so suddenly, and having to quit the cosy cottage he'd made his home. But to shop his friend and former employer like this just to rake in a bit of dosh from the trashy end of the press was not what he'd expected from a man of Alan Baker's calibre.

With the revelations made and the nature of the attacks launched on him by the press, Jon realised just how much his situation had changed. Two years and more he'd been trying to persuade people he really was Jon Chandler from Vissan, and now the situation was so totally turned around. Now it was vital he kept his real identity secret. If anyone ever discovered that the life-force of Jon Chandler was still alive he'd be extradited back to Vissan to stand trial. And then what, spend the rest of his life in jail? So much for going home.

Now it was all becoming clear. He knew why Michael Heathersett had been so tricky on the phone. The man knew the conversation would be subject to surveillance, and far from dismissing him as a delusional girl who claimed to be the man she'd hosted, his real message had been to warn him not to try too hard to prove that Jon Chandler was still alive. Michael had known exactly who he was talking to and he'd proved to be a friend, right up to the end.

And now he was dead. Despite sitting here in a comfy chair finishing off a cup of tea, he was dead. He thought of the fabulous wealth he'd once enjoyed, and of course the will he'd left. The fortune he'd amassed over the years would have been split up and distributed to everyone he'd put down for a cut. There wasn't a bean left even if he was stupid enough to demand a deep scan to prove to the galaxy he was still alive. First it had been his body, then his reputation, and finally his fortune. Everything he'd ever had was gone.

By the time he'd finished reading all the poisoned words that had been written about Jon Chandler it was long past midnight. Whatever the future was going to bring it wasn't going to start till tomorrow. Tonight he'd sleep in his own bed, and in the morning he'd face up to whatever life held for him in a very different new world.

★★★

That night he slept fitfully and the little sleep he did manage to get brought with it the most vivid of dreams. Dreams of a bullet that had screamed through the skull of a low-life. Dreams of a girl, drowning in the deep. Dreams of an elegant woman, and the horror as she'd turned into a monster. Time and again he'd woken in a cold sweat. Then he'd lain awake for hours - sleepless and afraid to venture back into the nightmare realm. Finally, exhausted, deep sleep had claimed him. If only it could have been the long final sleep. Maybe it was Jana Kell who'd been the lucky one.

94

The Hyperion Leaves Darius

It was already lunchtime next day when Jon finally awoke, and even from his bed he could feel the shift in gravity that told him the Hyperion was accelerating away from Darius and the hope of salvation he'd waited so long for.

Another hour passed while he lay there with his eyes wide and unblinking, staring at the ceiling, staring yet seeing nothing. Slowly he came to his senses and remembered back to the day before, the day when the last vestige of the hope that had sustained him on the long journey through the void had suddenly been whisked away. Everything he'd ever known was gone. There was no home, no life as he'd known it. His tall, powerful male body nothing but a handful of ashes, strewn somewhere out in the countryside beyond Jackson's city limits. He'd even read his own obituary, but what was that old saying, "The rumours of my death have been greatly exaggerated"? But for all he was still alive in this body everyone in the galaxy called Jana Kell, he might as well be dead. Was there any life now? Was there any point carrying on living?

There was no point to it anymore, no point to anything. Without even a battle the war was lost. The strange, almost alien life that was all he had left was little more than an insult to prolong the agony of a death he'd suffered, and yet failed to experience. The promise of death no longer had any sting. His thoughts turned to how he could end everything right there with nothing more than a blade and a warm bath. He pictured himself looking down from on high, seeing the girl's body below - a ghostly white spectre in a tub of swirling scarlet.

But for all his eagerness to end the round of suffering and experience everyone called life, somehow he knew he couldn't do it. The will to live, whatever the consequences, was too strong. Maybe if he'd been in excruciating pain, or if he'd been badly disabled, maybe then he could have done it. Maybe God would have forgiven him for arriving too soon. He wondered just how bad life had to be before a person could take the decision to bring their own existence to a close.

He needed to clear his head, he needed to get outdoors. At last he dragged himself out of the bed. He looked around, the room was stark and bare, waiting for an occupant destined never to come. All he had to wear were the horrible prison clothes, and even the ship's eagle eyed security force would spot him wearing those.

***

Jon stepped out of the door pulling it closed behind him. Sliding his cleaner's access card into each slot in turn he checked the other three top floor rooms, but each one lacked any sign of occupation. The next floor down was the same, and even on the fourth floor only two of the rooms were occupied. From checking the wardrobes Jon could see that both housed men with far larger frames than the body he still occupied. The third floor was no better.

In the first room he tried on the second floor he found the occupant taking an afternoon nap, but fortunately he didn't stir. He stepped quietly back into the corridor and pulled the door closed as gently as he could. But the next room was what he was looking for. How old the woman who lived there was he could only guess, but from the cut of her clothes it was clear she'd seen many more seasons than Jana had. And she was taller too, though that wasn't difficult, even for a woman. Unsurprisingly for a woman of her age group most of the clothes in the wardrobe were skirts and dresses, but salvation came in a single pair of cropped trousers that didn't quite reach down to the girl's ankles. The tops he found were all flowery blouses that looked quite wrong on Jana's young body, but he had to wear something so he chose the least offensive article from the collection. Fortunately the woman had one pair of shoes with quite a low heel, even if they did clash badly with the trousers.

With only two flights of stairs to go there was no point bothering with the lift so he walked down the stairs and into the lobby. It was only a few minutes to the park but as he thumbed the money in his pocket he decided on a different course of action and caught the shuttle-rail to the shopping street.

***

Warning bells sounded in the girl's head as Jon made a purchase for the enormous sum of 37 Phen. He remembered back to a time when money like that would have bought him enough to eat for a fortnight. And the shop-keeper had looked at his latest customer with noticeable concern, wondering if she was old enough to even be in his shop let alone make a purchase. But business was business, and with the scant number of people making the trip back to Phoenix he needed all the trade he could find.

TranzCon

Out in the park Jon picked his favourite bench overlooking the pond and sat the girl's body down. He pulled the foil off the top of his bottle, a twelve year old single malt, and took a swig that was possibly just a little on the ambitious side. It'd been so long since he'd tasted whisky he almost fell off the bench in a fit of coughing.

The next glug of the golden liquid was more carefully controlled and he really began to appreciate the quality of his purchase, and as the afternoon passed the level in the bottle went down and down. The hologram ducks out on the pond swam about in their usual way. A newly added kingfisher sat motionless on a branch before darting down into the green water of the pond. People came and passed by, though he noticed no-one stopped to share his bench. Maybe it was because he'd kicked off his shoes and pulled the girl's legs up onto the other seat. But what did he care? He wasn't rude to the stupid fuckers, though God in Her wisdom knew they deserved it.

Time passed, more comfortably with every moment, and as the lighting level dimmed towards evening life had actually become fun. Even the pain of knowing his life had ended was starting to dull. He giggled. Trying to follow the motions of the ducks was getting harder and harder, and there was even a time when he'd dropped the bottle on the grass and had had to watch as a few precious drops of the liquid gold leaked away. Some little bug down there was going to have a wild evening tonight.

But all good things come to an end. When Jon finally spotted the friends he'd expected hours ago he swigged the last drop from the bottle and threw it into the pond. Annoyingly neither of them even noticed the open display of anti-social behaviour. With bleary eyes he watched them as they approached.

For Bill and Doug who'd spent their whole shift searching the ship, it came as something of a surprise to find their quarry sitting there in full view. Maybe it was the older style of clothing that had thrown them.

Jon had known they'd come eventually, but it had taken such an age he'd almost got bored, and now he felt like a bit of fun. The lubrication provided by the whisky had at least some impact on his judgement as well. In the girl's bare feet he jumped off the bench and ran hotfoot along the side of the pond, or at least he tried to but in his unsteady state he overbalanced and stood teetering on the stones that marked the edge for what felt like an age, before he finally fell backwards into the murky water. Bill and Doug gave thanks for the blessing of a pond that was home only to virtual waterfowl as they hauled the girl out and carried her back to the security office.

***

In his inebriated state Jon was only slightly aware of what was going on around him so he never made sense of anything as Steven Prentice walked into the SA Block. The man pulled up a chair next to Ms Lincoln and looked down at the girl as she sat there, smiling and giggling.

'We're not going to get anything out of her while she's like this. Might as well put her in a cell and leave her to sober up. Ten tomorrow morning, OK for you?'

Ms Lincoln nodded.

95

The Morning After

When the light in his cell came on to indicate that daytime had returned Jon had the hangover to end all hangovers. Even Dougie Smith would have given him gold for his latest effort. And he had a raging thirst too. He put his head under the tap to take a drink, but the room started to spin and the girl's stomach started to heave. It was only the complete lack of contents that saved him from making a mess of the cell. He found a glass and filled it.

Time passed and the cell door opened. Jon watched as Ms Lincoln stood in the doorway.

'And how are we feeling today Miss Kell? Any better?'

The red eyes told the story better than words but Jon spoke anyway, though his speech was still slurred. 'Worse, much worse.'

Ms Lincoln turned her head out into the corridor and spoke to the man standing there. 'Sorry Steven, she's not up to it yet. Can you come back this afternoon?'

★★★

When the door next opened Jon was feeling quite a lot better. The throbbing in his head had stopped and the girl's brain was starting to clear. He smiled when he saw Bee coming in.

'Come on then Jana, let's get you something to eat.'

Eat, now there was a good idea. Jon realised he was absolutely starving and a tasty lunch was just what he needed. Only the more he thought about it the more nauseous he felt. Well maybe a cup of coffee to start with would do the trick. He stood up, still just a little unsteady and followed the big woman out into the main room. She sat him at the table and brought him the breakfast he'd missed five hours earlier. It was amazing what a microwave could do.

Jon was ravenous. He cut the sausage in two and pushed a whole half into Jana's mouth, only later realising the mouthful was still too big - his judgement wasn't up to full strength yet. The bacon and the egg were as if nectar for the gods and he wolfed down the lot in no time, though afterwards he wasn't too sure if the big fatty meal had been quite the right thing for Jana's badly abused digestive system.

The door into the Block opened. Jon heard the sound and turned to watch as Ms Lincoln and Steven Prentice walked in. They pulled a group of the metal and plastic chairs round into a circle and invited Jon to join the little get-together. And they weren't giving out rain-checks.

★★★

The humourless face looked even more serious than usual.

Ms Lincoln spoke. 'Miss Kell, we all know very well what you did yesterday and you'll be seeing the Captain about it tomorrow morning. But right now we're more interested in a breach of security you may have caused. Would you please tell us how you were able to escape from the SA Block?'

Jon thought about it for a moment - for once he was holding the trump card.

'What if I don't tell you?'

'If you don't tell us our only option will be to remove your privileges regarding use of the computer terminals, and you'll be spending more time locked in your cell.'

With threats like that Jon knew he should be shivering with fear.

The woman continued. 'Something we do know, and we think it relates to you, is that shortly before you escaped yesterday there was a rather unusual access to the ship's computer system using a high level authority log-on. We know now that the areas accessed included pages showing details of the security codes for locks on board the ship. Whoever accessed the system knew that it was possible to open the SA Block door without a swipe-card once the fire alarm had been triggered. It's too much of a coincidence to not be connected to your escape.'

Jon could see the game was up and he was going to have to provide something of an explanation.

'As you are all no doubt aware, the star-liner Hyperion was my first venture into the space passenger business …….'

Prentice broke in, 'you say "my first venture". Whose venture was it?'

'I said mine and I meant mine.' The words were slurred just a little.

'And who exactly do you think you are?'

'I'm Jon Chandler as I've spent a long time trying to tell people over the past two years.'

Prentice and Ms Lincoln exchanged glances.

'The Hyperion was my ship and I had a high level access code, and in all the years that passed, no-one bothered to remove it. There's security for you.'

Prentice pulled himself up straight in his chair.

'Well it's been removed now. We've looked at your record and we've seen what it says about spirit image retention and the fact that you also appear to have access to the late Mr Chandler's memories.'

Jon could see an interesting angle opening up here. He remembered thinking that his long term survival now depended on an effective denial that he'd ever been Jon Chandler, so he had to keep his real identity secret from now on, but did it really matter? They were still unwilling to believe he was really Jon and now the ship was back out in space another two years would pass before the shipboard authorities had the opportunity to pass on the news that a hunted fugitive was on board. Jon hiccupped and tasted the sweet flavour that rose up into his mouth. The girl's stomach rumbled uncomfortably and his head was throbbing again.

Prentice continued. 'You obviously knew you wouldn't be able to escape from a star-liner in flight, so even if you had access to the door codes, what made you think you could achieve anything by......'

Jon felt the bile rise in the girl's oesophagus. He jumped out of the seat to try and make a run for the kitchen, and he might have stood a chance if Ms Lincoln hadn't grabbed his hand and held him back. With his arm held firmly in the woman's grasp the girl's body swung round until Jon was almost face to face with the purser. And then it happened:

'WHAT THE FUCK! GOD THAT'S AWFUL YOU STUPID LITTLE COW!'

Steven Prentice jumped out of his seat trying desperately to wipe the foul smelling semi-liquid from his brand new uniform. Jon saw the funny side of it, and he was the only one who did. He burst out laughing. It took just under thirty seconds for Bee and Ms Lincoln to carry him back to his cell and lay him down on the bed, still barely able to contain his amusement.

As he lay there a thought came to him. In these modern days, crime and punishment were not quite what they'd been years ago. Punishment was based entirely on locking people away in small rooms, and removing their privileges. They'd never actually used any corporal methods for hundreds of years, and even for throwing up over the purser and his smart new uniform they couldn't do any more to him than they were going to do already. It was absolutely true, when you've got nothing, you really don't have anything to lose.

96

Solitary

The night was longer than some he'd known recently, but morning came as it always did. With no net intake of food for several days the girl's stomach was rumbling again, but this time Bee didn't come to let him out for the breakfast he so desperately needed. When she did finally come he saw she was carrying a set of handcuffs like those he'd worn the first time they'd taken him to see the Captain. It was no surprise to hear that this was to be his second visit.

★★★

The little courtroom was just as he'd seen it the time before except that now Steven Prentice sat in the Purser's seat. Liam O'Connor looked down at the girl standing in front of him and scowled.

'Read the charges please.'

It was Prentice who spoke, and from the tone of his voice it was obvious the man was enjoying it, though Jon no longer cared.

'Escape from the secure accommodation block, setting off a fire alarm when no fire situation existed, physical assault on a member of security, entering a passenger accommodation room, stealing clothes from a passenger, consuming alcohol whilst under a secure accommodation order: and there is currently an investigation into illegal access to the ship's computer system sir.'

Jon was impressed, that ought to be enough to get him keelhauled at least.

O'Connor looked at Jon. 'How do you plead?'

Jon looked up and smiled - but said nothing. The Captain was fuming now.

'Prisoner, how do you plead?' he repeated in a raised tone.

Jon smiled again before he spoke.

'Liam. I couldn't give a toss.'

That O'Connor was furious was obvious to everyone present and Jon began to wonder whether the old man was going to jump down from his seat and start smacking him about until he agreed to co-operate. But he managed to keep his cool. He spoke again, but this time his gaze was not directed towards Jon.

'Mrs Beeson, please take the prisoner outside until we call you. Ms Lincoln, would you remain in the courtroom for a few minutes.'

***

Bee pulled on the chain and lead him out. 'Jana, I don't know what you're doing, but you've got the Captain mad now. He's going to throw the book at you.'

Jon looked up at her. 'The charges sounded quite comprehensive. Surely I'd get the maximum sentence for that lot whether the Captain was mad or not.'

Bee shook her head in disbelief.

Some minutes passed before the courtroom door re-opened and Ms Lincoln's head appeared. She beckoned to Bee who tugged the chain again and nearly had to drag her charge back inside. The Captain glared down at him again.

'Miss Kell, we have established beyond any reasonable doubt that you are guilty of many of the charges laid against you, and your failure to co-operate has not helped your case. You have left me no choice and for the rest of the time while you remain on my ship you will be subject to a maximum sentence of solitary confinement. When we reach our destination you will be handed over to the authorities. Do I make myself clear?'

Jon looked up, gave a burp in the Captain's direction and smiled.

'Take her away Ms Lincoln - and don't ever bring her back.'

***

Jon sat in the tiny cell looking at the locked door, knowing it was going to stay that way for another month. "Maximum solitary", Bee had explained it to him. He would go into solitary confinement for the maximum permitted period, which as he already knew was twenty eight days, and then he would be allowed back into the SA Block for seven days of recuperation. After that he would go back into solitary for another twenty eight days, and the cycle would continue until the ship reached Phoenix orbit and he could be transferred to the authorities on the ground.

In his sober state Jon knew exactly what that meant and he was truly afraid. He remembered all too well the frightening feeling of being alone. The fear of being crushed by walls that closed in on him as the minutes ticked slowly by, the nightmares that haunted him each night, the boredom and the awful slop that passed as food. And he knew that the only way a person could face that sort of existence was to truly care nothing. Only a person with nothing left to lose could go through it and remain sane - but then it wouldn't be for long. He cursed himself for not taking his chance when he'd had it a few days ago in Juniper block. The door at the far end of the lift-motor room could have been his portal to the afterlife.

"Don't look down, you'll only chicken out. Just take a run and vault the wall". His own advice to himself rang inside the girl's head. Even in the reduced grav of the ship's accommodation doughnut the terminal velocity would have been enough to smash the girl's skull wide open on the concrete path below. Now he was going to have to do it the hard way. Nature's way. How many once proud hunters, knowing their last kill was already long past had slunk away to endure the agony of a creeping death? Maybe it was easier for their prey, at least their end came quickly.

★★★

Night came and after a few hours of broken sleep the horn blared to sound morning's return. Jon sat and stared at the wall knowing his mission and wishing things could have been different. Lunch would be coming in a few hour's time. He felt the girl's stomach, rumbling and aching for food, but he had to be strong. For just one brief moment he had to be strong.

He heard the sound of the flap as it dropped down. Two dark hands offered the tray of food and he took it. Without thought or hesitation he opened the two bowls and emptied them out into the toilet pan. He pressed the flush button and sat back down. It had begun.

★★★

Days came and days went. The pangs of hunger that had once been so strong had passed him by long ago and now it was easy to throw the disgusting slop into the toilet. And time was running faster with each day that passed. Recently he'd been sleeping quite a lot, sometimes while the lights were dimmed, and while they were at full brightness too. If he was sleeping when the daily ration of food came Bee just banged on the door until he awoke to take the tray from her.

★★★

At last the day came when Jon was barely aware of the banging. Somewhere in the girl's head he could hear the clang, clang, clang, but he was too tired, too sleepy to do anything. And after a while the noise stopped.

97

The Medical Centre

First there was a sound. Jon opened his eyes and saw fuzzy shapes that moved in front of him. He lay as if paralysed for several minutes, wondering where he was and how he'd got there. A sense of déjà vu suggested he'd just arrived somewhere as a TranzCon traveller.

From what he could hear he wasn't in the SA Block. After a few minutes his vision began to clear and he looked around at machines on trolleys, bottles hanging from stands, and a long row of beds. And the air was scented with something he recalled, but what?

He lifted his hand and something moved with it - wires and tubes.

'She's coming round,' a voice called, 'can you put a call out for Dr Keeble.'

***

Roan Keeble was a doctor, a medical doctor. A man who'd always felt a sense of purpose, a need to serve. Hospitals were fine, for some, but they weren't his sort of life. So at the first opportunity he'd branched out into general practice and had never regretted it. And that was almost 40 years ago.

He thought back to all the happy years he'd spent running his practice. The only doctor in the village, way out in the countryside, far from the bustle of the big cities. Surgery in the mornings, home calls in the afternoon, and walks with Samson when his work was done. Did a man ever get tired of a routine when it was a happy routine?

But perhaps humans with their century lifespans shouldn't associate so closely with ephemerals. When the faithful hound had taken to walking by his side rather than running on ahead he knew it was the end of the beginning. When the old dog preferred to lie on the lawn while he sat on his lounger with the evening paper in his hands he knew it was the beginning of the end. At last the inevitable happened and he was alone. He'd never bothered with a wife. Why did a man need a wife when the women of the parish queued up to see him each morning, even if it was primarily to tell him their troubles?

And then wanderlust hit him. After all those years.

Now on the return leg home to his beloved Phoenix Keeble knew he'd never leave his home planet again. Pay off the locum, get a new dog, walks in the country, smell the freshness of real air. This was the life he longed for, a life so different from the stainless, sterile interior of the big star-liner.

But it had been fun, and the ladies had, as the ladies *always* had, made him very welcome. Though fortunately they'd kept their troubles to themselves when they'd sat with him at his table in the first class restaurant.

And now there was this young woman. A prisoner in the secure accommodation block who'd tried to take her own life. Younger than most of the patients he dealt with but obviously very troubled. He'd have to see what he could do.

★★★

Half an hour passed and Jon watched as a broad built man stepped into the room and approached his bed.

'So you're back with us then Jana? You had us worried for a while.'

In the time that had passed since he'd opened his eyes Jon had remembered back to his half-life in the solitary confinement cell, and how he'd flushed his food away day after day. But then there was a time he couldn't remember.

'Where am I,' he asked.

'You're in the Hyperion's medical centre. You were unconscious and very thin when they brought you up from the Block four days ago. But you're getting better now and the tests show there's no permanent damage. An older woman might not have been so lucky.'

Jon considered the statement for a moment or two.

'Maybe an older woman might have been dead. That's what I'd have called being lucky.'

'Not after only 25 days, but she might have had some long term conditions arising from going for so long without food. I take it you were attempting to starve yourself in your cell.'

'I believe it is my right to choose to die.'

The doctor looked at him with a serious expression.

'Well yes - and no. As far as I understand it, Union law allows you to seek your own death, and even to have assistance doing so if you are unable to carry out the procedure by yourself. But on this ship you are under Phoenixan law which I am sure you know differs in many areas. There is also the consideration that the Captain has a duty to deliver you and any fellow inmates to your destination alive and well. The result is that, as a prisoner, you have forfeited the right to end your own life.'

Jon raised a hand to his face and covered the girl's eyes.

'And that's why I'm in here getting better?'

'You're making good progress. You'll be out of here in a few days.'

'So the Captain can put me back in solitary and we can start all over again? What's the point?'

'Well after making an attempt on your life you'll be on suicide watch for a while, so it won't be possible for you to go back into solitary just yet. And of course the ship's psychiatrist will need to talk to you to find out why you wanted to end your own life.'

Jon wondered if there was a world somewhere out in the unexplored part of the galaxy where they hadn't invented psychiatrists.

'Isn't it obvious? I've nothing left to live for. A few weeks ago I had very little, but as least I had hope. Now hope has left me as well.'

The doctor looked concerned. 'Right now Miss Kell we need you to recover your strength. We can address these matters later.'

★★★

A week passed and Jon was getting stronger. He'd moved onto solid food again and the girl's weight was getting close to what it had been before he'd gone on his starvation diet. And he was getting to like it in the medical centre. There was always something going on, the people there were busy all the time, getting on with their jobs, talking to each other, and what was most important, they were even talking to him. That was something he'd missed in his time in the SA Block.

He was in no hurry for it to happen but he knew that one day it had to come. Dr Keeble stopped at Jon's bed on his ward round and told him. 'Well then Miss Kell. You've made a full recovery, so we'd like to discharge you after you've eaten lunch. That's good news isn't it.'

Jon frowned. 'No it's not. I like it here and I'd prefer to stay.'

The old doctor gave him a kindly smile. 'Well I'm sorry, but it's not an option. You are well enough to leave now and we will be discharging you. Mrs Beeson will be here to collect you later.'

98

The Meeting

As Keeble had promised there was going to be an investigation into the reasons why an apparently healthy young woman with no history of mental illness had attempted to take her own life. Jon had hoped it might mean a few trips out into the ship, even if it did mean wearing the obligatory handcuffs and being lead around by his jailer in the awful orange suit. But it wasn't to be and he was even a little disappointed when Bee told him his sessions with the ship's psychiatrist would be held in the SA Block.

So it was with surprise that Jon sat at the table in the main room and watched as Dr Keeble walked in through the door. He came over to the table and started unpacking his briefcase.

'Good morning Doctor. I wasn't expecting to see you here today.'

The man raised his eyebrows as he pulled up a chair and sat himself down, face to face with his patient.

'No, neither was I, but we appear to have had a bit of a mix-up on the staffing front. Dr Wallis the psychiatrist never made it back on board after visiting Darius and we left orbit

TranzCon

without him. We won't know what happened to him until we reach Phoenix. But in the meantime it falls to myself to fill in as best I can. I acknowledge that I have only a basic knowledge of psychiatry, but I will do my best.'

Jon had been wondering how he was going to play the next few weeks. He freely admitted he was scared of the tiny cell and there was no way he wanted to go back and spend his life in solitary. The longer he strung the medical people along, the longer he'd be able to stay out in the wide open spaces of the SA Block. But maybe that was just prolonging the agony. If he played it the other way and persuaded them he was well there was no reason for them to delay putting him back in solitary. Then he could have another go at the task he'd tried before. After all, with every aspect of his real life lost and gone there was no reason for him to carry on any longer. But was that what he really wanted? Somewhere deep inside he felt a force that drove him on, an animal instinct for survival that required him to continue his life, or what unsatisfactory vestige remained of it.

When he'd settled himself into his chair Keeble got straight down to business.

'Miss Kell, I'm not a man to beat around the bush, so I'll ask you straight out. Why did you want to take your own life.'

Jon geared himself up to tell the story over again. 'Because my own body on Vissan is already dead. I'm just trying to join it. Do we need to discuss any more than that?'

'Yes we do. When I realised that I was going to have to take on the duties of the ship's psychiatrist, and that you were to be my first patient in that role, quite logically I read your notes. So I know about your connection with Jon Chandler. I also know that Jon Chandler died just after the TranzCon transfer when Jana Kell returned to her own body.'

Jon sighed. 'So you've already made up your mind then. The woman's suffering from spirit image retention even after years have gone by. I'd do better talking to a parrot than another psychiatrist.'

'Please Miss Kell. If you're going to be rude I *can* have you put back in solitary, and I'm sure that's not what you want. Now, I've seen what the other doctors have had to say about you, and after doing a little homework I know a lot more about spirit image retention now than I did before. You can't deny it's a reason why you'd know things from Jon Chandler's past. But if you're prepared to work with me, I'm prepared to approach the subject with an open mind. Let's just get to know each other and see what comes of it.'

'So how do we start?'

'Well we could go straight into the business I came here to discuss. Can you tell me why you wanted to end your life so much that you were prepared to starve yourself to death. Really it's an awful way to go.'

Jon drew in a long deep breath. 'In the absence of any easier way out it was all that was left to me. You'll have noticed that anything sharp has been removed from the SA Block, and of course, I'm supervised throughout the day now, even when I'm asleep. Someone wants me alive so much, it's just a shame they're not prepared to give me a reason to live. I should have gone off the roof in Juniper block when I had the chance.'

'What about just living your life?'

'I don't have a life anymore. My financial empire, my position in the government, my money and my body all went down the pan in one easy move. Exactly what's left for me?'

'There are billions of people in the Union and on Phoenix who lack the advantages Jon Chandler enjoyed when he was alive; people living a life of poverty, people in poor health. Just being alive is enough for most of them.'

'And do they have freedom?'

Keeble saw the way Jon was taking the argument, but knew there was no way round.

'Yes, they have freedom.'

'And that makes all the difference. Take away the threat of going back into solitary and let me out into the ship, and I promise, I'll take no further steps to try to end my life. At least not until we get to Phoenix and I'm not your responsibility anymore.'

Keeble looked deep into the girl's eyes and softened his tone.

'Most potential suicides aren't prepared to bargain for a better deal. They want out and there's nothing to discuss. But look Miss Kell, if we could just let you out, let you off scot-free, would you be happy with yourself knowing all the misdemeanours you're responsible for? If you accept your punishment and pay your debt to society, you'll be satisfied when the sentence is complete because you'll have earned your freedom. It's the same for all prisoners.'

'And how many jails have you been in doctor? It's an easy attitude to take when you're free. It might even be easy to accept for prisoners who've *really* committed a crime, but I don't admit to any guilt for doing things I *had* to do.'

'And you feel that justifies your actions? Even if we leave out setting off the fire alarm, how do you explain assaulting a member of the SA Staff. You've admitted that you did it, so surely it's something you have to accept responsibility for.'

'It was vital that I made contact with my people in Jackson. According to the agreement I made with the Purser long before we entered Darius orbit, Ms Lincoln was supposed to have allowed me to make my call from inside the SA Block.

But she didn't. I took the minimum action necessary to get out to somewhere I could make what I believed to be a very important phone call. All Bee got was a bit of foam in her face. I know it gave her a surprise but she's OK now, and she doesn't hold it against me.'

'There is no formal record of your conversation with the Purser, but even if I take your word for it, you have to agree there were things you did long before the meeting you claim to have had. You stowed away on this ship for a start. Anyone in the galaxy knows that's a crime. What was so important about getting to Darius anyway?'

'I presume you were aware that beam contact to the Union was lost?'

'Yes of course. It happened a couple of months before the Hyperion left Phoenix.'

'But it didn't worry you because you weren't trying to get home. Unless you were watching some of the TV shows from the Union I'll bet you hardly even noticed it was gone. Well I can tell you it was a damned site more important for me. At first they said it was temporary, but then things changed. The worry was that it wasn't going to be just for a few weeks or months, it was going to be permanent. And without the beam in service we had no way of knowing whether anything was being done from the Darius end to get communications back. So in the end I decided that spending two years of my life travelling through space was going to be a good investment. Transferring back to my own body from Darius would have left the real Jana Kell stuck there, but I'd have paid her compensation and paid for her to travel home as a passenger. I'd have made sure she didn't lose out.'

'But the body of Jon Chandler was already dead when you set off.'

'Yes, but I didn't know that because the beam was out of service. There was no way anyone on Phoenix could have known about my body dying. If I *had* known I'd never have bothered stowing away would I?'

'I take your point, but you have to accept that stowing away is a crime whether you had reasons to do it or not. Let me ask you how Jon Chandler would have felt about people riding around on his ships without paying?'

'No-one got hurt and I didn't steal anything. I was prepared to pay for my passage to Darius but without the beam in service I couldn't get proper access to my own bank account.'

'That's assuming you *are* Jon Chandler. According to the information I have about Jana Kell she couldn't possibly have afforded the fare to Darius.'

'But why would she have wanted to travel to Darius anyway? Her home was on Phoenix so she had no reason to want to leave.'

'Possibly she wanted to escape because the police were chasing her for identity theft.'

Jon shook the girl's head in disbelief.

'How can you steal your own identity? Maybe the authorities on Phoenix are the guilty ones because *they* stole *my* identity. And part of the problem was that Jana Kell had been in trouble with the law before I even travelled to Phoenix. Not declaring that was a crime for anyone offering themselves as a host. So don't try to put the blame on me for what went on before I even arrived.'

'And then you illegally accessed the ship's computer.'

'I know, and if they brought a prosecution I'd be guilty as charged. But as you know they're still investigating. The evidence is all circumstantial.'

'So you don't feel you've committed any crime at all?'

'That's not quite true, I did steal a sandwich from a shop when I was hungry. If you could get the sentence reduced to a few hours of community service then I'd accept it. But look, even if I could get out of solitary and the SA Block here on the ship that wouldn't be an end to it. They're waiting for me on Phoenix, they know I'm on the ship and they'll arrest me the minute I get down to the surface. I'm facing decades in jail even after being cooped up on this ship for years. For Belen's sake, all I did was let myself be talked into going on a TranzCon transfer. Do I deserve everything that's happened to me? Do I deserve *any* of it?'

Keeble stopped and thought for a while. He looked up from the notes he'd been writing.

'The way you make it sound Miss Kell, is that either you are Jon Chandler, or you are insane. If after all this time you are still suffering from spirit image retention then this is something we should treat you for and not something you should be punished for. How would you feel if I was to give you a guarantee that you wouldn't have to go back into solitary confinement? Would that make it easier for you to talk?'

'Easier to talk?'

'Either to admit that you really are Jana Kell after all, or easier to tell me things that might convince me you really are Jon Chandler.'

'Could you keep me out of solitary? Could you *really* keep me out of solitary?'

'I am the ship's chief medical officer. For many issues the captain has the power to override me, but when it comes to medical matters my opinion goes a long way.'

'Could you get me out of the SA Block?'

Keeble shook his head slowly. 'I'm sorry, but you'd have to be in some form of secure accommodation, and we don't have the facilities in the medical centre. We couldn't keep you chained to a bed for the rest of the voyage.'

'OK then, but do you have any idea what it's been like in here, virtually on my own for months on end. If I'm insane it's because this place has driven me that way.'

'Well the investigation of your condition is going to take some time, so you'll be seeing me on a regular basis. And maybe I could arrange for you to have visits from friends.'

Keeble looked at the girl's face and saw the way its prettiness seemed to drain away.

'In all the time I was free on this ship I avoided making friends because I didn't want there to be anyone who could pry into my situation. There's only one person on board who I really want to see, and I can't imagine that happening in a million years. Not while O'Connor is still the captain.'

It took less than a moment for Keeble to pick up on what Jon was saying.

'You mean the girl they caught you with.'

'Yes, and here's something else for you to consider. Have a look through Jana's file and see if there's any previous indication of lesbian tendencies. Then have a look through Jon Chandler's and see if he's ever been attracted to women in his squeaky clean life.'

★★★

An hour later Jon heard the phone ring and watched as Bee went to answer it. The big woman stepped out of the office and beckoned.

'Jana. Get over here quick. Phone call for you.'

Jon put the receiver to the girl's ear and heard Keeble's voice.

'Miss Kell. I've made a few investigations and regarding a stowaway matter the captain has the last word on the subject. On the face of it I'm not able to stop him putting you back in solitary, but we're not out of options yet. If you make a request to see the ship's lawyer, I think we can swing it.'

99

Outrage

Keeble settled himself into the chair the Captain had offered. Somehow it didn't feel quite as comfortable as it had appeared, but was it the seat itself or the way he felt knowing he was about to enter into a contretemps with the most powerful man aboard? Was it wise to take on such a formidable character? Without a doubt the answer was "No". And yet here he was, waiting patiently to plead the case of a woman he'd never even met before yesterday. Why was he bothering himself for a mere prisoner, an insignificant nobody?

O'Connor took his place at his desk. 'I understand you've come to discuss the case of Jana Kell doctor.'

Keeble was nervous and hesitated before telling what he knew of Jana's problem. He explained a few of the reasons why she'd done what she'd done, and why she'd felt justified in taking such action. Then he moved onto the claustrophobia she suffered from and how she was scared of being sent back into solitary confinement.

O'Connor had listened intently, the steely expression on his face betraying not even a hint of emotion.

'So what you're telling me Doctor, is that I've got to lavish more care and attention on this woman than I do on a paying passenger? Why can't you just force feed her once a day?'

'I'm sorry Captain, but force feeding prisoners has been illegal for hundreds of years. You can't ask me to do anything like that.'

'It might be illegal on the surface of a plant Doctor, but you're on board a star-liner, a Phoenixan ship operating under Phoenixan laws. As master of the vessel I have the power to take whatever action I deem necessary, so if I order you to force feed her, you will do exactly that. Do I make myself clear?'

'No, I'm sorry, even though I accept your authority as captain of the Hyperion, I cannot accept such an order. When something concerns the *safety* of the ship then the laws of both Phoenix and the Union are clear, you can order me to do anything you consider necessary. But when safety is not the primary issue I am obliged to act in accordance with the requirements placed on me by my own profession. I don't think anyone could argue that Miss Kell presents any sort of threat while she's detained in the secure accommodation block, and now that the Purser has removed her ability to access security codes I have every confidence she won't be escaping again. In any case our planet's pre-accession agreement means that many aspects of Union law now apply on Phoenix itself and also on spacecraft operating under Phoenixan colours. We have to accept that there have been changes to the laws applicable to ships in space.'

'Are any of these changes relevant in this case?'

'Yes they are. Many Union laws provide improvements in human rights compared to those previously applicable.'

'And no doubt they do this by undermining the authority of a ship's captain?'

'Compared to the regulations you were used to working with, I'm sure you might see them as a reduction in your authority. But I understand that Union captains have had no trouble working with them.'

'I expect you're right Doctor. I know there have been changes to the regulations, but its something I won't be getting to grips with until I've sorted out the stuff that built up while we were in orbit.'

'But surely Captain, as master of this vessel you are required to be fully aware of any legal requirements before your ship goes out into space.'

'Doctor, I've got manifests, health reports for passengers, health reports for the crew, security reports, bills of lading for freight, engineering reports and God only knows what else to deal with. When that's all sorted I can spend a few weeks with the new stuff.'

He pointed to a pile of papers pushed over to the side of his desk.

'Look at it! Three thousand five hundred and twenty seven pages of deathly dull guff to wade through. It's a good job these journeys take so long.'

'Don't get me wrong Captain, I do appreciate your situation. But you have to agree that workload does not absolve you of any obligation to comply with space transport laws.'

'And I suppose you're an expert then Doctor?'

'For the past two years I've served as this ship's chief medical officer and to get my ticket for the post I had to qualify in a number of areas which wouldn't apply to a doctor practicing on the surface of a planet. I'll admit to having a bias towards the medical side of the legislation, but you can appreciate that I know quite a lot about the general parts of the law as it applies to passenger space transport.'

'Are you trying to tell me my job Doctor?'

'I'm trying to help.'

'Well perhaps you could have helped a bit before we left orbit.'

'Was it a problem before we left orbit?'

O'Connor saw he'd been outmanoeuvred, it wasn't an avenue worth pursuing.

'Anyway I don't see how it impacts on how I deal with a stowaway. Surely any captain has the right to punish a prisoner who assaulted a security officer?'

'Mrs Beeson wasn't actually hurt by being sprayed with foam, and if Miss Kell hadn't done it there's no way she'd have been able to make her call to Vissan. She took the minimum action necessary to get out of the SA Block, and in her eyes it was something she considered to be of the utmost importance.'

'So you're attempting to justify her escaping from custody?'

'I'm trying to understand her motives. Do you know why she went to such extreme lengths to escape?'

O'Connor shook his head. 'No, I've no idea. It seems unlikely she'd get herself into so much trouble just so she could down a bottle of whisky and jump in the duck-pond. I presume you're going to tell me she had something more important on her mind.'

'I spoke with her yesterday and from what she told me she'd been promised that when the ship entered Darius orbit she would be allowed to make contact with someone on Vissan.'

'And who made a promise like that to a prisoner?'

'Stuart Robertson, the Purser.'

'The *former* Purser. You are aware of the fact that Mr Robertson chose to leave the ship at Darius and had to be replaced at short notice.'

'Regardless of Stuart Robertson's circumstances, the promise was made by him in his capacity as Purser of this ship, so it was made by the *office* of Purser. When Steven Prentice took over the role he became obligated to honour any commitments made by his predecessor.'

'And it was so important for her to make a single phone call?'

'Miss Kell insists that it was essential to make that phone call, although she won't go into any details about it. But look, it gets more involved, despite being a citizen of a Phoenixan state she seems to be well up on Union law, much of which is now applicable to this vessel. And she's had a meeting with the ship's solicitor.'

'And who the hell's paying for that?'

Keeble couldn't hold back a smile, but wiped it away quickly before the old captain had chance to notice.

'She has no money of her own, so Phoenix Intersolar will be paying.'

O'Connor thumped his fist down on the desk.

'And that's coming out of my budget for operating the ship as well as all the other trouble she's caused.'

Keeble ignored the remark and pressed on. 'After receiving advice, she's made an official complaint against the office of Purser, citing the circumstance of Steven Prentice refusing to let her make the phone call she'd been promised.'

O'Connor's face brightened. 'And the case will be heard by a tribunal headed by myself. When the complaint is not upheld, and I can tell you now it won't be, this inconvenient young woman will be able to take her appeal to higher authority when we reach Phoenix. In the meantime she can consider my judgement at length while she passes her time in solitary confinement.'

Keeble shook his head. 'It's not going to be as easy as that, Miss Kell is unusually afraid of going back into solitary confinement. She's prepared to do anything and everything she can to avoid being in solitary, and bear in mind that she hasn't got anything to lose. If you *do* put her back in there, then there's no doubt in my mind she'll go straight into another suicide attempt. And if starving herself to death is the only method available to her, that's what she'll do.

'On my ship she'll do as she's told. New legislation or not she is still a stowaway and that gets her no rights at all.'

Keeble was nervous again. He knew the captain was unlikely to be happy to hear the next item of information he had to offer. He dropped his bombshell.

'Technically she's not a stowaway.'

It took a moment for the news to sink in. O'Connor almost shouted when he next spoke.

'What in hell's name. Of course she's a stowaway. She came on board by stealth and hid herself away. How can she be anything other than a stowaway?'

'She's not a stowaway because Union conventions on space travel now apply to this ship. When you manage to get up to date with your reading you'll see that the rules changed the instant the Hyperion entered orbit around a Union planet, either habitable or airless. Ever since that moment, and whether you knew it or not, you've been obliged to handle stowaways under Union law.'

'So how does that differ from Phoenixan law?'

'It means you have to hand them over to the land based authorities when the ship next docks at a habitable planet. So it was your responsibility to send Jana Kell down to Darius to face prosecution there. By keeping her on board, at best you invited her to remain here as a passenger, and at worst you kidnapped and falsely imprisoned her.'

O'Connor shook his head in disbelief. 'But I kept her on board in accordance with company regulations, and they state quite clearly that stowaways have to be returned to the port where they embarked. If we didn't do that they'd achieve their objective of travelling somewhere without paying the fare.'

'For the present, the company's regulations still apply to travel within the Phoenixan solar system, but along with any other companies running services to Darius, Phoenix Intersolar have to bring their regulations in line with Union law. It's not the first time the rules have ever changed is it?'

'So what am I supposed to do then, offer her an upgrade to First class and beg her forgiveness?'

'It'd be cheaper.'

'What do you mean?'

'Compared to the cost of keeping the SA Block open for a single prisoner, it would be cheaper if you put her in First class. Drop her down to Standard, which I'm sure she'd be more than happy to accept, and it'd be even less. You said a couple of minutes ago you were concerned about how much she was hitting your budget. In fact if you really wanted to save money you could just let her go back to being a stowaway. From what she told me she survived for a year and a half on next to nothing, and I might add without stealing anything, even from the restaurants' waste bins. When we got to Phoenix the security team could round her up ready for you to hand over to the authorities.'

'Doctor, that's hardly an option is it? She's committed crimes so she has to be detained in the ship's secure accommodation.'

'And that's something we can all agree on, but surely she doesn't have to go back into solitary. She's had one session as punishment for getting drunk and being rude, and that's as much as you'd normally give a member of the crew who did the same. All you need to do now is keep her confined, and at the lowest possible cost. And here's the deal she's offering, if she can stay out of solitary confinement for the rest of the voyage Miss Kell will agree to live peacefully in the SA Block and will make no further attempts on her life. If you agree it means we can stand down from the 24 hour suicide watch and reduce SA Block staffing to its normal level. The safety of the ship will not be affected and the impact on your budget will be minimised.'

O'Connor grunted.

'But there's just one more thing.'

'And that is?'

'For her mental well-being she needs company. Being the only prisoner in the block for most of the journey to Darius was almost like being in solitary, and that's tantamount to sensory deprivation, something which is illegal if you impose it for longer than the permitted 28 day period.'

'She had Mrs Beeson for company.'

'Mrs Beeson was under strict orders not to talk to inmates for anything other than essential reasons. She is by nature a friendly person, but she wasn't allowed to provide company for the prisoner.'

'So what does the woman want?'

'If there are other prisoners in the SA Block with her, then they'll be company for her. But if she's on her own in there, she wants the right to be visited by a friend.'

O'Connor stopped and thought for a moment. The already concerned face deepened to a scowl.

'And don't tell me, she wants conjugal visits with that dyke she was doing something with just before we went into orbit?'

'She wants to sit and talk with her, and she'll accept the presence of a member of the security staff while they're together so there's no question of anything "conjugal". If you're prepared to agree to her requests, she won't initiate any proceedings against you, the Purser, or Phoenix Intersolar when we arrive at our destination.'

O'Connor sat and weighed things up for a moment or two.

'I feel like I'm being held to ransom on my own ship, but tell her she can have her demands. Just make sure I never have to set eyes on the little bitch again.'

100

Getting Close To Phoenix

Jon studied the image on the monitor and was amazed at how the software had been able to pick out one particular white dot from the tens of thousands available. One tiny white dot, so small and insignificant from this range - and yet the mighty star that gave life to the planet which human-kind called Phoenix. More than 23 months into the journey, and still so far away. If the ship's drive system failed that afternoon they'd all die, in sight of their destination.

But still, it was a destination. The arrival would be something to celebrate for almost everyone on the ship. But not for the solitary resident of the female section of the secure accommodation block.

So what would the homecoming mean for Jana Kell? Transfer from a tiny prison to another much larger prison. The chance to walk out in the exercise yard and smell the freshness of the air. Perhaps the chance to die.

Dr Keeble had been fantastic. The story of how the man had stood up to the Captain's wrath had become almost a legend on the ship. Never before had a man done so much, getting him out of solitary, getting him visits. It had been easy to solemnly promise such a man he would not seek to take his own life - while they were on the ship. Could he somehow manage to do it once they'd arrived? Perhaps not. Could he stand the idea of decades in jail? Not that either.

Maybe it would be better if the ship's drive system broke down.

And now there was just another fortnight to go before the Hyperion entered orbit. So much endured, so much still to endure. The deathly dull life where nothing happened - yesterday, today, tomorrow or the day after. Like a parrot, chained to its perch. Jon sat and quietly sobbed to himself. Yes sobbed, it happened quite a lot these days - bloody female hormones. If God could have granted him one wish right then he'd have chosen a bottle of whisky, and finished it in a single hit.

God! Where was God when he needed her? Maybe this was all her doing. Maybe this was punishment for the sins of his life on Vissan. An upgrade of the heavenly IT system - "fast-track karma" - you no longer had to wait for re-incarnation to pay the price.

101

Arrival At Phoenix

The day finally came. Jon glanced at the screen. The images of the planet's surface, once a boundless source of amazement were no longer of any interest. He couldn't be bothered to watch the TV. As a mere convict he was immune to anything on the news.

Gerry the guard arrived and summoned him. One ring closed around the girl's left ankle, and another round her right. Two more clicked shut on her wrists and now the prisoner was ready to go. But at least it meant being able to leave the SA Block, to pass the guarded door that had been closed to him for almost two very long years. To walk out into the wide open spaces so passengers could gawp at the girl in the orange suit, shuffling along in her chains.

"They say she killed a man when she came on board". Funny how rumours always spread.

★★★

The elevator reaching way out into space above Phoenix had only been commissioned a month ago, so Jon was privileged to be one of the first to ride on it. And he had to agree, even in his state of not caring a cent for anything that might happen on the world below, that the view was amazing. For a few minutes he even forgot his predicament.

***

Down on the planet a van was waiting for its sole passenger. Sixteen identical coffin sized rooms, all for one prisoner. The smoked glass window let a little light in though it prevented the occupant from seeing out. But at least the motion of the vehicle was fun. A stimulus to the senses dulled by years of inactivity.

***

Jon noticed the way the light from the window dimmed slightly, as if the van had entered a tunnel. After a while the engine stopped and the door of his tiny cabin opened. Gerry ushered him out and helped him down the steps onto solid ground. Not easy to negotiate with feet joined by just 400 mm of shiny steel chain.

Gerry got a signature in his book and left taking the set of chains with him. Job done - commodity delivered. The man had actually been quite friendly and had even tried to initiate a conversation, but Jon wasn't interested. Nothing that anyone said made any difference anymore.

The reception committee took away his orange suit, orange socks, and orange underwear; and replaced them with an almost identical set, though he couldn't help noticing that the bra and pants were white. Someone was going to be in trouble.

After they'd photographed him, taken a set of fingerprints and scanned the girl's irises he was lead along a corridor and out into a hall that stood three storeys high. A hundred pairs of eyes watched as he followed the guard up the steps and onto the first landing. Then they went along to the end of the walkway and into a cell.

'You'll be in here on your own until you've been assessed. Meals will be delivered to your cell. You get one hour of exercise at 10.00 tomorrow morning.'

'What time is it now?'

'16.30. You'll get your meal in two hours time.'

The big door swung shut and the key turned. Now Jon looked around at his new world. Bigger than the cell he'd slept in on the Hyperion, but smaller by far than the open spaces of the SA Block. A grey steel door, unpainted walls, a tiny barred window high up in the wall opposite the door, a stainless toilet - no seat, stainless washbasin, stainless cup to drink water from the stainless tap, two painted metal framed beds on either side of the cell. Bolted down to prevent abuse by the inmates. A pair of light tubes buzzed like an insect on the grey ceiling.

If he could make it till ten next morning he might still be sane. The chance to stand outside in the open air, for the first time in 49 months. A tiny ray of hope for the hopeless.

★★★

After a fitful night's sleep Jon was only slightly refreshed. "Fitful", "sleep". Somehow the words failed to go together.

All through his life he'd never slept right through on his first night in a new place and it had only taken the first half hour after "lights-out" for him to work out that prison was not the place where old habits were about to change very soon. The mattress on the bed was thin, the sheets were too small, the frame creaked whenever he moved. And the noise that came from outside the cell was endless: screaming, crying shouting. Most of the racket seemed to be the warders, shouting at the tops of their voices for the women to be quiet. Even the thickness of the big steel door had failed to damp out the noise that just went on, and on.

When the bell finally rang to announce the start of the new day and people started moving around it was a relief, and it was only then that he'd really settled down to sleep. The warder who'd brought his breakfast was outraged to find a prisoner still asleep and now he was on report.

Because of the infringement of the rules his exercise period had been cancelled - "just when you think it couldn't possibly get any worse ……". He couldn't be bothered with the rest.

★★★

After lunch had been delivered to the cell the big door banged shut again, but only for a few minutes. A large woman in a warder's uniform stood outside on the walkway.

'Kell. J?'

Jon sat on the bed and waited for whatever came next.

'Kell. J. Confirm your identity.'

'Jana Kell, dressed and ready to kill. Ma'am.'

'Don't be funny Kell. Come this way.'

★★★

The woman lead him back along the walkway and down the steps he'd climbed the previous afternoon. As he walked he noticed the nets, strung out from side to side. Waiting patiently to save the lives of those who couldn't bear to live life any longer.

At last she opened a rather lightweight door and showed him into a room.

Jon looked around at the same old grey walls, with matching floor and ceiling, that he'd seen so many time before, though the wall with the door in it appeared to be formed mainly from wooden panels and large glass panes. A violent prisoner could have smashed her way out in a few minutes. There was a table in the middle of the floor, bolted down of course, and complete with rings set into the top to anchor down prisoners who looked violent enough to smash their way out. The four very solid looking chairs set two each side of the table were mobile. Jon felt the weight of one and wondered about chucking it through the window.

After a while a slim woman walked into the room carrying an armful of lever-arch files.

'Jana Kell?'

Jon confirmed his name and watched as the woman selected a file with a label to match.

Listening to her reeling off the list of charges he had to face was depressing. As if anything could be more depressing than what he already knew about his prospects here on Phoenix. When she told him he was entitled to the services of a publicly funded defender, assuming he lacked the money to employ a more satisfactory lawyer, he actually began to perk up. A ray of hope filled his mind when the woman presented a list of names and a sheaf of CVs.

He spent a few minutes scanning through the list. And then he found what he was looking for:

"J. S. Kamar. Hollins and Whitecroft, Solicitors at Law".

Jon point out the name. 'He's the one I want.'

The woman remonstrated. 'But you haven't read any of their CVs yet. How do you know?'

102

J. S. Kamar

Jon sat patiently in the interview room and looked around at the stark grey décor. When he'd started out in adult life he'd never even seen the inside of even a police station - a man from a respectable background such as his didn't expect to. But since the first tussle with DI Bennett when his nephew Robert had been kidnapped, cells and prisons had become familiar places.

A few minutes passed before he heard someone at the door and the warder ushered in Mr Kamar. For the first time in years Jon felt a sense of elation though he knew he was only a client his lawyer was representing. For all the man's friendly nature he was an associate rather than a friend. But the man's face betrayed the signs of a smile he tried hard to hide.

'So, Jon, or perhaps Jana. After you disappeared last time I thought I'd never see you again. I assumed you'd get home to your real life on Vissan.

'And like a bad cent, here I am. And as I'm sure you know, my situation hasn't improved.'

Kamar sat himself at the table and pulled a pile of papers from his briefcase.

'It's the same charges as before, but with failing to comply with the requirements of a bail order, stowing away on an intersolar flight, and escaping from custody added in. You're probably aware that each of the new charges is worth more than all the old ones put together?'

Jon lowered the girl's face towards the table. 'I know. It's pretty hopeless.'

Kamar's face was still bright. 'It's tough I'll grant you, but don't give up too easily. We might be able to do something. I've got a few ideas, and I've got quite a bit more experience of how the law works than when we previously met. In the last four years I've won more than my fair share of cases, and it was because of that I got an offer to join a very well respected legal firm. My career's really looking up at the moment.'

'Until you agreed to take me on.'

Now the smile was for real.

'How could I turn you down after everything we went through?'

'And after your performance then, I wasn't interested in being represented by any other lawyer. You know, apart from Jana's sister who saw through me in a moment, you were the only one who was prepared to believe I was actually Jon Chandler.'

'And I suspect you're going to tell me that the life-force there in Jana's body is still Jon Chandler. No sudden realisation you were Jana after all.'

'It might have been easier if it *had* happened that way, but no, I know exactly who I am. And I'm sure you've kept up with the news, so you know all about me and the things I did.'

Kamar nodded. 'Anyone else might have just breezed through the headlines about you and turned to the next page.

But after having you as my client I read every article they published.'

'So you'll have made your mind up then?'

He shook his head. 'Not so. Something you learn in this job is that things are rarely black and white. There's always another side to any story and I was well aware there was no-one sticking up for you. Perhaps if you told me your side of things I might be in a better position to make a judgement.'

'It's a bit of a saga. Does your fee for defending this case run to it?'

'I'm interested to know the truth, even if I have to listen in my own time.'

★★★

'So what do you think Mr Kamar. Do you still want to represent me now you know the whole story?'

Kamar drew in a breath, considering what to say. 'I know who you are, I know what you've done, and now I understand why. I'm your counsel, I'm here to get the best deal for you whether you've done right or wrong.'

'But you know I killed two men?'

'It's a funny galaxy Jon, because murderers are sometimes the most ordinary people. Burglars, thugs who mug people out in the street, professional criminals who're in the business for big money. They live a life of crime and all jail does is to stop them for a few years, then they're back out doing the only thing they know. But murderers are often quite different, people who commit a single crime of passion. They don't suddenly become career criminals who're going to offend again and again.'

'There are some who might.'

'If they killed people as part of some other crime then yes. Or perhaps there might be someone working as a professional hit-man. But most of the murderers we see in the courts are single crime offenders. I don't know if you remember your old pal DS Mills?'

Jon bared his teeth at the thought. 'How could I forget that bastard?'

'Well he brought a guy in for murder last week. Respectable man, sales manager with a major corporation. Came home a day early from a business trip and caught his wife in bed with a friend they'd known for years. In the heat of the moment he pulled out a gun and shot them both dead. Well that's my job too. I've got a week to cook up some sort of defence or he'll be going down for 40 years.'

'Seems like a long time for murder.'

'20 years for one murder, another 10 for the second, and 10 more for possession of an unlicensed firearm. There's no point pleading anything other than guilty. All we can do is to ask for the circumstances to be taken into account. If the judge is having a good day he might get off with 25.'

'A quarter of a century, just for one moment of anger. And to my mind, quite justifiable anger.'

'And the rest. He loses his job, his house will be repossessed because without any income he won't be able to keep up the payments, he won't be back out on the street till after he's retired and then after not working for so long his pension will be peanuts. All those years inside and nothing to look forward to but an old age of poverty and hardship.'

'So if you had the choice, getting him off or getting me off, who would you choose?'

'I'd try to get you both off. I *will* try to get you both off.'

'But if you could only get one of us off?'

Kamar thought for a moment before he spoke. 'I'd get you off Jana.'

Jon wondered for a moment whether his lawyer was being truthful, or whether he'd gone for an answer to appease his client. Perhaps he'd spin the same story to the other guy.

'Any reason for choosing me?'

'Just one. When he landed the man went straight home from the airport. He didn't phone home the moment he got into the airport terminal like most business travellers do.'

'Do you think he suspected his wife and wanted to surprise her?'

'It's possible, and I'm sure the prosecution won't overlook it. The story he's telling is that his phone wasn't working because the battery went dead while he was playing games on the flight.'

'And was it?'

'No-one will ever know. He called the police on the house-phone but the stupid pratt put his mobile on charge before they got there. Destroyed the one flimsy piece of evidence that might have helped him.'

'And what have we got?'

'We've got more than nothing Jon. I've put a few ideas together. For starters we've got Option 1, what I consider to be your base option. You can tell the authorities the whole story you've just told me and make a claim to be Jon Chandler. They'll deep-scan you and prove you really are Jon Chandler, or at least they'll prove that the life-force in charge of your present body is Jon Chandler's.'

Jon broke in. 'It didn't work when they did it before. They said they hadn't got anything to compare the scan with.'

'Technology moves on, even on Phoenix. They've got mass storage here now, and in any case they can get scans sent across from the TranzCon centre in Jackson. There's still a delay because of the need to route via the courier ships but the turnaround is six weeks. And in a few months when the relays are commissioned we'll have full service.'

'Including travel by TranzCon?'

'Even travel by TranzCon.'

Jon shook the girl's head. TranzCon was what had got him into this mess in the first place.

Kamar continued. 'The charge of stealing money by fraud would be cleared, and it would explain why you stowed away. Everything that cop was after you for would drop out.'

'But it's a classic case of "Out of the frying pan and into the fire". Now that the things Jon Chandler did years ago are public knowledge they'd want to extradite me back to Vissan on murder charges. I'd have another seven years in an SA Block and then more time in jail. It'd be thirty years before I got out.'

'Some of the deaths they laid against you weren't even your fault. There's no law against hiring an investigator - you didn't know he was going to turn out to be a hit-man. And then you had some quite understandable motives for killing the man who mutilated your nephew, and you didn't have much choice about disposing of the hit-man who was blackmailing you. There are plenty of grounds for asking for a lighter sentence.'

'And how long would I get?'

'Full disclosure, pleading guilty, good behaviour, you'd still be looking at 15 to 20 years. They'll say you should have come forward with the truth years ago when it happened and not waited till now when your only choice is to ask for compassion.'

'You called it the base option.'

'Just consider it. You've already spent over three years in custody on the Hyperion, you'd be in the SA Block of another star-liner for another seven, and bear in mind that if you wanted to get home to Vissan one day you'd have to spend those seven years in space anyway.'

'I'd normally have travelled first class.'

'But seven years in space is still seven years regardless of how you spend it. The point I'm making is that after arriving back on Vissan you could be out of jail within five years.'

'Or still inside after another ten. So let's say I went that route, would I be able to get my fortune back because I'd been proved to be Jon Chandler?'

'I guessed you were going to come up with that one so I looked into it, and the answer isn't in your favour. If someone makes a claim within one year of being incorrectly registered as dead, everyone who inherited from them has to give back the whole of the inheritance, less a reasonable allowance they can claim they spent. The guideline figure is 90%.'

'And if it's longer than a year? Bear in mind that I was out of communication for the whole of that time.'

'Unfortunately, the law as written is the law. They never envisaged the situation of someone being out of contact for so long.'

'But part of the problem was that people on Phoenix wouldn't recognise my claim to be Jon Chandler. Couldn't I sue them for what I'd lost.'

Kamar looked unhappy and Jon soon saw why. 'To press your claim against people here on Phoenix, you'd have to pursue the claim here on Phoenix. That would mean another seven years in space, and then when you'd finished you'd be here on Phoenix. And there's very little chance you'd get anything out of them anyway.'

'Isn't there anything else I could do?'

'You'd be fully entitled to *ask* the people who'd inherited from you to return at least some of the money. Assuming you'd left your money to loved-ones, it would seem a bit mean for them to leave you in poverty while they enjoyed the wealth you'd once had.'

'But there's no guarantee?'

'None at all. The only thing you can rely on is the property you owned, in particular your house at Rosemount and your apartment in Jackson. For non-corporate holdings of real-estate left in a will, good title never passes to a new owner if there's the slightest chance the true owner might still be still alive. When the new owners bought the properties they would have had to take out insurance to cover themselves against the previous owner turning up.'

'And is there a timescale involved.'

This time Kamar smiled. 'A whole century has to pass before your claim finally lapses.'

Jon smiled as well. 'The house was worth perhaps a couple of million, and another million for the apartment. I'd have money but I wouldn't be rich.'

Kamar sighed. 'Some people would feel very rich indeed to find they had property worth three million HUC. You're sitting very close to one of them right now.'

Jon looked sheepish. Despite everything that had happened to him, he still hadn't come fully to terms with the way ordinary people lived.

'I'm sorry Mr Kamar. I should be grateful to have money like that. But the point I'm making is that, if I thought I could go back and re-establish a life something like the one I used to enjoy, then perhaps the journey through space and a few more years in jail might make it worth it.'

'Three million's not a sum to be sniffed at. What could you do on Phoenix to make money like that?'

'Well, I know a lot about Union business and financial systems. That's got to be worth something when you consider that the planet is supposed to be coming into the Union.'

'If it ever happens, because right now they still can't agree on the accession terms. There are some things both sides see as non-negotiable.'

'But it will happen. There's too much at stake.'

'Well, assuming Phoenix does finally make it into the Union, do you think you could make more money here than you'd have on Vissan if you got your property back?'

'I'm up for the challenge. All I need is freedom, and then I could get started on a new career.'

'So freedom's more important than money?'

'The last few years have taught me a lot. If you'd asked me five years ago I wouldn't have agreed, but after living here four years ago I learned how to be happy with hardly a bean. Money oils the wheels and makes it possible to do things that *can* make you happy, but money on its own doesn't buy you happiness.'

'I wish you'd come and explain that one to my wife - and the bank manager as well. But look, I'm glad you can see things in these terms. I'm glad you can value freedom above money because that's what Option 2 is all about.'

'And that is?'

'If you don't like the idea of being Jon Chandler because of the jail sentence that goes with it, it follows that you have to be Jana Kell. So if you went along with the idea of adopting Jana's identity instead of fighting against it we might be able to do something.'

'Like what?'

'When you were here before the doctors and the transfer specialist told you the spirit image retention condition would correct itself if you gave it long enough.'

Jon nodded.

'So if you told them you'd been delusional when you claimed to be Jon Chandler, all the fine learned specialists who were involved back then would have a vested interest in believing you. It would prove they'd been right all along, and people like that are very happy indeed to be proved right. Do that and they'll have to accept you've recovered. In fact they'll claim *they* were the ones who cured you, it just took longer than they'd expected. And once you've been cured, they can't really put you in jail for things you did when you were mentally ill. Or should I say, when you were *temporarily* mentally ill.'

It was too much to take on board and Jon didn't know what to say.

Kamar continued. 'Something they'll want to do is to observe you to confirm they were right, so Morris is going to want to check you into his clinic, and the answer is to go for it. OK you'd be locked up for a while, but it'd be in his private place and it's a damned sight better than any jail they could send you to - and that *is* the alternative whether you like it or not. After a while he'd have to decide you were well, and then he'd have to let you go. Remember that he's working for TranzCon and they're obviously going to be keen that you appear to be well. They don't want the media telling the population of Phoenix that anyone who volunteers to be a host for them risks ending up as a hopeless psycho case and going to jail because of it.'

'You really think it would work?'

'In short "Yes", though the authorities might still want their kilo of flesh. They might want it to appear that you didn't get off entirely scot-free, but that one's easy. So far you've spent over three years in custody on the Hyperion, you're in jail right now, and it's likely you'll spend some time in a secure mental unit. If a court passes a sentence on you that's less than you've already served, you'll walk free.'

'But are you as a lawyer prepared to go ahead with a case we both know is based on a lie? We both know that underneath my external appearance I'm Jon Chandler, and yet my only real defence is to prove I'm Jana Kell.'

'I've thought about it quite a bit, and it's OK, mainly because to my mind you deserve a break. If they'd listened to you four years ago when you were claiming to be Jon Chandler there'd never have been any question of identity theft, or stealing from your own bank account, or using your host's bank account. Mills couldn't have pursued you for Jana's crime, not that she ever committed a crime anyway, so there'd never have been any need to stow away on a star-liner. And if you hadn't been on the star-liner you wouldn't have needed to escape from custody on it. Am I right?'

'You're exactly right. None of it would have happened. I'd have had money available, so I could have paid for my passage to Darius.'

'Taking Jana Kell's body with you.'

Jon pursed the girl's lips. 'I see what you mean. Taking the body off-planet would have been a breach of contract, but that's not in itself a criminal activity. I'd have paid financial compensation to Jana as well as buying her a ticket home.'

'You might still have been guilty of a crime though because you'd have been abducting her from her home planet.'

'*Money* Mr Kamar, would have settled the issue. Believe me, I know about these things.'

'But it didn't happen that way, so I'll come back to the point I was making, all the so-called crimes you committed followed on from the actions of others rather than from your own intent to commit a crime.'

'That is indeed the case.'

'And that's what's important to me as your lawyer. I know that winning the case is dependant on proving something we both know isn't true, but the only way I can get you a decent deal is to prove something *we* know isn't true, but *they* don't. So I can tell you in all honesty, my conscience is clear.'

'So where do we go from here, now we've got a plan?'

'Later today they'll transfer you from the prison to the holding cells next door to the court-house and you'll stay there overnight. Tomorrow morning we've got a brief hearing where you have to confirm your identity, and I can ask for an extra week or so before charges are made. That's so we can fit in a psychiatric evaluation, but I've got to clear it with Dr Morris first. But I'll tell you this, I've dealt with him before and I'll bet he's really anxious to see you.'

'What about bail?'

Kamar stifled a laugh. 'Jon, you've skipped bail once. You don't suppose they're going to grant it again do you?'

'I suppose not.'

103

The Hearing

A trip in the back of a van with blacked out windows was hardly inspiring, but it was the best fun on offer that afternoon. The food at the holding cells was better than in prison, with only a handful of inmates the place was very much quieter, and one small room with a locked door was very much the same as any other. After years of isolation on the Hyperion Jon was better at withstanding boredom stoically than he'd been in the far off days when DI Bennett had first locked him up.

★★★

Morning came and brought with it a breakfast to rival those he'd eaten on the Hyperion. That was the thing about breakfast, it was easy to put on a good one.

A short walk handcuffed to a policeman took him to the court-house where Kamar stood waiting. The hearing passed quite quickly with the lawyer doing most of the talking. Jon even wondered whether he'd needed to be there at all. But then, any sort of outing was better than jail-time.

While Kamar had been discussing the arrangements for the psychiatric study Jon had stood in silence. Like a child, the court had wanted to see him rather than to hear him, so he'd had plenty of time to have a good look around. Like jail cells, courtrooms looked pretty much the same wherever you went - wood, wigs, protocol by the barrow-load, and an air of authority. Up at the back two reporters, both women, had sat tapping notes into their laptops, but on the other side of the room he'd seen two men in dark suits. Generously sized men, with mid-brown faces to match their dark suits. People from the Union? Maybe, but what were they doing on Phoenix? It was only a small exaggeration to say the larger one was built like a brick outhouse - the other was just big. The two of them had sat side by side and said nothing. Two impassive, poker playing faces were all they'd showed to the world. They had to be police, but what exactly did they want? Were there more players in this game?

★★★

When the hearing was over, Kamar walked with Jon and his escort back to the holding cell to pass on his news. He'd been on the phone to Dr Morris the previous afternoon, and it was exactly as he'd said, the psychiatrist was eager to see him. He would be admitted to the clinic the morning after next.

104

Hospital

When breakfast was over the warder came to Jon's cell and escorted him out, along the walkway and down the steps. Endless corridors, endless doors and gates to lock and unlock, and to bang shut as loudly as possible. Perhaps that was what made life as a warder worthwhile, no-one to tell them off when they made a bit of noise. Bobby aged ten would have loved it.

It had been an easy guess there would be handcuffs involved somewhere along the line, and there were. But the van he'd expected wasn't there. Instead, a man in police uniform signed a piece of paper and lead him out to an unmarked car parked in the yard. It was nice to sit comfortably in the back and watch the countryside go by while his chauffer managed the driving. On reflection he decided that the car trip alone was quite the nicest thing that had happened to him in over three years.

But all good things come to an end and after motoring for about half an hour the car made a turn off from the main road into a pleasant driveway flanked by opulent rows of flowering bushes. The top line of the sign visible from the road had read simply "The Marion Clinic". The rest of the text had been too small to read from the moving car.

About 200 metres down the drive the car stopped in front of a set of tall metal gates. The policeman leaned over to speak into a microphone grill fixed to a pedestal by the side of the road, and after a few seconds the gates began to open. The car moved forward, but only into a holding pound confined by a second set of gates. And then, just like an airlock on a spacecraft, the second set of gates began to open when the first set had closed. For all the pleasant surroundings Jon knew this was just another prison.

***

Inside what must have been some minor stately home from a bygone era the cop lead Jon in through an impressive doorway before they stopped at a more recently installed internal door. Again the man spoke into a microphone and almost immediately the lock on the door began to buzz.

Inside the hallway the two of them walked up to a window set into one of the walls where a middle aged woman peered out at him. The policeman handed over his sheet for signature. Once again the commodity had found its destination. The man unlocked the handcuffs and clipped them to his belt. He hadn't said a word.

The woman leaned out from her window. 'Take a seat over there Miss Kell. I'll be with you as soon as I can.'

Jon did as he was told. After all, this was one time in his life when he had to be on his best behaviour.

About ten minutes later the door to the side of the window opened and the woman walked out into the hallway. She didn't introduce herself but the badge she wore told him she was Mrs A. Price, Receptionist. She went through a few details on a form clipped to a board, then held a photograph up to the girl's face to check she had the right person. She dashed back into the office and sat herself at a computer for another half-hour, occasionally answering the phone when it rang.

From where he was sitting Jon could see there were two women in the office, the other one much younger than Mrs A. Price. Neither of them bothered with him, but while he was doing this he was doing nothing else. Patience was obviously the watchword.

At last Mrs Price reappeared. 'Right then, Jana. There's a room just through here where you can change into your own clothes.'

She headed off so Jon got up to follow. Just as they were about to go through into a corridor she looked back into the hallway.

'I didn't see where your bag went.'

'I didn't bring a bag. I didn't have anything to bring in it.' Jon gesticulated towards the orange suit he wore. 'This is all I have in the world, and even this sartorial elegance belongs to the state. If you saw me in what I actually own you'd probably call it a birthday suit. I assumed you'd be handing out hospital smocks, or something like that.'

The woman shook her head. 'Oh no, we prefer all our patients to wear their own clothes. It helps them to be more relaxed. You certainly can't wear that uniform. This isn't a prison you know.'

Jon wondered what he was supposed to do. Perhaps it was his own fault he'd turned up without a change of clothes. Trying to be helpful he made a suggestion.

'Well if you give me the bus fare and lend me a few HUC I'll go into town and find something.'

The woman scowled but let the remark pass.

'Andrea my junior's about your size and she only lives in the village. I'll ask her if she can lend you something for while you're here. Do you prefer skirts or trousers?'

'Trousers, please.' It was an automatic response.

'Are you sure, it's such lovely weather. Don't you want to get some sun on your legs?'

'I still prefer trousers, if that's all right.'

'Yes, of course. But I'll ask her to look for something light and summery. How would that be?'

'That'd be fine.'

Andrea was dispatched and while they were waiting for the clothes to arrive the woman took Jon through to an examination room where a woman in a nurse's uniform went through all the usual processes and procedures - height, weight, a quick look in the ears, a look in the eyes, in the mouth. For a finale they filled in a two page form that asked all manner of questions about the girl's state of health.

Just as they were finishing the paperwork there was a knock on the door and it was Andrea, already back from home with a holdall full of clothes. Two pairs of trousers were white and off-white. The tee-shirt tops she'd brought were plain blue, white with a bit of embroidery on it, and one where the pattern was just a little too flowery for Jon's tastes. For Jana's feet she'd brought what was quite obviously her best pair of trainers.

'Oh, and I've got another bag with some knocking-about stuff, and a pair of wellies.'

Jon looked puzzled.

'In case you want to help out on the farm.'

★★★

Summer clothes were always a problem - too revealing for comfort. The trousers fitted well but for the other garments Jon couldn't help thinking that either Andrea was half a size smaller than Jana, or else she liked to wear her tops a little on the tight side. The white one with the embroidery was the loosest so Jon chose that for starters.

The room he'd been taken to was on the first floor in what the position of the sun told him was the east wing of the complex. The single window looked out onto a large well cared-for open space set to lawns and flower beds. Further over to the left he could see the fields of a small plantation and a collection of outbuildings.

The room itself was nice, and painted in white with just a hint of green. Over towards the left stood a single bed. To the right hand side was a matching pair of wooden framed easy chairs with a small table between them. A small TV set was fixed to the wall to the side of the chairs, but if he turned one of them round it would be just right for viewing. Next to the window a door lead through into a shower-room with a separate washbasin and toilet.

It really was very pleasant and could have been a room in a country hotel, though as Jon had already found out, the door in a hotel would be locked to people trying to get in, not to the occupant trying to get out. And as he'd also found, the windows only opened to a ventilation position. But what the heck, it surely beat being in prison.

With the rest of the borrowed clothes hung up in the fitted wardrobe Jon had nothing to do now, so he stood by the window and watched.

★★★

It was Andrea herself who came to fetch him about half an hour later to show him round. She admired her clothes and told Jon how pretty he looked. As always that was the other "P" word he disliked quite a lot though somehow it seemed easier to accept when it came from a woman in the same age group as his host body.

She apologised about the door but told him it was normal practice to keep new patients confined until they knew their way around. Normally it would be unlocked until night-time, and then next morning it would unlock automatically from seven o'clock onwards. But *she* could press the call button to summon an orderly if she needed any help.

Stepping outside the building, the grounds were as he'd seen from the room, neatly manicured lawns, bedding plant in profusion, rose-bushes just coming into flower. The rays of the morning sun passed on their warmth, and if there was any wind at all the garden was shielded by the walls of the building. Patients sat around on benches, some chatting, some just watching in silence, one with a big ginger cat on her knee. The residents were obviously very happy here.

A short walk took them to the farming area. Small fields were filled with green of all descriptions. Perhaps in a few weeks the little plants might show themselves to be cauliflowers, or cabbages, or the tops of carrots or potatoes. Jon really had no idea about plants - gardeners grew them and botanists knew about them, but growing things had never been his bag.

If the fields of green had been peaceful, the farmyard was anything but. The smell was "rich country", but only lightly so. The sounds he'd heard as they approached came from a menagerie of pigs, chickens, sheep, and most of all - goats. It had clearly been goat-season just a week or two ago because dozens of the busy little animals scurried in and out or ran across the yard. And just before a patient managed to scoop one up it darted back through the open barred fence to the safety of its mother.

Jon wondered about the animals. Obviously the vegetables were destined for the kitchens and the dining room tables, but the little goats, so playful and funny with their antics, what would become of them when they were no longer a source of amusement? Would they make it to the table too?

He'd heard the argument before. "Oh poor little goats. Poor little baby goats. You wouldn't really eat one would you?"

But Jon suspected the truth. Served up with gravy, potatoes and veg, who would know they weren't eating lamb? Poor little lambs. No-one would suggest they weren't a fit animal for the table.

★★★

When the tour was over Andrea left Jon to get acquainted with his fellow patients. The hospital was obviously mixed sex because more or less equal numbers of men and women sat around the gardens, or worked on the farm. And meals would be taken communally, though Andrea had told him there was strict segregation when it came to bedrooms - women were in the east block, men were in the west. The main block that joined the two accommodation wings contained the offices, doctors' surgeries, kitchens and the dining halls.

★★★

The first day passed quite pleasantly. The warm sun made life easy to live and the gardens were beautiful, though Jon's first impression of his fellow inmates was not so good. He'd quickly sussed they were not his kind of people, though who were his kind of people? Now he was back on Phoenix his thoughts turned to Jasmine and Gary and he longed for one of the "take-away supper and too much to drink" evenings they'd enjoyed more than once.

But the food here was good. Lunch had brought a tasty chicken salad, dinner a full three course that would have satisfied a queen. All that was missing was a nice glass of wine to wash it down.

Later that evening, after watching the sun slip down over the west wing, Jon was watching TV in his room when he heard a "click" from the door. And sure enough it was locked again. Half an hour later the TV went off part way through a programme he'd just got interested in. There were no books in the room so clearly this was the message that the time for sleep had come. And what a night's sleep he had, a world away from life in prison. The night was tranquil and the peaceful dreams that ran through the girl's mind a haven.

Next morning he woke refreshed and ready for the new day. But the new day of what? Watching the sun slowly wheel round the immaculate gardens? Though as he reminded himself, the alternative was going back to prison. This was time to be enjoyed.

Breakfast comprised a selection of cereals, fruits, toast and hot drinks. Cooked breakfast was served on Sundays when the meals for the rest of the day were sandwiches prepared the previous afternoon because the staff needed some time off. And on the table he found waiting for him an envelope addressed to "Miss J. Kell". Dr Morris had made an appointment for him at 11 o'clock that morning. Room 213.

★★★

Jon was curious to see what was inside the main building of the Marion Clinic and had a walk around. Most of the corridors were open to the residents though one was blocked off by a glass-windowed door and a code operated lock. The sign read that it was off limits to patients unless accompanied by a member of staff. It didn't seem unreasonable that some areas were private.

Exploring further and with still plenty of time before he was due to meet with Morris he found the doctor's office on the 2nd floor as the room number had suggested. And then he wondered as he sat on the chair thoughtfully placed in the corridor outside, was it an office or a surgery, or perhaps a consulting room?

Whichever it was, when the door opened at 11 precisely and Morris invited him inside he found he quite liked it. There was none of the dark wood panelling he'd somehow expected to find in a building of this age. Instead the room was freshly painted in a pastel yellow, the furniture was modern and the chair the doctor invited Jon to sit in was more than just comfortable, it was sumptuous. Morris himself pulled up a leather upholstered office chair, its five black wheels clattering across the polished wood floor.

'So Miss Kell. How nice to see you again. I have to tell you I was quite distressed to hear about everything that happened to you since our last meeting. I do so wish you'd been able to come and stay with us before. I'm sure we would have been able to do more to help you.'

Jon was beginning to wonder himself. Perhaps he had been just a little hasty in turning down the doctor's offer.

'Now Miss Kell, or would you allow me to call you Jana? We like to be on first name terms here at the Marion.'

Jon smiled, making sure he showed a little more of the girl's teeth than normal.

'Jana's fine.'

'How are you finding life here? Are you having a nice time.'

Jon wondered about the question. Anywhere was a nice time compared to being in prison. The clinic could put many a hotel to shame - it was just the other residents he wasn't so keen on.

'Very nice thankyou.'

'Good, good. But something I have to mention is that various members of staff have told me you've not made much of an effort to fit in yet. You haven't interacted with any of the other patients.' He paused, probably for effect. 'We put a lot of emphasis on how people perform in a group situation. We like the clinic to be, shall we say, a microcosm of real life.'

Jon realised this wasn't just polite chit-chat. He was on the spot and some sort of response was clearly expected, some reason or excuse why he hadn't performed as well as expected.

'I've spent a lot of the last three years almost on my own Doctor. I think I've forgotten how to fit into society.'

Morris nodded knowingly. 'Well we'll keep you under observation. I'm sure it will all come back after a day or two.'

"But not with this bunch of loonies" was the thought Jon kept to himself. Still, it was a warning, he'd have to make an effort to socialise.

Morris got down to business. 'So Jana, the last time we met you believed you were Jon Chandler, the man you hosted for a few days. How do you feel now, are you Jon, or are you Jana?'

Jon went in with guns blazing. Morris had to hear the answers he needed to hear, not necessarily the truth.

'I'm Jana. There's no doubt in my mind.'

'And yet last time you were so sure you were Jon. When did things start to change?'

Jon had had plenty of time to work out his story. Now it was just a question of remembering all the details.

'For quite some time I still believed I was Jon Chandler.'

'Was this before or after you were taken into the ship's secure accommodation block?'

'Oh, a long time after that. I think it was sometime on the way back from Darius that I started to realise I'd been wrong.'

'And did it happen all of a sudden, or was the change more gradual?'

'I just started to have doubts. For so long I'd been sure I was Jon Chandler, and then one day it dawned on me I was actually myself.'

'Yourself?'

'Me, Jana Kell.'

'You have no doubt you are Jana Kell?'

'I'm absolutely sure.'

'What was it that made the difference?'

'Well I could still remember everything about Mr Chandler. I knew all about his financial empire, I knew about his family, his wife, his friends. Somehow the knowledge of my own life had just been swamped by everything I knew about Jon Chandler's life.'

'You were, shall we say, overwhelmed by his presence in your mind?'

Jon smiled to himself, the right boxes were getting ticked.

'I really thought I was him for so long. Then, I think it was because of all the time I had to myself that I was able to push his memories out of my mind and remember who I really was. You probably know they put me in solitary for weeks on end.'

'Until they had to take you into the ship's medical centre. A most unfortunate episode. I'd like to ask you about that time, but you're with us for two weeks so we'll have plenty of opportunities. Maybe later in the week.'

The "consultation", as Morris liked to call it went on for exactly one hour when the man swiftly drew things to a close. Jon was quite annoyed. To have poured out so much of himself, and then to be cut off in full flow was frustrating. But he had to acknowledge that this was Morris's empire, a land where he ruled supreme. When the master said "jump", the patient had to ask "how high?".

★★★

When lunch was over Jon knew he had the whole of the afternoon to pass on before dinner. A pleasant existence of course, infinitely preferable to life in the SA Block, but still the question of what to do. At least on board the ship he'd had his routines to follow - little ways of getting mindlessly through another day that was just the same as the one that had preceded it.

Morris had made it quite clear that joining in with life here was expected rather than recommended, so on his walk around the garden Jon made a few attempts to get to know the other patients. Too many of the men had a scary look about them so he stuck mainly to the women. Some had clearly found all the friends they were ever going to need years ago, and just ignored him. The woman with the cat on her lap looked his way and smiled, but then looked back down at the cat and said nothing. Another woman talked incessantly about her life 30 years ago, and was still talking when Jon got up and left. He wondered if she'd even noticed that he'd gone.

The only person Jon had found he could relate to was a girl called Esme. Just 17 and as level headed as any woman her age out on the street. Jon had asked what she was doing here at all.

'I might be in for murder.'

Jon was surprised. 'Might be?' People usually knew when they'd killed someone. He knew.

'They found my father's blood on the blade, and my finger-prints on the handle.'

'Does that prove you killed him?'

'It proves I used that knife to chop up tomatoes for lunch, and then someone stuck it in my father.'

'Did you actually kill him though?'

'Who knows? The last thing I remember he was laying into my Mum, and after that he was dead with the knife in the back of his neck. I blanked out.'

'What did your mother say? Does she think you did it?'

'She didn't say anything - he killed her. He'd tried hard enough over the years. I'm here for observation. They keep doing hypnotherapy. They think they'll get to the truth one day.'

Jon could see it wasn't a happy situation for a new orphan. If they proved she'd done it then jail was waiting, and if they didn't she'd probably be here for quite a while. In contrast his own situation seemed clearer, even preferable.

★★★

Days came and days went. Jon knew Morris had his practice in town to run and the doctor was only there three days of the week. So it was always on alternate days that Jon found an appointment letter waiting for him at breakfast.

Each time the doctor dug deeper into his mind, probing out the truth of what Jana must have felt in the time immediately after the transfer back into her own body, then when she began to realise the truth, and how she felt now when some people were not entirely convinced it was Jana's life-force inside the pretty female body.

Each time when the consultation was over Jon felt he'd understood a little more about the techniques the doctor used and actually began to respect his profession better. The doctor obviously believed he was learning a lot about Jana, but Jon was learning too, and with every session he was able to prepare himself just a little better for the next interrogation.

Some of the consultations were more difficult than others.

'Are you happy Jana, being a woman?'

'I've always been a girl, a woman. It's what I am.'

'Did you ever have a brother.'

'No, only a sister.'

'So you didn't see much of boys' lives when you were young?'

'Boys were different. They liked to play their own games.'

'And did you ever want to be a boy? Didn't you wonder if boys had more fun?'

'Maybe they did, but we had plenty of fun as girls. I never wanted to be a boy.'

'Because they were smelly? That's what girls think isn't it?'

'That's what we always said. I never really thought they were smelly, but they did seem to like getting covered in mud. Maybe they were cleaner than us because their mothers had to keep finding them new clothes.'

'But you never played with them?'

'Not when we were little.'

'Do you dislike boys?'

'No, not at all. Not now, not since I started to grow up.'

'Did you and your friends like it when the boys started to notice you?'

'Well we certainly noticed them. We used to fantasize. Used to have these ideas of what it would be like to be with a boy.'

When Morris finally called time Jon was exhausted. The barrage of questions had been non-stop and every single one had needed an answer turned around from what his own male thoughts told him. Thank heavens for Mandy, without the stories he'd heard every day from his sister he'd never have had the slightest idea about what girls thought or did.

★★★

Jon was getting a bit more into the life of the hospital and had taken the old clothes out of the bag Andrea had given him. Together with Esme he'd found some gardening tools and they'd been through the rose-beds hoeing, digging over the soil, and clearing out even the tiniest weed that dared show its leaves to the sunlight.

Other patients had joined in and Jon soon came to realise this was how the gardens managed to be so precise. It was therapeutic too, it was easy to forget the world and all its troubles while you worked in a garden. Without a doubt he was far closer to God than he'd ever been in any office.

And the consultations went on. Pregnancy and childbirth were hardly his subject, but he knew a little, and the rest was bull. Or maybe "cow". He could hardly believe what he was saying when he'd told the doctor about how, if his mother could do it, and his gran, then when it was his turn he'd be ready to bring a new life into the world.

'It's what women do. We play, we practice. We're getting ready for motherhood right from being little girls. I wouldn't expect a man to understand.'

The doctor lapped it all up, but Jon knew his own thoughts on the subject and they were quite different. Oh boy, when they were doling out the film and stage awards that autumn, did he ever deserve one?

★★★

The first week had passed more quickly than Jon had expected, and now the second one was drawing to a close. There was one last consultation and next morning he'd be off back to prison. But at least that was getting on with things.

Kamar had asked for the identity hearing and the trial to be put back an extra week so there'd be time for the Dr Morris's evaluation, and fortunately the judge had appreciated that this was not something that could be rushed. But now it was time to go back, time for the hearings. The time was coming closer when he would find out exactly which path his life was going to follow. Was he going to be free and poor, or rich and incarcerated for years?

The appointment letter had been on the breakfast table as always, and at two minutes to 11 Jon was sitting outside Morris's room. And at a quarter past he was still there. Just before half past Mrs Price from reception came up holding a note in her hand. The doctor had been called to an emergency and sent his apologies. He would not be able to make it today.

Jon was almost livid. Despite all the play-acting, he'd learned more about himself than really he'd been prepared to admit. He'd given his soul to this man - come to trust him, come to rely on him. And now he was cast aside, like a toy discarded after Belenfest when a new ensemble of playthings had arrived.

★★★

Next morning brought his last day at the clinic. Jon looked out onto the gardens, bright in the sunlight rising behind him. Beautiful, and just a little more prefect thanks to his own intervention. Later that day he'd be lucky to see even the grey walled exercise yard. Lucky to be there during the brief half-hour when the mid-day sun rose high enough to shine down onto five special square metres of concrete. Not that he could ever get onto that tiny patch of holy ground when women twice his size jostled for the right to feel their star's warming rays.

Breakfast came and Jon ate his fill. It was better by far than anything the prison could offer.

Back in the room the orange suit was waiting. Washed and neatly pressed, but still more orange than he preferred. With sadness he slipped out of the nice clothes Andrea had lent him. In the prison suit he was anything but pretty.

105

The Visit

The warder turned the key and opened the cell door. The message was that Jon had a visitor and had to be ready in a few minutes time. On the way down the stairs he wondered about it. He hadn't expected Kamar to call again quite so soon.

So it came as a surprise when he walked into the interview room to see Jasmine's lovely form perched on the grey-painted chair. Over four years had passed since the day he'd left her looking after Arnie, and Jana's little flat, and yet she'd been in his thoughts almost constantly. The one who'd shown him friendship, the one who'd believed his story when everyone else had denounced him as mentally ill, the one who Jon Chandler just wanted to push down onto a bed and make love to. Was it because she was beautiful, or was it just that a woman in her profession was available? Whatever the reason, there was no doubt that her reversion to a more conventional appearance had improved her looks. With the long blond hair that hung down over her colourful sun-dress she was nothing less than a delight. It came as a shock for Jon to realise that his own host body, if clothed differently to the orange suited apparel his days of captivity forced on him, would look the same. Somehow it was easier to be androgynous.

***

When the initial greetings were over Jasmine got down to business. Jon saw the way the smile that only moments before had appeared so natural had vanished from the lovely face.

She'd already told him about her change of circumstances. Her Mother had died not long after the Hyperion had left for Darius. That should have lead to her giving up the work she'd done for so many years, because after all, she'd promised Gary that when she no longer needed the money to pay for her Mother's care, she'd never work that way again. But it's not easy to give up the only way of making a living you've ever known, and for a girl who wasn't on drugs the living could be good. So after one last blazing row Gary had given up and left. With no pets allowed at the flat the two of them had shared there was no way she could keep Arnie once the rent on Jana's flat ran out. So it was with sadness she'd handed the little dog over to her aunt who lived on the coast 300 km away. At least he'd get plenty of runs out on the cliff-top paths.

'I'm in trouble Jon. That bastard Mills has got the drop on me.'

Jon thought back to the policeman who'd given both the Kell sisters so much trouble. 'DS Mills?'

'Who else? Lord knows I've tried to be careful, knowing what's in store for me, but I got caught in another sting operation. I'm going down for a year I know that, and I suppose I deserve it. But it's worse than that, that's why I had to come and see you.'

'Well prison's not nice, we both know that. But you'll survive. Why should it be worse?'

'One year's not a problem Jon. I've already done a six month stretch so I know what to expect. But that's not the end of it – Mills says he's got more on me. If I don't declare all the other offences he knows about he's going to re-arrest me when I come out, and then I get a mandatory two years for the next, and four for the one after till I've spent the rest of my life in jail. If I *do* ask for other cases to be taken into account at the trial I get another six months for each of them, and that means I spend the rest of my life in jail. I'm screwed either way.'

Jon knew this sort of approach. You had to keep your nerve, sometimes with your fingers and toes crossed.

'He could be bluffing. Maybe he knows sod all and he's hoping you'll provide him with the evidence he needs.'

'If it's a bluff then I'm not brave enough to call it.'

'Ever thought of stowing away on a star-liner? Being on the game's not illegal on Darius.'

'For fuck's sake Jon. This is serious.'

'Sorry. But that was my first thought. If you could just get away from Phoenix .....'

'And how am I going to do that? Where does someone like me get the money from to pay the fare to another planet? I've got 400 HUC saved for the rent at the end of the month and then what? People like you Jon, you just don't know you're born.'

Jon remonstrated and pointed out that his days as a rich man were long gone, faded memories slipping away into a dream.

'Anyway, the first thing they did when they arrested me was to confiscate my passport. Not even all the money you once frittered away so freely would get me off Phoenix.'

'Is there nothing you can do?'

Jasmine looked straight into his eyes, fixed his gaze as if she was trying to say something without using words – hoping that somehow he'd understand.

At last she spoke. 'I know you're in a lot of trouble Jon, and I know they're trying to say you're Jon Chandler.'

Jon shrugged the girl's shoulders. 'Ironic isn't it? If they'd let me be Jon Chandler four years ago I wouldn't be in this mess now. What's more I'd have been able to get you away to Darius too.'

'And I know you're in more trouble if they decide you're Jon Chandler than if they decide you're Jana.'

Jon nodded.

'So now you're trying to prove you're Jana.'

Jon wondered whether the last comment had been a question or a statement.

'Does it bother you? I mean, everyone in the galaxy's been trying to force me to be Jana, and now it's in my interest to be her, I somehow feel entitled. But I'd understand if you felt I was being disrespectful.'

'Two points here Jon. No it doesn't bother me if you want to be Jana. I've had nearly four years to come to terms with the knowledge that my sister's not coming back. You were involved but it wasn't really your fault, so if having her identity does you any good you're welcome to it.'

'And the other point?'

'I'm afraid this one's not so good. I'll be at your identity hearing, and I'll be testifying that you're Jon Chandler.'

Jon couldn't believe what he was hearing. 'But why. You just said you're OK about me being Jana.'

'I can sum it up in one word - "Mills". After everything that happened, after all the protests you made, after the way you stowed away on the ship, after what you did just to make *one* phone call, Mills finally started to realise you were Jon Chandler after all. And what do policemen do? They lock people up. It's in his blood, if he can't lock you up for one reason he wants to lock you up for another. The deal with

Mills is that if I testify that you're Jon Chandler, he doesn't come after me when my year is up. Do you see Jon, I don't really have a choice?'

Jon thought for a moment, let the news sink in. 'We can both see this is what you've got to do. There's nothing I could do to stop you, and I wouldn't anyway. My only question is, why. Why are you here telling me? Why did you take the risk of meeting me, face to face?'

Jasmine was looking down at the table, her fingers fiddling with one of the shackle rings set into the top.

'I felt I had to. I know I don't really owe you anything, but we've been through so much and we've got Jana in common. I just wanted to explain why I'm doing what I have to do. Maybe I shouldn't have come.'

Jon drummed his fingers on the table, wondering what to say.

'I don't blame you, really I don't. All my life I've tried to be a good guy, and it didn't work. Just one twist of fate and it all went wrong. Now I have to take what life sends my way and make the best of it. You know that if they decide I'm Jon Chandler they'll certainly send me to jail, but then they'll have to admit I'm entitled to claim what's left of the fortune I had. Even if the beneficiaries of my will won't give anything back I'll still have a few million to my name, and these days I appreciate the value of money in a way I never did before. And I'll send some to you.'

'Jon, we've been through this before. I don't want your money. Certainly not if I'm going to testify against you.'

'Well think of it as payment. You won't ever have to work, you know, like that again. Get back with Gary, have a life.'

'But what about you Jon. Maybe you deserve a life too.'

Jon laughed. 'When I took over this body it was just 22, so that's 37 years younger than the one I left behind. Even if I end up spending 20 years in jail I still get more life than I could have expected. I'm still a winner, in a very minor way.'

★★★

Back in the emptiness of his cell Jon felt more alone than ever, and yet he was elated to have met Jasmine again. He was sorry for her of course, but she'd survive a year in jail - even if this new turn of events was going to cost him dear. The real question was, would *he* survive?

★★★

Kamar came next morning and was waiting in the interview room when Jon arrived. He told the lawyer about Jasmine's visit and the trouble she was in, and the trouble it put him in. The two of them agreed that while there was a strong chance they might be able to overcome the testimony Mills put forward, anything the court heard from Jasmine would carry more weight. There was no way Jana's own sister could be fooled, and the jury would know it.

But something was puzzling Jon. 'Why are we going through all this rigmarole? You know, putting it to a court to decide who I really am? Why don't they just do it the easy way and force me to have a deep scan? That would sort it out one way or another.'

'They don't do it that way, because they're not allowed to. Not here on Phoenix, even now when we're on the verge of becoming a full member. It's one of the opt-outs the PCC won from the Union.'

'What's a PCC?'

'Sorry, I'd forgotten you're not up to speed with everything that's happened on the accession front. The Phoenix Co-operation Council was set up to be a sort of planetary government that could represent the Phoenixan states that want to join the Union. They've been through all sorts of wrangling this last four years and what started to become clear was that, while the four major states all wanted to join, there were some states who were never going to agree to any of the terms, including some that the Union saw as non-negotiable.'

'Sounds like an impasse to me. Have they made any progress at all?'

'What they finally agreed on was that the states who were vetoing the process wouldn't be part of it. They'll still be states with their own sovereign rights, and of course they'll still be physically present on Phoenix, but they'll be outside the Union.'

'That's a whacky arrangement.'

'It's going to work though. The five states that want to stay outside of the Union only represent about 3% of the global economy, so really they're insignificant. The four biggest players on the planet want in and they control 87% of the economy, and between them they have 53% of the population. The smaller states who could have gone either way worked out where the smart money was and they're on board with the accession process.'

'And how does all this fit in with a court demanding that someone should have a deep-scan?'

'It all comes down to religion, something you know is pretty big here on Phoenix. Even in the major states there are religious movements who wield far more power than they ever would on any existing Union planet. There's a lot of superstition and one of the main stumbling blocks was that a lot of people simply refused to accept the idea of tinkering with the mind. They won't travel by TranzCon, they won't allow their bodies to be used as hosts, and they won't allow scanning of the brain except for compelling medical reasons. And the *serious* hard-liners won't accept even that.'

'And these people, are there enough of them to swing the decision to join the Union?'

'They're in a minority, but it's a big one. It would be suicide for any political party to ignore such a large minority.'

'How large exactly?'

'42% of the population in the four major states. And consider this, there were 13% who didn't vote either way.'

'A minority facing a minority. So have they come up with a solution?'

'It's one of the points the Union has conceded on because they knew if they didn't there'd be no accession. And this is the deal, no citizen of any of the Phoenixan accession states can ever be forced to undergo a deep scan of the mind, either here on Phoenix or anywhere else in the Union. It applies to anyone who presents themselves in a body which can be proved to be a citizen of one of the Phoenixan accession states.'

Jon thought for a moment, then smiled.

'But what about the mind of a citizen of an accession state in a body which was not from one of the accession states?'

'A pedantic point, but one which deserves a reply. The assumption is that anyone who has transferred from one body to another couldn't possibly be an objector, so they could be forced to undergo a deep scan.'

'So what you're saying is that because I'm in Jana Kell's body, I don't have to allow them to do a deep scan.'

'No you don't, but the news isn't all good. If you wanted to prove your point to a court, then obviously you could volunteer to have a deep scan. The fact that you'd refused to volunteer would be seen by the court as a significant fact.'

'The implication being that anyone who avoids a scan must have something to hide.'

'Exactly. Some people would never voluntarily undergo a deep scan, even if their liberty depended on it, but someone like that would have to be a strong objector. Almost certainly someone with an established connection to some religious body.'

'And don't tell me, the Kell family only get as far as a church for weddings and funerals.'

'I'm afraid so. If you don't volunteer to undergo a scan it will go against you. But, and this is an important point, the usual situation is that someone would try to avoid being associated with an identity that was guilty of a crime that would end them up in jail.'

'I get you, the other possible identity being innocent.'

'It's different for you because whichever identity the court settles on you, that identity will be tried for crimes that either could or would result in a jail sentence.'

'But being Jana Kell would result in a lighter sentence than being Jon Chandler.'

'But being Jon Chandler would result in you becoming entitled to money in excess of what most jurors would earn in a lifetime. A lot of people would endure a few years in jail if they knew they were going to come out rich.'

'So what you're saying is, the case to establish my identity could still come out either way.'

'It will depend entirely on the witnesses called. Mills we know wants to see you identified as Jon Chandler, and we can call up Dr Morris and some experts from TranzCon who'd prefer you to be Jana. But you know as well as I do, everything rests on Jasmine. Her testimony's going to be worth more than all the others put together.'

106

Charged

When mid-afternoon came round again it was the same routine Jon had experienced before. The warder came to the cell, escorted him through the prison and down the steps. Back through the endless corridors, the need to stand and wait time and again while the endless doors and gates were unlocked, and locked again behind him. Never once did the warder fail to get the sequence right. Jon had seen movies where the stars of the day, mistakenly convicted and incarcerated of course, had somehow found a way to escape. How they'd managed it was completely beyond him.

And then it had been on with the obligatory handcuffs and out into the van with the blacked out windows. But the holding cells at the other end were OK as prisons went, and as before the food was actually quite good.

★★★

Next morning Jon ate a hearty breakfast before being coupled up to his escort, this time a woman. Kamar was standing in the morning sun just outside the holding cells and together they walked over to the court-house. Again the big courtroom was only sparsely populated. The judge, his clerk, the two counsels, the reporters at the back, and to Jon's surprise, the two men in dark suits were here again.

This was the first time Jon had come across Christopher Richard Ludlum, a senior member of the state prosecution service. Jon looked the man up and down. The well-set face, the short-cropped hair, the blemish-free skin all made the man a picture of health. And something about his stance indicated that the muscular body of an athlete stood inside the all-concealing robes. Jon looked again at the colour of the man's face and hands, perhaps a shade darker than the average Phoenixan, and wondered whether the man had blood from Kamar's race or whether the richness of tone was no more than a sun-tan.

Kamar had known Ludlum from years ago and while it was clear the two adversaries could never be friends, there was an obvious sense of professional respect between the two men.

Ludlum stood up and addressed the court. He outlined the fact that the defendant standing in the dock had once been the host to Jon Chandler, a TranzCon traveller from Vissan, and how there was a possibility that the body of Jana Kell was still occupied by the life-force of that traveller.

The judge asked whether Kamar was hoping to make an application for bail on the grounds that, with an identity question at stake, the assumption had to be that the defendant was in fact the innocent identity. In such cases the granting of bail was automatic.

Ludlum advised the court that in this instance, serious charges were set against both identities. Any application for bail would have to take into account at least the lower level of charges set against the Jana Kell identity, a woman who had on a previous occasion failed to comply with bail requirements.

Kamar confirmed that his client was not requesting bail on this occasion.

Ludlum stood up again and read out the now familiar list of charges against Jana Kell. He then moved on to reading out the charges against Jon Chandler, which Jon noted now included causing the death of a TranzCon host by making a false statement on a health declaration form. Hearing the eloquent way the man spoke Jon wondered whether he'd ever be free. Somehow it didn't seem to matter which identity they landed on him, he'd go to his grave in an orange suit, and probably in handcuffs as well.

Kamar spoke only to acknowledge the charges and to confirm that the defence accepted there was a challenge to *her* identity. The choice of pronoun did not go unnoticed by Jon.

★★★

Next morning Kamar was back in the interview room waiting for Jon, and the grin that spread over his face said louder than words that he'd got some juicy bits of information to share.

'The wonderful DS Mills. He was absolutely out to get you wasn't he?'

Jon nodded.

'No thought for himself or his private life. No effort was too much. He just wanted to see Kell girls in behind bars, and no worry about whose life-force was there inside them.'

'A wonderful servant of the public I'm sure.'

'Well Mr "can't do too much for the community" has decided to retire, and he's done it with immediate effect. The day before the identity hearing to be precise.'

Jon couldn't believe what he was hearing. 'How close to retirement age was he?'

'He's 57.'

'And what's retirement age on this planet?'

'Well it's 70 for most people, but the police retain a legacy right to go at 65.'

'So it's still a few years early. Any reason for this sudden decision?'

'The story I've been getting is that he decided to go because of some money he's just inherited from an old relative who died a couple of months back.'

'Did she leave much.'

'Well at first they thought she'd only left her house, the furniture and a bit of cash in a bank account. It's been going through probate for weeks and until a few days ago the whole lot wasn't worth more than about 150,000. But then they had her jewellery valued and got quite a surprise. Everything they thought was just cheap costume stuff turns out to be real stones, and real gold. The total value of the estate so far is well over a million.'

'So far?'

'It doesn't finish there. They've already uncovered one savings account they didn't know she had and they're looking for more. Seems the old duck was better off than anyone had thought.'

'And how many are sharing it?'

'Four of them. Two daughters and a son were in for fixed amounts and between them they'd have taken most of the legacy. Mills was the sole surviving nephew and was just in for whatever was left.'

'And now he's getting the lion's share. Doesn't sound like the old lady knew what she was worth does it? So what will Mills get? Is it really enough to make him want to retire?'

'He'll get just under a million.' Kamar watched Jon's face for an expression. 'I know the Chandlers of this galaxy don't think that's very much, but as I've tried to explain, to ordinary people it's a fortune.'

Jon thought about this one. If Mills had supported him in his aim of establishing his true identity four years ago he'd willingly have dashed the guy a million or two. If only they could have done a deal. If only he'd known the man could be bought so cheaply.

'But the Mills we know and love wouldn't have given up just because some money had come his way. I'll bet he didn't have any family did he?'

'Two sons, both grown up and gone. His wife couldn't hack being married to a cop so she divorced him and married someone else 30 years back.'

'Just himself to think of then. Exactly the type to have carried on to the bitter end.'

'The word is, he was acting very strange just before he went. Seemed to have lost the plot completely. Couldn't wait to get through to the end of his last day.'

'And how does this affect the case? Who'll be representing the police tomorrow?'

'They've passed his work onto another officer, DS Whittaker. Young, smart, on a fast-track to the top, but he knows sod all about this case. What's more, he doesn't like getting involved with stuff he can't win - might hold back his career.'

'But he's got to appear in court, surely.'

'He'll be there, but whether he's inclined to do much is another thing. I'll bet he wants to drop the case like a hot potato.'

'But there's still Jasmine to worry about.'

Now the smile had vanished from Kamar's face.

'And she's the big unknown. The police still want to put her away for being on the game, and they can't drop the charges just because one officer's retired. But whether

Whittaker's pushing her to testify against you is something different entirely. We won't know till tomorrow.'

107

The Identity Hearing

It was the same court-room as before, only this time just a little more full than on the previous occasions. In particular the twelve members of the jury sat to the judge's left hand side had increased the numbers. Jon and Kamar took a good look at them, five men and seven women who in their everyday clothes looked dowdy in comparison to the group of learned practitioners who filled centre stage in the big room. Seated at the back were a few members of the press - and the two men in dark suits. Almost as one the occupants of the court-room leapt to their feet as the judge entered and took his seat.

When the other participants had re-seated themselves Ludlum remained standing and opened the proceedings with a resume of Jana Kell's two possible identities and the charges which had been laid against each of them. Jon could see the man looked just a little worried when he called DS Whittaker to the stand - and immediately sat down. The action told its own story.

Kamar was surprised but he rallied and stood up, hurriedly arranging his papers.

'Detective Whittaker. Could you tell the court how long you have worked on this case.'

The man was calm when he spoke. 'I took the case over yesterday.'

Kamar scribbled a note on one of his papers, probably more for effect than any real reason.

'And can you tell the court how long you have known, or been associated with the defendant, such that you would be able to judge his or her identity.'

'Today is the first time I have met Miss Kell.'

Kamar looked up at the judge. 'The defence has no further questions.'

What Dr Morris told the court was rather more helpful. The psychiatrist described in detail the effects of spirit image retention and how he had never been in any doubt that Jana Kell would eventually regain the knowledge of her true identity. He agreed it had been surprising and entirely unprecedented that she had suffered from the condition for so long, and it had been most unfortunate that circumstances had forced her to take the drastic action of stowing away on a starliner. If the police had been just a little more understanding four years ago, most of the alleged crimes would never have taken place. Now he was pleased to report, that after two weeks of observation in his clinic he could tell the court that the defendant standing in the dock was herself, and not the mere body of Jana Kell occupied by the life-force that had once been known as Jon Chandler.

With a testimony like that Kamar knew there was little need to call the witnesses from TranzCon, but he'd wait until Jasmine had had her say.

While Morris had been speaking, Kamar had noticed how a junior aide had entered the court-room and whispered in Ludlum's ear. If the man had looked worried before, now he was positively nervous. But he continued. 'The court calls Jasmine Kell.'

Everyone heard the words repeated in the waiting area outside.

A hush fell over the room and Jon drew in a breath he held for just a little too long. He heard the call issued a second time, and then a third.

With a frown clearly visible on his face Ludlum approached the judge and asked for a recess of one hour. When the court re-convened the prosecutor announced that a key witness was temporarily unavailable and asked for a further recess while investigations were made.

The judge agreed to put the case on hold until after the weekend. The look he gave Ludlum as the court rose said more than words could ever have conveyed.

★★★

Kamar arrived at the prison just after lunch the next day. The smile was back on his face.

'They can't find Jasmine.'

Jon gave a look that said "incredulous". 'What, not at all?'

'She's disappeared off the radar. I met with Ludlum and the judge, and the old man wasn't very pleased at all. Ludlum accepts that without Jasmine's testimony he hasn't got a case. He knows we've got more witnesses ready and waiting, so if he tries to go ahead he's going to get cut to ribbons. The judge has given him until tomorrow evening to find Jasmine, or drop the case.'

'What if he finds her?'

'If he does, then we've got a problem. But I don't think he will. If she *wanted* to be found, they'd have found her by now. OK, she can't hide forever, but lying low till after Monday is easy.'

'But when they find her, she'll be in worse trouble. Failing to appear in court when she's been subpoenaed will get her an even longer sentence.'

'She could be in hospital somewhere. Or there's something else that's prevented her from getting here. Or maybe there could be another reason.'

Jon looked up, wondering what Kamar was trying to say.

'Maybe she cares about you enough to put herself at risk.'

Jon shook the girl's head. 'But she told me, I'm nothing to her. It's like she said, she has to put herself first.'

'Well she's not here and that's doing you a lot of good. If they still haven't found her by tomorrow evening Ludlum's going to call off the case. I'll see you Monday morning either way. We've got a trial to prepare for.'

★★★

Monday morning came, and Monday morning went. The fact that Jon hadn't been transferred to the holding cell at the court-house told him the case wouldn't be going ahead. Or perhaps Ludlum had persuaded the judge to give him longer. That was the trouble with prison, never knowing what was going on in the real world.

It was mid-afternoon before Kamar finally arrived to bring some very welcome news.

'They've still not found Jasmine, so Ludlum's throwing in the towel. That means the court has to accept your claim to be Jana Kell, and that means we do at least know what charges you'll have to answer.'

'And is it like you said, am I really going to get off?'

'Morris is going to speak on your behalf again and he'll tell the court that the condition you were suffering from made you truly believe you were Jon Chandler. Then I'll come in and tell the story of how you felt you had to do the things you did. You were desperate to get in contact with people on Vissan, so desperate you had to escape from the SA Block just to make a single phone call. And we've got a witnessed statement from Stuart Robertson on Darius to say he did indeed promise you would be allowed to make that call.'

'Open and shut then?'

'We could probably go for getting no sentence at all, but I've spoken to the judge and he agrees it would be easier if he gave you three years, and that's the three years you've already spent in custody. Hand on my heart, it's a rubber stamping exercise. You walk out of that court-room, and then you can buy me a drink.'

Jon smiled. But for a moment the thought of finally being free was too much. Tears welled in the girl's eyes and the emotion left him unable to speak. After a minute he calmed a little.

'But I haven't got any money. You know that.'

Now it was Kamar's turn to smile.

'Oh yes you have. TranzCon have been very embarrassed that a person who worked for them as a host has been through so much trouble, apparently as a direct result of a mind transfer. So they've offered to pay compensation, and that's on top of the money they've already paid you for working as a host.'

'How much do I get?'

'50,000 HUC. OK, I know it's not much in Chandler terms, but for a new life it's a good start. It would pay the rent on a flat here in Celebration for ten years, and you've said yourself you'll be making real money long before that. Now do you want the bad news?'

'Bad news? I thought it was all good.'

'There's always bad news, you just have to hope it's not *too* bad. I'm a public defender and the state pays me if my clients can't afford it. But now you've got some money, I'm afraid you'll have to contribute towards my fees.'

'How much?'

'5% of your total after-tax wages from the past two years.'

Jon laughed. 'That's nothing at all.'

'And 3% of your savings, if any. That's 1500 HUC which I'm sure you can afford.'

Jon leaped forward and hugged his lawyer.

'Mr Kamar, you've been worth every cent!'

108

The Trial

Jon was excited. The day had finally come for his trial. How many people had ever woken up in a prison cell, knowing their big day had come, and yet were just raring to get into the court-room? A tingle ran down the girl's back when Jon thought of how the day was going to play out. By the time the sun went down it was almost certain he would be free: free to walk out in the street, free to come and go as he chose.

★★★

The heavy set police-woman clicked the cuff closed around the girl's right wrist and attached the other cuff to her left. Jon looked down at the steel ring that encircled the soft flesh and thought "for the very last time".

Outside in the corridor Kamar was waiting. The beaming smile on the man's face said it all, nothing could stop them now.

The two of them chatted as they walked from the holding cell block across the open quadrangle to the courthouse building. Even the sun was on Jon's side that morning and shone brightly down on the path and the neatly mown grass.

The mid-summer warmth made it one of those "good to be alive" days.

The trio passed into the shadow of the courthouse building but after a moment Jon's eyes adjusted to the gloom, and he made out a shape. Somehow he wasn't surprised to see the dark suited man standing to the side of the double doors ahead of them. Watching as always, but not his problem.

As they drew closer to the line of stone columns that surrounded the open area the man stepped out into their path and flashed some sort of card towards the police-woman. She stopped straight away.

'Miss Jana Kell?' the man asked.

From just three words the man's Darian accent was clear for anyone to hear, though that wasn't exactly a surprise, he'd guessed the men were from somewhere in the Union and Darius was the nearest habitable world to Phoenix. His whole case rested on being Jana so there was no reason to deny what had become almost a fact.

'I am Jana Kell. Who wants to know?'

'Agent Roth of Trans-Union Security. I have a warrant for your arrest.'

Kamar looked at the man in alarm. 'Miss Kell is already a prisoner and is on her way to stand trial. If you'd step aside please, we don't want to upset the judge by arriving late.'

The lawyer gave a shout of surprise as a big hand came from behind and pushed him easily aside. He looked up at the mountain of flesh and knew there was no point attempting to retaliate. But he wasn't defeated. Doing his best to regain his dignity he shook himself free, walked back to Jon's side and took the girl's arm.

Ignoring the two agents he spoke calmly to the police-woman. 'Come on lets go.'

She shook her head. 'I'm sorry Mr Kamar. These men are Union agents. They have authority.'

Kamar looked up into Roth's face, he was shaking just a little but he kept his voice steady.

'Can you tell me exactly why you want to arrest a woman who is already in custody?'

A grin came to Roth's face. 'This lady has business on Darius. She has to stand trial for a number of crimes.'

'But she's standing trial for them here. There's no need for extradition to Darius.'

Roth grinned. 'Mr Kamar, would you agree that most of the charges against Miss Kell relate to crimes committed before the Hyperion arrived in Darius orbit.'

Kamar thought for a moment. 'I agree, but I don't see what that has to do with it.'

'Well think about this. According to Union law, anyone who has been arrested for a crime on board a space vessel is required to be disembarked at the next port of call at a habitable planet to face trial there. The Captain broke Union law when he kept her on board to return her to Phoenix.'

Kamar shrugged. 'That's the normal procedure with stowaways. They are supposed to be returned to the port where they boarded.'

'Not in the Union.'

'We're not in the Union.'

Roth grinned again. 'What time do you make it Mr Kamar?'

'What's the time got to do with it?'

'What time do you think it is on Vissan right now?'

Kamar shook his head. 'I'd need a computer to work that out.'

'Well I'll make it easy for you, it's five minutes past midnight. That makes today the first of July, and that's the day

Phoenix becomes a full member of the Union. This planet and everyone on it are now subject to all Union laws and legislation.'

Roth turned towards the police-woman. 'If you'd release Miss Kell to our authority we'd be very much obliged.' Then he called to his partner. 'Willis, get your cuffs ready will you.'

The man fumbled in his pocket, opened the handcuffs and held them ready as the police-woman pulled her keys out to unlock the cuff already round the girl's wrist. Jon weighed up the situation and wondered. If he pulled free the moment the handcuff was unlocked he'd catch them all off-guard. He knew the girl's small body made him no match for two big men, but she was fast, and nimble too. If he could make it to the courtroom he might still be safe. Even Union agents wouldn't dare challenge the authority of a court, especially now it had become a Union court.

The key slid into the lock and started to turn. Jon waited for his moment, the cuff swung open and he jerked the girl's arm free. But he wasn't fast enough. A big hand snapped closed around the slim wrist with a grip that could have been made of iron.

Roth looked down at her, shaking his head in a chiding way.

'Don't even think about it Kell. Resisting arrest by a Union agent will get you another two years, on top of the rest.'

David Hulett Wilson

More TranzCon

This book is just the first of a trilogy which might even have something every good trilogy should have - a 4th book. The 2nd book is well advanced, the 3rd book is planned and partly written but they are in many ways still fluid so your feedback could help to mould the stories. If you can spare the time to send an email I'd like to hear anything you have to say. And when I say "anything" I mean it, comments ranging all the way from derogatory remarks about how much of your time I've wasted to glowing praise will be accepted (and I guarantee to read <u>every</u> word).

If you'd like to know more about how this book came to be written, or anything about myself as author, please have a look at my website:

www.davidhwilson.co.uk

Please send any feedback to my email address:
mail@davidhwilson.co.uk

Getting Published

If you've ever written a book and tried to get it traditionally published you'll know just how difficult it can be. The acceptance rate is tiny and only the lucky few are ever accepted by an agent and sold to a publishing house. So more and more debut authors are turning to self-publishing to at least get a foot in the door.

But just getting the printing done isn't the end of the line - far from it. You've got boxes of books filling up the spare-room and now you need to find an audience, people who might be prepared to spend their hard-earned cash on a story written by a complete unknown. Sounds difficult? "Impossible" would be a better word.

**Well I'm making it as easy as possible,
I'm giving away my books**

(insert reactions of shock and awe)

"What" you ask? You're giving away books? Where's the money in that? How can you afford it?

Well this initial print-run is very much a promotional venture to break into the market - an attempt to get noticed. I suppose I could have paid out for a milli-second of advertising on prime-time TV, but everyone would have fast-forwarded through it because they'd recorded it earlier on a PVR. In fact financing an initial print-run and distributing the books without charge is probably the cheapest advertising that money can buy.

And that's where you as readers come in. If you enjoyed TranzCon please can you help me as much as possible. When you've finished with your copy can I ask you to pass it on to a friend you think might enjoy it.